Seward Bound

A novel by **C.A. McJack**

Published by
Red's Ink and Quill Publishing
www.RedsInkandQuill.com
www.AidanRedBooks.com

Acknowledgments

This had to be one of the toughest stories to publish if it was not for the helpful folks involved.

I want to start by thanking my husband's patience. I am usually his right-hand gal for our main business as real estate investors and educators. Whenever I lock myself away to write, he has to shoulder the entire workload.

To Candice Gilmer for showing me other possible platforms that were much easier for me to understand after a major upset on getting my book published and marketed.

Aidan Red for being a calming mentor when it comes to writing stories and the technical skills involved in getting a novel published. For being a partner in crime in sharing tons of booths at book events. For his sharp eyes on first round edits. His precision for perfection is like no one else's. His ability to explain software to a non-technical author who can barely use one program to write and edit to his assist in formatting my pieces into several products from eBooks to audios to paperbacks. His knowledge is endless.

To my content editor Trenda London and to my copy editor Amy Jackson for patiently working with me and continuing my education in the English language.

To some of my top fans: Michele Danin and Mark Danin for wildly and blindly believing in this latest novel and for purchasing my prior novel Fate's Twisted Circle and falling madly in love with the series. To Krisann Smith who loves being my beta reader and for being the whip cracker to keep me on task.

There are many others, I know, and I only have so much space. So, know that everyone of you is truly appreciated.

My many thanks to my editors.

Content Editing by Trenda London,
Facebook: ItsYourStoryContentEditing

Copy Editing by Amy Jackson,
Copy Editing and Proof Reading, http://AmyJacksonEditing.com

To D'Arcy.
Here's to all of the wonderful year we spent together,
sharing all of our fears, tears and cheers.

Chapters

Chapter One	1
Chapter Two	15
Chapter Three	45
Chapter Four	74
Chapter Five	104
Chapter Six	120
Chapter Seven	146
Chapter Eight	155
Chapter Nine	168
Chapter Ten	175
Chapter Eleven	196
Chapter Twelve	206
Chapter Thirteen	210
Chapter Fourteen	230
Chapter Fifteen	250
Chapter Sixteen	270
Chapter Seventeen	277
Chapter Eighteen	297
Chapter Nineteen	327
Chapter Twenty	343
Chapter Twenty-One	347
Chapter Twenty-Two	356
Chapter Twenty-Three	389
Chapter Twenty-Four	397
Chapter Twenty-Five	420
Chapter Twenty-Six	427
Chapter Twenty-Seven	430
Chapter Twenty-Eight	458
Chapter Twenty-Nine	471
Chapter Thirty	482
Epilogue	490
Other Books	495
Preview from *Fate's Twisted Circle*	496
About the Author	507

CHAPTER ONE

Tasha stumbled over the door's threshold, her gear spilling onto the floor in the dark cabin. The lock stubbornly gave after what seemed like a good fifteen minutes exacerbated by the damp early fall air. It felt like the dead of winter, with its hazy bleakness and patches of white fog.

She shoved grumpily against her gear, standing up, her arm reaching out in the general direction for a light switch as she closed the front door to stop what little warmth there was in the cabin from escaping into the cool twilight. The cold air seemed to roll off the snow-covered mountains that guarded the tiny town's flank, with Resurrection Bay on the town's opposite side.

She was tired after her long journey, and her side hurt like hell from where she had taken a bullet a few weeks earlier. She knew she had to take it easy after being discharged from the military hospital, but she didn't want to go to her parents' house only to lounge around for weeks under her mother's watch, subjected to endless questioning about her injury and what she intended to do with her life.

Instead, she had found the first job that would immediately accept her, allowing her to use the military's final travel orders to get her to Seward, Alaska. The job not only paid her a living wage but came with pre-arranged living quarters for her. The job acceptance letter came with a key to a cabin taped to the paperwork. She was happy enough that it was a two-bed, one-bath cabin that came with running water and electricity. She did not want to end up in an Alaskan dry cabin. But anything was better than living in a tent out in the desert heat. She had her privacy and that was all that mattered to her to 'recover' not just physically, but emotionally, from the last tour in Afghanistan.

Her neck hairs didn't have a chance to stand on end before her hand came across something not related to a light switch. In the next millisecond, her arm was painfully wrenched up behind her back and she was back on the floor again, fighting an unknown assailant as she struggled to swing her body around to free herself.

She felt half her stitches rip just above her hip from the exertion, the sharp pain overtaking her fear, and her knee jerked up instinctively. She heard the assailant swear and then groan. She tried to finish the attacker by headbutting the tall dark figure. Her skull made contact with a loud crack, and stars flashed in her eyes. She knew she was going to have one hell of a headache after this maneuver.

He rolled off her but then blinded her with an intense light as she struggled to separate herself from her stunned assailant. She kicked at the light—another noise, more like a curse—as she dove, grabbing the knife from her backpack. The flashlight spun noisily on the wooden floor, creating the swirling lighting effects one sees in horror movies just before the victim either loses or wins the battle against the evil.

She saw a figure on the ground, took a deep breath, and did a full body slam just as the figure caught the spinning flashlight. He illuminated her face as she pressed the knife tight against his heavily bearded throat.

He tried to move. She pressed the blade harder against his throat and made a guttural warning noise before ordering, "I wouldn't make another move if I were you." Her eyes flashed. "I will cut you wide open and have no qualms about it since you are trespassing in my cabin!" The knife's pressure made his skin indent on his throat.

"*Your* cabin?" he spat back at her. "What the hell, lady?" Blood was oozing from where she had nicked him on his Adam's apple. "Who the hell do you think you are barging into *my* cabin?" He tried to back away from her knife, then groaned in pain as she leaned more of her weight into him to keep his movements minimal. Her adrenaline was masking the pain of her torn stitches, giving her more strength and courage than she felt.

"Listen, asshole, cabin nine is mine and it was issued by Black Raven Aviation! So if I were you, I would highly suggest you leave before I slide this knife across your neck, or if I am feeling just nice enough, call the police on you—you pervert! Your choice, Grizzly Adams!"

Egads, this man is big! she noted to herself. If it were not for her knife and her knee in his gut, there would be no way she could have kept him down with just her weight.

His dark eyes nailed her visage after her threat. She was glad he seemed to believe her, for she did not feel very convincing and she was not even sure if they had 911 up here to call. "So, which is it?" she asked, shoving hard against him but keeping her knife firm against his throat.

"Jesus!" he swore. "*You're* the electrician?" Giving her a wolf-like grin, he asked, "They hired *you*?" He started laughing. "What the hell?" His large, bear-like body erupted in deep laughter before he began coughing and swearing at the uncomfortable weight of her knee in his gut.

"Hunh?" was her only response as she watched him choke on his mirth.

He moved to extricate himself from her, but she leaned into him with her other elbow pressing into his upper abdominal, determined to have his explanation. "Not so fast…Just who the hell are yo—"

In one motion he grabbed her hair, snatching her head back. With his other hand he dropped the light, thus grabbing and twisting the knife out of her grasp, deflecting it away from his throat. It had to be painful, grabbing the knife by its blade.

"No one holds a knife to me," he growled.

He literally swung her around by her mid-length hair as he stood up and moved toward the cabin door. She kicked, clawed, punched, and screamed at him, fearing that he was going to throw her out of the cabin and into the cold air, or worse, use her own knife against her.

Instead, he threw her up against the wall. She yelped, hitting the wall as he snapped the elusive light switch on—the one she could not find earlier. She squinted against the bright light and grimaced from another sharp stab of pain from the recently torn stitches. She felt warm blood begin to ooze from the exit side of the wound, dampening her undershirt. The front of her pants and shirt felt sticky too, where the entry wound had been oozing from the initial attack.

With the breath knocked out of her, her head swimming, she forced her lungs to suck in the desperately needed air.

The large mountain man, his back side to her, his hair and beard resembling the fur coat of a brown grizzly, slammed her knife onto the kitchen island's butcher block, his hand leaving a bloody mess on the countertop. He turned, taking a menacing step toward her.

She instinctively raised her arms, protecting her head and upper body in self-defense. But nothing came. She peered between her arms, only to see him studying her. Then he turned to grab a dish towel and threw it at her, telling her, "You've got blood on that sweater."

Tasha caught it, slipping it under her shirt, and held pressure against her entry wound while she watched him go to the kitchen sink to rinse the blood from the palm of his hand.

He looked back at her from his task. "I meant for you to wipe most of my blood off so it won't ruin your sweater, lady," he said, as if she was not too bright.

"First of all, my name is Tasha Lazar. Secondly, it is my blood because you busted my stitches from my wound, Griswald!"

"Wound?" He stopped and half turned to her, interrupting his task. He found another towel and eventually wrapped it around his hand. "What wound?"

"My would-be-golden-bullet wound," she growled in annoyance. Tasha pressed her backside against the wall, stemming the flow of blood from her exit wound. Her hip was killing her, and she was desperate for a painkiller at that point. But she refused to show her weakness to the strange, wild-looking man.

"You still haven't explained the reason you're here," she told him, digging into her jeans pocket for her phone, glad it was still there as she pulled it out with her free hand. She frowned at it when she noticed that it still had no signal. *Just freakin' great!* she thought.

"You won't get a signal with that phone"—he squeezed the towel tightly in his palm—"and there is no 911 to call, if you are seeking the police."

She reluctantly put it away, keeping a wary eye on him, sagging wearily against the wall. From the corner of her eye, she noticed something glinting in the light on the floor and realized it was her key.

He followed her gaze over to the key. "Cabin nine?" he grunted. "Well, you got the right place."

"Damn skippy, I got the right place." She indicated with her head where her key lay on the floor near the front door. "Still doesn't explain why you're here attacking people."

"Well, wouldn't you attack someone breaking into your home?"

"*What!*" she sputtered, stunned at the accusation. "*Your* home?" She was unable to move from the wall, still applying pressure to her wound, afraid the seepage of blood on her backside hadn't stopped yet. "First of all, the letter in that pocket of my backpack is the one stating *my right* to be here. It did not say I would be *sharing* this cabin nor living in *anyone's* home!" she spat out.

The grizzly bear's head turned to look at her gear on the floor. Before he went over to it, he reached across the island to grab her knife, obviously not trusting her, and lightly pitched it into the sink behind him along the back kitchen wall, ensuring it was far away from her. However, she did not move, still in a lot of pain from their struggle and too exhausted from the two-and-a-half-day journey up the coast from Seattle, Washington. She hadn't gotten much to eat or sleep on the barge coming up here, her car being her only sleeping berth in order to conserve what cash she possessed.

He lumbered awkwardly over—*from some unseen pain she had inflicted upon him?*—and deftly plucked her letter with his good hand from the outside pocket. As he opened the letter and began reading it, Tasha took the opportunity to assess the rather large and hairy man. His hair was long and as unkempt as his matching beard. A beard that was cut lopsided, either from his piss-poor grooming habits or by her knife to his throat. She suspected the latter, spying some matching tufts of hair lying on the floor—the only evidence of their struggle.

As he came near her, she slid up to her full height, still pressed against the wall. He towered over her by a good full head. He mistook her movement as defensive, and he spoke without taking his eyes off the letter. "Take it easy, I'm not going to hurt you. We both overreacted to a surprise."

"Golly gee, Beave, ya think?" she said rather sarcastically, and then grunted at the stabbing pain in her side. Maybe the VA hospital was right: they had reluctantly let her go too early and she wasn't ready to resume a normal life—but neither was she expecting to fight anyone stateside. Her head was throbbing.

He looked at her, studying her again before asking if she was all right.

Tasha gave him a pointed look as if '*really?*' Then she spoke. "I would be if I can get a secure and *safe* bed that is a lot warmer than my car and have"—looking at her wristwatch—"a good seven to eight hours of sleep before I have to report to Black Raven Aviation."

"I didn't hear a car come up here," he pointed out.

"That's because my car is *dead,* and I left it at the dock's parking lot. It wouldn't start for some reason after I got into port. The dockhands pushed my car off the barge and let me roll it into one of their parking spaces. I ended up walking partway up here after getting a lift from a trucker to the end of the neighborhood's main road just off the highway."

"You walked?" he asked incredulously. "With all that gear?" He pointed to the large duffel bag, the flight bag, and the hiker's backpack on the floor.

"And uphill too," she mouthed off, then shrugged a shoulder. "Minus the snow."

She separated from the wall, testing to see if she could feel anything seep

4

from her rear wound. She felt nothing, other than another sharp pain from the movement, taking a few tentative steps toward the kitchen island. "Now, if you would please leave or find a way to contact this Nathan Amsel fellow to help clear up this mess, I would be most grateful." She pulled the kitchen towel from under her sweater and placed it on the countertop, thankful that the bleeding had subsided.

"Well, he's not going to be back until tomorrow morning. He took a bird to Anchorage today for some business, and I don't have the company's satellite phone here tonight." He stepped back from her, dropping her letter dismissively on the kitchen island before continuing, crossing his arms in defiance. "And I am *not* leaving this cabin."

"Then fine! Get me to the nearest hotel!" She walked over to her bags, first picking up the lighter backpack without too much effort, but when it came to shouldering her much heavier duffel bag, she cursed herself for inflicting more pain. She winced to herself, losing control of the heavy bag and letting it dump back onto the floor. Too proud at that point to ask for help, her back still to him, she decided that she would just drag her belongings to the front door and figure out from there where to go, once back outside and away from this nasty man who was no gentleman in helping her with her things, given her condition.

She stood up halfway in her struggle and looked at him, finding him watching her with interest, arms still crossed over his chest and a smug expression plastered on his face. "What?" she snarled. "The least you could do is give me my letter back and give me a lift into town to the nearest hotel! It's what civil people do with any sense of hospitality."

"The nearest hotel is about six miles down the main road. However, I believe the owner has left for the season."

Her expression was dumbfounded. "What do you mean…*left* for the season?"

"Well, tourist season is pretty much over. Most businesses shut down for the winter and our town goes back down to our normal twenty-five hundred people."

"I'm not a tourist," she stated flatly, hoping her facial expression coincided.

"I know that."

"So where would you advise me to go?" Her eyebrows raised in anticipation for some reasonable answer.

"Can't really tell you, other than the hangar, and that is another two and a half miles down the road. However, it's locked up at this time of night." He smirked at her, or so she thought through the whiskers of his half-cut beard and mustache.

She let her backpack drop to the floor, deflated. It was obvious the man was not going to be helpful at all. Nor was she looking forward to heading back to her car to spend another night inside it. It was seriously colder here, and at that point she was thinking she would freeze to death before she bled to death, the front wound seeping again.

"Then is there a way to get me back to my car at the dock?" she asked, determined to control her anger so that it would not empower him into goading her.

"I thought you said your car was broke." He uncrossed his arms and leaned forward on the kitchen island, his arms and hands bracing him, one hand still wrapped in the makeshift bandage, flat on the surface, his fingers splayed wide, making him even more powerful looking.

Tasha sighed heavily with exasperation, letting her eyes look around, finally noting the interior of the now lighted cabin. "It is. But at least it is some shelter from the cold," she defiantly told him, as if the idea did not warrant much thought.

"You're going to sleep in your car?" The surprise was his first expression Tasha could read from his rather deadpan look.

"I have no choice, do I?" Her eyes flashed back at him. "Especially since you're of no help and your specialty seems to be hurting and scaring the hell out of people!" She now noted the living area of the cabin, decorated with hunting gear, pictures of wildlife scenes, and a stuffed caribou head among other small wildlife bodies mounted on the wall.

"You do have a choice, lady," he said, standing back up from the countertop and deciding to unwrap his hand to check if the bleeding had ceased.

"What choice?" she nearly whined at him, wanting so badly in her tiredness, pain, and frustration to stamp her foot at him like a petulant child.

"You stay where you're assigned by that letter." He pointed to the discarded letter.

"But you said *you* live here. There has to be a mistake."

"It's no mistake. I do live here, and so will you, according to that letter." He threw the blood-soaked towel in the sink.

"Well, what about your wife and family? It's only a two-bedroom cabin."

"It is a two-bedroom cabin, and it is just me, lady," he said rather nonchalantly as he half-flexed his wounded hand. If there was any pain, he didn't show it.

She cocked her head knowingly and waggled her finger at him. "Oh no...no, no...I'm definitely not staying here, Griswald," she said, half smirking at him, knowing better.

"Where else besides your car?"

"Not unless there is one hell of a lock on my bedroom door, I get my knife back, and you tell me who the hell *you* are."

"There are no locks on any of the rooms in these cabins, soldier. It's no-frills living. You can get your knife back when you promise not to cut my throat..." He absently pulled at his beard, his hand stopping when he realized part of it was missing. "Or cut the rest of my beard off, and the name is Jack."

The word *soldier* was a clear reminder to her that she was capable of sleeping with an entire platoon of men pretty much unharmed out in a big field tent. He would keep it professional. She eyed the woolly mammoth in his plaid flannel shirt in front of her, studying him, pondering her decision.

He wasn't having any of it when it came to waiting on her to decide, and he cleared the space between them in less than five steps, grabbing all her gear and easily carrying it to the rear of the cabin, past the main living area where the kitchen opened up and overlooked the living area with a large picture window. A bath was the only thing separating the two rooms in the mini hallway. He disappeared off to the left with her gear. She tentatively followed him, stopping at the doorway to the generous guest room, making sure he could not trap her inside with him. He had put the smaller flight bag on a chair and the large duffel bag on top of the desk. The queen-sized bed surprised her; she had expected much worse. She decided it would do for now, eyeing the non-lockable doorknob, confirming what he had told her.

He indicated for her to come in, but wanting him to leave the room before she went in, she backed away from the doorway instead under the guise that she was going to get her knife from the sink. He gave her a piqued look.

Sarcastically, she raised two fingers up at him. "Scout's honor, not to work on the other side of your precious beard." She turned for the kitchen. She was quick about it, rinsing the knife, drying it on her now blood-ruined sweater, and tucked it away in the backside of her jeans as he came back into the kitchen.

He gave way and allowed her to pass him, neither of them taking their eyes off each other, still leery of any further surprises.

In the kitchen, he gathered the two towels from the sink to take on down to the laundry, and he heard her go into the bathroom, the door closing quickly and quietly. When he turned toward the basement door, which was located near the front entry, he noted the blood on the wall where he had thrown her against it. She was not joking about bleeding, and he knew it was not his blood. He had hurt her. *But how was I supposed to know she was wounded? And of all things, a bullet wound?* he thought. She was lucky that he had just come up from the basement without access to his gun, for he would have given her another bullet wound. But now, thanks to her, he had only one good hand to work with to clean up the mess.

He was near done wiping it down when the bath door opened. He turned around but missed seeing her dodge into her room, her door closing quickly.

In the morning, he would see to it that all this mess would get straightened out. Tasha, as she called herself, was not the 'Tosh' as both Nate and he thought when they had hired their new electrician. It would be interesting when he turned her over to Nate in the morning. Most likely, the following morning he would be helping her get shipped back to wherever it was she came from.

He threw the blood-soaked towels back into the sink basin and wetted them down to keep the blood from permanently staining them. He would throw them in the wash in the morning, then take her into work with him at 8:00 a.m. It was late, almost bedtime, and he was tired and sore from his encounter with this little hellcat. He was quite sure he was not going to have any kids now, the way his balls throbbed where she had kneed him hard in his groin. It was just as well. The next day he had to pick up Drake before going into work. He had sure missed having him around that day.

The pounding matched the one in her temple, the place where she had headbutted the nasty man that had 'come with' her cabin. Slowly, she realized it was not her head, but a heavy fist on her bedroom door, and someone yelling that it was time to "get moving and go to work."

Tasha had fallen asleep in the same clothes she had arrived in. She got up to answer her door. She felt like crap and a bit woozy in her stomach. But it was not the time to have that problem and she did the only thing she knew how. Ignore it and drive on. A good hot shower would do the trick, and then dress to impress her new boss.

His frame blocked her entire doorway when she opened her door. He looked almost as foreboding as he had the night before, save for his evenly trimmed beard and the smell of an enticing men's cologne. The spiced woodsy scent of autumn leaves and forest of the great outdoors assailed her nose. His attire was pretty much the same: what looked like a shirt layered with a flannel shirt over it and work jeans. "You've got fifteen to get ready before I leave for town to run a quick errand and drop you off at the hangar."

"Fifteen?" Her voice was rough and heavy with sleep. "That's barely enough time to shower, dress, and eat, much less pack my gear!" She squinted her eyes against the one light in the main room.

"Then I suggest you best be movin'. Don't worry about packing your gear until the boss decides what to do. Now hurry up. I won't be waiting on you forever."

"Ugh!" She pushed past him toward the bathroom. "You know thirty minutes is more doable. Why in the hell get me up so late?"

"You said last night you wanted seven to eight hours of sleep. I honored that down to the minute."

Tasha glared spitefully at him.

He just pointed to his watch, saying, "You're down to fourteen."

She slammed the bath door on his morning smugness. She splashed water on her face to help wake her, put on deodorant, and brushed her hair back into a loose ponytail. She really needed a shower. She did the best she could by adding a little makeup to make herself to be more presentable.

She grabbed a Power Bar and her file with the acceptance letter and the various other important documents, along with her all-weather coat, nearly running, just as 'Griswald' was opening the cabin's front door. The sound of a sturdy, heavily used pickup truck was already running off to the side of the domicile, waiting. She did not remember seeing the truck the night before, but it was near dark when she had arrived and there were no outside lights to illuminate the area. The lazy sunrise was low over the southeastern horizon of Resurrection

Bay, where she spied the bay's water through a thick stand of pine trees.

The white mist raked her with its cold, invisible fingers as she shrugged on her coat, trying to keep the files from falling out of her hand.

"Is that the coat you're wearing?" he asked, following her once he had secured the cabin door.

"It's all I have at the moment." she told him, quickly jumping into the truck, grateful for the heater running at full blast—albeit an uncontrollable shiver shook her body before she was able to conceal it from 'Griswald.'

"Had you stayed in your car, you would have frozen to death," he said, looking at her before putting the truck into gear, "even in that coat of yours."

"I've been through worse." Keeping her eyes straight out in front of her, she tucked her hands into her coat pockets and found her gloves. She was determined not to let him get to her nerves today.

He ended up being a civil driver compared to the demeanor she had encountered the night before. She remembered the highway that she had come in on and saw the airport before he turned away from it to head into town. She had no idea why he just didn't drop her off right there and then. When she asked, he told her, "The guys won't be in just yet. I don't think you will like having to wait outside the hangar in the cold."

"Then where are we going?"

"To the doc."

"The dock?" she asked, slightly confused, still trying to rid her tired body of sleep. "We're getting my car now?"

"No, as in seeing a doctor."

"Hunh?" She wondered if he was being nice to her in seeking some medical attention for her but thought that it was a bit extreme even for him. She only needed a little more sleep and recuperation time.

"I have to pick up someone before dropping you off at work." Obviously, this was the only answer she was going to get, and she hated his vagueness. She hated feeling like a mushroom, being left in the dark and fed a bunch of crap.

Their stop wasn't far down the road. But then Seward was not a big town; it was just long and narrow, nestled tightly between the mountains and Resurrection Bay. It was another dismal gray morning, though she could see the sun's morning glow strengthening just under a scurry of low misty clouds.

The town reflected the aftermath of the summer tourism. It looked just as depressingly tired, blending seamlessly with the fall-like environment as if it was long forgotten by the summer tourists instead of being the latter part of August.

'Griswald' pulled into a gravel parking lot just outside a standalone building. The only nomenclature to the building was an ordinary sign declaring it was a veterinarian's office. He parked the truck, telling her to wait in the cab and that he was not leaving the truck running for her comfort, but to keep the old truck's engine from going cold and not starting, adding, "Don't do anything brash while I'm gone."

She rolled her eyes. He got out, walking hurriedly to the building's entrance. As soon as he disappeared behind the door, she checked her phone again to see if she had any reception. There was none; only the time displayed on her phone, and she was certain it was not correct either. She sighed, asking what she had gotten herself into when she signed on for the job. It was not starting out well at all, thus making her feel more ill.

She fought her inane desire to search the truck for more information on this man but had a feeling he would be watching her. She resigned herself to pulling open the glove box to see what she could find. But all that was in the compartment was the truck's registration and title in his name. He was not pulling her leg. His name was Jack—Jack Lassiter.

It was a good fifteen minutes before he reappeared again but with a giant—no, a small horse trying to pass for a dog! She had seen the breed before, but never realized how big Newfoundlands were! The black dog complemented the size of the man leading the way. He gave the dog a few moments to relieve himself and a chance to run around before heading to the truck.

Jack pulled open his door, telling her to make some room, as she realized that the dog was going to be riding in the cab with them.

"There is no way that dog will fit in here!" she exclaimed.

"Now, listen, lady. Drake will fit just fine! In fact, he'll help keep you warm and he is a lot nicer than me. Otherwise, you are free to ride in the back of the truck."

Ugh! Sooo typical! The last thing she wanted was to smell like a dog when meeting her new boss, but did not have a chance to answer before Jack whistled and Drake came bounding inside the cab. The dog immediately took to her as he filled the entire cab, squishing her against the cold metal of the passenger door.

Drake, like any happy-go-lucky dog, was in her face, greeting and licking her. She immediately defended herself from the slobbery onslaught to keep from looking any further disheveled in the day-old clothes she wore and with no shower to boot. Thankfully, it was just way too cold for a body to stink.

Jack ordered Drake to settle down and mind his manners, as Jack put the truck into drive. The dog reluctantly settled, but not without hounding her for the protein bar in her jacket. She gladly fed it to him, since her stomach rolled over again, the pain in her side finally awakening and letting her know that she was still not up to speed.

They headed back to the airport, and within five minutes he was pulling up to the biggest hangar with Black Raven's logo over the hangar's bay. He stopped by the smaller entrance cut into the main hangar door, telling her that after she stepped in she would need to walk a few yards and then swing a left at the first hallway she came across. There she would find Nathan's office halfway down the corridor.

She got out—more like fell out of the truck's passenger side—as 'Griswald' drove away before she could steady herself, her legs having gone numb sitting in the truck between the weight of Drake's one paw and the cold air. Her nerves were eating her alive and she told herself to get a grip. *I can do this.* She would get her cabin and get this 'Jack' guy out of her hair. She *wanted* her solitude. She needed space and some quiet time to think things through after her time in the Middle East with the Army.

The hinges squealed as she let herself in and tentatively entered the comparatively dark hangar space, letting the metal door swing shut again. She gave herself a moment, letting her eyes adjust to the dim lighting. In the muted light, she saw various airplanes ranging from a Cessna 172 to a 185, a small private older jet, an Otter, a Beaver, and a larger and older transport aircraft she did not recognize immediately. They were all haphazardly jammed into the hangar, with some in various states of repair or maintenance. It was rather quiet, but she heard the men's voices off to the far right and presumed that the small light spilling on the far side of the hangar was where the crew met for briefings. She continued down along the left wall of the open bay area, coming across the hallway she was supposed to turn down and then the door with Nathan's name and his job title of Owner. She was now thanking the heavens above that Jack had ended up being a man of his word, for she could have easily fallen victim to kidnapping or rape, not knowing this guy from Adam.

She knocked on the door. No answer. She tried the knob, only to find it locked. It was just as well. She would not make a good impression with the boss if he found her in his office, violating his private domain. She decided to sit down outside by his door, hoping that her stomach would settle and she could compose herself in the unexpected extra time.

She was no stranger to aviation, but she knew it was still a male-dominated world when it came to this type of work. She was competent enough, but these were fixed-wing aircraft, not Army helicopters. *Will the mechanics accept me? Or just give me hell, like this man Jack did?* she wondered.

An older man turned into the hallway, whistling a happy nondescript tune, a coffee cup in his hand and a mass of paperwork under his other arm. He was rather portly, but not sloppy. What hair he had left was salt and peppered, and his face was endowed with rather large jowls. It was not until she moved to stand up, using her legs to slide her backside up the wall, that he noticed her waiting by his door, and his whistling abruptly stopped mid-tune. "Good morning, how can I help you or who are you waiting on?" he asked, with a sincere smile that reminded her of a benevolent grandfather. She warmed to him instantly and her nervousness eased.

"Hi, I am waiting for Mr. Nathan Amsel, the owner."

"Oh?" He acted surprised.

"That wouldn't be you, would it?" she asked rather submissively.

"Well…that depends," he said, cocking his head at her.

"On what?" she asked, not sure if he was taking her seriously.

"If you are from the FAA."

"No…Do you want me to be?" she asked, now curious.

"Well, obviously you're not. They would've been at my throat already on Lucy being behind on her D checks, demanding to see her maintenance records."

"Lucy?"

"The Grand Caravan in the harbor." He handed her his coffee mug so that he could reach into his slacks pocket for his office key. "Yeah, the boys name each plane and the names have stuck over the years." He singled out the key he needed on his full key ring and unlocked his office door with a soft click. He pushed the door open, indicating for her to go in first, surprising her. He noticed her reaction as he went past her after she was inside his office and went to his desk. He dumped the files on top of the other massive stacks of paperwork that covered an old metal desk, a relic of the late seventies.

"You act like you never had a man be civil to you." He took his seat behind the desk.

"Not often. Especially when you work and live in their line of work." She remembered that she had his coffee mug in her hand; the warm ceramic felt wonderful in her cold hands. "Oh." She carefully put his coffee mug down on the coaster she spied, pulling the coaster away from under the paperwork, making sure the mug would not spill. "Sorry. Here you go, sir." She took a step back.

He studied her longer than he needed to, making her fight the urge to fidget. But she knew better. She maintained her bearing, putting her arms behind her back with her files in check, her military experience helping her through the momentary awkwardness.

"So, Miss…" He hesitated, not recalling her name.

"Tasha Lazar."

"Why are you here?" he asked as he steepled his fingers, his elbows on his desk, and leaned forward, curious to her presence.

"You hired me," she stated flatly. "You needed an aircraft electrician and avionics technician."

"We did?"

"Yes," Tasha insisted, swinging her file in front of her. She opened it up and pulled out the rather worn acceptance letter. She took a step forward, handing it to him. "We also have a slight problem."

"We do?" Now confused, he pursed his lips, reading his own company letter congratulating the applicant on being hired. He dropped it on the desk without reading all of it.

Tasha asked about a reassignment of her living quarters.

"Yeah, we do," said Nathan. His fatherly voice had a light western accent.

"So, you know about the mix-up at the cabin then?" She was relieved but not entirely surprised, given how small the town was and that she was sure *the word had spread*, even though it had not been even a whole twenty-four hours since her arrival.

"The cabin?" He shifted in his chair, not saying anything as if he were still trying to wake up from a dream.

"The cabin assignment," she continued, ignoring his need to reflect. "There must have been a mix-up. You see there is someone else living there

12

already, and I understood that I would have my own cabin—unless I am being presumptuous?"

"Wow! Now there's a ten-dollar word there." He shifted back in his seat and his hands now held onto the edge of his desk, giving her a small grin.

"Excuse me?" She was now confused.

"My guys and I barely use two-syllable words." He cleared his throat before continuing. "Do you have ID on you and your military records?"

His comments were impeding her point, but she diligently pulled out the necessary documented paperwork he requested. He leaned toward her, reaching for the requested items, and began a more thorough inspection. As he continued to peruse, he told her to take her coat off and indicated for her to have a seat.

Tasha took her coat off as requested, although it was the last thing she wanted to do, given her state of attire and how cold she still felt in the office, even though she was beginning to break out in a cold sweat. Something was amiss for the boss to act as if he had made a mistake. She was praying that it was not the case. She needed this job. She had nowhere else to go and she was not about to call her parents to help bail her out of this jam, should he decide at the last minute there was a mix-up.

However, an even more grave thought popped into her head when she realized that they may have thought she was a guy and not a girl. She knew of a few men named Tasha, but they were from Russia. In the US, girls were usually named Tasha. It was a male-dominated field, and often women were not hired for fear of HR issues. For most companies it was just easier not to hire women and not have the problem in the first place.

She was not able to find a chair to pull up without moving a lot of stuff off another chair, and so she remained standing before his desk. She could not bear the silence any longer, her stomach flip-flopping. "Sir?" Tasha hesitated a moment and then realized he was not paying attention to her. "Sir," she said a little louder, "is there a problem...with my paperwork?"

He looked up, as if stunned she was still there. Then he cocked his head, looking at her—more pointedly at her side, just above her hip area at her sweater. It was then, when she looked down, that she realized she should have changed out her sweater, for there were old blood stains from last night's fight with 'Griswald.'

"I can explain—"

"Is that blood?" He got up from his chair and leaned forward for a closer inspection. Nathan put on a pair of glasses to get a clearer view of what he was trying to discern, as she tried to hide the stain with a casual hand. "It looks rather fresh. Are you hurt? Are you feeling well?"

"Yes, I'm fine. It's nothing, sir," she said, dismissing it as casually as she could. "Is there a problem with my paperwork?" she asked again.

He was still caught up in his inspection as he said, "Ah—no, but it says here you're a Tasha Lazar, not a Tosh Lazar. We were expecting a guy, not a gal—especially a college-educated one."

"I assure you that I can do the job—" She moved her shielding hand to prove her point. But Nathan interrupted her.

"Oh, I am sure you can do the job." He squinted more at her sweater. "It says here that you were wounded in combat and that you were just recently released from the hospital and discharged from the Army." He took his glasses off as he came around his desk, walking toward her. "Sweetheart, I think you are bleeding," he said, pointing to the now damp and growing bright red spot on her sweater. "I think you need to get that checked out. It looks serious."

She did not want to look down and tried to dismiss the issue. "Look, I understand your concern about hiring a woman, but you obviously need an electrician"—she pointed in the direction of the main bay—"and I really need a job," she persisted. "I promise not to let you or the mechanics down.

"All I ask is if you can fix my living arrangements. You see, there was this strange man that attacked me when I got to the cabin and—"

"And he did this to you?!"

"Yes…No! I mean…we got into a mini brawl…"

"I would not call that a 'mini brawl' given the state you are in, my dear." Again, he pointed to her sweater.

She was quickly losing it and hurried to finish the whole story. "The 'Griswald' man—"

"Griswald?"

"His name isn't *Griswald*. It's a nickname that stuck since he's so big, with long hair and a full, mangy beard. The point is, he attacked me after I entered the cabin you assigned me, thinking I was some sort of intruder. He's currently living there, and I just need to get a new cabin assignment." She hurriedly prattled on, leaving herself breathless, her heart beating more than it should be. "I…I think his name is Jack something, Jack—" She stopped as the room swayed.

"Anyway, he's a bit caveman-like, not a real nice guy for scaring me like he did when he attacked me," she continued, and a warm hand caught her shoulder and steadied her. "I was just wondering if you could get me a new place."

"I can't believe it," he said, scratching his head. "That's not like him. Hold still, all right?"

She nodded affirmatively but lost her balance, suddenly feeling tired. She heard Nathan yell down the hall for someone and something else before she heard another man's heavy footsteps come in behind her and them talking about something not related to her.

"Is this the man you are talking about?"

Griswald's face appeared before hers, her peripheral view gone, and she ended up passing out before his image, more sickened than she had ever felt, her body numb, her vision fading, and unable to respond but hearing voices.

"Dear God! She's even bleeding on her backside! What the hell did you do to her?"

"Nothing! I didn't think it was that bad!" a man's voice said, heavy with

14

concern—a voice she was certain she recognized, although she still couldn't seem to open her eyes against the darkness.

"Get her to the hospital! Pick her up and let's get her into my car."

"No!" she murmured. "No hospital," she insisted through the darkness.

"Young lady, you have to be checked out." It was the last thing she heard as she passed out.

CHAPTER TWO

Jack carried her in his arms and then held her in the car up against him, applying pressure to both sides of her wound to keep her from bleeding any further; his boss drove like a madman to the town's emergency room. Had he had known she was still bleeding, he would have driven her there himself earlier that morning.

As Nathan checked them in, Jack carried her to the ER, where she would get prompt attention. He laid her gently down on the examining table, ensuring she lay on her good side so in case she did vomit she would not choke on it. He pulled up on her sweater and then tried to peel her first shirt layer off only to find it sticking to her. Thankfully, a nurse and doctor rushed in to take over, pushing him aside.

As the medical team ministered to her upper hip, he was able to see the mess of the exit wound where indeed she had been shot. Her barely healed stitches had been torn. The raw wound gaped open. He now blamed himself for hurting her, swearing under his breath.

"She's lost a lot of blood," said the doctor. "We need to know what blood type she is." He looked over to Jack, as if he would know. He shook his head no. Not wanting to take the extra time to get a blood check, the doctor tried to get Tasha to wake up enough to tell him. Then Jack realized how he could find out—that is, if she still wore them. He walked around to her head and pulled open the neck of her sweater, his fingers reaching in, coming into familiar contact with a set of dog tags. He pulled them out, laying them out in plain sight. All the information they needed on her. The doctor nodded gratefully for his quick thinking. "We got her. You can go to the waiting room now."

Jack hesitated, turning at the door. "Whatever you two do, don't use the shorter secondary tag."

The spry and shapely redheaded nurse paused, not understanding.

He clarified: "The tag is only to be placed in her mouth upon death."

"She's not going to die, Jack," assured the calm doctor. "She'll be fine. But I do need to know how she busted her stitches open and why she's still not in a hospital or under someone's care at the moment. I'll see you in a while," the doctor told him, then turned to his helper. "Get Jessica to pull up anything of her military medical records."

Jack walked back to where Nathan was still doing his best at checking Tasha in at the nurses' station. He spied the file folder he held. It was the same file Tasha had with her that morning. He asked for it and Nathan mindlessly shoved it over to him. Jack went through the paperwork in the file folder. It was her life in a nutshell. He pulled out her birth certificate, her DD214, and her passport. He shoved them in the direction of Nathan, helping him answer all that the hospital needed to know about their newest employee.

Once done, both men took a seat in the waiting room. Neither of them spoke, lost in their own thoughts, staring out into the waiting room's space at having taken this wayward stranger to a hospital—a girl that neither of them were expecting.

The receptionist called to them when she was done with Tasha's paperwork. Jack realized he still had her file in his hand. He retrieved them from the station nurse, tucking her life history back into the solitary file, stopping midway to pull them back out, now curious to learn more about their new employee. He glanced at the forms before resuming his seat next to his boss, Nate, the Big Raven.

That aroused Nathan's attention, both men realizing they did not know anything about the person they had just hired. Jack perused the files. Nathan leaned over just enough to read some of the information, before asking, "Did you know we hired a woman?"

"Nope."

Nate crossed his arms, letting them rest over the girth of his gut. "Did you confirm this one?" he continued asking.

"Yup." Then he added, "But so did you, Raven," calling him by his nickname.

Nate shifted back upright in his seat, thinking more. Nate's last name Amsel meant '*black bird*' in old German. Thus, the locals eventually nicknamed the old local bush pilot Black Raven. His crew called him Big Raven, or Raven for short.

"Which one of us finalized it?" asked Nate. He uncrossed his arms and shifted in his seat to lean toward Jack, keeping their conversation between them low although the waiting room was empty.

"You did, Raven."

Nate muttered to himself. "I swore I hired a guy. A guy named Tosh. And he wasn't supposed to be here for another month!"

"I thought so too. But we will have to get back to the office and see the original paperwork and her resume." Jack flipped through more of the paperwork and whistled low to himself. "I figured her a soldier, but not a wounded combat vet. College educated too. A degree in business management."

Nathan grunted. "Kinda figured that out when she used more than a two-syllable word in my office. She's going to kill our guys at Scrabble."

"Who the hell plays Scrabble in our crew?"

"Yeah, you got a point, kid." Nathan sat back up and crossed his arms over his pot belly and sighed, staring out into the room, although Jack knew what he was thinking.

Out of the blue, Nate asked in his usual gruff voice, "So, whadda ya think… of her?…so far? Besides the fact that you beat the snot out of her last night." He shifted his corpulent body as if he suddenly remembered something from earlier that morning, re-crossing his arms again, this time with the left arm on top of the right—a sign of his agitation over his next question. "Now what in the hell made you go ballistic on her?" Raven uncrossed his arms, putting a hand on Jack's shoulder. "I mean, I know you suffer from PTSD on occasions, but how in the hell did she remind you of a jihadist?" Nate's thick eyebrows shot up in earnest surprise at Jack.

Jack sighed. He knew he was going to catch hell for this. "Drake wasn't with me last night. He was at the vet's for his once-a-year physical and his grooming. I was in the basement when I heard the noise upstairs. She was already in, and it was dark in the cabin. I thought she was a thief when I tried to seize her in mid-action." Jack rubbed the back of his neck, swearing to himself, before continuing. "In fact, I didn't know it was a girl! I thought it was a young kid...and..." Jack hesitated to say it, more out of pride. "Um...well..." But he was amazed at what she was able to do. "She kicked my ass in the process...more like my nuts, Nate, and I got a terrible beard trimming in the process when we ended up with her holding a knife to my throat."

"She did what?" Raven's eyes were wide with surprise.

"—In fact, I'm fairly certain I won't be able to have kids now. They're still swollen," he admitted, grumbling more to himself over the prior ordeal.

"It explains the sudden change in your beard length then. Not a bad job, if she did that to ya."

Jack reached up to smooth down the shortened whiskers. "Nah, I had to finish trimming it this morning."

"I think she made you look better. More man than a wild critter." He chuckled to himself. "What's the name she called you?"

"What name?"

"Grizzly...Gris..." Nate fingered his lip, looking up, trying to remember. "Wall."

"Griswald?"

"Yeah...that's it! That's the name...Griswald." He laughed to himself.

"What's so funny about that name?"

"Oh...it just suits you. The crew has been trying to figure out a nickname for you for the past year." Seeing Jack's dark look, he continued, "Aw...come on, son. Everyone has a nickname. Hell, even my planes have nicknames! Especially since you have been growing that God-awful unkempt beard. Come to think of it, maybe that is why she attacked you, since she just got back from...where is it that she just got back from?" He scratched his head and then remembered. "Oh yeah, Afghanistan. Maybe you reminded her of a jihadist." He lightly smacked Jack's shoulder with the back of his hand and chuckled. "You're just missing the rag on your head, son."

Only his boss would call him *son*, but not in front of the crew. Nate Amsel was like a father figure to the entire crew. A good man. He had been flying most of his life. It was in his blood and he had worked hard to start his very own charter services so late in life. Living in Alaska was tough. It was the last frontier. It was a place where folks came to escape or find themselves. Some folks just blended in with the majestic surroundings, never to return. Others...well, if they didn't die up there, they left as soon as possible, weather permitting.

Jack was hired to help oversee the entire crew after his service time. Nate needed someone dependable and not afraid of the long hours. Nate knew he needed to lighten up his workload as he grew older but having no one to pass the family business down to, he now was looking for his replacement outside the family. Nate wanted Black Raven Aviation to continue as part of his legacy to the town of Seward. In fact, Nate's German surname was synonymous to the Alaskan Native Americans iconic god-bird, the Raven.

Jack was the airport's fueler when Nate had come across him one day, impressed with his ability to be authoritative with others in the general aviation world of Seward's only airport. When Jack first arrived, he, like so many others, had come with just a rucksack on his back and was camping out until he could earn enough to afford rent. But like most Alaskan towns, rent was just too high for those starting out.

Thus, Jack took the job when Nate told him it came with housing. It was one of the bonuses that came with working at Black Raven Aviation. Nate and his wife, Nora, had been smart a few decades earlier, investing in some land and building cabins for visiting summer hunters as side income. However, in the following years, Nate and his wife found out that they could make more money by renting the cabins full time, all year round, when housing became a premium. So half of the cabins they had built were rented long term, and the short-term rent paid off the land and the construction of the cabins. Seward was not a big town. Nor was it a highly sought-after place to live and work in, but there was still a housing shortage. Nate, being a small company, could not afford the normal wage of the average Alaskan aviation worker, so he offered 'free' housing in addition to the meager wage to attract skilled workers.

Learning to fly, for pennies on the dollar, was the other incentive for his workers.

The free housing for Jack was the deal sealer. He worked hard and was extremely loyal to the 'old man.' Yet the last thing Jack wanted was to share his place. He wanted his space and did not trust himself when it came to his 'war-mares.' He had been ground security support for a helo group and was one of three survivors in his fourth squad after a roadside bomb had gone off. The military doctors, having patched him up for the fourth time, had highly suggested it was time to seek a new career. He had completed four tours of duty before calling it quits. He was tired of seeing new faces rotate in, replacing the ones that didn't make it. Why he had not perished, when he should have several times, he would never know.

With Tasha showing up, well…it had gone bad. It only reinforced why he needed a place to himself. And he was one of the luckier employees to have a home to himself. The rest of the crew doubled up in each of the three two-room cabins that were available. The other seven vacation rentals paid for their living quarters. Those were usually full year-round by the summer tourists, and then in the fall and winter by the hunters.

Nate peered at Jack's pensive face, concerned for the man, not understanding what was going on in his head. "Hey, Nora and I do worry about you, son. Like I have said before, my door's always open." He swore to himself, unable to get Jack to respond.

Nate re-centered himself in his seat before continuing. "This messed-up war in the Middle East…We have no business being over there, getting our sons and daughters maimed and killed. For what? They say it's a fight against the terrorists threatening our country as their cover story, but most of us know better. It's definitely for controlling the oil fields. What the hell are Alaska's fields for then? The real effort needs to be not in drilling oil but more for alternative energy resources like tidal energy and solar energy during the summer months." He turned his head slightly at Jack, trying to gauge his reaction. Nothing. "Don't get me wrong, son. You did good over there and you survived. I just have my opinions."

"I know," Jack said flatly. He knew Nate was right. Being over there…he didn't want to think about it.

Nate's thick salt-and-pepper eyebrows shot up in surprise. He did not think Jack had heard anything he said.

"So, what's your decision on this Tasha?" Jack asked, switching the subject and curious to know Nate's intention, even though it was a bit late in the game to be changing their minds. It would not be legal, for one thing—firing her for being a woman.

"Oh…I—"

Nate was interrupted by the doctor walking through the double doors, approaching them. He took a seat adjacent to the two men. "Well, Tasha is going to be fine. We had to re-stitch her back up. She's been through a lot, I suppose. Records show she was shot. But there is recent bruising as if she had been in a fight." He looked at the two of them, as if hoping for an explanation. Neither of them said anything to the doctor, and he continued. "In addition, we took a quick internal look to make sure there was no further bleeding. But we need her to stay for a night or two at the clinic. We want to watch her for any further complications. Afterwards, she's going to need to be taken home and have someone look after her in addition to redressing her sutures daily, keeping them clean for about two weeks, and then bring her back for a quick check-up. Is her family here to do that?"

Nate sighed heavily. "Nope. It would be us, since we just hired her." Then, looking at Jack and giving him an encouraging hand on his shoulder, he said, "But I know Jack here can keep up with her and see to it that everything gets done."

Jack's head swiveled sharply in shock at Nate. For they had just been talking about whether to keep her on as an employee just moments ago! Obviously, Nate had made up his mind on keeping Tasha.

"Great!" came the doctor's response as he stood up and indicated for Jack to follow him. "Let's take you back and have the nurse show you what needs to be done once we release her. She's still heavily sedated after she regained consciousness and threw up on us. Nor happy about being here and started

20

fighting us about remaining in the hospital until we sedated her again."

They had gone past the first set of double doors, past the room where Jack had first taken her. The staff had wheeled Tasha into one of the rooms further, past another set of double doors where they had hospital beds for the long-term patients.

"I believe you will find the recliners next to the beds most comfortable to sleep in."

"Excuse me?" Jack stopped, forcing the doctor to turn around to further explain himself. "What do you mean for me to sleep in? I'm not staying here overnight."

"But you volunteered," the doctor stated flatly. "Tasha is not being cooperative when she is awake. All she wants to do is leave. We need someone to assure and keep her here for an observational night or two."

"What makes you think I can help you do that?" he sputtered. "Don't you have restraints or something like that for those patients?"

The doctor tilted his head at him. "Are you or are you not willing to help?"

Jack stood with his hands on his hips. He had not signed up for this, but he would do it for Nate for tonight. Afterwards, they needed to have a long discussion about their new employee. "Fine."

"I need to know now if you can do this or not, Jack." He waited, wanting to be sure about Jack's intentions.

"Yes, yes," assured Jack, nodding his head.

The doctor then turned, continuing to the second set of double doors leading to the long-term care section of the clinic with Jack in tow.

They approached her room, where the nurse had just finished checking her vitals. The staff had gotten her out of her clothes and into a gown and pretty much tucked into a bed. She was definitely knocked out. The doctor had them roll Tasha to her good side and the nurse proceeded to show him how to dress and care for the two wounds.

"How long will she be out like this?" he asked the nurse.

The petite brunette smiled at him, telling him that he had roughly four to six hours before she would come around again.

"Good, it'll give me enough time to get Drake a babysitter for the night, work assignments rearranged, and get some lunch."

"Don't forget to bring her a change of clothes, since we had to cut off the other shirt and sweater. It looks like she's been wearing these for a while." She gave Jack a neatly folded pile of Tasha's old clothes for him to take.

Terrific! he thought sarcastically. He certainly did not want to be going through her things back at the cabin.

He took a long look at her before the nurse interrupted his thoughts. "She's a pretty thing you boys hired. About time, too," she said, winking at him before leaving the room.

He smirked, realizing that the nurse had mistaken his expression. He turned to leave, knowing he had truly little time to get back before Tasha would be awake.

Jack went back to the hangar with Nate, checking in on the crew to see if they needed anything. Luckily, it was one of those slow days with not much work to do until a few parts arrived to fix the planes. He let two of his men go for the day. The other two remained and queried after their new hire. The guys were curious. He refused to fill them in until he would know more.

"Aw…come on, Jack," Jarvis whined. Hank nodded in agreement.

"Some other time, guys." He smiled dismissively at them.

Jack gave them further instructions, picking up his satellite work phone from the charging station as he left. His dog, Drake, greeted him warmly in his office, and Jack whistled to him to follow.

He stopped by Nate's office, looked in from the door, and almost missed seeing his boss behind the stacks of paper and aviation books. He gave his customary double-tap knock before entering.

Nate looked up and smiled. "You were right. We did think we hired a guy." Nate picked up the paperwork with the typo that was submitted by his secretary and bookkeeper, his wife Nora. Nora had made a serious transposing of the name.

"So we have an issue then, boss."

"Oh?"

"Where are you going to house her?"

"We can house her in…in…" He realized he did not have any more cabins. And like hell he was going to pay for a hotel. He looked at Jack a moment. "It is just you in cabin nine, correct?"

"Yeah, just Drake and I."

"Drake?—Oh yeah," Nate said upon spying the large black dog just behind Jack's leg. "That's right." To the dog he clapped his hands, beckoning to the gentle beast to come to him so he could pet him. "How's my good boy? Man, you got yourself just as cleaned up as Jack here. This girl must be really something for you two boys." The Newfoundland happily gave Big Raven a 'big kiss' as he gave the dog a good head rubbing.

Jack was not liking the sound of the conversation with his dog.

Raven separated from the ginormous dog. "Well, I have nowhere else to put her. I certainly don't want her to bunk down with the other men unless they offer to trade with her and come live with you," he commented as he leaned forward on his desk. "You two can't civilly share a two-bedroom cabin?" his boss asked as the black dog leaned into him with his whole body.

"It's just that—"

Raven interrupted Jack before he could come up with a lame excuse.

"Hell, where do the women bunk nowadays during wartime or in the field?" Nate shrugged his shoulders in question. "I mean times have changed since Vietnam, but don't you all eat and sleep pretty much in the same areas? I mean both of you are combat vets and you should get along just fine. I can't see her rooming with the other four hounds, nor would I trust my own daughter with any of them."

"You don't have a daughter," Jack commented drily.

"The point is, I feel she would be best in your cabin. At least you have some integrity." He raised an eyebrow at Jack. "At least, I hope so."

Jack rolled his eyes at him. "Fine. You need to take care of Drake for me, since I have to babysit our new hire at the hospital for the next two days. And she can stay with me, if that is what you've decided, but the moment she uses my razor to shave her legs, she's out." He jerked his thumb toward the door behind him.

"A razor?" Nate asked, looking at Jack's bearded face. "You don't even shave. Why the hell would you care?"

Jack's serious look melted into a slight smile and they both laughed. Then it occurred to Jack: "What happens if she doesn't want to stay?"

Nate pursed his lips a moment before answering. "Well, from what little I gathered about her this morning, she really has no choice. But I really can't foresee you having any major problems with her. She doesn't strike me as the petty type. Once she meets the crew, I can't see her wanting to trade with anyone—not that the guys are bad, mind you…" Nate was wanting to say more, but decided to say, "But…oh hell, once she gets to know you a bit more, she'll warm up to you. Just keep from beating her up again, all right, son?"

Jack bit his lower lip to keep from saying anything. The jibe would be a constant reminder of how much at fault he was for her current condition.

"Look, I know you didn't mean to hurt her. I'm not faulting you for it. But do tread lightly, mind your Ps and Qs with her until she is at least healed, and we get to know her more."

"Fine. We'll go with the current arrangements for now." But Jack was sure it would be the start of World War III. Jack commanded Drake to stay with Nate, after verifying that the older man would babysit his dog for as long as need be, and turned to leave his office.

"Jack?"

He stopped and expectantly looked back at his boss.

"Drake's in good hands, I'll go pick up some dog chow for him for the next few nights. Now go look after my newest investment."

Jack raised an eyebrow at this comment. But Nate did not expound.

"Heard you got a new hire in town," Kate commented to Jack as he busily stuffed his face with a late lunch of meatloaf and mashed potatoes. The warm meal was desperately needed. She stood, looking over the roomful of customers, with a pot of coffee ready for a refill should anyone call upon her.

Kate was a tall, busty woman in her mid-thirties. She had been around the block a few times and had been keen on Jack since his arrival in town. However, she knew better about Jack ever looking her way. But she could not help but flirt with the young man. "Say, did you trim your beard?"

Jack kept chewing as he looked up at her.

But she continued. "Oh yeah, you did. It looks a lot better, although I find you looked far better without a beard. You know the beard makes you look older." He lowered his fork, as if he was going to say something, but Kate continued. "Slow down there, you'll have indigestion before you know it, with Tom's cooking—if you can call it cooking. Anyway, bring the new hire in soon. I could use another customer. We need more business at this time of year."

A customer a few booths down waved, getting Kate's attention. She smiled sexily at him, giving Jack a small squeeze on his shoulder, and left him in peace. He turned his head to watch her walk down to the other table. She wasn't a bad-looking woman, just too big and a tad old for his tastes. Yet it had probably been close to a year since he'd had anyone in his bed. The last one was rather obligatory and went against his tastes.

During his travels through Alaska, he had encountered a few places where he was welcomed in a home only to have the host 'share' his wife or other female family member for the night. Women were few and far between. He could have his fair share with those that threw themselves on him, just because he was someone new and interesting. But he seemed to have lost his appetite when it came to sex. He wasn't sure if it was because he was just getting older, had been diagnosed with PTSD, or lost his girlfriend to another man while he was away in the Middle East—or a combination of those three.

But he decided it was the long gray days that seemed to keep him in some sort of a repressed mode. Not like he resented it. He was okay. He did not mind the 'numbness.' He still had not found what he was looking for in his life. He had a fantastic job and a simple life in the *wilds of Alaska*. He enjoyed the outdoors, especially the fishing and hunting. He hung out with a few of his co-workers from time to time. But he spent most of his time with his buddy Chad, learning about sled dogs and helping his friend train for the Iditarod. He enjoyed, most of all, sitting outdoors and taking in the views of the sea and mountains. It was when he felt the most complete and at peace.

He took his dinner roll, tearing it into two pieces, and mopped up what was left of the gravy and mashed potatoes. By the time Kate got back, he stood up, not letting her engage him in any more one-sided conversations, and generously paid his bill, telling her to keep the change. He sweetened it by giving her a quick kiss to her overly made-up cheek and promptly left her beaming at him.

He burped his satisfaction of the hearty meal as he jumped into his old pickup truck to head home. As his truck rumbled along the main highway, he noted the time on his watch, knowing he had only two more hours to go before she would possibly awake. A nap was in order, along with a shower and then to tackle the process of finding the girl a new change of clothes in her unpacked gear.

Once home, he was grateful for the quiet solitude of the cabin. He flopped onto his bed and set the alarm on his watch. The previous night had not been a good night's rest, with all the pain he'd had to deal with from their fight. He did not think his balls would ever stop stinging. His fingertips found the small welt on his head where she had slammed her head against his, and he paused, remembering how hard she had fought. He exhaled heavily at the memory, embarrassed. He did not need to be plagued with more guilt at having hurt her, which had kept him up most of the night, wondering about this new stranger, and a lady at that. With these thoughts racing around in his head, he fell asleep.

An hour later his alarm went off, and he begrudgingly got up. He sat at the edge of his bed and rubbed his face a couple of times to stimulate blood flow. He felt like he had slept for hours instead of the allotted one hour. He got up, made his way to the shower, and then changed into new clothes.

He stopped at the second bedroom door, hesitating, realizing that it would be the last time he had the cabin to himself. In addition, he felt weird having to go through someone else's stuff—much less a girl's personal things. But curiosity got the better of him.

"Ah, what the hell." he grumbled, and went to her duffel bag on the desk first and upended it on her bed.

"Bingo!"

The girl packed tight, but she had all her military gear and about five days of civilian clothes. He unrolled the clothes only to find that they were too lightweight to be worn here in the North. The girl was going to freeze to death if she remained for the winter. He finally came across her undergarments, slowing down to examine them more out of curiosity, only to chastise himself for ogling. It wasn't like they were lacy, fancy, or colorful. In fact, they were thin, feminine 'whitie-tighties.'

"By golly, I didn't even know that they made these for women," he mumbled, thumbing the material absentmindedly.

Jack grabbed a pair of military sweatpants, a flimsy sweater, a T-shirt, and a pair of clean socks. He then shoved all the rolled clothes back into the duffel bag; the few that were unrolled, he haphazardly shoved in on top, closing the bag, and then put the duffel bag back on top of the desk. On his way to the front door, he grabbed another winter coat from the nearby closet. The one she was wearing that morning was not enough to keep her warm.

He pulled into the clinic's parking lot after he picked up a six-pack of beer, some snacks, and a sudoku book from a gas station on the way over. He shoved an unopened bottle into a koozie, along with another bottle, and put it into the grocery bag full of snacks. If he was going to pull guard duty in a hospital, at least he would do it in comfort and style in the big recliner chair awaiting him.

He checked in at the nurses' station and then made his way to her room. She was still out. Good. He wasn't ready to deal with her just yet. Jack settled into the large recliner, found the lever, and raised his feet up. *Perfect,* he thought to himself. He seriously needed to think about getting one of these chairs for the cabin. He popped the cap on the bottle and opened his bag of beef jerky and commenced on his first puzzle, trying to avoid looking at the sleeping girl close by.

It was not long before she shifted in her slumber, her movement a respite from the monotonous number puzzle he kept plodding at. Her face was serene, her hair the color of pale honey. He really could not tell how long her hair was, for it was always pinned up in a messy double ponytail in which the tail of her hair was northward instead of ending southward. Her eyebrows were full and unadulterated. She did not look like she wore much makeup, from what he could tell. Her lips were well-proportioned and the color of light salmon. *She isn't bad looking*, he thought, taking in more details of her as she slept.

He looked down at the puzzle book as she murmured in her sleep, shifting again. The last thing he needed to be doing was staring at her. He took another long swig of his beer, placing the bottle back on the floor out of sight between the recliner and the nightstand, and decided to finish a puzzle as he aimlessly fingered out another beef strip from the packet on his lap. He was pretty much at home and comfortable. He had had worse jobs.

A good hour had passed, or so he thought, in that he had completed twelve puzzles. Now full and contented, he shifted in his recliner, pulling the one throw from behind his head, spreading it over himself, and reclining the chair for the long night. He was bushed after the past twenty-four hours. Since her arrival, he had not had any decent amount of sleep, and tonight was not going to be as easy, being in a recliner instead of his own bed.

"Incoming!" The shout rattled him awake.

He searched the darkness, thinking he was back in Iraq. Then, he slowly recognized things in the dim light of the room and remembered where he was. He saw her prone form in the hospital bed, trying to protect itself from an unknown attack. Then she jerked, her hand going to her hip, whimpering in pain as she talked out loud in her sleep. "I…I've been hit!" A moment's hesitation. "No, Sergeant!" And then some more anguished throat sounds.

The nurse came running in as he was trying to protect Tasha from her own jerky movements. It was obvious she was reliving the day she was shot.

"Tasha! Tasha, wake up," he coaxed her.

The nurse came over to make sure she had not pulled the needle out in her arm—the one they had left in in case they needed to take more blood or attach an IV bag again. Between the two of them, they got her to wake without further thrashing.

Tasha awoke with a jerk in their grasps, not recognizing her environment. "How did I get here?" She looked around, searching, catching sight of the nurse first. "I was in an office earlier…" Then she turned to Jack and recognized him. "You…" she said heavily, cocking her head at him. She tried to back away.

The nurse told her to take it easy, that he was not going to hurt her.

"What am I doing here…What is this place?"

The nurse answered her questions.

"What? No. Oh no. No, I am not staying here." She struggled to get up, suddenly realizing she had a hospital gown on and a needle still in her arm from the earlier transfusion. They both held her down in the bed. Jack ended up pinning her down with his hand, careful not to hurt her again, nodding to the nurse that he had her.

"Now, listen," Jack told her as she pushed against his hold. "Stop, just stop! You need to stay…at least one full day to satisfy the staff that you are in the clear after losing so much blood and busting those stitches of yours! So, quit being hardheaded and just do as they say."

"Hardheaded? You of all people would know who had the harder head! What in the hell did you do to me?"

"He actually carried you in here," the nurse interrupted, doing her best to ease the tension.

Tasha swung her head around to the nurse in surprise, and then back to 'Griswald's' visage. He tentatively lessened his weight on her when she did not attempt to sit back up. She could not imagine him doing that, given the way he had initially acted toward her. *How long have I been out?* She did not realize that she had spoken her thought out loud when they answered her.

It had been nearly a day. She sat there stunned. Until her brain, again, registered her predicament and that she could not afford the hospital stay, much less comprehend that she was hired or had even been on the job for one whole day! She started to push aside the bed linens, getting back up slowly now that the pain in her side reminded her to sit still. She winced.

"I'll get you another pain pill, hon. Just stay put or have Mr. Lassiter help you to the bathroom." The nurse left the room.

"Easy there, champ. No need to mess up those new stitches."

"I can't stay here."

"Why not?"

"I can't afford something like this! Not without a job, which I am certain I no longer have! That man, I was in his office earlier, just witnessed me being weak and unable to do a job."

"That man saved your life by noticing how much blood soaked through your sweater. That same man also hired you as of this morning, and your job does come with medical care and health insurance. It will cover this," Jack reasoned with her. He looked pointedly at her, then tried to push her gently back down when she resisted stubbornly. "What?" he asked, exasperated.

"I *do* have to use the restroom," she said, holding up a finger at him, "but… without you."

"That's fine. But how do I know that you won't bolt the second you turn that corner?"

"I have no idea what you did with my clothes," she commented more to herself, looking around for them and not seeing anything. "It's probably thirty below outside by now. So I'm trapped until I can find my clothes."

Jack smirked, telling her that would be highly advisable and was glad that she was capable of some common sense. She gave him a gimlet look. He came to the other side of her bed to give her a hand up. It was a tentative peace offering on his part.

She placed her hand in his large steady hand. Straightening up proved to be somewhat difficult for her, making her gown fall open on her backside. "Crap," she said indignantly, not catching it fast enough. But he moved to catch it before letting it fall forward any further, pulling it back into place, with her more in his protective embrace. Without looking, he found the strings to retie them, as she placed a hand on his chest to steady herself with his aid.

"Thank you," she said, rather embarrassed by the large, hairy stranger in front of her.

"I know these gowns are the number one reason I wouldn't want to be here either."

She smiled weakly, embarrassed to look at him in her current state.

He seemed to recognize this and prodded her, "Let's get you to the porcelain altar before you have any more problems." He helped guide her the few steps to the room and closed the door for her privacy.

She did not take long, and he helped her back into bed. After both settled back into their respective places, she turned on her good side to face him. At first, he ignored her as he thumbed through the book for the next puzzle. But her gaze eventually made him annoyed enough that he said, without looking up from the puzzle, "What?"

"Why are you staying?"

"To keep you from leaving."

"Okay, I promise to stay as long as I know my gear is safe at your cabin and the dock workers don't decide to push my car into the bay."

"Your stuff is fine. Your car we will take care of later." He was able to at least get two numbers jotted down.

She kept staring at him.

Acting disinterested in her, he continued to work the sudoku. "Now what?" he finally asked, unable to take it any longer.

"You don't need to stay here. Obviously it's not by choice. You have my word"—his eyebrows raised at this— "about remaining here. I just need to know where to report to as soon as they release me."

He put his pen down and studied her. She did not flinch that time. She only watched. The dim lighting of the room made her eyes a deep, difficult-to-read gray green. The only light was the reading light over his recliner. He took his time appraising her form that lay beneath the bedlinens before coming back to her face. "You will be reporting to me in the morning with any luck if you behave yourself here and do as they say."

She was not satisfied. "Then where do I report to you? I need a bit more details than what you're giving me."

He sighed. "You won't be reporting to work anytime soon. That's for certain." He noted her stiffening at this news. "It's only temporary. Besides, we weren't ready for you for at least another month!" Putting aside his book, tucking it between the side of his leg and the chair's arm, he leaned over to grab his beer for a quick swig before continuing. "I am to take you home with me for the next two weeks." He added, "I have the wonderful new job of babysitting you."

"What?" she exclaimed. Then he saw her sniff the air. "Is that beer?" She propped herself up further on her elbow to look.

"I'm not sharing, and you can't have any with the medications they've pumped into you."

"I don't want any, and I'm surprised that they let you in here with that."

"They don't know I have it and I don't care. I am making this job as comfortable as I can while I am 'assigned' to you." His voice showed his exasperation.

"Trust me, I don't want it, but I am starving. I suppose you have something decent to eat. I haven't eaten anything since getting on that ferry in Seattle coming up here. Do you have anything to eat?"

"Just some beef jerky." He pulled out the bag. He was willing to share those as he remembered his time spent on the ferry getting up there, only to realize that it was a two-day trip.

She greedily snatched the bag from him.

"You mean to tell me you haven't eaten in two days?"

Over a mouthful, she said, "More like three." Her first priority was chewing on the dried meat. "It wasn't like I was able to grab something to eat since I arrived here." She grabbed another fistful before handing the bag back to him, empty.

He sighed heavily. "Do I need to go get you something more substantial?"

"Nah"—still chowing down on the meat—"I'm good for now."

He watched her polish off the rest of the jerky in her hands before she asked for some water. He obligingly got her water from a large pitcher provided by the hospital and poured some in a glass that came with a straw.

"Thanks." She watched him resettle back into the recliner, appraising the man in front of her, not meaning to stare.

"Now what are you looking at?" he asked, mildly disgruntled.

"You."

"What about me?" he asked, watching her avert her eyes momentarily, but decided to forge on in their conversation.

"I just don't think I have ever seen anyone as hairy as you," she added lightly, looking down at her hands, as if wondering how the strange and obtrusive needle got into the back of her one hand.

"Wait—you mean to tell me you've never seen a man with a beard? And you spent time in the military?"

Tasha stopped in her self-observation. "Well, never seen one with as long a beard and hairstyle like yours."

"I just cut it this morning to even out the bad trim job you gave me early last night."

"I thought it looked different. But you are still pretty grizzly looking." She smiled coyly.

It was the first smile she had bestowed on him since their initial meeting, nabbing his full attention.

"Any man outside the military is going to look hairy and unkempt to you until you readjust to the civilian life," Jack commented drily, shifting in his recliner, placing the sudoku book back in his lap, and making a decisive mark in a blank square.

She was quiet again in the pregnant pause between them. "You're prior military too," she commented as either a second thought or trying to change the subject.

"Huh?" His head snapped back up at her.

She pointed to his one ring. It was his military service ring. "And the way you fight," she said, referring to the previous night when he had jumped her. "Which branch?"

"Does it matter?" Jack responded tiredly.

She shrugged a shoulder at him. "Just trying to get to know you, since it's obvious I am going to have to work with you on the flight line."

"You won't be working with me. Now go to sleep so we can get the hell out of here."

"How come?" She stiffened on her supporting elbow, making her raise a tad higher from her bed.

"Fuelers and schedulers don't normally work side by side with electricians." He closed his eyes, hoping she would follow suit.

"Oh." He heard her shift in her bed. "Can you tell me more about the place?"

"Go to sleep."

"I can't. I'm up now."

He grabbed his book and tossed it lightly to her so that it landed just in front of her. "Do a couple of puzzles. Some of us need sleep after watching over you." He watched her facial expression turn to surprise and then into a more serious and annoyed expression. He chose to ignore her, again closing his eyes for some shuteye. Jack felt her eyes on him, remembering their unforgettable gray green color. When he heard the pages rustle, he let go and fell asleep.

The next morning the nurses' commotion of doing their routine monitoring caused him to start in his chair. Recognizing the male nurse, he motioned to Jack that all was okay, especially after Jack noticed that Tasha's bed was empty. "She's in the bathroom. I'm just here to check her stitches and change the bandages."

"So, are we good to go home this morning, Chad?"

"Not yet…still waiting on the doctor's final approval. He should be here sometime around ten."

Jack sighed heavily and lay back in the chair. He knew he had gotten some serious sleep—better than he thought he would get—but he still felt like he could use more as he slowly let his body awaken.

"So, man, this is like a new thing for you." Chad smiled brightly at him. "Never dated girls in this manner. This one"—he looked at the board for her stats—"Tasha, she must be serious enough to stay in a hospital all night," Chad joked.

Jack gave him an annoyed look.

Chad held up a truce hand at him. "Hey, I call it how I see it."

"Then you need to learn to take better assessments of the *entire* situation," Jack came back grumpily.

"Oh?"

"Don't you start, too. I had to clamp down on the flight line guys."

"I bet. She's pretty cute if you ask me."

"An angry female grizzly is cute to you, Chad. Just do me a favor and stay away from her."

Chad raised an eyebrow at his grumpy friend.

"—at least for now." Jack ran a hand through his thick hair.

Chad was one of the first citizens in Seward that Jack had become friends with when he had arrived. Jack had run into Chad and his father, Malik, out in the woods one day on one of his many fishing trips. They were Alaskan natives, in which his dad was passing on the hunting and gathering traditions of their people to his son. That day, Jack watched how they caught salmon with their handmade nets and then bare hands for added sport. Fascinated, Jack ended up tagging along, learning more about what to eat and not to eat off the land and the tidal plains.

Since then, Jack had been adopted by Chad's family. Chad's mother did make the best gooseberry pie in addition to his father making the best smoked salmon. Jack's mouth watered in hunger. He was hungry.

"Mom's been asking about you. She wants to know when you are going to show up again. What have you been doing lately? Haven't seen much of you these past few weeks."

Jack didn't answer as Tasha stepped out of the bathroom. Chad turned to look at her, asking if everything was okay and if she was needing anything for pain.

"No, no more pain pills, they put me out. I don't want to sleep right now. More than anything, is there any way I can get something to eat instead?"

"Sure," said Chad. "It's better that you have something in your stomach before you take another pill. You will be wanting it soon. It's been a while since the last one." He patted the bed for her to take a seat while he took her vitals and then asked her to roll on her side so that he could check her bandages.

"Meals come from the diner just down the street. I would suggest you get your eggs scrambled, though," Chad commented has he continued his inspection.

Jack watched them from where he stood near the recliner. She faced him again, giving up her bad side to Chad as he drew up her bedsheets for some moderation of dignity, and then he told her he was going to slide her gown over her hip after undoing the lower drawstring. Jack shifted his stance when Chad exposed her hip to examine her exit wound. Jack noted the smaller front entry wound, the only mar on her fair and flawless skin. No doubt a tiny hole by comparison, as his eyes followed the curvature of her hip up until the bedsheets prevented him from further exploration.

Chad was professional about it, but Jack swore he was taking way too long for his tastes, as if he was teasing him. "Okay, let's have you roll onto your back a moment to let me see the front one."

Tasha did as she was asked.

"Yeah, this one is not so bad. We are going to keep from covering this one since it is smaller. Giving it air will help it heal faster, but you will still need to keep an anti-bacterial ointment on it when you have your helper attend to your backside every day."

"My helper?"

"Yeah, you are only allowed home if you have someone to watch over you for the next two weeks to clean and change your dressing. Kinda strange you pick the man who shot you to be your helper," Chad teased, with a knowing grin.

Tasha shifted uncomfortably, being on her back, trying to keep her body weight off the more tender rear wound.

"He didn't shoot me—"

"I didn't shoot her—" They both corrected Chad at the same time.

"Just joking with you two. Let's get you back on your side again. You don't seem comfortable on your back," noted Chad. He covered her hip with her gown and turned her back on her good side, facing Jack.

"No. You're right, the pain is starting to kick back in," she told Chad. Jack had gotten the subtle hint as she flashed her eyes at him.

"We'll get that taken care of soon after you eat something. And from what I can tell, you should have no problem going home around noon. Anything else from me?" Chad asked as he walked to the door.

She shook her head at Chad.

"See ya 'round. Try to keep from getting shot again, will you?" he reminded her, pointedly looking over to Jack.

Tasha swiveled her gaze back on Jack. When she was sure Chad was out of earshot, she said, "Should I be worried about hanging around you for the next two weeks?"

By now Jack had folded his arms over his chest and just gave her a smirk of *as if.* "Just be glad I chose to attack you and didn't have my shotgun available to use." He grabbed his stuff from the hidden side of the recliner to take out and dump in a trash bin.

"Now, what do you want for breakfast?" he asked after he returned to her room.

She gave him her order—an order fit for about three men to eat.

"What?" she asked when he did not move right away.

"I'm hungry too, but I don't even think I can eat that much."

"You probably haven't had to go without food for any longer than a day," she commented drily, looking him up and down the length of his bulk. He was not going to enter this *pissing contest*. She had no idea what he had gone through.

"Fine, stay put."

"Like where am I going to go?" she asked, throwing her arms up in the air and letting them drop, just as infuriated with him, as she indicated her current attire. "You have my clothes somewhere, and I haven't even been able to locate my shoes!"

He smirked at her. He was grateful that he had slid her shoes underneath his recliner. Her comment was the ultimate telltale sign that she had been up most of the night looking for her personal effects. The rest of her stuff was most likely frozen in the cab of his truck. He was glad he did not leave his keys out for her to find, for he would have been without a vehicle.

"Hey, Jack. There you go." The waitress slid the take-out order to him. "Who ya feeding, anyway? The Army?"

He paused, smiling at an irresistible response. Tasha *was* the Army. Fresh out from serving her time. "Ya, you could say that," he replied, not wanting to expound on who was sharing in the large breakfast order, and taking the double-bagged meals with him. He dashed to his truck in the light drizzle and made the short drive back all within the half hour.

Jack came back to her room only to find Chad chatting with her. Seeing their easy camaraderie instantly erased his good humor and he inexplicably wanted Chad to go jump off a cliff.

"Hey, there!" Chad exclaimed. "You brought us breakfast! Smells great."

"What are you doing here?" Jack asked.

"Ah—my job?" Chad stated the obvious, giving his buddy a puzzled expression that only Jack could see.

Jack gave him a hard look as Chad opened his hand on his lap to reveal a mini paper cup with Tasha's pain med in it.

Chad raised an eyebrow at his friend before getting up from the edge of the bed. Chad turned to Tasha. "You need to have at least eaten a bellyful before taking this pill. Otherwise, you will end up upchucking the darn thing."

"Trust me, she ordered enough for an entire squad." Jack moved the rolling tray table to deposit their meals. "Hands off the biscuit and gravy, lady. That one's mine."

"Still a Southern boy at heart, aren't you," commented Chad. "Well, I gotta do my rounds. I'll be back to check on you, Tasha." He winked at her and she beamed a hell of a smile at him, making Jack clench his jaw before resuming his post in the recliner.

She sat up and eagerly tore into the bag, pulling out the various covered trays. She handed him his, along with some silverware and his puzzle book, and then tore into hers as fast as she could without being unladylike.

They ate in silence. He opened the book she had returned only to find that every puzzle had been completed. All fifty plus of them. There was no way she could have done them all and still had taken her time looking around the room for her personal things all night unless she had stayed up the entire night.

"Did you even sleep?" The accusatory question shattered the cold heavy air between them.

She contemplated him sitting there before answering. "Some, why?" She shrugged a half-hearted shoulder, then noted the puzzle book at his side, which he had opened and was resting on his lap. "Sorry for not leaving any puzzles for you to work on." But she wasn't. It was her way of getting back at his nasty demeanor, and to be honest, she had been bored out of her gourd the previous night, unable to sleep. Like hell she was going to sit up all night looking at this grizzly-looking man. She had kept occupied with the book at first, until she had heard the first small snores coming from him. Only then did she get up to search for her clothes in all the closets and dressers in the room, only to find none— not even her shoes! She had then taken a walk around the ward to scout out the place they had taken her, only to find that the nurses' station was in full frontal view of the escape door and the two night nurses on duty had stared her down until the urge to bolt decided to retreat. She had returned to her room and settled back down to do more puzzles until a nurse gave her another pain reliever, and it knocked her out for the rest of the evening.

He sighed heavily before scraping up the last bite of his breakfast and closed the lid. Their eyes met—his blue to her green ones.

"Look, you don't have to sit here the whole entire time. I'm a grown adult here."

"Really? That's funny, I wouldn't have known that," he said sarcastically, pointing at her with the box in his hand, "since you arrived unannounced, got yourself hurt, and then didn't tell anyone you needed help."

She twisted some to face him but found she couldn't go far with the two sets of fresh, stiff stitches sending pain up through her side, making her wince and more annoyed.

"Don't you even dare place the blame on me, buster! First of all, I did send word back of when I was hoping to arrive over a week ago. And that cabin of yours was supposed to be mine. It was my cabin only...not...not with some asshole taking up residence there. And the last thing I expected was to be assaulted and have my stitches torn open again. It wasn't like you even gave a flip in the first place to give me enough time to get dressed and check out the damages on myself!" She swore, the effort to raise her voice at him causing her muscles to pull more on the new stitches. She eased back slowly on her backside, shoving a pillow to the rear of her hip to cushion the rear wound.

"I wouldn't even be here if it wasn't for you!" She folded her arms over herself. "What in the hell is your major malfunction with me?" She turned her head to look at him.

Just then, Chad returned as promised, asking if she had taken her pain reliever. The pill had still been untouched, since she had been eating. But now she had lost her appetite, the air thick with tension. Chad was either oblivious or just ignoring the silence, and after scouting her tray and seeing over half of it devoured, he picked up the medicine cup, shaking it, to remind her to swallow so that he could verify that she had taken it as directed.

Tasha did not want to take the darn thing, even though her side hurt like hell, her pride standing in the way with the man who made her life a real pain in the arse—or in her case, her upper hip. If the job description would have included him in the picture, she would have never taken the job. But what has done was done. She could not back out now. Besides, where was she going to go?

She loved her parents, but she did not want to move back in. It was important to her to show them that she could be on her own. She did not want to be like other typical women who were well cared for, unable to function on their own. Sometimes she wished she was like that, but most times she was grateful she wasn't, thinking how crazy it was to live a life that sheltered and not fully experience it.

In fact, joining the military had been her way of showing she could handle the worst, be tough, and with any luck find a husband. But that last part had failed too. Just like college. Just like high school. She was not lucky like the other girls, who had it made in the shade. She knew it would have made her parents happier had she found *Mr. Right* right away. She had been swept off her feet a few times, only to be hurt. But she had fallen madly in love with one of them, although nothing serious had happened between them. But he was now dead because of her.

Staff Sergeant Herrington. Her squad sergeant in Afghanistan. He was everything she had been looking for in her ideal husband. Problem was, he was married—and because of her he was killed when he had tried to come back after her when she had been shot, too stunned to move during the ambush near their base.

"Hey there, you all right?" Chad asked, breaking into her errant thoughts. He had been standing there waiting on her to take the damn pill.

In one determined movement, she snatched the cup, popped the pill, and chugged down a large gulp of water, deciding it was not worth pursuing the current conversation with a man unable to talk much more than a grizzly bear could to a human.

She tried to lie back but was uncomfortable, lying on her good side for now, unfortunately facing *his* direction. She glared warningly at him, then broke her gaze by closing her eyes, hoping to block him out of her mind. She felt the effects of the medication taking hold of her body, numbing it, including her brain. With a full belly and the meds spreading through her, it was not long before she was out.

All she wanted to do was sleep more, but the noise and someone insisting she wake up made her start again. It was the doctor that had attended to her, and she immediately checked for her grumpy guardsman, only to find his chair empty.

"Don't worry, Jack will be back. He's gone to get you a change of clothes from his truck, since we had to cut on your shirt and sweater to gain access to your wound. I just wanted to look again and to see how you're feeling with these pain meds." He indicated to her hip that he was going to expose her again. She gave him a *go ahead* nod and he started to move the gown aside.

"What time is it?" she asked groggily.

"It's a little after noon. We got you through the first twenty-four hours." He pressed a little too hard near her exit wound and she inhaled sharply. He apologized before continuing. "It's going to hurt a while longer. You managed to re-tear some of your inside sutures too. I would highly advise you to lie still for a while, at least two weeks. No heavy lifting, no side-to-side movements. Make sure both wounds get cleaned and dressed every day, especially your rear one. All right?"

She nodded her head as she stared ahead, her future as empty and as void as the recliner near her bed. *What in the hell did I get myself into?* she wondered. Now she would be living with an unbearable man in a remote cabin in the Far North.

"Did you catch all that, Jack?" asked the doctor.

The mention of his name made her swing her head around, looking over her shoulder to spy him standing just behind the doctor, making the room spin on her as if she were buzzed from too much alcohol. He, too, was looking at her backside, her buttocks exposed to this strange man, much to her discomfort. She pulled at her gown to cover herself.

"Yup," he drawled. Tasha was not sure if Jack was really answering the doctor's question.

"Take it easy on her for the next two weeks. She's good to go home now, and we'll contact Nate to let him know that she's in your care." Turning back to Tasha, he said, "I'll see you in two weeks for a quick checkup, okay?"

She nodded. *If I survive this beast's ministrations*, she thought grumpily.

Jack laid a pile of folded clothes at the end of her bed along with the shoes she had worn on her first day at Black Raven. It was her Army workout grays and sweats, and a coat that was not hers. "Get dressed. And meet me outside your room." Then, he rattled a small prescription bottle at her. "Then I need to get one of these down your throat when we get home." He left, giving her the privacy to change.

She sighed heavily, still tired.

The entire trip home, including a stop at the world's tiniest grocery store, was like watching a movie underwater. She felt like a zombie the entire time. It was not until they reached the familiar cabin that she perked up some. She was eager to fall back into a warm bed.

"Hey…you all right?" Jack asked when he had turned off the truck's engine and she continued sitting there staring out the front windshield.

She groggily turned her head at him as if her body was propped up and immobilized by some invisible constraint. He could sense the drug still had its grip on her. She hadn't said a word since they had left the clinic.

"You need help getting out?"

In her world she answered immediately. In his world, it took a half minute to register and then she nodded she could handle it. She opened the passenger door; the heavy door swung wide open and the cool Alaskan air swooped in, flooding the cab. She slid out, only to disappear straight down and out of his sight.

"Shit!" he cursed. *Stubborn-assed woman!* He jumped out his side and ran around his old, battered pickup truck, only to find her struggling to stand back up off his running board.

"I'm fine, just slipped on…on…on some ice?" she murmured, confused, now noting the patchy wet spots around the front yard, if one could really call Alaska's native brambles and small trees that, and the driveway area as if it had just appeared out of thin air.

He grabbed her arm and got her back on her feet, not letting go of her until he had her seated on the sofa inside. He would get her in bed later, but not until he could get the few bags of groceries in, preferably before the wildlife could grab ahold of it. One had to be quick in those parts: even though a town had sprouted there and existed for the past one hundred plus years, the animals still roamed as if it was just another bump in the wilderness.

It wasn't even ten minutes tops that he had gotten all the groceries unloaded and into the refrigerator, before he came back around the sofa to retrieve her, only to find her passed out asleep on the couch. He decided to leave her be, grabbing a heavy fur throw to cover her and keep her warm. They were home and she would be out for a while, so he thought he might as well work on a few things around the place, as he started a fire in the hearth.

She would be awake in a few short hours, needing another pill. He had to admit she woke like clockwork every six hours. He headed over to the kitchen where he had bought enough supplies for them for a week, and he started making a large batch of chili in a crockpot. He had nailed a deer a few months earlier, and he had plenty of venison on hand. It would easily last them for a while, since he had no intentions of leaving the cabin other than to check on the crew from time to time and ensure that they remained on schedule.

After getting all the ingredients together, he diced and added them to the crockpot to simmer for the next four hours. He decided to go over some paperwork he had brought home with him to help keep Nate on top of things.

It had been a good summer of flying. That year's booming tourism had made the company a lot of money doing chartered flights through the Kenai Fjords— enough to almost buy another plane and expand their operations. Yet all those built-up flight hours created a lot of maintenance checks on most of the fleet. Come the dead of winter, they would be busy flying again, but mainly doing supply runs to the smaller outlying villages. They would be needing all the help they could get. The last thought reminded him of their newest employee. Would she be up to the challenges of learning to fly? And would she be able to pass the flight physical? That is, if she was willing to learn how to fly.

Now he wished he had access to her files again, but Nate had taken them from him the previous afternoon. He thought he remembered her resume stating that she already knew how to fly or was just short of having her license. He was hoping that would be the case. It would take too long starting from the ground.

They would have to wait and see what the girl could or couldn't do. From where he stood in the kitchen, he heard her make a small sound and then shift on the sofa. It was silent again. He waited, not wanting to have to attend to her just yet. He picked up the pile of paperwork and took it over to the sitting chair adjacent to the sofa, using the coffee table as his makeshift desk. He looked over at her, noting her facial features as she slumbered. They were right, she was not a bad-looking girl. She was feminine, but tomboyish without being 'boyish,' so to speak. From the few short hours since encountering her, Jack knew that her prior military experience would help her stand up to most men, especially their oddball crew that Nate had managed to piece together. But he knew how the guys could be. Only time would tell.

Twilight took over, and when he woke up several hours later, the fire had turned to embers, leaving a red glow in the room that was reminiscent of an extremely late summer sunset. The smell of chili filled the room, with its wonderful promise of warm comfort food.

And then he remembered, jerking up in his chair to spy an empty sofa with the fur throw left aside. It had been the sound of the water being shut off that had awoken him. She had gotten up to shower and attend to her needs. The door opened, the steam escaping into the rest of the cabin on the hard-edged shafts of light from the bathroom. He did not turn his head. He just waited, sitting there. She went into her room and then padded softly back out in the main room to grab the fur throw, taking it with her, stopping when she realized he was awake.

"Sorry…for waking you," she said, pulling the throw up close to her chin and hugging it close to her upper body. "Thank you…for your help." When he did not answer her, she turned to walk back to her room.

"I need to make sure you didn't soak your bandage." His firm voice stopped her in mid-route.

"They're fine. I can take care of it from here. You needn't bother."

He stood up and walked over to her, pushing her into her room, making her nearly fall face-first onto her bed, and pulling up on the back side of her sweatshirt and down a bit on her pants, physically thumbing the dryness and the security of her protective bandage.

"Hey…ouch…Cut it out, you bastard!" She turned to slap at his unwelcomed hands. But he turned her around and he checked the front side, ensuring that the stitches were dry—but he saw no ointment residue.

"You forgot your ointment. At least have the decency to do your front side if you don't want me messing with you." He yanked on her arm like she was a small child, to come with him to the bathroom so that he could give her the cream, pulling the medicine cabinet door open and revealing all that was inside.

"Backside looks and feels good. But I will attend to it in the morning," he told her, giving her the cream to apply to herself.

"Are you done terrorizing me?" she asked, applying the cream as instructed to her front side.

"Nope."

"No?" She jerked her head up at him in mid-application.

"Got another pill to shove down yer throat."

"Jesus H. Christ! I think that would constitute as drug abuse!"

"Meet me in the kitchen. I'll have it ready for you."

"Why do I need a pill so soon?" She was speaking loud enough for Jack to hear her as he walked away, heading to the kitchen.

"So it will knock you out and keep me from getting a headache."

Tasha gave him an exasperated look and muttered, "I'll give you more than just a headache," as he wandered back to the kitchen island.

"You're already a pain. My balls are still hurting," he grunted back from the kitchen sink along the back wall. She could not believe he had heard her. The man was part animal, with the sensitive hearing and the uncanny ability to sneak up on unsuspecting folks.

"I can't take one of these," she protested as she came into the kitchen's light. "I have to have it with food, and I don't think my protein bar will be enough."

His eyes pleaded with her as he dumped something into a hot skillet.

"I'm not going to eat your dinner and then be blamed for your constant misery!"

"I've enough for the both of us for the next two weeks. And you will be grateful for whatever comes your way."

"Good God, you sound like my mother on liver and onions night!"

This comment stopped him in mid-flip of the sausage he was cooking, smirking at her snarkiness. He continued pushing the meat around in the skillet. She had spunk. He'd give her credit for that.

"Grab the cheese in the fridge, will ya?"

Tasha did as she was told. She was hungry again, with all the cooking smells.

"While you are in there, grab me a beer and whatever you would like to drink—minus the beer."

He's going to drive me to drink, she thought, grabbing a bottle of cranberry-grape juice for herself and a bottle of beer, as well as the bag of shredded cheese.

She popped the cap off with her thumb, handing him the beer as he continued to brown the meat.

She pulled out a barstool, from the four there at the island, to sit on and wait, watching him cook and then dump the meat into the crockpot next to the stove, putting the pan in the sink to wash later. Taking the same spatula, he stirred the contents, making the aroma in the kitchen intensify. Without looking up, he said, "The dishes are located next to the fridge in the upper cupboard. Grab two." Then he added, "The large soup bowls."

She got up, retrieving what he wanted. Jack generously spooned out the concoction into each bowl, her stomach growling in anticipation. He must have heard it, smiling underneath the beard and hairy mustache, and a barely noticeable dimple? It appeared, but disappeared as fast as it had shown itself. "At least your tummy won't be complaining and turning it down."

"I haven't complained much about anything other than being attacked, but I haven't tried your cooking yet to see if I can survive it," she countered. He gave her a stern side glance.

He reached into a drawer just near where she stood next to him, grabbing two large spoons and handing them to her. Tasha grabbed them both and put one into each bowl. She took the bowls back to the kitchen island where she had been sitting earlier, skipping a stool to leave him a place to sit. She opened the bag of shredded cheese and added it to her bowl. He had grabbed paper towels for their makeshift napkins, and a bottle of hot sauce, before joining her.

His frame filled the entire space plus some, and she scooted over, giving him elbow room to eat without feeling crowded. Unbelievably well mannered, he offered her the hot sauce first—she shook her head no—before he dumped a large amount into his bowl. It was clear he had no taste buds left as the vapors of the hot sauce assaulted her nose, making her eyes water where she sat.

She did not eat at first, the chili being fresh hot. She stirred her cheese into it, trying to get it to cool down, and took a swig of her drink while waiting, hoping the cool cabin air would quickly disperse much of the meal's heat.

"And?"

"Will you hold your horses?" She stirred the spoon around more. "It's too darn hot to eat. Some of us still have our taste buds and would like to keep from suffering heat blisters on the roof of our mouths! If I drop dead from your cooking, you will have your answer."

He took a slurp from his spoon. Making an appreciative sound that warmed the immediate air around them. Her body inadvertently shivered at the contrast. Tasha quickly gained control over her body, hoping he had not noticed. But he got up, leaving her at the kitchen island to add another log to the fire, poking the red embers around it to catch the fresh log afire.

"You didn't need to do that."

"What other clothes do you have?"

"Come again?" she asked, not expecting that question.

He strode back to the island to reclaim his bowl of chili. "Warm clothes. The stuff I went through in your duffel bag will not get you through a winter here. Those long-sleeve shirts and sweaters are way too thin."

"Look, I will have to make do until my first paycheck. It's all I have, and I will double up if I have to."

He looked incredulously at her.

Her brow furrowed. "They should be enough, honestly." Then, more concerned, she asked, "Just how cold can it get in Hell with you?"

His head dropped in disbelief.

"Look, I know you think I am stupid, but I do what I can. Right now, I have to focus on getting my car to start and out of dockyard's parking lot before those ferry guys decide to push it into the bay. Secondly, I need my phone to work. A few folks are probably worried sick about me not calling in the last few days. The last of my cash is about two hundred bucks, and I must make that last until my first paycheck. So, sorry, I'm not rich enough." Exasperated, she placed her hands on the countertop, pushing away to leave, when his hand came down on hers, stopping her.

"Sit…eat," he told her in between a spoonful of chili. It amazed her that he was not burning his mouth between the actual heat of the cooked meal and the hot sauce. The man either had to be Special Forces or Marine to be that darn tough and not feel any pain. "Look, yer not stupid. Just amazingly naïve about your environment, especially at this time of year when our winter starts in October.

"I'll see to it that your affairs get in order during the downtime, but I will need you to be able to handle a two-and-a-half-hour drive to Anchorage sometime near the end of this week in the condition you are in. We have to get you outfitted or you're going to freeze to death just walking outside to the truck." The hand that held his spoon jabbed in her direction, reminding her to eat.

It was the most he had ever said to her, and for the first time, he was cordial. She sat there stunned, taking in the protectiveness of his large hand over hers. They were without a doubt working man's hands, she noted, along with long, strong fingers. She wanted to prove that she could be just as tough as these men. He gave her hand a reassuring squeeze, surprising her, before letting go.

Feed the beast and he becomes a pacifist, she thought. "It's only a gunshot wound. I think I can survive a long car ride. Just lay off those pills you keep wanting to shove down my throat."

"It's for yer own good," he said, grabbing a bottle out of his pants pocket, opening it with his thumb to dump a pill out and shoving the pill to her, reminding her to take it midway or after dinner.

"They make me sleep."

"They'll keep the pain at bay."

"I don't feel that much pain. Honestly!"

He looked back at her. "It keeps the pain in my ass down," he said pointedly.

She made a face at him. "I haven't been that bad other than I was weak and tired." She twirled the spoon in her bowl, aimlessly making figure eights in the thick chili. "The only thing I have done to you has been invading an anti-social person's private space. I don't know how I could have messed up anything more than your eagerness to go fuel planes."

He chewed on his chili. "Weak?" he asked, letting his spoon drop into his chili. "I'd say pretty tough to have made it all the way to the boss's office with half your blood supply missing. You've managed to impress him."

"But not you."

"My opinion doesn't matter. And you took a bullet for our country."

"I didn't take one for the team, you know. I just wasn't able to dodge this one because I never saw it coming."

He smirked.

"What?"

"The ones that nail us are the ones we never see coming." Pointing to her lower body, he continued, joking with her. "But you do have a hellaciously wide pair of hips that I don't think you would ever be able to hide entirely from an enemy."

"My hips aren't that big, are they?" She looked down at herself as if discovering her body for the first time.

"You're fine." At the risk of sounding like a pervert, he continued, "You have all the right curves in all the right places, lady."

Tasha looked back up at him as he turned away from her, picking up another spoonful of chili.

"Hell, I don't know how I could be a pain to you, giving you a show of hip every day. Most men I know would be ecstatic."

"Oh, I am ecstatic."

"A whale jumping out of the ocean is more ecstatic than you are. I don't think you even know what the word means."

"Wearing my emotions is not my style." Pointing to her chili, he asked, "What's wrong with it?"

"Nothing, just letting it cool down. Some of us aren't Satan's siblings when it comes to handling caustic stuff—in addition to adding more hot sauce, as if it weren't already spicy enough. I treasure my taste buds."

He scowled at her and shoved the pill closer to her, getting up to put his bowl in the sink for washing later, and then he sauntered off into his room.

The chili was finally to the point where she could eat it. It was perfect. She could not have done any better. But then she realized it had been darn near a week since she'd had a decent hot meal—not just a microwaved sandwich on the run or a protein bar.

As she was nearly finished with her meal, Jack walked by her with a large basket heading toward the front door.

"Where are you going?" she asked, noting her clothes that she had arrived in and had lost at the hospital. "Those are my clothes…"

"I'm going to do some wash."

"At this hour? What laundromat is open now?"

"Laundromat? The machines are downstairs."

"This place has a basement?"

He cocked his head as if she had lost it.

"I thought that door was a pantry." But she now realized that was how he had surprised her that night. He had been coming up from the basement when she literally burst in on him.

"I guess I need to give you a full tour of the place since you will be here for the next two weeks."

"Where will I be going after that?" She hoped he could tell her. She could not wait to get her own private cabin. There she could unwind and gather her thoughts after a hard day on the flight line. Time to reflect. With any luck, she could convince her childhood friend Artie to come up and possibly rekindle something. She wanted to settle down. She was ready, but Mr. Right never came; in fact, he had died trying to save her. She was always going to be guilty of that.

Jack saw the light in her face fade some after she asked, and he was not sure what to make of it. "They haven't decided, and I really don't know where you are going to end up. I guess it all depends on if you even survive the winter here in the Far North. Most don't make it past their first winter, much less the first year."

"What do you do to them?"

"It's not what we do, it's if they can adjust to a simpler, solitary lifestyle." The weight of realization seemed to change her into a lifeless statue as she paused to think about what he'd just said. She was an entirely different person than the more animated one he had been seeing since they first met. The first persona was the one growing on him. She was almost entertaining. She was going to be a handful, trying to keep the guys at bay, since women, especially handsome ones like her, were so far and few in the North. Then, hoping to get the original Tasha back, he assured her, "You'll be fine if you keep your head on your shoulders and don't eat any yellow snow." The last piece of advice was a joke.

"Yellow?" Then it hit her. "Eww!" She got up to follow him. "Seriously? You have to remind people of that?" A quiet pause, but he knew her brain was thinking. He heard her mutter more to herself, "I would think certain parts would freeze and fall off first, if it's as cold as you say it gets."

With his back to her he smirked, nearly laughing at her guttural thought process. He flipped the light switch on and she followed him down the bare-bone wooden stairs; he didn't need her falling. He showed her where things were kept so she would be familiar with the space. He noticed that she took her time taking in the dank, cooler surroundings, her gaze hesitating on the various exercise equipment, the extra desk and its various piles of books and papers, the shelving that held camping gear and an assortment of various tools, an old forgotten floor rug that took up most of the room, and an exceptionally large deep chest freezer. Otherwise, there was not much down there. He was not a pack rat, but then, he

43

himself had only been in Alaska for the past two years, with only just the last year having his very own place. Even then, it was looking like she might be a permanent roommate if Nate couldn't come up with something soon.

Jack dumped their clothes into the washer, adding soap, and started the machine. He then turned to watch her literally touch everything as she further inspected all the things there in the basement. "You can use the exercise equipment if you want, but please put the weights back on as to how you found them."

"I think the treadmill is more up my alley, if you are okay with that."

"Intending on running?" he asked, raising an inquiring eyebrow.

"Just walking for now. It helps me think."

"Suit yourself."

He turned to walk back upstairs. "Everything down here is yours to use as long as you put things back where you found them."

"What do you do…for fun?" She crossed her arms over her body, the dankness chilling her. "I mean you can't be all work, workout, sleep, and no play." She forced a chummy smile.

"I'm usually working."

"And when you're not?"

"I'm out fishing or hunting."

"Oh."

"Anything else?"

She shook her head no, not knowing what to think of the Grizzly Mountain Man standing in front of her. She did not want to joke with him further for fear of upsetting his recent cordialness. She took another scan of the monastic storeroom. It was pure function. Pure purpose. Not even a marker showing what branch he had been in, a family photo, a girlfriend photo, or childhood memorabilia.

She followed him back upstairs; starting to tire again, just climbing the steps back up to the main floor wore her out. She moved her bowl to the sink after popping the pain pill. She began to handwash the dishes, mainly to warm up her hands under the warm water and to ease the dryness of her skin. She made a mental note to buy some lotion soon. She did not pay attention to what he did behind her, if he was even behind her at all. She no longer cared at that point, drying her hands off with the kitchen towel and hooking it back *where she found it*. She did not want to upset this man any more than she needed to. It was bad enough, and two weeks would be almost too long for her with someone who had no desire to talk about himself, much less tell her what to expect on the job.

She plodded back to her bedroom, pushing her door somewhat ajar. Tasha grabbed the luxurious fur throw and pulled it over the bedcover as she tucked herself in for the night, sleep swiftly taking over.

She woke to daylight, and from what she could tell from the angle of the rays, she had slept well into the late morning. Groggily she relieved herself, only to crave more of her bed. It was super comfortable, and most of all warm, compared to the floor and the air around her. *'Mountain Man' was right, I'm going to freeze to death.* The Middle East heat was looking more and more inviting again, even though she was certain she did not ever want to sweat again.

She jumped back into her bed and pulled the covers to her chin, trying to reclaim that elusive warmth, calmly settling down again, only to jerk back up as she sensed she was not alone, and found Jack standing there by her desk next to her duffel bag. He held another pill, along with a glass of water and a plate with a biscuit sandwich.

"Shit!" She sat up, startled. "You really need to announce yourself!" She jerked the covers up more after dropping them when she'd scooted up against the headboard in surprise. "I could have been undressed!"

"You?" He smirked. "Not in this cold." He deposited the plate on her lap and put the water glass and pill on the nightstand next to the bed. "Eat up before it gets cold and…well, you know the routine."

"I can say this much about you…you're more efficient than a butler," she told his backside as he left to attend to whatever it was that needed attending. She looked back down at the breakfast sandwich on the plate and decided that she was hungry. She did not eat all of it, but enough to take the pill and fall back to sleep. Snuggling down into her bed, she had to admit, the lodging was not as bad as she had thought it was, as she drifted off into another deep, medicated sleep.

CHAPTER THREE

The last two days had been peaceful, and Jack needed the time to catch up on some light reading and office paperwork. However, he found himself often peering in on Tasha as she slumbered, just to stare at her. Her pale hair spread across the pillows in a tangled mess, seductively obscuring part of her face. At one time, he had brushed it aside to view more of her face. She was fair in skin-coloring yet weathered from the desert sun. She was not much younger than he was—about two years, from what her records reported. He did not dare move her bedcovers; it would be something other guys might do, but not him. He had some standards, or his mother and dad would have disowned him for not raising him better.

Every six or so hours during the day, he would be back in to make her eat something and then take another pill. It was during that time that he went to pick up her car, with Hank's help. He had found her ferry ticket, her driver's license, and her car keys to take with him. Luckily, most everyone knew each other in town and the dock workers often worked side by side with aviation; if a boat broke down, they were the ones in town most likely to fly cargo there if it didn't go to Anchorage via the highway.

After dropping off his paperwork with Nate and checking in with the guys, he got Hank to break away long enough to drive her car back. Hank was pretty much an Alaskan native, since he had arrived with his parents at the tender age of three. How in the world he still had the typical Southern redneck drawl and the garage mechanic look so far north was beyond Jack. Hank eagerly jumped into the truck with him, his toothpick moving from side to side as he picked his teeth with it using just his tongue. The toothpick's movement was the only indication he was excited and eager to meet their newest employee.

When they arrived at the dockyard's office, the only car to be seen in the guest parking lot was a Prius—a rather new one, at that. Hank whistled low.

"Are you kidding me?" He turned to look at Jack. "A Prius?" Hank burst into gales of laughter as he got out of Jack's truck. "Say it isn't so," he said as they both headed into the office to claim her car. Much to Hank's mirth, the car did indeed belong to the one and same Tasha. "What the hell, man? Is she only intending to drive during the summer months?"

"Tell us about it," said the operations manager in the dingy office—that had not seen a good cleaning in roughly thirty years—as he gave them the second key to her car. "We told her that there was no way that car was going to drive in the snowstorms we get. She better hope that global warming is here to stay." The gruff dock manager tore the pink sheet he needed and gave them the yellow copy. "How's she doing since she arrived? Certainly took you fellers long enough to pick it up."

"Haven't seen her as of yet—"

"She's fine." Cutting him off, Jack nodded to Hank to come along. He was not about to let Hank yak it up with the guy, both being old timers, part of the good ol' boy system. There were going to be issues soon enough.

"Wow, coming from the man that slugged her. You sure have become tight-lipped, Jack."

Jack gave Hank a *what are you talking about* look.

"So, what's she like? Heard she's staying at your place," asked the dock manager.

"Yes, she's staying until her next doctor's appointment, and then I am sure we will be finding her another place shortly," he off-handedly told them, walking away with the key to her car outside, desperately trying to get both to stop their pestering questions.

Jack inserted the key into the door of the car, only to find the entire car opened itself up.

"Sweet! This car got all the bells and whistles...remote entry, alarm, heat, GPS, a/c...hey man, what's a/c?" Hank winked at him, joking.

Jack tried to find her ignition, only to discover it was a push-button ignition. It barely turned over.

"Battery," they said in unison.

Jack popped the hood and Hank went to check the engine for the battery. Hank yelled back to Jack. "Man, I thought these cars were half battery and half gas. Where's the battery?" High-school-educated Hank was a good mechanic, but only on older styles of cars and planes. The newer computerized models usually threw him for a loop.

Jack reached over to her glove compartment to locate her owner's operator manual, after having to shove some of her things back into the passenger seat to allow the compartment's door to drop open. He flipped through several pages until reaching the battery section, reading momentarily on how to locate and possibly jump start the car.

Hank stood outside looking over at the newfangled engine, absorbing whatever new technology that could be gleaned from it.

Jack poked his head out the driver's window. "Batteries are under the rear passenger bench seat." He turned to look back, only to see the rear two seats piled high with her personal belongings.

"Did you say batteries...as in lots of them?"

"Yeah, two main ones." He had gotten out and opened the hatchback of her car to put some of her things in the back. However, it, too, was filled with more of her belongings. She was here to stay. If this was her entire household, she lived lightly.

Not thinking, he said, "Hank, open the front passenger door and put all this stuff in there."

"Ah, we really can't," came Hank, as he looked in her front seat, noting it

47

was just as packed.

Jack swore, having remembered shoving some of her possessions back in the seat.

"I think she's here to stay," Hank concluded, saying out loud what was on both of their minds. "I hope she's a decent electrician besides the rumor saying she's smoking hot." Jack looked emphatically at him. Hank backed up with his palms held out *in no harm done* to him, just reiterating what he had heard in the hangar.

"How do you know she's not psycho?" Jack asked him, trying to throw him off.

"Seriously?"

Jack rolled his eyes at him. "Come on, let's get her stuff into the cab of my truck."

Together they unpacked her hatchback, getting access to her car's batteries just under the rear bench seat. It was just as he had feared when he opened the case: one battery looked like it had exploded within its section.

"Jack, if those are all the batteries, why are there two different sizes? They're the funkiest looking ones that I've ever saw, if you ask me."

"That's because a few of them exploded. She'll need a new set. And that'll take a few weeks to get here, if not all winter." He ran a hand through his thick hair, sighing heavily. "Grab the chains. We're going to have to tow this little hockey puck back to the cabin."

They were able to put her car into neutral, and Hank had the honors of riding in her car as brake man while Jack towed it with his truck. It was a slow process, but they got it back to the cabin, dropped the chains, and pushed her car into a more permanent parking spot until she could get a new battery and a battery warmer for it, if they even made them for Priuses.

Hank got out of her car along with a box that he had opened only to find more paperwork, but mostly photos. He had been going through her things, curiosity getting the better of him, while Jack retrieved and looped his chain to return it to the back of his truck's bed where the rest of his tools were stored.

"How old do you suppose she is, Jack?" he asked as he helped himself to another photo to inspect—a photo of her in her military class As next to what he presumed to be her dad. Jack nabbed the photo and put it back into the box, closing the lid and dropping it back into the car's front seat.

"Most likely the age of your grown daughter!"

"I'd still like to meet her," Hank told him to his backside as he watched Jack close her car door.

Jack sighed at him. "You will, in time. Just behave for now." He added, "We really need an electrician this winter—please don't do anything to make her regret coming here." Jack walked past him toward his truck, motioning to him to follow.

"Oh, we boys thought you did a good enough job doing that with your lack of edi…edi…can't remember how to pronounce that word."

"Etiquette," Jack answered impatiently.

"—And your lack of conversational skills. I was going to say."

"Get in the truck, Hank."

"Why are you in such a hurry? There's not that much work to do. Hangar floor's been Zambonied twice now. Hell, the floor is cleaner than the break table is!"

"Well, Hank, I guess there's a break table needing to be cleaned."

Hank ignored him. "Why did you beat up our electrician?"

"I didn't beat her up," Jack replied somewhat tersely, tired of being reminded of what he had done to Tasha.

"Then why did you and Nate take her to the hospital?"

"She tore open her war wound again."

"War wound?" Hank pulled the toothpick out of his mouth in surprise before reinserting it to the opposite corner of his mouth. "You mean she's a combat vet?"

"Yup." He tried to leave it at that. Hank swapped the toothpick back again. Jack knew it would give his guys another few more hours of entertaining gossip—of that he was sure.

"Well, I'll be a monkey's uncle. We got ourselves two combat vets," he said, pulling the worn toothpick out of his mouth and tugging at his salt-and-pepper beard. "Explains the fighting. I wouldn't be surprised if she could kick yer ass then." He clicked his tongue.

Jack half smiled, thankful that his beard did not show much of his facial expressions as he drove Hank back to the hangar.

The following morning, he found himself in a bit of a quagmire. She had clutched onto him with an arm and a leg thrown over him, her head cradled in the crook of his shoulder. He was pinned. He moved slightly, only to have his open book slide off his chest, landing noisily on the floor. She rolled onto her backside, freeing him, save for his shoulder and arm. So far, so good.

It was when he heard his front door open and the familiar sound of Drake padding in that he knew he was in trouble. It was not long before Nate located him in her room. Jack put a finger to his lips as he watched Nate's surprised expression turn into a barely confined rage. Jack, with his free hand, indicated he would join Nate out in the living room as soon as he extricated the rest of his arm out from underneath her head without waking her. He breathed a sigh of relief when he was successfully free.

Closing her door, he silently motioned his boss to follow him downstairs to the basement so that they would not wake her.

Once there, a furious Nate whirled on him, literally blowing up. "Are you *trying* to wreck what little business I have?" he cried, his finger emphasizing his point at the floor. "First you attack her and I have to spend money on her medical bills for reopening a wound." He held finger number two up at him. "Now you are working on a sexual harassment case by lying in her bed with her! When I told you to look after her for these two weeks, I didn't mean lie in bed with her!" His hands went to his hair, pulling at it. "My God, son, she hasn't even worked one day for us as of yet!"

It was just best to let Nate, the Raven, bellow until he ran out of air and things to yell about. "Jack, do you realize I have two possible lawsuits that would wipe out not only all of your jobs, but the business as well? What has gotten into you, son? I hired you because you have some common sense, plus some leadership skills in you—or so I thought. Please tell me I am wrong. I saw a promising future for you and Black Raven Aviation continuing for years to come. You are a hard worker and you have truly expanded our business. But what in the hell happened to you at work as of late? I mean, I know the guys find you distant at times, unable to lighten up, but this...this is a bit extreme even for you when it comes to this...this..."

"Tasha," Jack offered her name.

"Tasha." He grumbled, "Don't treat her any differently from the guys, you hear? Favoritism doesn't play well, and I don't need a war in my hangar between the mechanics and the only electrician."

"I'm not treating her any differently than the guys, and you misinterpreted what you saw. She is still untouched by me, other than dressing her wound daily as *ordered* by the doc. I just happened to fall asleep there after trying to calm her in the middle of a restless night. She seems to relax once someone is nearby."

"What do you mean a 'restless night'?"

"She dreams. Probably has PTSD."

"What?" Nate unfolded his arms. "Great! I now have *two* of you to worry about losing it on the flight line?"

"Naw, it's not that bad. It'll take time to let the memories recede. She's fresh out from the military."

"But look at you, it took you...what...close to two whole years?"

"I was security...she was aviation and probably just got caught up in something that went wrong, most likely. It's not like she saw or went through as much as I did or any other infantrymen. She's fine. I just don't need her thrashing around with a second set of fresh stitches on her. And if I remember right, you *were* the one that *assigned* me to her when you should have given that duty to one of the mechanics."

Nate gave him a gimlet look. "Jack, can you honestly see Hank, Jarvis, Emanuel, Nick, or Sam looking after her? The guys would have bent over backwards to help, but still...seriously? Hank treats his dog better than most humans, and he lives in a human junkyard of a home. He's...he's a borderline hoarder. Besides, Hank's married and I am sure his wife Sybil would not like to take care of a stranger in their home—especially a young woman like Tasha. Nick or Sam would've been in her drawers in less than an hour after meeting her. Emanuel or Jarvis…I'm not entirely sure if they would have taken the responsibility seriously, with the way those two still act like college freshmen and yet are in their late twenties."

He did have a point. But taking her on was the last thing Jack needed as he tried to settle into the cabin and begin as normal of a life as he could, being a single guy who enjoyed hunting and fishing, living the single man's dream life. He had his choice of women, but not one made it worthwhile to pursue. Tasha maybe, but she was off limits in his book since they would be working together. So far, only a little more than a week left before he would be dropping her off at her checkup.

Nate continued. "My request remains about taking care of her. *But please*! *Please* do not give her any reason to file a harassment suit, will ya? Stay away from her in the cabin and treat her just like the other guys…for your sake. The last thing I need is to lose a good, hard-working employee. It's because of you we have done so well this year. I don't want to lose the momentum, and most of all, our company desperately needs an electrician."

Jack sighed, telling him, "You have my word. I'll see to it that she is content here at our company, but only after she proves she's worthy enough. And…she will need to move out, eventually."

"Why?"

"She's a girl. She'll want her own space," Jack stated with certainty, then adding, "Or when I get myself a wife, I will not be sharing a cabin with two women."

"You're dating?" Nate said with surprise. "Who?"

"No one, for now," Jack said, rubbing his beard absently. "But when the time comes, I want my space."

"Fine." Nate shoved his hands into his pockets. "I'll see to it to give her a pay increase to cover the expense of not having enough lodging for my employees if you two are so insistent on not sharing a two-bedroom one-bath cabin." Nate looked Jack in the eye for a long moment. "Just keep your nose clean with this one?"

Nate took in a long breath as he looked around the basement of the cabin. He noted the exceptional cleanliness, the sparse furnishings, and the few things in storage. This was a young man who wanted to keep his life simple, and putting Tasha on him placed a speed bump in the road he had chosen to currently travel on.

"Well"—he headed toward the stairs to the main floor—"gotta get back to the hangar. Give that dog of yours an extra treat today. He's a damn good dog. Wife's going to miss him."

Jack followed him, then showed him out the front door, seeing him off, and hopefully getting him to feel calmer about Tasha and him.

He retreated into the cabin's dry warmth and decided it was time to make breakfast. He grabbed two potatoes that looked like they were a tad beyond shelf life, but they would do. He did not have everything he needed to cook anything too fancy, like a waffle-maker or a handheld blender. But he saw no point in having them since he could go to the diner when he fancied something other than his bland cooking. That day it would be some bacon, to add grease to the pan, and frying up some country potatoes with some eggs he had, enough for two servings of nicely scrambled eggs.

"Do you want some help with that?" Tasha used her nose to indicate all that was on the countertop by the stove. Tasha's arms were wrapped defensively around herself. She was standing between the corner wall where the kitchen jutted opposite of the main living area and the kitchen island in her sweats, sock-covered feet, and with a bad case of bedhead.

Jack turned around, surprised to find her up. But he knew he should not have been, given the fact that he had her drugged heavily for the last few days and she had pretty much slept around the clock. And with the previous night's refusal to take any more pain meds, she seemed perkier.

He slid the egg crate over to her. "Sure, crack however many eggs you want, plus three for me, and scramble them in a cup while I get the bacon started and the potatoes cut up."

"Sounds good," she said, her voice rough with disuse from the night's sleep.

He felt awkward with her looking around his shoulder as he found and retrieved the pan he needed. He felt her eyes watch every move he made, making him feel like he needed to disrupt her observations with small talk. "Did you sleep well?"

"Yes," she answered rather slowly, an indication she knew there was something else behind the question.

He turned to look over his shoulder at her, to see her expectant face for him to continue. Jack got the meat in the pan and set it over the burner. He nabbed the potatoes, along with a plate to cut the potatoes on, and came over to the island where Tasha had now taken a seat. Jack used the time to think while he got her a cup to crack all the eggs in and a fork to scramble them.

"You got any milk?" she asked as she expertly cracked the eggs.

He nodded and reached into the refrigerator for the half gallon, sliding it over to her along with another cup. He started dicing the potatoes as she added a little milk to the eggs and then whisked them. By the time he was done with cutting the potatoes, he found her staring at him again.

"What?" he asked, as he turned to place the potatoes into the large frying pan alongside the bacon that needed to be turned.

"Why are you being so accommodating?"

"Accommodating?" he echoed her question, giving him more time to think of what to say next in his defense.

"You have gone from being the 'Grizzly Mountain Man' with no manners to being actually quite a nice human, 'Griswald.'"

He gave her an exasperated look, as she gave him a more pointed look to explain himself. "First of all, my name is Jack, not 'Griswald.'" He emphasized his point with the fork he had used earlier to turn the bacon over. "I was ordered to take it 'easy' on you while you're recuperating. Trust me, I am not going out of my way to accommodate you. I am doing everything possible to get you out of my hair."

"It might be easier to get me out of your hair by trimming and shaving everything." She pointed to her face where he had his very full beard and then to her head where he had let his hair grow in long layers almost to his shoulders. He was not amused. He knew he was scruffy looking. But up there and in the fall, all men stopped shaving, the hair and beard giving extra warmth to their exposed faces. And it was not like he had to impress anyone—especially a girl.

"What do you have against the beard?"

"Oh, lighten up," she said, getting up and delivering the raw eggs to him where he stood at the stove. "I'll be gone before you know it, and I will pay you what I owe you in meals, if that is what you're worrying about."

"Well, get dressed while I finish up here."

"What? No more shoving a pill down my gullet?" she asked, suddenly suspicious. "Where are we going?"

"We're going to take care of your cellular service today so you can have a working phone up here."

When it registered that he was offering her more help, she beamed at him with those perfectly white teeth, squealing a muffled delight before hurriedly walking into the bathroom to shower and change into some clothes. Drake followed her to the door and waited on her, now taken with their new guest.

Breakfast was a feast in which she heartily chowed down with him. At least her temporary roomie was a decent cook. Afterwards, she followed him like a happy puppy out to his truck, stopping momentarily. She had spied her parked car from afar as he unlocked the passenger side of the truck. Within minutes they were bounding down the main road into town, toward several of the strip malls that lined the street.

It did not take long to change her service, and she was able to keep her old phone. Once back in the truck, she commented, "I can't believe there is just one service company out here."

"This ain't LA, lady." He gently steered his truck back onto the main road. "Speaking of the lower forty-eights—where is your hometown?"

"Palm Harbor, Florida."

"Florida?" He looked at her to verify she wasn't joshing him. "What in the hell made you come up here when you could've had any aviation job down there?"

"Aviation jobs aren't that easy to come by, and the pay isn't close to meeting the standard of living down there."

"Well, it's not much better up here either, unless you go to one of Anchorage's big companies."

"But it was one of the first to offer lodging with the job, and the first to hire me straight out of the military and hospital without question." He did not say anything, so she continued. "Besides, I wanted to escape the heat for a while and go to a small place that was far as one could get from the Middle East."

"How long was your tour?"

"Two years," she stated, as she checked the town's sights out her passenger window.

"Two—why so long?"

"I volunteered the second time to let another go home to his newborn. I was single and it wasn't like I had anyone to go home to. Just Mom and Dad, and…an old high school friend."

At this piece of information, Jack was shocked. Shocked that she did not have a significant other. But he knew it would not be long before the local males would be seeking her. She could have her pick, since men still outnumbered women two to one.

"If you're up to it, I need to stop by the grocery store again for more food. Come inside with me this time and pick up things you like to eat. We can eat at the diner first for a quick lunch."

"Yeah—sure."

He slowed the truck to take on the rough transition between the main road and parking lot of the small grocery store and diner. The diner was a separate building, forming an L adjacent to the main grocery store.

Together they entered the diner, sitting down at his usual booth by the window. Upon seeing him, Katie waved to him and immediately came over with a pot of coffee, filling his cup. He introduced Tasha to Katie and she greeted her, welcoming Tasha to their small part of the world. It was clear to Tasha where Katie's interests really lay in regard to the big man sitting just across the table from her.

Tasha was soon forgotten, but it didn't matter: she was still feeling the effects of her pain medications and wasn't as hungry as Jack—not after such a huge breakfast that morning. Tasha had to conserve what cash she had left. She ordered a cup of soup as he ordered a full sandwich and a side of fries. He asked if she was going to eat anything else, and she shook her head that it was enough for now but did ask if she could have a few of his fries to dip in her soup. He shoved his plate toward her so she could take what she wanted. There wasn't much banter between them, mainly because as soon as Katie was done with the other customers, she was back to talking about what was happening in town, asking how the flight line guys were faring, and what he was up to as of late. His attempt at including Tasha was lame when he told Katie that he was helping her get settled in before starting flight line work.

Although Katie noticed her, again, the conversation remained one-sided, with Katie doing most of the talking. Tasha sat there silently, taking it in, hoping to glean more details about who she would be working with and what to expect once she got to Black Raven Aviation to do at least one full day's worth of work.

Once Jack finished, the entire plate now devoid of every scrap of food, they got up to pay for their meals after dropping a cash tip on their table. He allowed Tasha to lead them to the register, where she paid for them with her credit card, and Katie gave her an overdone smile and a wink at Jack. Tasha must have surprised him; although she could not see him behind her back, it was definitely reflected in Katie's face. Their next stop was the grocery store.

With her in tow, they went up and down the aisles picking what each of them wanted. But he noted that she did not pick up much, and he asked if that was all she was going to eat for the next week.

"It's all I can afford in cash at the moment and I don't want to augment my credit debt further," she dismissively told him over her shoulder as she walked past him.

He sighed at her.

"What?" She stopped and turned back, looking at his expression. "Oh no, don't give me that! Look, I don't want to be any further indebted to you."

He picked up her celery sticks. "This isn't enough to sustain you, and you have no idea from one week to another when we will get snowed in for a week or more."

"It's late August!"

Ignoring her, he went on: "We have to stock up the pantry and the freezer for two of us." He looked at her yogurt containers and then dropped her celery sticks back on top of her peanut butter. "Don't worry about groceries. I'll take it out of Nate's hide later. Besides, you can make it up to me by doing some of the cooking."

"Cooking? What if my cooking sucks? What then?"

"Something tells me you can cook if you put your mind to it. I won't take that as an excuse. Cleaning comes to mind, also."

"Well, don't blame me if Drake keels over from food poisoning or you start having indigestion issues." Warning him, she added, "I will stop at the first verbal complaint."

"First of all, Drake doesn't get table scraps. He has dry feed and his doggy treats. Secondly, I'm not a picky eater."

Her blatant disbelief showed plainly on her face. He gestured with his hand for her to lead the way, telling her to pick up ingredients for at least three meals that would last them three or four days a week in terms of leftovers.

"You don't seem the type to like leftovers," she commented. "Anything I need to know in terms of what you like, don't like, or have allergies to?" She looked back over her shoulder as he pushed their cart along just behind.

He shook his head no, telling her he was pretty much game for anything if it had meat and it was hot. She was quick about coming up with three different options, but unorganized when it came to going up and down the aisles for each recipe's components, still unfamiliar with the store's layout. He could tell she would have a dinner option, but then only get the items for that one meal and then repeat for the next meal. Her way of thinking was literally one step at a time

55

under sub-categories. But he had to admit, she did not forget a single item after they left the store. In fact, he was certain that their cart looked like they were getting ready for the storm of the century as they walked back to his truck to unload their goods.

They made short work of it together, the wind coming down off the mountains stinging the backs of their necks and cutting through their jackets. They hopped in and started back to the cabin before the liminal lighting would settle in the valley for a couple of hours.

Once inside the cab, he caught her shivering, trying to gain control over herself without saying a word. She was not one to complain, as most women were apt to. He instinctively tried to protect her by turning the heater to full blast, even though the drive back wasn't long.

Although she was cold, she stuck it out with him, bringing in the grocery bags until he ordered her to remain inside the heated cabin and just unpack everything; he did not want her getting the chilblains—at least not so early in the season. As she continued putting things away in the pantry and the refrigerator, he brought in more wood and got the fire going again, the crackling of the logs quickly melting what seemed to her to be frozen air in the cabin. He hoped she would soon adjust to the cooler lifestyle. She would need to do it fast, since winter would soon be knocking on the town's doorstep. She sighed when she was done, leaving just a few things out on the countertop for her to put together in a slow cooker for the next hour or two.

"I need to lay down again. Just give me an hour if you can, Jack."

"Take all the time you need. Rest while you have the chance. I still have leftover chili from a few nights ago that I can heat up for us for dinner." He came over to the kitchen island that divided the living room from the kitchen in the open part of the cabin. Jack pointed to her hip again. "But first, I need to get at your wound."

"Can it wait?" Her arms were still wrapped around herself, trying to conserve her body heat. "I…really need a chance to warm up before unwrapping myself." Her green eyes pleaded with him.

"Go sit by the fire a moment while I get the things I need to take care of it."

He was not going to delay it. She scrunched her nose as she passed him, her hands rubbing up and down her arms, trying to stimulate more blood flow. Tasha planted herself obediently on the river stone hearth, facing him, and watched him disappear into the bathroom. She noted the way he walked with a sense of steadfast purpose. He was a man who knew what he was doing and where he wanted to go in life. For a man who was about her age, he acted way older than he should have, and he looked older than dirt with his unkempt whiskers and rather long hair. It wasn't curly, but the dark auburn layers seemed to naturally lie in wavy layers. The only real part of his face you could clearly see was the large prominent forehead. Even his eyebrows were rather full—but not so thick as to overshadow his eyes, and his eyes were the color of the bay waters on an overcast day.

She shifted in her seat so that another part of her body could warm. She closed her eyes and drew in a deep breath, savoring the smell of the burning wood, finding the scent comforting. It occurred to her that it was the first heated scent that did not seem to remind her of the Middle East.

"Are you all right?" His voice was close, startling her. He indicated for her to stand up before him, handing her the rubbing alcohol after placing a few drops on a cotton ball as he sat down on the hearth, the two of them exchanging places.

"Yeah, I'm fine."

He indicated to her to expose herself. She pressed her lips into a thin line before complying. She lifted her sweater and her first layer of shirt while simultaneously pushing down on her sweatpants to expose her one fair hip to him, turning before he could see any more of her front side.

Tasha could feel his breath near her skin as he removed the big bandage that lay protectively over the entire suture area. He worked on cleaning the stitches and then applied the ointment before placing a large new bandage over it.

"You *are* really cold to the touch," he told her. He did not dally, but he was not racing to get it done either. As he stood back up, his movement away from her left her skin in a cold void when she realized how his presence made her feel warm and protected.

"Here." He reached over to the coffee table, where he had picked out a couple of folded clothing items from his room and brought them out, tossing them to her to catch. "Put these on."

She nearly missed them since she was still trying to get her own clothes back into place.

"They'll be big on you, but I think you will find them much warmer than the clothes you do have." He had walked over to the refrigerator to grab himself the usual dark lager he favored, popping the lid off and flinging the cap neatly into the nearby trash can as he walked back to the sofa to plop himself down for the rest of the day. He whistled for Drake to come sit by his side on the sofa, where both could soak up the heat of the fireplace. Jack acted like a brooding king in his castle, dismissing his wench for the afternoon.

She did not have enough energy to make a comment, much less a smart-mouthed retort. A nap would do her good. Her bed called for her and her body moved on its own accord, clutching the extra clothes to her body for warmth. She headed for her room where she softly pushed her door closed, changed into the new clothes, and fell into her bed, snuggling down into the thick covers.

Jack held off ordering a new battery for her car. It would have to wait for now. He agreed with Hank that her car was not going to handle the onslaught of winter like she thought it would. He took out her other battery, hoping it was still good, and brought it into the cabin and stored it down in the basement. He would eventually help her with her car, but for now she would just have to catch a ride with him or one of the other guys to the hangar.

In a few days he would take her to get her cell phone carrier service changed over to their only area provider. He worked on unpacking her things from her car, putting all of it in the living room for the time being. He wanted his truck back too. Luckily, she had packed most of her things in a bunch of plastic milk crates or cardboard boxes. An errant pillow or two had been left out and he surmised that she had indeed slept in her car a time or two.

He decided to take her pillows to her room where she would be sleeping, only to find her up, still groggy, quietly standing there watching him load up the sofa as if not registering that they were her things.

"You good?" he asked. When she did not answer at first, he wondered if she was sleepwalking. But she nodded that she was fine.

"Do you want me to move your things into your room?"

"You got my car to work?"

"Sort of."

"Sort of?" she questioned him.

"Well, we got it here, but it doesn't work. You have a few exploded cells. The other battery I disconnected and brought inside and put down in the basement to keep it from freezing when the weather turns colder. We will have to order you a new one, in addition to a plug-in battery warmer... That is, if they even make one for your car."

"Seriously?" she asked, shocked. "But I am going to need my car just to get back and forth from work!"

"Well, you get the honors of carpooling in to work with me for a few weeks."

"Weeks?" She eyed him suspiciously. "Why weeks? How long does it take to get car parts?"

"Sometimes I've seen it take until the first spring thaw."

"What!" she exclaimed, and then resignedly sighed. "I've gotten myself into one hell of a mess with everything deciding not to work all at once," she muttered more to herself.

"No, your phone works, but you're not with the only carrier we have in town, so you'll need to change the network provider whether you like it or not. And we will do that tomorrow. But for now, I need you to take another pill and let me look at you to clean and dress that bandage of yours on your backside." He pointed to her side and then swirled his finger to indicate that she needed to turn around and march herself back into bed.

"Can it just wait? I want to know what it is like to be awake for longer than an hour, please. Besides, I'm thirsty and want some hot tea."

"How about coffee?" he offered.

"Hot chocolate?" she countered.

"That I have. Give me a few..." He picked up a box of hers to take to her room.

She came over to the sofa and took the two pillows he had just dropped there. One was a normal pillow she had brought just in case the cabin did not come furnished and she would be sleeping on the floor in her sleeping bag. The other was a body pillow—a pillow that was treated more like a giant stuffed animal to make her feel not so alone. She put both on the rumpled covers as he deposited her first box in the corner of the room.

"The milk crates are stackable on their sides and will make a quick-access shelf for my things," she told him, as if he didn't know, but she needed all the assistance she could get in this constant drugged-out state. And she would need to be ready to move on again when they found her another place in just a few more weeks.

Jack did not say anything, especially since she complied with his request by sitting back down on the edge of her bed. She just stared off into space at that point, not seeming to care much about her surroundings. He made short work of her personal things and then went off to microwave her some warm water for cocoa.

He returned with the cocoa and the medical items he needed to attend to her, finding her still sitting there staring off into space. "You all right?" he asked as he set the hot chocolate on the small nightstand. He touched her shoulder to get her attention.

She nodded her head, saying, "Just sleepy," and lay down on her side to offer up her backside to his medical assistance.

He raised an eyebrow at her compliance but went ahead and pulled back the bandage, checking for any increased redness or swelling. There was none. She was healing fast, with as much sleep as she was getting. "Any more pain?" He pressed lightly around the wound with the cleanser pad and then applied the ointment.

She grunted a little but said it was about the same, if not a little less.

"Let's get you another pill."

"No." She turned onto her stomach. "I don't need another one; I'm tired enough." She wrapped her arms underneath a pillow, dragging it back to her, nestling her head before turning away from him, exhaling heavily.

He did not push the issue, leaving the room with the hot chocolate cooling on the side table.

Her night was restless as she tossed and turned. Periodically, when a muffled sound came from her, he would look in to see if she was awake, only to find she was dreaming. If she kept that up, he would not be able to sleep either. Eventually he settled onto the empty side of her bed, bringing with him a book to read. It seemed the minute he sat next to her, she quieted.

She awoke several hours later only to find that she had slept until the next morning, the sunlight filtering in through her sole window. Aghast, she immediately sought out her phone's clock. It was ten o'clock in the morning! She jumped out of bed, nearly yelping in shock as her bare feet touched the cold floor.

She quickly tucked them back under the bed covers for warmth, realizing that she had not put on any socks when she had changed her clothes.

Tasha scanned the room to determine the best and shortest route to access her socks. Then she saw the packed box that contained her fuzzy animal slippers. She literally jumped into her desk's chair just to avoid touching the floor and nabbed one pair of socks, donning them and then braving the floor again to reach the box, where she grabbed her animal slippers. She did not care how ridiculous she looked. She wanted warm feet. If her hands and feet were warm, the rest of her body would be warm. She sighed once she slipped them on. From there, it was going to be the hottest shower she could get after she saw what this *Jack* was up to that day.

There was no sign of him, and the cabin was eerily still. Nothing in the already neat and spotless cabin had been moved or rearranged since the day before. She checked the basement, calling out to him. No answer. She then went to knock on his bedroom door. It swung open with her first knock, revealing his empty room. She took a moment then, for she had never seen the front bedroom where he slept. The bed had been slept in recently, and she could still smell his scent. His room was a bit larger, but it had the same furnishings as hers, save for the extra dresser drawers. The room was bare of all personal items that she could tell, other than a pile of books and a few men's outdoor sports magazines. She let her curious hands wander through them to the few papers that were tucked in a few of the books, marking the place where he had interest or had stopped reading. The papers were worn photos—photos of Marines in desert fatigues in full combat gear standing in front of an armored Humvee and other base locations. She was not sure if one of them was Jack, since she had never seen him without the beard nor in a high and tight crew cut. But the more she looked at the last photo, she was certain the guy on the left was him by his stature. Jack was a large man, not just in height but in structure. He was not a bodybuilder, but he was not your runner's build either.

Her body was reminding of her morning's ablutions. She quickly thumbed through more of the other books, finding other photos tucked in here and there. *Photos of family members? One of his girlfriends, perhaps*? she thought, catching a glimpse of a pretty, nice-looking girl, not entirely sure if she could have been his sister, with similar-colored hair. She put the books back as she found them, reminding herself it wasn't any of her business, and that she hurried for her morning needs.

Tasha took her time showering, soaking up the hot water until every single joint and muscle was no longer stiff. By the time she finished, the entire bathroom was a sauna. She inhaled deeply, getting as much moisture as she could back into her heater-dried lungs. She preened in the mirror, not wanting to put her clothes back on, enjoying her privacy and the sheer pleasure of being in the nude. It was the first in a long time that she'd had a private spot to call her own and without having to worry about another person needing the same room at roughly the same time.

On that thought, she began to wonder if she should be looking for another place while she was getting a full two weeks to 'recover.' She counted back, realizing that she had a little over a week left to find another place to live. Surely he would not be giving up the cabin to her. Would he? He had pretty much settled in for the long haul. In fact, he looked to have been there for a while, although he didn't have much in terms of personal belongings.

She made a mental note to ask him next time. She had dallied enough. It was time to put on her 'face,' with some light makeup she usually wore and lip stain. She dressed before opening the bath door back to the main part of the cooler cabin. Though a heater was running, it did not seem to take the entire chill out of the air. But she reminded herself that she needed time to adjust to the environment. She needed to start exposing herself as much as possible to the cold outside. She shivered at the thought.

Tasha padded back into her bedroom, finally noting that not even the dog, Drake, was inside. She presumed that he must have taken the dog for a walk or gone to the hangar. She didn't need him around the clock twenty-four seven.

She changed into her everyday work clothes before heading out to the kitchen to make herself some breakfast and then to start working on the slow cooker recipe she had wanted to make late the previous night. At least they would have barbecue pork roast, veggies, and some mashed potatoes for lunch or dinner. For breakfast, she helped herself to bacon and eggs.

While everything was cooking, she familiarized herself with the kitchen cupboards, noting what she would be working with and finding there was not much. It was truly backwoods cabin eating. Plain and simple. Foods that didn't require marination, chopping, dicing, sautéing, or pureeing. Eventually she would need more kitchen cooking utensils, storage containers, and mixing bowls. After flipping the bacon over, she began cutting the onions and other veggies to place over the meat in the crockpot before dumping the sauce in on top, smothering the entire entree to cook for the rest of the day. After her breakfast, she would work on making the mashed potatoes.

She stood at the bar to eat her breakfast while she fiddled with her cellphone to familiarize herself with the new service provider. She organized her phone as she needed it before making her first phone call to her parents, letting them know that she had arrived and was all right. *God forbid I tell Mom everything that's happened so far,* she thought, cringing.

As usual, her mother chastised her for not calling sooner and Tasha remained quiet, eating her meal through the entire barrage until she could get a word in. It was when she was washing her breakfast plate that she was able to get in her apology to her mother, rather than explain the useless and unwanted reasoning, and then ask if Dad was all right.

"He's fine. But he's out playing golf this afternoon."

Her mother insisted on knowing what had been going on, and Tasha knew not to let her mom know about having to go back into the hospital. She wasn't even too sure if she should tell her that she was living with a strange man in a cabin out in the middle of what seemed like nowhere.

Eventually her mother would find out, so Tasha decided on telling her half of the situation—the part where she was living with some strange man in a two-bedroom cabin.

"You're what?" exclaimed her mother. "Tasha, I thought I raised you better than that!"

"Mom! Listen, there isn't much housing up here to choose from, especially when it is provided by your employer. For some reason they were expecting a guy to show up, not a girl! Besides, it's only temporary until they can find me another place." *Or build one for me,* she thought. She had begun peeling the potatoes to cut up. "He's not entirely bad—he's a veteran too, and he bunks in the other room." She chose her words carefully to get her mother to calm down.

"Besides, I refuse to have any relationship with a co-worker, especially with an aircraft fueler. Give me some credit here. I need someone I can hold a serious conversation with—at least someone who can not only fix an airplane but is smarter than that, if you know what I mean. Most fuelers and mechanics…well, they aren't the conversational types to hold my attention for long." Her back was to the main room, facing the stove as she tossed the cut-up potatoes into the hot water and stirred them randomly. Occasionally she would get on her tiptoes to look out the small window over the kitchen sink, peering at the mountain backdrop. She noted that the tops were snow covered already and had been steadily growing thicker, the white boughs sliding to a lower elevation as the days had passed.

"You know I worry about you, especially after the Army sent our little girl home with a bullet hole in her. I still feel like I should have gone with you to help you settle in until you started work."

"Trust me, it's like living in a military barrack, just log-cabin style. Dad would love it, but I doubt you would." She was hoping to discourage her mother from even thinking of coming up to see her. Going to Alaska was part of the plan of keeping her folks at bay from interfering with her life. Both were hoping that she would have settled down by now and be producing grandbabies for them to love and adore. She and her family had always lived in sunny and warm Florida, and she was pretty sure that none of them until her, for at least two to three generations, had seen or lived in snow. "It's nothing but pure cold and hard wilderness out here, Mom. *Really* cold," she emphasized to her mother.

"Is there snow there yet?"

She peered out the window again when the sunlight diminished suddenly, to see thick clouds coming over the mountaintops. "Not yet, but I have a feeling it is coming soon. But it feels like the dead of winter already, with it always damp and cloudy."

"I don't know how you stand it, sweetie. I need the sun."

"It has its own beauty, Mother. It really does."

"There's no shopping malls or anything out there?"

"The town's small and I am sure it has most amenities. Besides, Anchorage is only a two-and-a-half-hour drive from here."

"Oh good. That means we can come and see you then?"

Tasha mentally kicked herself for her last comment, her eyes squeezing tight enough to start the first of her crow's-feet. "Sure…sure you can, but why would you want to come see me in the dead of winter with snowdrifts that are at least six to eight feet tall and temperatures in the negative digits?"

"I guess we can wait. I just want to know that you are in a safe place. And now that I know you are living with a man—"

"Mom!" she interrupted her. "I'll be just fine. He's just another co-worker—a fueler, like I said before." She was stirring the now vigorously boiling pot of water and potatoes. "It's not like he's a monster, even though he looks very gruff, like Grizzly Adams. Again…not my type. Please let's not discuss this. I don't need a husband. I am not anyone's type and I have lost out on ever finding one." She forked the potatoes to test their softness, finding them tender. She had switched the fire down to low, nearly dropping the pot of potatoes as she turned, her peripheral vision catching sight of Jack just standing there watching her on the far side of the island.

"Jesus!" she yelped in fright, dropping the pan loudly into the metal sink and nearly spilling the potatoes.

"Are you okay?" her mother asked over the line.

"Yeah, I'm fine." As she drained the water off the pot, then put the pan on one of the other burners, she gave Jack an annoyed look for sneaking up on her. "Just tripped on something, Mom." She made a *what* on her face to him, only to watch him tread silently off to his room.

"Are you sure?"

"Yes! I'm fine. It's the dog's bowl of water," she flat-out lied. Now curious to see where he had gone, she leaned on the kitchen island, craning her neck to peer in the direction he went and to see if he was still eavesdropping. He had gone into his room and closed the door, and now she wondered where Drake was, since he was not prancing around inside.

"A dog?"

"Yes, there's a dog that lives here too."

"Not a husky, is it?"

"No, Mom," Tasha dragged out sarcastically. She wondered if he was leaning up against the door, listening in on her conversation. "I'm not living in an igloo with an Eskimo and his dog team," she said, exasperated.

"Well, Arthur says to tell you hi and hopes the best for you. I do wish you would have stayed and at least given him a chance. He's *such* a nice young man."

"Artie?"

"Whatever happened to you two? You two were as thick as thieves during your college years."

"Nothing happened between us, Mother." She didn't want to go down that memory lane, either. "It just wasn't going to happen, and it never did happen. We were *just* friends."

She heard her mother sigh heavily. Tasha rolled her eyes heavenward.

"Well, I think you do need to call him and let him know how you are doing.

Maybe you should invite him up to visit you," she encouraged.

Artie was not a man who would tolerate much, especially the cold. Tasha was certain the man didn't even own any other shoes than two pairs of flip-flops. There was no way he was going to follow her to Alaska.

"I hear that his business of selling hot dogs is doing well. You know he started out with just one wagon and now has hired three girls to roll around three more wagons this year on the beach."

Tasha could not picture herself helping Artie and his beachside hot dog business. And knowing Artie, he was *doing* all his employees! Not that he was some disgusting pimp, but women usually would throw themselves at *nice* men and it was not like he was going to say no. He was the type of guy you hung out with after your dream guy dumped you, and then you moved on when another hopeful male prospect came along.

She loved aviation and flight line work way too much. She wanted more in her life than selling hot dogs. She wanted to see the world. And now, seeing more of the world meant not getting oneself killed—or wounded, like she had in the Army. She wanted to expand her piloting skills to not just private pilot, but to a cargo or passenger transport pilot.

Besides, Artie would not have wanted her anymore now that she was physically flawed: a large, disgusting hole, in not just one side, but on both sides of her body just over her hip. There was no way she would be wearing a bikini anytime soon, if ever.

"He thinks he will be able to expand all up and down the bay area beaches by next summer."

"Hmm?"

"Are you sure you are okay, sweetie?"

Tasha moved her cell phone to her other ear; her first ear had gone numb.

"All you have to do is say the word, and I will be up there before you know it."

"No, Mom. I am fine. I will soon be working a ton of hours before you know it. Just let me get settled in and into a new place before getting here, okay?" Tasha had gotten the butter, milk, and garlic into the pan to beat into the cooked potatoes, sliding the pan over to the active burner. "Hey, I gotta go now. I'll call soon. Love you." She made a quick kiss noise into the phone before hanging up.

She needed to concentrate on making the mashed potatoes before burning them. Also, she wanted to know how long Jack had been standing there listening in on her conversation with her mother. She took her agitation out on hand-whipping the potatoes.

"What is it with you and mountain men?" came the gruff male voice, making her jump a second time, turning back to him, facing him squarely.

"What is it with you sneaking up on people and listening in on their conversations?" Tasha shot back, turning back somewhat to her task, yet able to keep an eye on him.

"I asked first." He slid into one of the tall chairs at the kitchen island, peeking at the contents inside the crockpot and then replacing the lid. "Besides, what was so fascinating about my books on my dresser?"

She nearly stopped in her whisking but managed to keep her actions unaffected. "Books? What books? I didn't think you were a reader," she smarted off to him.

"Oh yeah, that's right, I'm just an aircraft fueler," he said, repeating part of her phone conversation with her mother.

She turned to look at him. "I'm pretty sure that is what you told me you do." She kept fluffing the potatoes, adding, "Did you not?"

He nodded, picking at some imaginary flaw on the countertop. "So, did you have fun going through my underwear drawer?"

She put the pot down on one of the unused burners and came over to the island, bracing herself with both hands on the countertop. "Oh yes, I have nothing else better to do than go through men's underwear drawers to see if they have a pair of black lacy boxers or briefs. Personally, I am into the man-kinis. Blue ones, preferably."

She pushed away from the countertop and crossed her arms before continuing. "It's not like you didn't have several opportunities in going through my things." She raised an eyebrow at him.

"Only to get you a few things you needed while you were in the hospital," he shot back at her. "However, I do think we need to expand your horizon on just 'whitie-tighties.' I think you wouldn't look half bad in some colorful briefs yourself," he said, half pointing to her bullet wound.

She scowled at him. "You would." She decided it was time to put the mashed potatoes away. They could heat them up later in the day. It was another way to sidestep any further conversation. But he was not going to let her.

"So, your parents know you have made it to Seward and that you now live with some grumpy bearded Neolithic man?"

"Wow, that's a big word for you," she said sarcastically, jabbing a large serving spoon at him after getting the potatoes transferred into a storage container. "And yes, they know I am fine and not having a lewd and lascivious relationship with you." She snapped the lid on and shoved the container into the refrigerator.

"Hmm...I do know what those two words mean too, you know, for being just a flight line worker like yourself."

"Don't you even dare—"

"So, what did you glean from the photos and my personal stuff?"

He wasn't going to back off. He was like a rabid dog hell-bent on holding onto his prey.

She turned back to him, squaring her shoulders at him, ready for his full fury. "Not much. You're a rather boring person. An ex-Marine—"

"Always a Marine."

"Fine, always a Marine." She gave him a placating hand. "With a mom and dad, like me, and a sister. Because there is no woman in her right mind that would ever date you, given your current conversational skills and limited abilities for affection."

His eyebrows raised up on that last bit.

"Oh, don't give me that look! If you had a girlfriend, I would have surely met her by now. And by the way, where the hell did you go and where's Drake?"

"I'm fine," he said, as if she cared, "and so is Drake. He's with the boys."

"The boys?"

"Yeah, had to attend to my 'fueling duties'"—he made air quotes when he said his job title—"and the flight line guys wanted Drake around for the day. So, I take it you missed me?"

"Sure, whatever." She waved a dismissing hand at him.

She made to leave the kitchen to head back into her room, wanting to get away from having to discuss her life and his heavy watchful gaze. The tension in the air was a bit thick for her taste. If he didn't want to discuss his personal life with her, then she shouldn't be obligated to either.

He got up and crossed the space in one giant movement, blocking her attempt to escape from behind the kitchen island.

"What?" Her body went on full alert, sensing a possible physical threat from him, as she moved her gaze from his chest to his menacing bearded face, now certain he was her mother's worst nightmare.

"I don't need you to be in my affairs."

"Well, neither do you, listening in on people's conversations!" she snarled at him, her hackles up, leaning into his personal space. She was familiar with his brutish type from the military, and fought back by invading his personal space, standing up to his challenge. "Maybe my mother is right about living with a strange man in a cabin out in the backwoods. Are you going to prove her right?"

He didn't budge. Seconds ticked. Only a faint twist at one corner of his mouth was all it took for her to know he was backing down and of no threat to her.

"Here's a bit of advice." His low voice was almost inaudible. "First of all—"

"First? You mean you are going to enlighten me with several?"

He ignored her comment.

"The reason you may be unqualified marriageable material is that you think no one is good enough." He bent down to get in her face, squinting as if he could discern something from her eyes and see right through her very soul. "And I am pretty sure no one will ever measure up to your impossible standards." And then he stood up, backing off from blocking her. "But hey, what do I know?" He gestured to himself theatrically. "I'm just a fueler."

"You don't know a thing about me to even assume that!"

"Don't I?" He smiled knowingly. "Time will tell when we get you on the flight line and see how you treat the rest of us 'dumb mechanics.'"

"Oh yeah? You think whatever you want to. Go ahead. You're entitled to your opinion! But *so* am I!" She raised her voice at him, angrier than hell at his smugness. She knew he had been listening to her entire phone conversation. She headed back to her room to be alone and to get what little privacy she could get from him.

The better part of the day was spent organizing her things and taking mini breaks from time to time with the games on her phone. She was about to go stir crazy if she did not move or get out of the cabin. It was cold enough being still, but she knew that if she walked, she would warm up a bit, even though it would be colder outside. As soon as she was done unpacking and repacking a few things, she decided she would dress for a walk before what little daylight was left disappeared. It was during her repacking of her duffel bag that Jack knocked, but did not pause before admitting himself.

"Sure glad you give someone enough time to put themselves together before entering there, 'Griswald,'" she told him sarcastically. Still peeved, she looked up at him expectantly from where she stood by her desk, stuffing the last few items into her duffel bag. He looked to say something else when he spied her activity.

"Where are you going?"

"Nowhere...yet." She squeezed the opening shut and slid the locking ring into place. "Sorry to disappoint you." She slid the heavy bag back against the wall, giving her some space to use on the desktop. "What do you want?"

"I needed you to pack an overnight bag for our trip tomorrow."

"Hunh?" She gave him a confused look. "What trip?"

"To Anchorage."

"I thought that was just a two-hour drive from here."

"It is, but the weather at this time of year can be a bugger."

"Haven't you driven in snow before?"

His sarcastic expression said it all. "Yes, I *do* drive in snow, but not in white-out conditions, should it happen to storm while we are gone."

"First of all, why are we going? Second, wouldn't you want to wait until there was a longer period of good weather?"

"The mountains change the weather conditions very quickly and are unpredictable along the highway."

"But why do I need to come to Anchorage with you?"

"I am still in charge of 'taking care' of you, and secondly, you need better clothes than what you have."

"I have cloth—"

"You don't have any boots, and you will need coveralls with a hood. Trust me on this."

"Fine." She crossed her arms. "I suppose you are paying for this up front too?" She uncrossed her arms to reopen her bag. "Well, at least I know I have a guaranteed job for the next six months to pay it all off."

"Just pack enough for two days. I am assuming dinner will be ready by five?"

She turned her head sharply at him, narrowing her eyes, hoping that her searing look would burn him into a pile of ash. It didn't work.

"Smells good and can't wait to try it. Later," he said with a twisted half smile, closing her door.

"Where are you going?" Tasha asked to the back of her door; otherwise it was clear that he wasn't going to listen to her.

She put together a small bag for the following day, then pulled on her mini boots and grabbed her jacket.

She crossed the main room to the front door, surprised to find him still in the living area, sitting on the sofa. He looked back up over his shoulder at her, astonished that she had come out of her room.

"Where are you heading off to?" he asked, watching her march over to the coat closet.

"Hey, you don't have to answer to me, why should I answer to you?" She tugged on her jacket's zipper and then pulled out her gloves to don.

He quickly got up, barricading her from leaving, a bottle of honey lager in one hand.

"I won't ask again," he warned her.

She stopped in her actions and looked up at him and then pointedly at the beer bottle in his hand. "I have cabin fever, I am cold, I am angry, and I need to go for a walk while someone continues to drink themselves to death." Then she added, with distaste hanging on each word, "I'm not fond of drunkards."

"Oh, for Christ's sakes!" He grabbed her by her elbow, turning her around and dragging her with him. "Woman, you're a pain!"

He shoved the bottle at her, meaning for her to take it. She hesitated, not taking it from him.

His breathing was haggard as he tried to control his temper. "I'm not a drunkard, nor am I currently drunk." Instead, he sighed and placed his half-empty bottle on the fireplace mantel and walked over to the coat closet next to the basement door with her in tow, letting her go momentarily and grabbed his coat, donning it. Then grabbed his boots to put on.

At first, she just watched him. "I don't need you to chaperone me on a simple walk!" she snapped before heading for the door without him.

He stopped her before she could open the door, one boot on and the other almost on. "It's not to chaperone you. If anything, you just might make my day if a bear or a moose decided to make mincemeat out of you. No one," he said, shaking some sense into her, "No one goes walking by themselves unless they are familiar with what to do when a large wild animal comes across their path."

"I think I could take on a bear at the moment if I keep on getting more crap from your arrogant egotistical self!" She tried to yank her arm from him, but his hold was firm on her coat sleeve and she feared he would tear her sleeve in two if she tried pulling again.

"Of that I have no doubt, given your state of mind." He smiled wolfishly at her. "But I will not lose someone under my watch due to their own stupidity. And with your wide-open wound, the scent of your blood will attract things you do not wish to encounter."

"Fine," she huffed. "Hurry up, before some of us grow old with age."

He gave her a harried look, then shook his head as he finished lacing his boot. He stood up, and she opened the door and took off walking, her usual fast pace, hoping he would give up on following her. But his long legs easily matched her stride and he stayed by her side.

The day was still heavily overcast and the air damp. The mist lent a gray pallor to the world. It matched her mood and her frustration at the man *assigned* to her. She turned to walk uphill toward the mountains. She needed the workout. She had been bedridden for too long, and her money-tight journey up here, literally packaged into a car with all her worldly possessions, had allowed her no room for movement. She was wound up and needed a good run to relax her again. But the minimum movement of walking bit into her side, and she knew the jolting of running would hurt even more.

Her silently stewing private bodyguard towered protectively near, taking to the road side of her as any gentleman would have done. She walked on the paved road leading up the hill, finding that it led farther into a rather sparse neighborhood of tidy little homes and their outside toys of covered boats, ATVs, and camping trailers. The trees were comforting, and she eventually felt the tension leave her body as she deeply inhaled the pine-laden air. It was quiet. Incredibly quiet. They continued until the road ended in dirt at a construction site where machinery sat.

"Bears?" she asked quietly.

He did not answer right away, as if he was lost in his thoughts, and she wondered if he had heard her, but then he answered. "Yes, it's a possibility." He smiled lightly at her jest at the construction equipment. But then he tapped her other shoulder to look back down the road they had just walked. He was pointing to something along the tree line. It was only when one moved that she spotted the large mule deer emerging from the tree line. In fact, a small cluster of them eased forward from the trees, feasting on the tall grass near the road.

She found herself smiling in pure delight at the wildlife so close, and not from inside a car or at a zoo.

"Think those would harm me?" she whispered.

"Think again." He was close to her ear and spoke low. "They could, if provoked. Never underestimate them, either. Getting this close to winter, animals become desperate as their food source becomes sparse."

They stood there watching them graze. When the cold began to settle deep into her bones, it was time to move again to keep warm. She tapped him to indicate that she needed to walk. He made her cross to the far side of the road, giving the cluster of deer their space to continue eating. It was fascinating to see the deer not bolt but continue grazing as they passed by. Alert, yet not scared of their passing.

As they retraced their steps, she saw a beautiful fox dart across the road and disappear into the thickets again. She was amazed to see so much wildlife so close to town. Jack reminded her that it was the hour where the animals were more active: either in the early morning or in the late afternoon just before the sun set behind the mountains. He guided her down a different road, letting her know it circled back to their cabin area. That side road was part of a much larger neighborhood, but the housing still sparse and heavily wooded in between the homes. Where the trees were thin, she caught glimpses of the dark gray tidal area. It was beautiful country. Rugged, yet so fragile.

By the time they made it back to the cabin, the sun was almost gone behind the mountainous ridge line. Although it was still the late afternoon, evening dusk had arrived to stay awhile. The lack of light made her body feel more tired than it should. She realized that she may have difficulties staying awake during the winter months. It was clear that her body's active rhythms matched the amount of time the sun was up. But then, it was a perfect time to test her private theory on human hibernation. At some point in her early twenties, during one particular harsh winter at Fort Drum, she had sworn that somewhere along the human ancestral lines, one human had messed it up for the rest of them by not hibernating like they should have during the winter. When it was cold and dark, all she wanted to do was sleep and snuggle down. No work, no play. Maybe get up enough times to eat, but that would be it. Alaska and this job would test her. She would soon know whether she could survive so far north.

As they neared their cabin, just down the hill from them, they saw a car stop just in front of their driveway. The rear passenger door opened, and Drake bounded out of the car like a Jack-in-the-box. She did not know the driver nor the front seat passenger through the semi-dark tinted glass on the sedan, but saw the driver give Jack a cordial wave before making a quick U-turn and taking back off toward town. Jack whistled for Drake and the large black dog came happily bounding toward them. With a short greeting and then a toss of an errant stick picked up near the roadside, Jack tossed it for Drake to go fetch as they made their way to the front door, and he let her inside while he went to the side of the cabin to continue playing with Drake in the yard.

He came in a few minutes later with a fresh stack of wood for the fire. Drake followed just behind him. She had yet to remove her coat, still waiting for the cold to dissipate in the cabin's welcoming warmth. While she spied on them playing outside from the main living room window, she had removed Jack's beer bottle from the mantel and placed it on the kitchen island, their evening dinner scent signaling that it was ready. Even she noted his demeanor had calmed with their walk. She took off her coat and hung it up in the coat closet. While Jack fed the fire and got out of his jacket and boots, she decided to heat up the mashed potatoes and spoon out the main dish onto two plates.

She was tentative about sitting down to dinner with him, for it had been an off-and-on day for both, each of them riling the other. She pushed his half a bottle of beer over to his seat, in part, as a peace offering to him for making him mad prior to their walk.

Without a word, he sat down to his place as she finished making herself a hot tea. She decided to sit adjacent to him so that she could face him rather than have him to her side and be so close to her. She wasn't ready to open herself up to this man, she thought, taking a few bites before putting down her fork to rest. In fact, he was more familiar with her than he should have been, especially when it came to her body. *Damn wound,* she thought as she picked up her cup and sipped her hot tea, watching him eat with gusto over the barbecue-flavored pork roast and veggies. She thought he would have hated the heavily garlic mashed potatoes until he hummed his delight at his first forkful.

He caught her watching him, chewing more and matching her stare before asking, "What?"

"Hmm?" She acted somewhat distracted, as if she were in her own thoughts.

He put his fork down, although his elbows were still on the countertop, and waited for her comment. She didn't say a word. He wasn't sure what to make of her, much less what to expect next out of her mouth, other than something disdainful.

Pointing to her plate, he said, "Are you going to eat? I thought it was pretty darn good home cooking. Not bad." He was trying to keep the peace with his last comment. *In fact, it was damn good cooking!* he thought. The finest he'd had since leaving his family for the military eight years before. No…that would be ten years, after living in Alaska for the past two years. If this kept up, he would be the happiest man on earth. He figured it might be worth it to keep her content in order to keep from having to eat out at the bar or diner every other night. Most likely though, she would drive him insane in keeping her appeased. How she managed to stay out of trouble in the Army with a sassy mouth like hers was beyond him.

She had not even dished out half of what she had served him. Tasha pushed her half-eaten dish over to him to let him finish hers. She took his empty plate and her empty cup to the sink. Next, she put away the leftover mashed potatoes and found another container to store the leftover main course. He continued to eat, although under a quiet, watchful eye. She made herself another cup of hot tea by just making more hot water in the microwave before starting on the dirty dishes. He eventually came over with her plate, finished with his seconds, and dumped it into the soaking bin side.

"Here, let me finish this for you."

She looked at him in astonishment, not moving from her station.

"What? You think I can't wash dishes?" Jack asked her with a smirk.

"No, just surprised you're helping me." She acquiesced to his takeover at the sink.

He dunked his hands in the warm water, grabbing a dish to wash. "No, I just need to warm up my hands too in this hot water."

Tasha thought she witnessed a small dimple appeared briefly just within the bristles of his beard line before he dropped his lopsided smile.

"You? The mountain man, cold?" she asked in surprise, toweling her hands dry. Then she turned to dispense the crockpot leftovers into the waiting container. She snapped a lid on it and placed the container in the refrigerator.

"Yes, I get cold too. But unlike you, I don't complain about it," he stated, turning his face to her, his eyes watching her intently.

"Complain?" She watched him take the cumbersome crockpot and wash it for her. "I am still trying to adjust and stating a fact."

"Which everyone already knows…"

"Fine, I won't say another word about it." She tried to remember when she had last complained.

He turned the crockpot upside down to dry on another dish towel on the countertop next to the drying rack full of dishes, then drained the sink.

She changed the subject. "Where are you originally from?" she asked, taking the clean sponge to wipe down the island countertop while he turned to face the island and her, leaning against the cabinets, drying his hands with the dish towel absentmindedly.

"Louisiana."

She looked at him when he turned long enough to hang up the dish towel, but resumed concentrating on cleaning when he turned back around, asking him, "Where's your Southern accent?"

"It was educated out of me at LSU." Then he added with a Southern drawl, "Sorry, darling."

Her expression was priceless.

"Yes, this backwoods mountain man does have a college education."

"I haven't said anything to the contrary."

"You didn't have to. Your expression says it all."

She hesitated again in her wiping of the island's countertop, before resuming her action and her next question.

"So, what made you join the Marines?"

"Wanted to see the world," he said. "What made you join the Army?"

"They paid my college tuition off, and like you, I wanted to travel some on someone else's budget," she said.

Jack scoffed. "I bet those were the last places you wanted to travel to then?"

She ignored his jibe. "What did you do while you were in the Marines?" she continued, wiping the last of the countertop, using the tentative truce to see how far he would let her into his private life.

"Combat Specialist."

Finished, she just sighed, giving him an obvious look, knowing that all soldiers were 'combat specialists.' "Not really original are you, Staff Sergeant?" she told him, exasperated.

"Ah, gotta love a girl who knows her rank." Her comment verified that she had indeed gone through his books and photos on his dresser earlier in the day. He went around her to the refrigerator to grab another bottle of beer, again using just his thumb to pop the cap off and chunking it into the trash bin on the far side of the kitchen island against the wall.

"What did you do in the Army?" he casually asked her.

"I think you already know what my background and rank are."

He raised an eyebrow at her before passing her to go to the sofa to sit in front of the fireplace. He sighed, putting his feet up on the wooden coffee table in front of him. She followed with her second cup of hot tea, taking the chair to his left. He eyed her a moment. She matched his blue gray eyes with her green ones. His lips were pressed in a line, nearly making them invisible in his beard and mustache whiskers. He was waiting on her to answer his unspoken question.

"The papers in my file were out of order when I went through them today," she told him, adding, "organizing my things." She tentatively sipped her tea, testing how hot the tea was in the cup. She was trying to relax, but still felt like she had to remain alert with him around.

He was impressed, as he followed her moves by taking a sip from his bottle. She was definitely detail oriented. "True. We went over your files while the hospital staff stitched you back up. But I want to know why a college-educated 'whirly girl' is here working in a small town such as ours." He took another sip from his beer.

"Why would you be just an aircraft fueler?" she countered back.

"Maybe I am not just a fueler. I do have other duties on the flight line. We all fly the aircraft from time to time."

"So you're a pilot too?"

"Not as dumb as I look?"

She didn't answer him. Instead, she said, "Like I said before, the job was the first to offer housing and a decent paycheck." Then she added, on second thought, "Can I add ratings to my private pilot's license?"

"You already know how to fly?" He was astounded by not knowing that earlier.

"Yes." She gave him a confused look. "Why?"

"That'll be a relief for Nate."

"Why would that be?"

"We needed another pilot, and with half of the training already done, your ratings will be a piece of cake once we get you familiar with the landscape and the ports we go to for supply runs. IFR rated?"

"Never finished it."

"We need to get you finished on that rating first. Alaska's weather doesn't permit much time for VFR flying." He watched her as she became entranced with the fire's light. The kitchen light over the sink area, the only lighting in the main room, had cast the living room in heavy shadows. "Who taught you?"

"My dad. He was an air traffic controller when I was going through high school. Haven't flown much since then. A rich man's sport." The fire's light was dancing over her face. She was tiring again, from the way she was answering him. Her defenses weren't up as she cupped her hands around her warm tea mug.

He grunted to himself as he kept looking at her. Noticing things. Little things. The line of her high cheekbones, the natural blush to her cheeks on her fair skin, slightly mottled with a smattering of light freckles that had been sun-faded over the last few years. Her neck was long and slender, like the fingers on her hands, the length making her graceful without the airs. Her time in the military had grounded her. Her pine green woolen turtleneck sweater matched her eyes. Her pale blonde hair shimmered in the fire's light.

"Go to bed, Tasha," he stated flatly.

At the sound of her name, she turned her focus to him. "I'm fine. I'm just…" She paused when she remembered what she had told him earlier at dinner, that she would never 'complain' of it again. She was doing everything not to shiver as she grew colder.

He pulled the throw from behind him on the sofa and gently tossed it to her.

Tasha nearly spilled her tea where she had held the mug close to her mouth when he expertly tossed the throw neatly into her lap. She set her cup down and pulled the throw around her, closing her eyes in relief at the additional warmth. She was tired but was not going to give in too soon. She sat up as long as he did. But somewhere between staring into the hypnotic flames and the gentle scooping up of her body, she had fallen asleep. She groggily awoke as he carried her to her bed, laying her down on her good side, checking her bandaging and applying more ointment to her backside. She felt the warmth of his hand remain there momentarily on her side before he pulled her shirt back down and tucked her in for the night.

CHAPTER FOUR

It was the pounding on her door that awoke her in the dark. *It can't be morning yet!* But his voice came through the door telling her it was time to get up and to get ready for the drive to Anchorage. She heard his bedroom door shut, knowing that he must have just finished showering along with the rest of his morning's ablutions. *The man is a drill sergeant!*

She dragged herself out of her bed, getting ready for the day. She decided that she could get away with the clothes that she had on from the day before and had slept in. She was going to have a coat on anyway, she thought as she grabbed her overnight bag and purse. It was not like anyone would know—until she met Jack's steady gaze, going over her whole attire from where he sat eating breakfast at the kitchen island. He didn't have to say a word for her to know that he knew she hadn't bothered to shower or change into different clothes as he passed her a plate with some cooked eggs, bacon, and some potatoes. She chose to ignore him.

They ate quietly. He had made himself coffee and offered her some. She graciously refused, saying that she would make herself some tea shortly. But he surprised her by pushing a travel mug over to her, already filled with her brew. He poured the rest of the hot coffee into his travel mug, then turned off the coffee maker. He saw her empty plate and asked if she was ready to go.

"Wash the dishes while I get Drake's things ready."

She did what she was asked to do.

"Drake's coming with us?" she asked, thinking it would be an uncomfortable two-hour drive with the three of them in the cab of the truck.

"No, I'm dropping him off along with a few of his things for the guys at the hangar to pet-sit him for the day."

As she prepared to plunge into the cold air outside, Jack went outside to start the truck, letting it warm up before he was back again, whistling for Drake to follow as he picked up both their bags. She picked up their mugs and followed them outside. Jack watched as Drake clambered in the driver's side, then turned back to the cabin door, closing and locking it.

After leaving Drake behind at the hangar with Hank, the drive along Seward highway proved to be uneventful in the early morning hours. However, the further north they went there were patches of snow already at the higher elevations, and the surrounding mountains grew thick with the white coating. Ever since she had arrived, she had been watching the increasing white patches of snow on the town's surrounding mountains as it inched downwards. The stark scenery did not diminish her enjoyment of taking in the sights of the great land. Her face was plastered to the passenger window, and if she were not careful she would find her skin sticking to the cold glass.

Neither spoke. Jack often looked over, finding her drinking in the sights of Alaska as it began to unfold itself, showing her its entire beauty in a dangerously beguiling way. He smiled knowingly, remembering his first time. The long early morning light illuminated the low tidal waters and the mountains in a multitude of warm golden-to-purplish hues like some of the artwork he had seen in some of the shops during the summer tourism season. Tasha's face reflected the liminal light. Periodically, she would sip on her hot tea, enjoying the warmth it provided with a small, delightful sigh.

He shifted in his seat to settle in for the long drive. He found the moment relaxing, if not enjoyable, and with a woman, at that. He liked that she didn't chat his ear off like other girls he had previously dated. Nor did she bore him with girly interests such as fashion, clothes, material things, or the latest everyday gossip. In fact, he was curious as to what things did interest her. He had never bothered to ask her until the previous night, only to discover that she had a clue when it came to flying.

What was it she told me last night, her reason for joining the Army? Ah, yes, she wanted to travel on someone else's budget, Jack mulled to himself. *Except that she paid a price by acquiring a bullet hole in her side.*

As if hearing his negative thoughts, she turned to him and changed the topic by asking him how far it was to Fairbanks by car and if she could drive at that time of year.

"I would definitely not recommend your car, much less my truck," he said, looking back at the traffic ahead of him. "However, we can fly up there periodically and give you a sense of the place for a few hours while they reload the plane."

"The company flies there?"

"We fly to wherever someone needs us to fly, whether it be a private charter or supply runs for the smaller towns. Flying becomes more necessary during the wintertime since the roads become mostly impassible with snow and ice."

"But not so much during the summer?"

"We slow down a bit, mostly taking hunters out into the wilderness or giving tourist flight tours of the Kenai Fjords. Most of us do the heavy maintenance when the aircraft needs it at that time of year. A few of us go on long vacations or hunting trips around April and May."

"I see."

"What things would you like to do or see while you are here?" he asked, hoping to find what interested her.

"I want to go camping, try my hand at catching a salmon during their runs…" She shrugged her shoulder, thinking more. "I want to see a glacier up close, touch the ice. I know that sounds silly."

"No, it doesn't. I came from the South and I never saw snow until I was at least twenty-two years old." Then it occurred to him. "Have you seen snow? I mean, actually experienced being in the snow before, Tasha?"

"Once, but it was the artificial snow. You know, the kind they blow on the mountains in the Poconos when they don't get enough snow at the ski resorts."

"Oh, boy, you are going to be in for a real treat then this winter, aren't you?"

She gave him a quizzical look.

"It's not the same, trust me," he assured her, smiling. He took a swig of his coffee and then clutched his thermos between his legs again. "Somehow I have this feeling it will be fun watching you experience your first true deep snowfall."

She did not ask any further questions, mainly because she thought he was making fun of her again and the last thing she wanted to do was encourage him.

"What else do you want to see?" he asked.

She looked at him, studying him a moment. Then, as if deciding something, she said, "I would like to do a lot of hiking, see the bears, fish in the rivers, but I like…" She did not want to bore him with what she really liked to do. It was too girly for him to even relate to.

"What do you like?" he pressed her.

"Nothing that you would find of interest," she said, turning her head back to her passenger window, not really seeing the view.

"Try me." He looked at her, trying to figure out what she was too timid to tell him.

She looked back over her shoulder at him. "I don't need you poking fun at me for my interests, and most likely you will find them dull."

"Why?"

"Because you are a *manly-man* type of guy whose interests lay in doing outdoorsy, rugged things."

"Okay, so I like camping, fishing, and hunting. I think every man up here is living the backwoods dream."

"I'm not a big fan of hunting or killing unless it is absolutely necessary. Sorry. Hunting them to track them down to watch or photograph…then yes."

"Then you should be fine with my hunting, for I only hunt for what I need each winter. I do not hunt entirely for the sport of it, wasting wildlife. In fact, you seemed to enjoy the chili a few nights ago. That was ground venison that filled your belly." He grinned at her.

She lifted an indifferent shoulder at him. "Like I said, I don't mind hunting for food, but you will never see me do it unless it's necessary. Heck, I get squeamish over someone wringing a chicken's neck to prep for dinner. Which—oh God, where do you dress your kills?" She shoved her hands deeper between her legs, either needing more warmth or in pure fear, her concern sincere, her face visibly pale.

He *hmmphed* before telling her to relax; he took his kills to the local butcher shop and not inside the cabin. He got the idea that she saw him as a typical 'Bambi-killer.'

"Okay, then, let me guess what you like, since you hesitate to tell me. And I get that it is very 'girly' in nature." He patted and pulled down on his beard with his free hand before returning it to the steering wheel. "It must have to do with clothes or art of some type."

"Not into clothes."

"So I can tell." He nodded to her morning's repeat attire.

She immediately looked down at herself, trying to gauge what was so wrong with what she wore in terms of the coat, sweater, a pair of jeans, and boots. "What's wrong with my clothes besides that you have determined that they are not good enough for Alaskan winters?"

"No woman I have ever known wears the same clothes two days in a row, much less sleeps in them."

She sniffed. "I don't think they stink. And I did change my undies this morning."

He lifted one eyebrow at this piece of titillating information. "Nice to know." He tapped a forefinger on the wheel. "More than I needed to know." He grinned at her. "No woman I've known would have admitted to that either."

"Well, I guess I am no ordinary woman, then." She hugged herself before shoving her hands back between her legs, holding onto her travel mug still half full of hot tea.

He studied her a moment. She knew he was watching her but ignored him. "Well, I think it must be art. Performing arts? Theater? Dance?"

She made a moue. "I do like art, but more like going through art galleries for fun." She caught his sly smile. "If you insist…I like doing stained glass. I myself do not dance but would kill for a date to any play or musical. However, I was born fifty years too late to find any man willing to suffer a night at the theater. Otherwise, yes, I love going to movies, but better yet, watching movies online in the privacy of my home is more fun for me."

"Movies?"

"Yeah…movies—it's like watching TV. By the way, I've noticed we don't have a TV."

"It's a mind killer. Wastes a lot of time when life's too short," Jack answered, putting a lazy arm out to drape over the steering wheel, yet partially to stretch his long limbs.

"Agree, but I still like things on the History channel where I can learn things."

"That's what your smart phone is for, isn't it?"

She rolled her eyes at him. "If you get the right service provider for your area."

"Stain glass art?"

She nodded her head at him.

"And that's all?"

"Quilting and reading," she told him rather quietly, trailing off, as if she was embarrassed by her simple interests.

"My mother used to do that. Father helped her plan her designs. He even cut out the pieces for her to sew," Jack said rather wistfully to himself.

"Are your parents still alive?"

He looked at her, startled that she had even asked a question about his family. "Yeah, they're alive. They live in Baton Rouge. Both are retired. But Ma works part time with her home business, selling soaps and dried herbs. Dad was a career military guy. But did end up being a high school football coach for a few years."

"Ah…explains you joining the Marines then. He was a Marine, too?"

Jack nodded affirmatively.

"And?" she prodded him, curiosity clear on her face.

"A younger sister. You saw her photo in my books. She's four years younger than me. Still working on her master's degree. Something in science, I believe. She keeps changing her mind. Last time we spoke, she wanted to be a zoologist. It had changed from being a veterinarian, and before that a marine biologist."

Tasha saw his faint smile through his whiskers as he spoke of his sister. "You said you went to college too. What's your degree in?"

"I have a degree in business management just like you," he answered flatly. His smile had disappeared by then.

She raised an eyebrow at him.

"Need a break?" he asked, without turning to look at her.

"Hunh?" At first she did not register his out-of-the-blue question.

"There's a rest stop with facilities. I need to stretch my legs."

"Yes!" she said eagerly. Between the cooler air and the hot tea, she had a bladder to unleash. "I thought I'd never get a chance."

Jack looked at her for her odd remark before commenting that he had no intentions of making her hold it all the way to Anchorage, as he parked the truck at the entrance to the public restrooms.

"Gosh, and here I thought you would do the typical man thing and pee in a beer bottle while still driving! I thought that's why the Marines were called Jarheads. They can go while on the go!" She grinned at him before scurrying off to the restrooms.

Damn the girl is imaginative with her taunts! he chuckled to himself. She was a pure mix of bashfulness and yet not afraid of anything, refreshingly new in his book of dealing with women. Not like he dealt with many of them. His last serious girlfriend was just before he had left for the corps. However, his decision to join broke that relationship. Jessica was not having any part of being in a long-distance relationship. Especially with a soldier, where she would be worried all the time about his safety—whether he would come home alive, if not permanently mangled. It was *too much* for her to handle, she told him. When he did return home after his tours, at last being sent home to recover from the shrapnel wounds, he had located her only to find that she had gotten married and already had two kids. There was no going back. It was time for him to move on. He blamed himself for losing *the catch of his life* and thought there would be no other girl out there that gorgeous and smart. He liked the college-educated ones, especially ones that wore office attire and worked professional jobs like accounting. It was one of his biggest turn-ons in women.

He got out of the truck to use the facilities and then to walk the boardwalk along the marsh where the rest stop was located.

Tasha was pretty, but not in your office kind of way. She was your Girl-Friday type he supposed, just low-key in terms of professionalism. Not really tomboyish per se, until you released the girl inside, allowing her to surface. She was mechanically inclined. Tasha understood the terms of various machinery, military terminology, and other guy-like things.

He had spotted her looking out over the marshlands when he came out of the restrooms. She had bundled herself up in her coat with the hood up. It was only her size that gave her away to him. She was neither short nor extremely tall. But she had long legs, and those hips—he remembered her curvature as he dressed her wound daily—those hips were generously curvy, giving her a waist that was not altogether petite. She was average but taller than the average woman. She was 'do-able' in his book. Not that he was picky when he needed his 'needs' to be soothed for a night.

What am I thinking? "Christ!" he swore to himself. This girl was going to be one of his co-workers. He was no better than one of his crew members on the flight line. He ran a hand through his long layers to help wake him from his daydreaming.

"It's just gorgeous here!" she said when he reached her side where she was leaning forward on the wooden railing. She was genuinely happy being outside in the cool air, even though he saw her shiver from its sharpness, her shoulders coming up protectively to her neck and then back down.

"Come on, let's do a quick walk, get you warmed up while we are out here." He indicated for her to follow him along the boardwalk that allowed visitors to view the wildlife that nestled out in the tall grasses and then to an overlook view of the surrounding mountains. The walk helped keep their blood flowing against the insistent wind that tunneled down the road and river between the two mountain ridge lines. He pointed out a few of the different birds he spotted, giving her tidbits of interesting information about each species. Birds were becoming few at that time of year, most wildlife having settled down in their dens or nests, the rest having flown south.

Their walk ended back at his truck, which he unlocked and started the engine, letting it warm up again, giving them a chance to reorganize their personal effects as they buckled themselves in. He put the truck into gear and they continued their journey down the other side of the pass.

They arrived in Anchorage at the end of the second hour and he decided to park the truck in one of the downtown's local parking garages nearest the mall so that they could remain inside to do most of their shopping. He needed for her to adjust to the weather in increments, not get her sick and weak before starting her job. Most everything they needed would be there, in addition to going to the bank and finding some books and magazines to keep him occupied during their roughest winter days.

He hoped that they would not take long finding her warmer clothes and clothes that would fit her. He had her get them a light brunch while he went to the bank to talk to a loan officer to see what options he had available to him. It did not take long and now all he needed was to locate a few sales magazines.

He caught up to her at one of the tables, where she had occupied herself with a cell phone game. She was not one to just sit there without something to fidget with in her hands. *But doesn't everyone do that these days?* he wondered.

She looked up momentarily, greeting him with her usual bright smile, where her eyes lit up too. He knew she was comfortable and relaxed, not on guard, as she resumed tapping on her phone screen. He thought it was because they both needed the space to move around, the cabin being tiny and cramped in some ways with the two of them occupying it. It would have to be that way for the time being. He knew his boss did not have the financial capability to put her in separate housing nor increase her wage to afford decent housing. He just didn't want to break it to her nor look like the jerk forcing her to remain in their cabin. He figured Nate would be the one to tell her.

"So, you're a big game player?" Jack asked her as he grabbed his unwrapped breakfast sandwich.

She pressed a few more times on her phone's screen and then put her phone down to talk. "Naw, just bored. It keeps my mind active and engaged until I can settle down and do things that are more important."

"What are you playing?" Between mouthfuls, he asked, reaching for her phone.

"Mostly solitaire or a few crossword-style games. Nothing major." She scrunched her nose at him.

"No, shoot-'em-up arcade games?"

"Ah…that would be more your style, I believe."

"Ah, yes, that's right, you don't believe in hunting or killing." He sat back in his chair, pushing her phone gently back to her and stroking his beard down a few times before taunting her: "What kind of soldier does that make you in the Army?"

Her green eyes sharpened at him. "A good one, I hope." She leaned forward some, her hands folding together. "I had a choice when I signed up…I could either blow things up or fix them." Her long fingers entwined. "I chose to fix things. Be a problem solver."

He tilted his head in deference. She knew what she wanted to do. There was no hesitation on her part. He was impressed.

"What did you do?" Tasha asked him.

"What did I do?"

"Yes!" She felt exasperated again. "There's a terrible echo in this state when it comes to talking with you!"

"I blew them up." He smiled at her.

"That still doesn't tell me much about you and your history."

"Why would you want to know my history?"

"Well, I figure we will be working together. It's nice to know the guys one will be working with. Besides, we will be roomies for, what? A few more weeks?" Her hands moved when she talked, emphasizing points.

He was tickled with her avid personality when she did let go of her defensive shield. He chuckled. "Roomies, huh?" Jack questioned as he crumpled up his wrapper, putting it next to the other trash on the tray.

"Well, whatever you want to call it. It sure would be nice to have a cool roomie to chat with and not have the roommate from hell." She chatted casually to him, picking up their brunch debris from their mid-morning break to dump it in the nearest trash receptacle. She turned to look back at him, still sitting there in his seat. "Well? What are you waiting for? An invitation to shop? Let's go, soldier!" she ordered him, and waved him to come hither.

He smirked. "Just typical."

She turned to lead the way but looked over her shoulder at him.

"Tell a girl you are going to take her shopping and it becomes an operation."

She grinned back at him. "I'm not stupid. You offered and I am taking you up on it. So hold your tongue."

He rolled his eyes at her as he lumbered up from his comfortable seat, dutifully following her.

As it turned out, she was not hard to shop for after all. She had passed by most of the current and irresponsible fashion trends that most women would have pored over, ignoring several women's stores. She was a no-frills type of girl when she looked for clothing items. He remained dutifully behind when she went to try on clothing, thankful that she only carried a large wallet and not a purse when she made him hold it and wait. At one point he stood by a bulk display of discounted and colorful sexy underwear, picking one up to figure out what it covered and if it was even worth the discounted price for the elastic string and tiny speck of cloth. He discovered that she was a quick-change artist as well when he looked up to find her standing there with her head cocked, arms crossed in front of her, watching him inspect the various panties. Her expression of *so-not-happening* was enough to make him drop the offending article and follow her out of the store, egging her, "You know you should try a few of those on."

"Only in your wet dreams, buddy," she retorted, walking by a few more stores, then stopping to turn back on him, making him pull up short, the bags he carried the only cushion between them. "Besides, you told me to pick out things that would keep me warm."

"Well, those might be more practical to wear." He tilted his head toward a window display of an Alaskan kitsch store in which was displayed a matching furred 'his' and 'her' bikini set. She recovered from her initial amazement of the items, smiled at the impractically of it, then mercurially glared at him, annoyed, only to burst out into laughter at him and his antics. Her laughter was infectious, and soon he was caught up in the moment, laughing with her.

Calming down, she continued, "Well, I hate to break it to you, Jack, but I already have one of those." He was stunned and confused at first, trying to glean the meaning from her cocked smile. His expression had to have been clear, before she said, "Unfortunately, it comes naturally, if one doesn't do their manicuring of one's private parts."

"Oh?"

She wagged a warning finger at him. "Don't go any further." She left him behind again, grinning devilishly, in her pursuit of warm, protective clothing at the next shop. At least she was making the shopping trip interesting.

She picked up a few more winter heavy-weight jeans, two insulated leggings, a pair of good work boots, heavier socks, and sweatshirts. The last item she needed, according to him, was heavy duty coveralls.

Her coveralls and work gloves ended up coming from an outdoor clothier place where he liked to get his hunting and camping gear. It was there that he helped make sure she got the right fit and quality protective gear. He would try to keep her inside the hangar as much as possible, and she should be, considering she was an electrician. Mechanics and linemen were the ones who would be outside the most. But there was no promising, since the work they all did varied daily.

After zipping her up in the suit and leaning low enough to her face under her fur-lined hood, he asked her, "Can you move?"

"Just barely." She tested her arms by swinging them around a bit. "I feel like a Yeti," she said, trying to talk around the brand-new fluffy fur that nearly covered all her face.

He laughed. "You'll get used to it, I hope."

"What do you mean 'I hope'?" She walked around to test the freedom of movement in the bottom half of the suit, doing a combination of lunges and squats.

"Many end up not liking the winters here and leave within the first year."

She stopped and turned around to look back up at him. "You seriously don't think I'll make it through this first winter?" she asked as she began to strip down, her hair being the only sign of her ruffled feathers from having the hood on.

"It's not a judgment or insult," he said, giving her a placating hand. "Not many realize how bad it can be up here for seven or more months."

"It's Alaska, you know. We're on top of the friggin' world!" she commented flatly back at him. "One would expect that. Going dark for the next six months will be the challenge for me."

"And?"

She stopped once she was free of her coveralls. "And?"

Remembering her sarcasm, he said, "God, I think there's an echo in here again."

She rolled her eyes at him. "And…I am a little worried about the darkness."

"You're scared of the dark?" he teased her.

"No…I just come from the sunshine state and then two years of freakin' sunny desert life. I do run on sunshine! Not that you'd understand."

"Oh, I do. Like you, I come from the South—albeit a bit hazier with humidity."

"So what do you do?"

"Do what?"

"In the dark?" She realized it was a loaded question and raised her hand up for him not to bother with an answer. Only it was too late.

He gave her a wolfish grin. But he scratched at his head, playing it out. "Ah, I can name a few things."

"This isn't going to end well." Picking up the coveralls, she took them to the cash register.

"You set yourself up, ya know?" Jack chuckled behind her as she passed him. Her eyes threw him razor blades. "Don't forget to pick up some gloves."

She was not entirely happy with any of the gloves they came across and ended up not purchasing anything. It was just as well, for she had decided to use her credit card on her other purchases only to find out that she had maxed it out and could not pay for her coveralls. He stepped in and paid for her purchase.

"Thank you," she said rather softly to him, blushing in her embarrassment.

"No problem. I said I would cover this day until your first few paychecks." He elbowed her to follow. "We still need to get you some decent work gloves that you can work in."

"My old ones can make do," she assured him, holding up the ones she possessed from her coat's pocket.

He did not have to look to know hers would never hold up to the duress of the work they did. "Those will fall apart before the month's over with, especially if you get Skydrol on them. You're getting another pair."

They wandered around in a few more stores, letting her check out a few more curios before they came across a bookstore where he wanted to stop and browse for a while. They easily spent an hour in the store. Tasha browsed through the jigsaw puzzles, enjoying the pictures, along with a few of the books. At one point, she found one that captured her interest enough for her to drop down into one of the many chairs to start reading it. Since Jack had found the magazines he wanted, he was ready to go. She said for him to hold a minute while she took a photo of the book she wanted to read for future reference.

"Seriously?"

"Yeah, it looks like a good one. And I want to be able to buy it eventually."

"Come on, I'll get it for you," he said, nodding with his head since his hands were full of shopping bags and his book choices, "and grab a puzzle. One that will take us a while."

"You do jigsaw puzzles?"

"It's something different, and I haven't done one in long time. My sister loved them when I did them with her. It'll keep you occupied in the dark," he taunted her, giving her a cheesy grin.

She gave him a momentary annoyed look but did not hesitate to grab a thousand-piece one of Alaska's natural wonders, the Kenai Fjords. Jack paid for their purchases and then dragged her into a barber shop at the last minute.

"What are we doing here?" she asked him.

"I could use a little cleaning up on my beard and hair, since it bothers you," he told her, indicating for her to take a seat in the waiting area and then proceeding to cover her with all their shopping bags to guard.

"You don't have to get a shave or…or a haircut on account of me," she sputtered to him, stunned.

"Who said I was going to lose the beard?" He pulled at it and then turned to the man waiting to take him in the chair. "It's too cold to take it off."

She raised an eyebrow at him. "I gotta see what you will be asking for then," she said as she took out the book he had just purchased for her.

He grinned at her before he told the man what he would like to have done, but she was unable to hear the instructions clearly from where she sat.

Several minutes later the barber shook off the cover, dumping the excess hair from Jack's beard and hair. He had gotten his long layers shorn to a nicer layered look, a high-and-tight without being military short, his neckline shaved, and last, his beard did remain in place but cut to a close-cropped sea captain's style of beard about an inch long.

The barber had asked if she was pleased with his new look when she looked up and over to them. She nodded her appreciation. He looked entirely different. More presentable. More of a man than a wild one. And then there was the smell of men's aftershave that nailed her senses, one of the few weaknesses about men she had: her sheer love of cologne and aftershave.

As Jack paid for the services, she got up and configured their bags more efficiently to carry, only to have him pick up the others, sharing the load between them. She could not help looking at him constantly as she tried to keep up with his stride through the mall.

He did a double-take, catching her staring at him as she followed, but he didn't say anything; instead he just smiled, flashing those white canines of his at her. He was quietly laughing to himself and then it hit him as to the last time he had been so happy. It had been a long time. *Too long*, he said to himself mentally, pausing and then dismissing the errant thought. It was getting close to dinnertime and they had not eaten any lunch, and his stomach was going to start rumbling if he did not find something soon.

"You hungry?" Jack asked her. He wanted to make the day last a while longer.

"Getting there. What would you like to eat?" she asked, being considerate of him. Her green eyes glittered as she kept adjusting and taking in his new clean-cut visage.

That's a first! A girl asking him what he would like. "Tell you what," he said, looking around them as if determining their location, "how about we unload our bags into the cab of the truck and then decide what we both feel like eating for an early dinner? If you see anything of interest as we head to the parking garage, we will come back to it."

She nodded in agreement.

They unloaded their goodies quickly. She had a hankering for anything original that one would not find in the South. He was on a mission for some Italian food, since he had told her that there wasn't anything particularly terrific in Seward for pasta.

The idea of pasta sounded terrific. Great comfort food. "I'm definitely sold if they have a tortellini dish."

"I do believe they have one." He turned her around to lead the way by placing a hand at the small of her back, guiding her forward to the mall's entrance and from there walking just ahead of her, toward the specialty restaurant.

The hostess sat them in a secluded corner booth where they could sit side by side and watch the other patrons come and go, yet still sort of face each other for conversation. Tasha scooted in but made sure to give Jack his space to stretch out his long legs. She still could not take her eyes off him, inhaling deeply the scent of his aftershave as he looked at his menu.

"Is it to your liking?" he asked her, without looking up from his menu.

"What?" His words cut into her dreamy thoughts over his new visage and her noting the newest exposed details, such as a prominent dimple. "The restaurant?" She picked up the menu, realizing she had been caught staring again, inwardly chastising herself as she quickly read through the menu's items.

"I meant my good looks."

"Hunh?" She chewed her bottom lip before commenting. "I know I complimented you before at the barber shop," she reminded him.

"Ah huh," he commented.

She gave him a quick side glance, pretending to be focusing on the menu, only to find him staring at her.

"What?" she asked.

"I just thought I may have had something amiss on my face." He was egging her.

She put her menu down, folded her hands over it, and gave him her full attention.

Ah, here it comes, he thought, waiting on her next smart-alecky remark.

"The visual change on you is quite dramatic. Kinda like an aircraft getting a new paint job and a new avionics package. You look incredibly different, and yes…very handsome for a man of your age."

"A man of my age?" he asked, in utter shock. Then, letting go of a bated breath, he said, "Christ, woman, how old do you think I am?"

"Facial hairs always make a man look way older than they really are." She sniffed indifferently, having picked up the menu again to peruse the fare a second time. She looked back up at him to find him watching her. It was his silent way of not letting go of the topic.

Exasperated, she dropped the menu. "What?"

"You still haven't answered my question."

"I'm not going to play 'guess your age' with you."

"Hmm."

"Besides, you can't be that much older than me if you toured the Middle East like I just did."

"You make it sound like a vacation."

"You and I both know that isn't true, unless you are the adventurous type, love action and long, hot, boring days playing in a sandbox along with dodging a few bullets here and there."

He guffawed at her comment before continuing.

"How old?" he asked, not letting her change the subject as he leaned forward, his arms crossed on the table's edge.

"You look old enough to be my father." Pointing along her jawline, she said, "You're just missing the grays."

"So, you like being a cougar?"

She gave him a double-take and a look that ended up with the expression of confusion.

Jack leaned toward her. "You like your men to be young then?" he taunted her.

"A cougar, I believe, is usually an older, drop-dead gorgeous woman in her forties who dates younger men. I am a far cry from being forty, 'Griswald,'" she growled.

"Ah…there's the kitty in you." he joked with her, minutely shifting on his elbows, his forearms still on the table, as he leaned closer to her, goading. "But that doesn't mean you like your men just turning the tender age of what? Twenty-one?"

"Oh, for Christ's sakes! Jack, you are not twenty-one years old!" Her eyes flashed at him, even in the dim lighting of their table. "You've been around the block a few times," she said, shaking her over-sized menu somewhat as if it were the morning newspaper instead.

"Twenty-nine. Is that better?" Jack grinned, answering for her.

She did not respond as she tried to continue reading the menu, though both knew she was not concentrating on the list in front of her.

Jack kept watching her, his silence prompting her, as he reclined in his seat, exuding that he had all the time in the world to hear her answer.

Defeated, she sighed. "Seriously?" She was aghast at him. "If you must know, I like men around my age preferably—somewhere within three years of my age, ideally. But that all depends on the guy, his personality, his charms, being responsible, hard-working, good in be—" She paused.

"Do go on," he encouraged with a Southern drawl and a crooked, knowing smile that he could barely control as he drank in the sight of her in the dim restaurant lighting.

She pressed her lips into a tight line, wanting to downplay her remark, and found herself grinding her back molars. *Why on earth would he care, much less want to know?*

His large hand motioned for her to continue.

"Why would it matter? Are you applying for the position?"

He threw back his head and roared with laughter. His teeth were flawless. He was a strong man—not just large, but pure power. His voice, his deep, masculine laughter bellowing from somewhere low inside his torso. A commanding voice that people noticed and listened to without question.

Gathering himself, he said, "Well, that depends…are you offering me the job? I'm still waiting to hear the rest of the qualities you're looking for."

"Now, what would your girlfriend say?" She cast a fishing line to get more information about him. "That is…if you even are civil enough to have one."

"Civil?"

"Yeah, civil. I mean, *recently* you have become hospitable in the last few days. Originally, you were a ball-breaker, and I didn't even have any balls for you to break!"

"You busted mine!" He grinned at her, showing her that dimple that only made him more frustratingly handsome.

"You deserved it for attacking me," she said flatly.

"You were in my home."

"It's not like I broke in! And"—she held a finger up to him—"I was assigned and had a key to that cabin that you're living in!"

"Are you two ready to order?" the waitress interrupted.

Tasha had not noticed her approach during their little tête-à-tête. She gathered herself, only to realize she had no idea what she wanted to order and that she had been too busy trying to avoid his inquisition.

"She'll have the tortellini dish," he said, looking at her for assurance, "with the white cheese sauce. I'll take the sausage and cheese manicotti."

"Salads?" asked the waitress.

Jack continued with their order, ordering them a bottle of wine. She was grateful as her mind raced to prepare where their conversation might be going. *But then, what's the harm?* He just wanted to get to know her. But she knew better: often the guys wanted more than just friends. *Is he just as typical?*

"Now, where were we?"

"I had busted your balls."

"Ah yes...." He shifted in his seat, a more instinctive protective stance on his body's memory.

Tasha did not fail to notice as she put her chin in her upturned hand, her elbow on the table, watching him intently. In fact, she swore she saw him blush, although he was still pink in the areas where no sunlight had graced his freshly groomed skin. She raised her eyebrows, waiting.

"And you asked about my girlfriend."

"Uh hunh."

"Like you, I don't have anyone serious."

"*Say* it isn't *so!*" she said sarcastically. "A burly manly-man like you?" She pretended to be surprised, ignoring the jab at her own status.

"Yeah, it's amazing that an incredible, winsome girl like you doesn't have anyone either!" he jested, taking a sip of his water and then setting down his glass gently. "So, what gives?"

"Nothing. Mr. Right isn't out there. But I'm not going to waste my precious time looking for him either. I spent enough time during my high school and college years...and then in the military."

"You have got to be kidding me."

She took a sip of her water, buying more time, figuring a way to shift the subject back to him.

"You probably didn't give them the time of day, much less a chance," he said, offering his advice.

She gave him a dirty look. "As if you made it any easier for a girl to locate you this far north, in the backwoods!" Her index finger lifted from her water glass that she still held. "But wait, that waitress at the diner is *very* much into you, if I recall. Now there's a cougar for you! That is, if you are into older women." Tasha cocked her head at him, giving him no time to answer. "Have *you* given *her* a chance?" She added, "Seems really personable and chatty."

He smiled at her deflection, giving him a taste of what he was dishing out to her. "No, and not too interested in her." Their wine came, and he poured them each a glass. He continued: "So, no one of interest to you and thus you start another adventure far in the North with the lot of us." He put the bottle back down and slid her glass over to her. "He must have really wrecked your heart, whoever had it first."

"No one ever had my heart—not even a guy I really liked."

"Ah...now there's the story I have been trying to dig out of you."

"No story. He was married and it never went anywhere, for he was loyal to his wife to the very end. The end," she said rather hurriedly, to keep her emotions in check. "Now your story."

He gave her a curious look, but she refused to divulge any further. He sensed that there was more but was not going to push, noticing the sudden change in her tone. "You want my story?"

"Why not?" She shrugged one shoulder. "No educated military man like yourself hides himself away in the Far North without something making him go off the deep end."

He finished a healthy sip of his red wine. "Such as yourself?" he asked her, gently swirling his wine in the large glass, his obvious attempt to remind her that they were both in the same boat.

"All the Mr. Rights I know have been taken by now," she stated flatly. Jack stopped agitating his wine at her next comment.

"I see now," he said, slightly tilting his head to the side.

"Do you? And your story?" she pressed.

"Like you, I served in the Middle East. Did four tours."

"You *did* like playing in the sand, didn't you? Must have been someone special for you in the armed forces to have stayed."

"Nope, *very* few females in the Marine Corps." He smiled. "And those few females are very scary to deal with."

"A special someone back home, perhaps?"

"Bad luck there. She wanted no part in a long-distance relationship nor waiting that long to marry. Basically, lost her to another man. Sometimes I wonder if she was the catch that got away. Smart, beautiful," he told her wistfully.

"Ouch," she sympathized.

Jack reached over, covering her hand with his and giving it a quick reassuring squeeze, before letting it go and draining the last of his wine.

"I guess I need to take it easier on you," she said apologetically.

"Nope." He poured himself another glass and then topped hers off again. "Keep your spunkiness. It's been refreshing." Their dinner arrived, and he raised his glass, toasting her "a welcome to Alaska" and wishing her the "best of luck."

She added, "To new endeavors!"

He grinned at her part on their toast. For that was what Alaska was: the place to find one's own North Star. The true dream-star.

The rest of the leisurely evening was spent chatting about each other's time in the military, focusing on the good times, their times in college, and their childhood dreams. Those were safe topics.

"I always wanted to start or buy my own business but have always been too broke—nor have I been able to borrow the money to do so," he said, rotating his wine glass on the table as he continued. "In addition, I wasn't entirely sure what I wanted to run…if it would be a good fit for me."

She watched him take the last slice of bread from the breadbasket, mopping up the rest of his meal's sauce.

Content with her full belly, she now lay back against the booth's chair, her arms partially folded across herself, yet holding her wine glass, nursing what was left. "What about a retail store in hunting equipment? You should run a business that aligns with your hobbies to make it worthwhile."

"Good point, until I wonder if running a 'hobby' business would ruin my hobby in the long run," he said as he sat back from the table. He noted her partially eaten meal on her plate. "You don't eat much, do you? Or was it not to your liking?"

"The meal was terrific!" she told him, shifting in her seat to shield her meal from him. "I just can't eat so much in one sitting. So I will be taking this home for another time, probably eating on it again later tonight. I always eat leftovers."

"Thrifty," he commented.

"Can't afford not to be."

His phone rang, interrupting them, the sound harsh in the din of the early dinner crowd that had gathered in the restaurant. Yet Jack nimbly answered it, quieting the ringer. "What's up?" he said, not giving a clue as to who would be calling him other than one of the flight line members. "Yup, got here just fine and been shopping all day. She's doing fine, holding up well," he continued, looking over to her and giving her a reassuring smile. "We got all, save for her work gloves."

Their waitress stopped by to clear their dishes, asking if they had saved room for dessert, but Tasha was unable to vouch for Jack while he was on the phone, instead asking for a to-go box for the rest of her dinner, thus giving them time to decide on the ending of one fantastic meal.

Jack listened to whoever it was on the other end for a while, pouring himself another glass of wine and topping Tasha's off for the third time. She did not shield her glass fast enough to refuse. At two glasses, she was feeling buzzed. But the third glass would put her over the edge, for she was not used to drinking alcohol. She had never acquired the taste for it, like so many did to nip off the daily stress. Instead, she found stress relief in her reading, phone games, sleeping, or walking.

"...No, I haven't checked the weather as of yet." He pulled out a pen from his pants' cargo pocket along with a small worn notebook. "I was expecting to leave here in another two to three hours to drive back." Jack switched the cell phone over to the other ear to write. She watched him jot down a few shorthand notes, nearly illegible, but the lighting in the restaurant made it difficult to read from her viewpoint. "Yes, we will stay put—and you want a dozen bagels from the Sweet House in addition to picking up the tire you ordered? And they'll have it ready for pick up at eleven tomorrow morning?"

Tasha had spied their waitress walking back to them with her box. Jack grinned at her as he asked, "Anything else?" Another pause. "All right, we will see you late tomorrow afternoon then." He returned his phone back to its clip holder on his belt. "I guess we have a bit more shopping and errands to do. We are staying here for the night, since bad weather is rolling in the mountains," he told her, sighing heavily.

"Here you go, miss." The waitress handed her the to-go box. "Any desserts?"

she asked.

"Sure," Jack purred at her, making the girl gush at him. "I'll take one of those tiramisus and..." He paused for Tasha's order.

"Oh, no...I am done for the night," she deferred, only to have him insist on her ordering. "Seriously!"

"She'll have the chocolate spoon cake you are known for here."

The girl giggled at him and hurried off to get their dessert order fulfilled.

"I know you will find some room. You're a big girl."

"You are going to make me bigger than I already am!"

"Trust me, you will need the calories for the winter."

"I'm not a bear who'll be hibernating!"

"True, but you will be up working in a cold hangar." He drank more of his wine. "We have time to kill—lots of it now." He set his glass down and began to spin the narrow neck around.

"How much time?"

"Until tomorrow afternoon when the aircraft part we need to pick up will be ready and the weather has passed, giving the highway maintenance folks a chance to clear the roads again."

She took a large sip of her wine, the liquid having become sweet, now that she was used to the taste of the semi-dry red wine. They were going to stay overnight at some hotel, and she hoped she would be in her own room but feared they would be 'sharing' as usual. He had been a gentleman so far. And he certainly did not have a 'thing' for the same sex, as he had made that obvious when he'd talked about his first love.

Their dessert arrived, and they took their time savoring each morsel. There was little talk between them. Jack was right: there was always room for dessert; the dark, rich layers of chocolate were smooth and divine in her mouth.

Jack took his fork and snared a piece off hers, asking her, "Was I right in guessing you were a chocolate hound?"

"What woman isn't?" She swallowed another morsel. "Watch it, there," she said, wagging her fork in warning. "You might lose a hand on the next steal. When it comes to chocolate, I don't share well with others."

"I'll keep that in mind," he said, wiping his mouth with his napkin now that he had demolished his dessert with nary a crumb on the plate. It was nothing new to her, since she was used to seeing military men eat the last few years. It sometimes reminded her of a pack of wild dogs gorging. Jack watched her with a smile as she continued to savor hers. "You haven't said much over dessert. What's going on in that head of yours?" he asked.

"Nothing." The quietness between them grew thicker. "I've been too busy with my chocolate cake to think much beyond that."

He seemed to doubt her but snorted a laugh before draining his wine, observing the dinner crowd before them as she finished her dessert. "From here we will go hunting for a pair gloves for you and then check into a hotel for the night."

There it was…in the open. She was not going to let it bother her. He knew she had no more cash nor room on her credit card. She would be at his mercy, financially. There was no way she could afford a room on her own. They were both grown-ups and most likely the hotel would have two beds. It wasn't anything different from being out in the field with her platoon. They all slept in the same tent in their own cots. *No biggie,* she tried to assure herself.

As Jack paid for their meal, she came up to ask him how much she would need to owe him in the future; she was keeping a tally on her phone of all she had spent on his dime.

"Nothing, Tasha. This is on me. It was nice to take someone out and enjoy a good meal. Stop your worrying. I'm beginning to think Nate hired an accountant and not an electrician."

"I just don't like the position of 'owing' anybody anything," she stated firmly, still wondering when the strings attached would be pulled and put her in a position that she did not want to be in.

They left the restaurant, taking their time walking up and down the grand corridor of the mall, stopping wherever a store gained their interest.

"Tell me more about the crew and Mr. Amsel, our boss. What are they like?"

They stopped at a window display as she checked out more Alaskan curios.

"Let's go in here and let you look," he offered, giving her a gentle nudge in the direction of the retail shop's door.

As they slowly walked down the packed aisles, he told her, "There are six of us, all guys save for you, in which we will now number seven. That'll give us two per plane and hopefully lighten our workload. But most of the time everyone will be flying at this time of year. The only one who doesn't fly is Hank. He's never liked it and thus he's the radio communications man with his walkie-talkie when working in the hangar, or he sits in our flight-planning room, reading."

"When will I be earning the rest of my ratings if you all are flying?"

"Each and every day. You will be going with someone who is licensed and getting your hours in, until we feel you're ready to get checked out. You normally won't fly alone unless you are taking one of our smaller birds, like the 185 or the Beaver."

"Tell me more about each crew member." She picked up an ulu kit to inspect it more closely. "What the hell does one do with this?"

"It's a cutting utensil that the Inuits use for cutting herbs and other food items," he explained.

She put it down, continuing up the aisle.

"Hank is the oldest of the crew. He's pretty much an Alaskan native, having lived here since his parents moved up here back in the early sixties from Louisiana. But you wouldn't know it from his Southern drawl and redneck tendencies. He's a lot like a junkyard keeper. Good mechanic."

She gave him a curious look. "Is everyone from the southern United States?"

93

"Pretty much. Global warming's becoming a bitch for most of us," he joked.

She smiled at him. "And the others?"

"There's Emanuel—or Manny, as we call him—a mechanic and pilot too. He hails from Panama City, Panama."

"Christ! What's his story for leaving the tropical beach life?"

"He hated the heat and wanted a better life."

"Seriously?" Her voice raised a pitch higher at the incredibility of the idea.

Jack laughed at her response. "Emanuel and Jarvis are our two youngest and newest mechanics. Those two are like a couple of college kids having a field day up here, constantly playing practical jokes in the hangar. They're good guys. Been inseparable since Manny arrived three years ago. Jarvis has been here nearly five years. They share cabin number eight, just up the road from us. Of course, when you go to visit them, don't be surprised at the frat house they've created."

"And this Jarvis?"

"He's originally from Seattle, Washington. He doesn't talk much about his past. From what I gather though, he came from the streets and made his way to Alaska eventually. He has no past criminal records, but he has ended up being a quick study as a mechanic. He's working on getting his Airframe and Powerplant rating. He's tired of having to get one of us to sign off on his work."

Now she realized she did not have one either. "I will have to have my work signed off too. I don't have the mechanic's license. Do you have one?" She was suddenly curious about this aircraft fueler and pilot.

"Yup, that too."

"*My*, you are a *Jack* of all trades!" She smiled more to herself as she turned away from him again to turn the corner at the back of the shop.

Jack had caught her smile, mesmerized by her 'ubiquitous gravitational field' that pulled at him to know more about her. He could not place a finger on it. It wasn't that she had feminine charms beguiling him. But she was no 'butch' either. *Pragmatic* was the only word that came to his mind. And it was a piss-poor description for her. She was attractive, but not out of most guys' leagues. Yet if she 'cleaned up,' dressing up in office attire or evening wear, she would be drop-dead gorgeous.

"The others?" she asked once he caught up to her as she took in the framed wall pictures.

"Sam and Nick—also known as St. Nick and Dr. Seuss or just Seuss. Those two are thick as thieves too. Both are pilots and mechanics. However, those two do most of the flying. I can't say they are great mechanics. But they get the work done when it is needed. They hang out at the bar a lot, playing pool, watching the latest hockey or football game on TV. They've been with the company for six, maybe seven years. They're just happy flying. Nothing more, nothing less. Those two are playboys and I would definitely watch out for them." His expression grew more serious. "Let me know if they become a problem for you on the line," he told her rather protectively.

She turned her face up to him, nodding her head somewhat. "Why not the others?"

"Well, Nate and Hank are happily married. And Jarvis and Emanuel don't strike me as your type of guys to hang out, to be honest, although I wouldn't put it past them either."

"What about yourself?"

He smiled wolfishly at her. She didn't need an answer.

"Un-hunh. Sometimes I feel like I've been thrown to the wolves," she sighed.

"Maybe. Maybe not. All depends on you and how you handle yourself," he commented.

"Me?" She moved down the aisle. "You know there *are* two sides here."

He followed her, noting her golden hair shimmering in the store's light. She had worn it down and not loosely caught up in a hair clip at the base of her head.

"True, but I think you will do fine on the floor."

"What about the boss?" They made their way out of the store and back onto the promenade to walk to the next store.

"A nice guy. Firm, by-the-book guy. Old-fashioned." Jack remembered how Big Raven was worried over Jack taking advantage of her that one morning. "He's a father figure to many of us, being so far from our homes. His door is always open.

"His wife, Nora, she's his bookkeeper and secretary. She's there about half of the time to help out and support his business. Otherwise, she is busy with their rentals and selling real estate. I think you will like her."

"How long has he been running the business?" They stepped into another camping supply store.

"Oh, I'd say he didn't get serious about it until about ten to twelve years ago. He's worked hard to get this far."

"And you have been there for only two years?"

"Yes. We are the newbies, so to speak."

"At least we have something in common besides our military background. We'll have to stick up for each other should the crew decide to gang up on us newbies."

Jack snorted blithely at the ridiculous notion. She would fit in just fine and there was no need to defend themselves from his guys. He would see to it.

She had finally found and bought her gloves, and they were off to find lodgings for the night. The sun had dropped behind the mountains and the air temperature was considerably cooler as they hurried to his old pickup truck. After several moments trying to start the truck, the engine finally rolled over and he let the truck idle to warm up. Jack put it into gear to head to the hotel that Black

Raven Aviation used regularly, and where they had an account.

He wasn't ready for what might happen next. He hoped she would not be the typical girl when she found out that they would be sharing a room, but there would be two queen beds like normal. They pulled into the parking garage and he plugged the truck's battery warmer into a nearby receptacle. He told her to grab her overnight bag and anything that might be damaged from freezing overnight in his truck. She picked up her bag and her travel mug obediently, deciding that her leftovers would do okay being frozen.

He got their room. But to his dismay—more like Tasha's dismay—it had just one king-sized bed. It was the only room left; the incoming weather had made other travelers stay put too. Looking over to Tasha where she stood by the tourism brochures, perusing through the various flyers, he thought Tasha's comment may have been right when it came to being thrown to the wolves. He was just like any other of his guys. Yet a wolf could be protective and not a predator. *Right?*

He pressed his lips together, trying to get ready for her to balk at the company's lodgings as they got into the elevator to get to the fourth floor. "There's a free continental breakfast downstairs in the morning between six and nine. Help yourself," he told her, trying to break the invisible wall that was growing between them.

"Great," she said as they both stepped off the elevator and walked down the corridor to a door. "You got my room key?"

"I got *our* room key. We share a room, like we do a cabin, since this is on the company's ticket."

"Oh." She didn't say anything else, or even stiffen at the idea.

At least not yet, he thought.

It was when they got into the room that she stopped short. His body mass nearly toppled her, making her drop her overnight bag on the floor rather than on the low dresser where the TV sat.

Here it comes, he thought, sighing inwardly as he apologized for possibly hurting her.

Instead, she surprised him with just a sharp look, her green eyes having turned hard as cut emeralds. "Wolves?" As if she had read his thoughts earlier, it was the only thing she said as she looked at the single king-sized bed. "And this was the old-fashioned boss's idea?"

He picked up her bag and set it on the low dresser next to the TV, sighing heavily, then continued around to the far side of the room to put his bag on the chair by the desk at the room's only large window. "Look, I don't like the idea myself."

She folded her arms protectively in front of her, clearly not believing him.

"Unfortunately, we are not the only travelers holding out for the weather to pass and this was the company's last room. The hotel rented the other rooms we usually have, and we will have to make do, soldier."

She raised an eyebrow at him as she continued to stand there. Whenever Jack used the term *soldier* on her, it was his way of telling her to 'buck up' and 'drive on' as an equal and not as the opposite sex.

"I'm not sleeping on the floor, and the bed is big enough for us to share." He took his jacket off and threw it over a sitting chair.

"Our guys usually do this?" Tasha used her nose to make her point over the large bed.

Frustrated, he ran a hand through his hair, not answering. He continued to act as if it was no big deal, as he warred with himself internally on what to say or do as he dropped into the chair. He pulled off his boots where he had taken a seat in the chair by a small table, taking his time to come up with something to put her at ease, but the next thing he said ended up being an off-colored joke. "I will not violate you if you promise not to violate me." He picked up the TV remote and flicked it on to a news channel, the volume automatically on low. Next, he pulled out his toiletry bag. "Now," he said, waving a hand at her, "come here and let's see to your backside." He pointed to her bullet wound beneath her bulky sweater.

She pressed her lips together in disgust before going over to stand in front of him, turning her back, knowing her buttocks were directly in front of his face as he sat in the low chair. She wasn't going to put on the typical verbal fuss most women would. She refused. *What are my fellow workers going to think?*

"Come on, pull up that sweater of yours. You know the deal by now."

She could hear him rip at a new sticky bandage, getting it ready, and the smell of disinfecting alcohol from the bottle he had just opened. She did as she was told, unzipping her jeans to let her pants slide down enough as she held up her bulky sweater to expose her exit wound to him. She jumped at the intensity of the cold solution on the dampened cotton ball.

"Easy there, girl."

She felt his other large warm hand slide to her other hip, steadying her, letting that hand remain. It was dangerously warm and inviting, as she closed her eyes at the sensation. It had been a long time since she had really let a man intimately touch her.

Jack dabbed gently at the wound. "There's no need to get your panties in a wad."

"They are not in a wad! It's just the rubbing alcohol was cold." Next was the coldness of the antibacterial ointment. Thankfully, she had braced for that application. He was gentle, putting a thick layer of cream on, letting his finger slide slowly downwards. She heard the bandage ruffle off the protective packaging, both his hands now on either side of her hips, as he applied the top of the bandage with just his index fingers and thumbs above her wound and then thumbing the sides down smoothly, almost making her shiver in delight.

He must have noticed it because he tapped her gently to cover herself for warmth. She did not move away as she normally did, instead pulling her pants back up and lowering her sweater first, close up and in his space.

Before she stepped away from him, she was surprised to hear how thick his voice had become when he asked her if she was ready for her pain med. She looked over her shoulder at him, his eyes dark, unreadable, and almost animalistic in her mind. "It'll help you sleep comfortably and make the ride back home easier for you," he added.

She paused at the possible double entendre before answering, "No, thank you. I'll be fine." She knew that she wanted her wits about her with him that night in that bed. She was finding it difficult to behave, body-wise. She just wanted to let go and get her own pleasure as she pleased. But she did not want to become the 'easy girl' with just anyone—or everyone, for that matter.

She decided to leave him and head to the bathroom for what little private time she would have to herself that night. She decided it was best to strip down into a comfy, warm, oversized shirt, her underwear, and socks. She washed her face, erasing the makeup around her eyes and brushing her hair out to ease the growing tension she felt. She was tired, her belly full, her wound attended to, her body relaxing easier than she had thought. She blamed it on the wine: more than she was used to having, but not to the point of stupidly tipsy.

She walked back out to the room to find him still in the chair, apparently engrossed in the news, his long legs stretched out where his sock-covered feet lay propped up at the foot of the bed on the far side of the room. He had sunk low in the chair, draping his arms wide over the chair's high arms. There was a plastic cup in his one hand with water in it. The cup did not seem right; it should have been a glass with a quarter of it filled with scotch, for a man like him. He was still dressed in his flannel shirt, yet the top few buttons were undone where she could see his exposed undershirt, the first layer stretched over his wide chest just beneath his beard. He barely noted her coming out, much less her pulling the covers back and snatching all the pillows save for one on his side. She slid under the covers, arranging the other pillows into a long body pillow for herself.

"Are you *that* threatened by me?" he asked softly. His voice made her head jerk up at him, startled at him for breaking the room's thick silence.

"Come again?" she asked, uncertain as to what he was talking about, curious as to what had caused him to think she was on the defense when she wasn't. *Well, maybe a little defensive.* It was not like he had been out to hurt her since he'd first attacked her over a week before. He had kept his distance, although he had provided her protection just like any other soldier would over a wounded comrade.

He pointed to the long lump line she had formed under the covers dividing their bed in half.

"Ah, no! I just like having a body pillow to throw my leg over and to hug throughout the night. It helps keep my skin from stretching or pulling the stitches when I sleep on my side. I'm pretty certain you wouldn't want me to throw my leg over you or to snuggle into you, clutching onto you like a teddy bear." It was partially truthful, and the best passing excuse she could come up with.

He eyed her a moment, as if deciding something. Then he got up in one fluid motion, nabbing his toiletry bag to take to the bathroom. The TV still flickered images, the volume nearly inaudible. She snuggled down, pulling the covers up to her chin, clutching the row of pillows between her knees and calves and pulling the rest to her upper body in a reassuring hug facing his side and the dark window.

At first her ears picked up every sound and motion in the bathroom, the wall being the only barrier from him, the grizzled mountain man no longer. Once the shower started roaring, she felt herself ease some and sleep came plucking at her senses one by one.

She woke again to the lock latching on their door and to the room becoming dark. The TV and the one lamp turned off in sequence, and then she felt the mattress sink under the weight of his body next to her and him sigh heavily.

There was a pregnant pause before she heard him say quietly, "Go to sleep, Tasha."

"I was almost there," she told him quietly, shifting the pillow closer to her as she lay still on her side, facing him. "It's hard not to notice a giant bear laying down next to you," she told him quietly, then rubbed her face against the soft linen of the pillowcase before lying still again.

Her whole body was alert to his every move, the very deep breaths he took. "What?" his deep voice came softly after what seemed like five minutes of silence.

"Nothing!" she hissed at him. "Just how in the hell can you tell I'm awake in the dark? Do my eyes glow in the dark?" she asked.

"Because your breathing hasn't changed, along with your body still being tense." She felt him move one of his limbs. "Besides, I don't think any of those two pillows has a chance of fluffing back up again in the morning, the way you're clutching at them." She could literally hear him smile in the dark.

"Stop it," she retorted.

"Stop what?"

"You're laughing at me."

"I'm not laughing, just smiling at your nervousness."

"I'm not nervous."

"Bullshit!" He inhaled deeply, turning his whole body, from what she could sense from the mattress's movement.

"It's just…weird sleeping with a co-worker. What the hell are the guys going to say?"

"So you're telling me that you never slept out in the field with a bunch of your fellow soldiers?"

"Not in the same cot or hammock! It would have been a very uncomfortable and tight sleeping arrangement."

"We're in a king-size bed, Tasha." There was some more unidentified movement on his side. "There has to be at least another two to three feet between us." Then she felt his hand on the side of her face, cupping her cheek. "You see?"

It was a welcome warmth to her cold skin, and she drank in the fresh-showered scent of him, his thumb slowly stroking her cheekbone. She nuzzled into his touch then, kissing the inside of his palm, regretting it instantly, for his thumb stopped.

"What was that for?"

Her mind raced for the only thing she could muster. "For being nice enough to take time out to shop with me and to pay up front for a lot of it. And then, staying on to be my nurse when you didn't want the job." She pulled her face away from his touch, hoping to find the surface of her other pillow to cool the scorching hand imprint on her face.

His hand moved away from her face and found her hand, getting her to unclench the pillow from her body, clasping hers, entwining his fingers with hers. "I didn't take off; I am being paid to run this errand and to look after you for these two weeks."

"Really?" She lifted her head so she could see him better in the dark now that her eyes were adjusting, his form a darker shadow on the white linen's soft glow.

"By the boss's orders." His other hand came around, cupping the side of her face again. "As for any co-worker knowing...that is on you and me keeping our mouths shut should the both of us be obliging each other willingly." He reluctantly let go of her face. His first hand still held her other hand.

"You would sleep with a co-worker and not have qualms?"

"Only with you. The other guys don't do what you do to me. You're more of a pain to me. At least they would let me sleep." He squeezed her hand in momentary jest. "At this rate, neither one of us is going to get much sleep tonight."

"How am I still a pain to you?"

"First my balls, then my ass, now my cock won't relax."

"Are you sure it's just not frozen stiff?" She stifled a giggle. "I'm not sure my cold hands would help warm you much."

At that moment he let go of her hand. She felt him move, the pillows disappearing from along her body, and him covering part of her body with his, pinning her down with his weight.

There were a few seconds of stillness before she felt his beard, then his lips finding hers and giving her a slow, seductive kiss. Her mouth easily complied, betraying her, as she tried him for the first time.

He felt good. She had to be desperate, for he was starting to look good in addition to feeling heavenly against her. His body seemed to make her come awake with a need she had not felt in a long time.

He broke their kiss to nuzzle her. She felt his breath upon her lower face and neck before he spoke softly near her ear. "Tell me no before you regret sleeping with one of your co-workers." His breathing was more labored as he held himself back from her, his leg halfway up between hers. "You need to be sure you want this, there's no turning back once it's done. What happens between us stays here...between us." She felt his prominent nose at the side of her face, inhaling her scent.

Feeling him and his invitation made her heady. She gave him her answer between her breath quickening in expectation. "Yes, just here...Never at work... No one will know...Between equals. Just us co-workers. Promise."

At this, he squeezed her tight up against him as he lay most of his weight on her, careful not to press against her wound as he tugged at her panties then worked at freeing her of her shirt, using his body to shield her against the cold, pulling the covers over them. He had worn nothing to bed.

Her nipples came erect when his chest hairs encountered her flesh and she lightly squealed her delight at the sensation against his mouth as he continued to kiss her, wrapping her long legs around his hips and pressing more of herself against him, making him groan.

He rolled her over, pulling her on top of him. "It's time for you to warm my cock," he murmured, lifting her hips up and then piercing her deeply in one motion.

All of it felt good. Without moving, she let her inner muscles suckle him, the palms of her hands braced against his chest; wanting more of the sensation his body hair gave her, she let her hands slide all over him.

"Christ, you feel good." He pulled her head to give her another deep and penetrating kiss to match their coupling.

She began moving against him, an ancient rhythm, wanting more. He groaned his delight with her movements, letting her lead some, holding her tighter against him, his breathing barely under control as they moved steadily onward.

His body heat, which he shared with her, was everything to her at that moment. His warmth melted the ice that had built up in her from her tour in the Middle East and then had crystalized in Alaska. In that instant he melted it all, making her feel very much alive again. She shuddered her delight against him, crazy aware of how fast she had risen and then fallen spent against him, laying her head on his broad chest, his massive heart pounding deep down behind a wall of pure muscle. Even two years after, he was still military fit.

She wondered if she had warmed him or had hurt him when he had stiffened against her moments before. But from the slippery wetness between her legs, surely dripping down on him too, she was sure she had given him as much pleasure as he gave her. He exhaled heavily under her. She moved to lighten her weight against him, afraid of squishing him.

He grabbed her, pulling her back to him. "Where are you going?"

"I just thought I was too heavy to be laying on you." She let her fingertips glide over his chest more, idly dragging a finger in circles through the light dusting of chest hairs that she could feel under her fingertips. "I wanted to give you your space."

Squeezing her gently to him, his Southern drawl leaking out, he said, "Naw, you're good. You're too light to hurt me. Besides, you're keeping me warm…" He shifted again under her. "And getting me wet dripping on me like that." She felt his smile when his whiskers shifted just above and to the side of her face.

"Hey, now, this is a two-way street." She reached down between them, dragging a hand through their dampness and then back up to his neck, and then to his face, to leave their scent on his skin as she planted another tantalizing kiss on his newly clean-shaven throat. "It's not only me involved in this passionate rendezvous," she added as she broke their kiss.

He halted her wandering hand in his large one, bringing it back to his lips, where he took each of her fingers, suckling them. She let her head fall onto him, tucking it alongside his neck, murmuring her contentedness.

As they rested, she listened to his heart beat steadily. It was the first time she felt that all would be fine again. There was a new sense of confidence growing inside her as he drew lazy circles down her backside, at first stroking her hair, pulling it out and letting it drop, and then went back to sliding his hand down her backside, making her shiver at his touch.

He must have mistaken it for her being cold, as he rolled over on his side, gently dropping her onto the mattress next him and then partially covering her body with his. She sighed, reaching up to get another deep and long kiss from him, using both her hands to capture the sides of his face. He willingly gave himself up to her mouth's demand, the man-beast tamed for the moment, until she felt his need again rise against her thigh, anticipating round two.

"Oh my," she mumbled low against his mouth. "Am I lucky enough for a two-gun salute, marine?" she joked. She felt his laughter on his breath against her face in the dark as he took her again, but that time with her leading the assault of pleasure on each other's bodies.

He awoke the next morning, the most rested he had felt in some time. He had awoken on his side with her in his arms. She was still asleep, her body's curves graciously spooning him. Her body meeting his, skin to skin, every inch, all the way down. Her breathing shallow and slow. Somewhere in the middle of the night, she had moved her mid-shoulder-length hair under her head, the locks sprawled out like the sun's rays in front of her face. He could still nuzzle her hair, inhaling the scent of the shampoo she used, without the weight of his head pulling on her locks or itching his nose. He gently dragged his hand along the curve of her shoulders to her waist and then to those expansive hips of hers. He took his time, drinking in the sight of her, the comforter pulled up her frontside just under her chin, although the sheet did not cover any of her side and her back, where his body had kept her warm through the night. She was more than pretty. Her languid nudity put her in the gorgeous zone, like a centerfold dream come true. The thought made him go hard again, wanting more of her. He wanted that day to last as he laid his head back down, hoping to drift off to sleep again until she awoke, glad that she wasn't a morning person.

He lay there for as long as he could until his cock would not let him rest anymore. He silently prayed the litany of *don't let her regret this* over and over in his mind as he gently kissed her whole entire back side awake, pulling the comforter back up over him as he shifted down over her body. He heard her moan as she awoke, rolling onto her back before pulling his head back up to hers, face to face.

His thoughts must have been scribbled over his face when she asked him, "Regrets?" her soft voice husky with sleep, the sound of it like expensive whiskey to his ears.

"None," he whispered back to her. "You?"

"None." She smiled beguilingly at him in the morning's half-light from the window.

If there was a pin-up poster for the bedroom look, it was her in all her glory in the faint light from the window. He had to kiss her to remind himself she was real. His kiss turned into a maul, continuing to feast along the rest of her body, as he took her again under the covers. She welcomed him by rolling over onto her front side and then up on all fours. He had consigned his soul over, losing himself in utter primal joy, still careful not to hurt her.

Afterwards, she silently slipped from their bed to start her morning ablutions. He gave her a moment until he heard her start the shower. He got up to dress, doing most of everything he could do out in the room. Grabbing the room key, he was thinking of getting them some breakfast to bring back, but as he passed the bathroom door, he found it partially open. He stopped when he caught sight of her body through the clear plastic shower curtain. His eyes hooked, he feasted on just watching her bathe, every movement mesmerized and captured forever in his mind's eye. The eternal scene ended abruptly when she finished, turning the water off, pushing the curtain open, and catching him spying on her.

"I seem to have a Peeping Tom," she said to him, pulling down a towel from the stack on the wall shelf.

He came in, the wall of steam drifting around him in a welcoming warm damp hug. He took her towel from her and began to dry her off—anything to be near her exquisiteness again. Yet it was the one flaw, just above her hip, that gave him the excuse to remain, as he patted her down, turning her to inspect the secureness and the dryness underneath the bandage. Then he kissed her wound gently, like any parent would do with a child's bruise.

He remained there sitting on the edge of the tub, just holding her close to him, she wrapped in the towel standing there, her one arm snaking gently around his head holding his head against her, each savoring the moment, until her tummy gurgled, reminding him to get going or they would miss the continental breakfast in the hotel lobby.

"Come." He stood up and escorted her out of the bathroom. "Get dressed or else we will miss the free food downstairs." He grinned at her.

"Damn, you're a cheap date," she jested. "But you being in here isn't going to help me get ready any faster." She pulled him out of the bathroom, swapping places. He turned to her after she got him out, giving her a *promising-of-a-next-time* kiss. Her insides fluttered as if a thousand butterflies to flight.

She quickly donned a long-sleeved hunter green sweater and a pair of thermal fleece-lined black leggings that matched her black snow boots. She put half the makeup on that she usually did: finding the dark circles under eyes were not there like normal, she opted for just mascara and a little eyeliner. She brushed her hair into a loose twist and clenched it with a hair clip to keep the hair out of her face, having to adjust to wearing a hoodie with her coat to keep warm. It had become impossible to keep her hair composed between the static electricity buildup and the wind from the bay. She constantly had strands sneaking around her face and covering it, making her unable to see much, whenever she wore it down. It was always getting tangled, and she was not about to carry a hairbrush everywhere with her. The military pretty much broke her of her habit of carrying a purse. She now just carried a wallet with her that could be easily stored in a coat pocket or pant pockets…when she had pants with pockets.

She lived her life simple. She did not need much to enjoy life, thanks to the military.

They made short work of packing their overnight bags and headed downstairs for their breakfast. Next on their list was to find the bagel shop and to order two dozen bagels to bring back with them in addition to the aircraft part.

After securing the bagels in the truck, they had another two hours to wait until picking up the part. Jack decided to let her explore downtown Anchorage, letting her peruse all the street-side art and curio shops that were open. Luckily, the day had warmed again to the late summer temperatures, making it unusually warm for that time of year. They kept their distance from each other in public, but on occasions they had ended up reaching for each other's hands to hold. It was not until he had gotten her on the outdoor trail for a short jaunt along the coastline that he would nab her in a bear hug and kiss her, unable to keep his hands off her any longer.

"I feel like a teenager again," she laughed breathlessly after one of their rather long and heated kisses. She was sitting sideways on his lap on one of the many large park benches in a thicket of trees.

He smiled at her, his gray eyes sparkling in mischief. Jack had been having more fun *petting* her, matching every teasing stroke she did to him under his open coat.

"Yet…you know…I don't ever recall making out during my high school years." Thinking back, she realized how much she had missed out by pushing so hard to make something of herself.

"Now, I *find* that hard to believe." He thumbed the sides of her wonderful skin, her cheeks pink from the sun's rays on the clear day. He gently laid her over the bench, letting her upper body lie upon the seat as he moved out from under her to slide over her, bracing his large frame on either side of her. "You seem to be a pro at this." He gave her another teasing kiss and then tickled her into gales of laughter until she could not take it anymore, begging him to stop so she could catch her breath.

"Not any more than you are!" She attacked him like a playful kitten would do to a large dog. He won several times, mainly because she let him, and he was careful not to tear open her stitches as they enjoyed each other's company. When his cell phone rang their playtime ended: the aircraft part was ready. Together they sighed, gathering one long look at each other in the dappled lighting under the tall trees.

"It's done," she told him.

"For now," he admitted, giving her one long kiss before they separated to head back to his truck.

CHAPTER FIVE

They drove in contented silence to the warehouse at the Anchorage Aviation Park Center near the airport. She came with him to see where she had to go if she was ever sent up there to fetch parts for the guys. Jack introduced her at the counter, having her sign paperwork and give them her identification to photocopy for the future. He grabbed the nose tire and hefted it onto his shoulder to carry to the bed of his pickup truck.

Once on the highway, they settled down for the long haul back over the pass. The day was clear as the sun began its slow and low descent on the horizon. Even though they were driving into the midday sun, she would take what she could get on her face. For soon, come December, there would be little sunlight. December was less than three months away. She had arrived in the middle of August, and it was about two days before September. She placed her focus out the window, gazing upon the breathtaking scenery.

Tasha tried to keep her mind off him. She needed to keep it light, for they would be working together. Nothing serious could come of it until she was certain that it would not be an issue at work or among the other co-workers. The nasty wild man that had first attacked her had turned out to be one genuinely nice man behind now trimmed whiskers. An unexpected excellent lover. Her body shivered internally, blushing at the thought, and her shoulders came up, trying to staunch the warm blushing.

The truck's heater was on full blast, and Jack was amazed she still shivered as he periodically glanced at her. He needed to focus more on the road, checking for the patches of black ice. "I can't believe you are still cold. We are going to have to work on speeding your body's adjustment to this climate."

"Oh yeah?" she asked, now curious. "I didn't think that was possible. It's why the Army always gave us a month to adjust to any new place before doing a physical fitness test. Though there have been times I think I needed about half a year, especially when it came to living higher than fifteen hundred feet. I was born and raised at sea level."

He smiled and then patted the bench seat near him, indicating for her to move closer to him. "Snuggle up if you need to."

"No, I'm fine. I was just thinking…" she told him. The waters in Turnagain Arm began to roil, catching her full attention. "What the—"

Jack pulled the truck over to the side of the road, turning the engine off to let her watch. It was good timing on their part. "What you are seeing is the high tide coming in."

"Really?" She was stunned. "I thought for a moment that you all had some Loch Ness Monster making that kind of rippling wave motion. It's…dramatic.

So…fast!"

"Remember, our tides rise almost forty feet in difference in less than an hour."

Together they sat there watching the water roll in waves, quickly covering the low exposed silt bars. Watching her fascination was like seeing Alaska anew through her eager eyes. Hope had come back to him, expanding the crippled soul inside his body, making him know what it was like to be alive again. He could not help himself when his eyes sought after her instead of watching the water roll in, her back to him, unaware. He had always watched her before, but he never seemed to notice her finer points. Her oversized coat covered most of her body, but Jack's eyes were drawn to her legs. Her long legs, he noted, the leggings leaving nothing to the imagination. He knew he needed to go slow and to keep their 'new affair' on the downside from everyone. But he wanted more, to slide his hands over her body, especially her rump. He found that his hand had moved on its own accord to her backside, sliding up under her coat and settling on her covered hip.

She turned to him.

What am I doing? he thought. Jack instantly apologized for touching her, yet he physically wanted to drag her to him.

She smiled, asking why he was apologizing.

"It's just that…I've discovered something…fun," he told her rather hesitantly, and more to himself than to her.

Really? Is that all it was to him? she wondered.

After his comment, she found him thinking as if he were working on a Rubik's Cube. But she tried to keep it simple and light with him, reminding herself of their tenuous situation. "Well, God, I hope I've been fun. I'd hate to be dull and boring." She smiled cautiously, her concern growing as she watched his troubled features.

Is he having regrets? she wondered. Or possibly something more than just co-workers with fringe benefits? A man like him—if a girl could see past the gruffness, the semi-long hair, and thick, close-cropped beard—was something to behold. Like the Norse God Thor himself. It wasn't until she had the chance to really notice the night before, letting her hands slide over his bare body, getting the feel of him in the dark, that she was aware of just how good looking he had to be. She had yet to see him naked under the full light, save for a few parts, like his lower neckline and a hint of his upper chest. He was a powerhouse. A labor man. His body a furnace for her in the way he threw off so much heat.

She found him comforting yet exciting…interesting. But it was still new…to them both. She figured he would lose interest eventually. Men in her life usually did, once the sex was not enough anymore. Many had found her boring or too serious. She craved adventure, yet wanted it all with the perfect man, in a serious relationship. She didn't like going from one man to another, date after date. Even after a few dates, the men became all the same; she lost interest and never pursued it like she should have done. But forcing something that was never going to happen, well…it just felt…wrong.

She was certain that *love* clicked. *True love* would be effortless and seamless. As she bumbled along life's road of hard knocks, Mr. Right had appeared, but unfortunately he had been taken by another, had a newborn, and then died needlessly protecting her.

Tasha reached back to his hand where it had kept its distance from her after touching her on the bench seat near him. She gave it a reassuring squeeze, releasing it, but did not bring it back to her to lay upon her body. She resumed her watch out the truck's window, desperately hiding her doubts.

She continued to watch the water level rise, and at the same time she wondered if she had gotten in over her head now that she 'gave' herself so easily to a man...a co-worker, at that. However, this time she was grateful he was *not* her boss. The last thing she needed was to be falling in love with a supervisor. She had often seen other women blackballed over stupid things, only to find out there was more to it than met the eye. Especially when the man in charge of firing them became disinterested or vice versa, the personal affairs bleeding into the professional affairs.

She heard him shift behind her, and before she could turn around, he had started the truck's engine again, putting it in gear to get back on the road. It was rather terse and silent. He just drove, with a new sense of determination.

"Did I do or say anything wrong?" Her senses were on full alert, trying to get a feel of what could have possibly been going on in his mind.

"No," he said flatly.

"I call bull." She focused on his profile as he drove.

He peered over to her, as if trying to discern her true intent, then faced the front windshield for several moments as he tried to gather his thoughts before saying anything.

"It's not you. I am just mad at myself for taking advantage of you."

"You're having regrets?...Now?" She was unable to believe what she was hearing. "Oh, for the love of God! What the hell is wrong with me now?" She turned in her seat to face a full-frontal verbal assault that was now threatening their happy mini-adventure.

"You?" He turned his head in question at her before looking forward again, doing that several times throughout their conversation—if one could call it that.

"Yes, me! Now, what did I do...or didn't do?" Her one hand gestured at whatever was the cause for the sudden change in the obvious physical void between them.

"It's not you, trust me on this."

"Well, man, spit it out," she demanded. When he didn't answer her right away, she continued for him. "Well, then, let me take a gander at it since it is *not me*." She folded her arms over her chest and pulled her jacket closed. "You want more?"

He gave her a horrid look.

"Okay, you don't want more and are now regretting last night and this morning." She threw her hands up in the air, as if *fine, so be it!*

She eyed him wearily a moment longer. "Question is…are you capable of holding your tongue over this affair around the crew?"

"Oh, I can hold my tongue. Definitely better than most women can," Jack retorted.

"Aw—just bite me, will ya?" she snapped, rather tiredly. "Don't stereotype me. I am not your typical gal! For one thing, it's not like I threw myself to you or to anyone that easily."

He gave her a gimlet look.

"Oh, no you don't!" she warned. "Don't make me out to be easy!" She leaned toward him in anger. "I am no whore and I refuse to be treated like one. It was mutual, the last time I checked! A fling between co-workers. I felt the need as much as you did! Although I'd have preferred to have done the deed with someone I actually love in a more serious long-term relationship!" Tasha didn't want to jab him with her finger for fear of ending up in a car wreck. In fact, just not touching him was the safer option, as she could sense the defensive wall that had gone up between them.

"The last thing I want to be known for is *being easy*. I'm *certainly not* that girl! Nor will I be used as the occasional fling for you between the other women you have on your waiting list!" she hissed. She was so angry by then that she couldn't stand to look at him anymore and turned forward in her seat, seeing absolutely nothing out the windshield, clenching her jaw to keep from saying anything else she might regret, other than, "So you can choose, asshole: it's all or nothing!"

She wrapped her arms around her body, hugging herself protectively for the answer she didn't want to hear, her thoughts running amuck at not knowing until she could no longer bear his silence.

"Come on! Make up your damn mind!" When he didn't answer her right away, she continued, verbally rubbing salt into the wound. "Don't tell me you can't make up your mind because you act like a girl!"

"What do you want?" he finally asked.

"Oh no you don't! You're not getting off the hook! You decide. That is, if you're capable of it."

"I'm thinking."

"What?"

"I'm thinking!" he said. "Give me a second, will ya?"

She gave him a crazed look. "Well, you better think faster before I think the jet fumes have addled your brain."

He gave her an incredulous look at her feistiness. "Asshole?"

"Yes, that will forever be your new name."

"And just when I was getting used to 'Griswald.'" He sighed with a half smirk, incredulous at how fast her temper had taken off. *And she isn't even a redhead!*

"At least 'Griswald' could make a decisive decision!" she shot back at him.

There was a gravid pause, the only sound being the rattling of the truck's engine and the outside highway noise of passing vehicles, before she dared looked at him, only to find him studying her as best as he could as he drove.

"What?" she demanded.

His stern visage ended up cracking into a smile. Then his deep, bellowing laughter erupted, filling the interior of the truck's cab. She wasn't falling for it. This was serious. She wanted to know his answer.

When he'd had his fill of mirth at her expense, Tasha remained there, still as a mouse and madder than a hornet, her profile sharp against the window's backlight, ignoring him.

"Okay, you want this to be more serious?"

"It doesn't matter what I want."

"It takes two on this, Tasha," he said, throwing her own prior equality comments back at her.

She didn't answer, sighing heavily at having to wait for his answer that he was determined not to give.

"I can't make a decision based on a one-night stand with you when it comes to all or nothing. But at least I know where you stand when it comes to relationships."

She arched a suspicious eyebrow at him.

"I will tell you this: do not think I take this lightly." Jack pointed back and forth between them. Her look didn't change. "I do hope there are many more times to come because I wouldn't want it any other way," he said more seriously. "I've quite enjoyed myself"—he paused—"with you."

She didn't say anything to him. She just sat there, looking at him. God, she was a cantankerous crab. Difficult to get her out of her shell once threatened.

"That is…if you will let me to continue to do so." He reached out to her with his hand palm up in a truce offering. His arm was long enough to touch her, but he had to reach a bit further for she had sidled up against the passenger side of his truck, as he sought out one of her hands to assure her.

She remained silent as he finally latched on to her hand. "Hey." He pulled her toward him. "Come here."

She complied but stopped halfway.

He dragged her the rest of the way to him, hugging her. "Sorry." He kissed the top of her head. "Can I keep the name 'Griswald'?"

He felt her shake, worried she was crying, only to realize she was laughing, smiling.

An hour and a half later, in addition to some more aircraft-related talk, they arrived in Seward. It was around four that afternoon. They had reluctantly put space between them as soon as they had reached the outskirts of town. Jack took them straight to the hangar with the part. It was amazing that the pass had gotten close to three feet of snow, but as soon as they got into Seward, the temperature was milder. However, the misty clouds over the bay were heavy with more moisture.

Jack put the truck into park and jumped out, grabbing the nose tire from the bed of his truck. She got out and followed him, hoping to get a better feel for the place where she would be working. She brought the requested bag of bagels with her, thinking she would find the boss in his office. She figured most of the guys would be gone by that time, their work shifts mainly starting at eight in the morning and ending at three in the afternoon.

The human-sized door was wide open, and it was obvious that someone was still there. Once inside, Jack rolled the tire on the floor as she followed him into the hangar. Drake came happily bounding out of a makeshift hangar office to greet them. Stopping the rolling tire with one foot, Jack took a knee to return the sentiment to Drake for a few moments before standing back up. Hank was next, in overalls and an old, thick and worn flannel shirt, the radio on his hip occasionally squawking from time to time with aircraft chatter.

"Well, well, well, look at yew!" he said, the toothpick moving as he spoke. "Each time I see you, your beard keeps getting shorter. Got yerself a haircut too, I see!" He clasped elbows with Jack, man to man, then slapped him on the back of his shoulder. "Trying to turn into one of them modern-day pretty boys, I see." He smiled big.

"We still have guys out flying?" Jack asked, ignoring him and at the same time trying to block his view of Tasha behind him.

"Yup. Boys should be home in another thirty to forty-five minutes. Then we will be closing her down for the night. Them boys are making me miss my missus's fine cooking. She made her stuffed meatloaf casserole fer tonight. But it's just as well now that you have here my new tire I needed," he said, pulling down on his long, scraggly, salt-and-pepper beard where he flattened it against his neck.

Hank looked up to see Tasha's small figure just behind Jack's larger frame. He smiled warmly to her. "Well, who d' we have here?" He clicked his tongue at her.

Jack introduced her to the older man and watched as Tasha stepped forward to offer her hand to shake, only to have Hank realize that his own hands were just too dirty and greasy from where he had been removing the old nose tire, and thus deferred. "It's nice to finally meet the Prius owner. Darling, just what were yew thinking bringing a car up here like that? Our first snowfall and you won't see your car again until next springtime."

"Well, as soon as I can get my hands on another battery and a battery warmer, we will see how it goes. You may just be right, sir."

"Sir?" He looked at Jack. "Did I get promoted without being told?" He elbowed Jack. Then, to Tasha, he said, "Just plain ol' Hank'll do." He grinned at her.

"Well, if you guys don't mind, I need to drop off the requested two dozen bagels to the boss and then find a restroom." She held up the bag of goodies, and Jack told her she would find the hall restroom near Nate's office and that the office should still be unlocked—and if not, to just put the bagels in the refrigerator in the break room.

"Boss-man treating us to bagels and smoked salmon again, Jack?" Hank rubbed his large pot belly in anticipation. "Whew-wee! I can't wait for them tomorrow morn' then."

She gingerly left the two men to continue their conversation, quite aware of Hank's leering, but made sure to ignore it so as not to give him any 'mixed signals.' She wanted to be 'polite and well-mannered' when first introducing herself. Only when she got to know folks well did she let her guard down and let her sailor's mouth return.

Jack and Hank stood there watching her as she disappeared between two parked planes and into the hallway that led to the interior of the building where the side rooms and offices were located.

It was the low, long wolf whistle that Hank let out once she was out of earshot that brought Jack back to his senses, realizing he was staring at her backside too.

She had left her coat off when they had arrived in Seward's warmer weather, walking around in just her sweater and leggings. It was an absolute fatal attraction outfit, the ski bunny slope kind, that would send any inexperienced male skier welcomingly to his death over a black diamond slope.

Jack looked back at Hank, only to find Hank watching him watch her, too. He rolled his eyes at Hank, pressing his lips together to hold back from saying anything that would indicate that Tasha and he had anything more going on between them. "Oh, don't even start, Hank."

"I'm just sayin', man, if that's our new Sparky, us guys are in for a real treat. We should thank Nate and you for getting us some real eye candy up here in these parts," Hank said, shaking his head, smiling like a sly old dog, looking every part the dirty old man, with his scruffy old salt-and-pepper beard that grew down to his chest like a wanna be ZZ Top band member. "Wait till them boys see her!" The back of Hank's hand chummily thumped Jack's chest, then stilled as another thought occurred to him. "Holy shit, Jack!"

"Behave yerself!" Jack shot back, warning him.

"She's yer new roommate…" Hank's smile grew ever wider, showing off his heavily stained teeth for a man in his mid-fifties. He howled at that minute, "Oh man! You sly dog. Oh, oh, yew is one lucky bastard!" He winked at Jack. "What in the hell did you do to get Nate to hire that fine piece of work? Is it part of some promotional package?"

"It's not what you think and it's not all that it is cracked up to be," Jack said, trying to downplay it, pulling at his own beard, forgetting its new shortened length.

Hank, upon seeing this unconscious act, said, "Ah—she got yer by yer balls. Even made you clean up a bit?" Hank jested, laughing like one of Alaska's old rough Yukon goldminers.

"She's just another soldier, another co-worker, Hank," Jack reminded him as he started toward his office at the opposite side of the hangar as Drake trailed them. "You best be sure you and the others behave around her. I don't need to be firing good workers over bad manners. She's one of us and you treat her likewise." He reached over to give Drake a *good boy* pat. The large black dog offered a forepaw to him, which Jack gave a quick shake and ordered him to return to his doggie bed in his office.

"Hell, Jack! How're we supposed to treat her like one of us and not all be fired in the first five minutes?" Hank's question followed him as Jack rolled the tire closer to the aircraft on his right and let it roll the rest of the way to the spot just underneath the aircraft nose, where it rolled over on its side after several tilted merry-go-rounds, and stopped. "You know how the fellers are."

"Just be yourselves, minus a few lewd jokes, and you will all be fine. I think she can handle you boys." He stepped into his makeshift field office. "Just don't be grabbing her or touching her, unless you want me to do it to you."

Hank's beard-covered chin flattened at that comment.

And Jack added in warning, "And I promise you, you won't like the way I touch you."

Hank raised his matching salt-and-pepper eyebrows at Jack's last comment as he followed him into his office. "Can't wait ter see how this unfolds. Still, I *can't* believe she's just a soldier to you. You must be gayer than hell not to notice her and be living in the same cabin! Hell, mine hasn't been used in the last six months and its gone harder than when I was a teenager just lookin' at her," he said, rolling back and forth on his feet some, standing at the threshold of Jack's office, his thumbs looped in his overalls' suspenders. "You're not gay, are ya?"

Jack's head snapped up from the paperwork on his desk at Hank's preposterous question, giving him an annoyed look.

Hank put up a placating hand. "Hey, now, I know, I know...don't ask, don't tell policy." His thick, untamed eyebrows raised up again as he pulled a fresh toothpick from the pocket of his overalls and stuck it in his mouth.

Hank's head turned back in the direction of the main hangar, sighing. "Ah man, that girl will give electrical a whole new meaning to 'sparks a'flyin'."

Jack smirked at Hank's last comment as Hank took his leave. Jack took a few moments picking up what he needed in messages and work orders to bring home. He joined Hank just outside the doorway of his office to see Tasha taking her time getting back to them from across the spacious floor. She was pawing some of the aircraft reverently, as if saying hello to a few of them. She didn't notice them watching her.

"Christ, Jack! Yer a lucky bastard," Hank grumbled lowly. "Now, I got ter go home and screw the wife. And my wife won't know what hit 'er tonight." Hank slapped him on his back before turning to leave, making Jack laugh to himself at the picture Hank had just painted in his mind's eye: both past life's prime, and neither of them great shakes to look at. A good couple—typical white trailer trash people, but nice folks.

Jack snapped his fingers to get Drake's attention. "Let's go home, boy."

Jack whistled loudly to Tasha to follow him. She stopped what she was doing, obediently walking back to his truck, getting in the cab on her side as Drake jumped in the cab on his side. He looked past Drake at her a moment before starting the truck.

He knew now, he was *definitely* not ready to introduce her to the rest of the crew. But it had to be done, and soon. Normally he would have gone to the bar to meet up with the others that night. But she was far more tempting than a bottle of half-priced beer, and he decided to head back to their cabin.

They unloaded their shopping parcels, and she began to heat up leftovers—hers from the restaurant and his chili—along with a few buttered pieces of toast with parmesan cheese and garlic to mop up their meals. They ate in silence, both hungry after a long drive. She picked up their dishes as Jack got Drake fresh dog food and a bowl of water. She had started washing the dishes and he worked on making them some hot drinks for the evening and stoking a fire back to life to take the nip off the air.

He let Drake outside for his last bathroom break for the evening, giving the dog fifteen minutes to do so while he made them cups of hot tea. He set their cups on the coffee table in the living room and turned to let Drake back in. Everything was falling into place like they had been doing it for years, like he always thought living should be like, but now sharing it with someone that interested him. He smiled to himself as he watched her rinse the last of their dishes, placing them in the drying rack and then toweling her hands off, turning off the kitchen lights.

She canted her head at him, smiling, unsure of his thoughts. He indicated for her to come join him on the sofa in front of the fireplace.

He took his seat first, making room for her to sit next to him. But Drake beat her to it, jumping up on the sofa to be with his master.

"Ah...I think someone misses you," she noted, picking up her teacup and going to the adjacent chair to sit down.

Drake whined some, trying to crawl over his master's lap to get her attention too. She reached out, giving him a compassionate stroke on his head, making him squiggle more, until Jack reprimanded him to mind.

"You know, I would rather have you in my lap than Drake here," he told her, stroking the large dog on his lap.

"Drake might get jealous if I steal his master's lap," she commented, sipping her hot tea. She smiled at him contentedly and then placed her stockinged feet on the coffee table near where he had one of his propped up, curling her toes around his foot somewhat enticingly.

"He's going to have to adjust to sharing me or figure out that he can get twice the attention."

Looking at the big black eyes that Drake was giving her, she decided, "He'll figure it out sooner than later." Then she added, "You know, you're going to have to break the news to him somehow and hope he doesn't tell the others at work."

"I think he's trustworthy enough."

"So, did Hank figure us out?"

"Nope."

She eyed him a minute longer.

"Although...he did go on and on about you in a not-so-gentlemanly way. Let's just say his wife is probably going to see some action tonight after meeting you this afternoon."

She cocked an eyebrow at this.

"You woke up an old man and his pecker this afternoon with your outfit," Jack explained, pointing to her leggings. "I would highly advise you *not* to wear those on the flight line again."

"I say let the old man do as he dreams," she told him defiantly as she took another sip of her tea, lying back against the chair and soaking up the fire's warmth. She drew her leg back from his foot, stopping at the edge of the coffee table, with her knee defensively bent. "Besides, these are perfect. They're stretchy, comfy, no metal parts to scratch the aircraft's paint surface, and they will allow me the ability to get into tight spaces without my clothes getting hung up on anything. Most of all, no metal just in case I do end up electrocuting myself by accident. I think I even asked if there was a dress uniform or code, and I believe you told me there was none, other than 'no birthday suits and short shirts,' if I recall correctly from yesterday's shopping. I bought two of them just to go to work in. The coveralls will be over them, most likely."

"I'm just sayin'," he warned her, hearing the echo of Hank's expression and taking a chug of his hot tea, emptying his cup. She thought it was strange that he had decided on drinking that instead of his usual bottled brew.

She peered over her mug where it was doing double duty as a hand warmer, and asked, "How come you're not drinking your beer?"

"I want my wits about me tonight."

"Oh? Is there something I should be ready for?"

He smiled lazily at her as he stroked the dog's head, grateful for Drake's weight to keep her from seeing what she was doing to him, stretched out and relaxing beside him, the firelight dancing on her face in the room's darkness.

"That depends."

"On what?" She put her cup down.

"You," he said huskily.

"With or without Drake?" she asked, watching the dog lift his head at his name, knowing where Jack was leading. To the dog, she said, "Sorry, Drake, not into weird threesomes at the moment."

Jack patted Drake to move off his lap, standing up to pull her to him and against his body. He slid his hands down her sides from her waist to the lower half of her flanks, squeezing her rump as he tightened his hold on her and gave her a kiss that took her breath away.

"Please tell me that you want this as much as I do again," he told her, pulling one of her limber legs up, wrapping it around his waist. "Say you want it." He let one hand slide along her face, his thumb smoothing her cheekbone.

"Yes," she murmured, leaning her face into his hand.

Then she felt the swiftness of his hand disappear to her buttocks where he picked her up, carrying her back to his room, and gently dumped her onto his bed, all without breaking their kiss as he slid his pants off and then helped her out of her clothes while she took his shirt off. His needs far exceeded hers in his rush to take her again, no wine or beer to slow him down at taking pleasure in his dessert.

He awoke to the sensation of her breathing slowly next to him. He had never known such joy in waking up to someone until then. It was the newness in finding mutual satisfaction in each other's bodies that had to be the explanation for his newest addiction. He had never had such sweet lips like hers take him in the way she did. He was amazed that she possessed such *airs* only to be the *call girl* a man could only wish for in bed. The small throat sounds she made only made him desire her more so he could hear her satisfactory sighs. He nuzzled her ear before kissing along her exposed neckline.

She murmured to him, "I can't believe you are up again. Do you ever sleep longer than six hours?"

She pulled his arm to make him roll halfway on top of her like a blanket, telling him to go back to sleep. He acquiesced to her request, only to find himself nuzzling her more, not wanting to waste a minute of her presence.

She shifted under him in her half sleep. "Please, I beg you to stop. I don't think I have ever been this sore in my life." She turned to her backside to face him. "You're going to have to break me in a little at a time." She smiled at him, then closed her eyes as she stroked the sides of his face, letting her fingernails scratch lightly through his cropped whiskers, as if she were scratching a cat's face.

"What if I promised you not to go there but everywhere else?" Jack asked, kissing her slowly awake, starting on the other side of her neck and sliding down to her shoulders, then her breasts, and on to her tummy, making her squeal with delight as his whiskers made her skin come alive. He pulled the covers back up over them to help keep her warm. He could smell their lovemaking from the night before as he got closer to her womanhood. Her leg, bent at the knee, came up seductively, wanting its fair share of his kisses as he made his way along her inner thigh.

"You're insatiable!" she told him breathlessly.

He murmured something incoherent to her as he reached the arch of her foot, giving it a love bite and making her groan more, ensuring that she was fully awake. His hands snaked back up her legs, where his thumbs snuck their way back up into the forbidden zone, testing to see how sore she really claimed to be. She clamped her legs on his digits, trapping his thumbs, making him come back up from under the covers in the dark room.

"Hmm," he murmured in her ear. "I seem to have no control over my thumbs." He wiggled them inside her. She made a guttural throat noise as his thumbs moved around on her skin before continuing.

"After this, you owe me," she told him. He looked back at her. "You owe me some more downtime. Most of all…some sleep. Remember? I am supposed to be recovering from my vicious attack—or should I say several attacks?—from a certain man." She gave him a beguiling smile as she spread her legs wide for him again.

"I promise. Scout's honor," Jack said.

She awoke several hours later in her own bed. She called softly for him, but only the cabin's silence was her response. She had been asleep for quite a while and wondered if she had dreamed all the past twenty-four hours, unsure if it was real. Since when did she go from hating this wild man to fantasizing about a strong passionate man? But the stickiness between her thighs, along with some tenderness, was the proof in the pudding, so to speak.

It was very real. Tasha found her shopping bags covering her desk, still packed with her new work clothes.

It had to be the middle of the day, judging from the daylight streaming in from her bedroom window. She showered and dressed for the day, after peeking into his bedroom only to find the bed made and him gone. Drake was not around either, and she assumed that he had taken the dog out for a walk.

It was after she had finished showering and pulled the curtain aside that she found him patiently standing there with a fresh towel. She jumped, letting out a small, surprised yelp. He was fully dressed and looked like he had been up for hours.

"Relax." he told her. "It's just me. And I'm here to work on your backside again." He handed her the towel but didn't let her be free to towel herself off in private, the heavy weight of his gaze resting on her as he dried her.

"Where did you go?" she asked him, wrapping herself in the towel that she took back from him.

"Ah, you missed me?"

She gave him an annoyed look as he leaned lazily against the doorframe, allowing her access to the sink.

"Downstairs. Working on some paperwork for flight requests from work."

"Oh." She rolled on deodorant under each arm, then began brushing her teeth.

"You need any help?" she asked in between brushing her uppers and then her lowers, eventually spitting out the spent paste.

"Not really, but I would like to see where you are at in terms of IFR training—get you up to speed before you head back to the doctor's office in the next two days."

"Okay, let me get my makeup on."

"Makeup?"

"Yeah, my mascara and eyeliner."

"Skip it," he told her as he moved to take the towel back off her where she had wrapped it around her torso.

"Why?" she asked, turning her backside to him.

He put the toilet lid down to sit so he could attend to her wound. "Because you don't need it and it's your wound that needs attention again, not your already pretty face." Jack peeled back the rear main bandage to see her stitches.

"Well, it's nice to know you don't expect much out of your girls."

"I tend to like them natural."

"Seriously? With oxter hairs, no shaved legs and all?" She peered over her shoulder at him.

"Okay, I wouldn't go that far—especially if she exceeds me in terms of body hair." He smiled at her. "Some of your stitches have dissolved already. That's a good sign."

"I'd be curious to know what you would say when they are in their sixties, growing neck and facial hairs."

"By then I expect I will be half blind or trade out the old gray mare for a younger version."

She rolled her eyes, even though he could not have possibly seen it. "You would." She twisted back to him, catching him smiling.

He got her to turn back, facing straight ahead so that her backside was to him. "You'll stretch your skin and widen that scar of yours. Trust me, you don't want to make it any nastier than it will be."

"It's not like I am going to be attracting men anytime soon."

He stopped in his disinfecting of her wound.

"You got me," he said, grabbing ahold of her hips and planting a kiss on her backside, the good side. Tonguing her slowly, reminding her of his attentions from last night.

"Yes, but for how long before Mrs. Right finally shows up?"

"Mrs. Right? I doubt there's a person."

"You believe that?"

"Yup. No one's perfect. You make do with what you can get." He added the ointment to her. "You are going to have one hell of a scar there if we don't find you some sort of skin crème to lighten it."

She didn't say anything as he put on another new bandage.

"Hope the doctor likes my two weeks' worth of work." He turned her around to face him, holding her arms at her sides as he thoroughly inspected not just her tummy, but her breasts and womanhood. She could feel his breath upon her freshly bathed skin as he drank in the sight of her. She wondered if he was going to make love to her again right there as the seconds passed. She closed her eyes, using her other senses when one of his hands came to stroke her skin upon her tummy and up to the undersides of her breasts, thumbing her nipples erect, and then on toward her neck. He laid the side of his face against her, making her feel warm in the bathroom's rapidly cooling air, losing herself in his caress.

"Damn," he swore to himself, suddenly pushing her away.

She opened her eyes, wanting to know what caused the sudden change.

He gave her the towel back to cover herself. "You are as bad as a drug addiction." He got up to leave.

"What on earth did I do?" she asked, still not sure of them.

"Absolutely nothing." He cupped her chin, smiling. "Get dressed. I'll get breakfast going for us."

"This late in the day?"

"Why not?" He shrugged at her and headed off to the kitchen.

As usual, breakfast was a breakfast for champions, and Tasha knew she would be huge before long. She grunted, rubbing her full belly as she commented more to herself at how fat she would be if she did not watch it.

Jack must have heard her when he commented back, "You need to put on a few for the winter."

"I'm not a bear."

He smiled at her as he finished rinsing the frying pan, putting it back on the stove to drip dry.

She got up from where she sat at the kitchen island to put her dirty dish in the sink. He had started doing dishes when he had finished his meal, wolfing it down in half the time it took her to finish hers. He had to have been hungry waiting on her all morning to wake up. She offered to finish cleaning, only for him to tell her to go downstairs in the basement to find a workbook and sample test book for IFR training on his bookshelf.

"I need you to find them, read them, study them, so we can get you caught up on your groundwork. I want you upstairs working on this for me."

"Where are you going to be?"

"Downstairs…And before you ask, I don't want you in the same room where I am working."

She raised a questioning eyebrow.

"I can't have you distracting me," he told her, giving her a winsome smile as he got the last of the dishes rinsed and in the drying rack next to the sink. She smirked and left.

The next two days were the same, with her studying in the living room and Jack working in the basement. A few times, Jack had to physically tromp off to the hangar to attend to some aircraft work.

One morning Tasha came out of her bedroom, having gotten up out of bed, and she yelped in surprise at the 'peeping tom' in the picture window of the main room, her empty teacup and saucer clattering to the wood floor. She clutched at her chest as Jack's heavy footsteps raced up the basement stairs, matching the pounding of her heart. Her heartbeat slowed down as she realized the 'peeping tom' was…a moose! A giant one! An excessively big bull. The goofy but gloriously racked animal had stepped up onto the porch with is front legs, his head lowered enough to clear the low porch overhang, seeming to peer into the window, but had made no notion of noticing its occupants. Jack asked her if she was okay as he spied her disheveled night attire, and then noted what had garnered her attention. Drake had come up after him, barking at their intruder.

"Shit!" He went to grab the shotgun by the front door, getting Drake to quiet.

"Jack! No! Don't kill it, please!" she begged him, sprinting quickly across the room to nab his arm.

"I can't let him just stand there, Tasha!"

"Why on earth not?"

"Trust me, you don't want a bull to see its reflection. It will think it's another bull trying to challenge him. We'll have a broken window before you know it and a moose inside the cabin!"

"Are you kidding me?" she half squeaked, half yelped.

He nodded, putting a hand on the doorknob.

"Wait!" she ordered.

He looked back at her, annoyed at being detained for a second time.

"Can't you just *tell* it to leave instead of shooting it?"

He gave her an *are you insane* look as he opened the door, the cold air gushing in. Jack was unable to contain Drake inside their cabin, and the large black dog immediately went outside to bark at the large beast but kept his distance.

"It's a moose! Not a Canadian!" he said in exasperation.

Tasha headed to the refrigerator, grabbing a head of cabbage that they had bought a few days earlier, and ran after Jack in just her sweats and fuzzy animal slippers.

She went past Jack as he finished loading the cartridges in the shotgun, rounding the corner of the wrap-around porch. He swore at her as she went by him.

"Hey, Morris! Yo…you there, would you *please* get off the front porch? Look here, I bet you're hungry." She offered up the fresh head of cabbage as a peace offering, peeling off a leaf and tossing it to him, hoping he would catch a whiff of the fresh veggie. His head turned, barely tolerating Drake's barking. But when she tossed a leaf his direction, he took a step off the porch, heading her way.

"That's right, Morris, a nice fresh head of cabbage for you, if you would *please* get off the porch."

Jack yanked back on her, dragging her behind him, trying to level the shotgun just as she tossed the rest of the cabbage out into the yard for the moose to follow. She pushed down on the butt of the gun, forcing the barrel upwards. Luckily, Jack didn't fire the gun when he realized her attempt to coax the moose to move had worked. She clung to his back side, looking around him as the long-legged beast lumbered after the cabbage head at the far side of the yard where it had rolled to a stop.

Jack ordered Drake back to his side. He felt her hand squeeze his bicep.

"You see…you can be nice to them and just ask them to go away."

"You *bribed* him with a head of cabbage!"

"I said please. Besides, you don't have to be the typical aggressive gun-toting American when you meet strangers…suspicious of everything. You need to learn to smile, be nice…polite, it gets you much farther along in life, you know."

He rolled his eyes but kept watching the moose at the far side of the yard. The bull made short work of her green peace offering and he wondered if the moose was going to keep coming back now that she had fed it.

Its head popped back up and looked toward them where they stood on the porch, noting them.

Tasha elbowed him encouragingly, as if she was George Burns' Gracie on the comedy show. "Wave and smile at Morris. Tell him goodbye, Jack."

'Morris' decided it was time to walk on to the next point of interest. His dark brown legs, like tree trunks, lumbered on, and he made no notion of harming them, snuffing heavily at the air.

"Told you being nice works, no guns needed." She rubbed her arms gingerly, the cold air now biting through her PJs, and quickly headed back indoors to start making breakfast.

CHAPTER SIX

Tasha's follow-up for her stitches went well she thought, although Jack seemed a bit concerned.

"Well, Jack, you did a good job." To Tasha, the doctor added, "I think you are good to go again. Just take it easy and not overdo it. Listen to your side. If it hurts, then don't lift or do that action. Let it rest. Get one of the guys to help you when you need it." The comment was more for Jack to take note.

"But she will need to be able to work alone at times—is that still advisable for her to start her job?" Jack asked. He was not looking forward to introducing her to the crew—at least not yet.

"Yes, she'll be fine," he assured him. "Just make sure she doesn't get beat up again. I know how rough you guys can be over there. Make sure they are gentle with her," he joked with Jack.

Tasha turned to him with a concerned look on her face, now wanting to know what they did on occasions to merit this comment. Jack motioned with his hand not to worry about it.

As they were leaving the doctor's office, they ran into Chad coming in for his shift. The two men clasped hands in an elbow-to-elbow greeting with Chad asking where Jack had been since he had not been up at the bar as usual. Chad nodded his head in acknowledgement to Tasha, asking her how she'd been faring and if Jack had been treating her well. She kept it light, making sure not to imply that more was going on between them.

"Jack, you gotta bring her on up to the bar one week. Let her meet some of the townsfolk. Anyway, I gotta keep it short, I must get to my station. But my folks...mainly Mom, was wondering when you'd be back for a weekend to go hunting with us. Especially after you guys switch over to a four-day work week. You all are still planning on doing that for this season, right?"

Tasha perked up at this new piece of information, looking at Jack for verification and for some sort of an explanation. Chad then offered Tasha the same invite if she wanted to meet his folks too, saying she was more than welcome.

"Oh...I'm not into hunting. Fishing maybe, but not hunting." She made a face at him. "I...I can't do it."

"No sweat, just come anyway. You can help Mom and a few others with our normal winter stockpiling."

To Jack, he continued. "Hey, bring her along, she can learn about the old ways," he said, looking at Tasha. "That is...if you are interested?"

She smiled broadly at him and agreed. "Sure, I'd love it. It'll be something different than the inside of the cabin."

"Let's say in about two or three weeks? We should start seeing something arriving down here to hunt. Definitely bring her along, Jack. I'll give you a call then?" His hand made a phone motion at his head to Jack as he walked backwards at first, toward the double doors at the end of the building where she had stayed earlier in the hospital. Then he turned, disappearing behind the doors.

The following day was the big day. Tasha was ready ahead of schedule, being anxious about meeting the rest of the crew and hoping to reassure the big boss, Mr. Nate Amsel, that she was capable of working. Tasha was still embarrassed over having fainted in his office on her first day, knowing first impressions were everything and she hadn't made a good one on that particular day.

When Jack woke up, on his way to the bathroom to get ready for work, wearing a Henley undershirt along with a pair of winter work jeans, he found her already dressed and ready to go in her room. He seemed momentarily surprised but then drily commented to her, "Brownnosing the boss is not going to work, if that's what you're gunning for."

Her jaw dropped in protest, and she followed him to the bathroom doorjamb where she folded her arms across her chest, watching him wash his face to help him wake up. "And what makes you think I am trying to impress the boss?" she asked.

"Well, it certainly isn't the rest of the crew," he remarked, patting his face dry with a hand towel. "Just you showing up impresses the hell out of them."

"You say that as if no one in their right mind would have taken this position. What's so horrible about my job?"

He smirked at her as he set to work brushing his teeth, making her wait for his answer. Thankfully, he made short work in that step in his morning routine. He lifted his long-sleeved undershirt to apply deodorant. "Ah…nothing wrong with the job or the daily duties, just meaning that we hired a girl for the position. It's going to be quite a shock to them, even though they know of your arrival by now."

"You mean I wasn't supposed to be hired because I am a girl?" She bristled, now concerned.

Seeing this, Jack quickly assured her, "All right, don't get your feathers in a ruffle," brushing his hair and then smoothing down his captain's beard. "The truth is Nate swore up and down he hired a guy named Tosh. For some reason there was a typo on our files over your name. You showing up early was a bit of a surprise to us, too. Your resume is outstanding—you meet all the job requirements, plus some. I already told Nate that you even had your private pilot's license and that you just needed to finish your IFR and the various type ratings to fly for us."

He put the comb down on the side of the sink, turning to her, grabbing her on either side of her waist to give her a quick kiss. "You have the job. You're in for now. Keep up with the workload and you'll have the job for as long as you like or work your way up when the opportunity arises." He physically moved her aside to go into his room to finish dressing.

"I'll go start breakfast. The usual?" she asked, remaining there to give him space and to keep her wits about her, not wanting to think about the previous night with him.

"No, just coffee and a bowl of oatmeal," he said from his bedroom. "You'll find the oats in the pantry closet. Just follow the instructions and microwave it for me. Make whatever you like. But make it quick. I need to get you there early, but not as early as you *think* you need to be."

She got their breakfast and they ate in silence, each of them in their own thoughts. Oatmeal sounded rather good to her too, when it came to a jittery stomach. But she was not about to let him see her nervousness. His larger-than-life presence sitting next to her was calming. But once at work, she doubted she would see him much, since he was a lineman and a pilot for the company. She did not want to look needy, but she wanted a way to call him if need be, only to realize that she didn't have his phone number programmed into her phone.

"Is there a number where I can reach you?" she asked. She sounded desperate and then bumbled out a deflective reason for the request: "I mean…for after work…to let you know if I have to work late or can't carpool home with you."

He motioned for her cell phone so that he could punch in the information for her, as he continued eating his breakfast. She got up for some more coffee to pour into his mug, but he refused by putting his hand over his mug. "Just pour the rest into that thermos for me," he said, pointing to the thermos that was located at the back wall of the kitchen on the back countertop. Finishing his data entry, he slid her phone back to her while she poured hot coffee into the stainless-steel container on the far side of the island. He watched as she fumbled the cap on, hearing her curse under her breath.

"Will you relax?" he chided her, dropping his spoon into his empty bowl.

She sharply looked up at his command.

"Sorry," he said, picking up his bowl to drop off in the sink and then walking over to her.

She watched him come toward her, not saying a word.

He took the thermos out of her hands, setting it back on the countertop, and pulled her into him, reassuring her with a hug, amazed at her lack of confidence at various times. "Listen, you'll be fine. Just don't let the guys push you around. Stand your ground. Learn quickly because we need the help. We have three aircraft down that are needing electrical work and need to be ready by the end of the week for some routine deliveries. And most of all"—he placed his hands on both sides of her face—"remember what we agreed to…about us?"

She nodded her head.

"Then, good. No worries." He gave her another hug. "Now, let's go."

They were at work in less than ten minutes, the nicety of living so close to the airport in a small town. Rush hour traffic consisted of a couple of deer along the roadside and about three trucks running past their intersection, going into the downtown area.

She had just her coat, a file folder with her original paperwork, and her cell phone. Putting the truck in park after parking in his usual spot by the hangar off to the side, he turned to her, letting her know that that day she would be meeting everyone since it would be an all-hands meeting that morning. She nodded, opening her door, jumping out, and following him at a respectable public distance.

They entered the hangar via the side door, and she trailed after him in the dim interior. The overhead lights had been turned on, some still warming up to their full brightness. She followed, passing the hallway area that she had become familiar with for the offices and a breakroom, still deeper into the rear of the building where they came upon a group of men waiting at a large metal picnic table. A smaller spotlight shined over them as if they were poker players amid a high-stakes game. A few of them were eating, most had their mugs of hot coffee, and only two of them were reading newspapers, just waiting. All were younger than Hank, who had taken up the end seat of the table where his newspaper obscured his entire upper body as he immersed himself in the latest story. They were an odd-looking group. She recognized Emanuel; his Panamanian heritage and diminutive size among the larger guys was quite distinctive from the rest of his colleagues. But then Jack was larger than all of them, with his height and bear-like frame. The two *pretty boys* had to have been Nick and Sam, the *flying playboys* that Jack had told her about. Yet in comparison, Jarvis was just as handsome but not as well-groomed or as dapper.

One of the pretty boys' heads came up—the one with the dark blond hair and blue eyes—noting their arrival. He gave a long low wolf-whistle at Jack with Tasha in tow just behind him and slightly off to his side, causing the rest of them to stop in their morning activities. Even Hank lowered his newspaper halfway, at first noting Jack, only to end up folding it and putting it down on the table.

The other guy sitting across from him broke into a smile, saying loudly, "Well, holy cow, each time we see you Jack, your beard keeps getting shorter!"

"He's gotten himself a haircut too!" commented the dark-haired playboy.

"Man, Jack, you just might be able to get a date yet at the bar tonight. I hear the ladies love a sharp-dressed man," Jarvis said, singing the last part from the ZZ Top song. He high-fived Emanuel.

"What's the occasion?" the blond playboy asked, the others elbowing each other, laughing amongst themselves.

The young blond playboy that had originally whistled at Jack's arrival finally set his bright blue eyes on Tasha. "Hey, guys, this must be the reason, but surely

Jack hasn't won this gorgeous lady's fair heart, has he?" His gaze was now upon Jack, questioning him in jest, testing Jack to see if there was a possible courting opportunity as he smiled at her.

Hank finally spoke, his gruff Southern voice gravelly in the early morning. "Nick, this here's our new electrician that Nate hired. Mind yer manners, son."

Jack raised an eyebrow at Hank's unanticipated professional demeanor. Somehow, overnight, Hank had gone from being a lewd old man to being protective of Tasha in front of the crew.

"I think he could have had his eyebrows trimmed and added some highlights to his hair," the Panamanian commented and gestured on himself, making them all laugh when he stood up and struck a believable gay-male-designer pose that one might see on TV for fashion and interior home design. He smiled big at Tasha, giving her a Gumby-like wave.

The guy sitting next to him looked appalled and forced him to sit back down, yanking on his shirt.

Hank smacked his lips in distaste, clearly not impressed, yet shook his head, saying, "And to think I work with you guys."

She was grateful that Emanuel had taken the pressure off her as she remained quietly waiting.

"Aw, Hank, you gotta admit, it's been like watching those time-lapse images of someone changing in front of you. Before you know it, he's going to be prettier than Nick!" The auburn-haired playboy punched the golden-haired pretty boy in the shoulder.

"Who knows? Jack may steal Nick's herd of local women out from under him," jested the other guy sitting next to Emanuel.

The guys whistled low here and there, laughing.

"Enough! And yes, I have already stolen some of Nick's conquests," Jack jested, giving it right back at him. The guys did their typical low *are you going to take that* whistles, taunting Nick.

Nick smiled confidently at Jack. "But I am still younger than him." His eyes went back over Tasha's form, eyeing her up and down appreciatively. "Seriously, Jack," he said, using his perfectly square jaw, chinning toward her. "Is she for real? Our new electrician?"

"Yes, she's real, Nick. Just like Santa is, son," Nate answered, finally arriving at their meeting table, appearing out of the dim of the hangar and into their little bright break area. Nate greeted Jack and Tasha. He gave Jack a second look, indicating on himself if Jack had done something different with his beard again.

Jack nodded, adding, "And a haircut."

Nate's eyebrows shot up in surprise.

Jack turned to Tasha, gesturing for her to take a seat, telling the guys to 'make a hole' for her on the bench and to let her join them. His boss smiled at Tasha, courteously asking her if she felt any better since they had last met. She said yes and quickly took the empty spot the guys made for her on the bench seat.

Jack had stepped aside for Nate to talk, and remained standing halfway between the table and him.

"Everyone, I'd like to introduce to you, Tasha Lazar. She is our new electrician and avionics technician in addition to already being a pilot, so I am told, but just short of a few ratings." He looked at Tasha for confirmation and she nodded an affirmative. "Well, it shouldn't take you too long to pick up on each of these birds." He pointed just behind him.

A new hush formed around her as they all looked at her and she diminutively nodded her head in greeting to them.

Nate continued, "I don't need to remind you guys to watch your Ps and Qs. Men have been fired for way less in jobs where it comes to improper behavior. Yet please accept her as an equal. She hails from Palm Harbor, Florida, and has just finished her time with the United States Army as a helicopter electrician." He cleared his throat. "A whirly girl," he said off-handedly, checking his files again, adding, "and a combat vet."

Raven closed his files, looking at each member of his crew a moment before continuing when his eyes met Tasha's steady gaze. "I hear she can kick some ass, if any of you guys get out of line," he told the guys sitting there, and then he looked back at the golden-haired girl. "And Tasha has my full permission to do so, just short of maiming or killing any of you." He smiled at her, then added, "Jack nearly had his throat slit when he tried two weeks ago, and to think she was still recovering from a battle wound."

Tasha could hear a pin drop in addition to feeling the weight of every man's eye on her. She did everything she could to keep from blushing. The breakroom light, a harsh light, did not let anything hide in the shadows at the table. She cocked her head, giving them a half smile that hopefully read *for me to know and you to find out.*

Nate then introduced each of the guys to her and what they were known for in the company. She knew Hank already; the lead mechanic and flight radio and communications point man. Nick was the golden-haired flyboy and mechanic. Sam was the handsome, dark-haired, quieter pilot and mechanic sitting next to Nick's far side.

Then there was Emanuel the mechanic/parts runner, greeting her in his native language—and she, in turn, spoke fluent Spanish back to him. He patted his chest. "Ah, be still my beating heart, someone who knows the language of love."

"I thought that was French," commented Hank.

The others laughed. She gave them her first sincere smile.

"Jarvis is one of our best mechanics out here. He's been doing his best when it comes to electrical work, but he could use the help and I hope you will teach him all you know, Tasha. I know fixed-wing birds will be a bit different for you, but for the most part it's all the same."

She nodded at Nate.

"Jarvis will help you learn the mechanics, especially since he is the one needing to test out soon for his Airframe and Powerplant licensing."

"You already know our manager of flight operations, Jack. He's your go-to man if you have any questions and will give you your locker assignment in the locker room…" He paused, after slowing down on the last part of his spiel, looking at Jack a moment. "…We may have a problem, Jack," he said, upon second thought.

Tasha blanched, but it was not over the locker room issue. She had just realized that Jack was her immediate superior! Her stomach rolled at the thought…of them. She had broken her cardinal rule. A co-worker, no problem. Someone of equal rank in the military or on a job, no problem. But a supervisor? Her career, although just begun less than an hour before, was now precariously balanced, teetering on a pin head. The fate of her career was now controlled by whatever happened in their personal life!

Another low bomb-dropping whistle from Nick. "This is going to prove interesting," commented a smiling Sam, just low enough that only the immediate group could hear them as Nate and Jack discussed the issue just beyond their group. "They just realized there is only one main locker room and it has yet to see a girl since its inception during World War Two."

"Well, I don't think any of us would mind sharing the locker and shower room with you," Jarvis joked. "Manny is the only one who gets embarrassed by being seen in his shower cap."

"Am not!" retorted the Panamanian. "*No los escuches*!" Then he blew her a kiss and winked. It was becoming clear to her that Emanuel would be the least of her concern.

"Hey, Tasha"—Sam jabbed the air behind him and winked at her—"there's an empty locker next to mine you can have."

If her body had not already been claimed by Jack, she would have seriously given thought to the dark-haired man. But he was far more…gorgeous than her… and she was certain she did not want to be constantly fighting off other women for his affection.

The guys talked amongst themselves, waiting on the big boss's decision.

Nate decided it was not important for the time being, and to have her keep her things in Jack's flight-planning office in the main hangar. Facing her, he said, "Tasha, we'll get it worked out here shortly. This hangar and company has never had a girl work on the flight line until now." She nodded understandingly, and Nate assured her, "We'll make it work, Tasha."

Nate turned back to the rest of the group. "Any questions, guys?" he asked, having to raise his voice over the din of the group's hushed conversation. No one spoke up. "Then, welcome aboard, Tasha." Then he said to Jack, extending a hand to him, "I'll let Jack run down this week's priorities and the upcoming safety review training." He turned the meeting over to Jack, leaving for his office.

Jack stepped up, coming closer to the group where he placed a foot on the seat in between Jarvis and Emanuel, balancing a clipboard on his knee. "We will meet at the dockside in one week. Everyone's required to be there for this quarter's safety training."

A few groans came out.

"I promise to make it fast, simple, and painless so that you all can have the ample time needed to get these aircraft back in top shape—as if you all have that much work." He looked at each of them. "There are no flights scheduled for these next three days. However, by the end of next week, Sam and Manny will take Clara up to Tatitlek. Nick and Jarvis, I need the usual cargo run down to Kodiak with the Angelina. Make sure you do your due diligence on your load, your CG, the weather, and aircraft fuel."

He looked up at them. "Nick!" He got Nick's attention back on him rather than on Tasha.

"Heard every word, boss!"

"Tasha, you're with me for the morning as I will show you around the place."

A few of the guys looked at each other, but most eyes were on Hank. It was clear that Hank usually took the 'newbies' around rather than Jack.

Continuing, Jack said, "There's also a package in my office that was addressed to you, Tasha."

"Ah, that would be my tool caddy." She smiled knowingly, now relieved she would not be starting the job without her tools.

"Okay, let's get to work," he said as he pushed off the bench with his foot, standing back up and then turning to a whiteboard located on a wall that jutted out to shield the break area from the rest of the main hangar floor. He wrote a few notes on the board.

She came up to him, remaining patiently quiet, standing several feet behind him, as the others took their leave for the floor or toward the tall, narrow, metal lockers along the back wall of the break area. The bathroom and what seemed to be the locker room were just off to the left of where the group had met. That area was dark, save for a reddish light just under the door leading to another area.

Jack placed the marker back in the holding receptacle. He pointed to the board behind him. "This is where you can find the status of each bird, whether or not it is flying for the day, when it is expected to be back, and when and what kind of maintenance needs to be performed."

She nodded, not saying a word, trying to focus on learning as much as she could, even though her mind kept kicking her for her past week's actions with him. But then, she had every right to be angry at him for not telling her *he* was her *boss*! *'I'm just a fueler, pilot, and mechanic,' my ass!* she thought.

He led her around to the locker room, opening the door and calling in first before letting her come through the large anteroom. It was obviously an old military locker room with several toilet stalls, sinks on the opposite wall, lockers and benches in the middle, and a large common shower area on the far side. It was warmer due to two large extra space heaters mounted on the walls, their red coils giving off heat, and the red light source she had seen earlier coming from underneath the locker room door.

It would have been where she could change into cleaner clothes or shower if she needed to…had she been a guy. However, she doubted that she would need it, since her job did not include getting entirely dirty as a mechanic could, compared to working with electronics.

Next he led her around, showing her the other exits, fire extinguisher locations, first-aid boxes, and other various emergency stations. She remained quiet, letting him prattle on—not that he even knew how to prattle, given his solitary monastic tendencies as a Northerner.

They went back down the hallway to the break room, past a room with a few cots and blankets, much to her surprise. That room was for any of them when they had severe weather that forced them to remain inside their workplace. The battery room was next, where she would be charging and servicing the aircraft batteries. He told her that she might as well make it her office, or the next room where all the various wires and electrical small parts were kept along with a wire-labeling machine. Both rooms were generous in size and she asked if she could organize it better for her to work in. She was surprised when he said, "no problem."

Last, they entered the main office where she had previously met Nate. Jack dragged her in again, but this time to meet Nate's wife Nora. Nate paused in his work to look up at them, his eyebrow going up as if expecting something, but Jack just nodded at him and introduced her to Nora.

"So nice to see a face to the name, Tasha. It's even better to have another girl on board with us." Nora greeted her warmly as she got up, coming around her desk to shake Tasha's hand. The middle-aged woman was a tad stouter and shorter than her husband Nate. Her eyes shone like iced diamonds and her hair was frosted blond with black undertones that were neatly caught up in a loose coiffure. She was dressed in office attire and her makeup meticulously done to hide the developing larger wrinkles. "I can't wait to talk with you more and get to know you." Nora didn't let go of her hand. "My, our boys are going to have a field day with such a pretty young thing like yourself. If they get too rough with you," she said, squeezing Tasha's hand lightly in a motherly fashion, "you just let me know, all right?"

"Tasha," Nate said from across the room, still sitting behind his desk, eyeing Jack momentarily. "You do let us know if it gets to be too much. I don't need to be losing an electrician over something incredibly stupid."

"I think she'll be fine. After all, she's been to hell and back in the Mid-East and has worked side by side with other military personnel, who are predominately male," Jack reminded him. "Our guys will most likely be a walk in the park for her."

She looked over her shoulder at him, not sure if he was building her up or mocking her.

Then Nora tugged on her hand, pulling her closer so that only she could hear her whisper, "Come see me whenever you need to, and don't let them see you cry."

She nodded to Nora with a smile. Nora patted her hand again, and then released her to return to what she assumed was accounting work, by the ledger on her desk.

"That's right." Nate steepled his fingers. "We have another combat veteran among our ranks, Nora."

"Indeed, quite impressive!"

"Not entirely," Tasha played it down. "I just wasn't fast enough to dodge a bullet."

Nate cracked up at this. "Well, at least she has a good sense of humor and a good outlook on life. She needs to rub off on Jack here with all his seriousness. Get him to lighten up some," he told her with a smile, the last sentence an informal order to her as he leaned forward on his elbows more where he usually rested them on his desk, in order to look at his paperwork, before continuing.

"So, Tasha," he continued, getting her full attention back on him, "I hear you already know how to fly."

"I do. But I am out of date on my medical and haven't flown in a few years. I am afraid I might be rusty."

"What did you learn on?"

"A Piper. A Warrior, to be more specific."

Nate's lower lip stuck out a bit as he thought a moment before commenting, "Would you be willing to learn how to fly all of our models?"

She shrugged her shoulders rather indifferently. "Sure, but who's going to spend the time and the fuel to train me? I certainly don't have that type of disposable income to learn a rich man's sport."

He smiled broadly at her, telling her, "Consider it on-the-job training. I'll have each of the guys teach you and fly with you to get your hours logged. Most of the larger birds I require two people to fly, so you can acquire the hours as you are working the routes with them. Jack or I will check you out before sending you over to a certified FAA personnel for your official check ride." He sighed heavily. "That will be a big relief for me and a huge benefit to the company to increase our pool of pilots when we get busier in the summertime with the tourists and then in the wintertime for all the supply runs."

Then he added, "Jack, be sure she gets the right materials and stays on top of it in between her electrical duties."

"We're already on top of it, boss." Jack steered her back out of the office.

"Great! It's good to see you in top form, Tasha. Jack did a good job taking care of you."

She nearly cringed at his comment, for if he only knew.

Once back out in the hallway, they walked to the main hangar, where Jack called out the nicknames of the birds, getting her familiar with their company lingo. For her reference, he pointed out that all the planes had 'names' hand-painted on the sides near the cockpit area. The last place was Jack's desk in the 'hangar's control room,' even though he had a private office next door to Nate's.

It was obvious that he worked out of this one more. The giant, nearly outdated radio box squawking intermittently with pilot chatter sat on the low wall of filing cabinets. The room was lined with maps: one of the entire State of Alaska, another of bay water ports and their depths, and several smaller ones of

IFR routes to various other land ports. As she turned around, looking back at the wall where the entry door was, she saw the dry white erase board with taped-off sections for all their ports of call, where one could change the plane, the flight plan, the time, the date, the cargo load, and the invoice number.

This was his main job, besides fueling and flying: seeing that the aircraft work got done, the cargo assessed and loaded, and the guys assigned to the planes. She was impressed, to say the least. But still wary that he had turned out to be her *immediate supervisor*!

Jack pointed to the large and familiar box that had arrived for her. Her tools. She went to pick it up and take it with her, hoping to get as far away from him as possible. But he made her unpack it there, forcing her to crouch on the floor and pull her tool caddy out and organize the spilled contents of various specialty tools, and small electrical end parts that she would be using for her job. It took her some time to get her caddy organized again, where she could locate anything without having to visually see it when she had her head in some access hole.

When she stood up with her caddy, he had motioned for her to have him inspect her tools. He had only found two of her tools out of their yearly inspection date, having taken possession of them, tagging them, and readying them for a calibration inspection outside the company. With that done, he told her that her first assignment that day needed to be servicing two of the aircraft batteries in the battery shop and then on to the Cessna 560 for a split AHRS compass issue. He handed her the paperwork necessary to fill out.

He did not even look at her, his mind obviously occupied with something else, until his phone rang, forcing him to answer it. She headed off to the battery shop to officially start her job, the introductions and job tour now over.

She closed the battery room's door, exhaling heavily from keeping her temper in check until she could gather her thoughts and focus on the job. She started by matching job orders to the correct batteries. She donned the protective gear and apron and commenced working. It would take a while to service them, as they needed to be completely discharged, then checked, cleaned, and recharged on the trickle charger. There was only one trickle charger and only one hookup cable. The other cable was missing, and she could not determine the second one's location during her initial search of the room.

She ended up remaining in the room to deep clean it while getting acquainted with all the storage drawers and updating some of the paperwork in the room. Even the trickle charger would soon be due for its yearly recertification, and she made a note so the machine would get calibrated in time, along with finding the second charging cable. There were extra batteries sitting on the shelves that looked like they had seen better days and were in obvious need of servicing too. They were the ones to be used when an original battery needed to be serviced and the turnaround time was too long to meet the airplane's flight schedule.

Hours later, Sam stopped to check in on her, asking her why she was not at lunch with them, only for her to realize that she had never bothered to make herself a lunch in her agitation that morning. She sighed heavily, telling him that she did not bring anything and was at the mercy of Jack for carpooling. Knowing him, he had already left for lunch.

"At least let one of us buy you a Coke and a bag of chips out of the snack machine in the breakroom," Sam insisted. "We can't starve our electrician. Come on, join us."

She smiled gratefully, pulling off her apron and safety goggles to follow him down the hall to the breakroom. She was surprised to find the entire crew there eating their lunches.

"Hey, there's our girl!" exclaimed Nick, a big smile on his face, patting the chair next to him, offering her a seat.

"Cough up two dollars, Nick," said Sam.

"Why? You have your lunch, what else do you need?"

"An energy drink."

Nick reached into his wallet and gave Sam two dollars. Then, Sam turned to Tasha. "What's your poison?"

She gave Nick her order and smiled big, nearly laughing at Nick's mouth opening like a fish out of water in shock as Sam bought her a Coke and a soda for himself, then gave Nick his change back.

"Rat bastard," Nick commented. Then to Tasha, as she settled down next to him: "My pleasure at buying you your first drink. Although I would have loved to have done it in a better environment than this place."

"You mean the Yukon bar, Nick?" Sam asked as he took up his seat on the other side of Nick at the end of the break table.

"How in the hell is that any nicer than sitting here with all of us in this breakroom?" asked Hank between mouthfuls of his hoagie sandwich. "Tasha isn't the type of girl you end up taking out to a bar. If you want to impress the girl, wine and dine her at Chinook's or somethin' similar."

"You mean there are restaurants here?" she asked in mock surprise.

"You see, there, Nick. Take her out to one of them places," Hank encouraged.

"Why can't we all go out together?" she taunted as she took a swig of her soda.

They all stopped and looked at her as if she had said something not right, and she asked them, "What's wrong going out as a group to have fun?"

Quiet Jarvis spoke up. "I think we're just shocked that you are so inclusive. I think some of us were just waiting our turns to take you out."

"Oh," she said flatly.

"Aren't you going to eat?" Emanuel asked pointedly. "You can't live on just a soda."

Tasha shook her head at them, not wanting to tell them that she forgot her lunch, much less not being able to afford to go out and eat, though it sounded wonderful. A break from cooking lunches and dinners all last week would have been welcomed at that point.

"I think there are still bagels in the fridge," Hank added.

"No, I ate the last one yesterday," Sam said.

"How about Nick buys you some chips too," Jarvis suggested.

The guys snickered more.

Before she could answer, Jack rounded the doorframe to find her there with them, a bag in his hand. "Here, I got you a sandwich from the deli. You might want to re-heat it again," he told her, pulling out a wrapped offering from the bag. "And I have some chips for you too."

"Wow, where's mine, boss?" Jarvis teased, giving Tasha the extra time to pull out of her shock, standing up to get her lunch as she tentatively reached for the items Jack held out to her. Feeling the coolness of the sandwich, she turned to the microwave on the back countertop where the cabinets lined the breakroom wall just behind their table.

"Thank you." She turned back around, grateful for what he had done, only to find him long gone from the break room. "Wow, that man's quick," she said under her breath.

Lunch was leisurely, and she learned that on most nights the guys went to the bar for drinks but also to eat. She could not wait to join them. But with her tight money situation and then the extra workload of studying for her additional ratings, it would be a while before she could.

When lunch ended, she looked at her phone, checking the time, certain that she could now service the battery that had been discharging. She returned to her lonely little outpost to do what she could until the end of the day.

It was just about quitting time when she finished the second battery, charged and ready. She headed out the door with the paperwork to return to Jack and to let Hank know that one battery was up and ready for them. The next thing she was supposed to do was to check out the plane with the split compass issue. Luckily, the plane was parked just outside of Jack's office. Not finding Jack in his office, she laid the paperwork down on his desk and attended to the plane.

They had power on the plane, and she had found both Hank and Jarvis inside the cockpit checking for worn cables in the center console panel between the pilot seats. The plane was a newer Cessna 560 Bravo, yet it had seen some better days in terms of usage and mileage. She quickly scanned the flat screens across the main instrument panel, noting the forty-five-degree separation. She then asked Hank what their true heading was with the plane parked. She found the co-pilot's side was correct, with its heading the same as the whiskey compass on the windshield.

"Honey, we've changed that pilot's side out through and through with the entire system and nothing is fixin' the darn thing. Hell, Jarvis and I even degaussed the entire plane. So it is beyond our capabilities."

"Are the compasses back in the baggage compartment or in the tail section?" she asked.

"They're up in the tail on either side of the horizontal part just forward of the elevators. You'll see the small access panels for them. They're still open for you to check. But I'm not sure what you're going to get done in less than thirty minutes," he said, checking his wristwatch. "It's time for cleanup and going home."

"Can you give me that time, though?"

"Ah…sure…There isn't much to clean up between the rest of us. Just dumping trash, mainly."

"You have a magnet?"

"Jarvis, go fetch her a magnet from our toolbox," he called, since he was the younger and more limber of the two of them, it would've taken Hank a good few minutes to clamber out of his seat at his age and girth.

Tasha jumped out of the plane ahead of Jarvis and then followed him to their toolbox. He handed her the magnet.

"Could I have one of you stay up in the cockpit and watch the display a moment?" she asked him. "I'll be needing you to yell out the degrees it tracks when I get back up on the tail."

She walked back over to the horizontal, looking up and checking the entire aircraft for anything that could possibly be a cause of the problem. She climbed the maintenance ladder, noting its unusual sturdy construction. It was not the lightweight newer kind. But then everything was old in the hangar, including some of the aircraft being older than her.

She held the magnet to different points around the compass, gauging the readings that Jarvis yelled out from the cabin door, then tried to stick the magnet back in her pocket only to find it determined to stick to the ladder. It was then that the thought struck her.

She clambered back down the ladder in a hurry, reaching the bottom as Jack approached her, wanting to ask her something, but she held a finger up at him to hold his train of thought a moment as she tried to release the ladder's stop brakes and pull the ladder away. The stand was just as heavy as it was unyielding for her. There was not much space, given how they had parked the plane in between the corner wall and stored mechanical equipment.

"You do realize it's—"

Tasha interrupted him. "Listen, Jack, I know. Your paperwork is on your desk. Now don't just stand there, help me move this ladder away from the horizontal, will ya?"

He was not used to someone telling him to do something and making him wait. That had become foreign to him, having been in charge for a little over a year, unless one counted his leadership time spent in the Marine corps.

"Where do you want to go with it?" he asked, looking at the tight space they were in. It would take some finagling between the two of them. And moving it to the other side would be of no help either, she suspected.

"Help me lay the darn thing down on the ground as far away as possible from the horizontal. About a good three to five feet should do it," she explained.

Together they laid the tall ladder over, bit by bit, laying it down on the hangar floor except for another piece of equipment holding it up about two feet off the floor.

Jarvis yelled out the door, excited that compasses had lined up again! "She did it!" He gave a loud whoop that resounded throughout the hangar.

Even Hank clambered out of the plane, wanting to know what on earth she had done.

She handed the magnet back to Jarvis after she showed all of them standing there the magnetic attraction that the ladder's metal was causing. "You all either got to get rid of the stand or not park the plane so darn close to it."

Hank gave her a job well done clap to her shoulder. "Nate got us here one hell of a Sparky!" Hank told Jack, putting a new toothpick into his mouth. "Well, you will have your plane ready by tomorrow, Jack. Come on, Jarvis, let's clean up and go home." And they hustled off to put their tools away for the day.

She turned back to ask Jack what he wanted of her.

"I got my answer…for the paperwork I was looking for." He had his hands on his hips, relaxed. He smiled at her in appreciation of her good work. "Go help clean up and I will meet you at the truck in forty minutes."

The guys were done with cleanup and didn't need her help, thus she ended back in her battery shop figuring out where to store her tool caddy since the locker she had been assigned to wasn't big enough to hold her tray of personal tools. In the end, one of the cabinets in the room became her tool caddy storage. She would figure out a way to get it lockable in time, but then didn't see the point since she had now met the entire crew and couldn't fathom why they would ever want her tools, being mechanics.

Jack's head popped around the battery shop's door, telling her that he was ready sooner than anticipated. It had only taken him twenty minutes and they ended up leaving with the rest of the guys. Jack, being the last one out the door, pulled it shut and secured the hangar for the night. She continued walking to his truck as the others piled into their cars. Jarvis and Emanuel shared a car just like Jack and she did. The others jumped into their own cars and took off, and she watched a few of them head off into town, and others to their homes up in the surrounding foothills near where their cabin was located.

Jack unlocked his truck and she helped herself in. The air was warm enough that she had no need for her coat and had remarked upon the weather to him.

"We're in the middle of a heat wave, it seems. It'll be like this for another few days. It seems the cold and snows come later each year. But it allows us more time to get more training in and the work done on the aircraft before some major flying in the late winter."

He put the truck into gear and headed back to their cabin. She thought about asking him to take her out to the bars that the guys had talked about earlier but then quickly reminded herself that it was not her place to even suggest it. She was damn lucky that he allowed her to stay in his cabin. Thus she reminded herself about her uncertain housing situation.

"Looks like you had a productive day today." His statement broke into her thoughts on how to find new living quarters and how to handle the fact that Jack had turned out to be her supervisor, *not* just a co-worker.

"Hmm?"

"You got all I asked of you done in one day. Especially fixing a plane that had been down with the ARHS compass split issue for nearly two weeks while the guys tried to figure it out. You did it in less than thirty minutes."

"It was just a lucky guess, since I am not all too familiar with that model." And it was; she'd had no idea the ladder was constructed of metal that would pull the compass off until she'd had trouble with the magnet sticking to the frame.

"And the guys, did they treat you well today?"

"They did. I'm no longer worried about any of them."

"Even Nick?" He gave her a quick side glance, pulling up into the familiar driveway of their cabin.

"Nick's definitely a flirt. No sweat there either. What's the agenda for tomorrow?" she asked as she got out of the truck and climbed the two steps up to the wraparound porch to the front—or more like the side—door of the cabin. The front yard and side of the cabin were off to her right if one followed the wide porch around to where the large living room window faced the valley and overlooked the tidal area and airport, save for a thick swath of pine trees lining the property.

"Not much for you other than a few minor repairs and assisting with cleaning of the cargo areas. Most likely I'll have you sequestered in the battery shop for now. I need you to study for the rest of your IFR rating and familiarize yourself with twins." He unlocked the door to the cabin, letting her in as Drake raced outside, greeting them both happily and then promptly relieving himself in the front yard, afterwards sniffing the grounds for the next few minutes.

"Dinner?" she asked.

"Sure. I'll be back in a few minutes." He shut the cabin door to go play a few rounds of fetch with Drake, from what she could make out from the living room's window.

Tasha got everything she needed to get their dinner ready, grateful for the time before it would come down to the 'issue' she was having about Jack being her supervisor.

Using her time wisely, she made both their lunches for the next day as dinner was heating up. She decided to take it easy by heating up pre-cooked chicken, a few veggies, and a baked potato for each of them. Jack and Drake came back in fifteen minutes later, the dog coming back for a drink of water while Jack divested himself of his flannel shirt, throwing it temporarily over the sofa's arm.

"Smells good," he said as he wrapped an arm around her waist, pulling her into him and giving her a hug. But she did not reciprocate—only told him to grab the plates, pretending to be busy with cooking. He hesitated, complying wordlessly.

She could feel his eyes burning a hole into her back side. Finished, she turned the stove's gas off, grabbed the potatoes out of the microwave, juggling them between her hands to keep from being burned, and then dropped each one on their plates where he drew up a seat. When she picked up the frying pan with the main meal to split between them, he asked, "What are you mulling over?"

The question gave her pause before she could scramble, making a face, then she said, "Nothing."

He raised a disbelieving eyebrow. She ignored him, scraping the rest of the pan's contents onto his plate, giving him the majority, and then turning to dump the pan in the sink to soak while they ate.

She took her seat without a word and dove into her meal. Using her peripheral vision, she noted his quiet gusto with his meal. Being hungry, she chose to focus on her plate instead of the usual sitting back to relax with a meal and interact with Jack...that is now that she could interact with him, unlike when she'd first started cooking for him. She was certain he would be content to eat in silence that night for it was preceded by a full workday, given how busy he must have been to have disappeared from the breakroom as fast as he had when he had delivered her lunch.

"Now—"

"Thank you—"

Neither of them was able to take the silence between them for long, as they spoke at the same time. He motioned for her to continue, being a gentleman at home, but not so during work hours or out in public.

Not looking at him, she focused on her plate. "I wanted to say thank you, earlier, for the sandwich. I completely forgot to make a lunch for myself and you. But you left before I could tell you that." She twirled her fork on her plate. "Why didn't you sit and eat with us?" she asked, knowing most likely what the answer would be, either 'too busy' or 'bosses don't eat lunches with their crew.'

"I had things to catch up on over lunch," he told her flatly, then added, "You are welcome."

She scooted around what was left on her plate now that she was full. She looked up at him to find him watching her as he chewed his meal. She stopped herself and just got up, dumping the small leftovers into Drake's food bowl before settling her plate into the sink.

"Drake doesn't need to be fed leftovers. You'll end up spoiling him and ruining any training I have put into him."

"It won't happen again," she told him with her back turned to him as she began washing her dish. A few moments had passed before she felt his hand on her shoulder, adding his spent dish and silverware to the sink for her to wash. He coupled her as she continued washing, his body's heat giving her the much-adored warmth that seemed to have internally disappeared from her during the day.

"What's wrong?" he whispered in her ear. He remained to further his invitation that was soon to come, and that she was desperately trying to avoid.

She dunked her hands in the warm soapy water, grabbing the next dish. "I'm still trying to figure out a way to say it."

This is new, he thought, pulling back from her to give her room, as if what she was thinking needed the physical space to organize itself. "I take it I need to sit down for this one?" he asked her, concern coloring his voice.

She heard the barstool give some to his weight as he sat down again, feeling his eyes on her back side. She avoided looking at him as she worked on finishing the last of their silverware.

"It depends," she said with caution, and deposited the rinsed silverware in the drying rack.

"On?" he asked, his Southern accent drawling on the one syllable word.

"How you handle it," she said, gathering a little more confidence in what she had to say to him. There was no sound as he sat there waiting, before deciding on something.

Jack went over to the refrigerator and grabbed himself a cold lager, eyeing her carefully as he thumbed the bottle's lid off and dumped it in the trash. He sat back down at his usual place at the kitchen island, taking a swig from his bottle.

"Let me take a stab at it," he said, unable to wait, the silence too thick for him.

She turned to face him, toweling her hands dry, raising an expectant eyebrow.

"About us?" he asked her.

She turned to grab a cup to make a hot tea for herself. When she did not answer, Jack continued.

"Something made it change when it doesn't have to."

The microwave beeped, indicating the water was ready, and she dunked a tea bag into the hot water as she came over to her seat, not entirely ready to sit down.

He noted this preference, swearing under his breath. "That bad?"

"You're my boss!" There. It was out. Just like that.

He looked at her, his face expectant for her to continue when she didn't.

"And...?" Jack asked, knowing where this was going. It was a military taboo; in addition, 'not recommended' in civilian workplaces, either.

"Why on earth did you pretend we were co-workers?" She took a half seat on the stool adjacent to him at the island, her sense of flight taking over her sense of fight—a fight that she had no desire to have with him.

"We are—"

"But not equals!" she said indignantly. "Oh for God's sake, Jack, can't you see what this does to me? My career?" She had been about to take a sip of her tea to calm her turmoil, only to let the cup clatter disapprovingly back down on the counter. "My work, my career now has been placed on top of a pin's head, tottering precariously in the balance!" She sighed heavily. "Anything that you become displeased with…from me not fulfilling your sexual needs to breaking off this liaison, will ruin my career—a career I've only worked one day at!" She moved to put some space between them, only for him to reach out and nab her arm, forcing her to remain seated, facing him, his other large hand remaining on her knee to keep her still.

"Griswald," she growled in low warning.

He pushed his beer bottle away enough to keep from spilling it. "No." He leaned toward her, his blue-gray eyes searching her face as if trying to discern more.

"No what?" she asked unhappily, unconsciously folding her arms protectively over herself against his seductive and powerful presence.

"No. No, I am not going to let you beat yourself up over this and no, your career isn't precariously balanced on you pleasing me or not. We both said no regrets. Yes?" His large, square forehead wrinkled some at her, awaiting her confirmation.

She gave him a gimlet eye. He was trapping her with her own damn mistake. "Yes, I said it! But that was before I *knew* you were *my supervisor*! You told me that you were just the fueler, the pilot, the mechanic, and…and…" She turned her head away from him.

"And flight operations*,*" he finished for her. "No one else wanted the job. So I took the job, and hence the day-to-day operations of Black Raven Aviation. Yes, I *manage* everyone." He exhaled heavily; his other hand cupped her chin, forcing her to look at him. "I do many jobs, like you will eventually. I work on the line just like you do." He implored, "We *are* equals!"

He tried to kiss her but she refused him, averting her face.

"Tasha, listen to me…What we have done…or will do will not affect your job. I'm fine with what we have. Your performance in bed with me, good or bad, will not affect your job!" By that time she was shaking him off her, and he added to encourage her, "It's good enough!" he huffed out. He meant that for him it was just fine as it was. However, she took it the less positive way.

"Listen to yourself!" she snapped, finally getting free of his grasp, mainly because of his good graces, the stool she sat on nearly toppling over in her efforts to get away from him. "Just good enough?" She pulled her hair back in frustration with both hands. "Jesus, you sound like I am just enough until someone better comes along!"

He stood up.

She wagged a finger at him to stay the hell away from her when he started to move toward her.

"What then?" she asked.

He didn't answer, not knowing what to say next.

"Let me remind you what I told you earlier: I will not be your part-time whore!" she nearly screamed at him. "Just good enough, my ass! Fine! This part…this private life…your benefits. They're over! We're done! So you can fire my ass right now, Boss!" She snarled his rank to drive in her point, her finger pointing to an empty spot between them, daring him to cross that line.

She made for the coat closet only to have him spin her around roughly by her arm, facing him. Her eyes burned in pure anger at him.

"You will not go outside alone. You will stay here!" he snarled back.

"And do what?" she goaded him. "Just try and make me! I'll make you rue the day you were born!" she hissed at him, pushing him hard, only to have him hold on to her, pulling her closer to him. "I'm not your sex toy!"

"Ah…but you still owe me…Are you going to renege on that?"

Her disgust was clear that he even dared to suggest it.

"Or is it in your nature to leave debt and destruction behind you?" He sneered at her. *So typical!* he thought. "At least you can cook and clean to work off your debt." He released her, only to shove her away from him and toward her bedroom, so angry at her rejection, not knowing why he said the next statement when it wasn't true. "Your bed skills were just the icing on the cake!"

"You're a bastard! I knew you wouldn't understand. Anyone who screws their boss only ends up losing in the end. Even liars lie to themselves," she said quietly, stemming angry unshed tears before turning and walking away, slamming her bedroom door on him, the sound reverberating upon each other's wounds.

Sleep was elusive that night. Her tossing and turning were her exercise for the day. By morning, she dragged herself out of bed to get ready for what most likely would be her last day. She got herself dressed, her clothing's dark colors matching the dim day and what was to be expected. It was only a matter of time.

She opened her door, turning to use the bathroom only to find Jack standing in a pair of trousers and thin nearly see-through undershirt, trimming up his beard. The sight of his profile nearly took her breath away. He was still cut. His heavily muscled upper body had a dusting of chest hair that ran down to his lean stomach, and her fingers twitched at remembering how it felt in the dark with him. His left shoulder and arm blocked most of his body, since he was left-handed, as he worked his face. She hardly ever saw him naked in the light. With the same hand, he reached over to swing the door shut on her face, clearly still angry with her. She turned away, deciding to access the kitchen and make them both toast with a fried egg for breakfast. By the time he was out of the bathroom and had returned to his lair, she was done. Their plates were set out along with their lunches for the day.

She left it there so that she could get her turn in the bathroom to at least brush her teeth, hair, and wash her face, among some of her morning routine. By the time she was through, she had found that he had eaten…or possibly thrown out?…his breakfast. Had he eaten it that fast? He was making himself coffee to fill a thermos to take with him to work. The microwave beeped and he pulled out a large container with hot water.

Without any conversation between them, he made her hot tea, sliding the large travel mug next to her lunch. She choked down her lukewarm breakfast when he had gone outside to start the truck, afraid he was going to make her walk to work. She raced to put her dish in the sink, shrugged her coat on, and got at least one foot into her boot when he came back inside. She looked up at him, meeting his icy look. When their eyes locked, she tried to imagine what he was thinking.

In his voice gruff, he said, "Relax, I'm not petty enough to make you walk there and make you late to work. I'll have a more reasonable excuse to have you fired."

She narrowed her gaze at his blatant threat.

He chinned over to the sink, telling her, "Finish those dishes first."

"I'll get the dishes later."

"You'll get them done now!" The still air erupted, nearly making her fall over as she was donning her second boot. "Do it…if you want to keep your job!"

Her contempt of him was clear on her face.

"I don't need to explain myself, do I?"

She did his bidding, not bothering to take her coat or boots off. Tasha made short work of it, being done in less than five minutes. He had stood there, his arms folded, watching her like a drill sergeant does with his newest recruit.

As she dried her hands on the towel, he grabbed both their lunches, putting them in one bag, making her wonder if he was thinking both sandwiches were his, and leaving her without a lunch again. He opened the door, turning when she wasn't right behind him, asking, "What in the hell are you waiting for?"

She pressed her lips into a thin line, trying to keep from making an angry retort at him, for she was at his mercy since her own car was dead. Today she would find another way, she thought as she passed him on her way out, nearly side-swiping him. She got in the old truck, slamming the door shut, and waited as he called for Drake to go back inside from his morning outing, locked their cabin door and got in, then put it in gear and headed toward the hangar. She played on her phone, googling how far the distance was to the hangar from their cabin. She found it only to be two and a half miles one way. That was the same distance she had run each day when she was in the military. She could still do it; although she was still recovering, she could walk it. She had done so from the docks up to the cabin—albeit some of it was via a lift from a local trucker on the highway. By the time they arrived at the hangar, she figured she would need to be up an extra forty-five minutes earlier to get to work on time if she walked.

He turned off the engine and remained still. She shut her phone down and reached for her door to let herself out when his hand moved to her leg, making her stop and look at him.

"I'm sorry for yelling at you this morning. The reason all food needs to be put away and dishes washed each time is because of the possibility of attracting a bear. They have a keen sense of smell. Bears will easily tear down doors or break windows to get to the food source. Do you understand?" he asked softly, not looking at her but out the front windshield.

"Yes. But the only bear problem we have…is you!" She got her door open and slid out, closing it on him and leaving him in the truck, nearly running to the hangar door to escape him for the safety in numbers of her new crew.

Tasha hurried to the morning break table where the crew had gathered already in pretty much the same state as the day before. The light over the table being the strongest, a tiny spotlight in the massive old hangar—the light was her safety beacon from Jack. Everyone was waiting for the day's assignments and duties. Nick and Sam were looking at car magazines at the far side of the table. Jarvis was eating some fast-food breakfast, along with Emanuel stealing a Tater-Tot or two from him. Hank sipped his coffee, catching up on the morning newspaper at the end of the table as if he were the father of all four of the boys. She took her seat at the other end of Hank, not wanting to discard her coat yet, the cold morning air still lingering around her. She put on her work smile for them as she greeted those that noted her presence.

She could hear the opening and closing of the solitary door that everyone came through in the distance. A few moments later Jack appeared out of the hangar's dim light, invading the harsh light around their group. She did not look his way at first, as the rest of the guys shifted, putting down their reading materials, and turned their attention to the man.

"Mornin'," he started, looking them over as if trying to ascertain who was fit enough to work that day. "After the work put in yesterday, we are now caught up and will be ahead of schedule for the next week." He put his hands on his hips since he held no notes to read from. "I would like to start getting these birds closed up and begin setting our attention on getting them fueled and the cargo manifests readied with their prospective CGs figured for each load. In addition, I need to verify each of you are still good for the winter season in terms of your proper licensing. For example, Emanuel, I need you to go see the doc"—he pointed to Tasha—"and take her with you for the employee company medical. You will be due at the end of this month. Tasha will need one before she starts her flight training."

Jack continued, "Hank, see to it that the hangar is detailed at all times. I want this hangar in top shape before winter sets in and we'll be too busy flying. Next Thursday is training day. We will meet at the harbor dock around ten in the morning. So enjoy the extra two hours off in the morning, get some rest. I will be doing our company check rides next week for those of you that have cross-trained to another model bird. Any questions?"

The mood was different that day. She suspected most of them were tired from going out the night before. They were quiet, as if still trying to wake up.

"Let's get to work!" He clapped twice for them to move.

"Tasha!" he barked. She had finished hanging her coat on the nearby coat rack and had turned toward the battery room. She turned warily around. "Can you finish the other standby batteries in the shop by the end of the day?"

"I can finish just two a day, unless you can find me an extra charging cable for the trickle charger. Then I can get you four done in the eight hours."

"There wasn't one in the shop?"

"No. None that I could find when I went through the room, cleaning and organizing the battery shop yesterday."

He mulled to himself as he unconsciously thumbed down his mustache and beard. "I'll run it by Nate today and see what I can do for you in getting the extra cable."

"While you are at it, ask him to place an order for more distilled water and a bottle of lemon juice. I won't need it immediately, but it should always be on hand."

"Lemon juice?"

"For possible spills and cleanup of battery acid."

"Lemon juice it is," he said, making a mental note. "Then, if you can, between times, check into finding out why two of our interior lights aren't working on the Angelina."

She nodded at him on the new task. He then walked off, leaving her to her own specific duties.

Once inside the battery shop, she settled into her work for the next few hours and read some more on Instrument Flight Rules up until lunchtime when her stomach began to rumble. Unfortunately, Jack had her lunch that she had made for herself, and like hell she was going to go ask for it. She decided on grabbing something from the vending machine instead, making sure to pay back Nick for the soda the day before. She walked back to an empty hangar, the guys already at lunch, and retrieved some coins from her coat pocket, making her way back to the lunchroom, where she found Hank sitting there eating alone.

"Where are the others?"

"Aw—today is a Mexican special day. Them boys ran up there to nab themselves the twelve tacos for six dollars. I knew I should've told them boys to see if you wanted some!" He shook his newspaper so that it would fold easier before folding and laying it on the table. "Jack not got yer lunch, girl?"

"He has it...in a way," she said, not expounding. "He ended up taking mine thinking it was his, I believe." She put the coins in the soda machine.

"Never seen a diet of just soda for lunch before. Is it some sort of newfangled diet? It can't be good for ya." He leaned forward on his elbows at the table.

"Naw, it's pretty much all I can afford until first payday." She nabbed the can that had dropped in the dispenser.

"Do ya need a loan?" Hank asked, starting to dig for his wallet. "I can't believe Nate or Jack didn't fund you up front for a bit."

She shook her head no. "I'll be all right." Lifting one shoulder up, she said, "Jack, sort of did—"

They were both interrupted by the devil himself, and he looked annoyed at having caught her talking about him. He looked back and forth between her and Hank, a bag in his hand with their lunch.

"I sort of did what, Tasha?"

"Just telling him that you helped out some by footing me financially for some food until my first payday." It was the truth. She had told Hank nothing else of them, nor to anyone else. He looked at her as if he did not believe her.

He jerked his head back toward the hallway, just outside of the breakroom, for her to follow him. She followed him quietly and down the hall some, where he turned on her in a sudden small violent whirlwind of movement, quietly growling at her. "I will not have you talking to people about me or us! Do you understand? It was what we agreed upon…to be professional at work!" He nearly punched her with the lunch bag as he shoved it to her.

She shoved it back at him. "First of all, we were not talking about you because there *is* *nothing* to gossip about a boring bear of a man! So get off your high horse! All I knew is I didn't have a lunch because you took it, and I assumed that you thought both sandwiches were for you!" she hissed at him, trying to keep her voice down. "I only said that you helped me financially, and it was the truth, ya bastard!"

Disgusted, she went around him to get to the sanctuary of her battery shop and to close the door on him, her hunger forgotten in her fury. But he doggedly followed her in, opening and closing the door behind him, dropping the bag on her workbench, pulling out a sandwich for himself, and shoving the other one to her.

"Eat!" he told her, watching her don her work apron.

"You can feed it to the bear, 'Griswald!'" she snapped. "I'm not hungry and I have work to do," she added, keeping her voice controlled and professional to him. It was partially the truth, although she could have taken a two-hour break and still gotten the work done.

He suddenly smirked, then pulled one of her shop's work stools out from under the worktable to help himself to a seat. "A bear?" he questioned her rather simply.

"You're the only one to mention bears, where I haven't even seen one yet— mainly because someone won't let me outside long enough to explore a town, much less our own neighborhood! Hell, Drake gets more outdoor time than I do!"

He noted her open test booklet, pulling it to him, ignoring her sarcasm. "You've been studying, I see."

Jack asked her a test question and she answered it easily. He did another one and she answered it again. He pushed the sandwich over to her, indicating to take a seat and eat. Her anger had waned some, her stomach rumbling its displeasure at having to wait so long, betraying her as he looked at her, waiting when she refused to pick up the sandwich to eat. "I can't have an electrician passed out on the battery shop floor due to self-starvation. Besides, I have heard the noise of a bear's tummy growling." His fingers pushed at the sandwich more to tempt her into eating. "Yours sounds like one."

She gave in and resignedly sat down on the far side of the workbench from Jack to eat, asking him to pass her soda to her where she had set it down on the room's window ledge just behind him. His seat was between the window and the workbench and his long arms allowed him to span the short distance easily without getting up from his seat.

He thumbed through some more pages in the booklet without looking up and asked, "Where is it that you wish to go?"

Her mouth full, she shrugged a half-hearted shoulder at him. Then she swallowed, picking at her sandwich. "I don't know, anyplace that doesn't look like the inside of your cabin."

"Ours," he corrected her. "There's not much to do around here." He kept flipping through the pages.

"The guys talked about some of their favorite hangouts. They sounded interesting," she suggested tentatively.

"They're bars!" he said, somewhat annoyed.

"So?" she questioned, noting his ire rising.

"You're not the type to drink," he stated, finally glancing at her. Their eyes met briefly before he resumed his search in her test module.

"Says who?" she asked. Then proceeded, "One, they are *your* beers and two, I am not an aficionado of beers. Besides, there are other things inside a bar besides just drinking. Music, pool tables…you know…the rest, I presume."

"Not much into bars, but I do go from time to time," he said more calmly, still perusing through the questions in her booklet.

"Well, don't stop on an account of me! Hell, bring me along," she retorted cynically. Tasha took a bite of her sandwich.

He gave her a grave look as she chewed.

"What?" she asked, after swallowing the bite of sandwich, trying to figure out what was going on under that thick skull of his. She took another mouthful of her sandwich.

"The last thing I need is for our guys, and this town, to find something to chat about."

"It's not a date!" she said between mouthfuls. "And *definitely* not with you!" She put her sandwich down, covering her mouth politely. "You worry more about what others think than a girl does."

"I am trying to prevent it and protecting you in the process."

"I don't *need* your protection," she stated, and then hinted, "The only protection I need is from you."

Jack's glowering was the only warning that kept her from pursuing that direction.

"Okay then, let's start with you taking me out to an auto parts store and let's get me a new battery for my car. That way you don't have to deal with having to drive me anywhere," she suggested, trying for another solution.

"After payday," Jack commented drily, stopping at a page and looking up at her.

"When will that be?" she demanded, wondering if he would give her another vague answer.

"Two Fridays from this coming Friday. Once a month."

"Christ! I won't make it from month to month!" She was now realizing that she would be forced to stay with this man much longer than she had expected.

Jack tilted his head at her, expecting her to expound on her thoughts as to why not. But she didn't offer anything as Sam popped his head in, with no warning knock on the door, asking her if she had taken her lunch break, only to lay eyes upon Jack sitting there at the workbench with her test booklet in his hands and her with a half-eaten sandwich on the table in front of her. He immediately apologized for interrupting, pulling back out. Even Tasha could feel Jack bristle at Sam's intrusion.

"Just stop it, Jack."

"Stop what?"

"I know there is something going on with those guys. What on earth did you threaten them with? There is going to be some necessary social interaction with the crew and I. They are all stepping on eggshells around me."

"I have not threatened them."

She eyed him longer, hoping something would spill from his guts. His expression of *what* was her only answer.

He ran another question by her and she answered it correctly. "It seems like we can send you up to get the written test done and out of the way this week, if you think you are ready for it." He pulled out his phone to look at the time, determining that their lunch was over. Not waiting on her answer, he said, "I'll set up the ground test for next week or the week after," and left her sitting there to finish the last of her sandwich.

CHAPTER SEVEN

Less than a week later, it was training day. Jack had let her sleep in, since their day started at 10:00 a.m. She was getting ready for work when he asked her if she had gotten another set of clothing, in case of emergencies, in her recently assigned wall locker by the break table. Making the last of their sandwiches, she said she hadn't as of yet but that she could bring a set with her that day.

"Make a third sandwich, Tasha. One just isn't enough."

She paused in their lunch-making endeavors before complying.

"Drake, let's go outside." He opened the front door for the eager black dog and then followed him to start the truck's engine.

She got the last of their breakfast dishes washed and the food put away, grabbed an extra change of clothes to store in her locker, donned her coat and boots, grabbed their lunch bags, and went outside. She ran into Jack's massive chest as she tried to pass through the door. He stepped aside, allowing her by after the silent pause that occurs after an unexpected crash, neither of them blaming the other for the bumper damage. Drake slipped by them during those few moments, heading back into the cabin for his second helping of dog food before sleeping off his sentinel duties for the rest of their workday.

The harbor docks were another mile down the road past the airport. He pulled into the lot, parking his truck along with the rest of the vehicles already parked and waiting, Jarvis and Manny having pulled up just after them.

"Give me your phone," he told her, as he held his hand out for it.

She gave him a confused look since she had lost the most current round of solitaire due to his interruption. No way was she going to give her phone to him! It was her lifeline.

"Why?" she demanded.

"I don't want cell phones during my training class." His hand was still out, waiting for her to give the phone to him.

"You know I can turn the ringer off and put it in my coat pocket instead," she argued with him in the cab of his truck.

"Then leave your coat behind since it is not that cold. I'll need you to volunteer with some of the equipment."

She did as she was told, although a bit reluctant. But he was right: as she got out of his truck while he reached into his pickup's bed for a box, the air was moderate. The sunlight warm. She followed Jack onto the pier, where he ended up stopping midway along the slips used for the much larger boats, dropping a box of what looked like equipment and blankets.

Thankfully, the morning's weather was clear and sunny. The only visible clouds hugged the mountainsides around the bay. The guys that had been there the longest, Hank and Jarvis, did not wear their usual heavier coats, standing in nothing but their long-sleeved shirts. The others varied between a windbreaker on Emanuel and her pullover sweater. The guys huddled somewhat together, still making her feel like she was not a part of the crew yet. Tasha stood somewhat apart from them, but within earshot of Jack's voice as he began their day on cold-weather-related effects on the human body. Jack stood near the edge of the dock, where everyone could see the waters lap against the metal beams on the far side of the wide slip.

Tasha's interest slipped away from the lecture when she spied harbor seals frolicking in the waters below. She slowly inched her way closer to the pier's edge, where Jack stood giving his military-style safety class, making it look like she wanted to get in closer to hear Jack. She remained apart from the group yet ready to be the volunteer that Jack had requested earlier of her.

Those seals. They were something to behold. She wished it wasn't work time, just so she could watch them. It was the first time she had seen wild seals, and there was a cluster of them playing, from what it seemed—until she saw one with a fish in its clutches—their heads popping up where you least expected in the murky waters.

The next thing she knew, she was hitting the hard, cold waters below. It felt like she went through wet concrete. Shock had not registered as she sank down further, the water closing over her head. She was not sure if she had lost her balance or if something had knocked her over. It was the last rational thought before her reptilian brain went to work in survival mode. Her instincts kicking in, she swam back to the surface of the water where the light was brightest, blowing what precious little air she had left in her lungs and following the bubbles to the surface. Her heart and lungs spasmed in the sheer cold that stabbed through her entire body, stinging her senseless.

She broke the surface gasping for air and at the same time looking for something to grab ahold of as her muscles refused to obey her. She looked up dazedly at the pier, so much farther away from below than from above. The guys were shouting at her, pointing to something for her to see. A ladder. She shivered uncontrollably, the shaking helping her clear the initial shock of being in cold water as she swam as fast as she could to the ladder to get herself out of the frigid wetness, the air feeling much warmer, although still cold in her book.

Sam and Nick were the first to reach the top of the ladder, with Nick starting down it first. Her hand had reached the rusty metal only to slip off it. She tried again, that time nailing it, trying to pull herself up and out. But she found herself incredibly weaker than she gave herself credit. She was a strong swimmer, the best in her platoon, always acing that part of the physical training every quarter in the military. But what was happening here was not the normal Florida girl's swimming habits. First, she liked her ocean waters to be around bathtub temperature—not the melted ice water cooling beer bottles!

She tried to kick herself up farther until she was able to get one foot up on the lowest rung to push up, the effort nearly exhausting her. She felt herself being pulled up by the back of her shirt and then a pair of hands grabbing ahold of her waist as they hauled her up on to the pier, like a fish that had just floundered onto dry land, shivering uncontrollably in a pool of water, until she was further yanked up into a standing position. There she distantly felt the aid of guys taking the second layer of her clothing, her boots, and her socks off. The blankets getting wrapped around her as one of them held her up. Her senses coming back to her, rational and logical thoughts attempting to start up again. But her reptilian brain kept fighting for control as she spied Jack standing there next to Hank with Hank looking rather concerned, Jack's lips moving with unidentifiable sounds bashing against her waterlogged ears, the sound waves reverberating until the water pressure broke and the water drained out of them.

"Okay, guys, let's get her into the truck and back to the hangar for a warm shower," Jack ordered.

Her knees were spongy as she felt herself falling again when someone let go of her.

Her first linguistic thought surfaced: "YOU RAT BASTARD!" she screamed, her own voice making the pinpricking on her ears hurt more. Then time and space sped back up, and she felt herself scooped up by one of the guys—actually, it was two of them—as she continued to struggle within the confines of the heavy blankets.

"Hold still, you aren't making this easy for us to get you into a warm place!" Sam's voice told her.

"Jarvis, get a better hold of her, will ya?"

All she saw were various shifting and hurried viewpoints.

She felt more hands wrap around different parts of her body—the warmth of an arm wrapped around her lower legs, another under her bottom, and the last set under her upper torso. She heard the sound of a familiar engine, the truck, and then felt herself folded and shoved into the cab of the truck, the cab already warm with the heater going. Sam slid in next to her where he laid her wrapped-up form next to his, wrapping his arms around her as she continued to shiver, the wetness annoying her skin, as she closed her eyes to focus on restarting her body's internal thermostat.

She heard Jack telling her to stay awake as she felt the truck's movement driving them back to the hangar. Doors opened and closed. Bright light and then darkness. Her body jerking for what seemed like a half hour, and then red lights and warmth. Voices. Commands. More voices.

Then Jack's face in hers. "Okay, Tasha." His voice was soothing. "Let's get you out of these wet clothes." A seat. They put her on the seat, lying propped up against one of the rows of lockers.

"Sam, get the shower going. Make sure the water is warm—warmer than you would normally have it for yourself, but not burning the skin on your wrist. The rest of you...outside."

"You bastard!" she hissed between clenched teeth at his face.

"I know, Tasha," he said, yanking the warm blankets off her and undressing her. "I know." The locker room air was cold as he got her undressed all the way and then re-covered her protectively with the same blankets just as Sam rounded the corner, letting him know the water was ready.

"Go, I'll take care of the rest and meet you guys in a moment at the break table. Just need to make sure she can stand on her own in the shower." Divesting himself of his outer shirt, he picked her bodily up, throwing her over his one shoulder and carrying her to the showers.

"Question is…is *she* going to let you live after this?" Sam asked as she continued to struggle over Jack's shoulder like an angry burrito verbally spitting out jalapeño hot sauce at him, her grunts and yelps at him stymied by her body's uncontrollable shivering.

"Just go, Sam."

"Lucky dog," Sam said under his breath as he took his leave.

Jack got her to the shower, the steam billowing around them as he unrolled her from the blankets in one pull, shoving her in under the warm water and holding her there, getting just as wet to keep her under the shower head and standing up. She screamed her displeasure at him, smacking at him as he held her at arm's length, letting her get her anger out of her system.

"Are you done?" he finally asked her when she stood there spent, staring sullenly at him, the evil glare lurking just behind those piercing green eyes of hers. He tentatively let go of her to test if she could stand on her own, which she did, her muscles now responding like they should as her core body temperature normalized.

The drenched hell cat stared back, deathly quiet. Her eyes watched his every movement as he backed away from the water still soaking her through and through. Jack noted, *She'll be fine. She's definitely a fighter.* She looked small standing there in her full glory. Still fierce. He turned to another shower stand where there was soap that someone had left behind, and he reached for it to hand the bar to her, only to get a face full of water splashed at him, soaking the front of his shirt completely.

"Get away from me," she hissed.

"I will as soon as I can trust that you will not topple over and you wash yourself of all the glacial silt. You will find yourself itching later if you don't get it off your skin." He offered her the soap again, waiting.

Tasha grabbed it like a wild animal getting hand fed, then turned her back on him, not giving him anything more to appreciate, but he equally enjoyed watching her rump and long legs, her wound still there just above her hips, only better healed and smaller.

"Go away," she commanded, sensing he was still there. "I'm fine."

"I know you're fine," he told her in a soft, seductive tone.

She looked over her shoulder at him, the invisible knives thrown at him pinning him to the shower wall that he casually leaned up against. He unfolded his arms and turned to leave his personal private show. His cabin-mate. His irresistible cabin-mate was getting harder with each passing day that she cut off his supply of primal happiness.

As he walked away, he casually said over his shoulder to her, "Thank you

151

for volunteering today, Tasha," almost not rounding the corner fast enough as the bar of soap she threw missed him and continued to sail into the locker room, clanging loudly against the metal lockers, making the last row of lockers shake upon impact.

Jack whistled a happy anonymous tune as he got dressed in a new dry long-sleeved shirt and flannel overshirt, his pants still wet, but not enough to warrant a change for the day.

He heard the water shut off as he closed his locker door.

"Where are my clothes?" she yelled from somewhere in the room, and he knew she was still dripping off in the shower room.

"There's a towel for you, hanging on a hook just outside the shower," he called out to her from where he stood a few rows over. "The bag of clothes is on the bench just a few rows over from you." He was determined to behave and not go over there to watch her, knowing he had to get back out to the guys, who were already discussing the unusual relationship between them after the morning's event. It was a learning lesson, especially for their newest recruit. He would nip the gossip that morning as she got dressed.

"I don't have any dry shoes!" she shouted a few moments later. "Just my socks!"

She heard a locker open, the metal screeching its protest of having to open and then close on the old hinges. A pair of rolled-up socks came flying over the row, or rows, landing just beside her: his thick socks for her to put on top of hers.

Then she heard the door to the locker room open, with instructions to meet at the break table when she was finished. She snarled under her breath.

Jack opened the locker room door to find all his crew, including Hank, with their ears pressed up against the door, although they acted like they were just standing there waiting, minding their own business. He sighed heavily at them, ensuring the door closed firmly behind him, with him standing protectively in front of it.

Hank rubbed at the back of his neck, tentatively looking up at him, his height being similar to Jack's height. "Just making sure you'd come out not missing an eye—or worse yet dying in the process of getting her warmed back up. All that screamin' and fussin' and carrying on back there. She can sure make a sailor blush, man." He was being respectful of Jack's authority at that point, though he was beginning to question it.

"No doubt! Shit! She's like a wildcat when you get her riled up," joked Nick.

The others were smiling, trying not to laugh.

"Can you blame her?" Emanuel shivered, remembering the first time they had dumped him off the pier.

"I heard she kicked your ass," commented Nick.

"Guys! To the table, now!" Jack commanded, getting them to think and move in another direction. He trailed after them all as they gathered at the table waiting for Tasha to come back out, all of them prohibited from going into the locker room. He passed out the one-page yearly test on hypothermia and cold-weather-related injuries for his guys to work on. It was an informal test, and although they were not supposed to help each other, they continued to talk amongst themselves, teasing Jack here and there.

"Yup, it must have happened. Jack is not answering that one," verified Jarvis moments later.

"Where's she from?" Sam asked.

"Florida, bro," Jarvis answered.

"And to think she just came back from the Middle East, another hot damn desert," added Manny.

"It gets cold there too," Nick said.

"Did she really kick yer butt?" asked the grizzled Hank.

Jack had pretty much ignored their comments, but even he gave Hank a tired look, as if *you too?*

"Not surprised there." Hank scratched his salt-and-pepper grizzled beard. "I don't think you cut yourself shaving the first time. That looks more like a knife cut," he mused, pointing to the same location on his neck where Jack had been sporting a small nearly healed cut whenever he stretched his neck up and his beard did not hide it.

The rest of the guys stopped in their writing to look up at Jack's neck—all of them—their eyes prying to see the knife scar, making Jack shift in his stance to avoid their silent inspection, giving Hank a searing look. And then, Jack thought it was a good opportunity to make another point of leaving her alone.

"I will say it again," he warned them, "do not test her."

They were silent, expecting more from the guy who had only joined them a little over two years before, who had become their lead—a good guy, a natural born leader, yet still one of them, working side by side on the line.

"You will rue it."

"It explains all the beard trimming," Emanuel said, trying to lighten up the mood.

"Yeah, he got his ass kicked," confirmed Hank.

The guys laughed as some of them finished up and handed in their test papers to Jack, getting ready to leave for the day. Their training days were rewarded with a short day so that they could run errands during business hours or just go home to relax.

"She's living with you, man," said Nick, handing in his paper. "Isn't she?"

The two that had gotten up first hung back after overhearing Nick's question. Nick was always the class clown for their group. Jack and he had not gotten along at first, the two of them used to being top dogs, although Nick was more laisser-faire about it, not wanting to shoulder much of the day-to-day responsibilities of running a hangar and flight operations. However, Nick was the best of them when it came to flying.

"And?" Jack asked, guardedly and with a warning glare.

Nick smirked. "You're going to have to sleep at some point tonight. I wouldn't want to be in your shoes." Then he shrugged. "Women have an evil way of striking back when you least expect it."

"Ah…you should know, Nick. The last one keyed your car," Sam teasingly reminded him.

Gales of laughter erupted, all of them remembering some of his lesser and more unsuccessful exploits from the local bar.

Tasha appeared at their table looking none too pleased, her hair still damp and disheveled. No one had heard her coming, since she only wore socks. She had found another dry blanket to wrap around herself as she continued to warm up.

Jack's eyes met hers. She made no notion to take a seat at the table, nor did she say anything. Her silence was ominous. The guys had stopped chattering to turn and look at her. Hank was the first to offer her to come sit with the rest of them, attempting to get her attention off Jack. She took it, her level, steady gaze not letting go of Jack's from where he stood.

The guys closest to her patted her shoulder with an "attaboy" for a job well done in training, while the others cheered.

"Well, you're one of us now!" said Nick.

"You've been officially baptized into the Black Raven Aviation gang," came Sam.

Hank's peppered white grizzled beard shifted, the only indication of his smirk, nodding a silent assurance to her.

"Ya, we usually dump Manny each year, but bets were either with Hank or you getting it," added Jarvis as he clasped his hand on his roommate's shoulder. Manny did not say a word, just nodded to her that it was the truth.

Jack gave her a copy of the test that the others had been taking. "Got to have you fill it out and finish it for our records." To the others, he said, "All right, it's Thursday and you all know the deal. Use your time wisely."

The guys all left the area for their cars outside. Nick stayed behind to talk to Tasha, but he was more interested in watching Jack's response. "Hey, I can wait for you and we can go to the bar this afternoon."

"Nick, leave it! I'm sure she's not interested," Jack snapped.

Tasha's head popped up at him, glaring silently.

She did not see Nick's smile as he told her, "Maybe another time, Tasha," and took his leave.

"Just finish the paperwork and meet me at the operations office. I'll take you home from there. Training days are half days, and you'll have a nice long weekend to look forward to."

Her glowering expression remained fixed as he turned to leave her alone to her task.

The test was easy: typical government-style safety test. She was done in five minutes and got up to turn her paperwork in at his hangar office, dropping it on his desk, where she found him filing other paperwork, placing it back into the filing cabinet behind him. He closed the drawer, picked up her paper, quickly glanced over it, made a passing mark, and then put it in a tray on his desk to attend to later.

"Come on, let's get you home." He indicated to his office door for her to go first.

She went ahead, not bothering to wait and follow him the way she usually did, choosing instead to make her way to his truck, which had been parked just outside the hangar door.

The early afternoon had become warmer, yet she shivered in the damp air. He was quick to open her door, shoving a bag full of her wet clothes between them. He made sure to keep the truck's heater trained on her before putting the truck into gear and driving them home. Nothing was said until they had pulled up in front of their cabin. Jack turned off the truck's engine and turned to her, saying, "The weekend is yours. I will be gone tonight and the rest of this weekend. I'm going hunting."

She looked at him then, her expression deadpan.

"I'll get you set up before I leave," he assured her as he jumped out of his truck, leaving her in the cab to go unlock the door.

She watched his backside, still mentally boiling.

He turned to find her sitting in the truck as Drake came running outside to go attend to whatever it is that dogs do besides relieve themselves. He stepped back to his truck on her side, opening the door for her to get out. She grabbed her bag of wet clothes, dragging it across the seat to make sure that his seat became just as wet as her clothes. It was a spiteful thing to do, but she was no longer going to take his 'crap.' She was surprised that he had her wet boots in his hands, for he must have had them in the back of his pickup truck. He took the bag from her hands but did not help her close her own door, much less help her over the pebble driveway and up into the cabin, as he disappeared inside with her personal effects. The small stones were difficult to walk on with just two layers of socks on.

The whole day was like reliving a religious narrative. She suffered cold indignity, literally and figuratively. She was baptized in the waters of Resurrection Bay, tested by her fellow members into a new order (an order that aligned itself with the heavens in their daily toil), made to suffer a painful walk over stones, and last, locked her in the cabin, her final resting place out in the wilderness. She wanted none of this manmade organized theology. She just wanted to remain one with nature, a simple, wild, unorganized mess. And Jack was going to mess with her peaceful concept by hunting in it and putting holes into the very spirit of life.

As she got inside, Drake came in just behind her and she closed the door, sighing to herself as she leaned against the front door, closing her eyes. She heard the basement stairs creak just to the side of her and realized that he had gotten all her clothes into the washer.

CHAPTER EIGHT

He returned to find her leaning against the door, wrapped in her blanket. He was not entirely sure what she was thinking, uncertain if her next move was to leave the cabin or remain inside, or if she was still angry or tired. Swimming in cold water is taxing to an unacclimated body—especially a smaller, physically fit body. Though she was in the water for less than a minute, she had to have been tired.

He pulled her cellphone out, punching in the last of everyone's numbers that she could possibly have need of while he was away.

She opened her eyes again to find him just sitting on the armrest of the sofa, fiddling with her device. *My phone!* She glowered at him. *How dare he control my life!* she thought.

He looked up at her, then spoke. "All right, you should have all the numbers you need to reach anyone while I am gone this weekend. You should have more than enough to eat as you rest up for the following week." Standing up, Jack handed it to her.

She dropped her blanket as she reached for her cellphone, she smoothly grabbed the same wrist and swung him around, giving him one of her fiercest roundhouse kicks to his gut. The movement caught him off guard, slamming him bodily up against the door of the cabin. The force of his body's impact shook the cabin's wall, making him violently expel the air in his lungs in surprise. She had deftly caught her phone in the process when he had released it, intending for her to take it.

Now! Now, I feel better! she thought, and sighed happily to herself. She walked away from him, where he barely could hold himself up against the wall trying to suck air into his lungs.

Jack remained dazed. The guys were right: she struck when he least expected it. "What the hell?" he shallowly rasped out at her.

She stopped, looking dispassionately over her shoulder at him. "We're *even* now, asshole." She turned to get herself some hot tea.

Oh, yeah. She's still pissed, he mulled to himself, attempting to get his lungs to open back up.

Hank had warned him, after pushing her into the water. The act itself was his way of giving her a taste of what he had felt when she had shut him out that night after her first day at work. Rationally, she was right. Emotionally, she had wronged him. They should not have done what they did before she had found out he was her flight operations manager. What she failed to realize was that his job was on the line too. But to him, he felt she was worth the risk. He had given her more credit than most women he encountered. Although he had been somewhat disappointed when she drew the line to cease their personal affair as if it had never happened.

But it had happened, and as far as he was concerned, there was no turning back from the deed. He did not realize that his train of thought was more for him than for her. He tried to suck in another breath, but only sucked in sharp pain.

How is it that she can just turn herself 'off'? Just like that? Jack thought. *To go so cold and act as if what we had didn't matter.* But he had insulted her in his anger and disappointment that night with she was 'just good enough.' He inwardly groaned, squinting his eyes shut.

Payback. It was definitely hell. Jack had just stood there on the pier looking at the second hand on his watch, counting down the time. He gave her only a minute, figuring that she had to know how to swim, given her life near a beach and then her military background. All the while, Hank, the Nervous Nelly standing next to him, had jabbered restlessly about 'shit hitting the fan' as the rest of his crew scrambled toward the ladder, offering their assistance to Tasha, Nick and Sam climbing down to help her back out of the cold Alaskan waters, Jarvis and Emanuel ready with the thermo-blankets.

"Man, Jack…Really? Did ya have to push her in? Ya could've killed her! She's not like the boys!" commented Hank, the normally laid-back older man agitated, concerned that Jack had been too rough with her. "Payback is going to be a bitch." Hank had kept muttering the last comment repetitively.

Without looking up from his watch, Jack had said, "Hank, go get my truck started and the heater going," digging in his pants pockets for his keys and tossing them to him. Hank had hurried to his truck.

The seconds had ticked slowly by on his watch. Jack finally heard Nick say that they had gotten her out completely, hauling her wet form back onto the dock by the scruff of her clothes, Emanuel and Jarvis wrapping blankets around her. She had only been in the water less than forty-three seconds and the guys had done a good job responding and assisting in the treatment.

As far as he was concerned, all had to go through the cold-water experience at least once, to remember what they needed to do. No one was excluded. Even Tasha. He would make sure everyone knew what to do and was prepared for any emergencies. He would make sure he would never lose anyone under him again.

He finally was able to get another breath in so that he could stand back up to his full height and follow after her.

"Not—so—fast!" he tried to spit out, catching smaller gulps of air as he lumbered over to the kitchen island, clutching his stomach.

The microwave beeped that her hot water was ready, and she dunked a teabag into the mug. She paused, taking in every step he made toward her, seeing him stop when his arms braced himself against the countertop. She was ready, the warm mug putting more energy into her hands, pumping her up. She wanted nothing more than to beat the living crap out of him at that very moment. Everything she had ever been angry about in her lifetime surfaced and was rearing its ugly head at her newest and latest enemy that she had created after her first day on the job.

Thankfully, he caught more air at the island, pausing long enough to give himself more time to get enough air pressure to make his vocal cords work normally. "Damn, woman…that's a hell of a kick…you got there," he wheezed, pointing at her.

Drake whined, trying to come in close to his master only to be ordered to stay put.

It was obvious he had no intentions to pay tribute to her fighting skills. Jack was finding a way to hack at her defenses. It was not going to work.

As she sipped at her hot tea, he watched the green-eyed mountain lion standing in front of him. If she'd had a tail, the tip of it would have been twitching patiently. She silently watched the prey she had just wounded, the prey deciding whether to continue to fight to the death or try an escape. Jack was not taking the last option. He was a fighter. And he certainly was not going to back down. At least not from a woman!

"This morning…" He sucked in more air and repeated the beginning of his statement in explanation. "…This morning was to instruct you…on the dangers of hypothermia…and how to treat it." He was able to push himself back upright, his massive chest enlarging as he took in a normal deep breath.

She put her tea down behind her and off to the side, leery.

"Everyone"—he was finally able to exhale almost normally—"gets… dunked." He lifted a finger at her, wagging it. "You…You are no exception!"

"Fuck off, bastard!" she said in a menacingly low voice.

He smiled at her, still weak. His eyes raked the length of her body. "I would, but you cut that off last week."

She narrowed her cat-like eyes at him. He moved closer, only for her to adjust the distance accordingly, forcing him to rethink, each of them eyeing the other's next move.

"It was for your own good."

"The hell it was!" she spat back. "You just had a wild hair up your arse to take it out on me for 'cutting you off!'"

Jack lunged at her; Drake barked at him from nearby. She deftly pulled one of the large cutting knives from the wooden cutlery holder, flipping the large blade over a hundred and eighty degrees out into a deadly defensive striking weapon, the razor side out from her forearm, held backwards for better shredding of the opponent with her fists and arms. She stepped sideways, trying to put at least the short side of the kitchen island between them.

He tilted his head at her and clicked his tongue twice. "You don't want to go there. I'll win." His wolfish smile broadened, his fingers flexing on the edge of the countertop. "Besides, do you really want more blood on your hands? It's a hell of a mess to clean up. It gets everywhere!" He licked his lips in anticipation. "Then, there'd be a lot of explaining of what happened at work," he continued, trying to reason with her.

There was a sudden knock on the door, startling them, giving neither time to collect themselves as Chad bounded in, catching them in their standoff. She was still holding the large meat knife in her hand, poised to strike, and Jack ready to pounce on her.

"Hey, Jack! Are you ready yet?" Chad eagerly blurted out, stumbling upon the situation taking place in front of him. "Whoa…a…"

It took a second for the scene to register. He swallowed loudly, unsure of what to do next: either back out and pretend he had not seen them, leaving Jack at her mercy, or try to rescue Jack from an insanely knife-wielding madwoman, the real-life situation mimicking a horror movie.

"Ah…" he stammered, still deciding, "I can give you two a few minutes…if need be." He thumbed back toward the front door. "I'll just stand by outside with my medical kit…when you both are finished."

Drake, ever grateful, hurried over to Chad, unable to take any more tension in the room.

Jack used the opportunity to try to lunge at her again, but she was just as quick at evading him. This forced Chad to rethink his decision on going outside, getting Drake to sit beside him instead of being jittery at his legs.

"Ah Jack…I wouldn't mess with her. If you haven't noticed, she's got a really, really big knife in her hand. I mean a *really* big one." He rubbed the side of his nose and then put a nervous hand back on his hips, trying to be nonchalant. "I don't think she's happy…with you. Besides, now is not the time to be practicing your hunting skills indoors. We're losing daylight," he reminded Jack, hoping he would back down from her. "Now, Tasha, if you are angry at being left behind, we can make room for you and take you along on our hunting trip."

She blanched at the thought.

Funny. She has no issues when it comes to killing a man, but has issues with killing an animal, Chad thought.

Jack suddenly pulled back, making her jump yet quickly discerning he was not going after her. Only when he had left her standing in the kitchen, going to his room to gather his bags, did she put the knife back into its specified cutlery slot by the stove. Chad sighed in relief, looking down at Drake, patting his head, more or less to get the 'flight or fight' adrenaline out of his hand. Chad looked back up at Tasha, finding that she had picked up her mug and resumed sipping it, leaning up against the aft countertop as if nothing unusual had happened moments before.

Chad cautiously came over to the kitchen island. "The offer still stands," he told her.

"No, it doesn't," retorted Jack as he passed behind Chad to the front door with two bags over his shoulder in one hand and the rest of his gear in the other hand. He opened it, with Drake following him outside.

Tasha just remained at her spot near the sink, her head moving like an owl, focused only on Jack's form.

Chad pursed his lips before he silently mouthed *okay*. "Well, this is going to be an interesting weekend," Chad commented, more to himself than to her.

Jack stopped at the front door's threshold, not caring if he let out the cabin's warm air at that point.

"You ready, Chad?"

"Yeah, sure," he said as he took his eyes from Tasha. "What about Drake? Is he coming along?"

"No, he stays this time. Hopefully Tasha doesn't starve or hurt him."

She gave Jack an exasperated *as if* look and tsked. It was the only sound she had made so far, and Chad heard it behind his back as he went to the door where Jack stood.

"The shotgun's bullets are on the mantle," Jack told her, pointing to the gun by the door, "should you need to defend yourself from a wild animal or an intruder."

Chad gave him an *is that wise?* look, considering what he just had just seen moments before, then hurried past him to go back outside where the air was not so thick with tension.

Jack looked back at Tasha where she stood by the kitchen sink, with the mug still in her hands, looking like she was a lost and lonely soul. However, where she had kicked him still stung, reminding him. She could stew all she wanted, he thought, hoping that the cold air in the cabin would cool off her temper.

"Jesus, man!" Chad exclaimed, doing a double-take at Jack's stomach. By the next day, later that afternoon, the imprint she had made had grown two shades darker, turning blacker and bluer rather than the original swollen red. Chad leaned forward in the late afternoon light, trying to discern what it was that afflicted his hunting buddy. "Hell, man"—Jack quickly pulled down on the fresh shirt, covering the mark—"is that a footprint?" He reached out to Jack, only to have Jack pull back from his inspection.

"I don't need a nurse."

"The hell you don't!" Chad persisted. "What in God's green earth did you do to yourself?" asked Chad. "Did you get that looked at up at the clinic?

"You know we could have waited until next weekend to hunt. Don't tell me that's not painful, man." He noted Jack wincing again as he shifted his seat beside the log he leaned against, watching the fire.

"I'm fine," Jack said, sighing tiredly. "Grab me a beer, will ya?" He pointed to the cooler just behind Chad.

"Only if you tell me what's going on."

Jack gave him an exasperated look when Chad didn't bother to reach for the cooler. The last thing he wanted to do was get up, his abdomen stiff and swollen with Tasha's impressed reminder. He was beginning to wonder if leaving the shotgun behind for her protection was a good idea or not, not knowing what to expect when they got back from their hunting foray. *But then, she was good with the kitchen knives,* he thought, remembering his first encounter with her, and then the most recent one when Chad had interrupted their little tit-for-tat the previous afternoon. He was grateful for his friend's ability to disarm anyone with his humor.

Their drive to the new campsite had been entirely devoid of conversation. Chad had known better than to prod his buddy when he was in a foul mood. They had set up their campsite, wanting to retire early to get a head start the following morning tracking down the deer. The next morning Jack seemed to have cooled off, finally, letting go of the week's tension. Chad had decided it was worth a try to find out what was vexing his buddy, especially when it came to his new roommate.

Chad pushed further when he decided to help himself to his friend's favorite beer instead of giving Jack one as requested. He took a long and tantalizing draw on the long neck, studying his very moody and unusually quieter-than-normal buddy over the flames of the fire. Jack just stared at the seductively hypnotic warm flames.

Chad remained patient, for it was a waiting game when it came to Jack. He had all that night and part of the following day to see if Jack would open up. It pained him to see him like that, seeming more agitated in the past few weeks since Tasha's arrival. But then, what healthy male wouldn't be? Especially if they were into Nordic-looking blondes. She was near his height at least, but then, most girls were. Chad was short for a man, and stockily built like most of his people. He was only five foot ten, his native skin a shade darker than the white men, with black hair as thick and straight as a raven's feathers, for he was a child of the raven god.

He reached into the cooler for a steak to start cooking. He seasoned the steak with their people's seasoning blend, hoping to entice Jack into moving to get his own steak or to get him to talk. It would have to be Jack's choice. He reached into their tool bag for the metal grill used to enclose the meat and then lay over the fire, the flames now low. The light was fading and the sounds of the woods began to sing, the river's water just down the embankment burbling, singing in harmony with the popping embers of the campfire.

"You know, Jack, that girl reminds me a lot of my Aunt Sylvia." There was no response at first. "She has to be the craziest one in our family. She's into knives, too…whenever anyone wanted to mess—"

"A beer, man," Jack insisted in a low growl.

"Will you let me take you to the clinic to get that bruising of yours checked out?" Chad ignored his request in hopes of getting Jack some medical help if he wouldn't talk about what was bothering him.

"No," Jack grumbled, the flickering firelight illuminating his expressionless face, and sitting there like a propped-up ragdoll.

"Then no beer for you," Chad insisted as he twisted back to attend to his steak over the fire.

"That wasn't the original deal." Jack's dark eyes glittered ominously in the fire's light, the animal spirit in him awakening and showing itself to Chad, the bear's spirit sliding over the man's form seamlessly.

"True, but one or the other, brother."

"No doctor."

"Oh good, I think you and Tasha's story sounds much more interesting than taking you to the clinic," he said, trying to lighten Jack's mood.

"She kicked me." That was all he said. Then he added, "Throw me a beer."

"Seriously? That's it?" Chad stopped in mid-turn, looking back at his steak. "You have to give me the rest of the story. I was certain that was her size footprint on your abdomen."

"Beer."

"The rest of the story," Chad insisted.

Jack sighed in resignation. "It was payback. Beer. Please. I won't ask again."

Chad reached into the cooler, knowing that the next time his own butt would be kicked thoroughly by the marine. "What did you do to her to get that type of punishment?" Chad asked, lightly tossing the beer over the firepit to him.

"I pushed her off the dock during our hypothermia training," Jack replied, twisting the bottle cap off.

"Ya..." Chad nodded his head in agreement. "I would have kicked your ass too. Are you trying to kill the girl?"

"No, she just needs to know how to survive up here." Jack took his first sip, the brew giving him a false sense of warmth as it slid down his throat.

"Survive? Survive what? The next apocalypse?"

"She needs to know what to do during extreme cold weather."

"Doesn't she already know all this from her military training? I understand that Fort Wainwright employs a few of my people to help them with cold weather warfare."

"She was never stationed there. She would never have been trained. She needs to acclimate and get the exposure."

"God, Jack, you'd think she had hailed from the tropics, the way you talk about her."

"She does...Florida's close enough."

"I see…trying to take a beach bunny and turn her into a snow bunny?" Chad jested.

Jack smirked, taking another swig from his bottle.

"So I take it she didn't do this voluntarily?" Chad added, an eyebrow raised at him in question as he leaned forward more on his haunches.

"I told her she would be my volunteer."

"Somehow…I don't see her agreeing to your comment, 'Oh, by the way, I need a volunteer to jump into the harbor waters to demonstrate how fast hypothermia can kill a person, Tasha.' Knowing you"—Chad pointed a finger at him as he held his bottle close to his mouth—"I seriously doubt that you told her what she was volunteering for." Chad drained the last drop of beer and quarter-turned to grab another bottle from the cooler just aft and to the side of his seat.

Jack's hand unclasping his beer was enough for him to know that was the truth of it.

Chad swore under his breath at his buddy as he continued to blindly dig around for another cold one. "You really have it in for this girl, don't you?"

Chad shifted in his seat, taking the meat off the fire and setting it aside on one of the nearby rocks ringing the firepit to get at his pocketknife and find something to put the mouthwatering steak on as he ate.

"I mean, what in the hell did she do to you?" Chad asked, turning, as he dug around in their supply cache for a plate, adding, "Or does she remind you of something so unpleasant to be this harsh with her?"

"Nothing. Absolutely nothing," Jack mumbled, shifting uncomfortably to lean forward. A groan escaped from him after he got what he wanted.

Jack had helped himself to the entire piece of meat just as Chad turned back with what he needed, seeing his steak missing and in his buddy's hands. He made a miffed face at him but did not dare challenge the hungry bear sitting across from him. He opened the cooler to grab another steak and start it cooking.

"So, let me get this straight," Chad continued, placing another raw steak into the wire grate and placing it over the campfire, "you're giving her hell because she isn't putting out for you?" He looked at his buddy a moment, adding, "That doesn't seem to be your style, man. I thought you were more of a gentleman than most men and that there are rules about co-mingling with your co-workers."

"There are, and I am still adhering to my code of ethics."

Chad's smile spread slowly across his face as he finished his beer, watching the frustrated older man sitting across from him. "But somehow you want to break those rules or—" He stopped, seeing Jack's scowl. "—Ooh, I think you did, you sly dog," he said, beaming at him even more.

"No, I didn't break the rules," Jack defended himself. *More like her*, he thought, wanting to put the blame on her.

"Okay…you just want to break the rules, then. So what's the holdup?" He hesitated. "Other than you keep pissing her off." Chad reached for another bottle when Jack motioned for another beer. "You know you ought to just try taking her out…you know…wine and dine her." He popped the cap off with no intention of giving one up for Jack. "You might make more headway there." Chad suggested the obvious. "Wouldn't recommend a bar though."

Jack did not comment, now finished with his steak and downing the last of his beer from his first bottle, wincing when he leaned forward enough to toss the bottle into the back of his truck bed just a few more feet behind Chad. Then Jack motioned for the second beer that Chad possessed. However, Chad didn't make a motion to hand it over to him as he continued his one-sided conversation.

"You have it bad."

Jack pressed his lips together and gave him a silent *what?*

"How about some willow bark for the pain. It'll give you some physical pain relief"—his short-lived concern turned into a smile—"but not the 'pining-for-someone' relief."

Jack finally acquiesced to the pain medication.

"Turn my steak over, will ya?" Chad asked, motioning to him as he got up to get his medical kit from the truck's cab.

Their hunting trip was a flop. They mostly tracked, noting good spots for another weekend when it would be colder to nab a deer, elk, or moose. The weather was unseasonably warmer than normal, as if Tasha had brought it with her when she arrived in Alaska. Jack smirked at his wandering thoughts, always finding them leading back to her. Tasha's simmering temper was enough to justify the warmer temperatures of that week. She was good at keeping it under control for long periods. So far, she had only exploded in their private living quarters.

"You're thinking of her again, aren't you?" Chad asked, breaking into his thoughts. Chad had been leading the way through the forests on the third morning, up a minor embankment, after scouting out some perfect locations in the new area they were visiting.

Jack looked back up at him curiously, and Chad pointed to his own face.

"You're cracking a smile there, buddy."

"I'm not smiling," Jack told him, the corners dropping instantly.

"You could've fooled me," he said. "Must be some good thoughts. Her fine hips…" he goaded Jack.

"No! Other things, like her being the cause of this week's heat wave with her temper!"

Chad laughed. Jack had cracked a joke, which was very unusual, given his serious nature. "Well, for Alaska's sake, would you stop pissing her off then? We need the cold and the snows to return.

"From what little I know of her; I suspect she doesn't anger easily over little things. It takes a lot, just like you, to make her take action."

Jack just grunted, pulling himself up the steep incline with a low overhead branch.

Chad noted he was still hurting, the way he walked slow and determined. Concerned for his friend's welfare, he suggested, "Tell you what, why don't we go see Freddie? Let's get in a little fishing on the open ocean." He pointed to his stomach. "You seriously need to rest and nurse that temporary tattoo of yours."

Jack nodded his head gratefully. He wanted to go back, but not to a cabin with an angry woman inside. "You drive then," Jack said as the two of them neared the truck and their campsite.

They expertly broke camp and head back to Seward's harbor where one of Chad's relatives owned a boat that he used to take summer tourists out fishing. It would be a welcome respite from all the tracking they had done.

"What is it?"

"What do you mean?" Jack asked, looking at Tasha standing there with her fists on her hips. "It's fish!" he said, stating the obvious.

"I…I know it's a fish, but what the hell happened to it?" she asked harshly, inspecting the mass of white meat.

"What's wrong with it?"

"Did you two go fishing near a nuclear reactor? I mean *look* at the *thing*." Her hands gestured to their hard-won prize. It was a sizeable twenty-five-pound catch. "That one has been swimming around the in radioactive coolant tanks!"

Chad fell over the sofa's backrest where he had taken up a casual half seat, his legs up in the air in gales of laughter. Chad sounded like one of his race dogs howling in delight. Jack stood with his hands on his hips between the kitchen island and the sofa looking rather dejected that she would *dare* call his catch *defective*. He was still damp from their fishing trip, looking haggard after an all-day fight with the ocean assailant.

"It's halibut! You've never heard of halibut?" came Chad between chortles.

"Yes, yes I have heard of halibut. It is one of the healthiest cold-water fish to eat, but this one…there is something seriously wrong with it! It's defective! It looks like ocean roadkill! Its eyes are on the same side! Most fish, mammals, and other animals I know have eyes on either side of their heads!"

More howls of laughter ensued from the sofa's unseen occupant as Jack and Tasha's eyes testily met each other's.

"Our eyes are on the same side," Jack countered back at Tasha, using two fingers pointing back at his own eyes. "Are we defective?"

She pressed her lips together and crossed her arms over her chest, still not buying it.

Jack smacked at his friend's upturned feet, his laughter still coming from behind the sofa's backside, where Tasha couldn't see him from where she stood in the kitchen on the opposite side of the island.

To Chad, Jack asked, "Help me out here, will ya?"

His disarrayed black head of hair popped back upright. Chad was gasping for air, trying his best not to laugh, the occasional giggles still escaping as his shoulders shook silently. He wiped at the sides of his eyes, brushing away the tears. "To what capacity, brother?"

"Are we defective for having eyes on the same side of our faces?"

"I should think not." He chuckled more. "Seriously, Tasha…have you never seen fresh halibut?"

"No!" She stamped her foot.

"There is nothing wrong with it. Just prep it like any other fish and you will do just fine with our supper tonight," ordered Jack.

Tasha uncrossed her arms. "I will not!" She was tired of all the belittling of her, as if she were some scullery maid.

Her defiant outburst made him do a double-take at her. She had been doing great the past few days in terms of being civil toward him, cooking, and cleaning. Being a 'terrific housewife' in his book, save for the 'fringe benefits' since their last disagreement, the issue still unresolved and lurking silently between them like a clear iceberg that only they could see and feel.

Earlier that day, Chad and Jack had returned to a cabin that had been seriously disinfected and deep cleaned. The cleaning fumes had wafted out of the cabin when he had Chad open the door that late afternoon, cautioning his friend of the woman inside. Jack had left her alone to stew in her anger over the long weekend's hunting excursion. Tasha had chosen to spend her weekend scrubbing him clean out of the cabin in addition to out of her life!

Chad had found her already cooking something on the stove, looking the image of the contented, domesticated housewife. He had smiled at her, giving her the best greeting he could muster, to keep her cool for when Jack would shortly enter after him. When Jack had pushed him further into the cabin, she had promptly warned them that she would make them both members of the 'V' club should they mess up the room with the filth of their shoes and hunting gear.

They had taken her seriously, the silence deafening. Both men had shucked their boots off at the door, and Jack had taken their gear down to the basement to disassemble and clean for later. She had noted that Chad had something large tucked under his arm. He had hesitated, not knowing what it was that she was studying about him, until he had realized he had forgotten their catch of the day. He had dropped it onto the island's countertop and unwrapped the specimen.

The gargantuan flat white fish took nearly half of the countertop, a physical white elephant in the room. Its sightless eye—correction, eyes—stared heavenward as if saying *why me?* and thus reflecting Jack's exact sentiments as Tasha continued to defy him.

"Why not?" Jack asked.

"Because I don't eat fish."

"What?" Jack exclaimed, narrowing his eyes at her, not believing a word she said.

"I don't care for the taste of it."

"How in the hell do you not like fish? For Pete's sake, you're from Florida!" Jack argued with her.

Jack looked at his buddy for support.

Chad shrugged his shoulders at him from where he had put his chin on his folded hands along the sofa's back side, watching the drama unfold in front of him, utterly entertained by the two of them. "So she doesn't like fish. Lots of folks don't like seafood. Some even have allergies to shellfish..."

Jack, unimpressed with his help, interrupted Chad's diatribe. "Fine, then don't eat it. But still dress and cook it for our dinner tonight."

She whirled on him, grabbing a prep knife and stabbing the white beast squarely in the middle, leaving the blade sticking upright in her defiance. *No more!* She was not going to take any more of his manly crap. "You hunt and *you* dress your kills! I just cook and clean the cabin. That's the deal!" she snarled, stabbing the air with her finger at him.

"I'm done here," she said, pulling off her apron and throwing it to the floor. "Fetch yer own supper, bubba!" The water in the pot boiled over, matching her anger, making the gas fire hiss with its overflowing drippings as she left for her room, slamming the door on them.

"I don't think she knows how to prep a fish, Jack," Chad commented, disrupting his focus from the still wiggling knife, its metal sides reflecting the room's light.

Jack gave him a *ya think* look.

"And she's still pissed, man. Are you sure she's not a redhead?" Chad asked, coming around the sofa to the island.

Jack went over to the stove to remove the over-boiling pot of potatoes off the fire. "Just dress the fish, Chad. It looks like you and me tonight."

The weekend had gone from bad to worse in less than three days. Going back to work was going to be a respite for Jack.

CHAPTER NINE

Several hours later, Chad had left after their meal, taking half of the fish with him to his folks now that Jack knew Tasha was not going to eat any of the leftovers.

Jack made up a dish for her in a container, labeling it with her name on it, and then stashed it in the refrigerator. He listened for anything just beyond the kitchen wall to ascertain if she was still awake or not. It was silent. He was torn between barging in on her to face their issues and getting them resolved one way or another or just going down in the basement to clean and put away his gear. He ended up choosing the latter when he finished the dishes, chastising himself for being a lesser man. He knew that no matter which way things got resolved, it would still be a suicide mission. He was not taking any more chances, knowing the odds were against him.

It was near midnight when he finished dinking around in the basement: first his camping equipment, then his wash, and next trying to work out, only to find that Tasha must have used his equipment, for the seating adjustments had been changed. Adjusting everything to his settings, he started to lift weights only to have his sore abdomen bellow its refusal at the exertion. He still had to nurse the bruise she had given him. He exhaled forcibly, deciding it was bedtime. He went up the stairs looking for Drake, to let him go outside one more time, only to realize that he had not seen him since dinnertime.

Jack softly called for him, only to be met with silence as he walked around the main room of the cabin and his bedroom until he spied her bedroom door. It was standing ajar. He walked over to her door, careful not to make too much noise, knowing that she would have fallen asleep by then. He opened the door further to peer into the darkness and found her fast asleep with her arms wrapped around Drake, who was lying up against her like a giant teddy bear. Drake only raised his head up at Jack's presence, clearly comfortable in her arms and in her bed.

He smirked at the sight of his large Newfoundland black dog lying there, happy to be of service as a teddy bear. "Don't you want to go outside, boy?" he whispered softly to his dog.

Drake groaned lightly and laid his head back down, making it clear that he had no intentions of going anywhere.

Tasha sighed in her sleep, nuzzling her nose more into Drake's thick black fur and wrapping her arm tighter around the dog's body.

Jack stepped into her room to be by her bed. He reached down to stroke Drake's head, telling him he was a good boy, and then found his hand wandering over the softness of Tasha's hair, stroking it, remembering how wonderful it felt in his hands, the strands silk-like. He found himself transfixed with her as she slept peacefully on her side. He reluctantly pulled the cover over her form. If he hadn't done so, he would have found himself sliding into bed next to her.

He reluctantly returned to her door, leaving it ajar, thinking how easily he had been replaced by his own dog. *Lucky dog!* Jack grumbled internally, collapsing into his bed and setting his phone's morning alarm.

Monday morning, he woke up with a start at something and checked the time. It was five minutes before his alarm was due to go off. He turned the alarm off and lay back down a minute, trying to find any bit of motivation he could to face the challenges of a new work week. He got up and did his usual morning routine, getting showered and dressed before waking Tasha up. He knocked on her door only to open it wide when he got no response from inside her room. Even Drake didn't bound out of the room. To his amazement, her room was empty, her bed made. No sign of her or Drake as he gave the main room of the cabin a quick once-over. He moved into the room more when he realized the smell of breakfast that had been made, eaten, and cleaned up, save for one bowl of oatmeal on the countertop with a note telling him to just reheat it when he was ready. There was no other message.

He checked outside, knowing better. His truck sat in silence, waiting, her Prius just off to the side of it. He started his truck, letting it warm up as he reheated and ate his oatmeal. The morning meal was not nearly enough, and he raided the pantry and refrigerator for additional snacks to take with him, along with his lunch in the refrigerator.

What is she up to? He swore under his breath, putting his coat on, grabbing his lunch bag, and locking the cabin door. He got in the truck and headed down to the hangar. He did not see a sign of her on his way to work. That made him madder, yet more concerned, as he slammed his truck door shut and walked quickly to the hangar. If he failed to see her in the hangar, he would come up with some excuse to his crew to go hunt her and Drake down.

When he opened the hangar door, he was warmly greeted by Drake. Relief swept over him, but his anger returned the minute he saw her walk out between the planes from the offices toward the crew's morning break table and lockers. She had an armload of clothes as she made her way, not noticing him as she waved to Jarvis along with a few of the others sitting around the table. She was still in her black leggings, boots, and a sweatshirt. She looked flushed, as if she had just finished running.

He bit the inside of his cheek to help him bite his tongue. He would deal with her later. The crew meeting went as normal, her face brighter than the guys', making him realize that he found himself staring at her more than he should have. He was grateful that none of his men seemed to notice, until Hank lumbered up to him once everyone went their separate ways.

"Glad to see yer still alive after Thursday's training. I was certain I'd be visitin' ya up at the clinic this weekend." He elbowed Jack in his gut near where she had nailed him with her kick, causing him to flinch and lay a protective hand on his gut. Hank immediately drew a concerned look on his face. "Now I know I didn't elbow you that hard, Jack." He tilted his head to determine something through Jack's shirt and his protective hand.

Jack immediately dropped his hand, pretending it was nothing.

A slow, sly smile formed on Hank's grizzled face. "Uh-huh, she did git ya!" he said, his toothpick floundering at the side of his mouth. "I warned ya, didn't I?"

Jack twisted his mouth at Hank, wishing he would drop it.

"Nice to see that yer okay now that ye've finally arrived. Was kinda concerned just seeing her 'n' Drake walk in the hangar." Hank clasped him on his shoulder, taking the hint, and continued past him on his way to his assigned bird.

Jack made his way to the battery shop after wandering around the hangar checking in on each man's post and their progress. Flights would start that week, and the hangar would be mostly empty during that time of year, save for two of their birds down for maintenance. Nate caught him in the hallway before he reached the battery room, making him wait to have a word with Tasha.

Jack wondered, following him back into his office, if she had had time to talk to Nate, about them or about his training exercises. They passed his wife, Nora, where she was busy placing supply orders. She looked up and greeted him warmly like normal, asking if she could get him a cup of coffee. He nodded, still needing something to perk him up and out of his nagging thoughts.

It turned out that Nate just wanted to catch up on what was going on in the hangar and ask if Jack could take on another two more flight orders. Nate never spoke nor indicated anything about Tasha. Jack's hands automatically took the coffee from Nora as Nate continued to carry on with him half listening.

"Jack?" Nate snapped his fingers at him. "Did you hear a word I said, son?"

"Yes, we can take on the additional orders. Might have to make the clients understand they'll have to wait until the first set of flight runs are complete, weather permitting." As he thumbed through his paperwork, penciling in the two newest orders, he acted as if he had heard Nate, although his mind was elsewhere. Later, he would look at the cargo manifest to determine which plane would do best.

"Been lucky so far with this unusually warmer weather," Nate commented, his hands clasped over his gut. "Can you see to it that Tasha gets up in the air this week? Let's get her going. I think I would like to see her fly the Skyhawk for the little orders and as a shuttle for a few folks this season. If she does well there, I want her ready for the bigger cargo planes by the end of this year." Nate looked over to Nora, who had been engrossed with her orders, grateful for the woman of his life. She had stuck with him through it all.

Nate's gaze returned to the large bear of a man sitting in the chair in front of his desk. Jack seemed preoccupied. "All going well with you?"

Jack responded only after he had realized the silent pause had gone on too long, and said, "Yes."

"Are you sure?" Nate asked, motioning with a twirling wave of his hand. "You seem elsewhere this morning."

"Yes, we're good. Just a busy hunting and fishing weekend."

"Did you bag one?"

"No. Just tracked them to their hangouts. It's been too warm. Located a few good spots for future reference. Ended up going fishing on Freddie's boat and caught a good size halibut for a couple of meals."

"Good for you, Jack," Nate said encouragingly, although still noting Jack's absent-mindedness, as Jack did not continue their discussion.

"Well, I guess that'll be all for now, Jack," he said, dismissing him. "Keep your head in the game," Nate advised him with a mock one-finger salute from his forehead. Mainly, the comment was advice for Jack to pay attention to his work that day.

Nate watched as Jack stood up. A little slower than normal, he noted, as Jack stretched to his full height rather stiffly. He watched him leave, his frame temporarily blocking the doorway, as if he was undecided on which way to go first. Once he had left, Nate asked his wife if Jack seemed a bit remiss.

She glanced up, smiling to her husband. "I think his mind is on a certain employee of ours, if you want my opinion."

"You think so?" he asked, remembering the time he had found Jack lying next to Tasha in her bed when he was tasked with taking care of her. However, Jack had done as he was requested back then, and all had seemed to be rather cool and professional from what Nate had made out the few times he had seen them, which was not often. He made a mental note to pay more attention next time.

"I'm pretty certain about it. You once used to be that way, a long time ago." Nora smiled coyly at him.

"Oh, I still am," he said, putting his feet up on his desk, taking a moment to watch her. "It's why I insist on you working with me in the office. At least I can get some work done without having my mind wander about thinking of you when you're gone, hon. The more you're here, the more work I get done," he told her rather arrogantly.

"You mean the more work I get done for you?" she teased him, giggling.

The battery room door slammed open just as she was finishing the last battery. She turned her head, noting the intrusion, only to feign disinterest and return to her work. She had been expecting him. Turnabout was fair play. It certainly took him a long time.

"What were you trying to do this morning?" Jack demanded, closing the door behind him and tossing his clipboard onto her worktable.

"Trying?" She lifted the eighty-pound battery box over to the workbench, straining under the heavy load, looking at him to remove his paperwork from the table without a word said.

He acquiesced to her expectant look.

She let the box land rather heavily on the workbench. "I wanted a morning walk/run and decided to take Drake with me for the exercise, since you seem to have this aversion to me going out by myself. The hangar is a little less than three miles and it was mostly downhill. No sweat. I was here on time, if you hadn't noted that earlier this morning," she told him dismissively, reaching into one of the backwall cabinet drawers for a multimeter.

"A note would have been nice," he said as he leaned forward on the worktable, challenging her.

She did not flinch, as he watched her note each of the cell readings with her meter.

Without looking up at him, she told him, "Ah, but I did leave you a note that your breakfast was there. Please don't tell me you left it out for a *stray* bear to get it," she taunted him.

His hand came down rather hard on the table, getting her full attention.

She took off her protective eyewear.

"Don't be coy with me! There was no note saying where you had gone or what you had done with Drake."

She *pssfed* at him. "As if I am going to hurt Drake because of your asinine tendencies. Please, give me some credit. You're the jerk, not the dog." She turned to grab the tool that tightened the caps down on each cell.

"So you're doing this because I am a jerk that pushed you into the water. Man, you are something else. I've never known anyone to hold a grudge as long as you do over something so petty!"

She set the tool down, steadying herself. "Oh, it's not a grudge," she said, at first pointing to herself, then to him. "We're even as far as I am concerned about being thrown into near-freezing water." Her finger indicated to his stomach where she had nailed him. "I'm just tired of you treating me worse than your dog, locking me up daily, tied down to a cabin, and not having a social life, while you go off for your 'little jaunts through the woods!'"

She put the battery lid back on, snapping down the locks. "If you haven't noticed, I am a grown woman quite capable of taking care of myself! I don't *need* you to control my every movement and thought, especially while you get to go out and have your fun. Thank you." She pushed at the heavy box. "This battery is ready for Clara. Tell one of the guys to come fetch it and at least get it to the aircraft. I will get it installed shortly." She took off her protective apron.

"Just where do you think you're going?"

She shot him a hot look. "Unlike you, I'm going to my other job that is required of me. Some of us *work* for *our* living!" Tasha walked past him only to have him grab ahold of her upper arm, spinning her around.

"You better have one hell of a reason for holding me up," she snarled, looking at his hand on her arm.

He let go, exhaling in violent frustration.

She added, "Like you, I refuse to waste time writing notes to let others know where I am or what I am doing. The last time I checked, we were not married, much less dating. So if you want notes, I expect you to do likewise."

"I don't have to answer to you! I'm your boss!"

"But not at the cabin! And *not* on my personal time!" she pointed out to him, getting up in his face although he towered over her by a full human head length.

"Since when? I remember someone telling me something different about a week or so ago! Even told me that we had to—"

She furrowed her brow at him, shaking her head from side to side. "You're a damn jerk, 'Griswald!' And that's putting it mildly." She left him, opening the door, letting it swing wide and remain open. It was her way of telling him to get out.

He refused to follow her as he simmered over their argument. Eventually, in his disgruntled state, he picked up the battery she wanted and carried it to the plane where she would be installing it, the weight of the box helping to dissipate his need to physically throttle her.

He got the battery to a nearby table only to find that she had gone to another bird to work on its baggage light issue. She was already waist deep in the compartment, her hips and generous backside taunting not only him but some of his crew as two more came to pause to see what Sam was up to with a Cheshire cat grin too big to support on his handsome face. It was obvious he was being nice, handing her the tools as she needed them, her arm and hand reaching behind her lovely backside every so often without pulling out of the compartment.

Jack's determined walk toward them was enough to disperse Nick and Jarvis back to resuming their work stations. Sam's smile dropped, but he held his ground right next to her as he let his hand drop back into her tool caddy for the next tool she might need.

Jack took the tool caddy from him and pointed silently for him to go back up front and resume his work in the aircraft's cabin. Sam, not wanting to comply at first, backed off when Jack gave him a warning look.

"You'd think after blowing two light bulbs you all would figure out that it wasn't bad bulbs." Her hand reached back again, requesting her crimpers and giving him her dykes back. "But I've found your short. You had a small insulation tear where something must have moved up against the wiring. Now I just have to find a heat gun and your wire is as good as new, Sam. I'd like to put some extra protection wrap around this bundle if you fly with the luggage compartment exposed like this with no interior walls."

She pulled herself out of the small opening, climbing back down the stand some, coming face to face with Jack on the last step. Tasha recovered quickly from her surprise of Jack standing there. Her eyes searched for Sam as her face remained on Jack.

"I put Sam back to work where he belongs. It would do you well to learn to work more on your own and not distract the rest of the crew." His eyes raked over her form, especially from the waist down. He noted her form-fitting thermo-leggings to her boots. "I would suggest you wear coveralls or jeans next time." He handed back her tool.

"Then, fine…Do you care to show me where you all keep your heat guns, the Vari-glass wraps, and zip ties?"

"I would suggest the wire room." He took his leave of her. "You might want to spend some time in there getting familiar with that room. It could use some cleaning too."

She dropped her tool into her caddy, which rested on the top stair of the mini-stepladder, folding her arms across her chest, rolling her eyes at his backside when he mentioned another room for her to stay put in. *What is it with him and locking me up?* Her eyes followed him as he made his way back to his hangar office. But it was the battery sitting nearby at the other plane that eventually tore her eyes away from him. There was no way anyone had been told about bringing the battery back to the plane in the time frame after she had left him there in the shop.

She hopped off the bottom step and went back to the wire room to find what she could use to finish her job on the bruised wire casing. *So be it then, for the time being.* She was only going to take being locked up and separated from the rest of the crew for so long. Eventually he would have to get used to her having to work with the others.

CHAPTER TEN

Another week had passed. Tasha was now accustomed to both of her little workspaces. It afforded her time away from the guys when she needed the alone time, and a little stress relief from the constant tension between her and Jack. The cabin was another story, although it was picturesque of the ultimate vacation destination. The only time she could relax was whenever Jack left the cabin, usually taking Drake with him.

She was extremely happy to get her first two paychecks—the first one being so delayed that the second one came with her first one. She had found that her first paycheck was just enough to cover for her new clothes, her half of their groceries, and just about half to cover the cost of the car batteries she needed to replace in her Prius. She hoped that the next month's check would cover the rest. She missed her mobile freedom—a chance to escape Jack's overbearing presence, especially when he was not happy over something she had or had not done.

She needed to celebrate, reserving some cash for herself, enough to buy some extra supplies and make her favorite chocolate cappuccino cinnamon chunk cookies—even share them with the guys, since the recipe made four dozen. If her work was not enough to impress the guys, then maybe she could win more support via their stomachs. At least the baking would fill her time, keeping her occupied while Jack and Chad were gone hunting again over the weekend. She managed to get Jack to stop at the store after work one day to pick up what she needed without too much grief on his part.

As soon as they were gone, she was able to breathe a sigh of relief, the tension draining out of her body to let her pamper herself at their cabin with a long hot soak, long naps, and then to continue reading her *Fate's Twisted Circle* book before working on another slow crockpot meal of roast beef and potatoes to feast on for the next few days. By Sunday she had the cabin cleaned, her laundry done, and had commenced making the cookies so that they would be as close to being fresh as they could be for the Monday morning's crew meeting.

As the third batch had finished baking, Jack and Chad returned from their weekend hunt, filling the cabin with their noise and gear. Drake happily came in greeting her, his fur coat cold from being outside all weekend as she bent down to pet and greet him in the kitchen.

"Man, I smell something good! Like dinner and...is that dessert I spy?" inquired Chad as he made his way over to the kitchen island.

She smiled at him. "Yup, good old-fashioned Southern pot roast and potatoes. Along with my favorite cookies—chocolate cappuccino cinnamon chunk."

"May I?" he asked, taking one before she could respond.

"Sure, but be careful with eating too many or you will find yourself unable to sleep since there is real coffee in those cookies."

"You seem to be in a good mood this weekend, Tasha," Chad noted, munching on his cookie.

"I'm all right for having a bad case of cabin fever. But I needed the downtime to sleep, care for myself, and do what I love to do most, which is reading or cooking. Thought baking a few cookies for the crew would be nice for tomorrow. They have another busy week of flying."

Working on his second cookie, he continued, "Well, the guys should really love these. I can already feel the caffeine hitting me. Wow, these really do perk you up!" He shoved the last of the cookie into his mouth.

"Here"—she dropped four additional cookies into a ziplock bag—"take these home with you," she said as Jack came back upstairs from the basement after unloading his hunting gear and getting the wash started.

"I will, but unfortunately my shift at the clinic starts in another two hours and these will help me keep alert. Thanks."

Jack came over, inspecting what Tasha had given to Chad, the epitome of her tension, helping himself to some of the cookies without asking. Then he lifted the lid to the crockpot to inspect dinner, grunting like a caveman.

Tasha finished putting another cookie sheet in the oven, turning to Jack who was now invading her cooking space, the thick smell of him from two days of no showering out in the field nearly overpowering her.

She sniffed outwardly, avoiding another whiff. "Jack, why don't you go take a shower and dinner will be ready by the time you get out. In fact, both of you need one," she said, jerking her head over to Chad, who was sitting far enough away from her not to pick up on his two-day-old scent. "I need my workspace."

"You first, man," offered Chad.

Jack looked her over before lumbering away to the shower. In the meantime, Chad chatted with her and eventually dinner was ready when they both had gotten their showers. The cookies were still baking while they ate, causing her to periodically jump up and retrieve a baking sheet from the oven as the timer went off.

"How many cookies are you making?" Jack asked as Tasha put in another baking sheet.

"About four dozen. It should be enough for the flight crew as long as you guys don't eat them all."

"The crew?" Jack questioned. "Why the crew? Did someone put you up to this?"

"No," she told him, giving him a light, exasperated sigh. "I just thought it would be nice to do something special."

"Well, don't make it a habit."

"Why? You make it sound like I am feeding wildlife and not our guys at work," she said, her sarcasm dripping at his last comment.

"Yeah, Jack, let her spoil them. Stop being a killjoy. Lighten up, will ya?" injected Chad.

When Tasha was done baking, she got the tray prepped along with their lunches made. She bid Chad a good night since he had to leave for his shift, and promptly worked on finishing up the dishes that Jack had started. Neither of them said a word. He was moody, and from what she could determine, they did not have a successful hunting trip. For when she jested at the kitchen sink, "Maybe you should stick to fishing. You seem to do better with that than hunting— although I would recommend getting better at catching normal-looking fish," he didn't respond as he gave her an indiscernible momentary look before he grabbed another handful of her cookies as he got himself a beer to drink and then sat on the sofa to look at one of his magazines.

Not wanting to deal with his grumpiness, she decided to call it a night and go to bed early.

The next morning was a disaster. Jack had packed the truck while she got their breakfast ready, only to find out at the hangar that, to her amazement, the large pile of cookies on the tray had been reduced to about a half dozen. The pile was so small that it was not even worth bringing the tray in as she placed it in the middle of their break table for their morning meeting. She finally noted Jack's eyes when she sat down among the guys, noting he looked like he had not slept at all—and for good reason, if he had ingested all those cookies.

"Well, guys…there was about three dozen cookies for everyone to share all day, although I wouldn't recommend any more than two a day since they do contain real, caffeinated coffee in them," she said, eyeing Jack suspiciously, confirming what she knew about the other missing cookies by the way his eyes jerked away from her along with his movements when Nate caught him off guard.

She smiled to herself, thinking, *Serves you right, ya bastard.*

"There's only six here, Tasha. What are you talking about?" Hank questioned as he helped himself to one and the rest of the guys dove in on the tray.

"Wow, these are good!"

"Better than a donut and a cup of coffee."

"Hmm…"

"You have to make more of these, Tasha," came the various comments.

Tasha shrugged her shoulders. "Sorry, guys, I just don't know what happened to the rest of the cookies I made last night," she said, smiling weakly but looking over to her culprit. The rest of the crew's faces followed suit, including Nate's, who was standing next to him.

After several seconds, Jack admitted, "Fine, guilty as charged. Sorry, guys, they are even better fresh out of the oven," he told them, still fidgeting under their accusatory glares.

Nate ended up rescuing Jack before a coup could take place by starting the meeting and thus getting everyone started for the day. It was a no-fly day due to several areas getting bad weather at their destinations—especially those that were inland where the air temperature had begun its winter drop, creating various mixtures of rain and snow, making it difficult for flying.

About mid-morning, Tasha was roughly pulled out of an aircraft hellhole by a pair of hands on her hips, barely missing the wire she was crimping together as she made the minor repair.

She knew it was Jack before she was set down on the hangar floor, standing there facing him, watching him as he dug into his winter coveralls for his wallet and keys. The cold air wafting around him told her he had just come from the tarmac outside.

"Here," he said, thumbing his wallet open and pulling out a wad of cash and shoving it into her hands along with his truck keys. "Go get what you need at the store to make more of those cookies."

"What…Why?"

"So I can get the crew off my back. Take my truck." He shoved his wallet back in his coveralls.

"Ah, Jack…" She thumbed through the wad of cash, lightly counting it. "Making those takes quite a bit of time. I may not make it back in the time you think I can," she said, and then tucked the cash into her pocket. "And I don't think Nate is going to pay me to go to the store and then be at our cabin to make cookies for half a day…"

He ran a frazzled hand through his lengthening layers of dark auburn hair. "*Just Go!*" he ordered her in a low enough voice between them. "Do what it takes, and I'll cover for you for the rest of the day."

When she hesitated, his voice boomed at her, "*Go!*" making her jump into action like any soldier would.

Either he was experiencing a serious caffeine rush—or withdrawal—or the crew had spent half the morning hounding him for being selfish. She smiled wickedly to herself. It didn't matter. *Let him suffer for his treachery*, she thought. She was going to take her darn time baking the rest of the day, since there little work to do.

Before long, Veterans Day would be fast approaching, and a three-day weekend was coming up at the insistence of Nate. Nate, a firm supporter of the troops, announced to the others at the morning crew meeting that Jack and Tasha would be off that weekend.

She was not entirely happy with staying three days at the cabin with Jack. But knowing him, he would most likely be off hunting or fishing. She would rather work than be alone at their cabin. She cleared her throat before Nate could continue with the meeting.

"Sir, I have no problem coming in to work that Friday. It is no big deal for me. I'll just coordinate a ride into—"

"Tasha, you're not going to disappoint Chad and his family, are you?" interrupted Jack.

"Wha—" She was confused over this sudden interruption.

"Remember he invited us to come over for the weekend so you could meet his folks and see their community?"

She leaned forward on her bench seat, folding her arms to rest her elbows on the break table as he continued.

"You've been wanting to see some traditional native art, taste their cooking, and listen to their people's history and stories."

Not wanting to make a fuss at refusing in front of them all, she reluctantly acquiesced. Jack's eyes were her silent warning to behave, and she nodded accordingly at her new part in this farce. Her acting skills were B quality, along with the lack of sincerity in her voice. "I guess I forgot," she said unconvincingly.

She saw Sam and Nick exchange glances. Quiet Jarvis, who was usually half asleep, even looked up sullenly, as did his roommate, Emanuel. It seemed only Hank and Nate were oblivious to the underlying tension between them.

At the end of their meeting, Nate told the crew that a round of drinks was on the house that Thursday night before Veterans Day weekend and that they would all get off early—around three that afternoon. As for the Thursday approaching, he just needed two planes ready to fly by Tuesday before all could leave. There wasn't much work to be done, and Tasha knew the crew would most likely have it done by noon. She hoped she could get in a few more hours of flying in the Skyhawk that day with one of the guys, like they had done a few times with her here and there the previous week.

The crew refused her assistance on either plane, thus she ended up on Monday morning back in the battery shop to continue studying for her IFR rating. It would be a long day for her. She was finding it difficult to focus any more on the manual and the test questions. She was more than ready when she started to have guilty doubts for not studying more, although she was certain she could test out. About an hour later, Jack showed up at the battery room.

He found her sitting at her worktable with her flight manuals and test questions splayed out. She was rubbing the back of her neck, as if suffering from the strain of studying all night. Tasha looked up at him expectantly, but did not say anything as he pulled up the other stool to sit across from her. He was ready for any comment from her that time. He knew she did not like being told what to do on their time off, much less changing her plans for the long weekend without being told.

He indicated to her workbooks. "You think you're ready?"

"Been ready for the past week. But you're going to have to let me out of my 'rooms'"—she held up finger the quotes—"long enough to test out and fly."

He ignored her jab. "Then come with me."

"Now what?"

"We're going to see William."

"William?" she asked. "Who's he?"

"A consultant for our company. He's a few hangars down from us and someone you need to eventually know, should you have any aviation questions." Jack got up and indicated for her to follow him down the hall in the opposite direction of their main work area to another open bay full of planes in storage and then to a door leading outside to the flight line.

Tasha followed, now curious as to why she would just now be meeting this new person that was important to the company. The walk was short, but not enough to protect her against the cool air that came in off Resurrection Bay as they stepped outside. She shrugged her shoulders up protectively against the icy breeze as they passed two structures down the line, the fuel pit being further down from where they stopped at a similar hangar. At the access door he pressed a buzzer and waited, facing her. When the door unlatched with a buzz, Jack turned to let themselves in.

Upon entering, she found the bay well-lit in the patchy gray of the day. It was 'sunny' in the anterior bay as they made their way to some rear offices in the spacious building. They passed the only two planes housed in that hangar, each of them only capable of seating about four to six people and appearing new and nicely maintained.

Jack opened an office door and called out. "William!" He looked back at her and indicated with his head for her to precede him.

She entered a lavish office, militantly neat. The open space allowed for not just an office with a bookcase and desk for the user, but a nice seating arrangement comprised of a sofa and two chairs forming the conversational *U* for small meetings.

William was a man in his late fifties. He was a blond man aging gracefully into a full head of snow-white hair. He looked up, smiling warmly as he came from around his desk, greeting them when Jack introduced Tasha to him. William shook her hand.

"Wow!" he said, looking Tasha over. "Not often do we see new women around here, especially in aviation. I hear you are the newest employee of Black Raven. Nate can't stop talking about his newest 'Sparky.' It's nice to finally meet you, Miss Tasha Lazar."

To Jack, he asked, "What can I do for you?" William offered them seats in the sitting area before taking a chair to occupy.

"Do you wanna see if you think she is ready to test out for her IFR ground test?" Jack asked as he settled back into the chair opposite William, allowing Tasha to occupy the entire sofa.

William folded his hands, letting his fingers intertwine, partially obscuring his mouth as he studied Tasha. She felt like an exotic bird on display as she literally splayed her book and papers next to her, as if she had just spread her tailfeathers for inspection.

"You think you're ready, Tasha?"

"I believe so."

"You either know or you don't."

She closed her eyes a moment, knowing better. "I do know this," she said, and hesitated briefly. "I just have to fight off the testing nerves. It gets so bad that all I want to do is throw up."

William smiled at her. "What are you worried about?"

"Making stupid mistakes for over-studying and becoming complacent. You know, the typical pilot error mistakes when they become complacent from flying too long, or the same route, the same plane, the same everything."

He smiled at her comment. "Oh, I think you will do fine. Let's see…" He reached for her book with the test questions. William took his time going back and forth between several of the question pages, asking her a few of the questions for her to answer. A few times, she wanted further explanations on the some of the questions that bothered her by giving some made-up scenarios, and together they went over those that she needed help on.

After about an hour of going through her materials, William put her book down. "Pretty good job knowing your stuff there, Tasha. I think you're ready," he said, and then asked her when she thought she would be ready to schedule a checkout ride.

"Ah…I'm not entirely sure," she said, looking at Jack. "I haven't flown enough since arriving here to entirely familiarize myself with the Skyhawk."

"What did you learn on first?"

"A Piper Warrior."

"Have you ever flown a 172?" William got up and went to his desk where he flipped through his calendar.

"Yes, a few times, but still prefer the low-wing model planes."

"Well, Nate only has that Skyhawk. You better get used to it. It's just as easy as the Piper." He paused in his page turning. "I need to inspect his bird here shortly for its annual, Jack," he said, looking up at him. "Are you boys okay with me doing two things at once? I can inspect the plane and get her checkout ride done at the same time with her help."

Jack nodded. "She is due. I think we can have all her paperwork in order by the end of the week."

"But I still need to take my ground test," she interrupted. "I don't know if I can get an administrator to test me out on such short notice."

William paused in marking his calendar, looking up at her, then asking Jack if he had told her who he was.

"Well, not exactly the entire part of your job and your relationship to our company, Will."

Tasha looked at Jack and he explained. "You just took your ground IFR test and passed, Tasha. William here is an FAA examiner and inspector for our area."

Her mouth dropped as she realized what had just transpired.

"You're welcome," added Jack. "Now to get you back to the hangar and get you scheduled for a few more flights this coming week." He pushed himself up from his chair. Tasha followed suit.

"Sounds good. I got you down for the twenty-fifth, Jack."

"Noted, and I'll let the Raven know," Jack said.

William looked over to her. "Tasha…see you then." He smiled. "I'll meet you at your hangar that day and we will go over the aircraft's inspection first."

Tasha, still coming to terms with finding that not only she had been tested but had passed, nodded and smiled gratefully at William. Jack guided her out of his office, and they headed back to Black Raven Aviation in silence.

It was not until they had reached their hangar door, after Jack went inside, that she hesitated outside just long enough to let out a loud 'whoop!' of delight and relief. Jack's head popped back out the door again, looking back at her where she stood, feet shoulder-width apart, her book and papers in one hand, the other on her mouth, surprised at having shouted out loud. Jack shared in her delight, smiling at her, her happiness contagious.

"Come on." He jerked his head back toward the interior of their hangar. "Get out of the cold. I can't take you in for your medical if you are sick. Grab your coat while I give Nate the news."

"Hunh?" Then, realizing he was going to take her to get her flight physical, she darted after him, his long-legged stride making it difficult for her to catch up by the time she got inside the hangar.

Less than an hour later they were up at the clinic, seeing the doctor, with the paperwork needed to bring her current with her flight physical, the nurse having led them back to a room together after weighing and taking her vitals.

"Nice to see you're doing well, Tasha," the doctor said as he came into the room moments later. "Jack, good to see you again. You know you're due too." He shook Jack's hand.

"I know. Part of the reason I'm here with her. Thought you could do us both at the same time."

"Always the micro-minute manager, Jack." The doctor smiled. "Did wonder about seeing two sets of paperwork here." He set his clipboard down on the countertop.

"Okay, Tasha," he began, patting the examination table for her to hop on. "Ladies first." The doctor pulled a drawer out to grab the scope he needed to examine her eyes, nose, and ears.

"Jack, go find the nurse to get your weight and vitals for me while I check her out," he said, shining a light into her eyes. "Look up a minute." Jack took his leave. "Good."

After several mini tests along her body and a few more questions, he asked,

"How's your war wound doing?" He indicated for her to lift her shirt up. He pressed along the area. She didn't flinch, the tenderness having disappeared since the last time she had visited.

"I'm fine. Back to walking and running short periods." She flinched some on the rear side when he pressed again. "I feel it the most when I try to do a few sit-ups at times. It pulls to one side."

Jack came back in, knocking first, yet not waiting for a response and dropping a piece of paper onto the countertop next to her chart.

"Well, take it easy for a little bit longer."

She dropped her shirt back down.

"The walking is good, running not so much yet." Looking at Jack momentarily, he added, "And still get the guys to do more of the weightlifting of some of that equipment of yours on the flight line. We need you to heal correctly on the inside, although it looks good on the outside, Tasha."

He gave her an eye paddle to hold over her eye as he gave her a quick vision test. "So far, so good." He took a moment to fill out her paperwork. They both remained silent as he took his time making his notes. Picking up Jack's paper, he asked, "Are these your vitals?" He looked at him rather oddly.

"Yup. Anything wrong?"

"A bit high on your blood pressure," he said as he got up again to get the cuff and his stethoscope to retake Jack's blood pressure. "You working harder than normal?"

"Nothing more than usual," he commented. Jack's eyes locked with Tasha's as the doctor pumped the cuff, then released the pressure. "That's better." He wrote down the new readings. "But I think we are going to have to discuss some relaxation techniques for you."

At that information, Tasha raised an eyebrow at Jack. But she didn't get to see his subtle response, as the doctor interrupted them by sending her back outside the room to get her hearing checked. She left with her paperwork in hand, going down the hallway to the screening room, only to find herself running into Chad on the way there. He was just stepping out of the room she needed to go in for her test.

He smiled warmly at her, his eyes filled with mirth, greeting her in his normal cheery disposition, surprised to see her there, but then trying not to be obvious looking around for Jack.

"Yes, Jack's right behind me when the doc gets through with him," she answered his unspoken question. "*And*...I guess we will be seeing you and your family over the Veterans Day weekend." She smiled broadly at him, knowing for some reason that he would not have heard of this new development. Chad's surprised expression confirmed it, yet he quickly hid it from her, letting her know that they were always welcome to his parents' lodgings.

"What have you got there?" He pointed to her paperwork in her hands.

"I've got to have my hearing checked for a flight physical."

He led her back into the screening room, taking her paperwork from her.

"I can take care of this for you. Take a seat there." He pointed to a stool. "I'll get you a headset. I take it you have done one of these before?"

Tasha nodded affirmatively.

Chad walked to another room, where he dug around in the equipment cabinet for the items he needed. "So, what time are we supposed to expect you two, and for how long?" he asked, creating small talk with her.

"I really have no idea. He only just told me this morning at the crew meeting. Actually, I was *reminded* of something that was never mentioned." She sighed heavily.

"Really?" Chad came back, plugging in the headset and hand indicator. "Well, it's a surprise to me too." He saw her eyebrow arch up. "Don't take it wrong. You are most welcome, and I do hope you come. I'll just have to give my folks a call to let them know. Mom will be thrilled."

"Somehow I just don't see how *anyone* can be *thrilled* at seeing Jack."

"Ah, Jack is…well…" He rubbed his chin, trying to come up with something. "…just Jack." He grinned at her. "He's actually a nice guy. You just have to quit kicking the snot out of him."

She gave him an exasperated look. "I only fight when provoked. He starts it. Living with him is like living with a damn porcupine or…or a grumpy bear that just awoke from hibernation!"

He laughed at her remark. "Put the headsets on and let's see if you can hear me," he said as he walked just behind the glass wall, taking his seat and pressing something. "Can you hear me?"

Tasha nodded.

The conversation continued over the headsets.

"Well, you kind of awoke a grizzly bear, I suppose." He gave her a big smile. "But he needs it. Can you hear the first tone?"

Tasha nodded.

"Good. The test is starting. It'll take about ten minutes."

Afterwards, they found Jack standing just outside waiting his turn. And from there, she waited patiently for them in the waiting room, scanning over very outdated women's home and fashion magazines and men's outdoor and sports magazines. She heard them come out but didn't move, feigning interest in a houseplant article. She focused on their conversation, but there was not much for her to glean other than their plans on hunting and trapping crabs for the weekend feast. She acted reluctant to put the magazine down when they stopped just in front of her. She looked up when Jack's booted toe tapped hers while he and Chad continued to chat it up.

"…Is there any gooseberry pie?"

"Mom'll have it ready for ya." Chad knew his friend's first addiction, the second was sitting in front of him as he noted Jack's lack of social graces was not going over too well with her.

She got up when Jack motioned slightly with his head, *let's go*. Jack turned to leave with her in tow, strolling toward the door with their paperwork in hand. She rolled her eyes heavenward at Chad, then asked him, "Did you get your answers?"

"Yup." Chad grinned at her all too knowingly, causing her to give him an uncertain look before leaving.

"Anything I need to know?" she asked.

"Nope." Chad looked like the cat that had trapped an entire planet's canary population in its mouth.

Lunch was an entirely a different affair for the day. When Jack did not turn to head back to the airport, Tasha asked where they were going next. All he told her was he was hungry. Jack took her to the Chinook Waterfront restaurant for lunch. It was a nice change from their normal fare of packaged sandwiches with chips and/or fruit that she usually made the night before.

After being seated by the window overlooking Resurrection Bay, she finally asked, "What's the occasion?"

"Celebrate your passing of both tests," he said dryly.

"Nate's okay with us taking a long lunch break?" she asked, noting that this was the type of dining that took your time and a lot of money. She was almost paranoid at looking at the menu, since most of her last two paychecks had gone to pay the prior bills and she hadn't allowed herself much left over for the rest of the month.

As if reading her mind, he said, "Will you quit your worrying? When you are with me, you are fine. Now what would you like to have?"

"Ah…" She looked pointlessly at the menu and then put it back down. "I'll just order a hot drink."

"That's it?"

She nodded.

He sighed, then put his menu down as the waitress came over to take their orders. He looked at her after she ordered just her hot tea and then casually peered at what the other few folks in the dining room were eating. "She'll have the maple glazed chicken and I'll have the garlic shrimp scampi."

Her head snapped back to him.

She leaned toward him, sitting opposite her, after the waitress left. "Are you crazy? I can't afford the appetizer, Jack, much less a meal! I don't even have a way to budget it back on the next paycheck! What are you thinking?" she whispered harshly at him.

"Relax, it's on Nate and myself. No paying back."

She eyed him suspiciously.

"You've worked hard," he said, smiling at her. "You've made Nate an incredibly happy company man. Now it's time to enjoy the success."

"Then why isn't Nate here?"

"Because he and his wife are having their lunch elsewhere today. He values his time with his wife."

She raised an eyebrow at this information.

He sighed at her. "Put your hackles down. Nate's been running this business now for some time. What little time he gets with his wife is usually working together a few days out of the week in the same office. They rarely get any downtime together and I am giving him a chance. Eventually, I hope to give him more opportunities in the future. If you have any inkling of what running a business is like, especially by yourself, you'd know that you don't have much of a social life, you're chained to the thing you created and love most, and if you don't break away every once in a while, you will lose sight of the things that are most essential to you."

"So, you have been working more than usual," she pointed out to him.

"How would you know and why would you care?"

"You lied to the doctor."

"About what?" He took a sip of his water, then realizing what she was going after, he cut her off. "No, I didn't, the workload is the same. And you," he said, extending his index finger at her, "have no business in my health issues. My blood pressure is fine, and it is not from work."

"Well then, I guess it's long walks or short runs with me, your choice."

"You are not running, and you are to cease for the time being. You heard the doc."

"Now, look who's talking about being nosy in health issues?"

He gave her a beleaguered look.

"Okay, fine. I'll walk, but you come with me. Consider it free psychotherapy sessions and your time to 'relax.'" She made finger quotes on the last word.

He smirked at her as their meals arrived at their table. "We'll talk about it later."

Tasha waited until the server left. "Why not now?"

He looked up at her from where he squirted the lemon on his shrimp.

"Man, that looks good," she said as she eyed his shrimp.

"I thought you hated seafood."

"Not shrimp," she told him.

"Then I want some of your chicken in exchange."

"Deal!" Eagerly, she cut into her chicken and gave him a large chunk as he gave her a portion of his shrimp.

They didn't talk much as they gorged themselves on the upscale lunch, each of them savoring their heavenly meals. He did not rush them, which was nice for a change, considering how erratic the morning had been. With her belly pleasantly full, she was not in any mood to return to work. They were back at the hangar by one thirty, only to find the guys had finished earlier than expected. She was extremely grateful. The guys were cleaning and organizing the hangar for the rest of the time until three o'clock arrived.

She ended up riding with Sam and Nick up to the bar from the hangar for what she thought was going to be a normal night out with the crew, Jarvis and Manny in another car, Hank and Jack in his truck following behind them. Once inside the bar, they were greeted by Nate and Nora, who had already gotten the tab going for the entire crew for a mini celebration. Two rounds for all of them. Nate got everyone together in the corner, after they all got their drinks. He wanted to make a few announcements and a toast.

"First of all, let's congratulate Tasha. Today, she passed her ground IFR test and her flight physical." He lifted his frosted mug to her. "Congratulations!"

The guys cheered, toasting her with their glasses and slapping her a 'good job' on her shoulder just like she was one of them, finally. It was minor compared to weeks of what felt like being just slightly out of reach of being accepted, given how she was constantly separated from them by her singular job description as an aircraft electrician.

Nate continued, looking at Jack. "Next week, we will see to getting you up in the air more and obtaining some hours with a few of the guys on the bigger birds. Get with Jack, on finding out where he will be assigning you. And please… Tasha…whatever you do, bring back my birds in one piece while you are learning. The guys don't need to add to their current workload."

Nora, his wife, slugged him for his last comment as she added, "We know you'll do fine, Tasha."

"Wishing you the best weather always," Nate said, toasting her again, welcoming her on board.

Hugs ensued from there and she joined in, listening to the banter between all of them, Nora from time to time pulling her out of her 'quiet shell' and asking her what things she had done or not done as of yet in town and making a few recommendations, encouraging her to get out more when work was less hectic. Eventually, Nate and Nora said their goodbyes, calling it an early evening and leaving the crew in the big corner booth to hang out and finish their drinks.

Tasha was certain Jack would have made her leave shortly afterwards, but grateful for Hank keeping Jack's attention with indiscernible small talk in the far corner. The guys had grouped around her, almost protectively, from the rest of the bar crowd, Jarvis and Nick to one side of Hank, Sam and Emanuel with her in between them and Jack's side.

That night was the first time she was able to get a chance to get to know the crew better. There was no way she was going to let Jack keep her separated from them this time. The guys talked about everything, from the latest football scores and their favorite teams, to the news, their hobbies, the local gossip, and a few of the locals themselves—especially girls that passed by or entered the local establishment.

Most plied their questions toward her past and she gingerly touched upon her past highlights, being sure not to give out too much information about herself yet, steering the conversations back to them.

She was still trying to get a feel for her co-workers, their likes and dislikes. She learned their nicknames. Sam was called Dr. Seuss because the Cat in the Hat's name was Sam. But then Nick did tell her of the day of a very hungry Sam opening an old and outdated breakfast ration with eggs from one of the planes, the Angelina. The packaged ham and eggs had turned green over time from the tin packaging, thus making Sam gag. After Nick was able to check out the *Green Eggs and Ham* book from Seward's Public Library—or steal it...no one knew for sure—the crew had begun quoting the popular line, "Sam I am, I don't like green eggs and ham."

Nick was known as St. Nick, as in Santa Claus. Tasha thought it was because of his birthname. But it was due to a 'heroic' flight through a nasty blizzard over the holidays one year to deliver desperately needed winter supplies to a small outlying village. Their essentials and groceries had run dry a week earlier, and new supplies had been constantly delayed for several weeks by another flight company having several mechanical issues with their planes. Nick had included a few extra toys, rounded up by the Seward townsfolk, to give to the children to hold them over for the holidays until he could return and retrieve the second load from Anchorage, consisting of mostly mail and hardware supplies.

Manny was known as the Peacock because of the colorful artworks he did from time to time at his cabin and on all of Black Raven's aircraft. When it came to tattooing the aircraft's nickname near the nose of each aircraft, the names had a double entendre for his preferences for men and his eccentric personality.

Jarvis had no nickname; the group was still working on one for him. But he was not alone: Hank and Jack didn't have one either.

"No, Jack now has a nickname since Tasha came along," said Hank excitedly, reminding them. "I've been told it's 'Griswald, the Bear' or just 'Griswald.'"

Jack shot him a dirty look for betraying him. "Hey, man."

Hank laughed. "Even Big Raven said it fit you."

The crew ended up loving Jack's new nickname and unanimously voted it official that night.

"Now, we need to work on yours, Tasha," came Manny. "You got anything in mind or an old one that you have?"

Tasha shook her head no. "Electricians and avionics techs have always been known in the Army as Sparkies. But doesn't sound like it works very well as a pilot's nickname."

A couple of the guys mulled it over in their heads, from what she could discern.

"Well, don't rush it. Your nickname will come when you least expect it," said Sam.

She was hoping it would be a cool nickname and not being noted for having done something stupid on the flight line. She did wonder why Nate was called Big Raven, and asked them.

"His German surname is Amsel, which means Black Bird," Jack said.

"And up here in the North, the natives worship their number one god, the Raven," added Hank.

"Nate's been flying since…well…since before all of us were born, save for Hank here," added Nick, "it just made sense to call him Big Raven because he is the owner of Black Raven Aviation."

As the evening continued, Hank bid his adieu after his second drink to go home when his wife arrived to pick him up, leaving Jack to watch over them all. Eventually, someone found a stack of cards and a round of spades ensued between the crewmembers remaining. Tasha didn't know how to play, thus she stayed out of the game, watching over Sam's hand and trying her best to learn, yet more to keep from looking or talking with Jack, now sitting on her other side, quietly watching them.

She kept the banter light with guys, not wanting to provoke Jack for any reason, especially when it came to separating her from the crew as he did at work. Jack had no right to intrude in her social life after work, but she did appreciate his protective presence somewhat in case one of the guys became too drunk on two beers—but none of them did, being seasoned drinkers. She relaxed some when the night did come to an end and Jack handed her his truck keys, telling her to do the driving since she only had her one glass of wine the entire evening.

The following Monday, Tasha was assigned to Sam on his runs to Tatitlek. He was a good instructor on the twin-engine, the Angelina, that he normally flew with Jarvis. She filled in Jarvis's spot to let him keep working and studying for his Airframe and Powerplant test that he had scheduled at the end of the week. And she needed to log the flight hours, getting familiar with some of their weekly runs.

Maintenance became less as their jobs morphed into cargo loaders and flight line servicing. Nick, Sam, Emanuel, and Jack flew more as the week progressed, all of them flying supplies to the various smaller towns instead of tourists who wanted to fish, kayak, or hunt. Hank remained as their ground crew, manning the radios and meeting them with the aircraft tug whenever the crew returned from their flights. Jack fueled most of the aircrafts as they returned to base. Hank stepped in often, doing the same fueling job as their cargo runs became stacked back to back. In no time, she would rack up all the flight hours she could possibly want by late fall.

With her IFR test flight completed and passed, it was near the end of October when she finished her type rating for the Beaver. She still needed more time on Sam's bird and the other models that the rest flew, but that would take more time with each of them before she could finish all the type certifications.

She got her first solo flight job shortly afterwards, when Hank came upon her in the wire room one afternoon, telling her that she needed to report to the boss.

"Okay, tell Jack I'll be there in a second. Let me finish up here," she said, closing her book on Clara's—the Twin Otter—model and performance ratings in which she had been studying.

"No, not Jack. Big Raven," Hank corrected her.

"Oh?"

It turned out that Nate wanted her to fly to Anchorage with the Beaver to drop off his wife for an overnight stay to go shopping and visit with her friends.

"Why not have her drive up there?" she asked, rather puzzled. Then she explained the monetary costs for her reasoning. "Surely the cost of fuel and employee time outweigh the two-and-a-half hour drive up there?"

"Ah...my next bookkeeper!" He smiled as he leaned forward in his office chair, putting his elbows on his still cluttered desk, although much of the paperwork had been cleared since the last time she had seen it. "There is a rhyme and reason to you flying her up there, Tasha. When I send her up there to let her shop, she must be conscious of how much she buys since she cannot overload the aircraft. So I save a lot of money in that area. Secondly, she really hates driving by herself on the icy roads, and I would feel much better if one of us would fly her up there, knowing she is safe. Last, I don't have the time to do it myself this time, and it would not only give you more flight hours, but some girl time. Give you a break from the guys," he said, smiling at her.

She raised her eyebrows up at this information. "But the flight will only take about an hour at the most."

"Let's just say you get to help her all day, you stay the night, and then you return in the morning or afternoon, weather permitting."

"You're going to *pay* me...to go shopping...with your wife?"

"Well, I will also have you picking up your battery-charging cable for our battery room and some other small parts for our aircraft while you are up there. So you will be working some of the time, but while you are there, you might as well enjoy some downtime and do whatever it is you women do." He sighed. "Don't take this the wrong way, but I can't have my guys turning you into a complete tomboy." He waved a dismissing hand at her. "Nora doesn't bite. She would love to have another woman to talk to and hang out with for the day. She's quite fond of you and would like to get to know you better. We're family here at Black Raven Aviation. So, go...go have some fun." He smiled encouragingly at her.

The trip did prove to be enjoyable. Nora did her best to get Tasha to talk about her life. Tasha kept it to the safer topics, about her family and Palm Harbor. However, Tasha deftly kept steering the conversation back to Nora, who had no qualms in telling her about their marriage and the town of Seward.

After securing the aircraft parts needed by the crew and then their rental car, she drove Nora to wherever she wanted to go. Shopping with Nora was a polar opposite experience compared with Jack. Nora was excessively big into home décor, family items, and fashionable clothing. Yet the main reason Nora was there was more for the spa-like day. She had set up a massage, facial, pedicure, and hot tub soak appointment, not only for herself but for Tasha too.

That left Tasha flustering at Nora about not being able to afford the treatments, only to have Nora give her a dismissing wave of her hand. "Who else is going to keep me company while I am in there? Consider it a company perk."

At that remark, Tasha had slowed down in her stride next to Nora to adjust all the shopping bags between her hands, but kept up with Nora as she casually noted other shops around them, determining which ones to skip.

Then Nora turned on her unexpectedly, cupping her chin with her one gloved hand. "Besides, your skin needs help," Nora told her, inspecting her face minutely, "and I am sure the guys aren't doing anything to keep you in top form. A girl, no matter what she does for a living, needs to take good care of herself and for her special someone."

"I don't have a special someone, nor do I think the guys or the aircraft care what I look like. I was never meant to be a runway model," Tasha commented rather meekly. She would always be touchy on that subject because her looks had failed to catch a husband or at least a decent significant other. Her own mother thought that was part of her problem.

Nora, ever the '80s lady, 'tsked' her comment with a "Nonsense, lady." Nora dropped her hand from Tasha's chin, taking her hand instead and pulling her to a nearby bench to sit upon. Nora waited while Tasha found a way to rearrange all the shopping bags she carried for Nora. She settled into her seat before turning to Tasha to talk to her like a mother to a child. "First of all, you are a very pretty girl. Yes, aircraft don't care what you look like, but guys always will, whether you are single or not. Always have your best foot forward. Be proud of who you are and where you are in life. You still have the whole world at your feet, sweetie."

"I sleep with a dog at night. That's not much to be proud about!"

Nora's shocked visage said it all. It was not that Tasha wasn't proud, but that she felt her current life was all work, cook, clean, and sleep, and if that is what life would be like for the next twenty-five years, it wasn't going to be a very exciting life. Being financially tight and having her movements controlled by an overbearing roommate whose boss-like duties extended into her personal life had become stifling, to say the least.

"I wouldn't have thought Jack was that bad of a man to make you say something like that," Nora said, aghast at her comment.

Tasha gave her a tight-lipped smile before correcting her. "No, not Jack. We are *definitely* not sleeping together! However, Drake, his dog, has been more of a companion than he has. Jack mostly goes fishing, hunting, flying, or works downstairs on his paperwork, I believe. He's not your social guy that likes to hang out with a 'female roomie.'" She fingered quotes around the term. She shrugged a shoulder at her. "Besides, Drake has fur, he is warmer, and more lovable in bed then any man I've had before. In fact, I am taking to Alaska just like any native sleeping with their dog team to keep warm at night. I've settled in just fine, albeit without a man," she told Nora, assuring her that she was content and happy.

Nora giggled but sighed, "Oh Tasha, there's a lot more to life, although Drake is a darling dog. You really let him sleep with you?"

"I let him one time when the comforter didn't seem to keep me warm enough one night, and I haven't been able to keep him out since then. He only seems to mind Jack."

"Well, I'll tell Jack to fix that for you—"

"No, no," she interrupted her. "It'll be fine. And I like it that way, I feel protected."

"Protected?" Nora's manicured eyebrows shot up in concern. "Has Jack done something to you that we need to know about?"

Exasperated, Tasha sighed. "No, he hasn't done anything to cause me worry, other than he is very overbearing at the cabin after work." She held up a hand. "I just feel locked up after work. We go nowhere, we really do nothing other than I make dinner, read, or do whatever it is we…more like *he* wants to do in the confines of our cabin. But it's mainly because I have no money to go do anything anyways, after we get our weekly shopping done, my credit card bills paid, and me saving for a new car battery and battery warmer…there's not much leftover to go do anything. The last thing I want to do is tell Jack to take me places and let me sightsee. Heck, I can't even walk outside without him or Drake going with me."

"Well, with good reason not to let you out by yourself! He's being protective because you are a lady, and a pretty one at that. It's not just the wildlife, but even some of the men could cause a problem, too. You are in a man's world. They outnumber us by two to one, you know?" Nora informed her, patting her hand.

"That's because most of the women freeze themselves to death up here," Tasha added sardonically.

Nora laughed. "I think you will get used to it here in time. But I know that Jack really likes you."

Ah, the anchor drop, Tasha thought, but kept it light, saying, "Of course. He likes my work, for the most part, and that I do the cooking."

"No, I mean Jack *really* likes you, Tasha."

"You're a romantic, aren't you, Nora? I hate to burst your bubble, but we aren't romantically inclined, nor would it be a good idea to be having an affair with my superior."

"I hope not with Nate!"

"No! My *immediate* superior, Jack…the one you two hired to oversee the hangar's day-to-day operations?"

Nora winked at her, patting her hand, letting her know she was just teasing— but telling her she shouldn't rule out Jack just because of his job title, and that he wasn't altogether a supervisor.

"Nora, he has issues. Issues he's not ready to face. And to add to it, let's not rule out the other women throwing themselves at him."

Nora ignored her response. "Ah, we all have our issues. Mine is shopping. Nate's a procrastinator. Nick's a womanizer. Jarvis has a chip on his shoulder. Yours…not sure of yet." Nora lightly cuffed Tasha's chin, smiling broadly. "As for other women, I don't think there are any other women out there that Jack's interested in."

"But you think he's interested in me just because I am his cabinmate?"

Nora raised a shoulder, smiling at her.

"Or did he flat-out tell you?"

"Nope." She smiled bigger at Tasha, deciding to keep the secret to herself.

Tasha rolled her eyes at her, not wanting to further encourage Nora, adding, "I think we need to get you going. Your appointment starts in thirty minutes."

"You mean our appointment!" Nora corrected, grabbing her hand to come hither.

The soak in the hot tub was divine. It was the first time since arriving that Tasha felt like she was able to thaw out all the way, nearly declining the next part of the spa treatment, the one-hour massage, just to remain soaking in the hot water until she dissolved into a pile of human mush.

The rest of the day was spent, to Nora's delight, purchasing knick-knacks and trying on more clothes, making Tasha try something on from time to time, much to Tasha's distain. She was never much of a clotheshorse. Tasha was happy with simple, comfortable, casual clothes. It was only after Nora insisted they go out to one of the fancier restaurants that Tasha had to buy herself a dressier blouse for the evening. It was the final part of their shopping trip and Nora's girls' night out by checking into the hotel and then getting dinner.

The smooth landing of the Beaver was deflating after being up on cloud nine the day before, with all the luxurious shopping and spa treatments, although Tasha was more a lady in waiting to Nora, toting all the shopping bags she had acquired. Getting it all packed into the backseat area of the Beaver had proven interesting, making her wonder if her center of gravity would be slightly off due to the weight. But she had managed to get it all stored and balanced, grateful for a dry, cold, and clear morning, the perfect day for 'heavily loaded' aircraft to get off the ground.

When they taxied to the hangar, Jack was waiting on the tug, ready to pull the aircraft inside since weather was incoming, turning for the worse. She had seen the new band of clouds forming a line along the southwestern horizon as she had entered the landing pattern for the airport. He motioned for them to remain inside as he hooked the tug to the aircraft and began dragging them into the hangar.

Nora smiled, placing a hand on her arm, while Tasha was performing her shutdown checklist and putting everything in order for the next pilot to fly, stopping her, and jutting her chin in Jack's direction. "You see, I don't think anyone gets this kind of first-class service." Nora smiled and then opened her door when the aircraft was chocked.

Jack came around to the passenger side, helping Nora down, his eyes growing wide as he realized just how full the back of the aircraft had been stuffed with shopping bags.

Nora greeted him. "Jack, dear, could you help us with getting some of these bags unpacked and put into my car?" she asked, patting his arm after giving him a big hug and winsome smile.

He nodded and then gave Tasha a queer look, questioning her payload. She had just stuffed the checklist back into the pilot's side pocket and lifted an eyebrow, tilting her head as in *get to it, man.* He pressed his lips tightly together as he absorbed the bulk of packages filling the cargo compartment, nearly stuffed to the quilt-stitched blanket protecting the ceiling. He exhaled heavily and began unloading the first of the parcels to a nearby worktable as Nora walked off in the direction of the hangar offices.

"Are these all hers?" he asked quietly once Nora was out of earshot.

"Yup, save for one and that has my new evening dress blouse that she insisted I get."

"You bought a blouse?"

"I didn't have much of a choice, since she wanted to go to Crow's Nest for dinner last night."

Jack looked her over, as if trying to believe her, before answering her. "Yup, that sounds about right for Nora's tastes. I sometimes wonder how the hell Big Raven can afford her," he added, grabbing another fistful of shopping bags and dragging them out to the nearby worktables.

He came to her side of the aircraft where she had gotten out of her seat and back to the cargo door to get to the rest of the bags, only to let her grab a few of them before gently shoving her aside, saying he would get the rest of them. "The last thing I need is for you to stress out the muscles that are still healing from your wound."

"Are you kidding me? I carried over half of these around town with me yesterday, following her like her personal butler. I think if it wasn't for the hot tub and massage, I would have dropped dead from the workout."

"A massage and hot tub?"

"Pedicure and facial too."

"I thought you looked…" He paused as he looked at her face and hair.

"…refreshed?" she helped him find a word.

"…different," he said, deflating her.

She rolled her eyes. He smirked after he turned away carrying the bags, and then added more from the worktable to balance himself as he carried Nora's wares to her car outside. Hank was walking toward him as he made his way to the door, Jack stopping long enough to ask Hank for help, carrying the rest of the bags and to follow him, indicating with his head that he needed to take Tasha's armload too.

"Wow, you ladies know how to shop! I think you two bought an entire household here," Hank said, grabbing the bags from her.

"Nora did, not me. Still too poor and haven't found a *wealthy* Mr. Right yet to let me have that kind of a lifestyle. These are all her bags," Tasha informed him.

Hank chuckled at her. "Well, princess, you'll find one soon, I bet. 'Specially, up here in Alaska."

"You mean there are rich people here?"

"Oh, yeah…there are. Wait till you see some of the clients that hire us. Someone's gonna lay eyes on you and be a goner." The toothpick wiggled between his teeth, his grin widening, he winked at her as he turned away from her.

She trailed him, shaking her head at the thought.

CHAPTER ELEVEN

The next two weekends were the same, with Jack abandoning her in the cabin alone. She had had enough. She wanted her life back. Nora may have just spoiled her that past week with their outing. Thus, she decided it was time to go out on her own whether Jack liked it or not. It was time to strike out and have her own fun. Tasha started by finding the others with a phone call and asking what they were doing.

Jack found her late on Sunday hanging out with Jarvis and Emanuel when he ended up calling them after she refused to answer her phone. Jarvis knowingly texted back that she was with them and all was fine, but Jack tromped up the hill to Manny's and Jarvis's cabin to retrieve her. He came in after heavily pounding on the door, spying her at the main kitchen island—a similar layout to their own cabin, albeit a tad more lived-in and messier. The word 'tad' was an understatement when it came to Manny's choice of interior décor. It was practically eighty-five degrees in their cabin and the walls were nearly obliterated in brilliant colorful Panamanian canvases that Manny painted in his off time, painting just about anything. It had looked like she had spent part of the day putting a puzzle partially together on the table and chowing down on Manny's notorious guacamole dip and chips. Manny and Tasha had painted the latter part of the day, from the various paint spots that covered her hands and lower arms along with several paint tubes and two water jars holding brushes.

Jarvis was by the kitchen sink getting more drinks for them, along with doing a few dishes, since Jarvis was the neatnik of the two of them. "Hey, Jack, you wanna beer?"

"Nah, I'm here to get Tasha out of your hair and get her home." He sounded like an annoyed parent that had to track down their errant child.

"She's not in our hair, Jack, at least let her finish her artwork. She's as good as Manny is when it comes to colors," he said, drying off a glass to put away in the cupboard. "Come on, take a seat. Take a load off them dogs of yours."

Jack reluctantly lumbered over and sat down opposite of where Tasha and Manny were working. Tasha momentarily glanced up at him, not really acknowledging his presence and clearly annoyed at the fact that he had hunted her down.

Jarvis kept the peace though, sliding a beer across the table and indicating for him to help himself to the guac and chips. "What did you and Chad get on your hunt this time?" Jarvis asked as Jack watched Manny and Tasha dabbing art brushes at their own canvases, Tasha blatantly ignoring him but very much aware of his presence.

"Bagged ourselves a nice elk to share." Jack watched her cringe at the comment as he took a long draw on the bottle. She absolutely hated his hunting.

"Sounds like elk burgers are going to be coming soon," drawled Jarvis.

The conversation carried on for a bit, Jack not being all that conversational on his side with Jarvis as he stared Tasha down as he waited. He was seething underneath at not finding her in the cabin when Chad and he had returned from their weekend hunt. Although the cabin was clean and orderly, it had inexplicably bothered him that she was not there.

Tasha could not take it anymore, not bothering to finish her fun piece. She told Manny to hold on to it for the time being, making sure that Jack heard her when she told them she would be back another weekend to finish it when there was more time. She kept her temper in check as it continued to be stoked by Jack's relentless glare, determined to contain her anger, remaining well-mannered in front of Manny and Jarvis.

However, once outside and walking back downhill, her arms crossed around herself to stem the imminent explosion, she tore into him the moment he demanded from her why there was no note in the cabin or why she was not answering her phone.

She stopped, forcing him to come about. "First of all, I am not your child, nor your wife!" Unraveling her arms from her body, she told him, "I do not answer to you when I am off from work! So stop treating me like I am some delinquent!"

"I was just concerned that something may have happened to you!" he said, indicating with a general sweep of his long muscular arm in just the Henley shirt and sleeveless hunting vest he wore in the cold damp weather. He put his hands on his hips. "Christ, Tasha, it's just common sense and courtesy."

"I don't see you doing this to the other guys in our crew. Why me?"

He sighed heavily. "For one, you are a girl."

She scoffed. "...who's twenty-seven years old—"

"But acts like a spoiled teenager!" he interrupted her.

"Seriously? You're going to go there?" she spit back at him.

"Two, there are bears, and no one should be walking on their own."

"Well, Jack, you just did...What makes *you* so special?" She crossed her arms again. "What makes you taste bad to the bears? I certainly haven't seen one yet, besides yourself!"

"You make too much noise for a bear to come near us," he commented under his breath.

"Fine, I'll sing loud the next time I walk alone."

"Tasha!" Combing his hair back with his heavy fingers, he came back up the hill to her.

Tasha took a step back into a fighting stance, raising up her fists defensively.

He stopped short. "Everybody sticks together! Everyone. Each man looks out after his cabinmate, even after work. They're not just friends nor cabinmates... they are expected to be a two-man team even when they're not working. You just can't seem to see that."

Tasha dropped her defensive stance.

Pointing to himself and then to her, he reminded her, "Unfortunately, you are stuck with me and we're mates!"

"Roommates, not mates!" she clarified determinedly under her breath. But she knew he heard her when she marched on by him, taking the lead, adding, "Some cabinmate you are."

The following weekend, after his hunting, Jack found she was hanging out at Nick and Sam's place. That annoyed him even more, especially because she had taken off on her own again, walking further up the hill to the final cabin on their gravel roadway before the fork in the road.

When he phoned her, she snapped without a normal greeting, "What do you want? I left you a note as to where I could be found."

"You sound different." He had been unable to put his finger on it, until he realized that she sounded drunk and made a comment on it.

"Oh, how am I supposed to sound like?" she retorted.

Jack then heard in the background Nick's gruff remark of "…submissive, Tash. That's what he wants." Some laughter and some sort of noise.

He hung up on her.

Tasha looked at her phone, unsure if she had lost her signal but not caring to call back, as Sam said to her, "Give it five minutes," laying down his royal flush.

"No way! Dang, who shuffled this deck?" swore Nick.

"Give what five minutes?" she asked, still confused over Sam's comment, watching him get up for another beer. Tasha dropped her hand on the table, face up. Nick grabbed all the loose cards, arranging them before shuffling them again, having Tasha cut the deck several times before dealing the next round.

The familiar pounding on the cabin door was her answer, as Sam pointed at the door as if just finishing the drumroll, smirking a knowing smile as he took his seat again.

"What the—" escaped her as she stood up indignantly, stamping her foot in frustration. "Just what is *his issue*?"

Both Nick and Sam snorted in amusement.

Nick kept dealing. "Tash, you have him fit to be tied. He doesn't like his women running around loose."

Sam beckoned for her to go let Jack in. Tasha gave him a look of *what if I don't want to let him in?* making them both smile broadly at her.

"I am definitely *NOT* his woman, Nick!" she scoffed at them as she marched over to open the door.

No surprise there. It was Jack. In the flesh.

"Damn, you're fast. Too bad you're not the pizza boy," she said spat venomously, leaving him standing in the doorway for him to close the door. Only he managed to grab ahold of her upper arm and sniff her.

She backed away from him, aghast.

"You're drunk," he stated flatly, and then looked over to both Sam and Nick disapprovingly.

"What?" she questioned, trying to free herself from his grip. "I'm definitely not drunk! Buzzing...possibly." She held up a finger at him, making her point. It was the truth, the evidence on the countertop.

He reluctantly let go, and she rubbed her arm where he had grabbed ahold of her. She turned to walk back to her seat at the kitchen island where they were playing cards, to resume her spot. She tossed over her shoulder, "Since when did you become an AA sponsor?" She arranged her hand. "It would take one to know one."

He was livid. He overlooked her last statement. Tasha could feel Jack's eyes bore into her back side.

"Come on, Jack. Join us for a round of poker," offered Nick. "Sam, go grab him a cold one. I think he's feeling left out."

"No thanks." He motioned for Sam to remain seated. "Come on, Tasha. You've had enough."

She defied him, taking the last sip of her wine cooler.

Sam laid his hand down before anyone could draw again: a straight. Nick threw in his cards, unable to beat that, with Tasha following in disgust, biting her lip to remind her to maintain her manners in front of her hosts.

"Fine, it's just as well," she said, getting up to discard her one bottle in their trash. "Sam keeps beating us repeatedly."

"Aw, now, being a sore loser is not a reason to leave, Tasha," Nick told her.

Sam gave her a knowing smile.

"No...not a sore loser," she said, thumbing back over her shoulder at her annoyance. "According to my AA counselor, drinking one wine cooler constitutes me as an alcoholic in his book." She shrugged on her coat. "And Lord only knows what you two would do to me with just a second bottle."

"Maybe all hell would break loose?" teased Nick.

"Nah, hell will be breaking loose as soon as we go outside. At least the three of us amigos would have had fun the rest of the night hanging out," Tasha growled out through her teeth.

"You mean..." Nick, the ever-eager beaver, only got himself a stern warning look from Jack not to go any further.

Tasha rolled her eyes at both men. Sam took a long draw on his beer, knowing better not to offer her a ride home. The bear had come to stake his claim.

Tasha smiled weakly, giving them a simple wave. "Thanks for the fun of just hanging out."

"Sure thing, Tasha," came Sam, with Nick toasting a 'good luck' to her, then, adding "Hey Jack," making him pause as she went past him, going outside. "You need backup for when she kicks your ass?"

Jack just closed the door on them, catching up with her in the darkness.

Once they had made it into their cabin, she put away her coat and went directly to her room, shutting the door. Her silence was worse than their bickering. There was not going to be any dinner made that night.

Tasha was quickly finding out that she was a solar-powered human, as her normal perkiness subsided into a blasé attitude. As the weeks flew by, sunlight became a premium. It became tougher for Tasha to get up and walk to work in the mornings. The cold rains came more frequently, often sleet or wet snow, usually covering the ground but melting as soon as the sun was up long enough. As the daylight diminished, her 'cheerfulness' diminished.

Jack had noted her 'spunk' missing. She looked like a lost child in the passenger seat of his truck. But he attributed it to the long hours she had been flying recently. She was as tired as he had become, going through the motions of the day. He noted her sleeping longer. Frequently, she was asleep long before he came up from the basement office around nine in the evening.

Drake had long ago abandoned his doggie bed for hers, keeping her company through the nights. Often, he would caress Drake's head, telling him he was a good boy, amused at Drake for being a giant teddy bear within her tightly wrapped arms. Next, he would pull Tasha's cell phone out of her one hand or bedding to plug the phone into her charging cord on the nightstand. Last, he would pull the thick comforter up over her sleeping form, tucking her in before he found his own bed.

He was unable to stop taking care of her since Nate had first asked him to. Those last few weeks, so he thought, had been comfortable, each of them with their own routine after work, her being the 'compliant housewife' for the most part. He was moderately content, although longing for more with her. But he realized that she was not entirely happy either, and not just because of him getting on her nerves.

It had been nearly a month of flying for her. Their work hours increased as they raced against the incoming winter weather where many days would be too inclement to fly in, even in IFR conditions. Nate preferred their guys to be flying on clear visual days due to the mountain ranges they flew between and the open seas to the nearby islands. Doing that greatly lowered any unnecessary risks regarding equipment, cargo, aircraft, or loss of life.

By December through the end of March, there would be fewer flights unless there was an emergency. Snowfall would be heavier, and most airbases would be closed for the season. Only a few airports had the ability to clear and deice the runways around the clock.

Black Raven only had pontoons and skis to convert the landing gears of two of their landplanes, the Beaver and the Otter, unless Lucy, the Turbo prop Cessna

280 already docked in the harbor nearby, was included. Being the smaller of the main cargo hauling fleet, they were often used to get into and out of the smaller, unimproved airports during winter weather.

Changing Tasha's flight schedule and aircraft did not seem to lift her spirits either. It was not like she was unhappy about not flying with Sam or assisting Jarvis or Manny with their runs on a different model aircraft. Tasha was a fast learner and definitely pulled her weight when it came to working with the crew; Jack had no issues there. However, he was concerned with her withdrawal from them. At times, Jack knew he was harsh with her for socializing with the guys, but it was for her own good that he kept reminding his men to mind themselves; he wanted to protect her. *But did I go too far with the discipline and expectations?* he wondered.

Tasha was a fading bloom changing with the seasons. Catching her in the hallway on her way to the battery shop, he decided to step in after remaining distant from her the past few days. Thankfully, most of the guys were either in the air or just leaving for the day. It would be just the two of them.

Jack needed to see if she was one of those people who was affected by seasonal affective disorder. If she was, Alaska's winter nights were going to make her suicidal before it was over. At best, she would be sorely depressed and listless. He did not want to see her go down that path…not so early in the season. Winter had not even officially begun.

"Come with me," Jack ordered.

"Why?" she asked rather suspiciously, although without her normal disposition of extreme caution. "Where are we going?"

"Let's just say I have something different planned than just taking you out to a bar tonight."

Sighing heavily, Tasha said, "It's been a long day. I really have no desire to go to the bar, or anywhere else, for that matter. I just want to go home and fall into bed." She rubbed the back of her neck to wake herself up, waiting for him to move, or at least lead the way to his truck outside the hangar.

She found him standing there staring at her, his face expressionless. She held his eyes, determining if she could push him to just take her home. It would be dark within a few minutes.

Jack tilted his head in the direction to follow him. Tasha acquiesced begrudgingly, following him down the hall past her battery shop and the offices to a small room that had never been opened or shown to her since her arrival.

Jack took a key out of his pocket, inserting it into the knob, turning it, and gesturing for her to go into the dim room first as he switched the lights on, closing the door behind them. At first, Tasha didn't understand what the room was for. The room that had two long cylindrical objects, with two chairs and two side tables. Objects that look like long aircraft engine shipping containers. But what came next was a complete surprise when Jack told her to "strip."

"What!" she exclaimed. She turned, giving him a confused look.

"What's the matter? You've never seen tanning booths?" he asked.

"No," she told him.

Being from Florida, she never had any use for indoor tanning salons. "Why are we doing this?" she asked. "Why are they even here, of all places?"

"Let's just say Nate and Nora take care of their employees very well. Nora had found a tanning salon that was going out of business and was selling their equipment for heavily discounted prices. She thought they would help all of us combat our 'winter blahs' should we need to seek 'more daylight,'" he told her flatly, then added, adamantly, "and you, lately, are quite depressed."

"Depressed? I'm just tired," she said defensively. "I've been flying all day for the past three weeks, four days a week, Jack."

"Well fine," he said, putting down his clipboard with the day's paperwork on a table near the door. "You can get some sleep for the next twenty minutes and I'll catch some z's in the other tanning booth."

"What about the others? The strange looks that you and I are sharing a tanning room together."

"Most of the guys are gone for the day…and Raven knows about me checking out the tanning room key." Jack shrugged his flannel shirt off, exposing his white undershirt.

Jack explained that everyone had access to the room whenever they needed it, but that they had to check out the key from either Nate or Nora and return it the next day. "So get going, Tasha. Strip and get in the bed so that I can set the timer and get you started."

"Can I get a little privacy here?" she asked as she watched him kick off his boots.

"If I go and stand outside the room, it is going to look obvious to anyone who does happen by, so hurry up and undress. It's not like I haven't seen you before in all your glory," he antagonized her, playing on her concerns, and smirked at her before turning around and giving her some privacy.

"This can constitute for sexual harassment, you know."

"I haven't made a pass at you and I am not asking you for sexual favors," he told her, still facing the wall.

"I believe you are asking for a strip tea—"

"I'm taking care of a depressed employee," he reminded her.

"What…No! I'm not!" she insisted.

He sighed. "No one needs nine to twelve hours of sleep, Tasha! Nor do they sit aimlessly for hours in a chair, staring out into space."

"Maybe that's because part of that sleep is beauty rest!" she tersely defended herself.

He snorted a half laugh at her.

"Nor am I a speed reader," she added.

"What was the last book you just read?"

"It was…it was…" She was not entirely sure what the last book was. *Or was it a magazine?* But he was right. Her days had turned into one big weekday, after weeks of nothing but work and then home. It wasn't like she could go anywhere when he disappeared on most weekends with Chad on their outdoor excursions. Jack made certain of that each time he dragged her away from any social life.

"It's either this or I take you down to a psychologist and get you some light therapy, which is way more expensive than what Nate and Nora can provide, and these tanning booths work just as well. It's your choice. You know as well as I do that once you go see a psychologist you're temporarily banned from flying."

He turned his head slightly, asking, "Are you done with undressing yet?"

Tasha pressed her lips in annoyance. She was tired of being verbally held hostage. It was Jack's favorite technique, as far as she was concerned, for getting her to do what he needed her to do.

"No! I haven't even begun. But fine! Have it your way." She yanked up on her sweater, pulling it over her head, and then tossed it to the ground beside her. *Two can play at this game*, she thought. She took her time stripping down, hoping that it would torture him. It must have. Still half dressed, Jack quickly moved past her to open the tanning bed's top for her and setting the timer. Tasha smiled to herself when she was certain he didn't see her face. She turned to face him in her birthday suit, waiting. Jack's eyes glanced appreciatively over her as he gave her the protective eye goggles and she climbed into the booth. Tasha put them on once she lay down on the cold bed, her nipples becoming erect from the cold surface and room's cool air.

"You have thirty minutes. Do get a nap if you feel you need it. I don't need to be giving your fair skin a sunburn and having folks up here mistaking you for a lobster." He grinned, pushing the cover down, the UV lights coming on.

It was extremely bright, even with her goggles on. She closed her eyes and did as she was told, surprised at how fast the bed heated up inside. Sighing contentedly, she could literally feel her body melt into the bed, sucking up as much warmth as she could, her achy muscles cheering in delight, her skin drinking in the heavenly light.

She heard Jack's muffled sounds of undressing the rest of the way and getting into his own booth as she remained lying inside the bright, humming, warm cocoon. The experience lulled her to sleep. Tasha nearly sobbed when the lights suddenly switched off, the warmth quickly dispersing. She pushed up on the top, getting up and noting that Jack's bed was still on, having noted his timer still had another five more minutes. She quickly donned her clothes, noting the new redness of her skin, elated with the aftereffects of feeling more focused after weeks of utter numbness.

She had just finished lacing her boots when his lights went off and he pushed up on the lid of his bed. She had a mere second or so to appreciate his entire body in its natural state, lying there on the bed, as he pulled his goggles off, rubbing his eyes and getting them to adjust to the lower light.

Tasha quickly averted her eyes. The last thing she needed to do was encourage him. It was bad enough she still found her eyes betraying her as they followed him whenever he wandered into any room. She had done her best to act uninterested, placing him on the same field as the rest of the crew. However, she found that impossible; he stuck out like a sore thumb compared to the rest of them. It was like his commanding presence created a vacuum in the space he occupied, nulling everything around him.

She let him speak first, finally looking up at him, lifting her face up from where she had let it settle on her upturned hands where she sat studying the floor. He had just put on his long-sleeved undershirt. He smirked at her when her gaze ended at his family jewels, since he hadn't bothered to cover them first, then closing her eyes in admonishment.

"So?" He tilted his head at her. "You feel any better?" He looked over to her from his viewpoint, determining if she may have gotten too much light.

She nodded, giving him a slight smile, her skin flushed from the heat. He would be able to determine more, after their supper, if it had been the right amount of light for her.

Jack reached for the rest of his clothes. As he sorted through them, he instructed her to take the spray bottle that was next to her bed and spray down the entire inside of the bed and wipe it down with one of the folded towels on the coffee table that resided between the two large beds and two chairs.

When she finished, he took the sprayer and the towel from her to do his own bed. He was still partially undressed, wearing just a pair of jeans and undershirt. She immediately chastised herself for being physically deprived of nature's most basic drive.

Jack turned back to her where she remained seated in the small room, now finished with wiping down his bed. She waited on him, stealing side glances at his broad muscular chest outlined by the thin material of his shirt as he dressed. She swore he took his time giving her the 'eye candy' view, too, as she studied him bent over in his chair lacing up his work boots. She did her best to act unimpressed, but knew she was a horrible liar.

"Come on, let's get some supper," Jack said, picking up the spent towel to take with them. "Where would you like to eat?"

She raised an eyebrow in surprise. First, because he was giving her the night off from cooking. Secondly, he was asking her where *she* wanted to eat.

"Chinese?" she asked, needing something really different to add to this new 'light tanning therapy' session. She did not want what little spark that had come back to be snuffed out so quickly. And thus, Tasha accepted his offer.

The dull evening that she had originally planned on turned out to be much nicer than expected, although their uneventful discussion steered to safer topics, like their flight duties.

They had returned to their cabin, getting everything ready for the following workday before settling in for the night, neither of them speaking while they went through the automated motions. It was only after she made herself a cup of hot cocoa, taking it to her room, when she stopped at her doorway, that she looked back at Jack sitting on the sofa with Drake next to him as he stared into the small fire he had whipped up.

Something must have made him note her standing there, though he didn't turn his head in her direction when he asked if she needed something. Tasha wanted to say more but knew better, not wanting to fill his head with any ideas, making it more than it was: two roomies/co-workers going out for a relaxing evening. Part of her wished for more. Instead, she simply said, "Thank you...for the night off from cooking and most of all for letting me know there is a place to 'suck in more sunlight.' You were right about me needing sunlight."

He didn't respond. He knew it to be sincere and for just what it was. Yet he swore there was more to her quiet 'thank you.' It was suggestively seductive. He had to get a grip on himself and thus remained facing the fireplace, bracing himself against her charms should he have seen her sweet face and shimmering blonde hair in the fire's light—not after the afternoon's earlier delight in seeing her in the nude.

She added, "It was greatly needed. Goodnight, Jack." Then she closed her bedroom door.

It was the only time that he looked back over his shoulder to the place she had been standing.

CHAPTER TWELVE

The big three-day weekend arrived, and their boss had the crew meet up at the bar early Thursday evening to celebrate Veterans Day. He insisted Jack and Tasha, his two combat vets, take off some time for their country's service. She was far from looking forward to the weekend, but kept an open mind to being somewhere other than their cabin.

Besides, being with Chad was rather nice, given his disposition. She hoped Chad and his family would be the respite she needed from Jack's overbearing presence.

Nate's tapping of his beer bottle for his toast brought her out of her thoughts.

"Next, I want, as an American, to express my heartfelt thanks to both our soldiers here"—he waved a hand to get Tasha and Jack to stand closer, yet separating them from the rest of the crew—"for standing up to bat for our country whether any of us wanted them to or not…protecting our country's interest and her people. You both have—literally, in your case, Tasha—taken a bullet for us." The crew laughed some, and he beamed at them both, saying, "Once a soldier, always a soldier!"

They both instinctively "hurrahed" to Nate, who toasted them a "Carry On!" The guys clinked their beers with each other and with them before disseminating for a round of pool or darts or just lounging at the table watching football games on various televisions located around the bar's walls.

Hank wanted a round of darts with Jack. Sam and Nick pulled at Tasha to go play a round of pool with them. Jarvis and Manny talked to Mr. and Mrs. Amsel while catching the latest sport plays from the nearest television. The night passed as the beers took their hold. Tasha spent the night 'learning' more about pool while she studied how each of her co-workers played.

Sporadically, she would spy Jack from the corner of her eye when her turn caused her to face the direction of the dartboard area, Hank and Jack deep in conversation, although she suspected that Hank did the talking. She smiled at the thought as she sunk two balls with one shot. Sam and Nick looked at each other, saying "beginner's luck."

Not quite, she thought, reminding herself to play the game like a newbie. Jarvis and Manny joined them when Nate and Nora said their goodbyes for the evening, paying their crew's tab. She quickly ran over to thank them for the night and for the celebratory IFR and flight physical lunch, only to find out that the lunch was from Jack.

"Oh?"

"Well, he's proud of you. He treats everyone whenever they do an exceptional job or pass a milestone. Only a few weeks ago, he took Jarvis out to lunch for passing his Airframe and Powerplant test," came Nora. "He's carrying on the Raven's tradition. But thanks for letting me know so that I can get Jack reimbursed next month."

Nora pulled at her to give her a quick kiss on her cheek and a goodbye hug. She took her husband's arm and smiled at Tasha, telling her to be good and "do beat the pants off the guys at pool."

Tasha winked back at her.

It was hard not to laugh for that was what she intended to do much later.

Nate waved back at her and to anyone who had noticed their departure. She returned to the pool table to find Jack was giving them a thumbs-up. He was back to taking the reins over all of them. It was about an hour later that Jack joined them when Hank's wife came to pick him up.

Sam and Nick smiled when Jack came over. Nick asked, "Feel up to a few rounds of pool with us?" He was chalking the end of his stick. "Winning team takes all?"

"Up to five dollars from each of us," Jack said, accepting the challenge. "Let's keep this civil and not break anyone." He looked back at her and she knew he was talking about her financial situation.

"Good enough for me," Sam answered. "It'll give us gas money for the month," he remarked as he elbowed Nick. "Easy money. Whadda say, Nick?" Then to Tasha, clicking his tongue, smiling to her: "Sorry darling. I'm a desperate soul."

They teamed up by cabinmates, each of them laying five dollars down: Sam and Nick against Jarvis and Manny. She and Jack would be up next. Of course, the playboys won the first round. Then, Tasha and Jack played Jarvis and Manny. Jack turned out to be an excellent pool player. Obviously, he was military trained in the second profession as a pool hustler. She let him take the lead for their team, but she worked up to being better as they went. By the time it was their turn against Nick and Sam, she was ready to scoop up the cash. She let herself loose. In less than two turns, Jack and she had placed all their balls where they called them. Sam and Nick looked at each other. Sam blamed Nick. "You taught her too well."

"What? No man! No way."

Then they looked at each other again, as both realized they had been hustled.

Jarvis and Emanuel had a mini bet going, as Jarvis paid Manny out. Tasha hopped gleefully, high-fiving Jack, then bounced over to Nick and Sam, giving them a quick kiss on each of their cheeks, and then ran over to Jack as he scooped up their cash reward.

"That is so wrong." Sam sulkily stood there shaking his head.

"Tell me about it," Jarvis said as he watched Manny counting the singles in his hand.

"Well, Tasha, we better call it quits before we have to defend ourselves against these guys." Jack grinned at her.

"How did you know, Jack?" Nick asked.

Jack looked at his crew. "Never assume what a gal, especially a military one, can or cannot do. One of the many things that the military teaches us is how to play an exceptional round of pool during our off hours. Obviously, the Army teaches them just as well."

Emanuel muttered something in Spanish, clicking his tongue.

Tasha smiled. "You better share some of that fresh guacamole when you do make it."

"Goodnight, guys. Have a safe weekend and see you all on Monday." Jack gave her the crook of his elbow and she delightfully accepted it, after she blew them all a kiss. Jack laughed. "Let's get packing."

Once in the truck and back on the road, Jack told her, "Glad you enjoyed yourself back there."

She grinned cheekily at him, the alcohol swimming in her blood along with the giddiness from winning. "I *did* have fun. Thank you. That was a *very* nice change after these last few weeks."

"Well, get some sleep tonight. We'll pack in the morning for the trip."

"Are we staying the entire weekend?"

"Pack for two nights, just in case of weather issues. I only intend to stay the one night and then drive back late on Saturday night."

"Okay," she accepted as they pulled up to their cabin. Tasha got out to unlock the cabin door as he shut down the truck for the night. Drake bounded out, not bothering to greet them, having had to wait an additional two hours for them to get home.

"Who's going to look after Drake? Or is he coming with us?" she asked, taking off her coat and putting it in the coat closet.

"We are going to drop him off with Nate first thing in the morning." He came around her, Drake fast behind him as he walked over to the kitchen to give him a fresh bowl of water for the night and a doggie treat from the pantry.

"Well, Jack, did you get a chance to relax?"

"I did, but my bed is calling." He rolled his head around, stretching the tension free from his neck. Then, he yawned. "I want more than eight hours of sleep this time."

Tasha had been watching him, although he seemed lost in his thoughts or the beer buzz had a hold of him. Her face was still flushed from the cold air and from drinking.

"Get some sleep. I'll wake you."

She turned for her room, but only made it to the door when he called out to her again.

"Before I forget…" He came over and handed her all the cash and then turned for his room.

"Wait…don't you want your cut?"

"Nah, I betted against you at first. Just keep it. Put it toward that car battery fund of yours." He smirked. "Better yet, get us food to make more of those grand meals you've been putting together. I've been enjoying them," he said, adding, "but buy more meat, will ya?"

She sighed disgustedly at him. "Goodnight, Jack," she said dryly, closing her door.

CHAPTER THIRTEEN

The next morning, they were on their way after dropping Drake off at the hangar. She remained in the truck as he delivered his four-legged baby into the crew's capable hands. He was not long before hopping back in, rubbing his bare hands from the cold morning air, then putting the truck into drive.

Chad lived near Lowell Point. The small village was a few miles south of Seward. The coast road was just as pleasant as the Seward Highway. Tasha was never going to tire of the scenery. She could barely wait until the spring and summer months arrived so she could check out the hiking trails and rent a bike just to go explore more of the town and local parks.

She had found her piece of heaven even though Mr. Right did not live there—only Mr. Wrong. Wrong in that he was her boss. *What is my 'thing' with men who lead or are a superior?* she asked herself. Wrong in that he was a man who loved to do nothing but hunt and fish and grunt like a caveman on his good days. She loved his physique and the stereotypical look that went with his love of the outdoors minus the heavy, unkempt look of his beard and long hair when she had first met him. Thankfully, the beard had remained tamed after their excursion up to Anchorage. He wasn't so fierce looking as she noted his prominent Adam's apple moving just under his bearded chin. He had a wonderful profile, one that she could easily love. In fact…did. She had made love to him several times and enjoyed every minute of it. Her body awakened at the thought. She smiled to herself though she sighed heavily. She chided and told herself to stay away from the 'boss.' She looked at him periodically by pretending to be interested in the views on his side of the truck which was the bay view.

She was still trying to come to terms with his need for killing things, though she was not averse to eating meat from the kill. She just had no desire to kill, nor 'dress' the kill. She was grateful he had never brought anything home—yet. Just the thought made her stomach roll. It wasn't like he was doing it for trophies to line the cabin walls, but his ability to do so would let him survive and anyone else he decided to help along the way.

Jack was wrong for her in that she loved men who were usually more sociable and more along the lines of being a funny man—something he was not. 'Seriously driven' would be her description of him. He was an island unto himself who enjoyed hours of solitude. She, on the other hand, would have gone nuts after about three days…unless she got entirely caught up in a terrific novel. She loved music; he loved silence. He was sure about everything; she was doubtful of everything. So many differences between them.

Eventually, they pulled into the small community where they found a few men outside their homes working on various things from snowmobiles, cars, and boat engines to what looked like fish drying on racks. Jack parked the truck at one of the last homes along the coastline. The snow still hugged the ground the further one traveled the length of the peninsula. This community had gotten more of the snow from the last storm. Seward had been sheltered by the mountains and the warmer waters.

"We're here." He left the engine running, turning to her. "I need to say a couple of things before we go in. First, you will want to share the same bed with me."

Her mouth dropped at his audacity, and she blinked at him several times.

"Please don't argue with me on this. It is just for the weekend here and for reasons I'll explain later." His eyes caught Chad peeking out the window at them and he knew he had less than a minute to ask for the second thing. He switched the truck engine off.

"Secondly, whatever you do...do not eat the brownies his mother makes."

Chad came bounding out the door and hurried over to Tasha's side.

"What? Why on earth—"

Chad opened her door.

"Hey, you two...come on in!" He helped her out of the truck like an eager young boy trying to be a gentleman. "Are your bags in the back?" he asked.

She nodded.

"I got them, Chad. Take Tasha up into the house and get her introduced to everyone."

Chad propelled her up the stairs to his family's home. Once inside, she was surprised at how warm they kept the house; a roaring fire was going in the central standalone fireplace and the oven was doing its part in keeping the house warm by the smell of fresh baking, heavenly scents seductively enticing her tummy into growling its anticipation. Herbs hung upside down, tied in bundles, along the lower rafters of the back-kitchen area. Chad's home, more like his parents' home, was much larger, triple in size, compared to their cabin. But the arrangement of the living space was near the same. The kitchen and the living room made up the main room, with bedrooms lining either side off the main room. The master bedroom and bath were on the bay side of the home. Chad's room was on the front or road side of the house, just off to their right as they came in the front door through the enclosed porch area. The third room and hall bathroom were located on the bay side, to the far right of the master bedroom.

However, the house was packed—literally packed full of their furnishings and handmade décor from years of living there. There were more than three people living there; it turned out that Chad, his sister, and his parents all live in the house together. However, Chad's younger sister, Tiri, was currently living in Anchorage, attending college, so her room had been turned into the office and storage room for all the dogsledding equipment.

"Mom," Chad called to one of the women in the kitchen. "Dad," he yelled louder, toward the back of the house. "I'd like you to meet our newest Seward resident, Miss Tasha Lazar. She works with Jack out at the airport."

The mature, stocky woman at the sink washing cabbages was near her height and had hair as dark as Chad's, but she did not look as native as Chad or the older man that had just come from one of the exterior rooms. Chad's easy smile came from his mother, and the same humorous merriment was seen in her dark eyes. She nodded and greeted Tasha warmly, but continued to finish what she was working on. Chad's mother's eyes lit up more when Jack came in just behind them with their bags, dropping them to the floor by the front door.

The older man was distinctively native in terms of his flatter, wider face and his stockier build. His thick straight black hair had large streaks of white on the sides of his temples. He wore the traditional garb and lots of handmade strand jewelry. Chad, standing an easy head taller, took more of his features from his father's side. Tasha found her hand enveloped in the thick, square, heavily calloused hands of his father's as he greeted her in their native language.

"You're definitely Russian descent, with that blonde hair and very fair skin of yours," he stated more than a question.

She tilted her head at him, letting him know he was correct with her smile.

"You mean the surname Lazar wasn't a dead giveaway, Malik?" Jack jested as he grabbed a firm hold of the elder's elbow in a very masculine arm-to-arm handshake, and then pulled him closer to hug the older man. It was obvious that this man and his family meant the world to Jack.

"It's good to see ya, son. Still as tall and as thick as a pine tree. Glad to see you tamed that grizzly inside you," he said, pulling at his own chin, indicating Jack's trimmed look.

"Yeah, had to get it cut because I encountered a wildcat one night and it took half my beard off, making it uneven. And then I didn't like how I trimmed it to even it out...so I had to have it professionally trimmed more."

Malik's thick dark eyebrows popped up in surprise.

"Well," Chad's mother said, putting up the dish towel before coming over to him, her height becoming even more diminutive as she hugged him, "I think it made him even more handsome. It's about time you got yourself cleaned up. You would have scared off your prey before you even got a chance to shoot it. You all should have a decent hunting weekend." She placed both hands on either side of his large face, grasping his beard and pulling him down to kiss him on his cheek, beaming at him as if she were actually his mother. "You're looking well since the last time I saw you," she told him, patting his gut.

She finally turned to Tasha. "Welcome, dear, it's finally nice to meet you. Chad spoke about you a few times. He wasn't lying when he said that you are as beautiful as well as smart. You work on aircraft? As a mechanic?"

"No, I'm an electrician."

"Can you fly?"

"Yes, I do, but I don't have all the type ratings necessary to fly all the aircrafts they have. But with any luck, I hope to finish within a few more months." She smiled back at Chad's mother, whose smile was just as infectious as Chad's.

Chad's mother reached out to stroke her hair. "So fine and soft," she murmured. "I bet you have the entire flight line boys in an uproar since you arrived."

"You're quite right about that, Ula. It's been nonstop," commented Jack.

"What? Only in your mind," Tasha retorted. "Don't believe him."

"And what about last night?" Jack retorted.

"Okay, okay...so I hustled them."

Ula and Chad gave her the look to continue. She told them about their game of pool with their fellow co-workers. "I didn't break anyone. Spoilsport next to me kept the bets at five dollars max from each of them so it wasn't like I was going to be able to pay next month's rent with the winnings!"

"So...you have at least gas money to get the hell out of Dodge when the next sucker finds out he's been hustled?" joked Chad.

"No, I have 'Griswald' here to take care of any unforeseen roughness or ill-tempered folks." She jabbed a thumb at Jack.

"'Griswald?'" came Malik, chuckling.

"Oooh, I love it! That sooo fits you, Jack!" Chad clapped his hands in glee, laughing at his friend's nickname.

Jack gave him a *drop dead* look.

"It's a good name for his spirit animal," said Ula, smiling up at him, patting the side of his face again.

"Spirit animal?" Tasha questioned Jack, hoping he would inform her more but knowing better, since he only gave information on a need-to-know basis.

"You can't see it?" Ula asked Tasha.

"The only animal that fits him would be a grumpy bear," retorted Tasha.

"Is he *really* that grumpy?"

"Okay, cougar," Jack interrupted Tasha before she could continue. "Let's see where they would like to put us for the weekend...Ula?"

Chad and his father both eyed each other, the two of them putting two and two together when it came to Jack's new beard length. Tasha caught Chad's shoulders shaking in silent mirth as Ula led them to Chad's front room.

"I'll put you two in here," she said as she led them to his room.

Jack had his hand on the small of her back guiding her forward, the pressure increasing as she began to balk at having to share a bed with him.

"Ah...I...you see...Jack and I...aren't..." she stuttered, pointing back and forth between herself and Jack.

He pushed her enough so that only she felt it, trying to get her to stop.

"We're just roomies!" she said, for lack of a better description, as she looked back at him, her expression confused as to why it was so important to have her share his bed again.

"Oh!" said Ula, a bit eager and louder than normal.

Jack's face became set and unreadable as Tasha momentarily glanced at Chad, to find him putting a hand on his face and looking through his fingers at her. Her brow furrowed more, as she did not understand anything that was going on. The look on Malik's face became hopeful as he looked at his son.

"I didn't realize that! Sure, we can pull the sofa out into a bed for you," she said, pointing to a sofa at the far side of the great room.

"Thank you. The guys will probably get up earlier than me if they are going to go out hunting. I'd like to sleep in if that's okay with you all?"

"That's fine, dear." Ula smiled at her.

"Tasha, take the room and I will sleep out on the sofa." Jack quickly offered.

"Oh, she'll be fine, Jack," Ula happily encouraged. "You'll need your rest for the big day tomorrow! Stay in Chad's room."

Jack pressed his lips together tightly, the only sign Tasha knew when he was 'fit to be tied' on something.

What's the big deal? she wondered.

After depositing their bags in Chad's room, they all returned to the kitchen where the timer was going off on the oven and the other woman that Tasha had yet to be introduced to was pulling out two pies. They smelled delightful as she set them out on the racks on the kitchen island to cool.

"Two gooseberry pies just for you, Jack," said the woman in a gorgeous blue sweater that offset her lovely, thick, raven-black locks of hair.

"I can't wait. Nuka and you do make the best," Jack told Ula.

"When I told them you were coming, those two women immediately went to raiding everyone's cache of gooseberries yesterday," Chad said. "Oh, by the way, Tasha, please meet one of my aunts. Aunt Nuka is staying with us for the week while the tribal council meets. She is my father's sister."

"I'm pleased to meet you, and to see Jack again." Nuka smiled brightly at him. "After we finish doing our part in the feast, I hope we can spend more time chatting."

For only Chad to hear, although he knew Tasha heard him, Jack asked, "This isn't the aunt you talked about earlier?"

"Hunh?" Chad looked at Jack, then remembered, forgetting to keep his voice low, "Ah no, that would be Aunt Sylvia."

"Aunt Sylvia? Now why would he want to know of Aunt Sylvia?" asked his father Malik. "That woman's crazy!"

"She's not crazy! You only drove her to it, you ol' goat," retorted Ula defensively. "You didn't do a good job of keeping her happy."

"Who's Aunt Sylvia?" Tasha asked.

"Ah, someone you will eventually meet if you stay here long enough in Seward," Malik told Tasha.

"Someone you don't need to meet, nor take further lessons in the art of knife wielding," came Chad.

"Some crazy female family member," Jack said.

Tasha looked at all the men as they answered at the same time.

"Listen, she's a wonderful strong woman," Ula said, pulling on Tasha's elbow toward the female side of the home, "who won't take shit from any man. Don't let the guys tell you differently."

She looked back at all three men as they cowered together, that was…if you could call Jack's stance *cowering*, with Chad on one side, his father on the other.

She mouthed *okay*.

Ula indicated for Tasha to take a seat at the kitchen island while she returned to the prep station to insert another dish into the oven. Aunt Nuka just smiled.

The chatter was light as everyone caught up on all the news, how the downtime remodeling work at the resort his folks ran was going, the weather and its effect on the animals' movement for their hunting weekend. The ladies talked about the massive crab bake that was to occur Saturday night for the community event. Eventually Ula chased the men off to let them target practice for about two hours before their late lunch.

"Hey, I'd like to get you a few practice shots in while we are here," Jack told Tasha, "but stay in here with the ladies and keep warm for now."

"Do you hunt, Tasha?" Nuka asked.

"Ah, no…no I don't," she replied.

Nuka looked quizzically at her and then to Jack.

"I'd just like her to get familiar with using a handgun, especially the ones we take with us on our planes."

"Whoa! Wait. We take guns on planes?" she exclaimed, pushing her stool around some at the island to look back at Jack to see if he was joking.

"Yes, all Alaskan aircraft have to have guns on board. They are part of our emergency kits and supply rations," Jack told her before turning to go back outside with the other men. This she didn't know, and had somehow managed to miss it in her everyday work. But then, she was not allowed to hang out with her fellow crew members much, when it came to Jack being overbearing in her work life.

She turned back around to the ladies. "Well, that's news to me," she said to herself.

"There's a lot of things we do differently up here in the North," Ula said.

Jack called back into the house, "Meet us outside in about thirty," adding, "And make yourself useful. Ula, Tasha's a good cook. Teach her a few more things—especially how to make your gooseberry pie!" He winked at Ula.

Tasha's jaw dropped at his comment.

"I'm not sure I want to teach you that recipe," Ula complained, a hand on her hip. "He'll never come back." She winked at Tasha. "Well, then, help us make the stuffing we need for the feast tomorrow evening."

The two ladies were definitely endearing to listen to as they talked girl talk and agreed on how bad 'the boys' could be at times. Tasha ended up cutting up the peppers and onions as the women tore up a couple loaves of bread to dry in the oven. The aroma of baking was now beyond tantalizing. Her tummy grumbled its desire to seek out whatever it was Ula was baking. It turned out to be a batch of brownies that she was known for in the community. She had cooked up two large pans.

Tasha licked her lips as Ula pulled out the two pans of rich dark chocolate brownies. They were done to perfection, lightly crusty on the top and yet thickly moist when she cut into the pan to make the squares.

"Do you want one, Tasha?" Ula asked.

"You don't have to ask me twice. Brownies are my absolute favorite! My God, they look so good!" She inhaled deeply. "Are you sure…before anyone else gets here?" Tasha asked, her fingers twitching as she held herself back. "I…I can wait, if need be."

"Sure, you can. Help yourself to a few. Lunch is going to be awhile."

Tasha grabbed a napkin and forked out two brownies for herself. They were still extremely hot to the touch, but she did not care. In the Alaskan air, they would be cool before she could even blow on them.

She was just downing the second brownie when Jack came stampeding back into the covered patio. It was only then that she remembered that she was not supposed to eat any brownies, as she swallowed the last large bite—still too hot—before he could catch her.

"Come on, Tasha, grab your coat," he said, looking at her and then tilting his head at her just as she swallowed the evidence. He was just like a bear. He sniffed the air.

Quickly, she jumped into action, hoping not to be caught.

He stared her down, but she chose to ignore his glare as she came over, shrugging on her jacket and gloves, and then putting on her hat.

Once outside, he stopped short, bringing her around to face him. "Spit it out, Tasha!"

"What?!"

"Open your mouth," he demanded.

"Like hell!"

Jack lunged in close to her, his prominent nose sniffing her mouth, then exhaling violently.

"*Can't* you just *do anything* I tell you to do? You just couldn't leave well enough alone, could you?" he snarled.

As far as Tasha was concerned, Jack had no right to tell her what to do on her off time. Secondly, he had no right to tell her what she could and couldn't eat either.

"Just what is your major malfunction, boss?" She yanked her arm from his hand, hoping to misdirect him from her brownie guilt trip. "What'd I do? Bruise your ego because I didn't want to repeat another night in bed with you, especially in front of your close friends?"

"You ate the brownies too," he stated flatly.

She boldly lied…well, somewhat lied: "No! I helped cut them into squares! *You told* me to *help* the ladies and I did, you bloody bastard! So go to hell!" she hissed at him.

Chad had just come around the corner to find them facing off. His timing was always perfect, for she would have thrown a fist at Jack had he not just shown up, saving his buddy's face from being mutilated. She could tell that Jack didn't believe her, from the look he gave her.

"Come on, you two," Chad said, waving at them to follow him around the corner of the house. "Let's get some practice rounds off. Dad's got the targets set up again."

The two of them followed Chad around the house to what seemed to be a side yard or commons area. They would be shooting toward the bay, away from all the other houses and roads. The view was breathtaking, the gray clouds in the distance smoky against the dark mountains with bright white strains of snow and ice flowing finger-like into the bay waters.

The targets were cans or pieces of firewood propped on a couple of stacked logs where trees had fallen long ago along the beach. Malik was already propping a rifle up, sighting his gun. He took a shot and hit a piece of wood cleanly. He did that about four more times at the same log.

Malik nodded at her when he finished. "Jack thinks you need to practice with either piece."

She watched Jack expertly picked up a nine mil, locking the clip into place, and then he handed it to her. It wasn't anything terribly new to her, but it had been a while since she had flown with her unit and carried one. But it was an entirely different thing in that she had not shot one since training. She was more ground crew, and like the rest of the soldiers, they were armed with the usual M16 assault rifles.

He indicated for her to shoot the target. She sighed and did as she was bidden. She clicked the safety back and leveled it on the next target over. She took a single shot at the can, knocking it completely off the log. She took the next target, which was a heavier piece of wood, and fired another round, watching the wood splinter and without another second passing put two more rounds into the same wood in roughly the same spot as the first one.

She looked back at the guys. Chad's mouth dropped as he stood there. His father next to him smiled as he sat on his seat with his rifle propped up against him. Jack…well…Jack was his usual expressionless self, his arms folded across his chest, the only sign of a job well done his approving nod. For the first time since seeing one of his prior military photos, she could see the faint image of a Marine sergeant standing in front of her as if he were overseeing one of his soldier's training.

"Well, Jack, I think she can take care of herself," Chad said as he brought back the piece of wood she had shot into three times. The shots were very tight—less than a half inch apart.

Jack then picked up his rifle that he kept at their cabin as she clicked the nine mil's safety back into place before returning it to him. He took it, giving her the rifle. For only her to hear, he said, "I take it you fired an M16 before?"

She nodded affirmatively.

"This will be similar then."

She lifted the rifle, surprised that it weighed so little. Flipping the safety off, she took aim at the last target and exhaled before firing. She wasn't sure if she had hit the target. It was a high-powered rifle with little kick to it. She looked back at them to find Jack nodding for her to continue. Again, he stood there with his arms folded across his broad chest, and legs shoulder-width apart.

She turned back and sighted the rifle on the target. That time she hit it just right, for it toppled the wood. She sighted the last target and hit it as well, and then went back to the original wood piece that Malik had shot at, knocking it over. She clicked the safety back and discharged the last chambered round.

"Too bad she doesn't hunt. We would never starve with her marksmanship!" Malik said, laughing. "However, I'm glad you would never be my wife. I'd have to sleep with one eye open if I ever pissed you off."

"And to think, she's not even pissed yet," chimed in Chad as he walked to the logs to gather and reset their targets, neither of them aware of what had just transpired in front of their home between Jack and her.

Jack retrieved his rifle, his mood dark. He took the one loose bullet, snapping it back into the clip, expertly sliding the cartridge into place and then slinging the rifle onto his shoulder.

"I take it I didn't pass muster with you?" she asked, crossing her arms. "Am I done here?"

He looked at her, studying her as if deciding on something.

She narrowed her eyes at him, peeved. "You're an ass." She turned to leave them when Chad yelled back at her.

"Hey...wait a minute! Where you going?"

"Back inside and help the ladies where it's a little more productive creating dishes, and I can help myself to a few more brownies!"

Jack had grabbed her arm, his look stern, a deadly warning to her about defying him, but she was having none of it.

"Because standing out here in the cold putting Jack to shame just isn't my thing, and it wastes my precious time when I can be doing something better!" Tasha shrugged her arm out of his grasp and walked off back to the house.

Malik laughed heartily where he still sat. "Oh my, Jack, she's a feisty one. Although I am not sure just what transpired between you two."

"Ah, Jack…does she know that Mom laces the brownies?" Chad quietly asked, now concerned. "You did tell her, didn't you, Jack?"

Jack's look made it apparent he did not.

Chad swept a hand over his thick hair, pulling it tight against his skull. "Aw, crap! And I betcha she's never even touched the stuff before."

"I tried to tell her when you interrupted us, but she didn't listen. The woman is as stubborn as a mule! During our off hours, she thinks I'm telling her what to do just for the hell of it."

"Just tell her she's fat! She'll back off them," suggested Malik, laughing at Jack's frustration.

Chad sighed. "Let me go tell Mom to watch what she serves to her. One shouldn't hurt her. Just don't let her fly for the next forty-eight hours."

"Problem is…I believe she's already had a few," Jack commented.

"What?" Chad was stunned. "How many?" He turned a full 360-degree circle in place. "No way! Not when she shot like that!" he said, putting a fist to his mouth. "Are you certain she was stoned? And you handed her the weapons? Are you out of your mind, Jack?" Chad put his arms out in a helpless motion to him. "I sometimes think you like tempting fate!"

Malik burst into gales of laughter, barely able to speak. "I'd hate to see her fire when she's in her right mind…oh shit!"

"Trust me Dad, you don't. She can be a lot like Aunt Sylvia." He was now worried for Jack.

Chad took off for the house to let his mother know. The last thing he needed was to take care of a drugged newbie that would be high as a kite all night.

With lunch ready, Nuka called for the rest of the guys to come in, as Tasha finished getting all the drinking glasses into place. She ended up setting the table and getting all the main dishes out on the kitchen island, which doubled as their table. Everything looked so good, and still she found herself rather hungry—even after eating three of those perfect brownies beforehand. Being inside the warm home, her humor improved, and for some reason it seemed all her worldly cares had just dissipated. At first she thought she would be miserable when she was told she was going to sit next to grumpy Jack. Yet at this point, she didn't give a damn.

The women were enjoyable to be with as they told her aspects about their lives and what was to occur that weekend in the village with some of the other tribal members. She was looking forward to the storytelling and some of the dances for the hunt. She was not entirely sure about trapping crabs for the following day's activity while the guys were away. It would be something new, and she missed being near the water, playing in it, although it was bitter cold. She still remembered her dunking in the harbor so many weeks ago, and she shivered at the memory.

"Are you all right Tasha?" Jack asked. He had come up behind her, surprising her.

Now why was he so concerned? He seemed different to her for some reason as she looked at him in some confusion.

"Are you cold?"

"No," she told him.

"Then why are you shivering?"

Her response seemed delayed to her and she wondered if he had noticed it. "Just remembering how cold that water was, and the ladies want to take me to the docks for hauling up crabs tomorrow. Not entirely sure if it's worth being cold and wet for a slobbery piece of mollusk."

He smirked.

Why is he laughing at her? It was a serious concern to her. That water was... cold!

"Jack...here...sit with her," encouraged Ula, interrupting their conversation—if it could be called that. "Chad!"

"I'm coming, I'm at her other side, I know, I know," Chad told his mother.

She found herself swept up between the two men and dropped onto her stool at the dinner table. She felt like she could eat a horse as she tried to serve herself but kept getting passed over between the two men, each of them putting a spoonful of this and a little of that for her as if she were some helpless kid. Some of the dishes looked like the food they tried to serve the school kids; it was unidentifiable, until she saw the eyeballs looking back up at her. At first she screamed, or so she thought, and then went into gales of laughter as she poked at all the eyeballs.

"Yup," said Chad to her right, "I'd say this is the start of this state for next four to six hours." He looked at his wristwatch. "Jack, get her to eat something with protein in it and then this spinach should do the trick to help clear her system."

"I don't do eyeballs," she declared, pushing the forkful of the gruel away from her as Jack tried to get her to eat the herring. "Nunh-nuh."

"Crap, she doesn't eat fish," Chad swore.

"Oh my God! They're moving," she said, as she tried to back away from her plate, bracing herself between the two of them with a hand on each of their arms.

Malik spoke up. "It's a good thing she can shoot, for she would starve up here." He joined in with Tasha's alternating laughter and hysterics.

"She doesn't like the idea of hunting, either," Jack said, exasperated, as he tried to get her to eat something else from her plate. A difficult, finicky child at the dinner table would be his description of Tasha's current state.

"What a waste of marksmanship," added Malik.

"Maybe we should give her another brownie. It may put her to sleep," Nuka offered.

Chad shot her a look. "It's her first time, we believe. I don't want to know what her reaction is going to be like. I'd rather have her just high and laughing for the time being."

"I think she's scared of the fish." Ula pointed with her fork as she continued eating. She smiled at Jack.

"Well, at least she's having fun in between times," Nuka added as Tasha started laughing again.

Jack pressed his lips together, trying to choke on a nasty retort. He just growled inwardly.

The visit was turning into a ruckus, as far as Jack was concerned. He was sure, like the others, that he would never forget that day. There was a reason he never took others along for a hunting weekend—especially women. Tasha was proving no exception.

Thankfully, Chad was extremely helpful in controlling Tasha. Between the two of them they were able to eat their dinner, taking turns holding Tasha upright and a few times feeding her like she was a young kid. Chad was more successful with her, in getting her to eat some chicken and some of the spinach casserole. He was praying that the food would help absorb some of the marijuana-laced brownies' effect and shorten the drug's duration.

Otherwise, dinner conversation was fairly normal…as normal as one can be while trying to control an inebriated person. They asked a lot of questions about their newest guest as if she were not there, with Jack being as polite as he could be without divulging too much information. He did not know how much Tasha was open to sharing her personal life with others. He kept it to a bare minimum as usual.

Ula finally must have felt sorry for him, for she gave him quite the helping of her gooseberry pie when it came time for dessert an hour later. She took up his side of the task and helped Chad with Tasha, who had eventually seemed to go into a quiet stupor. They hauled her over to the sofa where Chad sat down and Ula helped lay Tasha down next to him, keeping her on her side, as he kept his watch over her.

"Well, she just might be a quiet druggie after all," he said, looking at his wristwatch again. "Got another two to three hours to go now. Just in time for bed by then." Chad grinned to his friend, who had looked back at him rather annoyed, chewing a mouthful of gooseberry pie at the dinner table.

Jack wasn't looking forward to that night, knowing what was coming next. *Why couldn't Tasha just do as she was told?* He sighed.

Malik brought out a deck of cards for the rest of them to play a few rounds for the late afternoon. Dinner, being even more casual, was lunchtime leftovers reheated as each person felt like they needed. The sun would soon set, and it would be dark around four thirty.

Usually, folks went to bed with the sun, taking in the extra hours of sleep or midnight delights—whichever folks wanted. He knew he would have both, being a favored guest of Chad's parents. He could not say no, for it would be rude to their customs.

As the hours passed, a few other villagers came and went, some joining in on the card games, others helping themselves to leftover food or drinks, especially the homegrown version of liquor. Plans were roughly made to meet at seven in the morning to go hunting up the way a bit from the community. It would still be dark, with a little less than two hours before sunrise. Jack played a few rounds and listened to the chatter about the following night's event. Malik asked if Tasha had connected to her spirit animal yet. Jack shook his head and said that most likely she hadn't, coming from where she'd lived, but that she might enjoy watching or participating in the event, since she wanted to know more about their way of life. He figured she was going to get firsthand experience there that weekend, since Chad's family was still heavily 'old-fashioned' in their way of life.

As Chad's folks left to go to bed, he joined Chad in the living room where he still participated in the conversations, yet never left his post in attending to Tasha should she have awakened in her current 'high.' From time to time, Chad kept himself preoccupied with his phone games, being more 'forward thinking' in his use of technology than some of his community elders.

Jack drew on his bottle of beer after taking a chair across from them where Chad and Tasha reclined on the sofa. He was jealous of the way Chad had become the lucky one, staying by her side, stroking her silky pale golden hair as if absentmindedly petting a favorite pet. He continued to stare at her languid features, finding her most beautiful when she slept. She could be a real pain in the ass, but as the days passed, she turned out to be of more value than he could have imagined. She was helpful in keeping the cabin, and a damn good cook. She even took care of Drake from time to time without him ever asking. At work, she proved efficient, almost too efficient, for there never was that much work for her after she got them caught up on the electrical maintenance. Now, flying might prove a different story. But that would be on hold now for a few days because he had to ground her for the next four days to let the weed clear her system. Now he realized how grateful he was for having gotten her medical done before that weekend, her drug testing already completed. He pulled a hand down his face in relief and frustration.

"Jack?...Hey there, Earth to Jack," Chad said, trying to reach him in his preoccupation.

Jack looked up, his blue-gray eyes flashing.

"She'll be fine, I promise you. I'll watch over her."

"But what about your dad?"

"What about him?" Then he realized what was troubling Jack. "He's already told me he doesn't want to mess with her, that she was better off with a younger and stronger man." Chad smirked at some internal thought. "I honestly think he's somewhat afraid of her after watching her shoot. Aunt Sylvia really did him in at one point. He's got Nuka or Ula for tonight if either of them wants him."

Jack continued eyeing him.

"Look man, they're expecting me to stay with her. They think she would be a strong wife for me. But she's a little too tall and intense for my tastes." He sighed when Jack still didn't say a word. "I won't touch her unless she wants it. She's our guest and I have to play by the 'old ways' here somewhat."

Jack grunted a growl as his eyes flashed Chad a clear warning.

"Okay, I'll play hard to get," Chad amended.

Jack finished the last of his beer, decisively tapping the empty bottle firmly against the chair's armrest, adding his last comment for the night. "Only if you want to live a long and pain-free life, Chad," he told him, the threat dripping from each word. Jack got up from his seat, grabbing another bottle of beer. He would need his beer goggles on tonight. He thumbed the cap off the bottle and took another long swig before heading off to his room. He just wanted to get the night over with.

Tasha stirred, causing Chad to move on the sofa.

Jack stopped at the doorway, looking back. It seemed Tasha needed a restroom break and a drink of water. He disappeared into his room, grabbing her night bag to let her have access to it when she got back from the bathroom. Chad genteelly showed her the way and let her have her privacy. Jack set her bag by the sofa, not letting go of it, as Chad opened the sofa bed for them to sleep on. Jack handed Chad her toiletry bag, his face still looking like a storm cloud, as Chad splayed the blankets and furs on the bed.

Exasperated, Chad said, "Will you heel, man!" He held up his hand to Jack. "I promise you, I won't touch her." Then he placed his hand over his heart. "I truly love my life, man."

Jack reluctantly let go of the toiletry bag so that Chad could give it to her while she was in the bathroom.

He returned to his room and had just gotten his first shirt off and his toiletry bag out when he heard her leave the bathroom. He decided to take his turn, walking out there, to find Chad helping her back to the sofa, holding her bag for her from the hallway to where they would be sleeping on the far side of the room.

She seemed like she was aware, as if she had just awoken from a deep sleep. She even noted him, stopping to look at him. Neither of them said a word. Her green eyes seemed lucid, but it was her beguiling smile that still indicated to him her state of 'high.' That smile that made him want to reach out and take her right there. Chad prodded her to move along, not letting that happen for him either.

He sighed heavily before going about his business. Coming back out from the bathroom, he found that Chad had gotten her into her sleepwear. His jaw clenched at the thought. He heard them talking quietly, but he continued to his room to finish getting ready for bed and for a visitor he *didn't* want to entertain, even though rejecting them would be most ungracious to their host.

The quiet knock on his door eventually came with a little giggle attached to it. He wanted it so badly to be Tasha escaping Chad. Upon opening his door, he found Ula standing in nothing but a large heavy quilt around her. He stepped out of the way and let her in, as was the custom, however it was not unnoted when he looked over to the sofa bed where Tasha and Chad were lying. Chad's head was propped up where he was facing Tasha, and she had been lying up against him under some of the furred covers. She had looked up at Jack and saw him allowing Ula entry into his bedroom, and he with nothing on save for his long john pants. He prayed that she was still 'high' and that the scene would not register with her when she'd come to her senses again.

Tasha had to blink a few times to make sure what she had seen in the dim lighting. Chad called to her, trying to get her attention back to their earlier conversation. Chad was telling her his people's stories since everyone had gone off to sleep when she woke up. He was nice in keeping her company and being her 'housewarming companion' since the two of them had to sleep out in the main room, which was currently the warmest part of the house but would soon become cold again when the fire died down in the wood stove in the center of the great room.

"You okay, Tasha?" he asked her when he felt her stiffen next to him. With no answer, he looked back over his head to where she was looking but didn't see anything amiss.

"I think I'm going to be sick."

Chad moved out and away from her side quickly. "Do you need help getting to the bathroom?"

She shook her head no.

He peered at her, trying to see her pupils in the dim room. She remained still. He got out of their bed. "Let me at least get a trash bin, if you think you can hold it a second." He came back with a mid-sized container before hopping back in bed with her. "Here, exchange sides with me," he said, trading places with her. "That way you have the bin if you feel you're going to lose it. I've never had anyone sick after eating the stuff unless they were a severe enough addict."

She turned her head in confusion, watching him settle back down flat on his back. He didn't see her expression.

"What do you mean, you've never had one get sick after eating?"

She felt him turn on his side, his movements a bit bouncy in the flimsy bed. The night had been so weird in so many ways for some reason, and now her mind seemed to pick up on something that was obviously important enough to explain the things she was internally experiencing—the brief unexplainable happiness and lack of care, which came to a sudden sickening stop when she had witnessed an undressed Jack allowing Chad's nude mother, wrapped in a quilt, into Chad's bedroom!

"Ah, you just ate something that disagreed with you, that's all." He tried to keep the peace, hoping she would accept his reasoning. It didn't work. She had metabolized most of her brownies.

"No…you said something about an addict," she pressed on rather drunkenly.

"Well," he said, laughing some, "you're certainly an addict to my mom's brownies. You would think you were a diabetic the way you tore into them. They usually get sick when they eat too much sugar."

It must have worked. He felt her shift next to him, as if letting her guard down. She did not press him further.

Chad still felt nervous though, yet comfortable. She made no moves on him. But if she did…ah, he did not want to go there. It was like sleeping with a seductive tiger that would eat you if you didn't get things right the first time around. She and Jack were just made for each other…that is…if they didn't kill each other first. They seemed to come alive whenever they were around each other. It was good to see Jack coming out of his 'personal world,' especially knowing Jack's background. Watching the change was entertaining, to say the least—though he was on the edge of his seat every time he visited Jack, wondering if he was going to barge onto a crime scene.

She settled back down, although he could sense something was off. He offered to continue another story for her and she accepted. From what he gathered, she needed the distraction. He was certain she had heard some of the noise from his room. They continued talking into the late evening about her family and background to his family and his sister, her time spent in the military minus the Middle East time, and what she thought of her new job.

He would be tired in the morning, he knew, but he had to watch over her for the sake of his buddy in the next room. She fell asleep again, snuggling into him as if she had replaced his sister. He smiled in the dark, thinking of all those nights sharing the warmth as his people had always done for centuries, for it was essential to staying alive in that Great Land.

Chad awoke the next morning, startled to find Jack staring down at him. *It can't be morning already*, Chad thought, groaning inwardly. The disgruntled bearded bear's face was so darn close to his that he could feel his breath from his prominent nose. He found himself lying on his back, Jack's hand over his mouth. However, he was pinned by the weight of Tasha snuggled up against him, an arm and a leg thrown over him—although he realized too late that his hand was happily holding one of Tasha's breasts, where his arm had snaked around her in the night. His hand let go immediately. With Jack's help, so as not to wake her, he extracted himself from Tasha's sleeping form. The minute he was free and standing, Jack smacked the back of his head, leaving him in a stinging haze of pain.

Chad wished he could do the same at times to his old-fashioned mother. But his mother adored Jack and it was his parents' custom, adhering to the old ways. White men, like Jack, were not used to 'sharing' their loved ones—especially their mates. If he did not know any better, he would have thought Tasha and Jack had to have been, the way Jack had been acting.

He headed to the bathroom to get ready, rubbing the stinging at the back of his head.

Eventually, all the men met outside in the early cold dark morning. Chad met up with his father near Jack's well-worn pickup truck with Jack leaning against it. Jack, still sullen, gave Chad a predatory look when he approached them. The men broke into four teams of three, and they took a total of four trucks to haul in their kills.

The morning stillness was most welcome for Jack's turbulent thoughts, though he was certain he could snap a tree trunk in half with his mind as they trekked through the reservation's forest. Malik led the way, with Chad just behind and Jack bringing up the rear. He kept boring holes into his best friend's back side, hoping he could feel his anger and frustration.

Jack knew it was his fault for not telling her what to expect, but he hadn't wanted to scare her from visiting them and learning more about Chad's people. He didn't have a better way of telling her that she would have to sleep with him if they didn't want the customary 'open sharing of warmth' from family members, which pretty much meant anything goes. Chad's mother was either not getting enough from Malik or she just loved providing everyone 'a little extra.' It even went against his normal parameters, and it took a lot out of him to return the favor. Jack obliged for fear of offending. The lack of sleep did not help either. Chad's mother was a snorer. He kept thinking the worst between Tasha and Chad, since no other noise came from the main room other than the hushed tones of Chad's voice in a conversation that he could not discern.

Not paying attention to the current situation, Jack ran into Chad, knocking him over, as Malik halted, getting down on his haunches. Chad swore under his breath. Chad was not even close to the size of his friend, as Jack's weight knocked him forward. Chad was more the height and bone structure of Tasha. He wasn't small, but he was lean and adept, quick, like his spirit animal the sea otter.

The grizzly bear erupted in Jack when Chad chastised him as he picked himself back up off the ground. Jack tore into him with a full body slam, wrestling him into a snowdrift. Chad punched Jack in defense, shouting at him about having lost his mind. Jack, marine trained, got a blow at Chad's face, his other hand holding Chad down on the ground by his neck. Jack had drawn back his fist again to deliver a third blow when a gunshot went off. Malik had shot into the air, getting their attention, making him stop in mid-action.

"Stop! Both of you!" Malik grunted rather heavily. "Jack, don't make me shoot you to protect my son." He leveled his rifle at him. "Now, break it up!"

Jack shoved Chad as he got up, then offered his hand to Chad to help him up. Chad, still not sure what the hell had happened, hesitated in taking his buddy's hand. Once Chad was up, he pushed Jack's hand away as if Jack was on fire, still pissed. Both picked up their rifles, cautiously watching the other.

"Thanks to you two boys' ruckus, I'm sure we lost our supper." Malik, like any father, was pissed. "Jack, get your butt in front and start tracking before I throw you into the bay waters to cool you down. Son, you're behind me until you two can talk amicably."

Feeling guilty for losing his cool, Jack did as ordered. They were tracking elk, from what he could tell from the snow prints, focusing on nothing else but on the empty prints in the snow. They spent another two more hours trekking until they came to a small herd of them in a clearing, all of them hugging the tree line, their long legs becoming one with the smaller tree saplings. Malik came up from behind to determine which ones they needed to kill, pointing quietly at the choices made. Then Malik reverently asked their gods for forgiveness and thanked them for providing them their sustenance, chanting a prayer quietly in their native tongue.

The elk's ears twitched at the whispered chanting, entranced by the sound, calming them in the frozen stillness. Jack followed Chad's lead on the other side of his father, taking his aim quietly. At the last three native words, they both fired their rifles, bagging two of them. It would be enough meat to feed their family for the rest of the winter. Even Jack would end up going home with enough to last Tasha and him through most of the winter, cutting down on their grocery bill. Now the hard part was getting their kills back to the truck. Malik remained behind to protect their kills from other predators as the two of them went to retrieve their gear from his truck to help them haul their trophies back to the roadside.

CHAPTER FOURTEEN

It was late in the afternoon before the guys showed back up at the house, faces reddened by the cold air, as they stamped the excess snow off their boots in the enclosed porch area. Chad and Jack were the first to step inside, shrugging off their coats, pulling off their hats, the static buildup only enhancing their disheveled look after a long morning of hunting.

What Tasha noted first was Chad's face, making her gasp. "What the—" She stepped closer to inspect him. "What attacked you?"

Ula made an exclamation in their native tongue which only made her suspect it wasn't a wild animal that had caused Chad's bruise along the side of his eye. Ula was on top of it, bringing him a bag of ice to lay on the swelling.

Chad tried to wave her off by turning his face away, and he was sporting another bruise along his cheekbone. "Mom, being outside in the cold air was enough to have tamed the swelling."

"But sweetie!"

"I'm fine." Chad squeezed her hand assuredly, giving her a quick kiss on her forehead. "Honestly, it just looks worse than it is."

"At least let Nuka make up a poultice for you," she begged him. "You shouldn't go to the festivities looking like you have been just chewed up and spit out by a wild animal."

Chad smirked, only to swear at the pain he caused himself. "Fine, I just want to take a quick nap before our community dinner. She can apply it when I lay down."

"Let me look at your pupils first," Ula pleaded.

Chad acquiesced to her request to put her more at ease, by leaning down to her height and making bug eyes at her. She batted at him for being impudent, happy to see that he was all right.

He stole a quick glance at Tasha before going off to stand by the fireplace to warm up. Tasha flashed Jack a heated look, and he didn't dare look at her as he sat down at one of the kitchen stools at the island.

The oven timer went off, alerting her that the two gooseberry pies were done baking. She made herself useful by grabbing them out of oven while Nuka gathered the herbs needed from the makeshift drying rack hanging from the ceiling to make Chad's poultice. Ula retrieved the oil, handing it over to Nuka.

Tasha, setting the hot pies out on the trivets, watched Jack rub the back of his neck as he sat there watching Chad warm up. Tasha gleaned that Malik was outside with the others as they took their kills to be dressed into the large work shed that stood between the last two homes. She was grateful that she did not have to witness that part, though she was curious as to what they had bagged.

When Ula left Jack at the kitchen island to attend to Chad, Tasha went up to Jack and said, for only him to hear, "The bruises reek of you, for some reason." She watched Chad's mother sit with him, speaking in their native tongue.

She turned her back on Jack, calling out to them. "A nap sounds pretty good too. How about I watch over him somewhat while we both sleep?"

Chad smiled at her weakly, but out of the corner of her eye, she caught Jack wince before getting up and leaving the house. Ula nodded her agreement to Tasha.

To Chad, she said, "Hey, soldier, come on, let's get you to the couch and just have you use me as a pillow to hold you upright for a bit. My turn to watch over you. Lord knows I've done my fair share of eating this morning. I need to do something else besides nosh on more food."

It wasn't long before they were both asleep, to be woken up what seemed like moments later by Jack saying it was time to go to community center for dinner. Chad moaned some before moving to get up off her, his body's weight a warm comforter for her. She found Jack's hand helping her up next, the usual warmth in his hand gone, his expression stony. Tasha, growing familiar with him each passing week, knew he was stewing over something.

While they had slept, everyone had loaded the car and had taken all the food that the women had made over to the large round community center toward the middle of the housing development. There was nothing for Tasha to help with, save for just showing up to the night's festivities. Jack had been sent back to retrieve them. The two of them donned their winter gear for the short walk to the community center.

She trailed along behind Chad after giving him an aspirin for the pain, certain that the center's bright lights and noise would only cause more pain. To her surprise, Jack hung back with her, just to her side, sulking in the darkness of the early evening.

The only noise was the faint music coming from the metal building. Chad, being the first to the door, opened it, letting Tasha go in before him and then himself next, leaving Jack to follow them.

The building was an expansive room with tables and chairs set up for folks to dine, a stage in the middle, and smaller rooms with their doors closed off to the main commotion—offices, she supposed—along with restrooms, as she spied a mother and small child exit from one of the facilities' doors. The people milling around wore anything ranging from normal winter wear to native attire. Chad filled her in on the night's purpose. It was a tribal meeting of several nations, but then to join in the celebration of welcoming the winter, where the animals and the land got their time to rest deeply and replenish for the spring.

Dinner was first. Chad led them to the buffet line, where all the food that had been made all day was lined up along the far wall near a kitchen area; Ula and Nuka's contribution among several other tribe members' dishes. Chad was helpful in letting her know what each dish was when it was unidentifiable for her. Between Chad and Jack, she had her plate filled, whether she wanted it or not. It was just as well: her uncontrollable appetite was lurking just beneath, grumbling for more food. It was the strangest sickness she had ever had. Usually, she rarely felt like eating after food poisoning or being plain sick.

When they came to the dessert part of the buffet, she grabbed two of the delectable brownies that Ula had made to add to her plate, only to find that both Chad and Jack had taken one each for themselves from her plate to put on their own. *The rat bastards!* Tasha thought. Having physically passed the large serving dish of brownies, locked between the two men, she was unable to retrieve another piece for herself as they continued down the line.

Ula waved them over to where she, Nuka, and Malik had sat with a few others that Tasha did not recognize. Malik made the introductions, touching briefly on what each person's position was in the conglomerate of the night's gathering. The last was the man who would help her find her spirit animal. She noted Jack stiffen beside her, in addition to his glance at Chad to her other side. Normally chatty on most occasions, Chad chose to ignore Jack.

She raised an inquisitive eyebrow at Jack as he quickly glanced her way, dismissing her silent question. Something was going on. Unfortunately, now was not the time and place to be asking Jack. Not in front of their hosts. Especially now that she had learned not many outsiders could participate in their gatherings unless married to one of the villagers or invited.

The night dragged on at first, and she was not comfortable with their hosts, waiting quietly to be included until they spoke to her and began to include her in their conversations. She let them steer their conversations with the usual barrage of questions about her past and upbringing, dazzling them with images of Palm Harbor and the white-hot sandy beaches of the Florida gulf coast, then her adventures in the military and in Afghanistan, down to where she had been shot and ended up in Alaska. She nabbed a piece of Jack's untouched brownie off his plate, popping it into her mouth before he could react, accenting the last comment she made. *By golly, Ula's brownies are to die for!* she thought, savoring the richness of the chocolate.

"I needed a cooling-off period," she answered, giving the reason she had chosen to go to Alaska, creating the laughter needed to lighten the moods of the two men sitting on either side of her. It must have worked, for Chad's hand landed on her leg, giving her a quick squeeze of appreciation. His smile created pain on his battered side, making his smile drop just as fast; however, the merriment still resided in his dark eyes.

"Jesus, Chad, I know laughter is the best medicine for most things, but in your case, I think you are going to hurt yourself more," she told him.

He let go of her leg, not catching Jack's expression.

"Do you need another aspirin?" she asked, concerned when he let his head drop, only to find him sniggering.

"I'm fine, Nurse Lazar." He looked at her with a sideways glance, his dark eyes shiny as normal, full of mirth. "Imagine, the both of us having to take care of each other for the same issue that got us in our sad states."

It was Chad's way of confirming her suspicions for what had done him in. There was no doubt about it…it was Jack.

231

Their attention was garnered as the council members stood to talk about their announcements, addressing pertinent topics to them and getting in the latest votes. The ceremony—entertainment for her, but serious for the villagers—began as the drummers started off with the winter calling, praying for cold and deep snow to put all life into a deep sleep, the rhythmic dancers enticing the winter spirits with their magical cadence.

Tasha could feel the pulse of her heart match the drumming, and she felt her body imperceptibly sway in her chair, trying hard not to get carried away, reminding herself to behave in front of their hosts. The dancing continued for a few more hours as she took in the various folks taking turns calling out to the spirits in their native tongue. Others observed, like Tasha and Jack, without any prayers and upturned hands. Chad, from time to time, would translate the chants and the stories they were hearing.

Near the end of the ceremony, the man they introduced to her as Tarife came to their side of the table, tapping her on her shoulder to follow him to the side of the main room. Chad followed them, for he would be interpreting for her, although Jack had delayed him momentarily to tell him something before letting him free.

Tasha followed the elderly man garbed in their native attire to one of the side rooms. It turned out that the rooms only possessed a few large pillows on the floor surrounding a mini fire pit in the middle of the room, the fire already lit, the smoke rising through a hole in the roof that one could mechanically adjust the opening to release the gray fumes. Tarife indicated for her to sit down opposite of him. Chad, ghosting just to the side of her, led the way by sitting down cross-legged, making her follow suit.

Tarife grunted, then smiled at her as he put some dried herbs on the fire, creating a scented smoke—a scent that reminded her of burnt spinach. Tarife waved another bundle of dried herbs to make the smoke spread out, speaking in his native tongue.

Chad whispered softly, "Inhale, Tasha. Take a few deep breaths and close your eyes. Find your center."

Tasha followed his instructions, stifling a cough as she took in more smoke than air. She found the deepest darkest spot inside her as she focused her mind to empty. It was not as tough as she had first thought it would be. It was like yoga. Usually, she had a hard time locking out the world and getting her mind to stop thinking, especially after she had come back from the Middle East. Yet she found the small spot that she had mentally made for herself a year ago. She took a few more deep, slow breaths, waiting, but not really caring either.

Somewhere in the far distance, she heard Chad's calm voice again, telling her to take a walk in a forest. She tried to imagine the forest he was talking about, but only found herself walking near an open field—a marshy field—the only trees she could get close enough to being a forest that ringed the nearby field. But for some reason she could go to the forest but not to walk amidst the trees. Tasha tried several times unsuccessfully, as if there were some invisible wall keeping her from walking between the close-knit trees.

She sighed resignedly, telling Chad in her mind that she could not do it. Something wouldn't let her.

Chad surprised her when he quietly told her, "It's all in your head. Nothing is restricting you to go anywhere."

Tasha could still hear the distant chanting, foreign yet familiar to her. She looked back at the forest lining the marsh and a nearby pond, and made another attempt to enter the thick woods, only to fail again. She ended up standing by the pond, deciding to wait on whatever was supposed to happen next. It was when she gazed upon the pond's still waters that she found it reflecting a rather large moose with a broad set of antlers—antlers that were wider than its head and body.

The moose image blinked as she blinked at it, stunned at first, but enamored with the magnificent sight of the usually gangly beast.

"Are you in the forest yet?" came Chad's voice.

"No…not really."

"Where do you find yourself?"

"In a marsh by a pond…near a tree line, but still can't go through the trees."

"Have you seen an animal yet?"

"Not for sure…" she said as she moved her head from side to side, noting the reflection of the moose doing the same as if checking out its rack.

"Take your time. Tell us the first animal you see."

In her mind, she looked over her shoulder to verify that nothing was behind her. The wide and expansive field was empty, insects and dust glowing gold in the sunlight, dancing heavily over the wild grass. The silver line on the horizon, the distant bay waters reflecting the sunlight, and the surrounding mountain ranges on either side of that line in the distance, cupping that fine silver line as if to keep the precious metal from slipping away on the earth's deceptively flat edge. She found herself snorting the air, breathing in damp earth, noting the various nuances of the wild splendor surrounding her. Her gaze fell back to the water's reflection for her answer.

"A moose?" She felt herself smile wide, physically feeling a peaceful spirit envelop her like a blanket.

"Where is the moose standing in relation to you?"

She delayed her first answer before saying out loud, "I think I am the moose. I see its reflection in the pond by the tree line."

The chanting stopped. Tasha's vision went blank, as if the movie film reel broke. She felt partly dismayed, but it was partly funny in that she heard herself laughing uncontrollably in the dark, and then nothing.

Tasha woke up to find Jack snoring near her ear, his body aligned with her side, his head higher than hers, her head tucked under his chin. She found arms embraced her, hugging her like a doll in the liminal light. She was locked in. Not because of his hold on her, but because her body felt heavy from the lack of use. She knew then that she had been out for hours, having slept in one position all night. She was barely able to turn her head away from Jack's face, where he continued to snore, only to realize that somehow he had brought her back to Chad's home. They were still in their clothes from the night before and were out on the sofa bed together.

For some reason, she did not remember the rest of the night. Her last memory was of a moose looking at its reflection in the pond, yet there had been no physical moose to create the reflection. She was the only one at the edge of the pond. Even now, she wondered if she had dreamed it.

She shifted her body in its need to move. The firm weight of Jack's arm moved easily when he was deep asleep. She turned from lying on her back to her side, spooning Jack, and closed her eyes again, inhaling his scent, content in the moment. Happy that the moment was real. She sighed, and his arm slid back over her again and he hugged her tighter, nosing into her hair, his breath heavy and warm, but no longer snoring. She found herself dropping off to sleep again for another few more precious hours.

"Good morning, you two!" Chad's chipper voice startled them both out of their deep slumber.

Jack jumped defensively, nearly dumping Tasha out onto the floor. Laughter erupted from Chad as both regained their senses in the bright morning light that filtered in through the high small windows in the kitchen where Ula had breakfast ready. The rest of the family was awake and had been eating at the kitchen island on the far side of the main room. They were the only two still sleeping.

"Jack, you take his head and I get his legs," Tasha said, rather annoyed at the rude awakening, her voice husky with sleep.

"Sounds good. I'll let you at him first, rip him up nice and good," he agreed as he crawled the rest of the way over her prone form in his attempt to get Chad.

Chad turned, dodging them, which was easily done, given he was younger than them and more awake.

"Kids," warned Malik from his chair, where he sat eating his breakfast, reminding them to behave inside his home.

Ula chipped in, "Come eat while it is hot."

The three of them walked up to the island table obediently, each taking their places. As they sat down, Tasha noted that the discoloration of Chad's bruises had faded rather quickly from the day before.

Chad, catching Tasha observing his face, remarked, "Yeah, you can thank Aunt Nuka for that poultice. It does wonders in getting the discoloration and swelling down."

"Nuka, you ought to sell that formula on the market! You could make some serious money!" came Tasha's first coherent comment.

Nuka laughed. "I wish I could, but unfortunately it has to be freshly made each time and applied about every three to four hours to get his results."

She scraped more scrambled eggs out of a frying pan for all of them to help themselves. "Being young helps, too," she added, turning to dump the spent pan into the sink.

"Chad's tougher than he looks." His proud mother beamed, reaching out to stroke his face lovingly.

"Mom." He blushed, exasperated.

Nuka steered the conversation back to Tasha. "So, did your spirit animal choose you?"

"Ah, did it ever, according to what she told us," snorted Chad.

"The spirit has a strong connection when it is inside her," commented Malik, knowing what Tarife had told him the night before.

"So what did you see in your waking dream?" asked Ula.

Tasha was grateful that she had her mouth full, chewing on a piece of toast before answering, giving her time to remember what it was that she had dreamed. "The last thing I remember was being in a very large marshy field trying to find the woods that they talked about and attempting to walk through the trees, and unable to go between them." She frowned. "I tried to go in the direction you told me to go, but couldn't. As for seeing the first animal…" She looked around at them, embarrassed.

"Ah, Tasha, your guiding spirit already found you from what you told us," assured Chad. "Go on."

She toyed with her eggs before continuing, "I only saw a reflection in the pond when I looked at the water's surface, waiting to see how I could either go through the trees at the edge or wait for an animal to appear, like you said would happen."

"What was the reflection?" Nuka asked.

"It wasn't a snake, was it?" joked Ula.

"Thank God, it wasn't," she sighed heavily, "but the way I have been eating, always munchie hungry…I think I am having a bad reaction to have seen a reflection of a moose. I am certainly eating like one."

At this, everyone erupted in laughter.

"I told you that's what she saw."

"So, after you saw its reflection, you saw the spirit animal behind you?" Malik asked.

"No!…That's what was *so* strange! I kept seeing the moose, as if I *was* the moose. There was no animal looking into the water in front of me, behind me, or just to the side of me. It was like I was a part of Shakespeare's *A Midsummer Night's Dream*. I *was* the moose!"

"It just means that your spirit animal chose you a long time ago. It has already been a part of you. We only showed you the image of what guides you and keeps you safe," Malik said.

"It's a good thing," added Nuka.

"It is?"

"Yes, it is an incredibly good thing. He's been a part of your life for a long time," Ula commented.

"Maybe that is why Alaska has called to you. You needed to come back home. Find your peace and your place in life," Malik supposed.

Tasha looked at Jack.

He smiled at her, "Maybe that is why you did so well with Morris that day."

"Who's Morris?" Chad asked.

Jack smirked. "Morris is the name she gave to the moose that visited us not too long ago at our cabin."

"Seriously?" exclaimed Chad. "After all that time tracking them that weekend, you had one just *drop* on by your cabin?"

"You were moose hunting?" Tasha asked, dropping her fork. "How could you? Don't you dare!" Tasha implored him.

"Okay, okay," Jack tried to calm her. "They don't necessarily taste as good as deer or elk."

"Jack!" she exclaimed, admonishing him.

"How do you think we get by in the winter?" asked Malik. "They are there for us when we need it, Tasha."

"I may end up vegetarian yet," she mumbled, and then another thought hit her. "But I am not sure if I can give up bacon," she said, nabbing two more pieces to go with her scrambled eggs. In between bites, she expounded, "I am okay with you all hunting, I just don't want to see the kill shot and the gore that goes into prepping them for food."

"It's understandable, Tasha." Ula patted her hand.

"Well, moose are herbivores," offered Chad.

She gave him a *you're not helping* look.

"Your spirit animal even visited you in person! That's impressive!" Nuka cooed.

"So what did the moose do?"

"It was just curious." Tasha shrugged a shoulder. "He was looking in the window at us," she told them off-handedly.

"She was lucky he didn't catch his own reflection in the window," Jack said dryly.

"Oooh...*that* would've been bad," Malik agreed.

"If I recall," she commented, sniffing at him rather indignantly, "you were going to shoot it instead of just asking him to get off the porch." She leaned her head on her hand where she had braced herself over her plate but could view all of them from her spot at the table.

"You were going to *ask* a moose to leave?" Chad asked, incredulous at the idea as he looked at Jack for verification.

Jack added, "Politely."

"Politely?" questioned Chad.

Malik stuck his lower lip out at the thought.

Jack nodded affirmatively. "She bribed him with half of our supper!"

Nuka laughed, nearly spitting out her food. As she recomposed herself, Ula had to ask, "What did you bribe him with?"

"It was just a head of cabbage I tossed out into the yard while I asked him to kindly get off the porch!" Tasha defended her actions.

"Yup, that'll do it!" laughed Chad. "And I betcha he'll be back for more." He jostled Jack with an elbow. "Since when did you like cabbage anyways?"

"Since she began cooking," he said, thumbing over to her. "Not bad either. Better than the diner. And a definite change of pace from the bar food."

"Ah...so *that's* why we haven't seen you up at the bar lately," Ula said. "Jack, here, used to be a bi-weekly regular," she informed Tasha.

Tasha raised an eyebrow at Jack with that new bit of information. He was not one to talk about himself. And even when she had questioned him a few times, he had always managed to deflect the question, or they were interrupted.

"So he did go out a lot then?" she asked of Ula. "I sure wish I could afford to go out more often. Going to work and then straight back to the cabin every night is getting old," she said, hoping Jack would get the hint. He did not acknowledge her one way or the other.

This in turn led Ula to chide him on not getting out more often and bringing Tasha along, thus inwardly egging Tasha's original annoyance of Ula's choice of sleeping partners. Outwardly, she plastered a smile at him as he flashed his annoyance at Tasha for encouraging Chad's mother and the rest of them about socializing more. She knew he was not one to socialize, and she watched him go down in the verbal brawl, losing the battle until he promised them that he would get out more often.

She would be sinking with him, she thought as she continued to stuff her face with more food.

It was nearing lunchtime when they got their bags packed and loaded into his truck's cab. He was making room in the back of his pickup for two big cardboard boxes of meat that they were to take with them. Malik and the men from the previous day's hunt had seen to getting everything prepped and divvied up between them all.

Jack made the excuse of leaving their company early due to the incoming weather. He did not want to drive during the heavy snowfall that was expected later that afternoon and into the evening, although snow had been falling lightly that morning.

All was good and she felt the weekend had gone rather well, save for the one hiccup of seeing Jack sneaking around with Chad's mother. But it was none of her business, she thought, mentally slapping herself again. Although she did wonder why he had chosen to sleep with her again out on the sofa bed the next night, and not with Ula.

Thankfully, it was not as long a drive as Jack made it to be. She pondered about the weekend, watching the large wet flakes hit the passenger window and stretch into long streaks on her side of the cab.

"There's smoke forming." His mellow voice punctured the silence in the truck's cab and into her aimless thoughts.

"What?" she asked, realizing Jack was talking to her.

"Smoke," he said, waving his fingers over his head.

She gave him a quizzical look.

"From thinking too hard," he added.

She arched an eyebrow at him.

She kept quiet, refusing to imbue him like he did with her on most occasions. He risked looking at her a couple of times as he continued to drive, knowing he had to be more cautious with the icy roads.

She prayed he would not pursue the subject, yet he did. "What are you thinking about?"

"Not much." She shrugged her shoulder as she kept her hands tucked warmly under her armpits, hoping that would be enough to deter him from furthering the conversation as she turned her head away from him again.

"A moose." He settled back into his seat, keeping one hand on the steering wheel and the other smoothing down his mustache and beard, absently preening himself. "Helluva a spirit animal you chose."

"I thought they chose us, not the other way around," she said, turning her face back to him. "Besides, at least I don't look and act like my spirit animal all the time."

"What's wrong with a bear?" he asked, intermittently looking back at her from his driving. "And how is it that I 'look' like a bear?"

"Nothing's wrong with a bear, until you act like one…" She interrupted him before he could protest. "Which is often with me."

"Well, if you would do as I tell you, I wouldn't be like one," Jack retorted, becoming defensive.

"I have done most of what you've reasonably requested of me. But when it comes to my off time…then no! You have to give me a damn good reason— something that you do *not* do! So don't even start that with me!" She wiggled a finger at him. "I am not one of your soldiers who you bark orders to or are on a 'need-to-know' basis. The weekend went fine, so what were you *so* worried about?"

"For starters you didn't stay away from the brownies, and two, you didn't just agree to share a bed with me and pretend to be a couple."

She gave him a crazed look.

"By the way, you're grounded."

"Come again?" Her mouth and brain finally engaged together. "What the hell? You think you can lock me up in a cabin like some teenager who got into trouble?"

"I should do that too."

"Whadda mean, I'm 'grounded'?" She was not getting the point.

"From flying, for at least..." He paused to count in his mind. "...at least until Thursday, and I would keep your mouth shut on the subject."

"For what? Choosing to not share a bed and sleep with you?" She unfolded her arms as her hands formed fists, grinding them into her seat. "This is unbelievable! You are the pettiest man I have ever met!" She grumbled, "Like hell you'll blackmail me with this...with what happened between us before I started the job." Her voice began to bellow, challenging him. "If you were anyone decent, you would have been honest from the get-go in letting me know you were my boss! At least I would have had the gumption to not have let it happen, saving us from this...this situation!" She waved a hand at them both in the truck.

It was taking everything she had to keep from reaching over and beating him while he drove. "Go screw yourself, Griswald!" Then she added, "This coming from the man who sleeps with his best friend's mother!"

He stepped on the brake, the truck skidding off to the side of the road, sliding onto the shoulder, and into an embankment of old packed snow. Thankfully there was little traffic on the road, for he would have caused an accident. A car passed them by after slowing down at first, but then continued once the occupant determined they were fine.

Tasha continued, "Yes, I did! I *saw* you let her in to Chad's room...of all places!"

Jack turned to her, but she refused to let him talk.

"What kind of sick bastard does that kind of thing?"

"First of all, it's not about that—"

"The hell it isn't!" she hissed at him indignantly.

"It's because you were still tripping on all the marijuana you ingested, in addition to inhaling the stuff while trying to connect with your spirit animal!"

Her mouth dropped at this new and incredible excuse.

Jack continued before her rebuttal. "And...I am going to excuse your attitude based on your current state of 'high' that you may or may not be still on." He held a warning finger up to her.

Tasha slapped at his finger. "Like hell I did any drugs! I don't *do* drugs!" Each word in the last sentence was ground out between gnashed teeth before she turned to glare out the front windshield. "You're something else! You know that? You really *do* want to get *rid* of me! You just try and lay that at Nate's feet and I'll tell them...I'll tell them all...Chad and Malik...what you did with Ula! Let's see who gets fired first! Because if I do...you are going down with me! That's not a threat...that's a promise!" She turned to let herself out, needing to get away from his overbearing arrogance in the truck's cab.

Jack reached for her, putting a stop to her frenzied action. She turned to throw a fist at his face. He deftly caught it with his other hand, encompassing her hand with his large one, squeezing it just enough to get her attention.

"Listen!"

She wiggled more but he applied more pressure, getting her to stop.

"Tasha! Listen to me!"

She let out a small whimper of pain before gaining control over her anger.

He backed off on his grip, trying not to hurt her. "*Listen*! I am not saying you took the drugs on purpose! You *didn't* know!"

She scoffed at him.

"Then why are you so hungry? Why didn't you feel like giving a damn when you should have?"

She gave him a surprised look, as if he had known she was craving chips and anything else to binge on in addition to her not giving a *rat's ass* attitude as of late. Her hand and arm went limp along with the rest of her body.

"Yeah, I know so," he added, sighing heavily at her and letting go of her fist. "I told you not to eat the brownies."

She turned away from him in her seat, her mouth trying to work something out, only to give up and close tight-lipped as she sat looking out the front windshield, stunned. In the next instant, she was out of the truck before Jack could stop her. She was desperately trying to process everything, running pretty much blindly across the street to the Lagoon Park area.

He swore, turning the engine off and getting out of his truck, chasing after her but having to wait for a car to go by before he was able to catch up with her.

"Tasha!"

"Go away, Jack!" She shrugged his hand away when he caught up to her, disgusted with him.

"Where in the hell do you think you're going?"

"Anywhere but near you!" she bellowed back at him. Her eyes had become shiny with unshed tears and he knew he was the cause. Seeing her that way only made him want to fix everything.

He nabbed her, yanking her into him to hold her, not letting her go, letting her fists pummel his chest in protest, suffocating her scream of frustration in his thick coat, steamy fog from their mouths enveloping them both from the heat of the moment, yet not protecting them from the cold wet snowflakes.

They remained there, as one, until all her fury was gone. She had gone limp against him, but he still held her close as her anger subsided. The main highway traffic rumbled by on its way to town, ignoring them as they stood by the wooden trailhead where folks could observe the Lagoon and its wildlife.

She finally found the strength to push him away. He reluctantly let her go as she muttered, "God, you really *do* hate me…enough to end my career."

"No…No, I don't, Tash—" He shook her, forcing her to look up at him. "I don't hate you. Quite the opposite. I want you to succeed in your career. I want"—he changed his wording—"I need you to stay." He dragged her over to the railing of the walkway to lean up against it with him. "Like I was trying to tell you before, you didn't know, and you're not entirely to blame."

"Jesus! You think?" Sarcasm dripped in her deadpan response as she got back up to stand in front of him. "So what happens when Black Raven Aviation decides to do a spontaneous drug test?"

"It doesn't happen. Not since I've been there."

"And the FAA?" she asked.

"Look, it will be out of your system entirely within a few weeks, according to Chad."

"And he knows this how?" She raised a helpless hand up to God Almighty above.

"He usually does all of our drug testing."

"Ah, great, at least he will lie or switch the test for me…I hope," she half laughed sarcastically at him, crossing her arms over herself.

"…And yours was done well before we left town this weekend. You will not be checked for a while."

"But can't they see this even a year after the fact? By taking hair samples?"

Jack nodded but assured her they only did urine samples.

"Your life better count on it! This is my career we are talking about!"

"I won't let a good man go down alone if I can help it. You have to *trust* me, in addition to keeping quiet, Tasha. From the way you're reacting, I take it you have never even tried drugs in the past."

"Never had the desire to lose my self-control. I have enough issues keeping my emotions in check when I am in control. I don't need any more help in that aspect."

He gave her a big grin. "Atta girl."

She didn't return the grin, still suspicious.

They remained still in the gray dim daylight, the snowflakes lightly hitting their faces, the Lagoon area entirely silent except for a few vehicles whizzing by on the nearby highway. Both were lost in their thoughts yet needing each other's reassuring—nevertheless tenuous—company.

"I still hate you for this," she said rather unemotionally.

"I know you do."

"I'm reluctant on pretending this didn't happen. I don't see this ending well." She looked up at him, her arms still wrapped around herself defensively. "You can't expect me to do everything you want me to do. At least not without a *damn* good reason behind it. You could've said something in addition to 'don't eat the brownies.' Especially since chocolate is king in my book, brownies being my favorite."

241

"Now I know *and* remembered from the first time we ate out in Anchorage."

"Kind of understand why you did what you did with Ula. For you, it's time to move on. But not sure why on earth you would have an affair with your best friend's mother. But…it's none of my business." She moved to head back to his truck before he could explain himself to her.

"Tasha, it's not what you think."

She looked over her shoulder at him before telling him, "Like I said, it's none of my business. It's over between us." She headed straight for the truck before he could see her tear up again.

He sighed heavily, swearing to himself, and trailed after her. It was clear that Tasha was no longer open to hearing anything he could say to get her to understand.

Like any normal Monday morning, the crew had assembled around the break table. Tasha took up her spot within the crewmembers at the table. Jack usually went to his office or got Nate to come out and discuss what needed to be worked on or who flew which assignments for that day.

The guys were in their usual 'just waking up' mode. Nick and Sam were checking out a men's soft porn magazine, chatting up a few of the images. They all had eventually realized that she was not going to jump them over those magazines, knowing better from working in a male-dominated field. Nor did she really care. She had once told them that if they didn't mind her looking at nude males at work or get offended by her plastering sexy male posters up in the battery shop, she was fine with what they read…as if she would ever do so, for she was more of a private person. She liked to think she had a bit more class than the mechanics. Electricians usually did.

"She can't be for real, man," came Nick, showing Sam the photographed model in question, inspecting it like he was an art connoisseur.

Hank glanced over his shoulder, now curious. "Too many tattoos for my taste," Hank said.

Sam shoved the magazine back to Nick. "I'm not into girls with tattoos or scars."

"Same here," said Jarvis. "I like them pretty and well kept." He shoved a paper to Emanuel, and Manny made a face at him.

"You can't expect me to pay all of this," whined Manny.

Jarvis looked to his cabin buddy. "Well, stop using so much water when you shower, man. I paid all the water and gas bill last month. It's your turn this month."

"Utility bills?" Tasha questioned, rather confused. "Why are you paying utility bills?"

"We all pay and share the utility bills," Nick told her.

"Haven't you seen and paid yours?" asked Jarvis.

Everyone looked at her in surprise. She lifted an eyebrow in a mixture of surprise and confusion, shaking her head no.

"Damn, I knew Jack made a hell of a lot more money than we did when he took over that position," Sam commented. He backhanded Nick's upper arm lightly. "Told you to take the job."

"Nah, didn't want to work all that extra hours and come home with a headache from planning all day. It wasn't worth it, and I like flying too much to give it up."

"Yeah but think about it...no utilities to pay!" Sam said.

"How much do they usually run?" Tasha asked, now curious as to why she had never seen a bill for their cabin.

"Water is about fifty bucks," came Hank.

"Ours was a hundred and fifty dollars," sighed Emanuel.

"Stop taking such long showers!" Jarvis reminded him.

"Well, you let water run while you do the dishes, you water pig!" Manny chastised in return.

"Our electric wouldn't have been so high if Panama Jack here didn't roast us out at eighty degrees in our cabin." Jarvis thumbed at Emanuel.

"Electric?" Tasha asked, wanting more information from the crew.

"Ah...ours was only fifty bucks last month, but during the winter running the heater usually costs us two hundred dollars," Sam answered.

At this information, her eyebrows shot up.

"It's our grocery bill...that's the killer!" Nick added.

But she didn't ask any more questions, since Jack arrived with Nate to begin their morning briefing. She glared at Jack as Nate began the meeting, her eyes narrowing when he finally decided to notice her glaring at him. He gave her a momentary confused look, dismissing her silent confrontation, and then eyed the rest of the crew at the table as if trying to discern what it was that had her feathers all ruffled.

The day was a normal fly day. She was assigned to Jarvis as his second for a short jaunt over to Boswell Bay, getting more flight time on Clara. They would be back within the day, especially since the weather was holding. The rest of the crews were assigned to other short-day flights with their cargo loads.

It was an uneventful day, though she enjoyed the view due to the clear weather that time more than trying to become more acquainted with the aircraft model they were on. Their banter was light. Tasha worked at finding out more about what was expected of them at the cabins in terms of their responsibilities.

"You mean that Jack hasn't told you any of it? Not even one utility bill?" Jarvis asked in awe.

"Nothing. This morning is the first I ever heard of anyone paying bills."

"Oh wow! You got in tight with Jack, you lucky dog! He must be paying all of the bills for you two."

"Well, I do buy most of the groceries to help out. Maybe that is why he makes me do all the cooking and cleaning," she pondered.

"Ah-hah, you won him over with your cooking. Explains why he is looking fatter these days," he told her with a smile. Then added, jesting, "Quite the cabin couple."

Her head snapped at him, giving him a questioning look. Then she asked, "Is that what everyone thinks?"

Jarvis grinned broadly behind his pilot's mic, not answering her.

"Seriously, it's not what you think," she said, defending herself. "It's been a damn nightmare since I arrived when it comes to living with him. You all get to go home or do whatever you want to do on your free time. For me, it's like taking work home, only it's the boss who still wants to dictate your private life at home and during your social hours, on what you can and can't do. If I had wanted that I would have lived with my parents and remained there until Mr. Right showed up." Then, more to herself, she said, "Unfortunately, I am a little too old now and all the Mr. Rights have gotten married or are gay. I have missed my opportunity." She sighed to herself as she checked their instruments and the GPS screen again.

When he didn't respond, she looked back over to him in the cockpit. "What?"

"There's no way," Jarvis told her.

"No way what?" she asked.

"You two aren't an item yet?"

"Well, not like you and Manny, if that's what you are meaning."

She got his surprised look. "Yeah, I know."

"Who told you?"

"No one." She lifted a shoulder at him. "I'm blonde, not stupid, Jarvis. I just figured it out on my own, especially given how Manny acts most of the time."

"That rat—"

"He adores you, Jarvis," she interrupted him. "I know you guys like to keep it under wraps, and I do understand why. My lips are sealed," she assured him with a smile.

There was a pregnant pause as Jarvis seemed to come to grips with her blatant knowledge of them. "You know that Jack does too," Jarvis told her.

"Jack is fond of all of you guys. But clearly not me," she corrected him as she adjusted the second communication radio to the landing strip's frequency.

"And you think he isn't when it comes to you?" Jarvis asked incredulously at her lack of perception of Jack.

Tasha shrugged her shoulders gingerly. "Well…eventually he'll find me worthy enough on the flight line."

"Ah-huh…I beg to differ with you on that one. And then there is the rest of the crew, who believes there is a lot more going on than you two are letting on."

"Well, hate to bust the crew's bubble…there's nothing between us, I assure you. I've met some of Jack's girls that he's been involved with over the years. I am not one of his and I refuse to be one of his conquests."

Jarvis's jaw dropped at that information, but he recovered quickly as he had to focus on turning for the final approach to the Boswell Bay's airstrip.

"I didn't think Jack was seeing anyone else. That's news to us!"

Tasha dropped the flaps at his request when they reached the proper airspeed, then called traffic to give their position. Their conversation lapsed while they concentrated on getting the twin engine down safely.

As the local ground crew came out to help unload their plane of their 'month's groceries,' Jarvis commented off-handedly, "Jack has got to be blind and senseless" —Tasha gave him a sharp look—"not to notice you and that you are a good cook! Are you going to make those cookies of yours anytime soon? How about some brownies?" Jarvis asked.

Tasha remained quiet, not sure how to respond, given her recent experience with the last batch of brownies and not knowing whether Jarvis even knew she had been doped. *Could they smell it coming off me?* she wondered.

The week had passed uneventfully, other than two nights before, when Jack had discovered that she was 'borrowing' his men's cologne to spritz her bed and body pillow every few nights before she went to bed. He caught her red-handed as she was returning the bottle to the bathroom cabinet when she least expected him to be approaching the bathroom so early that evening. Jack was usually the last to go to bed, usually an hour or two later than she.

"Why do you have my cologne?" Jack asked, the mirror reflecting his face when she closed the medicine cabinet door over the sink.

"I just borrow it from time to time to spray on my pillows. It's a terrific and calming scent for me." She turned, shrugging a dismissive shoulder at him.

"I thought that was lavender you ladies use to help you sleep," he said as he lined his toothbrush with paste. "I didn't realize you were having trouble sleeping." He began brushing.

"It can. But I really don't care for the scent of it. I like the smell of pine, the outdoors, and the woodsy scent…like your cologne contains. Besides, I only use it about every other night or so because the smell lasts so long. If you are worried about me using too much of it, I'll be more than happy to pay for half the bottle."

Jack spit out some of the paste's froth. "Not necessary. I don't use it much. But seriously…you're having trouble sleeping? You already sleep enough hours for two people, Tasha."

"Have you heard me have any nightmares as of late?"

"No," he answered, now thinking about her comment. He realized that she hadn't relived any of her prior nightmares for quite some time. "But I thought that was because of Drake sleeping with you. He sure is loving you for holding on to him like a giant teddy bear at night…The way you have your arms wrapped around him." He grinned at her, some toothpaste foam lingering on a few of his whiskers.

"I don't hold him like that…do I? Wait. When are you seeing me do this? Are you coming into my room at night?" Tasha watched him finish brushing his teeth, rinse, and then grab the hand towel to wipe at his face.

"Don't get your feathers in a ruffle, will ya?" He replaced the hand towel. "I only go in to check on Drake to see if he needs one more potty break for the evening before I retire, and usually your cell phone is not plugged in and I end up plugging your phone to its charging cord most nights. Your cell phone doesn't plug itself in on most evenings, Moose." Jack had leaned on the countertop using his arm to support him, his free hand on his hip, clear that Tasha had no intention of backing off and letting him finish the rest of his ablutions. "Just your cell phone being on the charger would have announced my 'intrusion' these past few weeks."

She gave him her best 'evil eye.' "My roomie is a pervert who likes to watch women sleep." She folded her arms over her chest in defiance.

"No, I'm not. But, yes…" He watched her green eyes go wide. "I do like watching women. Especially pretty women."

She clicked her tongue at him in dismissal.

"If I was a pervert, you would have eventually found me sleeping with you instead of finding Drake as your sleeping partner." Jack nimbly undid his shirt's buttons. "Now, if you don't mind, I would like to finish getting ready for bed." Then he stopped, looking back at her with a mischievous grin. "If anyone is calling anyone a pervert, it would be you at this moment. Not that I would care if you watched me undress and use the shower and toilet."

Tasha rolled out of the bathroom on her shoulder, where she had made herself comfortable against the doorjamb watching him do his ablutions. He did not bother to close the bathroom door as she walked toward her bedroom, flopping down on her bed, listening to his movements from where she lay. Drake helped himself up to his usual spot on the far side of her bed, clambering up instead of jumping due to his long legs for his breed, positioning himself alongside her with his back side up against her body. She plugged in her phone, placing it on the night table next to her head.

Jack peered around the corner at her and Drake before coming all the way out and calling to Drake. The dog didn't move, giving him a soft acknowledgement groan as if telling Jack he was good for the night.

Tasha turned her head back in Jack's direction, where he had stopped at her bedroom doorway, his arms stretched out and upwards against the door frame, holding his body back from intruding into her personal space.

"I don't think he wants outside, Jack."

"I can see that." He allowed himself in, noting her cell phone had been plugged in on her nightstand this time. Though he stood only a foot or so away, his presence put her body on high alert—not for defending herself, but for acknowledging his sexuality, her physical needs betraying her by desiring his touch in addition to his presence.

"I think we got this…" she said, pulling her comforter up higher but reaching an arm out to Drake next to her, using him as backup. "We're good."

"I see that, too." Jack took a step closer, making her scoot down even more under her comforter, when his long arm reached over her to pet his beloved Newfoundland. He stopped in his attention, sniffing a moment. "You got enough cologne on your pillows?" His nostrils heavily exhaled the strong scent as he stood back up to his full six foot plus height.

"Gave a squirt earlier to Drake too."

"You put cologne on Drake?"

Tasha tentatively nodded her head, pulling her arms back in and under the covers as she rolled over on her side toward Drake, giving him her backside, but regretting it when Jack decided to take a seat on the edge of her bed, nearly making her body roll back into him with the indentation his weight made in her mattress.

"Okay, I was fine with your pillows. But Drake?" He pulled on his short beard, smoothing it down neatly before continuing. "Why? Does he stink?…

Hold on…Haven't you been giving him a weekly bath each weekend?"

"Yes, I bathe him whenever I have my 'cleaning weekends.' We shower together. Makes it easier to do two things at once." She shifted her body more toward the center of her bed to counteract the force of gravity pulling her to where Jack was seated. "He doesn't stink, but it's nice, occasionally, to give him a squirt too so he can be more like a ladies' man. His presence is comforting, and I like to pretend he's the perfect gentleman."

Jack looked over his shoulder at her, where he still had his back to her. "The dog is Mr. Right?"

She stuck her lower lip out at him. "For now."

He twisted his upper body to face her more. "You know, I can offer that same comfort if that's what you are looking for." His smile became more wicked by the second. "In fact, I seem to remember that I offered that earlier…and I got rejected."

"You're my boss, for one. Two, there is no way you would just 'sleep' with me." She turned away huffily.

"Ah, but we did before, at Chad's house. You didn't seem to mind then. Your honor's still intact."

"I was stoned!" Then, turning back to him: "And I believe you had had your fill for the night with Chad's mother!"

"You were definitely stoned," he reminded her.

"Not *that* stoned, trust me!" She had rolled back over and propped herself up on her elbows, facing him. "I know what I saw, and I am still in awe of your audacity in doing your best friend's mother!"

"You know, we still need to talk about that night, Tasha."

"No. No we don't. I'd like to erase that thought from my mind, not reinforce it."

Jack ignored her, giving her the five-minute rundown on the customs of Chad's folks and how that was traditional hospitality in the old days.

Her mouth dropped at his explanation, but she recovered quickly by adding, "This has got to be the most despicable explanation I have ever heard in my lifetime! Using that as an excuse for your actions? Do you expect me to believe this? Do you think I am that stupid?" she asked when he did not answer. "I'm not one of your ordinary twits."

"No, you're definitely not. Believe what you want to believe, Tasha. But that's the truth of their ways."

Tasha was about to retort, but Jack held up a finger at her.

"And don't say I didn't try to warn you by telling you what you needed to do to save me from their customs."

"*Save* you?" She flopped back down on her bed, physically giving him a cold shoulder. She laughed callously. "As if...My God—you are *so full* of yourself!"

He sighed, knowing she wasn't buying it, as he got up from where he sat on the side of her bed. Before closing her door, he said, "By the way, don't spray Drake with the cologne again. Just your pillows."

Tasha didn't answer him during the pregnant pause, waiting, expecting something else to happen, until she heard her door close with a click. Only then did she exhale, her mind racing at his 'custom' excuse only making her madder until she punched her pillow, startling Drake where he lay, forcefully shoving their conversation out of her mind.

CHAPTER FIFTEEN

By Friday, her temper had built to the point that she wanted to go to the bar. It was time, she thought. Time to move on. Suffering under Jack's funk was slowly killing her. Then, with the guys at work talking and looking at the women in the entertainment magazines, she was starting to have her own personal concerns about her body.

Maybe Nora was right. She needed to take better care of herself if she ever expected to get a man to notice her. None of the crew seemed interested in 'dating' her. But her choices were limited to basically Nick or Sam. Hank and Nate were married and far older than she. Jarvis and Emanuel were a pair, and far from being interested in women.

Then there was Jack. Definitely off limits. She preferred Sam, since it was clear that Nick was a narcissist. Sam was just as handsome, more gorgeous to the point of making her doubt herself being in his presence, and the last thing she wanted to do was to fight off other women seeking his attention, especially those that were more feminine and far prettier than her.

By the end of the workday, most of it spent mulling over male possibilities, she decided that she needed to look outside their group. There were plenty of men. Most of them older. Many of them scruffy due to their jobs and being in a man's world. She barely looked at any of them when she first arrived. Now it was time to do something about it. Hell, Jack had moved on. *Why can't I?*

She got the guys on board with her during lunch break to get them to take her out to the bar that night, saying she needed to blow some steam off and do something different from just going home. As the crew was leaving the hangar, Jack was nearly out the door when he spied her jumping into Jarvis's car, with Emanuel hopping into the back seat. He called to her, asking where she was going.

"Going to the bar tonight, need a break for a few hours. Someone will drive me home," she yelled back, waving him off dismissively. "See you later."

Of course, this did not deter Jack. It was nearly an hour later when he arrived at the same bar with Chad in tow. She scoffed at him before he looked up, catching sight of her picking up another glass of wine at the bar before turning back to the pool tables where some of the crew were challenged to a few betted rounds with the dockyard workers. She ignored him by turning her back to where Chad and he chose to sit and play a few rounds of cards at their table.

Tasha tried hard not to look over to where Jack and Chad had recently sat down. A few minutes later a new, mysterious, beautiful, young, native and exotic-looking woman joined them. The woman sat way too close to Jack for Tasha not to notice. Often she found herself sneaking peeks, getting madder when she should not have even cared about who Jack saw.

She was about to call it quits when the dock workers challenged them to another around of pool. Nick joined in that time, saying it was time to pull out the stops on her playing and bag a good pot for them all. She reluctantly acquiesced.

"I think your ride showed up," commented Sam as she picked up her stick to play her turn.

Tasha looked at him as Sam chinned in Jack's direction. She glanced at Jack only to find the young woman sitting next to Jack giving him a rather intimate hug and a kiss.

She quickly turned away. "Nope, he's not giving me a ride tonight. I think he's here on a new date."

Sam's eyebrows popped up even higher. "Who's she?"

"I have no clue, Sam. Just another one of his conquests, I suppose." She lifted a half-hearted shoulder at him, trying to discern a good angle to shoot the cue ball.

"I didn't know he *had* any conquests. Were you one?" Sam tentatively asked her.

She nearly missed her shot.

Tasha gave him a sarcastic evil eye before answering flatly, "Nope. Not *his* type nor any of the *crew's* type, since I carry a permanent bullet hole from Afghanistan. No man is going to want me after they see my scar." She mocked him—more like the crew—from the few divulging mornings at the break table. She found her angle before pointedly striking the cue ball, emphasizing her aversion to their comments on the magazine women they looked over during their breaktimes.

A solid purple ball slammed into the far pocket. She stalked the table to find her next shot.

"So...either you are giving me a ride home...or, if I get lucky...some new guy will—especially one that can capture my interest and be able to handle my body scars."

Sam's eyebrows raised at her derisiveness.

Looking up at Sam where Nick had now joined them with his new bottle of beer, Tasha added, "Contrary to what the whole crew thinks, Jack and I are not an 'item.' We never were, and I am pretty certain it will never happen."

Sam gave her a doubtful *okay* look as she slammed another solid ball she called into the side pocket.

Halfway through the evening, one of the dock workers took a liking to her, and in his drunken state, flirted with her. He wasn't bad looking, but unfortunately not her type. *Will I ever find any man my type?* She doubted herself again. Thankfully, he was near her age and he could possibly grow on her over time. He kept trying to win her heart, making steadily increasing passes at her. It started with a pat on the shoulder, then to a few fellow-like hugs, then a heavily beer-reeking kiss or more, each one nearing her mouth until he plastered her with an attempted beer-stinkin' French kiss—the last one making her wipe at her mouth in disgust the moment he turned around from her, cheering to his fellow buddies and some of the local truckers about his conquest of her. Her fellow workers, the reality of it, were having none of it as the dock worker pranced around like a triumphant boxer, smiling.

"Looks like you have a new admirer tonight," Nick commented from the side of his mouth as he passed her to change up the teams again.

"He's just got his beer goggles on and can't see straight," she said, indicating an easy shot that could be made.

Nick laughed, knowing better as he watched their 'flight line runway model for Black Raven' line up for the shot.

"She'll always have admirers," Emanuel said tipsily where he sat on his stool up against the room's far wall. That made Tasha do a double-take at him before stepping aside to let Sam by for his upcoming shot.

"Well, I got the hint she's shopping for a new date," Sam disclosed, getting to the spot he needed to set up his shot.

"Really?" Nick perked up at this news, then turned to Tasha. "Seriously?" When she looked to him, he stood taller with his cue stick vertical like a walking cane, his one hand extending wide-open invitation to hug and pointing alternately at his puffed-up chest in possible hopes. "I'm available…What's wrong with me…or…any one of us?" Nick indicated to their crew.

She pressed her lips together before answering. "Well, Nick, I'm not *too sure* you could love another. You're too much in love with yourself. It's going to have to take a hell of a woman to make you think past yourself."

"Ouch!" Sam laughed. "At least she's honest!"

"As for Jarvis and Manny"—both men held their breaths, hoping that she would not divulge their secret—"they're a little too young for my tastes. Hank is a little too old…"

"And married," added Manny.

"Okay, that leaves Sam and Jack," Jarvis declared.

"Jack has some serious control issues. And Sam would be the closest to what I'd like to date…"

Sam stood up, smiling as if he had won the beauty pageant, giving them a Gumby wave.

"…but unfortunately for me, I am too scarred up for his tastes in women," she finished, instantly deflating Sam's ego trip.

"What?"

"Ah…you heard me." Tasha shrugged a dismissive half shoulder at them. "If I remember right, this morning you all were deciding what type of woman would be the most attractive, and most of you said one without scars or tattoos. I don't fit that bill, guys." Tasha smiled succinctly at them.

"Well, I think Anthony wouldn't mind." Nick indicated to the drunk dock worker who had kept grabbing at her as he flirted throughout the night. When she and a few of them quickly glanced over, the drunk Anthony gave her a grand wet smile and a wave to her. "You want me to ask him for you?"

Tasha gave Nick a scathing warning look.

"Really Nick?" she said, a little exasperated. "I don't even know the guy! Why he thinks he's going to score in his state is beyond me."

"Because, girlfriend, you are exuding desperation tonight," came Manny, making a *Z* in the air in front of him with snapping fingers at each direction change.

"Yeah, try not to act so desperate and you might be able to score tonight," said Jarvis.

"Who's desperate?" came the drunken Anthony as he came up to her from behind. "Are you, sweetheart...des-per-ate?" He enunciated each syllable, laughing at her and then firmly grabbing her rump and pulling her into a staggering bear hug.

Tasha had been caught off guard, her pool stick hugged up with her in his tight embrace as he dragged her over to the dockyard workers' side and none too gently slammed her up against the wall, stunning her. But the moment he let go, flipping her around to face him, to lean in for his next kiss, she slammed her pool stick hard into his upper leg, missing his family jewels by a few inches, and then used her elbow to strike his face away from hers. But it did not seem to faze him as he lunged for her.

She braced herself for the assault, only to find Anthony ripped off her as Jack tore him away and threw him up against the adjacent wall. Thus, the melee began as she watched her crew stand up to the other dockyard workers joining in. Jack punched Anthony square in the face at the same time Anthony struck Jack with a broken beer bottle near his temple, leaving a fresh bloody cut. Anthony sank to the floor, clearly knocked out.

A few of the other men came over in their buddy's defense to attack Jack, but Tasha swung her pool stick at one, catching him in his throat and knocking him backwards on his back before he could get to Jack. She saw Jack toss the other man, using his forward momentum, tripping over Anthony's body first and then headlong against the wall, stunning him. Jack walked away, coming for Tasha. But her eyes must have said all the warning he needed when the man he felled earlier stood back up and started for him, only to run into Jack's elbow rearing back into his gut hard, leaving him breathless and dropping him to the floor.

Jack nabbed her hand, yelling back to the guys, "Finish it quickly, guys, I got her!" Jack dragged her roughly out of the bar in pure anger; she was barely able to keep up with his long-legged stride. When they hit November's cold air, it felt like she had hit a wall, her flushed skin stinging. He pulled her around by her upper arm, sending her skidding on the blacktop's icy surface, nearly careening into a parked car. She was super cold without her jacket, having left it behind inside the bar. She pushed herself back up to regain her balance. She was going to say something, but he caught her shirt scruff and pushed her roughly forward to his truck parked further down the row of cars, until he got his driver's side door open, grunting to her to get in, and shoving her in when she didn't move fast enough for him, forcing her to slide over on the bench seat, making room for him as he got in behind the wheel.

Jack didn't wait for his truck to warm up, making the old belts squeal when he put the old, battered truck into gear and drove them hurriedly home. She was sure he was going to end up with a speeding ticket. The heater in his truck was unable to take the chill off her as she found herself shivering uncontrollably in her seat. She tried to stifle her body's quaking.

Once home, she clambered out of her side before he could haul her into their cabin like roadkill. But he only shut his truck off, got out, and opened the cabin's door, waiting until she scrambled inside before shutting the door behind them.

His cell phone rang as she took off her wet boots by the door. He walked toward the kitchen, putting distance between them as he took the call, picked up a towel, wiped at the blood on his face, and left it wadded up to his forehead a moment, holding it there as he listened to whoever it was that had called him.

"Good...That's what I needed to know." He paced in short turns. "And grab that for me too."

Tasha walked on by, heading to her room in the near darkness of the cabin. The work light above the kitchen sink illuminated part of the main room.

"Let me know the status by tomorrow morning." Jack shut off his cell phone, stopping her in mid-stride to her room, his voice booming.

"Tasha! Just what the hell *do you think* you were doing?" He took two steps around the kitchen island, putting him just by the main thoroughfare with his hands on his hips. He was pissed.

"What do you mean, *me*? I'm *not* the one that started it!"

"The *hell* you didn't!" He took a step closer to her. "Carrying on like that... flirting with the dock workers! What *did* you expect to happen?"

"Definitely not that scenario! Don't make me out to be some floozy! I just wanted to go out—maybe find a nice date, just like you did! Which, by the way, *you should* really get *back* to her!" Tasha snarled at him. She turned to go to her room, no longer wanting to thank him for helping her from that close call and let it go.

"Tasha!" he barked at her.

She turned around. "What? Jack! What is it?" She gestured overtly with her hands, using her full arms.

"Don't you dare walk away from this discussion!"

"Discussion?" She pointed to the ground between them. "There is *no discussion* here. It's always one-sided with you, Jack!" She raised her voice at him.

"I just want to know why you have my entire crew risking their lives in that bar for that crap back there! Just what were you trying to prove?"

"I wasn't *trying* to *prove* anything!" she told him determinedly, her voice raising, taking a challenging step toward him, defending herself. "I want to move on just like you did!" She pointed to herself. "I want to have a normal social life just like everyone else...something I haven't had since arriving here, with you being an entirely overbearing monster, not just at work but in my private life!"

She was now screaming at him as she continued.

"If you're so worried about me having a date…" She began unbuttoning her flannel overshirt. "—well, you needn't worry. Like you"—she waved her arm in a big arc, her other hand still working the buttons as she looked down—"and all the rest of the other fickle guys out there, once they find out I have this nasty scar, it's not like I am going to be making it to first base with anyone!" Finally she pulled her first and second layered shirts up over her head in frustration, her anger making it clumsy as she dropped them to the floor, one sleeve still hanging on her wrist, standing there in her bra and pants, pointing to the area just above her hip. She looked down at herself, as if *just look at me*!

"I could've taken him out myself…given enough time!" she snapped, stamping the floor with her foot at him. "Even if he did win, he would've vomited at the site of…" She looked back up at him, his face still obscured in the darkness of the cabin.

Jack had taken both his shirts off, exposing his entire chest to her, and the kitchen's work light fell starkly across his torso, making the various rigid scar lines on his skin stand in high relief on the upper left side of his massive chest. One nasty scar, the worst one, lay just over his heart. It was the first time she had seen him illuminated in the flesh.

"Oh…" Tasha stood there staring at him, the shocking reality settling in her wine-addled mind about his injuries. Then curiosity got the better of her as she took a step forward to get a closer look. "That one"—she pointed to the worse one over his heart—"that one should have killed you." She was thoroughly distracted, stepping closer, inspecting him.

How come she never noted this before? They had made love, but then… she had never seen him in the light. It was always dark. And then…wait…in the bathroom in a towel…but…his scarring was hidden from her view with his undershirt and arm when he was brushing his teeth. He was always dressed before her whenever she woke up, and she realized why she had never seen these scars until now.

She reached out to touch them, but before she could, he caught her hand, stopping her. "Now, what do you wish to complain about when it comes to scars?" He lowered his head to her eye level before continuing, "Scars are not going to stop anyone from taking advantage of you, especially if you are flirting with them." He growled quietly, like a bear warning an intruder.

"I *wasn't* flirting, ya blind bastard! You were too busy flirting with your own damn date to even notice me in the first place!" she growled back at him.

Jack hauled her up against him, proving his next point not only figuratively, but literally against her abdomen. "And somehow I don't think you could have gotten yourself out of that mess by yourself." Jack held her firm against him so that she was unable to move.

Her bare flesh was a shock to his after so many weeks of absence from their last intimate contact. It was testing his limits; it was darn near killing him not being able to have her. They remained that way, the seconds ticking by, but eventually his other arm slid around her body, especially after she began trembling from the cabin's cool air, offering her more of his body's warmth. He felt her body meld into his, her breath caressing his chest, and he pulled her in tighter, inhaling her scent, only to lose himself to her. She turned her face up, eager to kiss him, neither of them breaking eye contact. When their mouths connected, he slid his arms down the length of her, picking her up by her bottom with her wrapping her legs around him to carry her to her bedroom.

He deposited her on the bed, never breaking his hold on her mouth with his as they sampled each other again. Her hands worked the button on his jeans and then his zipper as she tried to push his clothes off, only to have too short of arms to succeed due to his long torso as he seemed to be helping her with shucking off his clothes.

However, he gruffly broke their kiss. Tasha, eager in her giddiness that only his presence seemed to do to her, felt the stinging cold surround her when he told her to go to sleep. As he closed the door, she was stunned by the sudden decision not to continue their pleasure.

She growled her displeasure as she flung herself backwards on her bed, throwing a book from the nightstand at the closed door. Then she rolled over to whimper herself to sleep, mentally chastising herself for falling for such a jerk, her sleep fitful.

Jack opened her bedroom door the next morning. The late morning sunshine shone in on the disaster area. Tasha's bed looked like it had exploded, between all the pillows and the rumpled bedding, Drake the sole survivor on top of the material rubble. Somewhere Tasha lay buried beneath. He spied an exposed hand peeking out from underneath a pillow, and the tip of a sock-covered foot showed where the comforter had been scrunched up from draping over the bed's edge.

"Get up, Tasha, I need breakfast."

No response save for a sleepy Drake jumping down to greet him as he took a step into her room.

"Come on, Tasha, wake up."

A small moan of "go away," emitted, along with the sounds of bedding shifting.

Jack only took another two steps closer to her bed before she popped up defensively, sitting up facing him, swearing, "Christ! Do you ever sleep?" Her hand pushed her hair back from her face, flattening the pale strands against her head. She looked around and then back at him before questioning him.

"It's Saturday, right?" she asked, locating her phone to check the time and date.

He answered her before she could check. "That's correct, and it's ten a.m. I need breakfast."

"Seriously?" She rubbed her face with her hands, trying to wake up. "You can't grab a bowl of cereal?"

"No!" he said, taking his leave. "I want something hot. I'll be outside splitting firewood. Get me when you're ready."

For fuck's sake! she grumbled to herself, not one to curse often with foul language, save for bad early mornings with hangovers and very annoying unbearable people. She flopped back onto her bed, trying to grab a few more moments of shuteye, but the sunlight, streaming in through her window, exacerbated the dull headache from the previous night's drinking, forcing her to get up.

After making herself a cup of hot tea, she spied him through the living room's grand window, chopping wood like he said he would be doing. She watched as he easily split each log with one massive swing, the slices falling neatly to either side of the large stump. Then he set another one on top to split asunder. For several more moments, Tasha watched him repeating the attack to each piece of wood. He looked haggard, but something was keeping his energy and strength in top performance mode. No—frustration. Frustration over something, she realized, taking another sip of her tea.

Jack turned, facing her momentarily, slamming the ax into the old stump before bending over and picking up all the pieces to stack neatly on the large stockpile at the far side of the yard. She winced to herself after noting the gash on his forehead just stretching from his eyebrow to his hairline. Dried blood had crusted on the fresh wound, making it stand out against his skin under the harsh morning's sunlight.

She had no idea what he wanted for breakfast and thus decided to ask him, donning a coat over her pants and shirt that she wore, swapping the mug in her hands as she shoved each arm through her coat's sleeve, and slipped on her snow boots without zipping them up. She stepped outside, tromping on the wraparound porch to where he was cutting wood. Her standing on the veranda did not get his attention. It was only after he had walked over to the large pile of stacked firewood that she got his attention by standing on the work stump, shaking off what little snow had accumulated on the yard during the late night from her boots.

Again, she asked, "What did you want for breakfast?" She was halfway bundled up, while he wore just a thick flannel shirt, work pants, and boots.

He stopped, looking at her disheveled state before taking her mug out of her hand to take a sip—only to discover it wasn't coffee, but her tea, his face belaying his disgust as he handed her mug back. "I don't care, as long as it's hot," he said, dropping another piece of wood to split just in front of her boots.

She refused to make way until he answered her question.

"Do you want pancakes, eggs, bacon…oatmeal?" she persisted in a congenial voice, one of her hands lifting from her warm mug.

Jack made a face at her last option, not verbally answering her question.

"Okay, then. Oatmeal it is," she declared, being just as sarcastically sweet to his dour mood.

When she refused to move, he chose to grab the other smaller pieces of wood to take over to the stockpile instead, not wanting to waste time. It looked like he had been splitting wood for a while, as if all his free time was spent chopping wood, prepping them for the next two years. At the rate he was going, Alaska was going to be denuded of trees within a few years.

"Are you having hot flashes?" she asked, trying to joke with him, making her joke sound serious. His mood certainly matched the symptoms that older women experienced, his actions fitting to what a few of them used to tell her when she was growing up.

He set the heavy load down on the pile, turning to come back, and then stopped in mid-stride at her comment, his face going ash white as he looked at her…or so she thought.

"You are, aren't you?" she jested. "The sulking mood swings, the redness of your face…" She indicated with one hand over her face as she smiled beguilingly at him, standing there atop her wooden podium.

"Tasha!" he interrupted her. Jack raised a tentative hand at her.

"What?" She was not liking the way he was admonishing her so early in the morning. "I was just joking with you…trying to lighten up the mood here on this glorious sunny morning," she said, making a sweeping, grand gesture at the day, squinting in the sunlight beating down on them. "Grumpy bear, did you wake up on the wrong side of the bed this morning or what?" She jerked her upper body dramatically around at him, while her one hand held her tea mug, still unaware of the color draining out of his face as he stood rooted near the wood pile.

"Tasha!"

"For Pete's sake! What's wrong now? Are you still pissed from last night?" She raised her voice at him, admonishing him from her perch, lifting her index finger at him from her mug, the mug she used as further emphasis of her point. "You know, it was your choice last night—"

"Tasha!" His commanding voice boomed her name for the third time. She gave him a confused look as she started to look around, and he stopped her with "Stand…rock…still! Keep looking at me!"

"Hunh?" She was not entirely sure why he told her to remain still, the confusion clear on her face.

Something from behind snorted just at the back of her head. Something exceptionally large. Warm and unpleasant, its breath made a thick white fog form in the cold air just to her side as it drifted upwards in the negligible breeze.

She hadn't heard a car arrive, nor any car doors slam as its occupants exited the vehicle. Her body went from barely being casually relaxed to high alert as she realized it had to be a wild animal—a large, dangerous animal, given Jack's concerned expression and his hesitation to come near her. He stepped very quietly and slowly toward her, yet keeping his distance.

Tasha stifled a whimper, her hands shaking as her mind imagined a worse way to die other than the bullet that had been meant for her earlier that year. Her tea mug fell to the ground, breaking on the stump before her feet, the dark shards of pottery splattering on the snow amidst the wood splinters.

"Tasha, just be quiet!" he whispered harshly. "Don't move…Don't make a sound."

She complied, although her mind raced at the thought of being brutally attacked by a large grizzly. She felt sniffing at her backside and then exhaling rather heavily at the back of her head—more like the top of her head. Whatever it was, the animal was giant! Not being able to see her attacker only added more fuel to the imaginary gore in her mind's eye. She had never thought she would die this way. *Being mauled! By a wild animal!* She cringed even more, her eyes squeezing tight, ready for the onslaught of strong sharp teeth and claws.

Just then, Chad and Jarvis walked around from the side of the cabin from the parked cars to encounter the situation. Jack held his hand up at them along with a harsh whisper of "Don't!" but was too late, with both exclaiming at once.

"Oh, wow!" Jarvis exclaimed, hurriedly digging for his cell phone in his pocket.

"Oh, my," came Chad, then softer, "Oh, boy…ah, a big boy, at that!" He whistled low under his breath.

Their comments made Tasha open one eye at them, only to glare at Jarvis when she realized he was taking photos of her life's final moments! Chad wasn't any better as he just stared up at the beast just behind her in absolute wonder, his smile like a kid in an overstocked candy store.

A muffled large footstep pawed in the snow behind her. The sound heavy in the damp earth, the movement reverberated through the stump she stood on. She nervously eyed as far as she could without moving her head.

"Someone…please…help?" she whimpered imploringly. "Jack? Chad?"

"Shhh…" the three of them scolded her.

Her shoulders lifted at the stern rebuttal, like a turtle trying to tuck its head in his shell.

"Don't move, Tasha! I need you to keep calm," Jack warned her, stepping closer to her with the arrival of Chad and Jarvis. He quietly added, "As long as you keep still and quiet, I don't think he'll bother you."

Tasha squeezed her eyes shut again.

To Chad, Jack commanded, "Get my rifle by the front door!"

She couldn't help herself. "What? Oh God, no!" She was suddenly close to tears. At least they would put her out of her misery faster.

Tasha felt the snuffle again, and then a slow warm wetness seeped through her hair and just inside her jacket's collar at the back of her neck. "Ew!" she whined, realizing that it was salivating, obviously ready to eat. She felt her hair being nudged by its massive muzzle, surprised at how soft and warm it was, yet so ready to feel the sharpness of teeth biting down on her head and neck. She whispered "please" more to herself. 'Please' to either leave her alone, or 'please' to hurry up and just make her death quick.

"What?" came Jack's angry whisper. Seconds felt like minutes.

Tasha did not open her eyes, still quaking in her boots. A second later, a small thump off to the side of the yard behind her, the beast's feet shifting away from her, and a command of "Go! Go! Go!" Feeling Jack's hand upon her forearm, dragging her forward and down to him, his body protectively surrounding her back side as he hurriedly shoved her back toward their cabin. She nearly yelped in surprise but kept her silence.

Chad and Jarvis were ahead of them, leading the way. Chad a shotgun in hand, Jarvis snapping more pictures just behind them with his cell phone. Like Lot's wife, her curiosity getting the best of her, she looked over her shoulder to see a large moose wandering over to the far side of the yard, going after what looked like the head of broccoli—the one she had bought a few days earlier for one of their suppers. She stopped in her tracks, having Jack nearly bowl her over now that all irrational fear had dissipated into reality. Jack pulled on her arm after going around her, dragging her with him, back inside their cabin, all of them sighing relief at the same time once inside. Tasha was pissed it wasn't the grizzly as she had imaged, but she knew better about being too close to a moose. And it was remarkably close! Then, she realized how damp her hair and jacket had become.

Jarvis went to the picture window to watch the moose, while Chad returned the shotgun back to its place by the front door. "Man, I couldn't find the rounds. The shotgun wasn't loaded, but then I remembered what you all told me before about the moose."

"What do ya mean before?" Jarvis asked, snapping more photos with his phone. "Man, this is way too cool! I can't wait to show the others. They won't believe it!"

Jack nodded to Chad to follow him over to the kitchen area, pushing Tasha toward the bathroom as he took her jacket off, telling her, "Go shower, Tasha. I'm sure you don't want moose cud all over you. I got your jacket." He dropped it by the basement door to take downstairs later to wash.

Tasha gratefully nodded to him and headed for the bathroom, deciding she might as well get dressed for the day.

Later, she found them still sitting around the kitchen island talking amongst themselves, all having a cup of coffee. Her sock-clad feet padded over to the kitchen and she decided that a cup of coffee would help to calm her down. She grabbed the pot where Jack had made some for themselves, the guys' conversation dying as she reached them.

"Hey, don't let me stop you all from talking," she told them, only sarcastically adding, "or talking about me."

Chad, ever the peace-keeper, "Nah, we were just talking about how it is that Jack and I have been out tracking game those last few weekends only to not come across any to hunt, and here it is you two have them trained to come here. It's a hunter's best dream come true, to hunt just off the deck of your cabin! From a rocking chair, much less!"

The three guys laughed.

Tasha scowled at Chad. "You wouldn't dare," she scolded him. "That's my spirit animal you are talking about. Shooting him would be bad luck, wouldn't it?"

"Not legal to hunt within the town's limit," came Jack, his index fingers tapping both sides of his coffee mug where the rest of his fingers had intertwined around the mug.

"If you ask me, I'd say the devil is taunting you two with that moose, especially if it has been around once before…Or…that you two are just lousy hunters," suggested Jarvis.

Ignoring them both, Chad continued, "To answer your question, yes and no. It seems to be *he is* your spirit animal, since he made no motions to hurt you with him inspecting you so closely from behind."

"Or he knows you're his next of kin, after that spirit animal ceremony," sniggered Jarvis.

"Are you calling me fat, Jarvis?"

"Oh, hell no, woman! No sane man would ever tell a woman she's fat! That is, if he wants to live!"

More chuckles at her expense.

"Ah, but she's got those same long legs," joshed Chad, indicating her legs ending up somewhere by his neck. "And Jack, here"—he backhanded his buddy lightly—"knows from personal experience that she can sure kick like one."

Before turning to retrieve a mug, Tasha rolled her eyes at Chad as she caught Jack's almost imperceptible half smirk. Jarvis gave Jack a questionable look before Jack shook his head, indicating to drop the question.

She poured herself a cup, deciding to ignore Jack as he intently watched her. She turned back to them all, her eyes darting back to the picture window, momentarily checking before focusing on the guys in front of her. She leaned back against the countertop as if she was the person being judged. They all remained silent, though Chad and Jarvis smiled broadly at her.

"Ah…Big Boy isn't out there anymore, Tasha, he's moved on," Chad said, being the first to note her quick searching glance out the window. "Say, Tasha… what did you call him before?"

"Morris," Jack said, his smirk growing, showing a partial dimple half hidden by his beard line.

"Morris?" asked Jarvis. "What kind of name is that?"

"I didn't name him, Tasha did." Jack indicated to her with his cup of coffee before taking another sip, his elbows on the countertop.

"Hey, it worked at the time," she retorted, casually fluffing the dampness out of her hair with her free hand.

"Did ya get all the moose drool out of your hair?" Chad teased.

She rolled her eyes at him before telling him no breakfast for him and commenced making breakfast by getting a pan out and the food items needed.

"Moose drool," Jarvis repeated, his smile growing even broader, looking over to Jack knowingly.

Tasha quickly looked over her shoulder, doing a double-take on catching the silent conversation going on between the two men. She stopped her preparations and turned back around to them, crossing her arms, waiting.

"Yup, I like that one."

Chad had caught on, saying, "Oh yeah, that one has a nice ring to it. I think that will definitely stick."

"Just what are you all talking about?"

"Your new nickname," said Jarvis.

"My nickname?"

"Yup," said Jack. "Payback is hell, Tasha. You picked mine when you first arrived, and now the guys won't let me live it down."

"I didn't give you a nickname…did I? When?" She was confused at first, but remembered. "Oh."

Chad offered up a toast with his coffee mug. "To Griswald and Moose Drool."

"That really does have a nice ring to it," Jarvis chimed in.

"Oh, no…No, I will not be called Moose Drool!" Tasha retorted.

"Well, you know, according to my people's customs, when your spirit animal drools on you it only means you have been blessed more—"

"Cut the crap!" Tasha said, not believing Chad with his usual mischief, his smile widening more at her refusal. "That's a bunch of bull, if I ever did hear!"

"That moose was definitely a bull," Jarvis added to the unintentional pun.

"Ah, Tasha, I do think I remember hearing something like that." Participating in the roasting of her, Jack's mirth seeped to the surface of his face, his foul mood long gone.

The sight of a humorous Jack was so rare those days that it kept her from being able to make a snarky comeback and was a good reason to be dubbed with such a dubious nickname.

By that time, Jarvis was laughing so hard he found it difficult to get a word in between breaths. "Ooooooh, I…can't wait…to tell…the guys at work." One hand clutched his stomach, the other covering his mouth.

She was not going to win with this new nickname, but at least she could try to get a compromise. Maybe a weak threat would work.

"Okay, fine, Moose—but *not* Moose Drool." She pointed a cooking spatula at

Jarvis. "No breakfast for you either, should you tell the others."

"Ah, no problem there. Chad and I already got our breakfast after he fixed me up from last night's fun."

Tasha cringed at that comment, deflating the jolly air some, having forgotten about the previous night's tiff. She had let it go because she figured everyone had been tipsy, emotions tending to run amok.

"I'm so sorry, Jarvis. I didn't think the guy would have gotten that stupidly rough to cause you all to go to bat for me last night," she apologized, sighing heavily, and looked down at the wooden floor. "I hope you didn't get hurt too badly. What about the others?"

"Ah…no worries. We all stand up for each other, especially for our fellow aviation sister. I just have a bruised rib, nothing broke. Everyone else is fine too. A few scrapes, bruises…a black eye or two."

"It's the damage to the bar that I am worried about," Jack said on a more serious note. "Big Raven's not going to like hearing about this past weekend."

"Ralph said nothing was damaged other than a few broken bottles, spilled drinks, and some badly bruised egos. He saw how it started, with Anthony grabbing you the way he did. He is putting the blame on the dockyard guys," Chad added. "Not your guys." He took a final sip of his coffee as he stood up, and then he took his cup to the sink. "That's why we stopped here on the way to Jarvis's place, to let you know about what went down and to return Tasha's coat that she left behind at the bar, since you had your hands full getting Tasha out of there. And then protecting her from a stray moose this morning," Chad commented. He chuckled to himself and then teasingly elbowed her as she attended to frying the bacon and eggs.

To Tasha, Chad joshed, "You're a popular girl."

Tasha took a tentative sidestep, still holding the spatula, and crossed her arms with her one free hand up, cupping part of her lower mouth, embarrassed by the previous night's mess.

Instinctively taking away the focus from Tasha, Jack sighed, "That's a big relief…But I still have to let Nate know before he finds out by word of mouth." He turned to Tasha. "Well, you definitely know how to put action into date night."

Her hand dropped. "It was not a date night gone bad, Jack!" she defended herself, placing both hands on the kitchen island's countertop, bracing herself as she leaned toward him. Her right hand still held the frying spatula and she used it to emphasize her point. "Get that out of your head. He was *not* my date!…Nor was I flirting with him—or anyone else for that matter!"

Chad whistled a low warning. "The Moose is on the loose, Jarvis. We better vamoose if you know what I mean." Chad gave her a quick hug and peck on the side of her cheek, quietly telling her, "Don't kill Griswald if you can help it, Moose. I kinda like the guy." Then he let go of her, smiling back, telling Jarvis, "If you want a lift back to your cabin, you better not miss the ride."

On his way to the front door, Chad told Jack, "I'll be back to take a quick look at that cut on your forehead there." He touched his own head. "It looks like you didn't do anything to disinfect it or clean it there, buddy."

Jack scowled at him, dismissively waving him off.

"Seriously, man. That cut looks like crap."

Jarvis hurried right after Chad and they let themselves out, laughing loud enough for Tasha and Jack to hear them, even with the front door closed.

Her gaze reluctantly returned to Jack's face. She was surprised that he was smiling. "What?" she asked.

"Moose Drool. I kinda like that." Jack ducked out of the way of a careening balled-up dish towel, heartily laughing, then pointing back at the stove. "Eggs!"

"Eggs?" Then, she remembered. "Shit…eggs!"

Tasha quickly got them off the burner, so as not to overcook them, and onto the bacon-laden plate nearby.

Chad returned as promised, as she was halfway done with her breakfast, Jack having inhaled his in less than a dozen bites. He had brought in his first-aid kit, setting it aside on the island countertop, and grabbed another cup of hot coffee, emptying the pot but not turning off the burner. Jack got up from where he sat at the kitchen island, turning the coffee maker off while he pulled out the toaster and a loaf of bread to make a few slices of toast, still hungry.

Chad knew better than to interrupt his buddy's feeding time, helping himself to his barstool again next to Tasha's free side. He peered over at her plate, taking stock of her cooking. "Looks pretty good. Just might have to stay over another day—at least long enough to enjoy the special treatment you give Jack here." Chad smiled at her.

"No special treatment, trust me…More like ordered to make it," she mumbled as she continued to chew what was already in her mouth, rather unladylike. Her mother certainly would not have approved of the ill manners she had obtained in the Army.

Chad raised a questioning eyebrow as he looked to Jack for an answer, only to be ignored when the toaster tossed the slices of toast up for him to retrieve. Jack generously applied butter and jam to the four slices. Chad knew he was not going to get an answer as he watched Jack savor one of the slices, pretty much eating it in three large bites, carrying the other toast back to his seat at the island.

Knowing he was not going to be allowed to attend to the wound until after Jack finished eating, Chad decided to help himself to a piece of toast, since watching them eat caused him hunger. They all ate in silence, no one disturbing anyone's immediate pleasure in the hot meal and coffee, the air neither hostile nor jolly. But something was weighing heavily on Tasha, from what he could discern from her body language. Chad was determined to find out while he worked on Jack's gash on his forehead.

By the time Chad had finished chewing his one slice, Jack had all their plates back in the kitchen sink waiting to be washed while he made short work of cleaning up the countertop, ensuring all the smaller appliances were returned to their rightful spots in the cupboards.

When Tasha got up to do the dishes, it was Chad's cue to attend to Jack's cut. "Okay, Jack," he said, opening his kit. "Well, Tasha, at least you didn't kill him. Thanks for leaving him unharmed."

"I'm not sure why you even bother with him." She told him, glancing over her shoulder from her task of washing dishes.

"Hey now, he just rescued you…twice, I might add," Chad reminded her, giving her a cocked smile.

"For what? So he could have one of my breakfasts?" She shrugged a shoulder at him without turning around from the sink. She rinsed a plate and deposited it in the drying rack. "It's not like I have a lifestyle worth living for at the moment, other than my job."

"Wow, you think so little of your life, Tasha?" Chad stopped in his cleaning of the dried blood. "What about us?" He pointed to himself and Jack. "Are we that horrible of company?"

"What company? You two are barely around…off hunting every weekend!" she blurted out without thinking first. "Sorry," she said, resuming her work at the sink. "You're not bad, Chad. But Jack…he's a whole other story." She had finished their dishes and now commenced scrubbing on the frying pan.

Tasha was having a hard time containing her frustration with Jack and could no longer keep silent on the truth she had been sitting on all these past days. She twisted her upper body to face them. "Truth be told—hell, I know if I was *his* friend, I certainly wouldn't attend to him after knowing what he did with your mother!"

"Tasha!" Jack growled quietly in warning, unable to move because Chad had by that time gotten down to the raw opening of the wound, making him cringe from the antiseptic's sting.

She felt moderately justified by watching him in pain, although it would have been more pleasurable had it been by her own hand.

"Hey!" He tried to grab for Chad's hand, but Chad held the gauze in place, letting the liquid soak into the wound.

Curiosity getting the better of him, Chad watched her take out her frustrations on scrubbing the frying pan as if she was going to flay its metal skin off its hide. He indicated for her to continue.

"Why don't you have Jack tell you himself, since he *is* your *best* friend."

Deciding the antiseptic had enough time to do its job, Chad took away the gauze, getting closer to inspect the wound, and then eyed Jack, asking him like a father would do to a naughty child, "Is there something I should know about you?" Chad cracked a wicked smile at him, trying to get him to lighten up again.

"Yeah, get out of my face before I rearrange yours!"

"Now, now, now, Jack," Chad chided.

"You see what I mean? He's an ungrateful bastard!" Tasha put the sparkling clean pan down on the cold burner to drip dry.

"Yup!" Chad turned away from Jack's face to dig in his medical kit, neither Jack or Tasha knowing if he was answering her or referring to something else instead. It was the latter. "You're going to need a few stitches if you want that gash not to leave a large, nasty scar, buddy."

Tasha was drying her hands on the towel while she leaned back against the sink basin, watching them. She smirked. "Yeah, you may want to think about getting that done so you can go back to your girlfriend. She may not be into scars." Tasha draped the towel on the cabinet door handle just behind her.

"Girlfriend?" Chad asked.

"You know, the one sitting with you two last night before Jack decided he needed to interrupt my social life? Then just left her there…by herself?" Tasha crossed her arms over her chest.

"You mean to tell me that you *wanted* that bastard to grab you?" Jack started to get up, but Chad shoved him back down on his seat, adding, "I'm not done here, Jack."

To her, he continued. "And…I now see what is going on here." Chad swabbed another ointment on Jack's wound. "At least…I think I do," he said, anesthetizing the skin before suturing him.

"Jack, you need to communicate better so these things don't happen." Chad began stringing up his needle.

"You try to communicate with her—especially when she refuses to listen to you, much less give you the time of day!" Jack retorted in frustration to Chad.

Chad looked back at her, the string and needle now ready. Jack seemed to be a pro at having to be stitched up, for he did not cringe from Chad. But then, the night before, she had seen the scars across his left chest and upper stomach from what seemed to be shrapnel.

"Get me an aspirin, Tasha. Two of them should do it."

She was glad to be doing something else, her stomach quavering at Chad's next step.

"Well, the shrink is now in session," Chad declared as he started his delicate weave on Jack's forehead. "Seems like she's listening now."

Tasha deposited the two aspirins on the countertop next to them before turning to go get herself a cup of hot tea.

"You see, she even got you a few aspirins to take after I finish with you, Jack."

The microwave buzzed and Tasha yanked on the door, grabbing the hot mug and dunking a fresh tea bag in it before heading back to her bedroom to hang out for the rest of the day. But Chad stopped her from escaping.

"Ah-ah-ah, where do you *think* you're going?" But before she could answer, he said, "Stay right here. I still need your assistance."

She sighed and took up Chad's chair just behind him, and near where his kit lay on the countertop.

She pretended to be bored, waiting.

Jack winced, swearing that time, as Chad drew on the string, the last stitch now done. "You see, Tasha…" He hesitated, tying a knot close to the skin without putting any pressure near the wound. "If Jack was dating, I think I would know about it. Who you saw last night was my sister, who had just gotten in from Anchorage. She's off from college for the coming Thanksgiving week." Chad cut the string. "Not that I would've cared if he dated my younger sister, but I doubt he is into a woman darn near ten years his junior."

"Ah, yes…that's right. He's into cougars!" Her last statement was caustic, reminding her of his preferences.

Jack frowned at her, making him wince again, from around Chad's body where he stood cleaning up his makeshift surgery area.

"Take the aspirins, Jack," Chad interrupted him, using his body to keep the peace between them. "Yes, Jack does seem to have a liking for older women." Chad caught Tasha scowling at Jack. "Not saying that you are old—and certainly not older than Jack here," Chad told her, appeasing her vanity. "So, nothing to worry about then when it comes to my sister."

"But *he shagged your mother*, Chad!" she told him rather indignantly, annoyed by his seemly oblivious nature.

Chad stopped in his actions at this piece of news. It was about time the truth came out, although she was not the one wanting to be delivering it, yet Chad needed to know the *real* Jack. The Jack he was so carefully taking pains to stitch back up.

Chad turned to Jack, forcing Jack to tear his focus away from Tasha and back to Chad when he calmly asked him, "Did she say *shagging*?"

Jack sat there not answering.

"Shagging? Is that an English term I missed learning?"

"Ah…it's an English term, literally, from Great Britain," Jack replied drily. "Archaic in the United States." Jack peered caustically back at Tasha.

"Is it what I think it means?" Chad raised an eyebrow at Jack.

Jack nodded with an "un-hm."

Tasha was waiting for Chad's first punch at Jack's face when the full realization would hit him.

"So…you *shagged* my mum?" Chad questioned in a rather good impression of a Brit.

Jack's head cocked to the side in a half 'yes,' before answering him, "More like she shagged me that night."

Only Jack could see Chad's smile broaden until he could no longer hold his laughter in from the absurdity of the description used for those nights that Jack stayed at his family's home. Chad spied Tasha's smug satisfaction on her face as she waited on what she thought should have happened next, only to see her expression melt into incredulity over Chad's laughter.

"Did you *not* hear what I just said?" Tasha scolded Chad as he and Jack both roared with laughter. She huffily stood up.

"Oh, yeah…I did…" Chad was clutching his side, gleefully smiling at her.

"Shagging…I mean…where in the hell did you pick up that term?"

"It means—"

"I know what it means, Tasha," soothed Chad.

"But honestly, what kind of friend shags his best friend's mother?" Her palm raised upwards, past Chad, at Jack. "Jack *bedding* your mother, much less treating her like another conquest in his long line of willing women?"

It took Chad a minute to get his mirth under control, his near-black eyes glistening with crocodile tears as he took in Tasha's incredulous, wrathful, angelic look.

"Fine…Don't believe me! But I saw her go into your bedroom that night and Jack was waiting for her!" She turned on her heels to take her leave. But Chad caught her arm before she could angrily tromp off. Jack took ahold of her other arm, making her face them squarely.

"Sit down, girl." Chad sniggered, exhaling heavily to quell his mirth.

She dropped heavily onto the barstool, each of them letting go of an arm.

"First"—he laughed a little more, pointing a finger at her—"yes, I do know about Jack and my mother."

Her jaw dropped at that information.

"And you're okay with that?" she asked disbelievingly.

"It's customary in my tribe to 'share the warmth with strangers.'"

"But your dad!" Tasha insisted.

"He knows! Even advocates it!" Chad's mirth bubbled again at her secondary and increased reaction to his statement. Chad reached out to hold her down again with his hand on her arm as he got himself back in control enough to answer her. "My folks are believers of upholding the 'old ways.' They carry on our tribe's traditions…yes, swapping themselves or have other family members 'share' themselves with our 'honored' house guests. It would be an insult to us if you did not accept their 'gracious nature' under their roof."

Tasha was backing away like an unwilling cat being held within his arms.

"Do you understand, Tasha?"

"Everyone?" she asked in an incredulous whisper.

Chad nodded again, hoping that she would understand the cultural differences.

The puzzled expression remained on her face for some time as she looked back and forth between Chad and Jack, and it was clear that she was trying to determine if they were both serious or just pulling a prank on her.

"Tasha?" Chad raised his right hand up, getting her full attention. "Honestly, I swear to our Raven God himself, that is the truth."

Her expression continued to make it clear that she did not believe him. "I can't believe you're still defending him, Chad."

"I'm not."

"But—" Tasha faltered.

"It is why I asked you to sleep with me before we went into their home, remember? It would have kept you from all this…this…this unnecessary anger," Jack filled in.

Both men watched as her thoughts kept running across her face, some clear, some not so clear. She crossed her arms. "But then why didn't you offer yourself," Tasha demanded of Chad, adding, "to me?" And then, upon second thought: "Ugh…never mind, I forgot, I am damaged. Got scars that guys can't get past." She got up to take her leave.

Chad reached out again, forcing her to remain seated. "No…no, that's not the reason. Not the reason at all, Tasha." Then Chad looked back at Jack, who had his entire focus on Tasha, his head sticking past the side of Chad's body, easily done given the length of his torso. "Trust me, I would have…ouch!" Jack had done something to him that Tasha could not see. "But you see, I have two things that kept me from doing anything with you that night. Your scar is not one of them. Trust me on this?" Chad placated her with his hand. Even Jack looked up at him in question. If it was not so serious for Tasha to know the truth, the entire scene was comical.

"First?" she demanded angrily, disgruntled about Chad having *two* issues with her.

"First is that you were as 'high as a kite' that night. I tend to like my women sober when I decide to have fun with them. Ouch! Hey! You two!"

They both punched him on the opposite sides of his torso.

"Secondly, I value my life and really would like to live to a nice, pain-free, ripe old age."

Tasha tilted her head in confusion. Chad jabbed his thumb backwards at Jack.

"The black eye and swollen cheek?" she asked.

"Him."

"Figured. Why?"

"I dunno…Ask him."

Tasha glared at a penitent Jack.

"He touched and undressed you," Jack stated flatly.

"Seriously, Jack? You punched me for that?" Chad pawed at himself. "I'm a nurse! I've seen her in all her glory before at the hospital…remember?" Chad looked to Tasha for support. "Tell him I was honorable with you!"

"You got worked up over that, Jack?" Tasha asked, surprised that he would be like that about her when she was certain she didn't mean anything to him.

"Was he honorable?" Jack asked.

She nodded, finally letting Chad off the hook, the tension between them gone as their eyes locked. She was still trying to process this new information, seeing Jack in this new and different light. *Do I really mean more to him than just a few flings?* she wondered, still grasping at this new line of thought. However, he still remained an enigma to her, never really opening up to her and allowing her to get to know him whenever she did try to be a friend the way Chad was to Jack.

"Hey, you two." Chad tried to get their attention as they had both leaned in, trapping Chad without any personal space to spare.

"Before you two go all gooey-eyed at each other, would you mind letting me get out of the way? Nothing is more dangerous than being caught between a bear and a moose."

Jack pushed him aside, more for blocking his view of Tasha, as she leaned back, giving Chad room to clear out. She returned to sipping her tea, her elbows on the countertop as Chad came around to her far side and repacked his medical kit.

"Thanks, Chad," Jack told him.

"Glad to be of service for you two." He smiled at them both. "I need to get going. Gotta get some shuteye after all the fun last night and this morning with you guys. Thankfully, no one was worse for wear. They should all be back to work on Monday without too many issues."

CHAPTER SIXTEEN

The week before Thanksgiving proved to be even more challenging when it came to dealing with Jack. Although their co-workers knew nothing about their prior involvement or the ups and down of their private life, it was becoming more apparent to the crew that something questionable was afoot. The guys were talking. And Jack was not helping matters when it came to him culling her from the 'herd' as often as he did with some reason or assumption on his part—reasons such as 'he works better alone' or he needed his guys to 'concentrate on other aircraft issues.' He made it impossible for her to work and socialize with the gang.

It seemed that no matter how determined she was to avoid him, he still sought her out. She was beginning to feel like hunted prey, realizing that he was not 'over her' as she had so thought. Having a relationship with the immediate man in charge still did not settle with her. It just was not right in the civilian or military world. Dating a superior was taboo. The last man—an exceptionally good friend that she 'crushed on' and admired—was her squad leader. Although there was no intimate relationship with the married man, he ended up dead on her account by taking the second and third bullet meant for her.

The following Monday morning had proven to be just another day at work. The meeting went smoothly, even with Nate pausing, giving his damaged and tattered crew a dubious look, and then deciding to deliver the pertinent information they needed—including another training session like the last one that she had involuntarily participated in, making her shoulders come up warily around her neck as she remembered the cold-water plunge. Only Sam smiled at her, assuring her verbally that it would not be the same training and that he would make sure that she would not be the next victim, thus ensuing Jack's black look at him, the stitches on his forehead making him look more menacing than normal.

Training turned out to be just an hour long on each aircraft's emergency kit and how to operate each item: the flare gun, an extra gun, the meal kits with their heating apparatus, a fire-starter kit, handheld radio, the water filter straw and purification tablets and so forth.

Their test was to go through each of the aircraft's emergency kits, to make sure all were within certification dates and that all was operational or tested. With six crew men, the work on all the aircraft was done within a matter of a few hours and the crew had to stretch out the rest of the day's work for another six hours.

It was not that the crew had to look busy. Jack and Nate knew better. Not that it was entirely enforced that they had to earn their keep, for there were days that they came in unscheduled or stayed overnight without any overtime pay. The crew had gathered for the most part at the one aircraft that needed a squawk to be worked on—a squawk that would have taken any one of them less than thirty minutes to complete.

Hank had been gathering the tools at one of the toolboxes scattered throughout their hangar, doing a toolbox inventory. Manny and Jarvis were standing apart, for they too had a hidden secret, just like she and Jack. Jarvis sat on one of the six-steppers facing the group, reading the left wheel weights as the rest of them gathered by the cargo side door with Sam and Nick inside, stacking and balancing the cargo. Emanuel called out the weights on the right and tail wheels from the electronic scale, with Tasha just outside writing down the figures on the manifest. All this was getting done while 'shooting the breeze,' as Jarvis would call it.

But obviously this was an issue with Jack when he came over to them to separate her from the group, this time to check on a battery status that had been already checked and was good to go, a known bogus request. But he insisted.

Enough is enough! she seethed, watching Jack take his leave. She had had it! She threw one of her jeweler-type electrical wrenches at him. It sailed cleanly through the air, hitting him square at the back of his head. Jack stopped. Tasha literally watched his hackles rise when his shoulders went back and squared before he half turned back to her.

His expression was part amazement and pure anger at being challenged by this pipsqueak of an electrician.

"You want a piece of me?" she yelled at the top of her lungs, thumping her chest with her fist.

The others drew back, murmuring amongst themselves, daring him to take her.

She took another step forward, pointing past him to the hangar door. "We can take it outside so you can save face from the others when I beat the hell out of you, ya bastard!"

A low whistle came from one of the guys behind her. Jack took a challenging step toward her, cocking his head at her like a taunted grizzly bear that had gotten its face smacked hard by a feisty salmon.

"Ta—sha!" came Nate's razor-sharp interruption. He had just caught her throwing her wrench at Jack and challenging him to a fight. "Jack!" he called, trying to get his attention.

Neither backed down nor seemed to acknowledge their names in their standoff.

"Both of you!" he ordered, finally getting them to look at him, Nate's face mottling to a serious shade of dark red. "Now!" He pointed to the ground, indicating that he wanted them to follow. "In my office!"

They reluctantly took a step each, wary of the other, Jack's eyes dark with anger and annoyance, Tasha's lips determinedly set thin to keep from saying anything further.

"Jack! Pick up the wrench and bring it with you!" Nate ordered over his shoulder, leading the way back to his office. Tasha, being closer, lagged after Nate while Jack picked up the small wrench, lumbering a few paces behind them.

Once inside his office, Nate took his chair behind his desk. Tasha came to a stop just in front of his desk, but with much more distance, giving her anger room to breathe. Jack passed her and went to his usual spot off to the far left side of the desk and remained standing, his height commandeering most of the area in the rather large office and turning it into a tight space. Nora was at her desk just to the right of them, looking up at the egos that had stumbled into their office.

Nate put his hand out to Jack, wordlessly indicating for the offending piece of evidence used against Jack. Jack took one step forward, firmly planting the wrench in the palm of Nate's square working-man's hand. Raven did not say a word as he leaned back in his seat, taking his time looking at both Jack and Tasha standing in front of him, twirling the small electrical-sized wrench a moment between his fingers. He unconsciously tapped one end of the wrench into the palm of his other hand as he took his time thinking, shifting his glance back and forth between them.

The sullen silence of both parties had Nora raising an inquisitive eyebrow at Nate, ceasing any work she was in the middle of doing. Sensing this was serious, she sat straighter in her seat, waiting. The scene they created was comparable to a small courtroom with all the necessary roles: a judge, a defendant, a plaintiff, and a one-woman jury.

Nate sighed heavily. "Tasha…"

She was going to say something, but he silenced her with a warning finger.

"First…no throwing tools."

The wrench was one of the smallest one she had — a 3/8. *How much damage could that have possibly done?*

"You could've have hurt Jack and that meager brain of his, and trust me, he needs all the brain cells he has left."

Tasha's mouth would have dropped, if it was not for her determination to stand up for herself. She caught, in her peripheral vision, Jack's eyes rolling heavenward as he stood with his arms folded over his broad chest.

"*Do not ever* throw a wrench *at anyone*, again, Tasha." Nate enunciated each word, continuing.

"Fine! Next time I'll use a pair of vise grips instead!" she blurted, interrupting Nate, as Nora snorted just to her right and behind her.

Jack's hands uncrossed from his chest and landed on his hips.

"Tools are used to fix things!" Nate stated firmly, ignoring her outburst.

"Well, then…he needs *fixing*!" Tasha directed an accusatory finger at Jack, making her point to Nate. "And I am using any tool necessary to *fix* him on my own!"

Jack's head snapped at her, his eyes glaring angrily.

Another snigger came from behind her. Nate eyed Nora, silently pleading with her to be still or leave.

"Oh my," she coughed in between her mirth, trying to compose herself. Without turning around to look at her, Tasha knew that her easygoing spirit was not going to hide that broad grin of hers, although she was supporting Tasha, woman to woman.

Nate rolled his eyes is if *why me, Lord?* before dropping the small offending wrench onto his desk, piled with the usual paperwork. Raven dragged both hands down over his face until his elbows settled on his desk, forming a triangle where his hands clasped in the supporting peak for his chin to balance on momentarily, like Justice with her scale inverted.

"Secondly"—Nate's index fingers pointed together at her—"I want an explanation as to why my entire crew, including Jack, all look like they have had a bad night out on the town, and you look like an unscathed angel that just sailed through the devil's sandstorm."

Now Jack interrupted him, but Nate jabbed a finger, silencing him.

"I asked *her* this time," he barked, looking at her, daring her to look him in the eye, "and I want the truth. I'm not entirely sure if what you told me is the complete truth after this morning's crew meeting," Nate said to Jack as he turned his full attention to Tasha, expectantly, motioning to her to continue.

"They all stood up for me at the bar last Friday night, when one of the pool players decided to"—she fingered the quotes—"*'hit upon me'* when it wasn't warranted." She gave a halfhearted shoulder shrug at him. "The crew all went to bat for me...defending my 'honor' kind of thing." She sniffed apathetically at him.

"I see." He steepled his fingers, looking at Jack's expression for her story's verification. She didn't want to offer anything more about last Friday night, crossing her arms defensively, her body quarter-turned with one foot forward, prepared for any possible further onslaught of his anger.

"That's so sweet!" Nora cooed. "We have such a good group of guys!"

"Nora, *please!*" Nate reprimanded his wife before turning his attention back on Jack.

Jack's expression did not flinch under Raven's scrutiny. A few seconds ticked by before Nate decided Tasha's version was more believable than Jack's version, or that hers concurred with Jack's version.

"Should I be expecting a bill of damages from the bar owner?" the Raven asked Jack, sighing as he leaned back in his swivel chair, pulling on his chin.

"No, sir." Jack's voice was deep and frighteningly level to her ears.

"I better not, for your sake," Nate told him.

Jack's eyes flashed.

"So what's the problem, Jack?"

He did not volunteer an answer right away.

"A problem so bad that Tasha wants to beat the living daylights out of you"—Nate leaned forward in his chair, squinting at her small wrench without his reading glasses on, reading the size—"with a three-eighths wrench?" He looked up expectantly at him.

"None, other than she won't do what she's told," he growled. It was taking everything out of him to keep from wanting to throttle her for putting them in this situation in front of their boss.

Nate gave Tasha a pointed look. She refused to answer.

"Would you like to tell me what it is that you didn't want to do?" the Raven asked Tasha.

"All sorts of things," Tasha sighed heavily and more to herself.

"Come again?" Nate asked.

"All sorts of repetitive and needless activities to keep me culled from the crew," she told him more huffily. "And after all this time, I am tired of it. From here at work to my off hours, too."

Oh, was the quiet expression Nate gave her with his raised eyebrows, expecting more information to understand the explosive scene he had just witnessed, starting where she had vehemently said "no" and pitched her wrench at Jack, nailing him square on the back of his head.

Tasha quickly side-glanced at Jack before continuing. "My free time belongs to me. But I am forced to cook and clean for him as if I was his wife! While he goes out hunting, fishing, or datin…."

Nate pointed to Jack. "He hasn't…" He hesitated, as if trying to find the best word for this awkward situation.

"No," came Jack.

"No, he hasn't demanded the 'fringe benefits' yet," uttered Tasha at the same time of Jack's response, surprising Jack some, although he kept it to himself.

Nate looked over to his wife, as if trying to discern the term 'fringe benefits.' She shook her head no. It was the type of silent conversation that takes place only after years of marriage between two happily married people. Nate pursed his mouth, digesting the information.

Tasha used the moment to continue addressing her issues. "Also, I don't care to be treated like a mushroom."

Nate's mostly pepper-colored fluffy eyebrows came together at her next comment, motioning with his hand to expound.

"By constantly keeping me in the dark and feeding me crap. Well, not necessarily crap…He hasn't lied, yet…but he doesn't tell you everything you need to know on why he wants something done or not done."

"Not everything needs an explanation," Jack retorted.

Nora made some sort of indiscriminate noise, or so Tasha thought, as Nate looked over to his wife's desk and then behind her momentarily at his closed door.

"For example," Tasha continued, "I just find out this last week that he hasn't been entirely honest with me about cabinmates sharing the utility bills. I've never heard of this, nor have seen one utility bill since I've been here!"

"He dictates who I can associate with here at work. I am tired of being left alone in a cabin. His dog goes out more often than I do!

"If he can see other women, I should be able to go out on my own and date other men! Without his approval! I am tired of sleeping with his dog!"

"Hey, I offered…" Jack interrupted, finally unable to take any more of it.

"I don't date my superiors, Jack!" she barked back at him. Then, to Nate: "I want my own life!"

"I'm not your superior!" Jack reminded her. "We're equals." He pointed to himself and her.

"Equals, my foot! When did you share in cooking and cleaning, or better yet, when were you going to let me know I had to pay my half of the utilities, *Jack*?"

"You were in no position to afford half of the utilities when you got here! You barely could afford to put your car back together at the time, much less pay for half of the groceries!" He jabbed his index finger to the ground between them. "I was being nice to you by helping you out by swapping chores for paying your half!" He crossed his muscular arms over his chest again before adding, "You said you would be open to dating a co-worker—"

"It wouldn't be kosher, Jack! It's nepotism, and I am fairly sure Nate would not tolerate it in their company!"

"Ah…Tasha, that would be hypocritical of us," Nora added, pointing back and forth between herself and her husband Nate.

"Permission to pursue her?" Jack asked of Nate.

"What?" came Nate, surprised at Jack's presupposition.

Tasha exclaimed at the same time, "He's *not* my father!"

"Sure, sure!" Nate waved a dismissing hand at Jack. Tasha glared at Nate and he added, "I don't care what you two do as long as neither of you kill each other in the process, the aircraft work gets done, no other crew member gets hurt in the process, and most of all, neither of you waste my time with harassment suits. I won't tolerate any less, and I expect better from you both!"

"I can't believe I'm hearing this," Tasha muttered angrily to herself, both hands pulling back on her hair in frustration. "This is so wrong…No, no…I want my own place to live. That's all there is to it!"

"And no!" she yelled at Jack. "I'm not dating you!" She was frustrated at having no solution, and in one motion Tasha stormed out to the only place she could call her own—the battery room.

She nearly stumbled on Nick and Sam as they had walked by…or had they? Then she spotted the rest of the crew walking away toward the main hangar, Emanuel looking guiltily back over his shoulder at the commotion of her exodus. The noise she had heard earlier had to have been them. They were all eavesdropping.

She walked huffily to the battery room a few doors down toward the hangar, slamming the door as she took her seat at the bench, putting her elbows on the table and her head into her upturned palms, wishing she could just shut out what had just transpired, all because she lost her self-control. She tried to will her anger under control enough to stop shaking. Now everyone knew…about them.

She did not hear Nick and Sam come in, until Nick asked if she needed help blowing off steam. Sam, being more delicate, asked, "Are you all right?"

She turned on her stool to face them, looking past them out the window of her shop, before answering tiredly, "Yeah."

She sighed heavily at them. They both raised their eyebrows in surprise at her deflated response, unsure what to make of it.

"If there's anything we can help you with…" asked Nick, as she spied Jarvis peeking in before allowing himself in, with Manny right behind him.

"I'm fine, guys. I…I just lost it." She tried to pacify them, not wanting to create a bigger mess.

"We think you should date him," said Manny, as Jarvis elbowed him in his side.

Hank had come in by then, overhearing what was just said, and offered his two cents. "I have to agree with Manny here. Jack's been a changed man since you arrived, Tasha." He cleared his throat as the toothpick he normally chewed on wiggled between his heavily mustached lips. "For the better, I mean. You might want to reconsider the idea."

"We know he's a hard-ass at times, but seriously, has he been that much of a jerk?" Nick asked, and he pointed to the crew. "I mean, we can put him in his place for you if you need us to." Sam and Jarvis, standing on either side of him, gave Nick a double-take at having been involuntarily volunteered by him.

"No…no, guys. Thank you. I'll fix this myself…somehow."

"We're here for you, Tasha," Hank offered. "There are enough ears between all of us to listen to you. Just not too sure if we have enough brains to understand the emotional turmoil you girls go through."

"Well, I still think you two would make a cute couple," came Manny. "Give the man a chance, girlfriend."

She smiled weakly at Manny. "It wouldn't be right, much less fair to you guys, if and when he starts playing favorites."

"Well, I think he already does that Tasha. It wouldn't change anything," Sam said, winking at her. "But then, I wouldn't mind having a chance for a date with you."

She rolled her eyes at him. "Get out of here!" She smiled at them all. "Just give me a while to gather myself."

They reluctantly left her.

When the door closed, she laughed. How could she leave them? She really liked those guys, and her job. She was not about to quit. But the idea had not crossed her mind in the first place.

CHAPTER SEVENTEEN

"Get in," he told her, having pulled the truck beside her, letting the engine idle the truck forward as she continued walking up the incline from the airport to the main road and then on toward their cabin.

The rest of the crew had headed home before she had made her way out the hangar door, stopping by his office, letting Jack know that she didn't need a ride. It had been a day since their 'public' argument.

"I'm fine. You go ahead." She nodded for him to go on without her.

He refused to go.

Jack sighed heavily. "Okay, what did I do now?" he asked from inside his truck's cab.

"Hunh?" She gave him an odd look, not expecting that question.

"I had to have done something today." Even though a day had passed, they were both amicable but at arm's-length distance from each other.

She did not want to discuss the previous day in Nate's office, much less the time that Nate had come into the battery shop to talk with her alone later that day.

She shook her head. "No...Just need to get my exercise."

"You didn't get enough from this morning's walk to the hangar?" he asked incredulously, doing a double-take of her, his hands resting on top of the worn steering wheel.

She gave Jack an annoyed look, then turned toward town, no longer heading toward their cabin when she got to the highway intersection.

Jack's truck zoomed forward, blocking her path on the road's shoulder. He opened his door, getting out of the truck.

"Jack! Please!" She didn't want to fight with him, tired enough from the long workday and the zenith of the previous day's final burning wick to the bomb, when she had blown up in utter frustration at him and her antagonizing situation that they were stuck in, just because she didn't want to become another work-related statistic in terms of failed relationships with a higher-up.

"You're upset! Now, what?" Jack got ahold of her arm, keeping her from walking away. His grip was firm but not in a possessive way. It was the touch of a really concerned friend, trying to keep her from doing something stupid like jumping off a ledge.

And she was, in a way.

"You are certainly working on it!" She sighed heavily at him, pausing as if deciding on something, but then shook her head no. "I'm going to be late to my appointment."

"Appointment?" Jack echoed, his head straightening up and back in astonishment.

"Yes, I have an appointment and I have less than"—she looked at her phone's clock—"fifteen minutes to get there on foot." She pulled her arm out from his grasp.

He partly let her go, stopping at her hand.

"Let me take you there." He tugged gently on her captured hand, encouraging her to take his offer.

"It would not be a good idea, Jack," she dissuaded him, as she pulled her hand free of his. He reluctantly let go of it and she began to walk away.

"Why not?" he asked her back side, causing her to cease after two steps and to look over her shoulder at him.

"I don't want to get into it," Tasha told him tiredly, not desiring another verbal standoff as she tried to resume her walk into town.

"Fine!" He ran a hand through his thick hair.

She stopped, turning completely at his vexation.

"I won't hassle you. I'll just take you there, okay?"

"Promise?" She eyed him suspiciously, folding her arms over herself.

"Why am I going to regret this?" he mumbled, more to himself than to her.

"Never mind," she said in a low, exasperated voice, and turned around to leave him standing there.

Jack took two hurried steps to block her from leaving.

He grabbed her. "All right, all right," he amended as he corralled her into his side of the truck, getting her to scoot over when he slid in next to her. "Where to?" he asked, putting the truck in gear.

"Benson Drive."

He gave her a quizzical look, but she ignored him and refused to expound, looking out the front windshield expectantly.

Jack drove her to the requested location, still unsure what she was doing. She pointed a little further up the street when he turned onto Benson. His gut acidified when he realized Tasha was apartment hunting. He sighed heavily as she told him to park across the street, and if he wanted to, to remain long enough to take her home when she was done.

"I'll come with you," he said, knowing that it was not the best place in town to rent. It was known for renting to the vagrants and to folks that other landlords refused to rent to for not meeting one criterion or another.

"I'd prefer that you didn't," she warned him with a stern look.

"I said I promised." Jack reminded her, turning the engine off.

"Not to give me any hell?" she asked, her eyes searching for any seditious sign.

Jack twisted his mouth, biting his tongue, his hands on the top of his steering wheel, then letting them slide down the inside of the steering wheel in surrender to her censoring eyes.

She nodded at him, let herself out, and did not stop to wait on him as he trailed her. She walked determinedly to the leasing office, entering after having to work at the sticky door. She introduced herself to the agent in the office, not bothering to introduce or explain Jack's presence.

The middle-aged woman looked up in surprise and immediately put on her biggest smile at Tasha. It was clear to Jack that the woman was just grateful for a normal person to have walked in, especially when Tasha made it clear that she was currently employed at their local airport during the small chat they went through as she was getting the keys for the two units that she had open and ready to rent.

She smiled at Jack. "You must be her other half?"

"Ah…no, he's actually my manager from work. He gave me a ride up here," Tasha corrected the woman.

"Oh…then verifying your employment will be a cinch." The manager's smile broadened so wide across her face that her lips practically touched her ears. The image bored into Jack's mind, making him cringe inwardly.

Jack did not smile back at her. He was not buying her sincerity as she continued to tell Tasha that it was an affordable and wonderful place. That it wasn't the Hilton was the only truth the manager spurted out. Tasha looked back at him, seeing his set expression, obvious that he was barely going to behave himself as he did his best to impose on the manager by making her self-conscious. Tasha didn't miss a thing as the middle-aged woman looked back nervously at Jack, excusing herself from going with them to view the two units, telling them that she trusted them to let themselves in, look around, and then to turn off all the lights and, upon leaving, to re-lock the units.

"Are you sure?" asked Tasha.

"Go on," she 'tsked,' and dismissively waved an overdone manicured hand with neon fuchsia nail polish.

As Tasha turned to leave, she glared at Jack, quietly imploring him to behave. He shadowed her. Once outside, she did not bother to wait, eager to look, as they made the short walk to the first of the two two-story buildings. Each building had six units. The first place to look at was the middle unit on the second floor. As they headed for the wooden stairs up to the main outside balcony and walked the length of the walkway, Jack could see her squared shoulders curve protectively inward as they came across a few of the seedier tenants sitting outside. There were two of them on the first floor, sitting in chairs and drawing on cheap booze and cigarettes by the parking lot area. They stared at her, giving her a warm catcall greeting like any extroverted ex-drug users would do. That only made Jack grind his molars. Tasha nodded politely, although cautiously, Jack noted. He, on the other hand, only tilted his head, acknowledging them.

She climbed the stairs, nearly falling on one of the bowed wooden steps, the plank tilting more than it should have. He skipped over the stair easily, avoiding the same fate—if not worse, given his heavier weight. He noted the two rough men looking up through the stairs' slots at them, their curiosity getting the better of them. Jack gave them the same expressionless stare, and the two men resumed their talk amongst themselves.

Tasha unlocked the middle unit and had walked inside by the time he caught up to her. He nearly ran her over when she stopped short once inside the darkened unit. The place had a moldy, damp smell of old cigarettes and other unpalatable smells that assaulted even his nostrils. They left the front door open hoping to air out the place—or at least for them to be able to breathe some untainted air.

Tasha seriously couldn't be considering living here—at least not for the asking $800 a month rent, although it was the cheapest in town. But that should have been her first clue, considering most one-bedrooms were about $1200 to $2000 a month.

Jack found a light switch, illuminating an even scarier place. Her living in the field as a soldier had been more hospitable than that neglected space.

It was evident that the unit still needed cleaning. The carpet, however, was beyond cleaning. Just throwing it out and exposing the subflooring would have made it look ten times better. The laminate flooring was peeling where there were no worn spots, although there were several of those bald areas. The refrigerator leaned to one side and there was only one working burner on the mini stove: the other three burners were missing various parts and unable to work.

He heard her sigh before proceeding to walk down the mini hallway to the bathroom and to the bedroom. He did not need to look any further when he saw the condition of the bathroom in the mirror's reflection when she switched on the light to see more. Jack was grateful when she turned all the lights off and came back to the front door where he stood waiting, hopeful that she would reconsider. Nate had told him that he could not afford to put her in another place. Her staying with him was fine by Jack, now that he had grown used to having her around. She had enlivened his days since her arrival because he never knew what to expect from her—although she had become more predictable as the weeks passed.

"Tasha."

"Don't!" She raised a finger at him. "I still have another to look at, and worst-case scenario, I can make it work with a little elbow grease."

"Seriously? Tasha!"

She walked past him, determined not to hear his tirade, knowing he was right.

"You and I even lived better than this in a war zone, for Christ's sakes!" he said, getting ahold of her sleeve and pulling on her to confront her. He lifted her chin to get her to look at him, knowing she was a bad liar when facing him. Her green eyes gave her away every time.

Her eyes flashed at him from the waning daylight spilling in from the doorway, her determination still there, although wavering.

"Is it that horrible…living with me in the cabin, Tasha? I realize I haven't been the most pleasant roommate," he said, sighing heavily and then pulling her closer to him. "I thought I had done most everything you have asked of me, including giving you your freedom to come and go as you please—although you had it all the time, I just wanted to know that you had someone with you and that I wanted to know where you were. Look, I am sorry if I seem overbearing."

Her eyes glistened as she heard, for the first time, the sincerest apology from him. It wasn't easy for him. She gathered that from his personality. "I've grown rather—"

A man's shaggy head popped in, interrupting Jack, followed by just as scruffy a body, confirming that both the man and his clothes had not seen a shower nor washing machine in months. He looked like he belonged to the apartment that they were standing in. He smiled, showing the few tobacco-stained teeth he had left. It was a starving and filthy smaller replica of Jack when she had first met him, although she would have made sure to put him entirely out of his miserable state. But somehow she got the impression that this stranger had no idea how miserable a life he had.

"Whoowheee! I was told there was a pretty girl wanting to rent here. They weren't lyin'. But I didn't know you had a boyfriend…er husband with you. Sorry for interruptin'." He winked at her. "Just wanted to welcome you to the neighborhood." He eyed her lasciviously.

Tasha easily fell into Jack's arms, grateful for his one arm sliding more protectively around her, feeling his body shift into fight mode underneath the palms of her hands. She prayed the man got the hint, hoping he would go away. But he didn't. She cleared her throat, and said, "We're just looking around at the moment and we have several other apartments to look at before deciding." She looked back at Jack. "Don't we, honey?" She slid her arms around him, squeezing his waist, playing along.

"We sure do. We can talk later," he responded automatically, being the physical protective barrier for her as he moved to turn the light switch off, moving first to make the man back up with his physical presence, and outside as Tasha quickly pulled the door shut, locking it. The man went on back down the original stairs they had come up on as they hurried down the other set of stairs to the next building, where the other unit was a ground floor at the far end.

Tasha quickly got the other door unlocked, letting them in and shutting the door before the man realized where they had gone. That unit was a replica. Jack switched on the light that illuminated the tiny one-bedroom. It was almost as bad as the other one. Not nearly as bad in terms of stench and cleanliness, but it, too, had seen better days…maybe thirty years ago.

Tasha sighed heavily at this one, seeing the years of thick dust on the wall vents and grease-stained ceiling by the stove area. She walked back toward the hallway, inspecting the bedroom and bath. The bathroom was still in pink tile and black-and-white flooring.

It was better, but not by much. She would take this one if need be, she thought, switching the light back off and returning to the main room, taking a detailed look around until her eyes came upon Jack.

He stood by the front door, still not pleased at the situation. It was clear he was doing his best not to give her hell. But it wasn't in writing yet, and she hadn't decided. His apology had caught her off guard. But he could be just not wanting to lose his live-in cook and housekeeper, saying anything to her get her to rethink her decision.

However, she kept wondering if it was the right decision. Logically and ethically, it was the right choice. But emotionally and physically it was not, and she found herself wanting more of him, the silent craving growing into a physical pain with each passing day. She refused to look wishy-washy by asking him to reconsider continuing the affair with her, a co-worker—and an underling, to boot. But then she remembered part of what he was going to say when they had gotten interrupted earlier at the other apartment.

She asked, "What were you going to say to me earlier, before we got interrupted?"

This seemed to pull him out of his thoughts. "I…I can't recall."

She stopped, studying him a moment.

He knew what he was going to say, but he seemed to have changed his mind. "So?" He indicated the apartment with his hands in his coat pockets, changing the subject.

"I think this one will work." She shoved her own hands back into her coat pockets, taking another all-inclusive look at the main room.

He didn't say a word, and she continued. "I'll let Nate know tomorrow that I will take this one and to give me about two weeks to make the transition. I'll be out of your hair in no time." She smiled weakly at him, pressing her lips together afterwards. She moved to pass him, not wanting to deal with the silent awkwardness.

Again his hand shot out, nabbing her before she could fully open the door, leaving the door ajar, and again finding herself standing in front of him. "You do realize that Nate can barely afford to let you have your own apartment? You are being truly selfish putting him in that position. This is costing the business more than you know, and could possibly cause a few of us to lose our jobs." His grip and voice were rougher than the last time, in the other unit. "Why are you doing this?"

"He said it could be done."

"It could be done, but not for certain, Tasha. There's a big difference." He jerked on her, forcing her into his space. "He's not going to give you up, but he's not going to give me up either. But don't force his hand when it comes to the others!"

"I'm not the selfish one!" she snapped, clearly indicating him. "Besides, I am doing the best I can to find the cheapest place, save for sleeping in my car again. And unlike you, I will not be camping out in a tent during the winter!" She got up on her toes to get into his face. "One thing is for certain—I cannot live with you!"

"Why?" He grabbed ahold of her face with both his hands, making sure she wouldn't back away easily.

She slapped at his hands on either side of her face.

"Why, Tasha?" He shook her gently, his voice more insistent. He saw her eyes fill with unshed tears while at the same time he moved to protect himself from that defensive knee of hers, twirling her around and putting her up against the wall by the front door leaning into her, nabbing her hands at her sides and blocking any further movement. He was firm but not rough with her. His strength was more than she was willing to fight, given her physical and mental exhaustion from their constant disagreements the last few days.

"You promised!" she hissed, reminding him.

"Yes, I did. But I want to know why. Why would you want to live in this hellhole instead of where you live now? What is so bad that you cannot stay with me?" He searched her face. "Tell me, Tasha!"

"Let go!" she growled back.

"Not until you tell me why, Tasha!"

The tears had started to pour down from her eyes. He could not take it anymore, wanting to make it better. He wanted whatever it was to be fixed. He knew he needed to do something to make her reconsider, and the only thing he could do, it seemed, was to kiss her, locking his mouth with hers.

The more she pushed him away, the more he wanted her. He felt her whimper and then comply with his mouth. His kiss had become hers, letting her take over. She cried out in anger, but not entirely at him.

"So…" he said heavily at her. "I still think you want me as much as I want you." He looked over her lovely face, only to end on her swollen mouth, wanting another kiss. "And…you have decided to run instead of fight." From the look in her eyes, he knew he had nailed the truth that she had refused to tell him. He wanted to verify that silent certainty, kissing her once more, although gentle that time, savoring her as he created a blazing trail on her face and down her neck and then back up to her mouth again, his hands releasing her hands, pulling her into an embrace. It was the truth, as she melted into his arms.

"Stop being so proud, Tasha."

"Not unless you do," she retorted breathlessly.

The front door opened, catching them in their embrace, as a man stepped in—a different one, but just as unnerving as the last scruffy one. He was bigger, about Jack's size, she noted as he said hello.

"Heard you might be moving in, darling." She looked at Jack and then back at him in question. "Is he bothering you? I can take care of him for you." The man clicked his tongue at her.

"Ah…no…ah, he's not. He's my…" she said, not wanting to lie but not wanting to let these men know she was single the way his eyes were taking her in even though she remained in Jack's arms, as if he was going to be next in line.

"I'm her fiancé," Jack answered for her, saving her, making her look at him rather sharply. But then she quickly composed herself to play her role.

"We were just talking and deciding. But we have a few more to look at." Tasha smiled at him, pulling on Jack to come along with her, covering her back as she walked toward the front door where the man stood. At least he made way for them, letting them leave. She wanted to get out of those apartments—now. Her potential neighbors were making her rethink in Jack's favor.

They made their way back to the leasing office and returned the keys. She politely made their excuses of considering some other apartments and would make her decision from there. Once back at Jack's pickup truck, and locked inside the cab, she exhaled, wrapping her arms around herself and feeling overwhelmed by so many scuzzy men who either looked like recovering drug users or just plain borderline homeless, a few degrees shy of being mentally unstable. She sank in her seat, thinking, waiting for Jack to drive them back to their cabin.

She looked at Jack when he did not bother to start the truck right away, finding him looking at her. She used her feet to push herself back up more in her seat. "What?"

"You mentioned you had other apartments to look at?" He looked back out the window a moment before resting his gaze on her again. "Where to next?" he asked with his fingers on the steering wheel, pointing indiscriminately as to what direction she wanted. He bit the inside of his cheek to keep from smiling when she told him that she had no others to go look at that afternoon and to just go home.

He started his truck and put it into gear, taking his time, knowing she was growing impatient with his casual manner. He made a quick stop by the grocery store again to pick up some beer, telling her to find something easy to make for their dinner that night when she told him that they had some leftovers that they could re-heat instead.

"I feel like having something Italian," he told her.

"You mean you want pizza," she asked as she watched him pick up another six-pack of his favored dark lager. She trotted after him, her one and a half steps to his one.

He smiled at her. "You read my mind."

"Let me guess…a meat-lover's kind too."

"Ah, very good…I'll have you trained yet."

She stopped dead in her tracks on that last comment, very perturbed.

He took a step back, grabbing her hand to come along as if she were a belligerent child, assuring her by lowering his head enough to have his beard brush the side of her hair and neck as he whispered, "Just joking." It made her shiver with delight at his seductiveness. He straightened back up. "Go grab a second one for yourself if you don't like the meat-lover's kind." Then he gently shoved her ahead of him to go to the freezer section while he went to another aisle to pick up a few other supplies to add to his basket. "I'll meet you at the cash register in a few."

Tasha went in the opposite direction, finding the pizza section. She made her choices decisively, closing the refrigerator door to find Sam approaching her, smiling that gorgeous casual GQ smile he was known for in her book.

She greeted him warmly. "Well, I thought for sure you would be up at the local bar with Nick and the others. What are you doing here?"

"Well, one of us has to be responsible enough to break our partying and resupply our cabin. A storm is coming in tonight. It's supposed to be a doozy, where we may be shutting down for a day or so."

"You're kidding—shutting down in Alaska? The land of ice and snow?"

His smile was infectious, and she smiled back.

"Even we need a break occasionally. Rule of thumb is anything over four feet and we declare a break."

"Crap, it only took an inch of snow in Florida to shut us down!"

"Ah, we can still play football in a foot of snow here."

"Now that I would like to see! I bet that gets very cold and wet," she giggled.

"Well, we do need a cheerleader on those days. You willing to be ours?"

She stood by Sam as he reached into another section for some pre-made breakfast meals.

"Of course. Who are you playing against?"

"That would be Jarvis and Manny." Sam closed the door and then resumed their leisurely walk back toward the front of the store.

"And Hank? You forgot him." Tasha tried to imagine the hangar doing a mini football tournament.

"He only referees when it is just the four of us wanting to toss the pig." Then he added, "More like Nerf football, since we have to play around all the parked aircraft."

"I see."

Again they stopped, as Sam grabbed a frozen bag of Tater Tots and a few other pre-made dinner meals.

"When do the others play?" She referred to Jack and possibly Nate.

"They play on occasions. Not often, though—"

"Tasha!"

Her head snapped around at the sound of her name. Jack called for her, rounding the corner of their aisle, interrupting their conversation.

"Speak of the devil," she murmured quietly to Sam.

"The boss comes a calling for you, gorgeous." He laughed lightly at her.

"At least you don't have to live with the boss," she commented under her breath at Sam.

Sam just smiled more, then nodded a greeting to Jack as the two of them approached him. "Hey, Jack. What's up? Found Tasha for you," Sam said, teasing him.

"So it would appear." Jack spoke with his poker face back on. "I didn't know she had become lost."

Tasha could not discern anything from his comment, neither hostile nor friendly. But knowing Jack, she figured on the former option.

"Where are the others?" Jack asked.

"Still up at the bar. Emanuel and I are shopping for the rest of us."

"Manny is here?"

Sam nodded at her question.

"He's over in the fresh produce department crying over the cost of an avocado at the moment," Sam jested.

"Seriously?"

"He likes his fresh guacamole, especially during the winter storms."

"That sounds good. Can I come over?"

"You sure can, if you can tromp through the whiteout." Sam nosed to Jack. "That is…if Jack will let you come out and play."

Jack responded, "I'm not her keeper. She can go anywhere she wants." The only hint that he still had control over her was in his next statement. "But one of you guys will pick her up in the snowstorm."

Tasha raised an eyebrow at this comment. As if Jack were her father!

Without further ado, Jack indicated toward the boxes. "I'm starving. You got the pizzas?"

Tasha showed them to Jack, and he took them from her as she spied the full basket resting in his large hands.

Sam had not missed any of it, evident in his smile at her. That part was clear, as Tasha silently rolled her eyes at him as soon as Jack turned his back on them, heading toward the cash registers.

"I better go feed the bear before he gets out of hand," she said sarcastically to Sam, following Jack's trail, looking over her shoulder at him, smiling apologetically. Sam was the only one who had any idea what it was like to live with Jack, after she had talked to him during a few of their flights together.

When she came to where Jack was unloading the basket at the conveyor belt, she harshly whispered at him, "You can be such an ass at times! What the hell gets into you?" She pulled out a box of her favorite tea to hand to him, one of the last items in the basket, making her assistance futile. She smiled at the cashier when Jack refused to answer her immediately.

Jack only looked at her before pulling his wallet out to pay for their groceries. The other store helper got their bags ready for her to pick up, only to have Jack take all but one for her to carry back to his truck.

The wind had picked up, making the air damper and colder. She could see the clouds gathering to the south of them, over the gulf waters. They were still low on the horizon in the low light of the late afternoon. It would be dark within minutes. It was not until they were both in the truck and Jack had started the motor that he spoke. "If wondering what happens to you makes me an ass, then so be it. I always find myself having to rescue you from the men and wildlife."

"Oh, for Pete's sakes! That was Sam! Not one of those crazies at the apartment complex!" She slammed her hand down on the bench seat between them, facing him as he continued to drive. "You know, our Sam? The Sam that works with us on the same flight line?"

She shook her head at him. "Since when is he a threat?"

He remained quiet as he concentrated on driving.

"Is that why you pulled me off his flights?" Tasha asked next, turning back into her seat, staring out at the highway.

His silence was the answer, as far as she was concerned. He turned onto their gravel driveway.

"I'll be damned," she said more to herself. "You think I am having an affair with just about anyone I talk to, the way you react."

Jack put the truck in park once they pulled up to their cabin. "Just like you do when I talk to other women, Tasha," he retorted.

"Me? No…you encourage and take actions with other women! You and I are different in that I just have normal daily engagements, which happen to be the guys at work, and while I am out having fun with a group of people…yes, I know they are mostly men, but I am not flirting or bedding them!" Her subliminal jealousy was taking over her, although she knew better than to become riled over anything Jack did because they had no discernable relationship. It was ambiguous to her.

Tasha turned to him before he could undo his seat belt, putting her hand on the buckle. "Shagging your best friend's mother? She was extremely pleased with herself the next morning, bud!" She got up into his face. "And that waitress."

He tried to move her hand so he could undo his seat belt, only to squeeze her hand hard enough, without hurting her, to get it to unclick. But she grabbed his belt, not letting him free.

"Yes, *that* woman who literally throws herself at you!"

His strength won out, and extricating his body from the seatbelt, he got out of the truck's cab.

Tasha whirled to her side, getting out, angrily marching around the truck to invade his space. She refused to be ignored while she tried to make her point to him. "That's a far cry from just talking!" she blurted in anger to his back side as he was retrieving their groceries. "She would bed you right there in the restaurant's booth since you do *nothing* to discourage it! But I have never once berated you or in front of her for the few times we have been there for breakfast or lunch. It's not my place to say anything about it to you since we are no longer…hell, I don't know"—her hands pulled up and out on her hair in her built-up frustration—"what we are in this relationship when it comes to your thought process." She exhaled heavily but held up a finger at him to make one more point as she was refilling her lungs, thinking to herself on how her mother could do her long-winded tirades she was known for. Realizing how much she sounded like her mother at that moment, she internally cringed at the errant thought. Tasha corralled her emotions.

Jack turned around with all their bags in his hands when she had ceased talking, her anger moderately subsiding. She stood there with her hands on her hips, looking at him.

"Unlike you, I can, on most occasions, control my reactions toward you much better than you can with me over the silliest minute things when it comes to me socializing with the crew!"

He just stood there, looking somewhat bored at her.

"You don't see any men—especially our guys—throwing themselves at me, do you?" She jabbed at herself with both hands for emphasis.

"The keys." His utter nonchalance disrupted her one-sided tirade.

"Keys?"

"Yes, the keys, take them." He wiggled them on his index finger that had separated from his grip on their bags of groceries.

She took them and carried on, for she was not about to let go of the subject. "So you have no right to treat any of your co-workers like crap just for talking to me, on or off work." She unlocked their cabin and he carried all the bags to the kitchen island, maneuvering around a happy Drake before the dog helped himself outside. She closed the door against the cold air. "It is *so* not your place to tell me what, when, where, or how I can go, especially when I am off work!"

He turned to her, folding his arms across his chest, waiting.

"You don't see me going after every woman you talk to, do you?" She crossed her arms to match his stance. "Even that waitress, Katie, you kiss each time we go to that particular diner! Both Ula and her must be better than just good enough for you?"

He still did not move.

At that point she just gave up, so mad at him that she found herself shaking and depleted to the point of crying. Her jealousy reared its ugly head at her internally and then she promptly smacked it deep down, refusing to let it get the better of her. Tasha realized it was a waste of her time trying to make him understand her viewpoint. She just wanted a hot tea before crying herself to sleep again. She threw her hands up in the air in defeat. "Better than me, obviously!" she said, her voice cracking on the last word.

Jack nabbed her as she turned to take her leave of him, pulling her to him.

Tears fell as she pounded her fist into his chest, still angry and frustrated at him for what his presence did to her. "Stop it!" she sobbed into his chest.

"Tasha," Jack said softly, stroking her windblown hair down. "I'm sorry. It wouldn't take much for you to leave and I guess I get a little perturbed over any guy talking to you. But then, it seems like every time I turn around I am having to pull you out of some nasty situations, like the bar that one night and then today with all those men looking at you as if you were going to be their next village whore. All because you want what I have to offer but refuse to take it because of our work status, even after I made my intentions clear a few days ago. I'm not a monk. I refuse to be one just because you decide you don't want me. If you haven't noticed, there's not much up here in terms of female companionship."

He shifted under her, pulling her to a stool in front of him, getting her to sit facing him on his chair at the island, still holding one of her hands in his. He cupped her chin. "You," he said, caressing her face with his thumb, "you are a

288

hell of a gem up here in these parts. I see men falling all over you, where you can't seem to see it." He let go of her hand to wipe a tear from the corner of her eye with his thumb. "I'm tired of fighting, just to keep you safe, and most of all, around me. I...I can't let you go." He grabbed her hand again. "I still want you. Here...with me...in this cabin."

Then they both heard his stomach rumble, breaking up the seriousness of their conversation.

"To cook and to clean for you, I know," she mumbled her fate.

"No," he said, and pulled her into him, "much more than that,"

He kissed her, tentatively at first, then, deepening as his carnal desire took over, pulling her off her stool and enwrapping her within his arms.

Tasha felt her legs go weak as she became one with him, leaning into his body for support.

In between, the kisses, he murmured, "I know you want it as much as I do, Tasha."

He slid her jacket off her as she did likewise to him. She sighed at the feel of his body underneath the soft flannel shirt he wore. She caught a trace of his cologne as she worked at his shirt's buttons, concentrating on just him, her body's desire taking over to her heart's content. Nothing was going to break that moment—or so she thought before the front door flew open. She felt him push her away, standing up to confront their intruder. She turned to see Drake bounding in with someone just behind him.

It was Chad. He had a rucksack with him as he came in, dropping his belongings onto the floor by the entryway. "Hey, you two, don't let me interrupt this"—he stopped, trying to gauge the scene before him, unsure—"*peaceful* moment between you two?" He took off his boots. Upon seeing no weapons between either of them, he said, "That's a nice change, to see you two *not* trying to kill each other." He smiled at them both.

Tasha recovered, grabbing her coat along with Jack's to hang up in the coat closet as Chad took his off, throwing it over the back of the closest chair that formed the horseshoe of the sitting area.

"You weren't trying to kill him, were you?" Chad asked her quietly when she passed him.

She gave him a stern look. He smiled crookedly at her, giving her a quick wink.

Then he turned to Jack, "Hey buddy, just needed to crash here since my shift ended and I have to be back in another eight hours to do another twenty-four-hour shift at the clinic. Mom and Dad said the storm is already hitting at home and told me remain here in town. They're expecting quite the whiteout. So I hope you are okay with me staying here for the night." Then he added, "You don't even need to share Tasha with me for the night."

She cuffed Chad now that she had finished hanging their coats.

"Hey, now." Chad smiled at her.

Jack laughed, now that he had all their groceries un-bagged.

Chad gave her a quick hug, the two frozen pizza boxes having caught his attention. "Man, I hit jackpot night!" he said, coming over to the island. "When's dinner?"

"Well," Jack said, picking up one of the boxes, "according to the instructions, about thirty minutes." He dropped the box and turned on the oven. "Make yourself useful, Chad. Get the fire going in the fireplace."

Tasha sidled up next to Jack, reaching up to the cabinets to grab them some plates and cups. He smiled at her, the smile reaching his eyes. He playfully tagged her rear end when Chad had turned around to concentrate on building a fire.

"We're not done, yet," he said, for only her to hear.

Her night off from cooking was nice, although they played host to their last-minute guest. They chatted amicably over dinner and then a few rounds of cards until Tasha yawned, tired from the long day at work, apartment hunting, and then a warm belly full of pizza and some wine.

She excused herself to attend to her needs before bed, going to the bathroom to shower and unwind. After her shower she peered out into the hallway, deciding it was safe to head for her room for the cabin was dark, the only light coming from the embers in the fireplace. She saw the back of Chad's black head propped up by the arm of the sofa. He seemed to have settled down for the night, twirling his beer bottle in his fingers as it rested on the coffee table next to the sofa, watching the embers die further. She quickly dashed to her room with just her towel wrapped around her and closed her door quietly. As she reached for the light switch, she felt her hand encounter something other than the switch and she nearly yelped, her towel dropping, only to find herself enveloped in Jack's arms, a hand initially over her mouth until she nodded that she knew it was only him in the dark.

"What are you doing?" she asked quietly.

"I'm sleeping with you. Chad has my room for the night."

She arched an eyebrow at him. No one had spoken of sleeping arrangements earlier.

"I'm not sharing myself with Chad," Jack mocked in a feminine voice.

Tasha smiled, trying not to burst into laughter.

His voice grew deeper. "Nor am I willing to share you."

As his eyes drank in the sight of her body, he inhaled sharply, picked her up and dropped her onto her bed with him falling next to her as he possessively got ahold of her and began his promised assault. She felt like she had died and gone to heaven in his arms. Starved of his touch for so long, she no longer cared, giving in, joining his need to possess her. His warm hands stroking her entire body, creating a world for themselves. But she still wondered if she would be just a fling, wanting so much more with a man that barely let her into his world.

The following morning, she awoke to an empty bed as she reached across her bed with a searching arm, noticing that he was not lying up against her. She sat up, noting the daylight was much further along than she had first thought, as the rest of her woke up. Not hearing anyone in the bathroom, she donned her sweatpants and matching shirt before plodding out to the main room looking for both men.

She only found Jack, who was just coming in from outside, stomping the snow off his boots with Drake running past him. Behind him, she saw a landscape thickly draped in white with more white snow falling.

"Mornin' Tasha." he greeted her, and smiled lazily. Contentment exuded from his soul. Tasha had never seen him as happy as he was until that morning, as he took off his coat, shaking the snow outside the door, then closing the door, and laying the coat over the chair to dry before putting it in the closet.

She stood taking in each moment, photographing those moments into her memory forever.

"About time you got up. I thought I must have done you in last night." Jack grinned even more at the thought of them as he came over to her, sliding his arms around her waist. The crisp winter air filled her nostrils, his arms large and long, giving her such comfort and security after weeks of what had felt like solitary life in the wilderness.

She sighed happily, glad he had convinced her to remain in their cabin as his roommate—not hard to do, given that her last apartment search had pretty much sealed the deal in remaining put. She closed her eyes, savoring every bit of him, enjoying the gift of his presence.

He surprised her by scooping her up, spinning her around as she wrapped her legs around him, and then placing her on the kitchen island's countertop. "Are you hungry?" he asked her.

"Are you cooking?"

"I can."

"Then by all means, I am ravenous!" she told him.

He left her sitting there to attend to their breakfast. His large frame had originally blocked her view of the winter scene from the living room's picture window, of everything heavily covered in snow. Tree limbs were bent downward under the weight of frozen water.

"It really snowed out there last night."

"Almost two feet," he commented as he got the bacon going. "Looks to be more coming. Another band of dark clouds coming in from the gulf. Might be here in another hour."

Then, she asked, almost having forgotten that Chad had spent the night, "Is Chad at work?"

"Yeah, he was up around five this morning. Wasn't entirely bad then, but he might have hell after he gets off his shift. We might expect him back again since his parents' house is a little out of the way." He looked back at her, sitting there on the countertop. She was still facing toward the living room, her luscious bottom enticing him again. "You all right with him coming back here?"

She turned to him, shrugging her shoulder demurely at him. "I'm fine with it, but now he knows about us. What keeps him from telling the rest of the crew?"

"He's not a part of our aviation team. And I trust him. He's not one to gossip."

"Even if he says something accidentally?"

Jack came back over to her, blocking her picture-perfect view of the winter wonderland. But she was just as happy with the warm, secure vision of him. He pulled up a stool to sit in front of, making him nearly eye level with her face.

"He knows better. I've already told him to keep a lid on it due to our respective positions at the hangar." He scooted himself between her legs and snuggled himself into her body, wrapping his arms around her as he watched the stovetop from his position. They remained, enjoying the quiet solitude of the morning until he had to flip the bacon.

It was not long before the smell of bacon was filling the air and her tummy was growling in anticipation. She twisted again where she sat, continuing to watch him, fascinated. She was now free to observe him without having to be aware of him or others noticing her staring. She ended up stretching out over the entire countertop on her tummy, her lower legs, bent at the knees, wagging in the air like two tails, her chin propped on her upturned hands.

He had a wonderful 'tushie' and long legs. For a large man in height, he was well proportioned. Not gangly. His was hair a thick wooly brown with auburn highlights. His beard matched accordingly. Since their trip to Anchorage, he had kept it cropped at a captain's length, although it seemed to have thickened along his jawline. His facial features were broad and angular, a high square forehead with prominent cheek bones and a square jaw that joined a muscular neck. His hands large, square, with long fingers that had uncanny strength, like a bear's paw. He still reminded her of a grizzly bear in his looks, yet it was mostly due to his temperament.

Although he was dressed as usual in the two shirts and wore the thick insulated pants, she could make out the lines of his body. She pondered how he kept his military form when he drank a beer almost nightly. He did have exercise equipment downstairs and she had found him on occasions using it—but never at the same time of day or for hours on end.

Hell, she knew the treadmill saw more of her than him. The weights…well, there was no way she would be able to pick them up or change them out. They were far too heavy for her. Just changing them would be all the weightlifting she would need.

Jack did a double-take when he caught her watching him. He smirked at finding her lounging across the kitchen island, her head propped up on her hands, watching him cook as he took the bacon off to do the eggs next. He leaned up against the adjacent wall in order to keep an eye on both the pan and her. "You're going to make me burn our breakfast if you keep that up." His blue gray eyes grazed over the length of her body, her legs lazily swinging in the air just behind that wonderful rump of hers.

She made a moue at him and rolled off the countertop, dropping lightly to the floor. "Well, I guess I better fix that so that breakfast is tolerable. And I, for one, would like a cup of hot tea, and you would like your cup of coffee?" she presumed.

She came by his side of the island to tease him more with just the closeness of their bodies in such a tight spot. He nabbed her, spooning her as he held her in a bear hug, planting a kiss on the top of her head, inhaling her scent, ruffling her hair with his breath.

"Forget the coffee, I think we return to bed after breakfast," he murmured into her hair.

"What about work?"

"There's none for today."

"You mean for just us? That will be a bit obvious to the crew as to what we are up to."

"No, we are officially shut down for the day."

"The storm isn't going to last that long, is it?"

"No, just need to give the town a chance to clear the roads and the airport authorities to clear the flight line. Meanwhile, I thought I would use my time wisely by having my way with you in addition to getting some more sleep. But somehow I don't see myself getting any sleep." His hands slid down her body, stroking her like a cat, her body reacting likewise in appreciation.

"Eggs," she reminded him.

"Eggs?" he echoed as he hesitated in his nuzzling her with his prominent nose along the side of her face.

"Yeah," she said as Jack moved reluctantly away. "I kind of like mine sunny side up, not overdone like these will be in just a few."

Jack released her, attending to their eggs as she went to grab them their cups. "Are you sure you don't want coffee?" she asked him again, microwaving some hot water for her tea. He nodded no.

They settled down for their meal, Jack's hand spread protectively over the top of her thigh as he ate, studying her. She smiled contentedly at the thought of many days spent like this and if she would succeed in having more moments like this.

"What are you thinking?"

She did not want to disclose her thoughts, unsure of resuming the relationship. It was still new, and she didn't want to push him when it came to thinking ahead. Would she be another in his long line of casual lovers? She shrugged her shoulder dismissively at him. "Not much. Just wondering about this moment."

"This moment?"

She wrinkled her nose at him some. "I like this…this hour…" She shifted uncomfortably at having to talk honestly with him, the act itself so rare between them. "Even last night was wonderful…"

"But?" Jack asked cautiously. She noted him shutting down and backing away from her, as the weight of his hand grew suddenly heavier on her thigh.

"—but how do we *keep* this?" She put her fork down. "I mean how do I keep *your* interest?"

Jack was not entirely sure where she was going with this, his brow crinkled in confusion at her. "You have my interest. You have me and for as long as you allow me"—he moved her thigh to separate her legs for his hand to slide up closer to her private part—"to have you." He leaned forward, his other hand reaching to cup her chin, bringing her face closer to enticingly kiss her. Jack eventually broke away from her addictive mouth. He laid his forehead against hers, the heavy weight of his hand on the back of her neck, keeping her still. "We can make this work. We are both professionals—prior soldiers, at that—and this private relationship we have…it can survive. What we do here has nothing to do with our work."

Jack searched her eyes for her answer. She nodded her agreement, then closed her eyes, disappointed. She wanted more, a future, and it was clear that Jack was simply happy to have her for the present, nothing more. She would have to accept that if she wanted to keep her tiny bit of happiness and to make it last a little longer than one day. She sighed inwardly.

She felt his hand squeeze momentarily on the back of her neck. "Come on"— he forced her back into the moment—"finish up, I've got plans for us."

She did not feel like finishing her meal. She picked up her hot tea to sip instead as she tried to gather all the blocks of her defensive wall together, trying to rebuild what was left of the protective wall she had surrounded herself in the past few weeks. Jack had torpedoed that wall in less than half a day, yesterday afternoon. She was not going to get it back up anytime soon, as she found him finishing her portion of her meal in less than two bites, picking up their plates to rinse and leave in the sink. He returned, taking her hand in his and leading her back to her bedroom where they ended up in her bed with him pulling the covers back over them. He pulled her in to his body, snuggling down in the warmth of the bed linens and letting her use him as her human furnace.

The snow day had become a perfect quiet solitude that most folks could only dream of as a vacation day in a log cabin. Very few would make it a once-in-a-lifetime vacation. But for her, she was literally living the dream as they spent the day napping, making love, and then snuggling with each other only, to repeat the process.

It was mid-afternoon, when the sunlight began to fade, that she found her fingertips tracing the lines of his various scars along his chest. The main scar, which had permanently blazed a darker red mark, started around his upper midriff and ended near his shoulder. She rested her head on her upturned hand where she had propped herself up on her elbow to look at him as he lay on his side, eyes closed, resting from their latest pleasure, his face partially buried in the pillow from the sheer weight of his head. He was still awake but he was slowly drifting asleep, his breathing slowing and becoming shallower on her.

"That tickles." His baritone voice lazily resonated deep from within his chest.

She stopped, but then continued a bit more firmly so as not to tickle him on the other scars. He stopped her hand with his, bringing it back to his lips for a light kiss, his whiskers creating an electric fire on her palm.

"Are you able to tell me what happened?" she asked.

"Hmm?" he muttered, reluctant to move his head in the pillow.

Tasha pulled her hand out of his grasp as she lightly tapped one of his scars.

Jack's blue-gray eye opened, focusing on her. He studied her before he answered her. "I did tell you." He exhaled heavily. "I survived a roadside bomb." He caught her hand again. "They're just shrapnel wounds." He gave her a concerned look before taunting her. "I'm beginning to wonder if you're a real blonde, the way you forget things."

She 'tsked' him before rolling away, but he pulled her toward him, hugging her. "What is it that you want to know?"

"Expounding more would be nice. Some details to let me know what you have been through."

"Why? It's in the past."

"Yes, it is, but talking about it helps from time to time," she tried to encourage him. She wanted to know more. There had to be a reason for the way he acted and rarely talked about himself.

He looked at her as if deciding what to say as he laid his other hand upon her face, his fingers stroking the side of her cheek, each finger tracing her features. Tasha was surprised to find him telling her.

"It was my fourth tour and another new squad under my command. The last squad was killed, save for me and two others, in the last patrol. We were doing our routine patrols around the airport's perimeter. Our jobs were to gain the upper hand, clearing the Taliban and their supporters out of the upper regions surrounding our base. This time it was a firefight, we were ambushed right on the street. Our driver tried to back us out of the area, only to hit an IED. Only three of the six of us survived that day. I ended up badly wounded from the shrapnel. The other two dragged me to safety until a backup unit could reach us. Pretty much end of story."

His lips pressed together as if he had tasted something bad—bad as in blood and/or the dessert sand. She did not probe further. But she was curious now. Jack had gone through four tours of duty. Most soldiers don't beat those kinds of odds, especially Marines out on the front lines.

"So your fourth tour was your final. You are incredibly lucky not to have been killed. This scarring looks like it was serious enough to put you out." She inspected the other scars, some light, others thicker and more intense.

"It's the main scar that put me out." He exhaled heavily, taking her finger, dragging it over the largest one she had originally traced. "The other scars are from the prior incidences. The last one came pretty close to nicking my heart, and the doctors deemed it was time for me to choose another profession." He looked at her a moment. "I agreed, since I seemed to have become bad luck." He laid her hand on the bed between them, still covering hers with his.

"Bad luck?" she questioned in surprise. "I would think good luck…that you survived."

"For the others, I mean," he corrected. "To the men under my command."

"Why the others? Soldiers die all the time in war, Jack," she assured him, having experienced some of it herself. She would have been one of them had it not been for Staff Sergeant Herrington getting in between her and the next two bullets.

"You had four tours. You had other squads in tours one, two, and three, right? They have gone on to either do more tours or go home, right?"

His silence was her answer, and she realized that Jack had lost every single member of each of his squads, save for two: the two that had saved him on the last mission.

Her eyes conveyed her understanding that words could never describe. Losing a squad was like losing an entire family. You got to know all your battle buddies when a group was put under daily pressure. You constantly drilled and trained, getting to know each other's flaws and strengths. Whether you liked them or not, you became a unit, a tight-knit functioning family. He had lost all of them, save for two.

"Don't!" he gruffly told her, pushing her away and getting up to leave her.

She jumped, from years of reactive military training, at his sudden change in demeanor, unsure of what to do next as the cool air sank between them. She protectively pulled the sheet up over herself where she sat watching him pull on his discarded clothes as he found them one by one.

"Jack, I'm sorry for whatever it is you think I've done."

"I don't need your pity or concern."

She got to her knees on her bed to give her some height as he stood up. "*Damn skippy*, I'm concerned! Because I know what *that's* like! *I've* been there and I've *seen* it! But getting angry at me for caring, or shutting me out, is not the answer! It's how normal people react, Jack!"

Jack turned to her. He was going to say something to her, his mouth opening a few times before his jaw clamped firmly, deciding not to say a word and leaving her in silence, closing the door firmly shut instead of slamming it.

Since arriving in Alaska, Tasha had never felt so cold until that moment. She remained in her room the rest of the day, not coming out—not even for dinner. It seemed she would never understand him and some of his actions. She wanted into his life, to know him inside and out. She was tired of the one-sided rollercoaster ride. *No more*, she grumpily thought to herself, tired of being made to feel like an idiot. She would shut him out for good this time.

CHAPTER EIGHTEEN

After the past week, Tasha was sincerely looking for some personal downtime away from everyone, including Jack. Neither had spoken since that afternoon four days before, other than what was necessary to keep their current lifestyle at home and at work civil.

She figured he would be out hunting with Chad or staying with Chad's family over the four-day weekend, thus giving her the much-needed space for her own whims.

Although the rest of the work week went on as usual after that snowstorm, and Monday's workday was typical with working on her flight hours and some light maintenance, it was only after work and a stint in the tanning booth for some more 'sunlight therapy' that all her plans went to crap that evening.

They arrived at their cabin after work, ready to eat a home-cooked meal and to settle in and to prepare their next day afresh. Jack greeted Drake as normal and went after him to play fetch in the front yard for a few minutes. However, Drake met them outside their cabin, and she was certain that Drake had been inside before they had left for work that morning. It was when she went to unlock the front door that she found it already unlocked, her key not meeting any resistance when she turned the handle.

Tasha walked in, expecting to see Chad, only to find a drop-dead gorgeous twenty-something dark-haired brunette sitting at the kitchen island eating a bowl of their dinner from the crockpot that she had started that morning. The woman immediately put her fork down, giving Tasha a big, wide, heartwarming smile, standing up at Tasha's entrance.

"Oh my…he *certainly* knows how to pick them!" She beamed, her Southern accent thick. "*My*…a *blonde* this time!"

Tasha looked behind her to double-check that this strange woman was not talking to someone else in the room.

"No, silly…you!" the woman reiterated as she came over to greet Tasha. "You are absolutely gorgeous!"

At that comment, Tasha's eyebrows shot up in surprise, as she was not entirely sure what to make of this tall young woman, but there was something familiar that she could not immediately put her finger on. She furiously racked her brain with *who is this woman?*

Cocking her head in *do I know you?* Tasha dropped her work bag onto the armchair closest to the door.

Tasha was neither hostile nor openly inviting, but the woman blithely ignored her as she continued. "I can't believe Jack hasn't told us about you!" She traversed the short distance, clasping Tasha's hand in hers in greeting.

Before Tasha could ask her who she was, Drake bounded past her with Jack in tow, and as he closed the cabin door, the runway model squealed in delight at seeing Jack, immediately dropping their handshake. She ran at him, jumping up on him as he caught her, the brunette wrapping her legs around him as he somewhat twirled them together, absorbing her full-impact greeting.

"Figured it was either Chad or you who let Drake out," Jack said as he caught the diminutive woman full-on in a massive bear hug, twirling around, lovingly enwrapping her body with his arms.

Tasha raised an inquisitive eyebrow at them, but quickly caught herself about showing her expression as Jack made the full circle with the girl still in his arms.

The intimacy was a little disturbing for Tasha, since her last intimate encounter with Jack had gone south in flames. She hurriedly hung her coat in the coat closet by the front door, no longer hungry after meeting this stranger and watching Jack eagerly kiss the woman. She turned her back on them, heading to the kitchen to drop off her used lunch containers in the sink and then head off to her room.

But Jack stopped her. "Tasha, this is my sister, Lela. One of the most important women in my life."

Sister? She repeated the word in her head, stopping her in mid-departure, in her struggle to hide her jealousy, and chastising herself for caring about what or who Jack knew. *That's right!* Tasha remembered seeing a photo of her tucked in between the pages of one of Jack's books. Inwardly, she sighed heavily before turning to face them with a plastered-on smile. "Sorry for not being more welcoming. I was trying to figure out who you might be and why you looked familiar." She compared the family features between the two of them, noting the same hair coloring and wavy thickness, the long torsos with near-matching heights, and their prominent noses. She let her inspection of them be the reasoning behind her comment, not because of her prying into Jack's private life when she could whenever he was not around and which he rarely discussed, even when she prodded him.

"Jack, why are you keeping her a secret from the rest of us? I didn't even know you were dating again! I'm so happy for you." Lela playfully slapped his broad chest, her hand palm upwards, indicating to Tasha. "And a blonde this time! Even that's *new* for you," she jested him.

"Ah..." Tasha hesitated, at a loss for her name.

"Lela," she filled in for Tasha.

"Lela," she affirmed, "we're not dating." She doggedly pointed a finger back and forth between her and Jack. "I'm just his roommate and co-worker. We just share this cabin."

Jack made a quick face at her that only she could see from her vantage point.

Tasha headed toward the kitchen, throwing a quick smile over her shoulder at Lela. "Sorry to disappoint. But I'm sure Jack will find someone soon—he has so many waiting for him if he would only make his move and be a bit more conversational." She knew she didn't have to look his way to see his frustration;

she *felt* it aimed at her back side.

Yet Lela chimed in behind her, "Aww…I think you two make a cute couple."

Tasha ignored her comment, picking up the lid to the crockpot to check on their dinner, stirring it to see if it was ready, even though that was obvious, since Lela decided to help herself to it.

"It's really good! I hope you all are hungry. I hate eating alone, although I did start without you." Lela walked back to the kitchen island to retake her seat and resume her eating. "I didn't eat lunch on the plane, and I was ravenous…and the smell of it was divine." Lela took another bite, savoring the taste. "Umm…This is terrific, Jack. But I'm telling you, I know it wasn't you who cooked this," she continued with her mouth full.

"Nope. Credit goes to Tasha," Jack said, having grabbed two more bowls from the cabinet for the barbecue stew. He slid the bowls over to Tasha to dish out their portions while grabbing a loaf of bread for all of them to share. Tasha did not bother to look at him as she took the bowls, dishing out their meals, giving him the physical essence of what he had done to her a few days earlier when he shut her out.

Jack noted her cool and aloof demeanor toward him. He knew he deserved it. But he had not been ready to open up to her that day—not with past war brutalities dampening what had been a perfect day in his book—and he was regretting it. He refused to saddle another, especially her, with his burdens and guilt. Leaders were supposed to be strong for others, not the other way around. But he had not bothered trying to correct it yet, not knowing how to tell her of the things that constantly plagued his mind. He didn't want her to know it was him, that he was the epic failure at being a leader. Yet there he was again, leading Nate's crew every day, concerned whenever something went to plan or didn't and fearing every day that he might end up losing one of their guys to some unforeseen and preventable accident.

After grabbing the silverware, he pushed one fork over to her as he took a filled bowl, sliding it over to his seat and leaving two barstools open between him and his sister. Jack studied her, trying to discern her next action or thought. He knew her temper was simmering under her placid demeanor. She was still angry at him, and now probably even more at the fact that his sister had shown up unexpectedly. That reminded him, and he turned to Lela. "So, sis…what brings you up so far north, and not at Mom and Dad's place?"

"Well, it's our Thanksgiving break and I thought it would be nice to come visit you instead. It was a last-minute thought to come see you. Mom and Dad get to see me all the time during all my other semester breaks."

Jack gave Lela a knowing look.

"Honest…I swear to God, Jack! I'm just here to visit my big brother!"

"Mom didn't put you up to this?"

At that question, Tasha looked up from her bowl where she stood just apart from them, leaning up against the back wall of cabinets by the sink and stove, observing the little family reunion.

"Tasha, come sit down and eat." Jack begged her to join them by patting the barstool nearest to him.

Tasha did not comply to his request. "I've been sitting in a cockpit for the past seven hours. I'm tired of sitting."

But Jack knew it was an excuse.

Lela twisted in her seat to look back at her, giving her a quizzical look before returning her attention to her brother and answering him. "No." She raised her right hand at him, swearing, "On scout's honor, I am not here on reconnaissance mission by Mom or Dad. Come on, Jack! Can't we just visit and have fun like we used to have?"

Tasha snorted to herself at the thought of Jack being 'fun' to hang out with, tapping her chest as if she had swallowed her meal wrong, momentarily distracting him from his sister, only to find her silently laughing.

"What's so funny, Tash?" Jack asked.

"Oh, nothing." She smiled sweetly, pressing her lips into a thin line, controlling her mirth.

Jack wasn't going to let it go, causing Lela to turn in her seat to look at Tasha in question.

"Something made you laugh. What is it?" Jack drilled her.

"Oh, fine!" she expelled heavily, exasperated. She took a seat next to his sister, dropping her bowl rather heavily as she hopped up on the tall chair. "I'm trying to imagine you being fun."

"And that's amusing?" Jack asked, clearly insulted by her comment.

"Jack, since I have known you, you have always been a serious guy. I hardly ever see you laugh or just have plain fun." Then she turned to his sister, and it was clear to him that he was going to be ganged up on by the two women. "Now...I am...curious, as to *what he did* for fun?"

Lela smiled in that grand Southern fashion. "He was fun to hang out with until after he came home from the war." She stuck out her bottom lip at him. "We used to hang out at parks, the mall, go see movies...do neat things...go places."

"I see," she commented, looking at his sister, now certain she could not be much older than twenty-three or twenty-four, especially if she was in college. Then she looked at Jack. "Explains the high blood pressure." She raised her eyebrows at him, and the corner of his mouth tugged into a smirk.

Lela continued. "He got worse after he found out Jessica got married."

"Lela!" Jack growled at her.

"It's true! She broke your heart."

At that, Tasha now focused her gaze on Jack, raising an inquisitive eyebrow at the new piece of information. Jack had told her about his previous girlfriend, but he certainly had not indicated *just how special* she had been to him.

"Don't give me that look. I told you about her before," Jack dismissed Tasha as he took another bite of his stew.

301

"I vaguely recall you mentioning her over dinner one night, but more in passing, as if it was a trivial matter. *So*, that *was serious* for you!" She put her chin in her upturned palm, waiting for more information. But it was not to be the case.

"I take everything seriously," he grumbled in his defense.

"Definitely noted since living here. In addition to the emotional detachment from people."

"How long have you been here, Tasha?" Lela asked, now curious about his roommate.

"Oh, abo—"

"Mid-August," Jack answered quickly for her. "Not long."

"Not long! Are you kidding me? You haven't mentioned her in any of our emails or phone conversations!"

"You don't call, Lela," stated Jack.

"Emails?" asked Tasha, surprised Jack even communicated to anyone in that format.

"Okay, I meant texting," corrected Lela.

Tasha's eyebrows went even higher at that information. "And here, all this time, I thought you never talked to anyone save for Chad, Jack," Tasha admitted.

"Chad's still around?" Lela asked.

Tasha nodded her head affirmatively.

She looked at Jack. "Can we go see his dog team?" she asked excitedly.

Jack had finished his meal, lightly dropping his spoon into his bowl as he got up to discard his empty dish in the kitchen sink.

"Sure, we can go visit him, if you want," Jack told his sister.

After grabbing his normal bottle of lager and returning to his seat, he asked, "How long are you here for then?"

"That eager to get rid of me?" Lela joked with her brother.

"No…you know better. Just need to know how many days you will be here so I can plan accordingly." Jack took a swig of his beer.

"I leave out on the Saturday after Thanksgiving. Is that short enough for you?"

Jack ignored his sister's taunt, sighing heavily. "Fine, I'll call Chad tomorrow and see what his schedule is and if he will be home over the holidays. But we are not intruding on his family's holiday activities unless invited, understand?"

Lela hopped in her chair with glee, clapping her hands excitedly. "I so love the dogs and how neat it is when they all line themselves up according to their rank. It's like watching the canine hierarchy in action compared to listening about it in animal psychology class!"

"I thought you were a marine biologist…according to what Jack told me," Tasha questioned.

"Not really. I am working toward a degree in zoology."

"Still the same major. Now, that's a first!" commented Jack.

Lela gave him a dismissing hand. "Some of us aren't like you, who were born knowing what they wanted to do. Besides, I have more of an open mind then you will ever have, big brother. I like a lot of things."

Tasha remained quiet, observing the arguing siblings—which was pure entertainment in her book—as they continued to verbally poke each other's 'terrible' differences, smiling at the polar opposites trying to find a happy frictional balance, neither dominating the other. Jack was the North Pole and she was the South Pole.

Where Jack had incredible singular focus, his sister was all over the place, doing multiple things at once. Thus even startling Tasha with her question: "Tasha, did you know what you wanted to do in life?"

Not wanting to upset the balance, she answered diplomatically, "Not entirely, but one thing, for sure, I didn't want an office job and I loved aviation. I knew I wanted more than just being some sorry housewife to an ungrateful husband or working some minimum-wage dead-end job."

At 'ungrateful husband,' Jack raised an eyebrow at her. She cocked her head as if *what?*

"Were you married before?" Lela asked.

"Lela!"

"What?" She looked at her brother. "It's not like I am asking her if she's a virgin!"

"Thankfully, no," Tasha muttered more to herself. If Jack was any example of men out there that were considered marriageable material, she was grateful that she was still single.

"To which?" Lela asked.

"Both," Tasha clarified for her.

"You act like marriage is horrible. Did something bad happen to you?" Lela drilled her just like her brother.

It must be a family thing, thought Tasha.

"No, it's just not in my life or I would have been married by now."

"She hasn't found Mr. Right," Jack mocked, adding, "yet."

"Jack's available." Lela tried to be helpful.

"Yes, I know, Lela, but I don't want to be one of the many women standing in that long line of his."

"Are you dating someone else?" Lela asked Jack.

Jack shook his head no at Lela. She remained quiet, studying her brother a moment and then looking back and forth between them, contemplating.

"Are you two *sure* you're *not* dating each other?" She pointed back and forth to them. Then she added, "In fact, you two *act* more like you're married."

Jack coughed over a laugh before gaining control. The mirth sparked in his blue-gray eyes at Tasha.

Tasha gave him an annoyed look before rolling her eyes at them both.

"Well, Lela, he's not my type." Tasha clicked her tongue at her wishful thinking as she got up to go do their used lunch containers and their dinner dishes.

"Well, what are you looking for in a man then?" she pressed on.

Tasha looked over her shoulder at them, only to see Jack leaning back in his chair, where his sister could not see him, giving her a minute toast with his lager, not helping to control his sister's inquisitiveness as she leaned eagerly forward on her elbows on the island countertop to hear more.

"Probably much of what you are looking for in a man, I suppose," said Tasha, hoping that would be enough to quell all notions of being a matchmaker. Yet stubbornness ran in the family lines and Lela would not accept her final answer.

"Aw…Come on, Tasha! Men must be falling all over themselves over you in this town. Seriously, you haven't found at least one guy here?"

"I've been working a lot of hours and your brother doesn't let me out of my 'gilded birdcage' that often, especially since my car doesn't work and I have to carpool with him."

She turned to her brother. "You should take her out more and do the things we used to do."

"She doesn't like hunting, and somehow I don't think fishing is her idea of fun either."

"Well, can you blame her? I guess you are a lame date after all."

At this, Tasha tried unsuccessfully to stifle a laugh, grateful that her back was turned to them as she kept washing the dishes.

"Besides, she hates the beard," Jack added.

"I agree with her, Jack. I liked you much better without the beard, even though this shorter combed length is way better than the last time I saw you… what…about a year or so?" She continued as she got up with her spent bowl. "Well, Tasha must have good taste." She gave Tasha her spent dish and then grabbed a beer for herself, making Jack press his lips together, either from not wanting to share his stash or still seeing his sister as being way too young to be drinking beer.

"Or she's holding out for a rich guy? Maybe a hot-looking pilot?" Lela kept speculating.

By that time Tasha had finished the dishes, wiping her hands on the dish towel before settling it back on its hook just inside the cabinet door. "Not necessarily." Tasha grabbed a mug to make some hot tea.

"Tall, strong, and handsome?" Lela encouraged.

"That would be nice." Tasha coyly smiled. "But then I would be happy to have a man that would not only warm my heart but keep me warm on these cold Alaskan nights." She shrugged a half-hearted shoulder. "Be open, honest, and understanding, and most of all be able to accept who I am, flaws and all.

"Handsome, strong, and tall would be bonuses. But there are two more important things he must have. First, he needs to be dumb enough to love me but smart enough to hold a conversation for the rest of our lives."

Lela and Jack looked at each other before bursting into laughter.

"I love it, you're right up her alley, Jack!" Lela exclaimed in glee, leaning back some on her stool.

"No!"

"No!"

Came Jack and Tasha as they rebuked Lela.

Extending her hand to her brother, Lela persisted with Tasha. "Seriously, what is so wrong with Jack! He fits your last description perfectly!"

The microwave beeped.

"But I didn't tell you my second important item," Tasha reminded them, taking out her hot mug of water to dunk a tea bag in.

"She wants a unicorn," Jack said sarcastically in a lowered voice to his sister.

Tasha snubbed her nose at Jack when she turned back around facing them, ignoring him.

"Yup, finding someone who wants an open and long-term commitment… something I am pretty sure Jack doesn't want."

He grimaced at Tasha, hoping that his sister did not see his reaction.

"Okay, you may be wanting the impossible," Lela said defeatedly at her brother.

Tasha smiled as she tentatively tested her first hot sip of her tea, watching them interact some both verbally and with subtle body language.

Finding her tea to her liking, Tasha made her excuse to leave them be. "True…so I bid you both adieu for the evening so I can at least dream about Mr. Right if I can't have him in real life."

"Really, this early?" Lela asked.

"Yup. Some of us have to work for our living, Lela. I need all the rest I can get before another flight tomorrow down to Kodiak. I'm sure Jack will take off tomorrow and spend some wonderful time with you these next few days."

"I think you should join us," Lela begged.

Tasha reminded her, "Ah…but I am *not* family. And it sounds like both of you need some family time."

"Tasha will have the rest of the week off starting this Wednesday," Jack assured Lela.

"You mean Thursday," Tasha corrected him.

"No, I saw to it that you got time off to go shopping and get what we need for the four-day weekend."

"Shopping?" Tasha was blown away with his assumption of what was expected of her without first asking her. "For what?"

"You're making Thanksgiving dinner," Jack stated.

Tasha raised an eyebrow at that new piece of information, considering she had never cooked a Thanksgiving dinner. Her mom usually cooked the dinners. "I've never cooked a turkey before, Jack."

"I know you can follow instructions that come with the bird. But we can always do a spiral-cut ham instead. They're easier and much more to our style of a Southern Thanksgiving meal," he told her rather lazily with an arrogant smugness as he leaned back against the back of his stool, taking things easy for the evening.

She narrowed her gaze for just him to note before Lela turned her attention back on her, causing her to drop the heated look.

"I promise I'll help," Lela added, assuring Tasha.

She sighed resignedly. "Fine. I guess my weekend has been planned out." *Again,* she thought, shoving her annoyance aside, behaving herself in front of his sister with a Mona Lisa smile. "Well, goodnight, you two." To Drake lounging near them, she said, "Come on, Drake, I need my personal bed warmer tonight," hoping that Drake would deter any notions of Jack making her share or give up her room to his sister, or Jack himself barging in on her during the middle of the night, using his sister's visit as an excuse. As far as she was concerned, she was off limits to him, annoyed at being shut out of his personal life.

And she wanted no part discussing any sleeping arrangements. Nor did she want to know.

The next morning, Jack delivered her to the hangar, having left his sister to get up, get dressed and ready for their time together by the time he returned. Jack remained until he was sure that their weather was clear for her flight and their pre-flight checks were completed.

"How's your fuel?" Jack asked, sticking his head just inside the cabin of the old plane.

"It's fine, Jack." Tasha looked back over her shoulder from her co-pilot seat. "Would you just go and attend to your sister? Sam and I are just fine here. Work will continue as normal whether you are here or not."

"Maybe...that's what he's worried about," Sam chimed in, pushing Jack out of his way so that he could take his seat up front next to her. "He's afraid his job might become obsolete." Sam grinned at Tasha.

Jack ignored him. "Do you have the manifest and cargo sheet with you?" he asked while Sam got himself situated in his seat, buckling in.

Only Tasha could see Sam roll his eyes at Jack's question. "We've got them all, 'Papa Bear.' And she'll be just fine."

Tasha was unsure if Sam was referring to the plane or her. She caught Jack's minute grimace.

"I think we're good to go, if you would be so kind to watch our engines upon start-up."

Jack's hand slapped the airframe, the sound reverberated along the interior's frame.

Armed with earmuffs, Jack's face remained stalwart during engine ground checks before Sam gave him a thumbs-up. Jack waved them off toward the runway. Sam told her to take over steering and to be ready to take off with his help. As she steered the plane to the end of the runway, she could still make out Jack, standing just outside at his truck, as he waited for them to take off before he would be satisfied to return to his sister.

"Ready?" Sam asked Tasha, with his usual grand smile.

"Yup, we are good to go," Tasha concurred, ensuring the flaps were down to the correct takeoff setting before she pushed the throttle full forward, reaching full power before taking her foot off the brakes.

Once in the air and in level flight heading southwest over the Gulf of Alaska, Sam asked her, "So what was all that fuss about back there?"

Tasha diminutively lifted a shoulder at him.

"I mean it's great flying with you—I get extra help and special treatment on the plane when you are with me on the flights. Not that I mind." Sam grinned at her. "But he was like a worried hen today. Is everything fine between you two? You're not fighting again, are you?" Sam asked.

"No. Just the usual causal relationship with a distant and uncommunicative roommate who just had his younger sister arrive last night," she told him. Still miffed at the previous night's events unfolding, she kept her face adverted from Sam looking outside her side window at the view below.

"His sister?"

She nodded.

"Did you know about her? About her coming up here?" Sam asked her.

"I knew he had a sibling, but I wasn't aware he was going to have company over the Thanksgiving week. Nothing was mentioned to me," she added. "I'm not entirely sure if *he knew* she was going to stay with us either. Surprising folks must be a family attribute," Tasha added sarcastically.

"Oh?" Sam knew there was more to come as he purposely watched her until she looked over to him, catching him waiting for more information.

"What?" she asked, doing a double-take at his expectant visage.

"You don't sound entirely thrilled with the idea." He smiled again. It was hard to stay miffed around Sam. "What's she like?"

She sighed. "I'm okay with her showing up. She's pretty, charming, and very eager on getting to know people. Completely different from Jack's personality, that's for sure."

"But?" Sam prodded her, double-checking their heading on the indicator.

"Somehow I had my weekend planned out, without my knowledge, by making the 'family Thanksgiving dinner'"—her fingers quoted the three descriptive words—"Southern style!" Tasha sighed heavily. "The point is...I've never made a Thanksgiving dinner, Sam!"

"Aw…you'll do fine! We've survived all your baking so far and Jack is definitely putting on weight since you've been cooking." He gave her his usual GQ smile, his perfect white teeth flashing at her just behind his mic.

"But the thing is, I had every intention of having some nice downtime to myself…not cooking for Jack and his sister!"

"You were wanting to be by yourself over the four-day weekend? You don't seem to be the loner type, Tash. What's wrong? The holidays get you down?"

She checked their altitude, adjusting for elevation. "Nah, just tired of all the emotional ups and downs dealing with Jack twenty-four seven."

"Ahhhh, are we still on the rocks?" he commented more than questioned.

"You could say that, Sam." She looked back at him. Sam was a patient listener. "I was hoping that he would leave for the weekend for some long hunting trip or join Chad's family or something. But now I am cooking all day and helping to entertain his sister, who wants to play matchmaker for her brother."

He scoffed. "See? Even she thinks you two are perfect for each other. It's not just *us* guys!"

"She's a hopeless romantic," she pleaded with him. "Besides, how do you keep a relationship with a partner that barely speaks to you and rarely opens up? It's like dating a dead possum! You're never sure if it is really dead or just playing!"

Sam threw his head back and laughed at her description, the sound nearly deafening over her.

Worried, she gave him a stern look. "This conversation is between you and me, Sam. Are we clear?"

Sucking in air when he could, Sam said, "Oh, no," drawing the 'no' out with the inflection of his voice. "The story is out…between all of us guys! Nothing is sacred when it comes to the crew, Tasha."

Her look was genuinely concerned, and Sam did his best to appease her.

"We all care about you." Then he added, "and Jack too."

She sighed heavily, muttering to herself, "I knew I shouldn't have said anything."

He patted her shoulder reassuringly. "You worry too much. Besides, wait until the guys know where we need to crash for Thanksgiving."

She gave him a double-take on the last comment. *Great!* she thought, smirking.

Sam hounded her on the rest of the flight as to what to expect for the grand dinner, and she was thinking that turnabout was fair play, should Sam be serious about bringing the rest of the crew over for dinner. At least the guys knew how to make it fun when Jack got the best of her. The crew was getting good at distracting Jack and taking his focus off her, usually grouping around her more and more as their bond cemented during her short time working with them.

It was an uneventful flight, their deliveries unloaded without an incident, and they made good time on the return trip with the strong tailwind. Jack was there waiting for her as promised when they landed, his sister standing next to him by the aircraft tug.

Sam whistled low as she pulled the aircraft near the hangar door. "You weren't kidding about Jack's sister being pretty. I will *definitely* be over Thanksgiving Day! Don't let Nick know about her just yet, Tash."

"Oh...I don't know, Sam...I just might have to tell him if you tell the others what I said earlier about Jack." Tasha blackmailed him into silence.

Sam clicked his tongue, smiling. "Okay Moose, you got yourself a deal." He shook hands on it while he continued looking at Lela.

"Hey, Sam." She snapped her fingers at him to get his attention. "Help me with the shutdown checklist and I promise that you can get to see her quicker and longer before he rushes us off to do whatever he has planned for us."

Jack hooked the tow to the plane and backed the aircraft into the hangar while they proceeded over the checklist.

Sam was pretty much out of his seat when Jack opened the cargo door of the plane. "Hiya, Jack, brought your girl back to you, safe and sound." Sam thumbed back to where she had freed herself from the seat restraints, standing up and grabbing her flight bag. "More like she brought us back."

Jack began backing down from the doorway until Sam clapped his hands together, rubbing them in anticipation as he asked Jack if he could meet his sister. His exuberance put Jack on full alert when it came to protecting his sister's honor, and he blocked Sam's exit process. Tasha smiled knowingly just behind Sam in the aircraft.

Tired of Jack holding up their progress of exiting, she said, "Come on, Jack. Sam's not going to hurt her. He just wants an introduction." She pushed Sam out of her way, and then Jack, so she could get out of the plane. He moved easily for her, but not for Sam. She added to Jack over her shoulder once she was past him, "Besides, you no longer have to worry about him and me getting it on together."

Jack frowned at her for even remotely making that suggestion. She raised a questioning eyebrow at him.

Jack turned to Sam still in the doorway of the aircraft, but Tasha did not catch what Jack threatened him with before letting him out.

Tasha headed to Lela, happily greeting her before handing her flight bag to her, asking Lela to hold it while she sought the restroom for her personal needs and to give Sam the extra time promised while meeting Lela. It was apparent that Tasha no longer held Sam's sincere interest.

When she came back, she found the two smiling twitterpated rabbits talking away, with Jack standing apart looking rather dejected and annoyed. But he remained quiet, a faithful sentinel with his arms crossed over his chest. She smirked at the sight of them all.

Jack noticed her immediately, cocking his head at her smile, the awkwardness vanishing as he walked toward her to meet her halfway. In a heated whisper, he said to her, "Now why did you encourage him to meet my sister?"

She smiled brightly at him. "Well, it was obvious he was taken with her and *he is* a *nice* guy. Nice enough to make me consider him as a possible Mr. Right at one time."

Jack's expression said it all.

She stopped, far enough away that they couldn't be overheard by them, wagging her finger. "So, yes…your jealousy was warranted, but not to the point of being a jerk to him. But now there is no excuse, since I have just officially dropped off his radar. So leave him be, and your sister is old enough to decide for herself if Sam's Mr. Right."

Tasha turned to walk toward Sam and Lela, throwing a glance over her shoulder at Jack as he followed her, "So look on the bright side—you have no competition save yourself."

"What's that supposed to mean?" He stopped her, making her face him.

"It means you stand in your own way when it comes to obtaining me. But after last Wednesday…the way you shut me out…well, you did that to yourself and I will not continue on that rollercoaster ride nor the crap with this arranging my life without asking me if I had any plans."

Jack tried to interrupt, but Tasha continued

"For example, this extravagant Thanksgiving dinner I seem to be making for you and your unexpected sister! This is the last time, Jack! I'm only doing it for her since she is nice, although she's an incorrigible matchmaker."

"Okay, fine, what plans did you have?"

She sighed heavily at him. "Does it matter now?" she asked, not wanting to divulge that she had nothing planned save for making it an exceptionally long spa weekend for herself and catching up on her latest good read, the second half of her *Fate's Twisted Circle* novel.

"Yes! What did you want to do?"

She looked at him. "I wanted a personal spa weekend with lots of sleep and reading time."

"That's what you normally do anyway when I'm gone, isn't it?" Then he asked, on second thought, "What's a *spa* weekend?"

"Same solitary quiet weekend paying attention to myself, minus the housekeeping and cooking."

"Fine then, I will do the dishes and cleaning for this weekend."

"You?" she scoffed. "And what about entertaining your sister while she's here?"

"We've arranged for you to join us, since you said you never get out much."

"I want to sleep in," Tasha added.

"No problem, Lela's as bad as you are when it comes to sleeping in," Jack told her, hoping to quell Tasha's objections.

"Speaking of sleeping, where *did* you sleep?" she asked, now wondering.

"Why? You missed me?" There was a glint in his eye along with a half-cocked smile with some hope just behind it.

"Drake is still warmer than you will ever be," she retorted, taking a good jab at deflating his outsized ego.

"I let Lela sleep with me since you were definitely in no mood 'to share the warmth' with me."

Tasha's eyebrows shot up in surprise, her mouth gaping open before she quickly clamped it with a riposte, "My...ain't we a true redneck...sleeping with your sister!"

"It's not like we hadn't done it before when we were little. Besides, I sleep in the master bedroom with the king-size bed. There's plenty of room even for you, if you care to join! I'm not so sure if Drake can fit in though."

She twisted her mouth at his matching sarcasm, now crossing her arms, fingers splayed on her upper arms.

By that time, Sam and Lela had seen them and were drawing close to them, interrupting their tete-a-tete, when Sam asked, "So, Thanksgiving at your cabin, I hear." He was grinning ear to ear, knowing it would annoy Jack even more, diverting Jack's attention from Tasha, making Tasha's smile grow in knowing anticipation. Lela barely controlled herself, hopping just behind Sam, in her delight of having Sam drop in.

"What time do I need to be there to help out?" Sam asked, looking over to Tasha, now gloating at the turnabout. It was not like Jack to say no, as he caught his sister's eager nod of her head and then looked over to Tasha's smug expression before she could drop it in time, and she waved a dismissing hand as if *I couldn't care less* and then pointed back to Jack for the confirmation on arrival time.

Tasha's extra day off on Wednesday had been Jack's gift to her for the extra time needed for all that she wanted to do. Tasha slept in and got her hour of quiet soaking in a hot bath while Jack and Lela made a late breakfast for them all. The rest of the late morning and afternoon were pleasantly spent at the Alaska Sea Life Center before ending their day grocery shopping for the big meal the next day. Lela and Jack helped her take the guess work out of what they wanted with their Southern-style Thanksgiving meal. The supplies were huge for just the four of them, only to have Jack make the comment at checkout, paying for their groceries, that he figured Sam would most likely not be alone in coming over. He planned on the entire crew to be stopping by their cabin, except for Hank and Nate, since they were already having their own family meals at their own home with their spouses. Tasha raised an inquisitive eyebrow at him, and at this he goaded her, "Your cooking has become legendary."

"No kidding! Don't you tell Mom I said this," Lela said, looking at Jack, "but Tasha is *certainly* a better cook." She picked up two of their grocery bags. "If you ever get tired of flying, Tasha, you should look into opening your own café."

Tasha picked up two more large bags, with Jack taking on the last four.

The previous week's snow had diluted with the warmer wintery mix that Seward had been getting in between with more of the sunnier days, making it easier to carry all their bags out to his truck without slipping on ice. As usual, Lela, being smaller and younger, slipped in between them in the truck's cab. Tasha was thankful that Lela was talkative, telling Tasha more about their family stories on the short way home. It was a nice break from the long 'silent conversations' that Jack and she often had—although many times, Tasha had found herself doing the talking to break up the more prolonged silences, making her feel like a mundane gossiper. But Lela outdid herself in that trait, making Tasha feel normal when it came to gossiping.

Once home, they refused to let her prep any dinner that night, much less work on the following day's grand dinner. Instead, between the siblings, they reheated leftovers for the night, getting her to imbibe in some rose wine and do a small jigsaw puzzle together. They talked mostly about what was new with Lela and what her goals were after she graduated, mainly to see if anything had changed or if she was planning on changing her major again—as she was given to do, according to Jack. However, what Tasha was learning firsthand about his sister was that she had a good head on her shoulders. Lela was not like Jack nor their father when it came to setting goals, immovable to interruptions to their progress until they had reached their final result. Lela had goals, but she took her time, smelling the roses—and the manure—as she traversed the hurdles in life, reaching her goals in a more leisurely manner. Lela was different from Jack in that she was living life to its fullest, and that proved true when a knock came at their cabin door that night.

Lela immediately jumped down from her stool at the kitchen island to go the door as Jack asked, "Were you expecting someone?"

"Yeah," Lela answered eagerly as she opened the door, greeting Sam, pulling him inside where the fire was crackling in the hearth. This was no surprise to either Jack or Tasha.

"Hi, Jack, Tasha," Sam said, noting where they were sitting at the island with the jigsaw puzzle.

Tasha smiled warmly at him, waving him over to where they sat. "Care for a drink? Something hot perhaps?" she offered, now seeing the flakes of snow on his dark brown hair.

"Sure. How about a hot chocolate?"

Tasha smiled and got a mug going for him. Sam squeezed Jack's shoulder in a quick greeting and took a seat next to him, looking at the nearly finished puzzle in front of him, then taking a piece and adding his part to the near completed work.

"Let me get a few things and I'll be ready in just a few," said Lela.

Jack gave her a *where are you going?* look, but she ignored him.

"Must be snowing again," Jack commented, but not really toward anyone in particular. More or less it was his way of saying *hell's freezing over*, not happy with Lela bailing on them, and giving Sam a wary eye about dating his sister. Sam, too, ignored Jack's darker look.

"Yup, that time of year again, and I think we officially have winter setting in," Sam admitted.

"Oh?" Lela questioned as she entered the bedroom, still half listening.

Sam continued. "Well, looking at this week's weather predictions for the weekend, it's supposed to snow every day and the temps don't rise much above freezing either. And it will be like this until well into April."

"Well I, for one, am sick of the slush we've been getting. Snow will be a nice change and make things look pretty for a while," Tasha added.

Jack gave her a surprised look, knowing she was always cold. But then, she had been dressing for the worst cold, in addition to adapting to the colder climate in the past few weeks. The only thing he noted was that the lack of sunlight was wearing on her upbeat personality. But he made sure she got into the tanning booth often enough for the UV light therapy. The lasting effects literally glowed gently throughout her skin and facial complexion. Even her blond hair shone brighter and lighter for a few days afterwards. It was as if she were a solar-powered light that needed recharging. Tasha gave an additional meaning to the aviation moniker *Sparky,* the slang reserved for a flight line electrician.

Tasha resumed her seat once the hot chocolate was made, setting it down where Sam sat. The break from the puzzle helped her immediately find two more pieces to put into place, with Jack and Sam finishing the last five pieces.

Lela came back out of Jack's bedroom wearing a fresh and fancier sweater for the evening. She had added a little more makeup and brushed her hair again, but not so much that a guy would have noticed. Jack gave her another silent look of *'behave yourself'* as he placed his large hand on Sam's shoulder, squeezing it in light warning at the same time when he asked, "When are you bringing *my sister* home?"

Tasha smiled into her mug to keep from laughing, catching Sam rolling his eyes after he adjusted his shoulder under the controlling weight of Jack's paw.

"I'll promise to be home before midnight, *Dad*!" Lela pleaded with Jack. "Seriously, are you going to do this to me too?"

Jack stood up, still not releasing his bear grip on Sam's shoulder, shaking him a bit. "Nope, but Sam has to work with me when you leave at the end of the week." Then he looked at Sam. "She comes home in one piece and no additional issues, you got that?"

Sam nodded, still trying to pry Jack's grip off his shoulder. "Relax, I'll treat her just like I always do with Tasha, if not better."

"That's what I'm afraid of," he grumbled.

Tasha just kept a tight smile, adding, "See?…And you were worried about me with Sam? I told you I was chopped liver."

Lela gave her a confused look, but Tasha waved it off dismissively so as not to worry her.

Sam quickly amended, "Chopped liver? Never, Tasha. Not in a million years. But come to think of it, chopped liver may just wake up a dead possum."

This comment led to both siblings looking at each other in confusion, wanting the other to clarify Sam's statement.

Sympathetically, Tasha hopped off her barstool, pulling Sam from Jack's grasp, and shoved Lela and him toward the front door.

Before Jack could ask, Sam threw over his shoulder, "We'll be at our usual hangout. We're meeting the rest of the crew there if you care to join us."

"I won't be joining you all. I have a big morning getting dinner ready for the day. But Jack may end up going," she said, much to Sam's momentary horror, where only she could see it as she spoke.

But true to form, Jack said, "No, I'll stay here with Tasha to help with any last-minute items."

Tasha gave Sam a reassuring *you see* look.

Once they were out the door, Tasha returned to her seat at the kitchen island where Jack had chosen to sit back down, taking a long swig of his lager, eyeing her.

Tasha put her elbows on the table, her chin in her upturned hands, looking at the finished puzzle, enjoying the feeling of a completed task, before looking back at him, finding him still watching her. She met his steely blue-gray gaze and studied him for a moment. She refused to give in to him by speaking first, as he drew on the last of his lager, then sat up and forward in his seat, twirling his bottle between his hands on the countertop before he spoke to her.

"So now what?"

She made a moue with her mouth, shrugging her shoulders at him as she stood up to make herself another hot tea. He, too, stood up to throw his empty bottle in the trash and to invade her space as she waited by the microwave, then turned to the refrigerator to grab another bottle, popping the cap off neatly with his thumb and flinging the cap in a perfect arch into the trash can.

"Come sit with me, Tash," he told her when the microwave beeped that the water was hot.

"I can in a minute. Just let me put this puzzle away," she said, not really wanting to spend time in his brooding presence.

"Leave it, Tasha. It can wait until tomorrow morning." He indicated with his head to follow him to the main living room area, and she watched his long legs lumber to his favorite spot on the couch. She dunked her fresh tea bag in the water as she gave him a studious look, not sure what to make of this invite.

"Hey, while you are at it, switch off the light in the kitchen, will ya?"

Tasha waited for Drake to get up, following his master to his seat just next to him on the sofa. Thankfully, the large black dog did before she came over, so she could take her usual chair adjacent to the sofa, in front of the crackling fire.

Tasha turned the light off. "Trying to set up a romantic setting?"

"Nah, just trying to cut down on the energy bill this month," he threw back over his shoulder and the back of the sofa at her.

"I see," she commented more to herself, sighing in relief. She came around and settled in her chair before turning her face toward the fire's light.

"Besides, I like the way your hair reflects the fire's light."

Tasha's face snapped back to him.

He sat there, his face smug, with his hand on Drake's winter fur coat, his long fingers twirling lazily within the swaths of fur. With his beer bottle, he indicated to his own hair. "It's like watching your hair move as it catches the shifting light from the fire."

It was a moment before she spoke. She was not entirely sure what to make of his comment, until she found herself asking out loud, "Well, if you were trying to romance me…that first part was one of the better pickup lines I have ever had heard, until the second part…a part that makes me sound like I have Medusa's head of moving snakes…Am I that awful to you on most days?"

He snorted at her comment. "It's a simple compliment," he said, taking another deep draw on his beer. "Are you always this tough to compliment without some sort of suspicion? Or is it just me?"

"You…because I am never sure where I stand with you."

"Let's talk about this."

"Why bother? I already know where I stand on the personal department. We are not going to date each other again. I refuse to be shut off when I ask or talk to you, Jack." She uncrossed her feet to re-cross them with the opposite foot over the other. "What I am not sure of is if you're happy with my work on the flight line or flight progress…in learning fast enough at picking up all the aircraft models."

"You're good there." Jack smirked, more to himself. "Always have your work done in half the time I expect it. You work hard and are detailed-oriented, and I have yet to find a mistake in anything you do. Why do you ask?" He tilted his head at her, waiting.

She took a sip of her tea, holding the mug close to her mouth as if hesitating on telling him. "I just get the impression that nothing matters in what I do." Then, putting down her mug on top of her knee, she turned it awkwardly in her hands. "I guess what I mean is that I see you complimenting others, giving them a 'job well done,' while I get the 'redheaded stepchild' treatment and culled from the herd at work. Something I do makes you unhappy. Not once have you said a supportive word to me at work."

He was about to defend himself, only to realize that she was right. He did everything to keep his crew from thinking he favored her at work.

"And let's add that note to my cleaning. At least I know you're happy with the cooking." She sighed. "I can only imagine what being married would be like…It would be a living hell. I guess it's a good thing you've been showing me what married life would be like, had I gone down that route. I have to thank you for saving me from such a miserable life."

"You're not going to marry based on our living arrangements? Seriously, Tasha?" He cleared his throat. "That's a bit rash, even for you."

She had brought one of her feet up to give herself a massage to ease the ache of standing and walking around all day with the siblings.

"I didn't know we were working toward a marriage here," he said.

"We're not! You're noncommittal. There's no point in having a relationship with you." She switched her foot to massage the other one.

"So you keep telling me." He ordered Drake down from the couch and patted the seat next to him, telling Tasha to come over to him so that he could massage her feet, knowing her love for 'spa moments.'

She reluctantly acquiesced, getting up to sit near him on the couch.

"But may I remind you that you are the one that gave up the relationship. I haven't, no matter what you believe."

At that statement she stopped just before sitting down, but he reached for her, pulling her down to sit next to him, waiting for her to throw her legs over his lap. When she didn't, he reached over to her legs, nabbing her calves in his massive hands.

"Determined, aren't you?" she commented more than asked.

"No, just committed, when you believe otherwise."

She sighed heavily at him, closing her eyes, leaning back against the crook of the sofa's arm. Jack was unsure if it was a sigh of contentment from his massage or due to his last comment.

"It's a bit past the point and it will be a losing battle, Jack."

"But at least I will go down with a fight." Jack smiled at her when she momentarily opened one green eye at him before allowing both her eyes to focus on him.

"That can be a dangerous flaw there, roomie. It may burn you in the end."

The heat from his powerful grip traveling from her feet and up her legs made her body relax yet come alive under his touch. Keeping in mind her determination to work against the flow of what everyone thought about them to knowing she needed her wits about her just to make the following day's Thanksgiving dinner go smoothly, if not flawless, Tasha would stop this intimacy before she would let herself get burned again.

"We'll see," Jack said as he thumbed the arches of her feet more seductively.

Tasha's studious gaze became more relaxed, her eyelids drooping some and the green of her eyes darkening. He had her out like a light a few moments later.

Jack got her up early the next morning, like they were going to work, but instead it was to commence the dinner preparations.

Tasha remained in her informal pajamas that consisted of a pair of sweatpants and sweatshirt with thick warm socks.

Jack grinned at her over his cup of coffee, her bedhead having taken on a life of its own with the static electricity that had built up in the cabin's dry air. Tasha was no 'morning person' but neither was she a 'night owl,' having gone to bed somewhat early and before his sister had come home from her date with Sam. She scowled at him smiling at her, coming over to where he was leaning against the back countertop next to the coffee maker, and grabbed herself a cup of coffee from the pot he made, taking the second cup he would normally have had.

Jack raised an eyebrow at that, for she rarely drank the brew, save for the times she needed the extra energy. Thus, he commented, "Did you have a rough night?" He had hoped that his foot massage had left her not just relaxed, but with any luck, perhaps dreaming of him.

Tasha didn't respond.

So Jack continued. "I'd think you would be more of a hop-to-it kind of morning person after…how many years in the Army? Ah yes: eight years, and two of them in the Middle East."

She gave him a gimlet look over her coffee cup and then set her mug down before answering him. "Unlike you, I gave up that nasty habit as soon as I left the military. No point in being hyper-alert around here—or should I need to know something else that you are not telling me?" She looked around the great room of the cabin.

He smirked as he added what little was left in the coffee pot to his cup.

"When did your sister get home?" she asked, now curious.

At that, he lifted an eyebrow at her before answering, "Right at midnight like a good girl, though she would have been ten minutes late when it comes to military punctuality."

"And you were worried about her with Sam. Told you Sam's a good guy."

"Sam values his life," he told her flatly, and Tasha rolled her eyes at him.

"You know there is life after the marine corps and war? It's time you move on and enjoy life at a much simpler pace and with less rigidity," she said drily.

"And here I thought I was reporting for KP duty this morning." He took his seat at the island, enjoying her presence and small talk.

"Oh, boy." She sighed, smirking into her hand as it slid down over her face, creating more color in her cheeks, waiting for the rest of her body to awaken. "Don't remind me of those days. The Army was good at butchering potentially great meals." She broke out into a radiant smile at him. "I'll cook up breakfast for us, if you start on peeling the bag of yams in the refrigerator and then cube them

317

into that large cooking pot for me to boil."

"Deal—after you and I finish our coffee first. I'll be generous enough to you to let you finish waking up, and give Lela a little more time to wake up and get out here, since she said she would help," he told her.

She thanked him with a tiny toast of her coffee mug.

The smell of breakfast cooking had Lela finding them both working in the kitchen together. She smiled brightly at them, especially at Tasha's morning attire. Her brother Jack, always the early morning riser, had been put together in his usual at-home casual attire of a Henley shirt and blue jeans. Only his beard and hair still had a wild, unbrushed look. "You two look like you had a good night together, even though I still found myself sleeping with my brother."

"Oh God, she's a morning person too?" Tasha stated to Jack.

He smiled, knowing his family members.

"And then proud to admit that she's a redneck from Louisiana to boot?"

"You certainly know how to make it sound worse than it is, Tasha," Lela replied.

"Well, at least I know better. But it does look a bit strange to go out with one hunky guy," Tasha started, eyeing Jack's response to her comment and finding him pouting some as he peeled the fresh yams at the far end of the kitchen island, "and then still end up in bed with your hunky brother." She smiled at him when he looked up at her in surprise, finding her teasing them both. Tasha slid the scrambled eggs out of the pan and onto Lela's plate, and then brought another plate of bacon for Lela to pick from when she sat down at the kitchen island.

"You two could remedy the situation by hooking up with each other. Especially after I learned more about you two last night."

Jack and Tasha looked at each other.

"Hey, I'm just sayin'…" She held up her hand at them. "It's not just me rooting for you two to hook up…You have an entire crew, brother."

Jack leaned closer to Tasha, and asked for only her to hear, "And who's fighting a hopeless battle?"

She scowled as if she had just been bitten by a mosquito.

"You are a hopeless romantic, aren't you, Lela?" Tasha retorted.

"No, it's just a matter of time—along with a little determination on both of your parts," she told them. "Besides, I can't wait to hear more when everyone stops by today."

"What do you mean *everyone*?" Tasha stopped in her task of whipping up the green bean casserole. Even Jack looked up at his sister eating across the way from him.

"I mean the entire crew from last night, including Chad."

"Chad?" they both said in surprise.

"Yeah, I invited Chad, since he will be getting off his shift late tonight at the hospital, around five p.m. Everyone else is coming around one p.m. since they all talked about Tasha's cooking and something about some coffee-laced cookies that she makes."

"Lela!" Jack scolded.

"I think I can make everything stretch for everyone. I just might have to make some normal mashed potatoes and possibly bake more bread," Tasha responded, still stunned at the change of plans. "Not sure on supplies for dessert…" she mumbled on, before turning to Jack. "Is the store even open today?"

"It may be," Jack replied, and turned to Lela. "Get dressed. You and I are going for some more supplies."

Lela downed the rest of her breakfast at his order, though she added, "Will you two relax? Manny said he would bring the guacamole and chips over along with some fried plantains for all of us. Nick said he would bring the drinks to share, and Chad said something about a gooseberry pie."

They both looked at her, stunned. Tasha was the first to say, "Well, gotta give her credit in knowing how to make a true Thanksgiving dinner by getting others to share, Jack."

"But she reminded me of those fabulous cookies of yours. Do you have everything you need to make those?"

"Unfortunately not."

"Then make us a list, along with anything else you may need, and we will go get them while you get ready. But let's get that spiral-cut ham in the oven first. It will take a few hours."

Tasha thought out loud. "Well, while the yams and the green bean casserole are cooking, I can make up part of the cookie dough and have it ready by the time the main meal is all cooked."

"Atta girl." He grinned at Tasha, giving her a notepad to write down what she needed for the cookie dough.

She warily eyed him, exhaling heavily, letting go of the pent-up frustration of having more last-minute things thrown at her. It seemed Jack's face had grown younger overnight. For a man that rarely showed emotion, his happiness was running amok just beneath the surface of his body. Given the way he normally carried himself in a poised militant and authoritative manner, his body remained casual and relaxed. It had become obvious that this was Jack's favorite holiday, and he was happy to have family and friends over.

With Jack and Lela's help, she was able to make the meal's deadline when the crew began arriving. Tasha exhaled slowly and deeply, now dressed and put together at last, letting the last of her stress slip away. Everything was ready and on the back countertop along the wall. Dinner was going to be buffet-style, given the size of their cabin's eating area. Her first Thanksgiving dinner done mostly by her own hands. Although her long weekend had not gone as planned, Tasha was determined to make the best of it, happy to be a part of the crew anytime.

Jarvis and Manny were the first to show up with the extra appetizers. Nick and Sam were next. It was a casual affair, as the guys piled their plates high with food and clustered as one big family—a flight line family—around the kitchen island. After making sure everyone got their fill and had commenced eating, without anyone dropping dead from possible food poisoning, Tasha and Jack got their meals last.

Together, standing side by side, they leaned against the back countertop, no chairs to be had, their plates in hand, dining *al a carte*, observing the crew shooting the breeze with the usual flight line banter. She watched as Jack happily chowed down on his meal, his manner watchful as he kept an eye on his sister, who was constantly exchanging glances with Sam. Jack smiled when he found Tasha looking at him, mouthing silently for him to 'stand down.' He locked eyes with her while they ate, though she tried her best to keep watch over their company, participating in their conversation intermittently, refusing to give the crew more fodder when it came to their relationship status.

Thankfully, Nick, Jarvis, and Manny were too heavily leading the group conversations to notice them, much less the other two brand-new lovebirds trading similar glances.

At one point she caught Sam and Lela looking at Jack and her, their heads together, talking amongst themselves. She caught the gleam in Sam's eye, when they locked with hers and she wagged a warning finger at him from the hand that held her plate, hoping it was imperceptible enough to the rest of the crew and to Jack. Sam just shook his head minutely and smiled brightly back at Lela.

When most of them were finished with the late lunch, they began to play rounds of Uno so that all of them could play as one group for a few more hours until Chad barged in an hour later, done with his hospital shift.

Tasha gave what was left of her hand to Jack, since he had managed to be the first to win that round—not just that time, but in several previous rounds. She saw to Chad, making sure he got his fill, and then he squeezed in between Lela and Jarvis where the group congregated around the kitchen island. Chad did steal a bear hug from Lela, much to Sam's raised eyebrows, looking back at Tasha and Jack for answers, only to find them grinning back at the scene.

Tasha then commenced baking the first batch of her requested chocolate cappuccino cinnamon chunk cookies so that they would be fresh and warm for the taking over the next few hours. Jack, still on KP duty, did the dishes without being told to do so, alleviating much of the workload. They made quite the team. As the cookies baked, she dried the dishes, putting them away and getting the next round of smaller plates out for the various desserts. She asked Lela to bring the desserts from their storage on top of the basement freezer, with an eager and helpful Sam in tow. Tasha noted Jack's concerned dark look when he watched Sam following his little sister, lightly cuffed him, getting him to mind his own business.

Her reprimand did not go unnoticed. Jarvis spoke up. "Yo, you two really act like a married couple instead of the roomies you are."

They both looked back over their shoulders at him where he sat smiling at them, the others following his lead.

"No, don't even go there, Jarvis. It's bad enough with his sister trying to matchmake us." The oven's timer went off, saving her.

"Speaking of the *matchmaker*, it doesn't take that long to retrieve ice cream and pies from the deep freezer downstairs," came Jack's comment as he looked over to the basement door, laying the last of the washed dishes in the drying rack.

The crew muttered amongst themselves as Tasha told him to mind himself again, trading cookie sheets out of the oven.

"Protective isn't he, Tasha?" Chad commented between mouthfuls of his reheated dinner, trying hard to stifle his mirth, and added, "Woe to any man pursuing a woman under Jack's protection."

"Yeah, I seem to recall a small bar fight a few weeks earlier for another lady," Jarvis said.

Jack had dried his hands and now shoved the dish towel toward the back of the countertop. "I'm going to see what is taking so long."

"No, you're not, Jack! Leave them be!" Tasha stopped him by grabbing a fistful of his flannel shirt, which kept him from going any further for fear of ripping the shirt's material.

"If I was Sam, I better hurry for fear of pain or worse," Chad chuckled, and the others laughed with him.

"Ah, so he wasn't just like this on the flight line with us too?" Nick asked.

"No, mostly with you, Nick, because I know your history," retorted Jack.

"But I remember Sam getting the brunt of it though," said Jarvis, seeing Nick nod in agreement.

"And I have no idea why he would have any reason to be like that," Tasha said, giving Jack a sideways glare as she stood by, holding onto his sleeve. Jack kept trying to pry her fingers off his shirt, finally winning, making his way over to the basement door.

"Lela!" he yelled downstairs. "Some of us are growing old with age up here waiting on our dessert!"

This sent all the guys sniggering, along with, "Sam's in trouble now."

"Clamp it, guys!" Jack pointed a warning finger back at them. "That's my little sister he's messing with."

"Argh!" Tasha strode past Jack. *"I'll* go get them," she said, and jogged down the stairs.

However, the guys could still hear her from downstairs, barking out, "Okay, you two spawning salmons. Stop sucking face unless you want an angry bear to make fish meal out of you two!"

This sent the guys into gales of laughter.

"Oh man, the moose is on the loose." Jarvis laughed, high-fiving Chad sitting next to him.

There was some scuffling noise down below, along with "we got it" and "we were deciding on which flavor ice cream to bring up."

"I think she outdid Jack," Jarvis commented.

"She's definitely scarier than my own mother," Manny commented.

"She'd make any drill sergeant proud," was Jack's only comment, barely audible, as he stood there, feet shoulder-width apart, waiting with his arms folded across his chest and a half-cocked smile.

Lela and Sam, with Tasha bringing up the rear, came bounding up the stairs, their arms loaded with pies, containers of ice cream, and a cake or two. Dessert was going to be buffet-style for the rest of the evening, along with the luncheon leftovers that were already occupying space along the kitchen's back countertop.

Jack relieved some of the desserts from his sister's arms as he gave her a pointed 'brotherly' look, her face still tinged with dark pink on her cheeks, either from Tasha's berating or what he suspected more—as Tasha put it, from 'sucking face' with Sam. Jack smiled to himself once he was free from his sister's annoyed look as she turned to grab serving utensils from another drawer.

The oven timer went off again, and Tasha quickly resumed her duties in baking, exchanging another cookie tray until all four dozen cookies were done and stacked neatly in a circular pyramid next to the rest of the desserts.

On round two, the guys did another mad rush for the back wall in filling their plates and returning to either the kitchen island for another round of cards or sitting on the sofa in front of the fireplace using the coffee table as an impromptu dinner table.

"You know, I just noticed something, Jack," Nick pondered. "You two don't have a TV in this cabin, do you?"

"Nah, never needed one," Jack answered as he finally helped himself to a few more desserts, piling them up dangerously high in addition to helping himself to four of Tasha's 'espresso-styled' cookies.

"Jack," Tasha warned him, having seen his quantity of cookies, "you need to watch how many of those you eat. The last thing I need is for you to be up all night long again like the last time."

"I'm fine, I need to be alert." His eyes sought out his sister where she was sitting in the living room, and Tasha's eyes followed his gaze.

She spied Lela sitting with Sam, a little too close for Jack's comfort, their heads bowed together in quiet conversation.

Jarvis spoke up, saying that they had a medium-sized TV in their car and that they could hook up their gaming system to it for all of them to take turns.

"Your car?" came Tasha. "Do you always carry a TV with you?"

Manny chimed in, "Yeah, sure. For the times we have hangar duty while someone is on flight. There's very little to do while waiting on someone to return. Not much maintenance to do during this time of year."

Nick elbowed him to go get it, going after him to help him carry in all the equipment.

"And I can only spend so much time in the tanning booth while listening to the hand radio," Jarvis commented, as if the dark-haired and tanned Heinz 57 nationality mix was too fair to be suntanning. He stroked his exposed olive-skinned forearms where his sweater sleeves were pulled up to his elbows.

"I'm in on gaming," Chad spoke up, around a mouthful of ice cream and cake, standing up with his dessert plate and walking to the living room area, where he literally butted in between Sam and Jarvis, making sure to bump more into Sam, where Sam was deeply engaged with Lela in a lovebirds' conversation.

Tasha took up Chad's seat at the island with her dessert plate, sitting down next to Jack where he was making another meal of the dessert portion. They watched as the guys settled in with all the equipment that was brought in, watching Jarvis and Nick setting up the equipment and collaborating on who would be on whose team.

The oven timer went off again, distracting Tasha to attend to the next batch of cookies. Jack got up with her to help in sliding off the fresh-baked cookies, coming around the far side of the island, opposite of her, so as not to get in between her and the oven door.

With one hand putting in the new sheet and the other clutching a hot pad holding the hot tray, she was about to set it down when explosions of gunfire rocked her into defense mode, causing her to drop the sheet of baked cookies onto the floor as she reflexively ducked behind the island, cringing at the realistic sounds of a battle.

It was a microsecond too late when she realized it was not real. She silently cursed herself, grateful for dropping the cookies, using the heat of the pan as an excuse for her 'clumsiness' as she had purportedly burned herself. Jack had only half-dropped to one knee, asking her if she was all right, helping her pick up the mess.

She mumbled a barely audible, "Yeah," having partially straightened back up, looking over the countertop to the living room and using the kitchen island as a protective barricade as she visually verified it was the video game, somewhat cringing at the next explosion before turning to him, nodding. "Yeah, I'm good." She exhaled heavily. She felt clammy and knew she had to get away before showing more signs of distress.

With the noisy clatter of the baking sheet, Chad asked, "Everything okay back there?" He looked momentarily over his shoulder from his seat with a game controller in his hand waiting for his turn.

Seeing Tasha's ashen face and Jack's concern, Chad noted both looking in surprised horror at the TV. Chad knew something was wrong as Tasha darted for the basement stairs, quickly disappearing. It was Jack's negligible nod of no that made him get up before Jack held up a hand, motioning for Chad to stay put before following her. Chad was not sure if she had burned herself or it was something else, before it dawned on him what the group had just done, and he quickly began taking steps to rectify it.

Jack found Tasha downstairs on the treadmill, her back to him, walking rather fast, a range-walking pace, as she hummed a nondescript tune to herself, her hands alternately fisting and opening, spreading her fingers wide apart. Jack came around slowly, making sure to call her name, not wanting to further surprise her in her current state. He had felt it too, although it was more of a twinge now, since two-plus years had passed since his days in the Middle East.

She did not stop nor look at him when he came around to the front of the treadmill, standing clearly in front of her. There was some color returning from her exertion, but she was still ashen.

"Tash…hey…look at me." He reached a hand to her face, getting her attention.

Her eyes shadowed with past fear, struggling to calm herself.

He knew what troubled her, though he asked, "What's going on?"

"Nothing!" she told him in a low, harsh voice, crossing her arms protectively over herself, tucking her hands under her armpits as if she was cold, although he could see her hands were trembling the moment she stopped alternatively fisting them.

"Tasha—" Jack softly called her name again in his attempt to get her to calm down, noting Chad's feet coming quietly down the stairs.

"I'm fine!" She quickly grabbed ahold of the two side support bars—with difficulty, since it looked like her arms and hands had a mind of their own, being indecisive on what to do next. "I…I just needed to get some exercise in after a large dinner."

Jack reached over the treadmill's control panel and pulled the emergency chip out of it, nearly causing her to stumble into the panel and him, his soft tone calling her bluff. "Bullshit, Tasha." Jack took her trembling hand into his large, reassuring, warm hands, attempting to quell her nerves.

"So you have it too," Chad's voice came behind her.

Tasha twisted her upper body, her one hand in Jack's, the other still on the support side bar, her knuckles white, as she nearly jumped at Chad's presence.

Chad put up both hands as if trying to calm a frightened mare. "Sorry," he said, putting his hands on his hips. "None of us were thinking."

Tasha gave him a confused look, knowing better. "About what? Apologizing for—"

"Post-traumatic stress disorder…Just like Jack," Chad clarified.

At that statement, her surprise was her first sincere expression as she looked back at Jack, tilting her head at him in question. He did not respond, his visage stalwart. He was never an easy read.

"Are you sure you're okay, Tasha?" Chad asked, noting her one hand on the bar still moving in an agitated state.

She caught his studious gaze and quickly hid her hand, only to have Jack catch her second hand protectively in his, hiding it in between his reassuring hands. Neither of them said a word to Chad.

"Yup...the tremors, the pallid skin, the nightmares, panic attacks, depression, sleeping too much..." Chad said, describing her symptoms. But then he started describing Jack's: "Or too little sleep, agitation, high blood pressure, issues with making emotional connections with others, angers easily...Need I say more?"

"That's your issue?" She shook her head at Jack, finally understanding some, but not believing. "He's a Marine...They're tougher..." But she knew better after she had said it.

Jack heartily squeezed her hand.

"It doesn't matter, Tasha," Chad said softly. "Jack is just as affected as you are. You want me to get you something to calm your nerves?"

"Nah, just give me a minute," she said, barely audible. A few seconds passed as she was thinking, then she added as an afterthought out loud, "The walking or running usually helps." She turned away from Chad, not wanting to look Jack in the eye, still ashamed.

The tension in the air was thick, causing them all discomfort. Everyone wanted to help, but preferably dismiss what had just happened. Thus, Jack moved toward Chad, but more to get the side support bar out from between Tasha and him, to embrace her, not pulling her off the treadmill entirely, telling her, "I got you, Tasha. If you—"

"Maybe Jack here should give that a try," Chad said, pointing to the treadmill. "It'll help his blood pressure in the long run," he added, in his usual jovial tone—his attempt to lighten the mood.

She pulled back from Jack to look up at his face, catching the mirth and exasperation in his eyes.

"May have to yet when she gets strong enough to go back to running," Jack told Chad. "She'll need a running buddy outside during the spring and summer time."

"Well, I got the guys to change the video game to something else, just so we can get you two back upstairs with us. Apologies, again, to the two of you—especially you, Tasha. None of us thought ahead."

She and Jack dismissed it.

"No need—"

"No problem—"

They both stopped.

Jack, the gentleman, offered her to continue. She nodded for him to continue, adding to the awkwardness.

"Just tell them we'll be up in a few," he told Chad.

"After I finish...whatever it is...I came down here for"—she spied the chest freezer—"in the deep freezer," she added deceitfully in her shame, half-shrugging a shoulder at Chad in a diminutive gesture.

Chad smirked. "Your secret's safe." He winked at her before heading back upstairs. Then he stopped to throw back over his shoulder, "You know you two are just perfect for each other. If you two would only talk to each other, you could help yourselves out, since neither of you will admit to having PTSD, much less being wildly in love with each other."

As soon as they were certain he was gone, Jack pulled her to him, protectively encircling her body with his arms, picking her up off the treadmill and hauling her to his desk, where he leaned up against it and tucked her into his embrace, giving her a kiss on the top of her head before placing his head on top of hers, sighing heavily. Neither of them said a word, each using the other for comfort, remaining until they both could go back upstairs. Tasha was unclear if he was more comforting to her or if she had become his comforting teddy bear.

Jack asked her a few moments later, "You ready?"

"Yeah…Let's go before they start talking about us 'sucking face.'" Tasha led the way back up. She felt his smile at her back side as he followed her up the stairs, finishing the rest of a perfect day with a perfect evening.

It was late as the last of the guys left, the three of them getting all the dishes washed and the food stored away. Jack had kept a wary eye on Tasha the rest of the evening, staying protectively close. Lela became quiet when Sam left. She was helpful but gave them the space to be their 'normal' selves. But Jack was not sure if Lela was being quiet because the earlier incident or if she was more engrossed with her own thoughts of Sam. He decided on the latter as he disapprovingly watched her giving Drake a bunch of leftovers, which the large black dog happily devoured.

Jack thanked Tasha again for the wonderful dinner as she bid her goodnights to them. The flashback earlier that evening had drained much of her normal spunkiness when in public and in front of him. His sister said goodnight as well as he pulled on his jacket to get some air, taking Drake outside one last time for a small game of fetch and a potty break before letting Drake perform his 'guard duty' over Tasha's slumber.

Drake's duty was short-lived when four hours later Jack was jerked awake at the shout of "Incoming!" He was not sure if he had been dreaming, reliving the few times his convoy was under attack, coming awake just before the ominous explosion that had killed his entire squad. It was an all too familiar sickly warning. Usually the warning was a much deeper voice belonging to a male soldier. This warning was strangely higher-pitched than it should have been, thus awakening him.

Another directional warning came, and his sister, sleeping on the far side of his king-sized bed, protested wearily awake with a "what's happening?" and Drake's whimpering small bark got him to his feet, realizing that Tasha was having another of her rare 'war-mares.'

He hurried to her room, pushing her door open, reaching for her as she screamed out, "I'm hit!" clutching her side where she had taken a bullet months earlier. Drake jumped off her bed, greeting him with a concerned whine, grateful for his presence, scared of her incoherent actions. Jack scrambled to get ahold of her, sitting just behind her on her bed and cradling her to him as his sister came into the room inquiring of them, the hallway light stabbing the room's darkness and throwing her form into a foreboding silhouette. He told her gruffly that Tasha was having a nightmare and waved her away, telling her to go back to bed and to take Drake with her.

He cooed to Tasha as she screamed to someone, "Stay back! Stay back!"—her team taking on heavy fire, he surmised. He watched his sister's realization as she took in Tasha's room, noting her old Army gear lying about in several places, finally understanding that Tasha was a vet too, as if she had not originally believed it. He was sure that Lela knew, but then he had never said anything to her, figuring Tasha would have mentioned it at one time or another. But then he remembered how intensely private Tasha was, never disclosing her past much to others unless directly asked and had no way of diverting from the question.

"Hey, soldier, I got you, you're okay," he said, rocking her slowly. "Shhh, I got you. Stay with me, Tasha." Jack stroked her hair back on her head, his arm securely wrapped around her torso, ensuring his hand covered hers where she protectively held it over her wound, more or less trying to keep from bleeding out as he could only imagine of what she had gone through. "You're fine… you're all right, hang in there, Tasha." Jack placed his head protectively on top of hers, still rocking her upper body with his. He twisted his head, noting his sister still standing there. He softly barked for her to leave them, that he had it under control. He would stay the rest of the night with her, just like he had on the other nights when her memory remained persistent in coming out during the darkest hours.

Eventually he got her down to where she was crying and calling out to someone, whimpering the person's name the rest of the night's hour, clutching on to him as he rolled with her, pulling her body up against his when he lay down next to her in her bed, covering them both under her comforter. Her hand releasing her distraught grip on his chest was his only indication that she had subsided back into a deep and near-lifeless slumber. Her grip had been painful where he bore the shrapnel scars, but he was willing to share, if not take all the pain she had experienced just to make her comfortable, and most importantly, happy. He lay awake on his side, his hand errantly stroking her stray golden tresses back in line with the rest of her hair. He was grateful that she seldom had that dream. She was much tougher than he had ever expected of her.

When she shifted in her sleep—throwing a leg over his hip, snuggling down into his chest, her arms folded and tucked between them—was when he finally closed his eyes. When he wrapped his arms protectively and loosely around her prone form, it was one of the few times he ever slept soundly, knowing she was by his side. He would get up before she awoke, ensuring she had her body pillow up against her for her to snuggle before leaving her side in the morning like normal. But then, Chad's comment earlier came to him, reminding him it was time.

CHAPTER NINETEEN

Tasha was sluggish to rouse from her sleep, feeling more tired than rested after what seemed like a long night. She squeezed her eyes against the sunlight that was streaming in through her bedroom window, trying to figure out what had awoken her as her mind quickly discarded her dreams, becoming incomprehensible, disconnected fragments. She threw an arm over her eyelids to shield against the intrusive light, rolling to her side and snuggling up against her body pillow that lay in the center of her bed, finding her hand underneath the pillow caught up with something she was not able to remember nor determine what it was, when she heard, "Who's Sergeant Herrington?" before realizing her hand was held by Jack's familiar hand.

Tasha's eyes snapped open against the light, her free arm slamming down on the pillow separating them in her bed when she heard the question. The sound of his voice made her realize that he was no enemy threat, yet she did not want him near her either, especially at that time of day, where she was not at her best.

"Good morning…About time you woke up." He cocked a devilish smile at her.

She sighed heavily in disgust, swearing, before demanding, "Now what?" She tried to roll away from him but found her hand underneath the pillow still imprisoned within his grasp. She rolled back toward him defeatedly as he determinedly asked again, "Who is he?" His face was only a half arm's length away from hers, the body pillow blocking him from being any closer.

"Christ, Drake, I've heard of pets looking like their owners, but you have taken it too far—and for the worse on your end of the deal."

Jack just smirked at her. "Ever the morning person, aren't you? Is there even a right side of the bed for you?"

"Let me guess, you're hungry and you want your breakfast? Has anyone ever told you that you are worse than a demanding cat or dog?"

Jack's smile dropped again when he commented and asked the question for the third time. "No…not really. Just curious as to who this Sergeant Herrington is and what he meant to you?"

She gave him a quizzical look, hoping to deflect his questioning and get out of answering him.

"He must have meant a great deal to you for you to have made such a fuss over him. Who is he?"

"What?" She shook her head at him, determined to keep her guilty secret to herself, and for the rest of her life.

Jack cracked a half-smile at her from where he laid his head on the body pillow separating them. "Who is he, Tasha?"

"Seriously?" She tried again to pull her hand free of his, only to stop when he squeezed it harder. She acquiesced. "I guess someone I dreamed about."

He was not accepting her answer. "Who is he?"

"I don't remember most of my dreams, Jack. Would you get out of my bed?" Again she wiggled her captive hand underneath the pillow. "Before you give your sister any further matchmaking reasons."

"She already knows I spent the night with you." He exhaled heavily, snuggling his face even closer to her on the other side of her body pillow, turning the pillow more into a fence between two neighbors.

"What?" she hissed at him, keeping her yelling to a harsh whisper. "Why?" She slammed her upper free hand against the body pillow between them in her building frustration of being trapped with him in her own bed.

"Let's put it this way: you did a great job late last night of warning the entire cabin of 'INCOMING!' and to 'TAKE COVER!' You even had me out of bed, practically low-crawling to your room with my sister on my heels, concerned as hell. Even scared Drake enough to run out of your room, seeking help. Thus us 'boys' thought we would do the manly thing and exchange beds."

"Why on God's green earth would you encourage her? Are you out of your mind? Must I remind you that *we* are *never* going to happen?"

"Ah yes, I need to ask why that is…But first…who is this Sergeant Herrington?"

"Oh my God!" she sighed, dragging her free hand over her face, sighing heavily. "You're now jealous of someone I had a dream about?" She focused only on various parts of his face, with him being so close, smelling his scent. He waited.

Like hell she was going to answer him! He didn't answer any of her questions, so it was only fair to not answer any of his, as far as she was concerned.

"Why should I answer you when you don't even open up nor answer any of *my* questions about you?"

"What would you like to know?"

"Your time in the Mid-East."

"It's in the past and I've moved on."

"Moved on, my ass," she growled. "Well, then"—she made her voice sound lighter, as she dismissed his inquiry—"I guess you answered your own question then. It's in the past and time to move on."

He raised an eyebrow at her, his silence determined.

She added, "No…not until you spill something."

He sighed at her. "What do you want to know?"

"Why are all your military photographs signed 'Suicide Jack'?"

Smiling, he said, "*So*, you *have* been going through my personal things and books in my room."

She ignored him, expectant of his answer.

"It's a nickname I got while I was over there after my second tour."

She waited for more, yet he wasn't forthcoming.

"Why?" she prodded.

"Ah…no…your turn, who is he?"

"A platoon sergeant. Why the nickname?" she persisted.

"Because anyone assigned to me, after losing two entire squads before, became suicide members in my squad."

She raised her eyebrows at this, asking, "Not because you were suicidal?"

"Nah…That's two answers for you. Now I want two."

Tasha rolled her eyes. "For Pete's sake…Go on."

"Why was he so important to you?"

"What makes you believe he was so important to me?"

"I asked first."

"Fine. I liked him," she stated flatly.

"And?"

"He was killed."

"That's not enough."

"What more do you want to know? Let's talk about your ex. What was so special about her that you have never been able to move on with your life?"

"I have moved on, but someone isn't willing to let me—in addition to answering questions about Sergeant Herrington…He must have been Mr. Right, I take it?"

She studied him. "No, Mr. Right, like every male out there, is either gay or married. And in his case, he was happily married with a newborn. So you're quite jealous of a ghost, I'm afraid." She used her free hand to emphasize the discussion points. "You know, I think you need to seek some counseling on these jealousy issues."

"Not jealous…curious." He nabbed her second hand, holding it, before continuing. "But there must have been something more for you to be fussing over him in such a way in your sleep. Is this part of the reason you won't date a superior?"

She pressed her lips into a thin line, biting her tongue, as he nailed it. Her silence betrayed her, convincing him.

"Ah…hunh. So *there's* the reason for you not wanting to date me."

"Nothing happened. He was honorable…to the end," she blurted out defensively.

"But you wanted more?"

"Yes…no."

"But you cried as if he was your lover."

"He and I flirted, we were close, like friends, even though I wish I could've had more," Tasha answered him, very much annoyed.

"So what happened?"

"I told you, he died."

His expression was clear that he not buying her entire story.

"What was she like that made you fall head over heels with her?"

"Jessica?"

"Yes."

"She was pretty, smart, and witty. Like you. Looked great in office clothes…a big turn-on for me—"

"Ah…something else that will never happen here, since I work on the flight line." Tasha clicked her tongue in tough luck.

"Ah…but you could…in the future."

"The future? Do enlighten me on what you foresee of my future." She smiled big. "This has got to be interesting."

"Maybe you will work your way up to owning Black Raven Aviation."

"What? What about Nate and his wife?"

"They are looking to eventually retire but not lose their legacy."

"Like I am going to afford to buy out a company anytime soon," she told him sarcastically.

"There are ways…ways around obtaining businesses."

"Like in…what…a hostile takeover? Sorry, I'm not into that. You can count me out."

"Nope. That's not happening, for I like Nate way too much to do that to him. You'll see one day, if you stick around long enough." Tasha's eyebrow raised again at that new piece of information. Is that what he did on those nights after work in the basement office?

"I'll stick around until I'm fired, let go, or worse, chased off by you," Tasha retorted.

"Chased off…by me?"

"I don't need you to make my life any more difficult than it already is, Jack."

"Difficult? I think I do a pretty good job of making it as easy as possible for you. Financially, I've never asked you to pay any utility bill—"

"More like you didn't tell me we had those…to share!"

"—and all I have ever asked for in return is to cook—"

"—and clean. But I guess you may be right," Tasha replied, disarming him.

"Right?" He was confused that she had agreed with him.

"You're not half the mess of the other four guys who share a cabin. So I lucked out. Oh, I guess I shouldn't forget that you *do* help out on laundry. You at least load the machines and then bring the basket of clean clothes back up for me to fold. Most men wouldn't even dare to be caught dead doing that for a woman."

"It's the least I could do." His response was smug. He studied her for a moment, his hand releasing her hand so that he could stroke her bed hair down, musing at the softness of her golden tresses. "So tell me…what happened and what made him your one and only Mr. Right?" His hand ended up caressing the side of her face where it remained cupping her chin, his thumb rubbing the side of her cheekbone. "What is it that I will never have?…as you keep reminding me."

"I would have thought that obvious to you."

Jack paused. His thumb stopped in mid-swipe. "I'm not asking again," Jack told her.

"The lack of communication, for one thing. Being more open, friendlier, and being more fun to be around," she continued down her perfect male checklist. "You keeping me on a need-to-know basis. I am not in the military anymore and I refuse to be your personal mushroom both here at the cabin and on the flight line. So there's a start for you."

"There's more?"

"Yeah."

"Well?"

"Nothing to complain about with the lovemaking sessions, other than too few and often end up in spats. I want long term, even if we have to duke it out a couple of times. You…you just make me *so* mad…when you shut me out. As silly as it sounds, I literally want to be inside of you…if that is even possible."

"No, not silly. Not being vulgar, but guys have been doing just that throughout history. But often we get dismissed as a perverts or sex maniacs trying to get inside of women."

Tasha gave him half a smirk from where she laid her head on her pillow, facing him.

Jack smiled at this, but he grew serious. "So what makes you think I don't want anything more serious?" He drew closer to her face, pausing before giving her an earth-shattering kiss—the kind that she still found herself hungering for since their first time.

Neither of them let go as he continued to let his lips explore down the side of her face and neckline to her shoulders, pulling down on her oversized sweatshirt, exposing her shoulder. She sighed in delight.

"So what was it that made him become an immortalized lover?" Jack asked, making her go cold again.

"Please don't, Jack." She tried to push him away, trying to roll out of her bed, yet unable to with her hand still held captive just underneath the body pillow that was between them.

"What is it that you are not telling me?" he asked as she lay flat on her back, looking defeatedly up at the ceiling.

"I'd rather not go into the details. He just didn't survive the firefight we encountered," she said sullenly.

"So who's keeping who out now?" he softly asked her. Jack let go of her hand and sat up on his elbow, facing her.

He studied her, watching the shadowy memories float over her pale visage. He did not know what he was looking for, but he did know it was what kept her from considering him as a potential partner. Every excuse she had was just false smoke, save for the *one* unspoken reason. The real reason.

Her face held pain again—pain that he had caused by wanting to know more about her past and this Sergeant Herrington. He let the back of his hand gently slide over her smooth skin along her cheekbones down to her chin, where he gently secured it between his thumb and fingers, turning her face back to him before apologizing to her and promising not to be as callous as he had been.

She reached up with her hand, covering his as she turned into his palm, placing a feathery kiss and sighing into it. Tasha surprised him when she whispered, "He died trying to save me when I was shot. He took the other two bullets meant for me."

He studied her a moment, watching her tears seep just beneath her eyelashes, as she kept her eyelids shut trying to staunch them. "Fair enough," he told her. Jack pulled her head toward him, cradling her as he let her cry it out.

She shifted under the covers, moving closer to him, sliding underneath the body pillow, aligning her body perfectly along his, asking to 'just snuggle' while she gathered herself. Her upper body had gotten cold from where she had been exposed. He knew she was seeking heat, if not protection from him. Normally, he was not a 'snuggler' by nature, nor was it his temperament to just lie around in bed once he was awake. But that morning there was no immediate need to get anything done or seen to during his off hours. The snow drifts outside shifted quietly against the cabin's exterior, muffling all of nature's sounds, providing them the atmospheric void to drop back into a dreamless morning nap, knowing that they were both safe and sound from the hell they had been through, sharing a stake in Alaska's frontiers and possible good fortunes.

The rest of the Thanksgiving holiday weekend was spent quietly together at the cabin. Lela and Sam had become inseparable, giving Jack and Tasha space and time for reacquainting themselves more intimately. Jack was even released from the duty of driving his sister back to Anchorage on early Saturday morning to catch her airline flight back to Louisiana when Sam offered to fly her there given the unexpected good weather. It had given him the idea to take Tasha out sightseeing by air just after he got the 172 ready for Sam and said his goodbyes to his sister.

As Jack gave Sam a warning look about handling his sister, Lela spied Tasha just past them all, holding back some distance with her arms wrapped around herself from the bay's cold breeze. Lela bounded to her, pulling her into their group. "What are you doing over there?"

"Just giving you all some space between siblings and now a new love interest." She gave Lela her best knowing grin, although somewhat saddened seeing her leave. Lela's obvious close relationship with her brother, the way she was able to bring out the best in him, had given Tasha a chance to see more of the rare intimate and gentler side of Jack in these past few days.

"Aww, come on now, you're family too. I expect you two to be married within the year."

Tasha raised an eyebrow at her insistency.

"Look, I know when my brother is in love. How he watches you when he thinks you're not looking…He's very protective of you!" Lela leaned in, giving Tasha's arm a squeeze. "I know he can be a bear! But it's his nature. You see how he is with Sam and me?" Lela stopped just outside of earshot of the two men.

Tasha quietly smiled at her and nodded reluctantly in agreement.

Lela pulled her into a big goodbye hug, telling her in her ear, "No more of those crazy nightmares of yours! Okay? He's always going to be there for you, Tasha…if you just let him." Lela released her, dragging her to Jack, either to distract Jack from being overbearing to Sam or to reinforce her desire to see the two of them together.

Sam personally gathered his newfound love into the passenger seat of the 172, strapping her in the seat's harness. He quickly swung into his seat from the other side, donning his headset and then helping Lela with hers. Jack pulled the chocks, giving Sam the start signal as he and Tasha backed to a safe distance, away from the propeller's arc.

After watching them take off, gaining enough altitude, they turned in the direction of Anchorage beyond the mountain ridge to the north of the bay, Jack pulled her to him, leading her to the Twin Otter he had pulled out telling her to get Drake loaded into the rear passenger area and to get in the pilot's side. He went to retrieve his large flight bag and carried two extra coats for them to load up just behind their seats.

"Isn't Big Raven going to be upset with us using the company's planes and fuel costs for personal usage?"

"Nah…I let him know so he can take the expenses for my sister's ride to Anchorage out of my paycheck. Besides, you've had a little time in Clara, and now it is high time to finish your checkout ride on this little gal. I need to get you signed off, so it's part personal and part work time," he said, winking at her and giving her a half-cocked smile.

Tasha pursed her lips before smiling back at him. She went through the checklist and before long they were in the air gaining altitude over the bay before she asked him where he wanted to go. Jack gave her the heading and she made the adjustments, swinging the aircraft around on the smooth cold morning air and settling into a comfortable cruise speed.

The Twin Otter was a solid plane, like all of them in Black Raven's fleet, a little paint-worn here and there, but mechanically in good shape. The cockpit had been updated, especially in the avionics area, and even had the dual control wheel configuration, making it much more suitable for check rides.

About five minutes later, his voice came clear over her headset, "Okay, Tasha, I have controls," as he gripped the control wheel.

"Controls are yours," she said as Jack banked the plane left.

"Now, there's a sight every pilot should witness at least once up here in Alaska." He pointed for her to look out her window, where she saw a clear view of a pod of beluga white whales in the clear, calm waters below at the mouth of Resurrection Bay. He slowly reduced power and entered a gentle descent as he saw how entranced she had become watching them swim. He gave her time to watch them, circling a few times around the group, descending until they were a few hundred feet above the water. Finally, he added power and began climbing again.

Her huge grin was his biggest reward. He returned her smile with a grunt of delight.

"I wish there was more to see," she commented.

"Ah, but there is. Alaska is the 'Great Land.'" His mood was infectious, and she delighted in seeing even the whiskers in his beard smiling, making her laugh. "Trust me... You want to see more?" Jack asked. "That is exactly what I have planned for today. And most of it by air." He had changed their heading to the northwest, crossing over the Aialik Peninsula. He was heading into the Kenai Fjords National Park, by her guesstimates.

"So I'm good with my company checkout ride, then?"

"Ah... you're not getting off that easy," he replied, his facial expression relaxed and happy. He was one with the plane, directing it with the calm assurance of an experienced pilot.

"Oh?" She should have known better, and gave him a cheeky grin, knowing she had to show him she could do a few more maneuvers, probably a few mock emergency situations, and a few landings at other airports.

"Patience, Moose. We'll get it done soon enough." He eased back the throttles to bleed off altitude again. Within minutes they leveled out just over the tops of the jagged rocks standing as sentinel at the gates of the glaciers, 'scud-running' between the higher jagged peaks, giving her the feel of being an eagle gliding by on the sea air.

He reminded her, "Only fly this low on very clear visual days." He quickly glanced over to her, making sure she had heard him. Their eyes briefly met, both alert to the terrain around them. "Remember to look at how the wind pushes the waves around for those signs of strong air currents coming off the mountains and the glacier up ahead, especially from Aialik Glacier at the head of the bay. Often you will hit air pockets and it gets bumpy up ahead. During our summer season is when you will find yourself giving flight tours to the tourists, and they will want you to fly low, and you can, but not to the point of endangerment. Thankfully, it is mistier at that time of year, making this place even more magical than it is today."

Jack expertly glided through the fjord's labyrinth. "I need you to memorize this place." The bump he had anticipated came as they passed through the colder air coming off the glacier, but he minimized it by adding more speed and climbing into the colder air. Beyond the glacier, he passed over the large Harding Ice Field, with just enough space to skim the ice with the aircraft's wheels. She was certain the tires were touching the icy surface. He was more daring than she was when it came to flying. He gained more altitude before making a one-hundred-and-eighty-degree turn, leveling out and centering the controls before telling her to take over the aircraft.

She was stunned, but took the controls, only to find him pulling back on the throttles, making her lose altitude. "What are you doing?" she asked as she advanced the throttles for more power to maintain their altitude. But he blocked her hand.

"I need to work on your confidence level when you navigate this fjord, especially at lower altitudes. You need to learn to fly low and slow. Remember, I am a paying tourist who wants to get great photos of this place."

"If they want great photos, they need to take a boat, Jack!"

He snorted at her. "Come on, Tasha, show me that usual spunk of yours. Put it into your flying!"

She twisted her mouth at him, not daring to look at him and possibly misjudge what was coming at them as she returned to the glacier, darting between the rocky and tree-lined tops. It was like a video air racing game.

"Atta girl! Keep the flight as slow as possible without losing your altitude. You will need to learn to fly lower."

"Hey! This plane doesn't have pontoons, or I would go lower! I won't do it."

Laughing, he placated, "No worries." He looked out the side of his window, his arms now crossed over his chest, appreciating the view. Jack chinned to the Alaskan Gulf. "When you get to the gulf, make another one eighty. I'm going to have you run the gauntlet again. But lower, keep it to five hundred off the water, Moose."

She was at eight hundred feet as she glided out past the inlet. She gave him an incredulous look as she pushed in the throttle, gaining speed and more altitude for the long turnaround. The back of his head was all she could see as he studied the view below his side window. When he turned back to look at her, he gave her a mute *what?* look.

When she headed back toward the inlet, her heart pounding, she hesitated.

"Come on, Tash, you can do it, it's a perfectly clear day. I have your back," he told her. As they entered between the two mountain ranges, he continued, "Lower your nose first, get your altitude set, and then work on slowing your air speed with power and pitch attitude. Give these tourists the ride of their lives. That's what you get paid to do."

She did what she was told, concentrating on the solid rock formations ahead. She did not once get a chance to enjoy the view that time around, getting a feel for the layout of the fjord as the glacier came into view.

He had her add power and climb into the area where the cold air pocket would be, intending to be stable and high enough that she would not hit the pocket as hard. She made it but refused to fly as low as he did over the ice field. The broken ice field and beautiful pure electric blue gullies were a foreboding place for any aircraft to land on.

"Good. Now again," he said to her. "We'll keep practicing until I feel certain about you making this flight with the summer tourists. Today is a great day to practice since the winter weather doesn't often cooperate for us."

She did a few more runs back and forth until it became instinctive and she was sightseeing again, enjoying the view.

"Good. I have another place for you to enjoy." He had her fly back out over the gulf and then gave her a new heading to the northwest and instructed her to climb to a cruising altitude of 6,500 feet to clear the snow-covered ridgeline of the next peninsula.

"Where are we headed to next?"

"To the town of Kenai," Jack responded.

She threw him a questioning look as she mouthed the town's name, trying to remember what it was remarkable for as a tourist destination. The only things she could muster was scenery and fishing. Fishing most likely when it came to Jack. She did not prod him, deciding to look out her window at the glorious view, no weather to worry about and very few clouds. A rare day indeed.

About forty minutes later, Jack instructed her to prepare for a landing at Kenai Municipal Airport as he changed the comm channel over to ATIS. The information service gave them the information for approach and the appropriate frequency. Jack selected the frequency and reached around behind him, his hand landing on Drake's head and giving him a good stroke, checking on him.

Tasha was on a left downwind to One Nine Right, checking for other air traffic when Jack told her they would be doing some pattern work. She contacted the tower and apprised them of their intentions. The tower cleared them for the touch-and-gos.

"Land on the numbers."

"Excuse me?"

"I want your wheels to touch somewhere on those numbers. Not the letter under them, but on the numbers. You're making a spot landing for me."

"But there's plenty of runway."

"I know. But I need you to be exact. Not all places you will be landing in the future will have long runways or have large areas for takeoff or landings. Almost every landing you make should be a spot landing."

"Crap," she mumbled. That was something she had never mastered. When she was learning, her instructor, her father, never made a big deal out of spot landings, and now it was about to bite her. She sighed and tried to figure the best way to set up the approach as she turned from base to final.

"You're too high," Jack told her loudly as they crossed the runway threshold. "Use flaps or slip the plane." He reached up and selected the flaps down. Then he quickly pulled back on the throttles. Jack's unexpected intervention seemed to suck the air out from under the plane, dropping it suddenly, her stomach abruptly in her throat. Annoyed, she slapped his hand away from the flight controls. She even heard Drake's concerned whine over her headset and the noise of the aircraft.

"Hey! Are you trying to rip the wings off this bird?" she retorted, giving him a quick, searing look before flashing her eyes front and center.

"Trust me, this bird can handle this way better than a 182. Now get your wheels to touch the numbers."

"We're too low, Jack."

"No, you're not. You need to aim for the numbers until the numbers don't move in your field of vision. It's perception. Know the size of your bird, Tasha."

"I don't fly this one that often!" She reached for the throttles to add air speed for fear of landing too short of the runway.

"Hold your airspeed with attitude," Jack said as he stopped her hand. "Use power to move your landing spot."

She kept the numbers centered on the windshield and swallowed hard, a guttural noise rising from her throat and slipping past her lips, helping to release some of the intensity that built up. She lowered the nose slightly to maintain airspeed, hoping Jack had not heard her.

Flaring late, the left main hit hard with the other main striking milliseconds afterwards, and she was certain that the tires had left some heavy marks on the runway. But before her nose wheel touched down, Jack shoved the throttles back into full power and reset the flaps to takeoff position, telling her she needed to go around and try again.

She was not sure if she had done it or not, but figured with having to take off again, she had failed. She heard Drake bark once in the back seat, and Jack said something to his dog that she did not catch over her headset.

As she reached the traffic pattern altitude, Jack got her attention. "Look down near the numbers."

She looked but was uncertain what she was looking for. "What am I looking for?"

"You hit hard enough there should be some new tire marks."

"I'm not seeing any other than a few others just past the numbers."

"Bank left a moment for me to look."

She did as she was told.

"Yup, just as I thought. You went past them."

"How can you tell from the rest of the other marks?" Tasha quizzed him.

"I look for the darkest one. You missed it by a hundred feet." He drawled out.

Men! Men and their inherent ability to judge distance and sizes. Just like the mechanics on the floor knowing what size wrench they needed on whatever nut they had to adjust or take off. Even after all the years on the flight line, she still had to take at least two to three similar-sized wrenches to test on the nut before getting the right one. It was a maddening eyeballing trait she hoped she would eventually pick up…and soon.

She lined up again, that time pulling back on the throttles and slowly dropping the flaps to make the drop less jarring.

"You're still too high," he said, and she pulled the throttles back more, remembering to use power to move her target.

She double-checked her airspeed.

"Still too high, Moose."

The ground was coming up fast. He assisted again, pulling the throttles back even more. She focused on flying the plane and holding her airspeed, but she steeled herself for the impact, completely surprised when the wheels touched down firmly and the plane bounced once gently.

"Clean up your flaps and let's do it again," he said, sitting back with his arms crossed.

She selected the flaps up, retrimmed the elevators, and pushed the throttles forward to full takeoff power, exhaling softly as the plane accelerated and lifted off.

"You all right?" he asked, and she nodded affirmatively.

It was a workout for her when it came to that type of training. It unnerved her, but she knew it was necessary. She understood his point, and appreciated his explaining how to do it, but she rarely got the practice time, and was afraid to ask for the time for fear of showing her weaknesses in some areas. But Jack was giving her the time, and she had not expected it, especially over the holidays.

She knew that she had to learn to take off and land in the water with the other aircraft that were capable of it, and she knew two of their birds could be modified with skis for the snow and she had to learn that as well, and soon.

Jack instructed her to check for signs of where she had touched down, and she banked toward the field so they could look. The best they could tell, the new set of markings were on the top edge of the numbers. "Better…Now get it right this time, Tasha. Drake needs to use the bathroom."

"So do I," she retorted. In her peripheral vision, she could see his smirk and short laugh as his white teeth flashed momentarily.

He sat there again, his arms folded over his chest, watching. She knew his eyes did not miss a thing, from the instrument panel to the flight control movements, and to the view outside. However, he acted like he was just a passenger, admiring the view and the runway expanding in front of them.

"Come on, Moose…watch your numbers. Set your airspeed and then put the numbers where you want them. They should stay in the same place, coming straight at you. Use your peripheral vision for everything else."

She heard him uncross his arms, expecting any minute for his assistance on the flight controls. But nothing came as she adjusted the throttles, maintaining the aircraft's angle of approach, ensuring the numbers did not move. As she got close, she flared and pulled the throttles back, the main wheels gently touching the ground. That time Jack did not assist, only said for her to take them to the next taxiway and head for the main building. He contacted Kenai Ground as she taxied to where he directed her to go. When she shut down the engines, Jack turned to her and told her she had done it.

"I did?"

"Yup."

"Can I practice some more?"

"Later, and at our airport when we return. But first, Drake needs to go as much as you do. And I'm hungry. Ready for lunch?"

Tasha nodded in agreement.

Brother's café was the unexpected fare they shared, discussing more about what she had learned and how to improve upon it. The airport was by far much larger and more active than Seward's, a pleasant and much welcomed surprise. He let her wander around the facilities, exploring some before returning to the aircraft to check on Drake. Jack had seen to it to have his water and food bowl out for him inside the plane's interior so he could chow down while they ate inside.

He clipped a leash to Drake, telling Tasha to hold on to it while he grabbed his flight bag. Jack waved to a fuel truck to indicate that their plane needed fuel.

"We're not leaving?" she asked, confused that he seemed to be locking up the aircraft instead of getting it ready for flight.

"Ah, I thought you wanted to see more of Alaska, Tasha."

"I do, but humor and enlighten me as to what we are doing next." He smiled broadly at her, giving her a moment of doubt, before she added disappointedly, "Oh, God. Please don't tell me we are going fishing or hunting."

He pursed his mouth, thinking, as she ended up turning away in disgust, taking Drake with her, making the dog lead the way. But he laughed, lunging after her, catching her elbow before guiding her toward the building again but through another set of doors. "That seemed like a good idea, but I won't torture you." He opened the door for her and Drake to go inside, "However, I have something better," he added, still not indulging her with his plans.

An hour later, having obtained a rental car and stopping for few groceries at a place Jack seemed to know well, he pulled into a recreation area where there was a nice expanse of sandy beach. He parked near a picnic area and unloaded a grocery bag filled with drinks and snack items in addition to a five-gallon bucket and two pairs of rubber boots. They got settled at a nearby table bench where they sat down, resting while watching the bay waters, sipping their drinks. Jack sat next to her, scooting in close to her, both soaking in the view.

After several minutes, she finally had to ask. "So, we're not fishing." She didn't bother to look at him. "And we are not exactly hunting. But taking in the view of a bay after flying an airplane to get here seems a bit excessive for a date with you on the beach." Tasha eyed Drake doing his normal roaming, sniffing at all the new scents. She added, "Mind you, I'm not opposed to long walks on the beach or having a picnic, but couldn't we have done this back in Seward?"

Tasha heard Jack as he turned his head, forcing her to look into his gray-blue eyes alight with humor.

"What?" she asked when he remained silent.

"Ah, but there is more to this walk on the beach with you and then taking you out to dinner."

She warily eyed him.

"There's a reason they call this Clam Gulch. I do intend to romance you with a long walk and a terrific dinner, but first we must wait a bit."

A movement at the tree line caught her eye, just past Jack, where she spied a moose with a young calf wandering toward the water's edge. Jack whistled to Drake, where he was upwind of the wildlife, to come back to them. The large black dog obediently came, sitting down next to them, where Jack placed a staying hand on him, petting him while he followed her gaze. She smiled in delight at seeing the two so close to them, especially a mother and her young.

"It seems your spirit animal has the same idea," he joked quietly, having leaned in toward her.

She laughed lightly, settling her chin on his shoulder, comfortable and content with his presence. "I can't decide if they are just plain ridiculously gangly ugly or just an unusual sight of beauty to behold."

She felt him smirk under her chin.

"What?" she asked.

"You know you are describing yourself?"

"I am?" she murmured, feeling sleepy with contentment. "Is that so?"

He shifted under her, pulling her body past him on the bench so that he was no longer sitting in front of her protectively with his back side toward her, making their jackets rustle in the movement. She now sat in front of him, where he leaned forward, wrapping his arms around her torso, placing his chin on her shoulder before telling her, "You definitely have their long legs and generously wide hips, to boot," he told her quietly by her ear. "Thus, very gangly indeed, but in your case, gorgeous to behold when you are walking across the hangar floor."

His warm breath tickled her ear as he lightly joked with her. She tilted her head toward him, where he gave her a light kiss on the side of her face. That moment, she treasured. It felt so right, yet she swore not to trust it to last long. Those rare moments between them. The open honesty and casualness between them comforting her, making her often rethink her future, and finding herself comparing him to the grizzly man on that late chilly summer evening when she first arrived at the cabin.

Tasha did not remember falling asleep in his arms. His embrace and body underneath her kept her warm in the cold air. Jack gently nudged her off him on the bench seat as he roused her. She was going to ask him how long they had been sleeping when she figured out the answer by noting the bay waters had disappeared, leaving a tremendously large expanse of wet sand, making the beach nearly double, if not triple in size.

Handing her a pair of rubber boots to put on, he told her it was time to go digging for their dinner. He showed her what to look for and the size she needed to take, enough for them to enjoy that night's meal. It was certainly a different kind of date than she had ever had before with a man. It was actually fun fetching the clams. Even Drake joined in on the fun of digging for them, barking when he had one exposed enough for them to pull out.

The day dissolved into an early night, as was usual for that time of year. Jack started a fire while he told her to do a quick rinse of the clams at a nearby water spigot to wash away the sand, and to fill a metal bucket up with fresh water to steam them. He did the cooking out under the heavily starry night while she opened a container of a pre-made chef salad and a mustard potato salad for them to share while eating the steamed clams, the light from the fire pit creating a romantic ambience while they ate. The only reason they had the place to themselves was due to the cold November night air and being so late in the year. After dinner he pulled out a bottle of wine, offering her some in a makeshift plastic cup that he must have procured from the grocery store owner. It was a beautiful and lightly sweet rose wine to end a delightful meal with as they shared the cup between them. With his cooking and packing duties over, he sat back down next to her, pulling her to him again, where she leaned against him, absorbing his body's warmth against the cold air. They leaned against the bench table where they sat watching the night sky giving up a few of its stars to the earth's atmosphere. She sighed contentedly, her belly full, and she made a quiet comment, "So much better than a spa weekend that I had wanted earlier this week."

She felt him grunting a half laugh as she turned to look back up at him, seeing his eyes glitter in the nearby dying firelight. His happiness was infectious. Tasha found herself thanking him, giving him an unexpected kiss, and he caught her mouth with his before she could pull away, prolonging what they both wanted.

At least so he told her, but she still felt uncertain, knowing Mr. Right had somehow taken over Mr. So-Not-Right's body just then in that perfect moment. Yet he pushed her away from him physically and she was unsure as to why he had stopped them, thinking it was somehow her fault and unable to determine what it was until he pointed up at the night sky toward the north horizon, pulling her up with him as he stood up.

It was just a lingering finger of light. At first she thought a thunderstorm was on the horizon, but the weather forecast for the next twenty-four hours was clear skies, and the only clouds were where the warmer air from the water began forming ground mists as the temperature continued to drop during the long night hours. She had almost missed seeing the light, for the glow was more subtle with a greenish hue only to grow brighter and stretch across the sky like visible high-altitude cirrus clouds, and she realized that he was showing her one of Alaska's most popular attractions...the Aurora Borealis!

Mesmerized, time slipped from Tasha, turning that moment into endless minutes. The Alaskan air danced with the Universe tonight. Her smile widened in delight. Only when her neck protested from the strain of looking up was she able to tear her gaze away from the sky's display, catching Jack's eyes, which mirrored her delight as if he were seeing the lights for the first time through her eyes.

"This is fabulous, Jack!" Her enthusiasm spilled over. "I...I don't know what to say. There are just no words to describe..."

"Amazingly beautiful," Jack interrupted, pausing long enough to study her as if he were making a mental photo of her, his comment a double entendre. His gaze made her self-conscious enough that she resumed her view of the light show. She needed to step on the brakes before letting her emotions show too much, before making a fool of herself. Or worse yet, getting left out in the emotional cold again when Jack decided to leave her in the dark when it came to personal and intimate things about himself.

She stole a sideways glance at his face now that he had resumed his watch of the moving display, the light casting a subtle glow over his hardened and resolute features, now catching a shadow of the Marine standing next to her underneath his beard and longer layers of hair. It made her realize that they had far more in common than she gave him credit for. She was getting a rare glimpse into a contented man who was quietly fighting his own post-war demons. Both were carving out a living doing what they loved most in aviation, and in between, trying to take in as much of the Far North's beauty as they could.

She sighed contentedly, causing his arm to snake around her, pulling her into his side before guiding her back to their bench seat where he reclined, his back supported by the edge of the picnic table. He offered her his lap so that she could spoon his body, lie against him, and make it easier for them to gaze upon the sky without straining their necks. Drake shifted in his resting position, coming over to their legs to lean up against them, offering more warmth against the outdoor temperatures.

When it got too cold to endure with just their coats and cold weather gear on, they reluctantly headed for the rental car, loading up their supplies and Drake, and Jack took them to a pre-arranged rented cabin for the night to rest before heading back to Seward the next morning.

As they snuggled down under the warm bedding, his strong arm protectively wrapped around her, pulling her to him, she thought there could not have been a more perfect evening as she drifted off into a deep and much needed sleep.

CHAPTER TWENTY

On Monday morning, after the crew meeting in the hangar and going over the work schedule, Jack could not have been happier after the Thanksgiving weekend. And it must have shown when Hank caught up to him with a second cup of coffee for him after everyone had gone off in their own directions for their task of preparing for another week's worth of delivery flights.

If there was anyone on the flight line that socialized with Jack, it was good ol' Hank, both being Southern boys with similar backgrounds. It was then that Jack's drawl would sometimes come out when he was relaxed, now that the work week was going smoothly.

Depositing a mug and sliding it over to him on his desk, Hank dropped into an old, battered office chair by the far wall in the cramped flight line office that Jack primarily used daily, preferring to be near the crew rather than tucked in one of the hallway offices by Nate and Nora's office. Jack's head popped up at the sound of the sliding mug, and he promptly dropped his paperwork, deciding he could attend to it later and enjoy the mini coffee break with Hank. Most likely Hank wanted to hash over his wife's Thanksgiving fare and what Jack had missed, since he was over at their place the year before Tasha had arrived.

"I say, Jack," Hank said, pulling at his salt-and-pepper whiskers, "I think this is the only time I have ever seen you this well rested….and I dare say…content?" Hank asked, waiting on Jack's answer by taking a cautious sip of his hot coffee before placing it back between his large gruff mechanic's hands, holding it in his lap where he had precariously tilted the old swivel chair back against the wall. Hank clicked his tongue before continuing. "In fact, if I didn't know ya any better, son, you look like yer glowing." He had a mischievous glint in his light blue eyes before adding, "Are ya sure you ain't pregnant?"

Jack smirked.

"Otherwise, I think ya choked a ton of chickens rather than one turkey!" came the bawdy punchline from Hank. "Must have been a hell of a Thanksgiving weekend fer ya, Jack."

Jack laughed before conceding to tell Hank what he wanted to hear most. Jack told about his weekend with his sister unexpectedly showing up on his doorstep and how he might end up as Sam's brother-in-law before the year was out.

At that comment, Hank's heavy salt-and-pepper eyebrows shot up. He smiled at Jack. "Aaah, that explains the boy's head being up in the clouds. I *thought* something was different this morning," he said, raising his mug up with a finger pointed at Jack before taking another sip of his coffee. "Not 'appy but not sad either. But if he keeps going at the pace he's using it now, that phone of his is goin' to have some worn-out keys and screen from all that texting he's been doing."

"Ya, I don't doubt it, given the way my sister is with her cell phone too." Jack leaned back in his chair to stretch his long legs out in front of him before settling with his ankles crossed. "I'm curious to see how long this long-distance relationship lasts." Jack took a long sip of the thick strong black coffee. The brew would help motivate him enough to go back to work when he really did not feel like working today—a first for him in an exceptionally long time. He had not wanted the last weekend to end, and his thoughts must have shown on his face as Hank kept clearing his throat in his feeble attempt to make Jack spill more beans.

At that reminder, Jack jerked forward, reached for his lunch pack, retrieved a ziplock bag of extra cookies, and tossed them over to Hank. He knew not to leave him out on Tasha's notorious caffeinated chocolate cappuccino cinnamon chunk cookies.

Hank realized what they were and immediately tore into the bag like a cocaine addict. "Ah, she didn't...did she?" He seized a cookie with his age-thickened, calloused fingers, taking a hefty bite of one, and savored the sweet morsel with a delightful sigh. He took a second bite and spoke around the mouthful of cookie, saying, "Damn, she's a great cook and a baker. You is one lucky bastard, Jack. I need her to get with my wife and share the recipe with her."

"Are ya kiddin'? The way you drink coffee all day and then eat those cookies, I am surprised ya haven't keeled over with a heart attack from all that caffeine in yer system!" Jack told him.

Hank grunted, having found another cookie to maim.

"Hell, I eat just four of them bad boys and I certainly don't need any more coffee to keep me up!" Jack told him.

"So...is that why you looked like the piece of crap the cat brought in the first time she brought that plate in that day?" Having finished the last of the batch of cookies in the bag, Hank reached up and scratched his beard. "I was wondering why the boys were fussing so much over how little she brought in the first time around."

Jack smirked at the memory of his mistake. "They're even better fresh out of the oven, Hank." Jack had eaten almost half of the four dozen cookies she had made for the crew while he had worked on some late-night paperwork down in the basement, not realizing the caffeine content in them. He'd had no sleep that night.

"Hmm...I bet they are."

"Anyway, you may have trouble getting that recipe from Tasha."

"Oh?"

"Yeah. I understand that it is a highly coveted family recipe." He remembered a few of Tasha's phone calls with her mother over the past few months. "But hey! Who knows? She may end up sharing that information, since she barely tolerates her momma, from what I can tell."

"Did she visit with her folks this past week?"

"Nawh, she stayed here and made us a Thanksgiving meal. And Southern style to boot, Hank! Honey-glazed ham, real yams, green bean casserole…the whole nine yards! I haven't had anything *that* good in a long…long time. I can't believe she pulled it off, especially when she wasn't planning on making a dinner, and it was her first time making a Thanksgiving feast." He interlaced his hands, putting them behind his head as he leaned back in his swivel chair behind his desk, stretching his back.

"What 'erbout my wife's last year?" Hank asked, then upon second thought: "Ah—never mind, she ain't no Southern cook. Just don't tell my wife I prefer Tasha's cooking any day."

Jack cracked a half-smile before promising him.

On another topic, Hank commented, "Noted that Clara and the 172 had been flown over the weekend."

"Yep! Sam took the Cessna to fly my sister to Anchorage for her return flight to Louisiana last Saturday, and I got Tasha checked out on the Twin Otter while at the same time giving her time to sightsee the Kenai Peninsula and then onto Kenai and Clam Gulch."

"She do okay?"

"Yeah, she's good to go. I just want to see her gain more confidence with each of these birds." Jack dropped forward, exhaling heavily. "She's not much of a risk-taker, which makes Big Raven happy."

"I'm sure that would," Hank chimed in. "But then, if I had to fly…I would fly with her then."

At that comment, Jack raised an eyebrow at him. This was Hank talking—the only man on the flight line that refused to fly any of the aircraft. He was a fine mechanic, the best of all of them with all his time and experience. The most he would do in any operational aircraft would be to taxi them around for engine and rose compass checks. But Hank never flew, nor would he tag along on a flight. Hank waved him a dismissing hand to keep him from inquiring further as to why he would never fly with any of them much less take the initiative to learn how to fly. Jack shook his head, respecting his secret, before continuing.

"In the beginning, she had a little trouble when I tested her on spot landings with the runway numbers. But after a few more attempts, she did fine. With more time and practice, she'll be just as good as our two main flyboys."

"How about the bigger birds? You'll need to test her soon, before winter settles in long and hard."

"Yeah, I need to. Just trying to adhere to Nate's requirements and do our flights in good VFR weather, but he has to let us fly IFR to keep all of our skill sets up to par. For Pete's sake, this is Seward, and getting clear flying weather is like playing golf with a softball and expecting to score several holes in one. He worries so much over his business insurance that I sometimes wonder if he has little faith in our team's flying capabilities."

"Yeah, I understand yer point, but I, for one, sure like Nate's reasoning for keeping most of his flights to good weather conditions. To me there's no point in flying if ya can't see the ground and water below."

Jack cocked his head at this other comment of Hank's, wondering if that could be another clue as to why he never liked flying. Hank didn't seem fearful of flying, but he sure didn't care for it either.

Jack picked up his scheduling paperwork, now rethinking some of the flight assignments. "I'm going to schedule Tasha to have more flight time with Jarvis and Sam on our bigger gals after this week. We could stand to have all of our people proficient with all of our birds by the time summer rolls around."

"Well I, fer one, think she can handle it. Tasha's a tough little wingnut," Hank commented, smiling around a fresh toothpick that he had just put in his mouth for the long day ahead of them.

"She may be little, but she's fierce," Jack said rather offhandedly. It was a saying that his dad would say of his sister when she was a colicky newborn.

Hank chuckled at the sentiment as he took his leave.

CHAPTER TWENTY-ONE

Later that day, Tasha came bounding in with paperwork that she had completed from Sam's and her assigned flight up to Kodiak. The cargo and passenger run had been fast and uneventful, putting her in a good mood since she was home early, making it a leisurely evening. She blushed at Jack when he caught her studying him while he looked over the papers. "Sorry, I'll go—"

"Nah, wait here. I'm done here for the night."

"Really? Are you sure?" Tasha thumbed over her shoulder. "You know I can catch a ride back with Sam or Hank."

"So eager to leave?"

"No, you usually have so much work that I didn't want to interrupt you... to just go home." Her hands were clasping and unclasping with uncertainty. Jack noted this, deciding he had been a jerk one too many times, causing her to have so many doubts when it came to them. He knew he would have to get his head on straight and fix that too.

"Nah, the paperwork is minimal at this time of year with all of our flights. It's the maintenance paperwork, FAA checks, and financial statements that keep me busy." Jack grabbed his coat, slinging it over his shoulder as he picked up his clipboard and a few files with his other hand, nodding for Tasha to lead the way, when the phone rang on his desk, and he realized he had nearly forgotten to take the mobile with him.

Tasha was closest and ended up answering his phone for him with the 'Black Raven Aviation' greeting.

"Yes, sir..." came her response. She turned to look at the whiteboard in Jack's office. "Your desired return?" She grabbed a sticky note to jot down more information. "I'll have to check." Another pause. "Is this a good number to reach you?" She looked down at the paperwork in his basket. "You're most likely looking at about fifteen to twenty thousand for the entire trip."

Jack's eyebrows jumped up at her quote, and he was motioning for the phone to talk with the client. Tasha ignored him by turning her back on him. By the time Jack freed his other hand, she had hung up the phone.

"What was that about?" Jack inquired, now curious.

"A Mr. Reynolds wants a flight to Kodiak for some ice fishing with a few of his co-workers."

"How many?" Jack asked as he came around to the side of his desk where she sat on the edge, and went over to the scheduling chart.

"Four guys," she stated to his back as he began to write on the whiteboard.

"When?"

"In two weeks from today," Tasha stated.

"Wait"—Tasha perked up—"You said Reynolds? Like in Mr. Reynolds of Southern Alaskan Energy Corporation?" Jack asked.

"If that is what those initials stand for." Tasha got up from her perch on his desk, handing him her notes. "He also wants a chauffeur and company van to pick him, his buddies, and their gear up to take to the aircraft, have an outfitter waiting for them, and then have us return about four days later to pick them all up and deliver them back here to their Airbnb."

"We don't have a company van, and a chauffeur, Tasha, much less an outfitter. I thought you knew that."

"I know," she told him.

He looked quizzically back at her.

"I have an idea…if you let me run with it."

He added, "And you overcharged way too much."

"Did I?" She shrugged her shoulders, looking at the paperwork in his basket. "We charge that in delivery fees when we bring in Kodiak's bi-monthly groceries. Why not them and all their extra requests?" She came over to Jack and stood next to him. "You get the aircraft you think we need, and the flight times booked, and let me take care of the rest. That is…if you trust me, Jack, putting it together."

At that comment he raised a brow at her, but she would not divulge any further information, so he told her that she could only spend five hundred of the company's funds.

"Jack!" Nate yelled to him at the hangar door where Hank had pulled the Twin Otter out for Nick and Emanuel to finish prepping for Mr. Reynolds' flight to Kodiak. Nate had broken into Jack's train of thought as he tried to figure out what Manny and Nick were doing so far away from the hangar on the flight line as they tended to the bird. He was just noting there was something different on the aircraft when Big Raven approached him.

Jack unfolded his arms, turning to meet Nate, when a somewhat familiar white van turned around the corner from the road and drove directly onto the flight line.

"Do you know what this eight-hundred-dollar bill is for?" Nate shuffled to another bill. "And this bill for—" He stopped speaking as he looked up at the van that had just pulled up halfway between them and the awaiting aircraft.

With the van parked, Tasha and Jarvis jumped out from either side of the van, with Jarvis opening the van's side door to let its guests out and then pointing to the aircraft on the ramp, which they were about to board. Nick and Manny had just finished adhering and rubbing down the Black Raven Aviation's new logo on the side of the Twin Otter's vertical, the same decal that covered both sides of the white van.

"We have a van?" Nate asked, the question trailing off in confused awe.

Neither was sure what to believe in as they watched the scene unfold before them. There was a big, bold-colored Black Raven Aviation logo on the side of the immaculate van, which neither had any idea where or how it was procured, and last, Tasha's incredibly sexy black tux pantsuit and matching black heels that looked eerily like standard issued military women's class A dress shoes.

As the men unloaded, carrying their personal effects, Jarvis promptly followed with their larger bags. He, too, wore nicer clothing with a standard black tie, as if he belonged to a high-class charter service.

The first man out stood there waiting as the others exited the van with Tasha leading the way, guiding them toward the plane, her high-class walk with a confident swagger a little too 'sexy' in her ladies' tux for Jack to handle, knowing men like those.

"What the—" Nate was speechless, getting Jack's partial attention. "Whose van is *that*? It's certainly not ours, is it?" Raven eyed Jack as if he had authorized the purchase of a new company vehicle.

Pointing past Big Raven, Jack remarked, "I think we may get our answer soon, boss." Jack prepared to handle a possibly heated argument with a FAA personnel coming their way.

"Jack, where is my government vehicle?"

It took only a second for Jack to put two and two together, as William caught up to them. He pointed to the exceptionally clean and neat Black Raven Aviation logoed van. Even the interior had been cleaned and altered, from what they all could gather through the open side doors.

"What the hell did you *do* to my van?" William stopped, his mouth agape right along with his boss, Nate, as they watched the first man smile and shake his head after watching Tasha guide his three men onto the plane. He waited for Tasha to return to the van, where he said something to her and she pointed over to them—or more to Nate—as William realized that it was Mr. Reynolds, the CEO of SAE, wanting to come over to meet her boss.

"Jack, you know using a government-issued van as your personal company vehicle goes against FAA policies, and sending Tasha to come borrow it—"

Jack held up a hand for him to hold his thoughts as Mr. Reynolds came up smiling tremendously, wanting to meet Nate in person. He began, saying, "My name's Mr. Todd Reynolds, sir." He handed Nate his personal business card along with an extra piece of folded paper. "And I wanted to tell you what a terrific service your company provides." He shook Nate's hand like any person of importance does.

Nick had started up the Twin Otter's second engine, much to Tasha's internal gratitude, hoping the sound of the aircraft would keep their conversation short. They were trying to time it down to the minute so that nobody would have known that she had the entire crew involved, save for Jack and Nate—and William, if you added in the FAA administrator. Unfortunately, Mr. Reynolds made it impossibly difficult for her to hide the 'special ops' with his request to meet Black

Raven Aviation's owner.

Mr. Reynolds looked over to Tasha appreciatively, somewhat ruffling Jack's feathers, but he maintained his bearing with his arms crossed over his chest and his long, jean-clad legs shoulder-width apart.

"You picked some competent folks, Mr. Amsel. So far, I'm extremely impressed with your company and hope to use more of your services in the future."

Tasha hurriedly interrupted with a lame excuse as she gauged all three men's disgruntled looks, knowing she was going to either get one hell of an ass-kicking, put on probation, or worst-case scenario, be looking for another job after this stunt. She wanted it low-key, without any of her superiors knowing, preferring to seek forgiveness than ask for permission, but Mr. Reynolds' insistence only made it worse.

"Mr. Reynolds, we need to get you on board with the rest of your group before any unexpected weather comes in. It's time to start your adventure." She gave him her brightest encouraging smile. "I'm sure my boss can discuss more with you after your trip." She extended her arm back to the waiting aircraft.

"Yes, yes," he replied, eager to follow her charms.

Right off a cliff to his demise, thought Jack.

All three men watched as he pulled out a crisp one-hundred-dollar bill to tip Tasha. They watched as she first demurred the tip, but he insisted, forcing Tasha to take it. She thanked him as she quickly folded it and tucked it into a hidden inside pocket inside the plunging neckline on her suit. Jack caught his boss and William staring incredulously at her.

The three men watched as Jarvis helped Manny assist Mr. Reynolds, and then Reynolds turned and handed two more bills to Jarvis. He closed the side door quickly and signaled Nick to leave. Each of them knew they had to be fast before the 'crap hit the props.' Nick started engine number one before taxiing.

The crew waved until Nick turned the bird onto the runway, and then the three of them ran over to the van to strip the decals and the seat covers off, denuding it back to its original state. William marched over to Tasha with Nate and Jack in tow, demanding an explanation. But before he could ask, Tasha spun around with the seat covers in her arms to face them, as the other two crewmen ran off with the rest of the gear.

"Hi there, Will, you're early, but I got your van back to you in time as promised, cleaned and detailed with a full tank of gas, as promised." Tasha dropped the keys into his hand and thanked him for his involuntary service for letting them 'move the cargo' they needed. She smiled, batting her overdone eyelashes innocently at him.

Her bribe rendered him speechless as he double-checked his van for any other issues, nodding his head in tentative approval.

"That *cargo* could qualify as human trafficking if it wasn't the CEO of Southern Alaska Energy Corporation, Tasha," William said to her back as she moved to return the bench seat covers that Jarvis and Manny had bought earlier that week with their own money. "But thank you for the extra care and the full tank of gas. You are excused from this one time, but not again," he said rather flatly, getting into the van.

William drove off.

Oh boy, she thought. She knew she was in deep doo-doo.

She approached Nate and Jack as Jarvis ran back to her to retrieve the rest of the seat covers and dash back off to wherever they were storing the gear for a possible next time. She came to a stop in front of the two men, knowing full well she would take all the blame for the rest of the crew's involvement since it did not go off as well as they had hoped. Both had unspoken questions clearly written on their visages. Tasha had scarcely heard Nate's muddled question as he was sorting the various paperwork on top of his clipboard. Jack held his hand out, and at first she was unsure of what he was wanting from her. Then she realized what he wanted her to give to him. She made a face at him, not wanting to give up her unexpected tip. She waited on Nate, his earlier question not clear, until he opened the paper that Mr. Reynolds gave him, then clutched his chest in surprise and inhaled rather harshly.

"Are you okay, sir?" Tasha asked, now concerned, as they both stepped toward him.

Raven just shook his head, getting them to stand down, unable to speak at first. Then he said everything was fine, turning away from them, stunned.

Jack quickly swiped the money from inside her vest just as Nate turned back to them upon second thought, deciding not to take his leave and catching Jack in the act.

"Son, I did not see that, did I?" Nate looked pointedly at Jack opening the single one-hundred-dollar bill. "Just for that, give it back to her."

Tasha swiped it back just as quickly, blowing him a raspberry.

"Tasha! You better share that with the others…that is, whoever else you conned into this stunt!" Nate chastised her.

"Yes, sir," she said dejectedly.

"She can keep it, sir," came Jarvis, with Manny just behind him on his heels, playing with his one-hundred-dollar bill, grinning from ear to ear. "For Manny and the rest of us are going to celebrate with our own little reward when Nick and Sam get back." Jarvis pulled his own tip out, showing another hundred, snapping it in delight. "I mean, no harm done. He did pay us…I mean…he did pay the company, didn't he, Tasha?"

Her face grew white, realizing that in their hustle she didn't get a check from him, and her mind raced, hoping that the man would at least pay them on the return home in four more days. She had put a lot of her own money on the line and was wondering when she would get the billing from the sign master for all the decals—the two magnetic ones and the six other vinyl aircraft stickers for at least three of the aircraft.

Jack, seeing her visage pale, told her to come with him to his office in a disappointed, gruff voice. Manny and Jarvis tried to follow her, but Jack barked at them to remain while he took care of reprimanding her over the billing or lack thereof.

"If anyone is going to reprimand anyone, that would be me, Jack," Nate the Raven reminded him, knowing Jack's mindset.

They stopped.

Nate paused, looking at each of them, studying them before asking, "If Jack can't explain the eight-hundred-dollar invoice I just got, along with another bill for customized new seat covers, then I am certain that someone in this group can."

No one spoke up, save for Tasha. "That bill was supposed to go to me, sir. I was the one that took Manny's artwork and had it turned into the company's placards." She reached into her pants pocket and handed him a stack of new company logo cards with their business name, website, business address, and contact information professionally printed. "I can pay the bill, sir." Now handing over her tip money, she said, "Just give me another day to round up the other seven hundred."

Jarvis nabbed Manny's bill and handed over their tip money to Nate, much to Tasha's surprise. She protested, telling Manny and Jarvis that they needed to keep theirs for all their hard work in creating the logo and taking care of the van. But Big Raven did not take any of their money as she insistently waved hers at him. Tasha reminded them, she being the ringleader, that it was her idea in the first place since their recent passenger had requested so much of what the company didn't have but that she wanted to see the company offer. Tasha had enlisted most of the crew's help. Hank was sort of in the loop, having approved Manny's artwork along with the others, but not knowing it was a part of a much bigger plan in those harried two weeks of prepping. But she had failed them all when she forgot to ask for the check when she caught sight of Jack and Nate together standing at the hangar bay door. Then seeing William, the FAA inspector, show up minutes earlier than anticipated had caused her to nearly lose sight of their mission.

Tasha reached out for the billing, but Nate did not hand it to her. Instead, he handed over the irregular piece of unfolded paper Mr. Reynolds had given him. She hesitantly took it, cringing at what it could have possibly been until she realized it was a business check written in the amount of twenty thousand dollars. Tasha yelped, instantly covering her mouth to restrain herself as she looked excitedly at the crew.

"Now, would you care to explain why we received this much?"

Tasha chewed her bottom lip a moment before she explained that some of it would need to go to the outfitters on Kodiak in a few days.

Big Raven's fluffy eyebrows went up in surprise, and then he asked, "And how much was that going to cost the company?"

Thankfully, the outfitters were only an additional fifteen hundred, since Tasha had paid a deposit of five hundred earlier last week, thus Nate blew out a bated breath, happy that Tasha had covered all the costs of the trip and more.

"Just what were you thinking, Tasha?"

She explained her reasoning, with Jarvis and Manny helping here and there, all eager to have helped in propelling the small company forward. In the end, Manny quietly asked if Nate was happy with the new company logo or if he should peel the rest of the placards off the other aircraft.

Big Raven looked down at the cards, rubbing at his face while taking in the new logo's design. None of them were expecting the next question. "Since when do we have a website?" Nate asked, looking at Jack, who just shrugged a shoulder. They only had a directory listing on the city's search engine. Not a professionally done company website.

"Nick and Sam got you a new domain name last week and built up a pretty nice two-page website." Tasha spoke up again, not looking directly at him, unsure if he would be mad that they started a new page for the company.

Jack just smiled at the way she was begging for forgiveness after having committed the crime. Nate glanced back at Jack, as Jack dropped his smile.

"And you didn't have a hand in this?" Nate asked Jack with suspicion.

"None, sir…It's news to me, especially when I saw the decals on the aircraft's vertical just this morning as Hank unhooked from the plane out on the tarmac, and when the van pulled up."

Nate grunted before turning back to Tasha and the ground crew. "Now…that I think"—he eyeballed each of them—"I have the full story, I will take care of all these 'explained bills' and another expected billing from a Kodiak outfitter." He turned away once again toward the hangar, only to stop momentarily to say, "Nice job…you all." Then he added, "Nice outfit, Tasha." Nate nodded his head in approval.

"I told you you would look great in it, Tasha!" Manny high-fived her hand.

Jack gave her a hard look, telling her that he still needed to see her in his office.

She begrudgingly followed him, her heels clicking on the tarmac, now that she knew Big Raven was fine with all that taken place. Well, most of it. Once inside Jack's office, he closed the door, giving them what little privacy they had with the open venetian blind covered door's window. His hand grabbed ahold of her upper arm, dragging her roughly away from the window and to the side of his office, out of sight.

"Have you gone insane? What were you thinking wearing something like that?" Jack indicated to her outfit's plunging neckline that exposed her fair and desirable flesh. She must have been cold, since he could see her upper body's reaction through the velvety black material, further inciting him.

It was not entirely outrageous, but it was professional enough, she thought. It was a tuxedo.

"Are ya trying to offer more?" He scoffed at her, at first taking a step back, flustered, only to get up in her face about trying to cause a scene, 'just asking for it!' and losing his self-control, he kissed her roughly to prove his point. She pushed him away, now realizing how angry he was at her dress attire, making it more than it should be. Then his office door suddenly flew open, with Hank's face peering around the doorjamb that made him stay put. She watched him as he tried to regain his composure, asking Hank what he wanted at just that moment.

"Boss just wanted me to ask you to put in more orders for the new logos now that Nora got a chance to see it, and says to run with all the logos on all our aircraft."

She and Jack locked eyes for a few seconds, and seeing the vein in his neck tick, she covered for him, telling Hank that she would jump right on it if Jack was okay with her doing so. Jack just nodded.

"Everything okay?" Hank asked tentatively, not sure what to make of Jack's silence.

Jack had never once looked back at him since his intrusion. He ran an agitated hand through his thick auburn waves, telling Hank, "Yup, all's good."

To Tasha, Jack said gruffly, "Go change your clothes before you go order more decals."

Tasha was going to argue that she could do it in that attire just fine, but his 'tried patience' look warned her not to disagree as she took her leave.

Tasha was not looking forward to going home that night with him in his current state.

It was hours later, and he was in a much better mood, when he found her in the battery room going over the twin-engine manuals and he asked her if she was ready to go home. Surprised at how fast the day had gone by after that morning's incident with Mr. Reynolds, she double-checked her clock on the wall off to her side, finding he was leaving an hour earlier than expected.

"Come on," he said, indicating with his head to follow him. Jack waited in the doorframe, his arms straddling the opening, holding the door open with his backside.

"But it's early," she protested. "Am I fired?" Tasha asked, taking off her protective apron that she had used to protect her tuxedo, then straightening her books before going to him.

Jack just smirked. "Far cry from it," he said as she went past him, "but you did a helluva job of making me look like an inept manager in front of Raven."

"I didn't mean to. You let me take the reins. You said you were okay with it."

"But you went over the company's budget and let the bills go to Raven instead of to me—or in your case, to you."

"I don't know why they didn't send the bills directly to us, as I requested. As for William, I am definitely on his doo-doo list."

"Ah, William will get over it. You were lucky there was no harm done to the van since he really is not allowed to 'loan out' government equipment to civilians. But I think you made his day with having the van detailed, cleaned, and gassed up. Jarvis even told me that he took time to change the oil and the oil filter, which I ended up conveying to him later, and asked if he needed documentation for the maintenance performed."

"And?" She looked up at him, walking by her side as they went to the door to go outside to his truck.

"Let's just say he's thinking it through more." He opened the passenger door for her, a first since they had been working together and keeping their relationship low-key. It had to be the dress suit she was wearing for him to automatically do that for her, she thought, watching him go around to his side, getting in and starting his truck. "In the meantime, I have to do another bidding by Nate before we go home."

Tasha raised her eyebrows in question.

"You have to order more business cards and make up a new brochure for our company."

"But where am I going to get that done?"

"At our cabin, in my office downstairs, online." He made the turn onto the main highway and then another turn to the main driveway to the company cabins up the hill, where their crew lived in the first three cabins. "It seems you have been promoted to a new and added position in our company." He caught her mouth dropping open in his peripheral vision. "You are to be our first Marketing Consultant. I am supposed to take you out for your bonus reward. But I'd rather celebrate with you by having my fun unwrapping you from your tux. I can't take it anymore."

Tasha sank back in her seat, smiling and blushing at the thought.

CHAPTER TWENTY-TWO

With the holidays looming over them and not knowing how bad the winter weather would be, Jack tightened their flying schedule and most of the crew was open to working the full five days to make all the supply runs happen. In between, there were a few folks wanting to be air taxied to a number of different areas, but even that demand was coming to a halt, the tourism season now far behind, giving them a little respite in the flying—enough for Jack to note that Tasha had been ignoring several phone calls from her parents as she was out flying as co-pilot to build her hours.

Tasha had just gotten in the shower one morning when her cell rang, and he decided to answer it for her. A distant and frantic woman's voice came over the line before he could even say a greeting as the woman, clearly her mother, began scolding Tasha for not calling enough or returning her messages before eventually settling with the question of "Is everything all right?"

Only then was Jack able to talk, his voice sending Tasha's mom into another sonorous rampage, thinking something bad had happened. He let her go on as if he were listening to a large herd of caribou stampeding across a remote tundra road. He could see why Tasha was not inclined to answer most of her mother's phone calls. She could never get a word in edgewise. His silence at his end was the only thing that got her to cease her barrage.

"If you could let me speak, Mrs. Lazar, I can tell you your daughter is fine. She's been flying most of her waking hours, and when she gets home it is usually too late to call you back in the continental US, since we are about four hours behind you," he soothed her mother. "She's been so busy with work that she's barely had time to get in enough sleep during our last big push before the Christmas holidays when our company will be shut down for a half week. I'm sure she'll be returning your calls here in another day or two."

"Is there anything I can tell her when she returns?" He was now wondering if there was an emergency, but since she hadn't called Black Raven Aviation directly, nor was there any Red Cross Emergency caller seeking Tasha, he figured there wasn't anything major. However, he was not expecting the next bit of information.

Tasha's mother promptly informed him that her husband and she would be arriving in Anchorage in another three days to spend some time with their daughter in order to see her, her new home and job.

Ah...the parental inspectional visit, he thought. He wondered if it had anything to do with him being her roommate. Although they had been more than just roommates on more than many occasions, the past work week and different hours had kept them sleeping in their own beds, trying to keep their exhaustion at bay. He had been hoping that it would change back to the way their last two days of the Thanksgiving weekend had been. However, with her parents' arrival that would also keep them apart and make living in the cabin a bit difficult during their stay. He was about to ask Tasha's mother when her voice cut back into his thoughts and he realized she was asking him a question after she had droned on about how they should go about getting to Tasha, what to see and do in the surrounding areas for the time that they had, and so forth.

"Did she get it fixed yet?"

"Come again?" he asked, pretending that he had momentarily lost their connection and had not heard her question clearly.

"Her car? Is it fixed so she can come pick us up at the Anchorage Airport? Or should we pick up a rental car and drive down?"

Jack realized that they had never taken the time to put a new battery in yet. "No, she hasn't, but I can meet you or send one of our guys to Anchorage to pick you two up from the airport."

"What about her? Is there something more than just a battery her car needs? Why can't she pick us up with a company car?"

Jack pacified her with his assurance that nothing more was wrong with her car other than the lack of time to work on it, which was not necessarily the case. It just wasn't a priority, and it made more economical sense to continue carpooling. He had teased Tasha a couple of times about getting her to sell her car, but she flat-out refused, saying she might need it one day and would have it up and running by spring so that she could do some more sightseeing whenever he decided it was time for him to go back to fishing and hunting all weekend long.

Jack re-verified when they were coming in, only to tell her that Tasha was scheduled to be flying all day with one of the other pilots and would not be back until much later that day unless there were weather issues. Jack told her he would see what he could do to rearrange Tasha's flight schedule for that day when she interrupted him with a few more questions.

"Mr...."

"Just Jack, ma'am."

"Jack...aren't you her roommate?"

"Yes?" he replied, unsure where this was going and bracing himself for what might be next. But he knew that Tasha had told her that she was living with him months ago.

"I thought you were one of the aircraft fuelers."

"I am, but I also do a few other jobs such as scheduling all my crew's flights, and fly planes, too. I thought Tasha told you we do all the roles involved in running a small flight company. We all perform basic maintenance, flight line duties, such as towing and fueling aircraft, and we all fly when needed. I ensure all crewmembers learn and know all their duties. Some of us are simply better in one area than another. But we all learn each other's jobs and pull our own weight. Your daughter happens to be an incredibly good electrician, yet she pilots and crews several of our aircraft. I have a terrific ground control guy and two very excellent pilots, yet they all perform maintenance from time to time."

It was then he could literally sense her bristles going down over the line, with the change in her demeanor toward him. "That daughter of mine doesn't tell her own mother much of anything. So much like her father. Trying to get information out of her is like trying to pry open a sealed jelly jar, I tell you!"

Jack smirked. Tasha was not one to talk openly about much of anything.

Jack could tell she loved her parents, but her mother usually put her on edge and he pretty much knew why just with this current conversation. But a visit from her father would make her happy, She was definitely a daddy's girl.

"Well…Jack, since I have you on the phone and she isn't one to return her mother's calls, is there any way I can get driving directions from you and see to a room at your cabin? That is, if there is enough space to stay for about a week?"

Then she added, "I think I'm too late in booking a room at a nearby hotel this late in the season, especially over the Christmas holidays."

"I'll do one better for you, Mrs. Lazar." He was now curious to meet her parents.

"Call me Asa," she purred.

Thus, Jack quickly suggested a few ideas to her and what he could arrange.

The Beaver touched down perfectly on the damp runway lined with two feet of piled old snow from the previous winter storms. Jack pulled up to the hangar, swinging the aircraft around so that Hank could pull it in for the day. His two passengers had been, for the most part, quiet, save for the few questions here and there as they flew south from the Anchorage Airport over the expanse of the mountain range. They were more interested in the scenery below them on the near flawless day: heavy low clouds where intermittent icy rains dotted various areas of the southern mountainous parts of Alaska where the Gulf of Alaska's water provided the moisture that was wicked up by the warmer southern winds, forming the 'mystical' clouds that shrouded Seward on most occasions.

Jack hopped out of the aircraft as Hank opened the hangar door and jumped onto the tug. He hooked the tow bars while Jack helped the high-maintenance woman out and down onto the flight line. The well-preserved, physically fit older man followed her with her handbag and a carry-on tote.

He led his guests inside the hangar and toward the hallway as Hank towed the Beaver in just behind them. He didn't stop to introduce them to his crew, where a few of them had popped their heads out from their aircraft, noting the new folks, before resuming their work. He preferred to drop off the two guests at Tasha's battery room, hoping to surprise her with their arrival, bringing her some delight and a break from her work.

When he reached the door, he stopped long enough to scout the large viewing window next to the entry door to see if Tasha was in the room. He smiled when he caught her, back side to him, as she added the water to the NiCad battery still attached to the charger. She was dressed in her normal work clothes along with a protective apron and safety goggles on, shielding her from any errant acidic spills.

"You two ready? She has no idea that you are here visiting."

The graying blonde woman nodded eagerly, putting on her grandest smile. The reserved man just tilted his head accordingly, just like Tasha would do to him and others.

Jack turned the metal doorknob, opening the heavy metal door, letting his guests in first as he called to Tasha, letting her know she had some folks wanting to see her.

Without looking over her shoulder, "Okay, tell them I'll be there in a sec. I gotta get this bad boy off the charger to rest for a few minutes," she answered, unhooking the large connector from the battery box, then turning around with the heavy battery to place on the worktable in front of her as she saw them.

"Well, that might be hard since they are standing right here," came Jack, grinning at her when she nearly dropped the battery in her surprise. It took a second for her to recognize them.

"Ah, sweetheart!" Asa clasped her hands together in joy. "It's *so good* to see you! Just look at you!" Her mother started across the short distance to give her a quick hug as Tasha unloaded the battery to the worktable between them, but her dad stopped his wife, noting Tasha's protective apron.

"Asa, you may want to give her a second to get out of her protective gear before you hug her. You may end up ruining your clothes," he warned her.

Jack nodded in agreement when they looked back at their delivery guy.

"True," Jack affirmed, getting the excuse he needed to get her folks out of there as soon as possible before anything else besides greetings could be said. He was going to use the time to occupy them with an introduction to Nate and his wife Nora, just further down the hallway.

Asa 'pooh-poohed' her husband Victor with a dismissive wave as she grabbed ahold of Tasha's now ungloved hand, maintaining a good bodily distance from her daughter while giving her a quick kiss on each side of her face. "Why didn't you ever tell me the good news, Tasha?"

Too late! Jack thought, cringing inwardly.

Tasha gave her mother a quizzical look as her mother continued gushing, "I'm so happy for you and I can't wait to help you with all the preparations for your big day!" Asa squealed her delight as she squeezed her daughter's hand.

"What are y—" Tasha looked at Jack as he quickly stepped over to pull her mother away, telling her mother that he would let them catch up later since their workday was nearly over, expressing his desire to show them around the company's headquarters and to meet the owner of Black Raven Aviation.

"Okay," Asa happily agreed. Rather too eagerly, Tasha noted, her father, Victor, giving her a knowing smile as he opened the door again, allowing for his wife and Jack to pass him.

As her mother stepped out into the hallway, saying, "We were so surprised to hear of your engagement and meeting Jack, your fiancé." Her mother winked, causing her makeup-covered crows' feet to become more pronounced. "I've been wondering why you haven't called and have been so quiet." Her mother gave a knowing up and down look at Jack and then back at her. Asa giggled like an excited schoolgirl. "We'll chit-chat later, darling," she continued as the three of them took off down the hallway.

Tasha stood in stunned amazement, not entirely sure she had heard her mother right, her mouth opening and closing like a fish out of water before she realized her new 'status.' *WTF?*

Thankfully, Tasha did not react—nor did Jack give her time to react, by quickly scooting her parents out the door and into Big Raven's office without so much as a warning knock that he was coming in, and with guests in tow.

Jack performed the introductions to both Nora and Nate, letting Big Raven gush about their daughter and her ability to contribute to company's mission and team as he got up and came around his desk to shake hands with Tasha's father, Victor. Jack watched as her mother Asa puffed with pride, even noting her father standing more upright, smiling, although it was quite obvious he wasn't one to be as openly outgoing as his 'social butterfly' wife. Jack hoped to get them out of there quickly as well, before Tasha's mother would open the lid further on the can of worms he had started when he airlifted them to Seward from the Anchorage Airport. He had not meant for it to come out that way at all. But in his current high from the past few weekends with Tasha, plus the few good work weeks, the company being ahead of schedule with all their delivery flights and showing better profits, his head was definitely in the clouds when he said he meant to *ask* Tasha for her hand in marriage in a few more weeks. But instead, her mother had misunderstood what he had said over the headsets and thought that Jack was already her fiancé. When she had begun her nonstop questions, he had made it difficult to hear by knocking the mic's connection by his side loose, causing static in everyone's headsets. Jack had gestured to his headset that he could not hear her. When he had landed, the opportunity to correct her never came up.

Nora offered them something to drink, along with pulling out empty chairs for them to sit and rest while they talked. Jack was grateful that her parents declined, saying that they did not want to keep them from their work for too long while Jack showed them around before taking them to the cabin.

Unfortunately, Nora kept talking about the company her husband had started and what their company provided for the surrounding area. Jack had pretty much remained quiet, letting them do the talking, lost in his thoughts, hoping to usher them to his truck. He could deal with Tasha's anger later, in private and away from everyone, hoping to nip the 'misunderstanding' in the bud before the entire hangar knew.

Jack noted Mrs. Lazar remaining politely quiet, listening, yet it was clearly obvious that she was not interested in the day-to-day company operations nor the types of planes being flown. Mr. Lazar, on the other hand, was the opposite and very much engrossed with the company stats Nate provided. The two men would have cheerily gone on had it not been for Mrs. Lazar reaching that short and imperceptible tolerance point where she caught Nora's eye, loudly declaring to Nora what was more important to her, stepping closer to where Nora stood in front of her desk.

"We're *so* happy to be here! Finally, a chance to see where my baby girl is working. I'm glad she's out of the Army and that *nasty* war. But I still wish she would have chosen some other job than the one she is doing. She's way too smart to be just charging batteries—"

"Honey, she's an avionics tech and pilot!" her husband interjected, hearing her disappointment in their daughter's career choice. "What's so wrong with being an aviation technician and a pilot?"

"That she is!" Nora chirped, being prouder than Tasha's mother, noted Jack. "And our best electrician and marketer!"

Even Nate stood up for Tasha. "She's as good, if not better than most of my men. She's the daughter I wish *I* had."

This caused Victor's chest to puff out with fatherly pride.

"Not only smart and hardworking, but beautiful too!" Nora cooed.

"Ah, don't get me wrong Mr. and Mrs.—"

"Just Nate and Nora, Mr. and Mrs. Lazar. We are pretty laid back here in the Far North."

"Likewise," said her father, stepping forward and placing a hand on his wife's shoulder. "Just call us Asa and Vick."

"Do understand, I worry about Tasha, and I mean all the time!" Asa grabbed ahold of Nora's arm, as if they were lifelong friends in an intimate girl-to-girl chit-chat.

"Oh?" came Nora. "Whatever for? Flying is one of the safest modes of travel out there—"

Jack had stepped over to the door, hoping that her parents would catch the subtle hint that it was time to leave. Nora caught it, and along with how eager they were to leave the men to their aviation talk, the older women led the way to the doorway. All was fine until Tasha's mother dropped the *F* word.

"You know, with her not calling nor telling me what's been going on with her life…" She sighed heavily to herself. "She's not getting any younger. I was certain she was just trying to scare away any available men, until Jack here told us. And to think that she never even bothered to call us to let us know she had a fiancé! Kids these days! They go through life as if nothing matters!"

Nora nearly tripped at the news, looking back at Nate as his head snapped up in surprise. Their eyes momentarily locked and then together they looked in Jack's direction, hoping for some clarification. Jack sighed and momentarily closed his eyes. He imperceptibly nodded, indicating he would explain later, before leaving, saying he needed to attend to some things in the hangar before taking Tasha's parents back to the cabin.

"Jaaaaaack!" The menacing sound came from the hallway where Tasha appeared, stepping into the brighter main hangar, catching up to where he was walking and talking with Hank.

"Ah man, she sounds like my high school teacher on the final straw with my bad behavior," snorted Hank. "Whadda ya do now, Jack?" Hank began turning to greet Tasha, catching her determined walk out of the corner of his eye, her mouth twisted in annoyance.

Jack's hand shot out, keeping Hank on their original course, ordering him to keep on walking with him and to ignore her. "I need to you to stay put," Jack quietly commanded.

"Jack!" Tasha finally barked loud enough to make everyone in the hangar stop what they were doing. When he still did not respond, she used her last-resort threat. "I know you can hear me, and if you don't stop this instant, I will use a much *bigger* wrench to knock some sense into that thick skull of yours!"

"Aaah, I think you need to stop, man," Hank advised. "Yer life may depend on it, and I've seen her aim. It's pretty dead on." Hank tried to move away from him to allow Tasha to join them, giving Jack and her some space to duke it out, but Jack growled, "Stay!" as if Hank were his dog.

"I'm not sure if that'd be safe..." Hank said in a worried tone as Tasha finally caught up to them.

"I need a witness," Jack whispered harshly as he turned to face her, knowing the inevitable. He placed his hands on his hips, a bracing stance against a possible bodily assault, surprised she was going to address her reason for being pissed off with him right there and then, rather than her usual—to let it simmer before exploding in the privacy of their cabin.

Tasha was barely in control with the volume of her voice as she separately ground out each word. "What the hell do you think you are doing!" She ignored their fellow crew members, who not only ceased their work, but became an impromptu audience.

Jack shifted, now that he had other witnesses to his possible death besides Hank, who had discreetly removed himself to avoid being caught up in the maelstrom that was about to occur.

Tasha glared furiously at him, her arms crossed, waiting.

"I thought you would be thrilled to see your parents, Tasha!" Jack did his best in trying to remain positive and quell the situation, shifting away from the *real* issue.

"Cut the crap, Jack!" her voice hissed in volume to the point everyone could hear her, augmented by the hangar's uncanny ability to amplify any and all noise. Although she was not fully shouting...*well...not yet*! Jack thought.

"*What* on earth *possessed* you to tell them we were *engaged*!" She emphasized the point with a pointed finger at the floor between them. "It's bad enough they surprised me with this visit, but to tell them we were *engaged*?" Her voice rose an octave higher on the last part of the sentence. She invaded his personal space, challenging him, although her head only came to his chin. "What in hell's bells *were you* thinking!"

A low, long warning whistle came from one of the guys—either Nick or Jarvis, Jack surmised. She no longer cared who heard. She had to make a point of showing the kind of crap she had to endure living with him. Now he had her mother—her own mother!—sappily cooing and ceaselessly blabbering on about the wonderful news, as she was prone to do: a habit that had driven her insane all her life. A mother who lived life utterly blithely and blind. Tasha was certain that if it wasn't for her dad, her mother would have never made it past her twenty-fifth birthday. She would have been eaten alive by life itself!

A pin could drop, at that point, and everyone would have heard it. Even the normal chirping cricket in the background did not dare make a sound as everyone waited for what the mighty Jack would say next. Jack looked pointedly at her, an errant hand coming up to rub the back of his neck before dropping back to his hip as he thought of what to say next.

"I know, I know…I have it under control."

"What?!?" Her expression contorted with shock at his calm answer. She was going to verbally lay into him before he interrupted.

"I was getting around to it…but just work with me here on…"

"Work with you? Work with you…" The second repeated statement was a near whisper, her expression clearly incredulous of what she was hearing, her mouth moving to form words—more like various sentences, as her brain spun to put everything into some sort of sense before hell and its minions broke loose.

"First of all! I don't recall being proposed to…" She looked like an arched cat, hopping and hissing around an intruder. "…much less agreeing to this insane idea! *It* definitely *was not* a part of the *job description*!"

Jack tried to get a word in edgewise. But this was where Tasha was very much like her mother. "It's the next logical step, Ta—"

"The next step? Oh, my, God!" She stepped forward, jabbing her finger into his chest as he leaned back from the woman who had turned into a snarling wolverine. "*We* are *nowhere* near that step, Jack! Sharing your bed just a few times does not constitute that *we* are *serious*!"

At that comment, Jack heard Jarvis and Manny high-five behind them to one side while he overheard Sam tell Nick, "Pay up, man." Jack rolled his eyes but stopped. He did a double-take, catching Hank's expression of *ya got yourself in deep on this one*, his thumbs hooked in the suspenders of his beige overalls, his toothpick wiggling just off to the side of his mouth, his beard's whiskers indicating his amusement.

Tasha raged on, "For fuck's sake! What am I supposed to tell them! I'm not going to *lie* to them, Jack! Never have and never will!" she shouted, hoping to make him retract whatever it was he said to her mother.

"Well, then we will make it the truth, simple as that, Tash. We're engaged."

"What?—No!" She stamped her foot at him, desperately trying to keep herself from taking a swing at him with her fist. "I won't do it! You need to stop this now—"

"*There* you *are*, darling!" Her mother's gleeful interruption made Tasha grab ahold of herself, spinning one-eighty, her backside up against Jack, plastering on the biggest fake smile she could. Everyone else could see, save for her own mother…and possibly her own dad? However, she found that hard to believe until her beaming dad came up, giving her his normal bear-hug greeting and kissing her on the top of her head, and she noted Nate and Nora past his shoulder, trailing a short distance behind them.

Tasha's mother gave her a quick peck on her cheek along with a similar two-handed squeeze—the way Southern belles greet other women and their female family members—before she graciously continued toward Jack. Clearly infatuated with Jack's charms, her mother, quickly feeling his large biceps, clicked her tongue at him as she intertwined her fingers with his one hand, standing next to him and placing her other hand on his upper arm. "If I was twenty years younger, I certainly would have been chasing him," she giggled.

Tasha rolled her eyes to her amused fellow crewmembers, thankful her dad was standing to her side, unable to see her facial expressions. She dropped her false happy face at Jack, her expression glowering at him. Her mother looked at her and she quickly changed back to a staged, delighted expression. She was not sure if Hank or any of the others could see her reactions, but she no longer cared.

"Tasha, you certainly hooked yourself a fine-looking young man here," her mother sighed dreamily, before noticing the other four men by the airplanes. She disengaged herself from Jack, adding, "But look at your crewmates, Tasha. They are all so handsome! How did you do it?"

"Do what, Mom?" Tasha wasn't sure where she was going with this question.

"Being able to work around such gorgeous men—"

"I'm usually not allowed to work around them much," she interrupted with controlled annoyance, eyeing Jack for all the times he culled her from them.

"—and decide?" Her mother's eyes came to a long stop at Sam and Nick, who were watching the entire family reunion with broad smiles. Nick had taken up his normal suave *Gentlemen's Quarterly* pilot pose, with Sam standing in a loose at-rest position, feet at shoulder's width apart, his arms folded over his torso, flexing his biceps at her mother.

Tasha couldn't *decide* if they were a part of this 'sick joke.'

"Decide?" Tasha asked in confusion.

"On whom to date, my sweet little girl," her mother gushed.

"Mother!" Tasha reprimanded hopelessly. "This is my workplace! Not a dating service!"

To Nate and Nora, her mother continued. "You two certainly know how to hire a good-looking crew." Her mother twirled partway around, her upturned hands gesturing to all of them, though her smile wavered some at Hank's older and much more unkempt gruff physique. Hank nodded politely at her.

Her dad finally rescued her from her embarrassing mother. "You look well," he said as he quickly glanced to Jack and then back to her. He let her have her space but left an arm draped over her shoulder, his hand squeezing her shoulder and alternatively pulling her into him in quick, reassuring half-hugs. She was certain that he was just as uncomfortable with his wife's flirtatious comments. Was there something going on between her parents that she didn't know?

Tasha smiled weakly at her dad before giving Jack another nasty look.

"Well, now that you both have had a quick tour of where Tasha and I work… Tasha or I can take you up to our living quarters and let you rest after your journey," Jack offered, grateful for her parents' intrusion for keeping him from being roasted by Tasha.

At that, her mother's head snapped back to Jack rather too eagerly for Tasha's taste. It was like her mother had become a Stepford Wife overnight! A near-perfect robotic rendering of her mother. Not like it was any surprise to her. Tasha's mother had always resembled an annoying dandelion on the wind, ready to mess up any perfect lawn with its weedy intentions!

"Yes, that would be wonderful, Jack! Tasha makes it sound so rustically quaint."

"It's a cabin, Mother!" Then, she added, as it just occurred to her, "Wait! What? You're staying?"

"Why, *yes*, you silly girl! We're staying with you and your fiancé at your home!"

"No hotel?"

"We've got room, Tasha," Jack added. "No sense in them spending money on a hotel, especially since most of the hotels are booked out at this time of year."

Some of the crew looked at each other, in addition to Hank taking a gnarled finger and scratching the side of his beard, all of them knowing better. This was her only indication that Hank knew a lie was on, whether it be from him or one of the other guys. At that time of year, if there was a hotel open during the non-tourist season, there would only be one, and that one was not even full. Seward was pretty much shut down over the winter months.

"We do?" Tasha asked incredulously, surprised that he would put up with her parents staying under the same roof, especially dealing with her addle-brained mom. She was uncertain as to which of them was giving up their room. But then she made the connection, not saying a word, her mouth twisting some, remembering how surprised she was at finding Jack laundering his own bed linens the night before. She had never seen him do that before. It was never as if he expected her to do his bed linens as she did the housekeeping. She always did her own bed linens, each of them taking responsibility for their own room's tidiness. It also did not help when Sam made an audible comment to Nick that only Tasha and Jack heard: "I need to try that when Lela's parents come town."

Jack threw him a nasty look as Sam smiled, giving Jack a thumbs-up and mouthing to Jack, *smooth move, buddy!*

"You have *got* to tell me all the details, sweetie!" Asa gushed breathlessly, still unaware of the silent conversations and expressions being exchanged around the hangar.

"Details?"

"Yes! I can't believe you've kept this engagement a secret for so long! Whatever *were* you thinking?"

At a loss for words, Tasha stammered, "Ah...well, I..."

"Honey, they've been working extremely hard. I am sure they've been extremely busy with flying," her dad added, coming to her rescue again.

"Honestly, dear, she couldn't even *bother* to call her own mother and tell me this terrific and life-changing news?" She was acting incredulous that her daughter would leave out an important detail as becoming engaged. "I mean... how many months since he's proposed to you?"

"I can't seem to recall, Mother..." she said, picking up on her father's last comment, looking at Jack for some sort of helpful input of whatever it was he had told them about their imaginary engagement. "I guess time flies," Tasha said with a half-shoulder shrug, not intending the pun. She was never good at improvisation, as she stole glances to see if her father was believing any of her answers.

Her mother shook her head in disbelief at her own daughter not being as excited over her own status. She did not note anyone else's expressions that stood around listening to their conversation.

"We'll talk about it more at the cabin," suggested Jack, unhooking Tasha from Asa.

Tasha released a bated breath, not realizing she had been holding it.

"I'm sure you both will want to rest a bit before we all come home for the day." Jack extended his arm out in the direction of the hangar door where his truck awaited parked outside, letting her parents take the lead. Hank handed over his truck keys, since he had taken their bags earlier from the aircraft and put them in his truck's bed.

"Tasha, I'll come get you after I get them settled in."

Still peeved at him, she said, "Don't bother, I'll catch a ride." She jabbed her thumb back at the crew with a smile. "Wouldn't want to waste your time being away from my parents," she said under her breath as she turned back toward the safety of her battery shop. She shook her head, seeing the bemusement on Nate's and Nora's faces, ignoring the rest of her co-workers as she heard laughter erupting from Hank, the humorous contagion spreading amongst her co-workers as she walked away annoyed.

By the time she reached the cabin, she realized it would have been better to have Jack pick her up so she could have made him explain himself. That was... if she didn't kill him first, before trying to come up with some sort of corrective action plan to 'right' the situation in front of her parents.

She declined a ride with Sam and smart-alecky Nick, not in the mood to be the brunt of their jokes. She chose a safer ride, making sure she got the back seat of the Jarvis and Manny's sedan so that she could continue to stew, her fingers drumming angrily on her arms where she had folded them over her chest. The ride seemed to take longer than it should for the short distance to their living quarters. Manny had turned to her in the front seat as Jarvis drove, watching her with a lopsided smile, not saying a word until she nearly bit his head off with a curt, "What?"

"*Gau!.. Nada*, curious as to why Jack would put you in this situation in front of your parents." His hand raised up lazily from the headrest he was holding on to while he was facing her. "I mean it's obvious that this was just as a surprise to you as to the rest of us."

She did not answer nor look at him, preferring the side window's view. She chewed her bottom lip in seething anger.

Manny only smiled more. "Well, he must have a reason, and usually it's a good one."

She snapped her head back at him, glaring, catching even Jarvis's glance at her in the car's rearview mirror. Manny just raised his hands up in a partial submissive truce, getting her to calm down before turning back around in his seat.

As Jarvis pulled up to their cabin, Manny called out his window as she got out of the car, relieved to be out from under their scrutiny. "Hey, do keep us in the loop, Tasha. I want to be one of your bridesmaids!"

Jarvis was smart enough to gun the car forward before she could charge Manny to rearrange his face, leaving her in a small cloud of dust and pea-sized gravel as they headed to their cabin, farther up the road.

When she let herself in, she was hoping to drag Jack downstairs into the depths of the cabin's basement where she could lay into him. Unfortunately, her parents were out in the main room chatting it up with Jack, having made themselves at home, waiting on Tasha's arrival.

Jack got up, coming around the sofa to greet her, taking her jacket from her to hang up, telling her to go freshen up so that they could grab dinner at the wharf. "The last thing I want you to do is spend your time cooking after a long day at work."

She raised an eyebrow, considering this was really a big splurge for either of them, wondering if her parents were going to be ready for the higher food prices up north. Then she decided not to put her father into that position of paying for all of them the way he usually did.

"That's all right, I can put something together for all of us. I'm not that tired and I need to catch up on the *latest* news, Jack." She gave him a warning eye.

"Oh sweetheart, come on, you need a night off! And your father and mother want to spend as much time with you as possible." Jack's helpful, positive demeanor should have been the *tipoff* that their engagement was not real. "Just do what you need to clean up while I chit-chat with your folks."

"We need to talk!" she hissed at him, for only Jack to hear.

"Later." Jack gave her a plastered smile.

"Now!" she insisted under her breath.

"Give us a moment?" Jack asked in a lighter tone of voice to her folks in the living room, the intonation similar to a 1950s television comedy show. He followed her to their rooms, where she hesitated trying to determine which room she needed to go to. Seeing Jack's room to her right, with her parents' luggage on his made-up bed, thus guided her decision.

He closed her door, knowing, giving her a placating hand to keep her voice down, and she slapped at his hand.

"What the hell's *wrong* with you?" she asked, grabbing her head in disbelief. "All this just to sleep in my bed with me while they're here?" She turned in circles in front of him, not giving him a chance to say anything, "What am I supposed to tell them? I…I can't do this! Especially when my mother persistently asks us when, where, and how did you propose!" Tasha put her knuckles to her mouth as she pondered, her mind racing to fix the situation quickly.

Then she paused, an idea forming. "I know. We can fake an argument, and all of this is over." She looked up at his face, catching a momentary glimpse of hurt before his normal straight-faced expression resumed home on his visage.

"What?" she asked.

"Is that what you want?"

"Yes! It would get everything back to normal! The truth!"

"And when do you plan on doing this argument?" he asked, stopping her in her train of thoughts. "I mean it shouldn't be now. I personally would like to go out to dinner and enjoy the evening. But I also wouldn't recommend anytime near the beginning of their stay, because it would put everyone on edge while they are staying here, and it may set your mother off to restoring our engagement. No?"

She opened her mouth about to say something, knowing he was right. Her mother would do that. Then she asked him, "Just how long are they staying?"

"A week. They leave on Sunday."

Tasha slapped a hand to her face, dragging it down, unsure if even she could handle that long of a stay with her mother. She had work, to boot. "What about me…us working?" she asked, pointing to them both. "I know I don't have any vacation time built up—not in this short amount of time with the company."

"Ah, Raven understands, he doesn't expect you to be at work much. It's not like you have much to do, and I made certain to lighten your flight duties this week so that you can spend time with them."

"How? I don't even know much of this town."

"Drive them around, let them see the scenery!"

"With what? Your truck? There's snow everywhere!"

"Got it covered," he told her.

"Got what covered?"

"Your car. I have your battery and warmer. I just haven't had the chance to install it. Maybe I can get your dad to help, give us some more bonding time."

She gave him a furrowed brow. "Bonding time?" She uncrossed her arms, then crossed them. "How long have you had a car battery and warmer?"

"About a week and a half. They came in while you were out flying. I just haven't gotten around to getting it installed."

A rap came at her door. "Come on you two lovebirds. We're hungry." It was her father.

"Jack!" she hissed. "We still need to come up with a way to set the record straight. By the way, what *did* you say?"

Jack shook his head. "Don't worry, I'll take care of this."

"When? How?"

Jack didn't answer her, opening the door and giving her dad a smile.

Jack was up early as usual when he headed to the bathroom before letting Drake outside and starting the coffee maker. He intended to have coffee ready for Tasha's parents, only to look up on his way to the front door to see Mr. Lazar—Victor—sitting quietly at the kitchen island already sipping coffee, the aroma of the inviting scent of bold roasted beans lingering by the countertop where the coffee maker stood, waiting for the next cup. He paused in surprise, his hand rubbing the back of his neck working out the morning stiffness. Before Jack could recover, Victor offered a soft, "Good Morning" to him, pausing to scan Jack momentarily, making Jack realize his shirt lay open, revealing his full chest of scars. Jack nodded in kind, quickly buttoning his shirt as he walked over to the door and let Drake out before turning back to the kitchen to grab a cup of coffee.

"I see you're a vet too," Victor said to his back side, his voice gruff from the lack of use over the course of the night. "What nailed you?"

Jack finished pouring his cup before turning back to Tasha's father, giving him an answer. He noted his age-worn square hands, fingers still thick with strength, his body mature but fit, by the contours of his forearms where he rested his elbows on the countertop; he remained upright but relaxed. Jack wondered if he had slept well. Rather than immediately answering his question, Jack asked Victor about his night.

Victor dismissively answered him, "Yes, it's just hard to adjust to a four-hour time zone difference at my age." Victor pointed back at Jack's chest again, not letting his question go unanswered.

He begrudgingly obliged. "Got a little unlucky with a few roadside bombs and ambushes with my squads."

"Unlucky?" Victor asked incredulously. "Son, you should consider yourself damn 'lucky' that you are standing in front of me entirely intact, from what I can see."

Jack cocked his head at him, and Victor continued.

"From that one scar on your chest, it's a miracle you survived. You're lucky to be alive! Let's not mention not being disabled! Am I right?"

Jack nodded, not entirely agreeing with him.

"Let me guess," Victor said, pointing with his forefinger that held his coffee mug. "You lost a few of your fellow combat buddies. All subordinates?" The elder studied him like an open textbook. "Hell, son, I've lost a few good marines." His gaze let up on Jack as he rambled on. "It happens...it's war. We are trained to expect it, but they never *train* you on how to *deal* with it." Jack's gaze met Victor's, pausing momentarily. "You'll never forget them for the rest of your life. That is the 'weight' you feel. But it shouldn't hinder what you do next in life. Most, like you, think it's a guilty curse or a cross to bear. But you need to rethink. To rethink that guilt by looking at it as the highest honor for any man. Only we, the survivors, will remember those men for the rest of our lives. Someone else besides their immediate friends and family to remember them. You remember not just their names and their ranks, but their personalities, their likes, dislikes, and what they were passionate about had they had a future.

"You understand that, son?"

Jack nodded, knowing Tasha's father was right. Yet the difference did not help in assuaging his survivor's guilt at having lost *so* many.

"Now, let's talk."

"Talk?" Jack was confused. "Talk about?"

"About this charade you have my daughter in, young man." He wagged a finger at him in warning, noting Jack's shifting stance against the countertop after he nearly choked on his coffee. "And to answer your question, no, Tasha didn't tell me. When she's flustered the way she was all day yesterday, it wasn't only from our surprise arrival."

Jack sighed. Obviously honesty was the best policy with her father. "You're right...in your assumptions. We aren't engaged."

"Please tell me, son, that you didn't get her pregnant out of wedlock."

"Ah...no. Nothing like that. Your daughter is still honorable."

"Is she now?"

"For our generation, she is."

"For your generation," he grumbled. "It should be for all generations," Victor told him, being the typical protective father. He took a sip of his coffee before asking, "Is she happy?"

"I think so, but not at the moment with me," Jack stated flatly.

371

Victor's eyebrow went up at this sentiment, but he was not entirely surprised. "What are you holding her hostage with to dream up this situation? It's not her nature not to tell me. But her mother, on the other hand…"

"She's not being held hostage. She's free to come and go, even though she is constantly complaining about me being overbearing or protective of where she goes…"

Her father wasn't letting him off the hook just yet.

"Both at work and in her down time."

Victor grunted a laugh. "She tells me the same thing." He sincerely smiled at Jack.

Their conversation, far from being over, was interrupted by the appearance of Asa. Victor indicated to Jack not to say anything further.

Asa was the exact replica of Tasha, only older. Neither of them was a morning person. However, she did not look nearly as disheveled as Tasha was on most mornings, her mother being more refined. She hugged her husband, planting a kiss on his temple, asking him and Jack if they had had breakfast. When both said no in unison, she offered to make breakfast. Jack offered to take them out for breakfast, remembering a prior comment from Tasha about her mother's not so great cooking abilities.

But first he had to work on Tasha's car for a few minutes to get the new battery installed, along with the warming block, in order to get them there or to drop Tasha off at the airport. Tasha's father offered to help him as his wife went to get ready and wake up Tasha so that the two of them could continue their conversation outside and out of earshot from both women.

The Prius started up beautifully with the new and the old batteries installed. Adding the block heater and battery heater did not take long either. However, driving the car around was dismal in terms of the tires having become flat-sided from being parked in one spot for too long since her arrival in Alaska back in late August. Victor insisted on taking her car on down to the nearest shop to install winter tires on her car for her after having breakfast.

Tasha had declined to join them for breakfast, not wanting to have anything to do with keeping up the charade. Jack knew she did not have to be at work until later that morning, having checked the weather and conferred with Nick on a 'go' or 'no go' status with the Angelina. They had deferred the start time, but he let her take his truck to work so she could escape from them for a while.

The previous night's dinner had been a challenge. Jack was certainly impressed at how Tasha could deflect most of the questions about them, given the disposition of her mother's logorrhea on just about everything and anything. They had kept it short, since her parents were both suffering from a little jet lag and had been wanting to see their bed soon.

Their conversation in her room, once they were by themselves, was nearly nonexistent. Her silence was her other way of showing anger, which was by far the scarier of the two anger modes she possessed. At least when she went on her diatribe like her mother, he knew where she was coming from and could sometimes defend himself or appease her with a solution. Her silence was not entirely 'golden.'

"Please tell me you have some decent coffee in here," Tasha said as she came into Nate's office that morning.

Nate pointed to their coffeemaker.

"I have no idea what Hank makes in the break room's coffee maker, but it's not coffee."

Nora looked up at the rather disheveled Tasha and gave her the biggest smile. "So, are we to assume there is a big day?"

Tasha scowled, refusing to answer, but the two of them noted her cringe as her shoulders came up at the question.

"You look tired, Tasha, is everything all right?" Nate asked as she gave them both a haggard look. "Pull up a seat, little lady," he offered. "You know we're here for you whenever you need to talk."

She reluctantly sat down and took a sip of the coffee, savoring the strong brew with her eyes closed.

"Why are you so tired? Did Jack and your parents keep you up past your bedtime?" Nate lightly joked.

"No. Jack can be a pretty bad snorer."

"You're not flying today, are you, Tasha?" Nora asked. "Please don't take this wrong, but you shouldn't be flying if you are this tired."

"I do fly, but not until later around noon with Nick on the Angelina. We gotta wait on some weather to clear." She thumbed the mug's handle.

Nate offered, "I can see if someone else can take—"

"No," she interrupted, "I don't have the vacation time and I need to temporarily 'run away' from an unbelievably bad situation, in addition to my mother driving me nuts. Right now, Jack is 'bonding' with my dad, and he promised to take my parents around to Lowell's Point later this afternoon." Tasha sighed heavily, keeping her gaze down at the contents of her cup.

"Ah, so the wedding is still on?" Nora teased lightly.

Tasha gave her a pointed look, not answering her with what she wanted to hear.

Instead, Tasha asked, "How did this happen? What started all this? Did I miss something?" Tasha asked to neither one, puffing her cheeks with an angry exhalation.

Coming around her desk to refill her own coffee mug, Nora placed a quick assuring hand on Tasha's shoulder as she walked past her to the coffee stand. "No, dear. Just the fact that Jack is wildly in love with you." She smiled at her tenderly.

"Well, he has a weird way of showing it." She caught Nate watching her as she took another sip.

"Jack hasn't gotten that badly out of hand, has he?" Nate asked. "Other than a surprise engagement, he's not forcing you to do anything against your will, is he? Even like that Mr. Reynolds escapade?"

Tasha gave him an *are you serious* look before answering, not certain what Nate may have been inferring when it came to Mr. Reynolds. "Not exactly. He's always been harsh. First with dumping me into the harbor waters within the first few weeks of being here, then constantly culling me from the crewmembers, then basically locking me up—without really locking me up—in a cabin that he didn't want to share in the first place…"

"I thought that was you not wanting to share the cabin," interrupted Nate.

"Yes and no," she corrected him, sighing heavily. "I just didn't want to deal with a hairy, grumpy, wild mountain man in the cabin who made it very clear I was unwelcome by attacking me, only to tell me he thought I was breaking in with my very own key."

She continued, "I'm having flashbacks to basic training, when it comes to training and getting things right repetitively, especially to all the things related to each aircraft and basic survival skills in cold weather that I am not really seeing much of." The statement ended more in a question as her gaze drifted out the office's window, searching for Old Man Winter.

"That's because there hasn't been much of a winter this year. Winters seem to be coming later and later," Nate pointed out. "However, it's January, February, and March that we see most of the cold and snow."

Tasha continued her side. "I think he trains a little too harshly, and I feel like it's a personal grudge against me at times. But he seems to relax knowing that I can pull my weight around here, that I can fire a weapon, fight hand to hand, et cetera, but he still doesn't let me out on my own for a basic walk or to go out and socialize with friends…okay, my co-workers…for I have no social life," she amended. "I just don't really see where there's trouble other than that one night at the bar where that drunk dockyard worker got out of hand and I was caught off guard in defending myself. But I think I would have handled it fine, and I had the rest of the crew there to help—which they did—but Jack went nuts, taking out the three men just to get me out of the bar that night and then blamed me for 'starting' it."

"Aaah—now the truth comes out," Nora commented. "I still think our boys are good to her, especially Jack," she cooed at Nate.

"Ever the romantic, aren't you, Nora?" Tasha smiled weakly.

"Well, I can see his point, Tasha. He cares enough to protect you, and without sounding like a dirty old man, you are too beautiful to be up here in this neck of the woods with so many desperate men out there. This is still America's frontier. Not enough women here, much less smart women" —he looked over to his wife—"like my wife, who is not only beautiful but helpful. You are more precious and rarer than the gold in them there hills of ours." He smiled broadly at her, although his eyes were on the love of his life.

"You both are romantics," she teased them, an endearing smile escaping her as she watched what a true and perfect marriage was in front of her. She felt so easy with them both and often found it hard to believe she had such a great boss. They were like her second parents and she was hopelessly in love with them, her job, and the crew. Even Jack, if he would ever figure out what he wanted in life when it came to them, or at least show some sort of commitment other than being a fringe benefit for him. The other fact of the matter was whether he was ever going to allow her into his past and more personal thoughts. She wanted in. She wanted to know more about the man from his own mouth. Not from outside sources and clues.

"Overall, he hasn't been ungentlemanly toward me…if that is what you are asking. Just too bossy in my personal life…like he forgets to drop work at work and brings it home during our off hours in the cabin…He brings a lot of it home, and my guess is that one day he's hoping to take over for you."

Tasha added, "He's even been working on obtaining another aircraft. He got mad at me, one day, for 'snooping around his desk' when I told him he would not be happy with a certain aircraft model because of the difficulty in performing maintenance and that getting parts would be more difficult due to its age. I told him he was better off purchasing a newer and lower flight hour bird even though he would have to pay more up front but have less cost in maintaining the bird in the long run."

"Ah-huh," Nate grunted. "Explains why Jack changed his mind on the purchase of that aircraft with me." Nate looked at Nora again. "I will definitely take it into consideration."

"So you *did* know about this?" Tasha asked Nate.

The Raven nodded yes.

"As for the extra stuff for Mr. Reynolds…that was totally my idea. Jack reluctantly let me run with that job. I just don't think he thought I—I mean—that we, the crew, could pull it off in two weeks. Nor did I tell him what I was up to, since he never explains why he does certain things to us. Jack had no idea on all the extras. I know I went over budget, but after he made the comment of who Mr. Reynolds was, I thought this would be a great opportunity to gain an important client for the company. Why would you think Jack forced me and the crew to do what we did?" She gave Nate a quizzical look.

It was a moment before he spoke. "Because he came back later to apologize for what the crew did and for not giving me a heads up on what was going down. He thought he failed me in not being a more competent manager."

"You mean he tried to take all the blame for my actions?" She was stunned that Jack would shoulder it. "He certainly wasn't to blame…It was all my doing."

"And for that I am grateful, because it shows us that you had the initiative to see our business continue to thrive, and it means a lot to this old man. Jack has been the only other person to show interest in keeping this company running strong and to keep everyone gainfully employed."

Clearing his throat, he continued, "Nora's my first love. My second love is flying and creating this company.

"And Tasha, my dear, you have given it a fresh breath of air that it has needed for a long time with all your hard work that you and the boys have put into our company. I thank you for that from the bottom of my heart."

Tasha flushed, looking down at her hands, not knowing what to say, other than to follow her mother's internal voice screaming at her to say out loud, "Thank you, sir. I'm glad to have helped."

"So," Nora chimed in, "other than you have no idea what date your wedding is, Jack's been pretty good to you?"

"Nora!" Nate reprimanded gently.

"Well, I *have* to know *this* so that I have plenty of time to go shopping with Tasha and find all the things a girl needs to have for that special day!" Nora replied haughtily to her husband.

"Do I need to tell Jack to fix this and remind him of his place, Tasha?" Nate fatherly placated.

"No. No, Jack said he would fix it while I was out flying today. I'm just curious as to how this is going to go over, especially with my mother. He wouldn't let me start a fight to break up the engagement last night. He wanted to do it another way, but I am almost terrified of what's going to happen next."

"That's too bad, my dear, I was really hoping for a nice wedding," Nora admitted with a sly smile. "I think you two make a nice couple. That Jack is certainly full of surprises as of late." Her head looked up even higher, smiling even more brightly at something behind Tasha. More like someone. Jack was standing in the doorframe. Tasha was certain that he had overheard some of their conversation because no one had bothered to close the office door.

Nate waved him in. Tasha moved to get up, but Jack's hand settled heavily on her shoulder, making her remain in her chair. She was uncomfortable knowing Jack's utter dislike of being gossiped about. This time his anger would be warranted.

She licked her lips. "So I take it the news didn't go over well back at the cabin?" she asked Jack where he remained standing just behind as she sat in her chair.

"Sort of," he replied, smiling to Nate and Nora where Tasha couldn't see it.

"What!" She turned to around to look up at him. "What do you *mean* sort of?"

"Well, your dad figured it out this morning. On his own...that is."

"He was all right with"—she pointed back and forth between them—"us?"

"Yes, he was fine with our arrangement even though he strongly recommend in the near future that I maintain your honor and do not leave you 'high and dry with a broken heart,'" he said, referring to his earlier conversation with her father while working on her car.

"And Mom?"

"We both decided it wasn't a good idea to let her know."

"Okay. But it really doesn't resolve the situation. You know she's—"

"—Like Nora, wanting to know a date," Jack interrupted. "I figure we just make one up for now and then decide down the road where to go next."

"But that still doesn't take care of how and when you proposed…" she said, exasperated. "My mother is going to want *these* details…as if I had even experienced it!" Then she added, "And amazingly, I don't even recall any of this craziness you got us into." She stood up to face him. "And by the way…what *did* you say to her to start all of this?"

"Your mother mistook what I said about eventually marrying someone like you over the headsets when I picked them up from Anchorage," he explained. "She just ran with it. I had no idea that she would be so excited over you *being* engaged."

Tasha gave him, a *ya think* look. She felt despondent and sighed heavily.

"Your mother acts like you are never going to get married, which I find hard to believe. Like her, I can't believe you're not engaged yet." He gave the back of her chair a gentle shake. "Someone will though shortly," he said dismissively, as if it was not going to be him.

"It certainly won't happen now that my mother has told all of Seward about our engagement by now." She rolled her eyes at Nate and Nora.

"I won't pretend anymore." She walked over to the coffee maker to refill her cup. "You have way too many other important things on your mind to even begin to deal with me," she said, remembering what Nate had said to her earlier. "I'm not willing to take second place in some strange man's life."

Then to all of them, she said, "If you will excuse me, I need to figure out a way to stay awake and alert for my noon flight."

"Tasha." She was surprised to hear Jack say anything to her. "Go get the sleep you need in the overnight pilot's lounge. I'll wake you when it's time to go."

"What about my parents?"

"They're fine, I dropped them off so that they could wander around downtown and do a little window shopping, plus your dad is insisting on getting your car new snow tires while I check in on everyone down here in the hangar. After you take off here in the next hour or so, they will pick me up and we'll go down to Lowell Point."

"The town will definitely know of our engagement by now," she muttered, more to herself. Tasha looked over to Nate, confirming that it was all right with him.

Nate nodded, telling her, "Good idea, go on, get your rest."

Later that evening Jack picked her up in her Prius, her parents waiting in the back seat. Knowing that she would be tired, Jack took them out to dinner, but that time to another restaurant.

As the four of them received their dinners, the conversation that Tasha was dreading came to the surface again. But knowing her mother's roundabout way of getting there only fueled the pent-up frustration raging inside. It was literally eating at her as her mother kept pushing.

"Oh Tasha, I'm so excited for you," she began, giving her usual small squeal of delight, normally pinched off with her raised shoulders. "I can't believe how caviler you've been about it, darling. You *must* give me details! I insist!"

Tasha looked to Jack for help, hoping he would fill in the 'missing details,' for if he did not speak soon, she would end it—right there, right then.

Her mother continued, "Jack's so modest and quiet. You know"—she waved her hand, flashing her own exquisite wedding band at her from across the table—"like the strong silent type most women can only dream of landing." She giggled at them both.

Tasha rolled her eyes.

"Oh, come on, darling…he's a fine catch!"

"Mother!" Tasha snapped, gritted out from between her teeth. "He's right here! Don't be making his ego any bigger than it is!"

"All right, sweetie," Asa agreed, making a quick pout with her mouth. "But I still want to know how you both met, when you decided you were right for each other, where did he propose, what time frame were you two looking at 'sealing the deal'…" She listed her questions finger by manicured finger.

Again, Jack was not taking the hint to play along or just tell her mother the truth about them. Her father took Asa's hand, giving it a gentle squeeze before telling her that they could talk about it later, noting Tasha's barely contained annoyance. But her mother was not having any of it.

"Why *not* now? We're *here* and visiting them in person. Oh, for goodness sakes! Victor, It's been nearly a year since we last saw her when she was in the VA hospital recovering from her incident."

Tasha gnashed her molars.

"Oh—and I want to know when and how many grandbabies I will get to enjoy and spoil!"

The last comment was more than she could handle. Tasha's hands came down heavily, gripping the table's edge, and as she leaned forward in her seat, Jack's hand shot out to her thigh trying to stay her, hoping to keep Tasha from reaching across the table and committing matricide.

"Mom!" she hissed, desperately trying not to make a public scene, grateful they were one of the earlier diners by the window, sitting far enough away from the few other diners. "We ARE NOT engaged!" Her hand lifted and indicated to Jack and herself and then to their table. "I'm not entirely sure what Jack told you, but *we* are *not* going to be married! He's made up this fictional situation in which I am the MacGuffin of this crazy story."

Blustering, her mother asked, "Why*ever* not?" She looked between Tasha and Jack in question. "What's wrong with him?" Then to Jack: "Or her?"

"There's nothing wrong with Tasha," Jack said, his only offer of help.

"I'm only a 'roomie' with fringe benefits until something better comes along for him and can provide him the kids he wants—something I will *never* be able to give him, since the war has seen to it that I am incapable of having any, Mother! Right now, his only love is for his career. I refuse to be his second love!" She got up from the table, shaking Jack's hand off her as he tried to keep her at the table. She walked away before she would rue anything else, slamming down on the exterior dockside door's handlebar, shoving it open to give her access to the walkway overlooking the harbor full of moored boats where the dock's lamp poles spotlighted a boat here and there.

It was freezing outside and she could see the steam coming off her body; her anger kept her warm as she put some distance between the restaurant and herself. She sighed angrily, turning toward the railing that kept her from falling into the harbor, resting her elbows so that she could cover her face with her hands, hiding the unshed furious and frustrated tears threatening to spill.

Her parents' visit would have been tolerable had Jack not decided to mess around with this ruse. Her mother would have done the usual nit-picking of Tasha's unusual lifestyle choices and her work after her military service, her tone always disapproving. A mother wanting the best for her daughter. Her mother, of course, knew what was best in her eyes.

Her father was her *go-to* man. She could tell him anything. They shared the same love for aviation. He made her feel like all was right in whatever she chose. But he, too, shared some of her mother's sentiments of wanting her to have found the love of her life by now. However, he was far from being pushy about it. He knew about the military's recommendation on not getting pregnant, given the way she had been wounded. At least 'not anytime soon—not in the next three to five years…if ever,' the doctors had advised her. The bullet's diagonal path from front to back, the entry about two inches lower than the exit, had caused serious damage to her internal organs.

Tasha was determined not to cry over it or her new circumstances. She had never had any real strong desire to have children in the first place, figuring she would have little time to be a mother, with her dream career choice. But she had never genuinely thought about it either—and now found herself wondering if Jack wanted them. Hell, Jack was not even the marrying kind of guy—at least not when it came to her. He was still hung up about his last girlfriend, from what she had figured out after his sister's visit. Although Jack kept telling her otherwise, she was not convinced yet, especially since they were just at the beginning of their more intimate relationship in these last few weeks. His actions outweighed what he told her. He seemed to be in no rush about anything, especially marriage! That was a given the way he had treated this current farce: it was just a joke to him.

But their relationship could easily be destroyed given that he never discussed much about himself. How *dare* she imagine anything with Jack? But now that Jack knew she was not capable of having kids, she was going to move on as best as she could, she decided, rubbing her hands over her face to warm it up and get her circulation going in her frozen cheeks. She should go back in, but what was the point? In her stubbornness, she would rather freeze than go back to their table!

She had not heard Jack come up, in her preoccupation, until she felt her coat sliding around her shoulders. Grateful, she shrugged into it, zipping it up fully to hunker down in it as Jack took up a position next to her, draping his arms over the railing in front of him, propping a foot up on the lower railing, and taking in the entire view of Resurrection Bay and its iconic mountain backdrop, not saying a word as the waters lapped the shoreline underneath the boards of the walkway.

He looked at her until she caught him, flashing those eyes back away and out over the harbor. "I'm fine, thanks for asking," she said sarcastically.

He huffed before continuing. "I must say when the horns come out, you have a hell of a way of gouging all nearby in your rampage. Heck of a wreckage in there, Moose," he told her softly, using her nickname. "I'll have to make a mental note not to let things go too far."

She gave Jack a skeptical look before resuming her watch, focusing on a boat detail that was moored close to them.

"I take it your mother didn't know"—he paused—"that you could never have kids."

She looked at him in surprise.

His lips twisted into a thin line, from the indication of his auburn whiskers. "Yup…you never told her." His ability to see minute details did not escape him, even when she was sure he was not paying attention. "Your father didn't seem all that surprised though."

"My father is more pragmatic. He doesn't push his beliefs and opinions like my mother does," she said laconically to Jack.

Jack cocked a half-smile. "You didn't tell me either, although I am not sure if you were taking precautions, and come to think of it…nor have I seen any evidence of you going through your monthly cycles since we have been living together." He turned to face her, waiting, finally adding, "Unless you are—"

"It's none of your business—"

"The hell it isn't!" he woofed low at her, stopping her. "It takes two, Tasha!" He reminded her of their involvement together.

"Why on earth would you even care if I got knocked up? It's not like you would step up to the ball plate should I have gotten pregnant. Most men don't."

"I do care, because it would be mine too."

380

"Well, Jack, you have no worries there. I'm about as much fun as you can get without any consequences." She turned to walk away but his hand caught her coat sleeve, staying her.

"Consequences?" He nodded, knowing full well the main consequence would be her wounding his heart more than just the physical scars he bore. "There are other consequences you seem to have forgotten—or do you truly not feel anything between us?" he asked, trying to drive home his point.

"Enough, Jack. Enough with the fantasies! Enough with me not knowing where I stand with you in whatever relationship we *do* have! I'm tired of having my heart dragged through the mud. Let's not mention what you did to my own obnoxious mother!"

At that, his full brown eyebrows raised. "True, but you did it to her by not telling her from the very start, too." He pulled her into him, hugging her, glad to understand that it was not just him having fallen in love with this fair-haired Russian beauty that had resuscitated his life, filling it with a quiet and interesting love when he least expected it.

"But I know better than to let myself believe—"

"Believe what—that I do care?" he answered for her.

She tried to push away from him.

"That I love you?" he asked, maintaining his hold on her, keeping her from bolting and running away.

It was the first time he had told her, making her cease her struggles momentarily. "You have no future with me, Jack. Are you willing to give that up? What happens when Mrs. Right does appear and can have—"

"Like I told you before, Tasha, there is no Mr. or Mrs. Right. There are no perfect people out there in this world." Tasha was going to interrupt him, but he bent his head forward to place his forehead to hers. "I'm no angel either. I know I have some things to work through when it comes to coming to terms with my past. I know I need to expound myself more when it comes to asking you things to do or to not do."

His blue-gray eyes pleaded with her, his voice low and sincere. "Know that I do love you, no matter how you are packaged. I love the entire kit-and-kaboodle, Tasha. I love you, and I can't find a way to make you understand that." His arms crossed behind her neck, shaking her gently to emphasize the point. "What can I do to correct what we started? Most of all, how do I convince you?" He let go of her, standing back up. "I can propose to you here, but I have no ring to offer you. Besides, I would rather it be someplace special—for the two of us. Maybe in front of your parents? The crew?"

"That would be a start. And hopefully in a more private setting with just them." She mulled to herself. "Even a date would be nice to know…"

He smiled at her, shaking her shoulder at first, then bringing her into his arms, hugging her. He knew all was good when she wrapped her arms around his waist.

Jack got her to apologize to her mother, who was still sniffling, her father sitting next to her with an arm wrapped around her shoulder. It was obvious that her father had done his part in calming her mother down and breaking the news that only Tasha and he had known all along. He smiled warmly at Jack, nodding to him as if acknowledging some silent conversation between them. They took their seats and tried to resume their meals, but no one ate much, thus all of them later got take-home boxes.

The following three days she spent with her folks, her mother was unusually quiet and clearly disappointed with her. She steered their conversations to safe topics, focusing on the things they did around Seward and at their cabin and what was new with them and her old friends back home in Florida. Tasha knew it was killing her mother not to say anything, her father having said something to keep her on a short leash.

It was when they had headed up to Anchorage to sightsee some of the downtown area, two days before her parents flew back to Florida, that her father was able to privately converse with her during a roadside pit stop. They were on a viewing platform overlooking the bird sanctuary, though there was not much to see with the thick snows blanketing the entire flat empty area. A thick dead-brown blade of sawgrass was stabbing through the snow, trying to entice the clear skies above with its silent lonely scream, as if missing its symbiotic relationship with the summer birds.

Her father nudged her shoulder with his. "Hey, kiddo."

"Hi, Dad." She smiled weakly at him.

"You going to be okay?"

Tasha looked back at him, uncertain, before answering him. "Yeah, I'm fine."

He sighed heavily. "I know you're fine. But what I want to know is…are you happy? I mean *really* happy?" He had reached out with a gloved hand to move a strand of her hair out of her face in the gentle zephyr, commenting off-handedly, "Man, it's cold out here!"

She smiled, remembering how cold it had felt so many months before and it was not even winter. She was adjusting bodily, but her heart had grown warmer too, discovering a new love—not just for her job and the people she worked with, but for a man that was doing his best to convince her he loved her.

"I'm…" She hesitated, trying to find that right term for the right level of her 'happiness.' "I'm content, for now."

But her answer only made her father's eyebrows raise.

"I am happy. I love my job and the folks I work with."

He still waited.

She added, "Jack too. But not the way you two are hoping for. Technically, it's still too early for us…for me to feel like it will go somewhere."

Tasha saw the disbelief in her father's face.

"Okay, okay…I'll try and work on it with him. Just don't get your hopes up on Jack."

"I think he's a nice man, Tasha. Rough looking—"

"God, you should have seen him when I first met him, Da—" Her laugh interrupted her words. "His looks are tame by comparison."

Her father waited for her to expound.

"Jack's fine…once I got to know him. I just was not hip on the beard, the backwoods-redneck look, his preferred hobby of hunting and fishing, and his overbearing attitude. He works a lot, whereas I prefer not so much…I mean, I want to work…just smart, not hard. But I want to enjoy life when I can."

"Ah, and you're afraid you have nothing in common with this man during your off hours?"

She gave a breathy half-laugh. "Yup, pretty much. I don't think I could keep his interest long enough for a marriage, to be personally honest about it. It's not like I have that much of an exciting life. I like simplicity. But what happens if he becomes bored? Or myself, for that matter? I just don't know if I can handle any more disappointments."

"Tasha, you have a lot more in common with that man than you think."

At that comment she raised an eyebrow at him.

"I doubt he'll grow bored with you." Then he added, "You have too much of your mother in you when you get 'spooled up.'"

"Dad!" she exclaimed, clearly insulted.

"You're both vets, you have a 'common experience.' You both love aviation, you two are both outdoorsy, and Alaska is the place to be…that is…if you love this darn *cold*!" He shivered against another light breeze, rubbing his mitted hands together.

"Come on, Dad, let's get you back inside the car. I see Mom has already let herself in. I take it she isn't doing well in this weather either."

"We just came from seventy-five-degree weather, what do you think?"

She smiled, remembering the sun kissing her bare skin even though it had been nearly three years since her last visit.

Victor stopped her before going any further toward her car. "You need to give Jack a decent chance. He's a man battling his own set of demons."

"I know, Dad—"

"Just like I know you are too," he added.

She gave him a questioning look. "You think I am battling demons?"

"I know you are. And just like Jack, neither of you want to confront it in order to deal with it. You two need to be patient with each other, especially you. You're better at overcoming things than others are. Give him time."

They had reached her car.

Her father winked at her over the roof of her car, adding, "Us stodgy Marines are a little slow on accepting help from others and new things." He opened the passenger side door and slid in.

The rest of the time spent in Anchorage did not feel like she had an anchor weighing her down, with all that had gone on between her parents and Jack. Even her mother eventually apologized to her, after spending about a day and a half 'in the dumps' with all the shocking truths coming out in the open a few nights earlier.

It was the late afternoon before she would be seeing her parents off at the airport in the early morning that her mother sat down on the edge of her bed in the hotel room, her father in the bathroom taking a shower. It was the first intimate conversation Tasha had had with her mother since that dinner evening. As Asa took her hand in hers, giving a quick gentle squeeze, her mother wanted her to understand that she genuinely wanted Tasha to be happy, and if Alaska was where she wanted to be, that she had to accept that it was Tasha's choice.

"And…"

Here it comes, Tasha sighed inwardly. Her mother caught her eye-rolling.

"*And*, I still believe Jack is a nice young man. You should honestly give him a chance, sweetie."

"I have, Mother. He's more into his career than he is into searching for a mate," she said, so her mother didn't get her hopes up, adding, "…and most likely a mate that will bear him children."

Her dad came out of the bathroom, overhearing them. "I wouldn't judge the man too harshly—not yet, especially in not being able to bear him kids, Tash."

"You could always adopt," Asa added wistfully.

"I'm not judging him. I am being realistic. Jack loves his career a little too much and really has no time to waste it on me, much less making a family life, Dad."

"Do you love him, kiddo?" her father asked.

"Yeah, I guess so," she said with some reservation.

"I know so by the way you are acting with him, kiddo," her father stated more firmly.

But Tasha told them why she had doubts. "But I am not diving wildly headlong into this relationship with a man who is a near stranger to me. I barely know him. He doesn't let me in nor talk about himself. He doesn't let me know how he feels or thinks. I find things out here and there, through his sister, his best friend, or his co-workers. I would like to know things directly from him, if he would ever open up about himself." Tasha looked at her mother, her concern showing just below the surface of her face. "I don't need the heartache, should it not work out. I've lost my heart a few times and it hurts too much for me to take such a risk again. At least not yet."

"Hmm…sounds like someone I know rather well." Her mother looked back at her father standing there before them, where Tasha and her mother remained at the edge of the bed, before continuing. "Your father is a quiet man, and especially after his time in the service. He kept many things from me in order to protect me. And obviously still does to this day." Her mother sighed to herself, although she smiled lovingly at her father.

Tasha was not sure if she was referring to her just recent glean or from a few other things in the past that her dad had done to protect her mother.

Then as an afterthought, she asked Tasha, "Who hurt you? It wasn't Artie, was it?" Her mother had just realized that there had been others, yet gave no indication of this new surprise.

But Tasha interrupted, nodding her head no, and patted her mother's hand reassuringly, adding. "I promise you that I will give Jack a chance."

"We just want to see you happy. You hardly smile since you came back from the war. And I apologize to you because not seeing you smile makes me worry, like any mother should." She hugged her daughter.

Relief swept over Tasha as she hugged her mother. "I'm sorry, Mom, for making you worry and for being such a disappointment to you."

"Nonsense, sweetheart. You are not a disappointment...I just think that your choices are rather strange at times. But I have to accept your choices that you've made in your life and in your career," her mother reminded herself more than Tasha.

Tasha's father had moved to the other side of the room, watching them both hold each other and giving her a silent questioning look.

She quelled him with another more confirming commitment. "I *am* happy and I promise to give Jack a chance, Dad."

The rest of the evening she showed her parents the town of Anchorage, taking them to places that held interest for them and for her. She realized that she had done them a disservice in not telling them things and for not assuaging all their concerns earlier. Her parents just wanted to see their 'baby girl' move on, obtain her dreams and a new life. For their past would be carried forward by her future.

Tasha accompanied her parents to the airport the following morning, waiting as they checked in with their luggage in a seat near the terminal's glass exterior wall. She noted a familiar figure approaching her, making her do a double-take, before realizing Jack was there.

"What are you doing here?" She sat up in her chair. "Aren't you supposed to be flying cargo to Whitter?"

"Yeah, I did, and I just had Jarvis drop me off here hoping that I could catch you and hitch a ride back."

"A ride back?" she asked, unsure she was hearing right. "To Seward? You'd have been back by now had you just returned with Jarvis. It's going to take me... what...about eight hours? Because I am not driving in the dark and I want at least six more hours of sleep before that two-hour drive back."

Jack took a seat next to her. "That's fine. It allows me to spend some more time with you." He planted a quick greeting kiss to the side of her head.

"What about work? I mean…don't drop things on account of me." She felt guilty for being jealous of his time spent at work.

"Work is fine without me, and my life isn't going to end without making it to my goal on time."

"You had a timeline?"

He nodded.

"So, what's wrong?" she questioned. His vague demeanor made her curious.

"Nothing."

He got up from his seat to greet her parents as they made their way back to where they sat, their tickets in hand, ready to get in the TSA line and to their gate in time.

Her father greeted him warmly. "Nice to see you again, son." He shook his hand again. "Take good care of her," he added, still holding Jack's hand. "I know she can be a handful but give it your best."

Tasha saw the minute stiffening in Jack's shoulders as her dad placed a heavy burden on him by putting him in charge of her. It was the last thing he needed, with all his past military experiences. She was not going to add any more hardships to him if she could.

"Dad!" She rebuffed him somewhat. "I'll be fine, I don't need anyone to take care of me. He's got enough on his plate with his work and dealing with the rest of the crew back home." She gave her dad and her mother a long hug, telling her that she loved them both, making her mother tear up even more.

"Mom. Stop, Mom! Please, you'll make me cry too. You'll see me soon. I just need to make it through this first year and this winter. I promise, I'll visit soon."

Asa nodded, giving Tasha a quick kiss before she leaned over to Jack and gave him a quick hug and kiss, telling him something that only he could hear. Jack nodded affirmatively.

"Are you riding back with her, son?" Victor asked.

"I'm hoping she gives me a lift back since I just sent my guy back to Seward with the Angelina. Otherwise it's going to be a long, cold walk back."

Her dad gave her a warning look. "She better! I'd feel better if she didn't drive alone."

"What is this? Is my driving that bad?" she asked, imploring her mother to say something in her defense, but of course there was no support there. "Seriously? Dad? Jack?"

Jack shrugged his shoulders at her. "Well, since I've known you, I think I only had you drive three times before the snows hit. So I honestly can't tell either way. But practice is always good." He gave her a mischievous grin before she playfully smacked his arm.

"Atta boy, tell her straight up." Her dad laughed as she rolled her eyes.

"Well, when you take off and you see a little car below doing doughnuts in a parking lot, that'll be us," Jack told them.

Tasha pulled on Jack, tearing him away from her dad as she waved both her parents off, encouraging them not to miss their flight home to warmer weather and waters.

Jack grinned as they turned, making their way back to her car, her hand in the crook of his elbow as he clasped his hands together nefariously. "All right, Mario Andretti, move over. Here comes Tasha!" His comment made her laugh.

"I can make that car fly if you want me to!" Tasha joked, and then giggled.

"That's what I'm afraid of." Jack grinned.

🐻 🐻 🐻 🐻 🐻

They spent the rest of the day and early morning enjoying each other back at the hotel until they both were too exhausted to keep their eyes open. Tasha stretched like a cat next to his side, enjoying the quiet before snuggling her backside into Jack's body lying next to her, already asleep.

They left the hotel just after lunchtime, nabbing a quick bite to eat before getting on Highway One, driving south to Seward. The weather was holding, but there was still a lot of snow in some areas of the mountain passes. She was grateful to her father for purchasing new snow tires. However, she still took her time, considering it was her first time driving on snow-packed, covered roads. Jack did not hound her, and told her there was no rush in getting home.

The drive proved to be good in two areas. The three-and-a-half-hour drive gave her the much-needed practice, stopping at a few empty rest areas where Jack did make her practice turning into the slides and getting a feel for the freezing conditions and how her car would handle. The second was the rare opportunity to have Jack tell her more in-depth stories of his past, especially his last ten years. It was then that she learned more about his life from the end of high school, his time spent in college, learning how to fly, earning his private certificate, all before joining the Marines as ground maintenance and security ops for the marine flight line.

What got her attention was when he confessed his most basic and current fear: his fear of not doing enough training for the folks he was responsible for and keeping them alive.

"I never want to lose another person to a premature avoidable death," he told her. "I would rather die first or for them…" He paused as he pondered the side view out his window, not looking at her, before adding, "…than to survive at the expense of another man's death." But it was his voice, the catch in it, that made her aware of how particularly important it was to him. "I have failed too many men as a leader. I shouldn't even be allowed to manage our crew and flight operations, at times. I can't promise to keep everyone safe or alive." His comment chilled her to the bone, and it felt like the interior of her car came crushing in on them at that moment, making her chest squeeze with suffocating grief, the gnawing grief that he carried with him forever.

Luckily, there was a rest area that she spied, slowing down to pull over and stop, using it as an excuse so that he would not balk from her for feeling unnecessary pity, which, of course, she did not. He said nothing as she got out of the car to use the restroom. As she mindlessly used the facilities, she wondered if he would do something rash at that point. Her uncertainty made her rush back outside, only to find him gone. She stood there stunned, unable to move, afraid to look to the river's edge alongside the road to find him having committed suicide, but she jumped out of her skin when he approached her from behind, having come from the men's restroom, and then she sighed heavily in relief.

"What's the matter?" he asked as his arms wrapped around her, standing outside in the frosty air, the snow in a hodgepodge of various piles around the parking lot.

"Nothing."

"Then why did I surprise you?"

She didn't answer him right away, making him pull away from her enough to let her turn around in his arms. She mitted his jacket down smoothly along his chest, not sure what to say next, curling her lips into a thin line.

"That was too much for you, wasn't it?" he asked, referring to what he'd just told her.

She shook her head. "No. No, it wasn't. But the last time I tried to say something and reach out to you, I got shunned pretty hard for showing compassion." Tasha stopped petting his chest, her mitted hand resting over his heart. Nodding her head at him but looking at his coat, she continued, "I...I just don't know what to say or do to share your pain without upsetting you. I'm grateful that you *finally* allowed me inside...to your most personal thoughts." She patted his heart lightly through his thick layers of clothing. "I want to hug you so badly, but I fear your rejection."

She smiled weakly, looking up at him, uncertain. "Tell me what you want me to say or do."

"I like the hug idea." He picked her up off her feet and tightly bear-hugged her before he set her down, and they stood holding on to each other for a long moment. He had buried his face in her hair. "I'm sorry for hurting you earlier. I was angry. Angry at myself for failing all those men. I took it out on you instead. You didn't deserve that. But I don't deserve the compassion for letting them die."

"But it wasn't your fault, Jack! How could you ever think it was your fault? No one can really train for bombs or ambushes! You didn't put them in harm's way," she told him softly. Her hand reached up to touch his face, pulling his down to her, giving him a solid, reassuring kiss before telling him, "They knew their jobs, and I am sure they were the best of best, because you were a part of the same team."

Then, trying to lighten the mood, she added, "Hell, your on-the-job training is tougher than my Army's basic and advanced training. I don't think they know it, but I'm certain the guys at Black Raven Aviation could even outdo some Marines. You run a tight ship, so to speak, soldier!" She smiled, using his terminology until he smiled weakly at her. Then she poked him in an attempted tickle-fest, rendered near impossible with their winter gear on, getting him to smile more until he nabbed both her hands, stopping her, finally laughing with her. With his winsome smile out, the one that made an irresistible dimple appear on the one side of his face, she could not control herself and flung herself at him, bodily knocking him off balance, and together they tumbled onto a snowdrift just behind him that softened their fall, where she enthusiastically covered him in snow bunny kisses.

When the wet snow got to them both, they extricated themselves, dusting off the excess wet powder as they headed toward her car. As they were getting in, he stopped, telling her over the roof of her car, "Thank you."

She nodded. "Jack, at some point you've got to have a little faith in us at Black Raven Aviation. The guys know their stuff. If I can believe and have faith in them, especially since I am the newest and weakest link in the group, then you should too," she advised him, and dropped down into the driver's seat.

CHAPTER TWENTY-THREE

Nick was the first to emit a low whistle from where most of their well-tailored group had congregated, sipping cocktails from the convention center's open bar before the show. Periodically, Jack glanced over to the exterior doors. The only sign of his concern was him pulling at the tie he was unaccustomed to, exposed by the open front of his dress jacket. Past the glass doors, the cold Alaskan night had settled heavily into Anchorage's valley and bay area, the bay's waters not wide nor deep enough to influence the air's temperature swings over the Great Land's landmass.

Raven did his best garnering Jack's attention, deciding Jack needed to be distracted with what they had already talked about on the flight up the day before, knowing Jack's uneasiness until everyone was together. There was not much time left before the theater doors would open, allowing the audience into their assigned seats. Only Manny and Tasha had yet to arrive. Manny had decided it was time to 'spice things up a bit' concerning Tasha's rather simple and dignified nighttime wardrobe.

Jack thought that would prove interesting, and smirked to himself, since he had seen Tasha shop before. She always had a list or something already in mind before she went, not being much of a window shopper, save for art and quilting stores. When it came to clothes, simple timeless comfort always won over fashion.

Time was in a battle with itself, taking too long for Tasha and Manny to join them. Yet it was ticking by swiftly once the auditorium doors opened.

Nate, standing next to Nick at the tall table, looked toward the front entry doors when Nick's low whistle made everyone's gaze follow his. Manny held the door for a lagging Tasha, but no one was sure which person he was whistling at as the sound lamely died off in the din of the surrounding crowds. Jack caught Nate's befuddled and comedic expression with a side glance as he set his empty whiskey glass down on a nearby table.

Nate didn't break his line of sight as he slightly turned his head to ask his wife, just behind him socializing with Hank and his wife, "Nora, honey...did you loan out your *entire* supply of Christmas wrapping paper to Manny?"

"No, hon, why would you *ever* ask that?" she asked, still nursing her glass of red wine, puzzled over his question as she turned around to look at what he was staring at. "Oh...oh my..." Rarely was Nora at a loss for words, ever the quick-witted 'lady' with exquisite conversational skills. She took a long, distracted sip instead, to keep whatever response—or lack of one—at bay. That caused Jack to raise an inquisitive eyebrow and finally allow himself to look toward the entrance.

"Well, I think you better check your storage room at home when we get back, honey. I think you're missing a few rolls."

Nora elbowed him to behave. Nate's deadpan comment caused Nick to finally lose control of his mirth, with Sam quickly following suit—but trying to be more polite about it after catching Jarvis's annoyed look.

Jack could not help it when he caught the loud display walking up to them. The material of Manny's evening jacket was the embodiment of blazingly bright Christmas wrapping paper. His bow tie clashed with the colorful motif of his jacket. Thankfully, Manny's soft pink shirt and dark navy pants did not add to the outrageous display of finery. However, the multi-colored jacket-and-tie combination did outshine his metallic dress shoes.

"Damn, Jarvis, no offense, but I think your date is a walking Christmas tree," Nick said softly so as not to let their boss overhear them, yet knowing that Jack had heard him by the way his shoulders were shaking from his quiet laughter.

Jarvis shot him a heated look, not entirely sure if he was madder at his roommate or at Nick. Sam pinched his brow in his attempt to control his mirth before dropping his hands back to his hips in an assured stance behind Jack, Nate, and Nora.

"He's just missing the string of lights," Sam added.

"He don't need any mo' lights, guys…he's blinding enough!" snorted Hank.

"I'm not sure I'll be able to concentrate on the show if he sits near me or within my view," commented Sybil, Hank's wife.

"Is he applying for a position as the airport's rotating beacon? If he is…he's got it. I always thought the airport needed a new one," Hank jested, chuckling.

The snickering continued among them all.

"At least he dressed up for the occasion," Jarvis encouraged, trying to be as supportive as he could, given the circumstances.

"Which one? Christmas pageant or the theater's show?" Sam countered.

The laughter subsided as Tasha caught up to Manny, grabbing ahold of his proffered elbow, still a step behind him as if she were using him as a human shield, though she was nearly a head taller. Manny, in his hurry, nearly dragged her. She was unused to walking in high heels, her long legs reminding Jack of a young gangly moose stepping out into the wilderness without its mother for the first time. He wondered how she kept her limbs from tangling when she walked.

Those legs, though, ended at the hem of her short navy-blue velvet dress, studded with a few matching stones that helped make the rest of her shimmer brightly, though not necessary, given that the cold air had made her fair skin blush and pale hair fluff naturally with loose tendrils framing her angelic face.

Tasha looked like the season's quiet angels of hope compared to Manny's ruckus of a holiday party drunkard.

Nora sidled up to Jack, catching his eye. "So…what do you think?"

Jack raised an eyebrow at her as Nora chinned over to Tasha. He did not answer, but turned to look where Manny had finally superseded Tasha's gait, dropping her hand from his elbow in his rush to greet Jarvis, who was holding out

Manny's drink.

Jack didn't hear anything else as his body strode on its own accord to the invisible, irresistible force emanating from Tasha. The blue velvet dress accented every part of her that made her more than different from the rest of their crew. Her skin glowed in contrast to the fabric, where it generously exposed her neck, upper chest, and part of her shoulders. If the crew had been mollified into accepting her as just one of them, as the 'little sis' of their group, then her evening attire would make it impossible for them to ignore the woman who was a part of their team.

When Tasha cleaned up, she was an entirely different person. Tasha was that out-of-your-league woman that would make even most playboys swallow hard at the sight of her. Whether he was imagining it or not, he was certain that every male in the house had stopped long enough to note this dazzling woman. His protective nature nearly caused him to run to her, using his body to shield her from the public's gaze as he joined her.

Jack stopped short of her in his hypnotized state, offering her his elbow, his other hand taking the coat she had taken off once inside the building. He paused at the coat check, finally telling her, "You look…nice, Tasha." He grabbed the ticket stub given to him, adding softly, "Really nice."

He not only felt her release a bated breath but saw her deflate as if she was relieved, making him cock his head. "Are you all right?"

She nodded her head, the few tendrils bouncing around her flushed face making her even more enchanting. "Yeah." She inhaled and exhaled just as quickly. "Yes." Her eyes scanned their surroundings before meeting his, as she looked back at him nearly level with his face in her high heels. He was not sure if it was just out of habit from her military training of being aware of her surroundings, or if she was fretting over something.

Directing them toward their group, Jack got in close enough not only to note, but inhale her intoxicating scent. He nearly lost his focus, again stopping them, and turning to her again. "Then why are you nervous?"

"Nervous?" Her face snapped up. "No…no, not nervous, just don't like sticking out in a crowd with a dress like this." She anxiously smoothed the front of her dress.

"Well, you have no worries there when you were preceded by the 'comic relief,'" he reminded her, indicating to Manny, who was standing by Jarvis.

She stifled a quick laugh with her long-fingered hands, hiding her beguiling smile with perfectly manicured French, white-tipped nails. But that smile wavered momentarily, causing Jack to hurriedly amend his statement. "A comic with an entirely gorgeous side-show gal."

"A side show?"

He sighed heavily, knowing that his additional statement had made his comment worse. In the past few weeks since her parents had left, he had grown familiar with her inner nuances. He finally decided to make it clear that she was never a 'side show' in his world, since the day she had entered it. He pulled a small box from his jacket's interior pocket and opened it, his offering causing her to do a double-take when she realized it was a ring.

He offered her the diamond and black opal ring that she had taken a liking to earlier that day in a local craft jeweler's store when they had decided to go walk around the local shops that morning. He was certain she had talked herself out of it because of its expense, saying, "it's too opulent for my lifestyle," thus reverently putting it back into the jeweler's hand with a heavy sigh after having tried it on. She had admired it with her hand flexed up, stretched out at arm's length, letting the stones sparkle under the store's lights. When she moved on to another part of the store, where she became entranced with a large glass-topped coffee table allowing her to view the innards of the pedestal consisting of half of a large amethyst geode, Jack told the jeweler to hold it, silently giving him his credit card, eyeing him sternly for the secrecy and telling him he would be back shortly.

Her hand's swift movements were her only signs of her surprise. Tasha was not given to gushing noisily. She had reached out and then hesitated, unsure if she should accept it or not. He offered it again, insisting. She shook her head tentatively no, her mouth covered by her hand.

She was not expecting this. But he had no doubts that he could no longer live without her. She had turned out not only to be a great cabinmate, but a terrific co-worker, a pilot, a beloved crew member, and his mate—his other goal in life. A wife that would work by his side. He wanted marriage.

"Tasha…" he began, exhaling heavily, not realizing he had been holding his breath. Jack began dropping to one knee, but Tasha's arms shot out, trying to keep him standing, but his sheer size and weight compared to her frame and dress attire had made it impossible.

"…What are you doing? No…wait…not here!" she said, struggling with him.

"Why not here?" he asked, his knee making contact with the floor.

"Be…because…Jack, no…"

"No?" he questioned, his voice huskier, at first not certain, but…he knew her. It was the grand gesture in public that was killing her, never liking the limelight. He moved to get up after he smirked at the thought.

"Yes!" she said, stopping him in mid-rise at her vehemently hissed answer.

"Yes?"

"No!" She abruptly realized his confusion. "I mean, yes…just not…" She looked around them. "Just not here, *please*!" she pleaded, her hand gesturing for him to stand up, yet still not taking the ring.

"So, which is it?" Jack asked, cocking a half smile, making sure to hold his mid-position stance, although it was severely testing his balance and his knees, his leg muscles quivering in suspense.

"Jack!"

"Yes?"

"Come on, work with me here!" she whispered harshly.

His muscles spoke for him. "You know the suspense is beginning to kill me—"

"Yes, yes…Just stand up!"

"I just want you—"

"Jack, YES!" she interrupted, tapping a twitterpated foot, her embarrassment flushing her face.

"—to be sure," he finished.

"Yeah." She nodded at him diminutively, throwing sideways glances as he stood up completely, in fact stretching taller to alleviate the aches in his leg muscles. Tasha's face was red from the embarrassment. Jack was about to say something, but she was lithe enough to answer him. "Yes. I said yes."

It made him laugh. His happiness rushed through his body. It was an awkward moment when he realized she still had not taken the ring. He immediately corrected the situation by slipping the ring on her left ring finger and kissing her forehead, telling her, "Later, then." He could feel the small shiver on her back where his other hand protectively encircled her and led her to their awaiting group, standing there the entire time watching him bare it all. "Looks like I just made you the main star," he commented near her ear, at the same time giving the group a *behave yourself* look so as not to embarrass her further.

"Congratulations, son," Nate grunted like an endearing father, patting Jack's shoulder. "About time. Hopefully, she will remember it this time around," he said, joking quietly as the two of them herded their small group into their seating section.

Jack took the saved seat between Nora and Tasha, with Nate sitting on Nora's far side, joining Hank and his wife, Sybil. The rest of them had seats in the row in front of them in the balcony area. The show was an enjoyable flight line comedy called *Cesspool Aviation*. However, his attention kept being drawn to Tasha sitting next to him, her long, stocking-covered legs beckoning his eyes to the hem of her dress and then back down the length of them to her beautiful feet tucked in a matching pair of blue velvet pumps. Whenever she looked at him, catching him a few times, he felt like a pervert, then a jealous lover, but realized it was Manny who had helped her shop and dress her like the Nordic goddess she embodied. She was more fetching than he could ever have imagined, and he could not wait until they were alone.

The night ended up being surprisingly incredible. At first, like the rest of the crew, she thought it would be a tortuous journey as it was a mandatory 'group fun night.' She wondered what had possessed Nora and Nate to take their crew up to Anchorage and enjoy a night at the theater.

The new play was an aviation comedy, and it was part of their Christmas bonuses for the extra hard work the crew had put in during the weeks between Thanksgiving and Christmas. Nora explained their reasoning behind taking everyone to the event to most of them during the flight. Of course, the only two not flying with them and carrying any excess luggage in the car were Hank and his wife. He went, but he drove there instead and met them at the airport to pick them up when they landed.

After months of reining in her more emotional side, hiding behind a daily practical side, Tasha finally let her romantic side out. Manny convinced her to buy the little racy blue velvet dress by tearing it out of her hand after she had tried it on, after what seemed like an endless merry-go-round of evening dresses that she would never be caught dead wearing. She sighed, exhausted from their afternoon shopping spree. Tasha felt it was not the right dress, but she gave up arguing with Señor Flamboyant. He did know fashion, she gave him credit on that aspect, in addition to being a top-notch artist.

Just when she thought they were done, he had dragged her to a shoe store, finding matching pumps and hosiery. Manny was right, the heavy-weight hosiery did keep her legs warm in the skimpy dress. Finally, he ordered her to take a nap, shower, and get dressed in the next two hours, handing her two cut cucumbers, clearly stolen from the large water dispenser in the hotel's lobby, to be placed on top of her eyelids as she slept, promising her he would be back for her since he was not finished with her.

What more could he possibly want to do with me to help dress up for the night? she wondered.

It turned out that he found a hairstylist to coif her hair while he applied makeup that he had bought—*or God forbid*, she thought, closing her eyes against the thought, *his very own*. Manny was like a zealous teenager helping a dowdy friend on prom night. She kept warning him that the last thing she needed was to look like she was some 'street tramp.' He just scoffed at her, saying, "*Nunca, señorita, nunca.*"

What made them almost late was him getting ready. As she stood waiting outside his room, she nearly jumped in horrid surprise when he met her in his evening attire. The bright colors bowled her over. Her only 'nice' comment to him was a question: "Are you *sure* you're ready?" Ever eager, Manny nodded affirmatively, racing to the hotel's elevators.

Tasha hoped no one would notice her skimpy attire as she took in a calming breath, letting all the tension out of her body in one long exhale. Manny already had a cab waiting. In his exuberance to get to their group, Tasha found herself paying the driver at the end of the trip and bringing up the rear as Manny held open the convention center's door for her.

Once inside, the brightness of the interior overwhelmed her, along with the throngs of people after months of small-town living and flying to even smaller towns than Seward. It looked like Alaska's entire population had shown up for the event. She wondered if they would find their group. But Manny did, faster than she could scan the crowd, offering her a last-minute elbow and then nearly dragging her in his hurry to join their group.

Halfway, Manny dropped her hand, walking faster than she could in her heels. She was grateful when she looked up, seeing Jack, looking incredibly dashing in his suit jacket and tie, walking toward her and taking her coat to have it checked at the coat counter. She couldn't take her eyes off him. To keep from staring, she continually scanned past their personal space. It was the first time she had ever seen him dressed in evening attire, which made her pulse quicken. She tried more deep breathing, only to release a bated breath. But his comment of 'being nervous' pulled her out of her inner battle with her nerves. Being in large crowds was not her preferred element. She was grateful for Jack's protective presence.

He escorted her the rest of the way to the second story of the auditorium only to stop, blocking her way. She was too busy with reining in her nerves, not listening to Jack at first, and then hearing herself being referred to as the 'side show.' She would not have minded the reference, normally. But when would she ever be the main attraction in his world? He was always busy with work, and when at home he was either sleeping or off in his basement office working on his grandiose goal of expanding Big Raven's business. Her thoughts must have shown clearly, as she watched him sigh heavily and pull something from inside his suit jacket.

Thinking it was a corsage, she relaxed. Instead, it was the ring she had fallen in love with earlier that day. Tasha did not expect that, nor could she react fast enough to stop him from going down on one knee in front of her in public, hurling her into panic mode, the two of them in an obvious time-worn ritual that she never expected in her lifetime. At least…at least, not with anyone she had been smitten over.

In her panic from her embarrassment, she tried to make him understand that she didn't want an audience. It was a wasted effort when she caught their group's interested gaze on them, now that Manny had joined their ranks, sipping his piña colada. The guys had had their fun with him by now, most of them smiling, laughter lingering in the air around them. She quickly averted her gaze, focusing on the giant man on his knee in front of her. Never had she been so swept away in such confusion with time being of the essence.

She agreed, just to get him to stand up, but he was making it difficult for her by questioning everything coming out of her mouth in the momentary chaos. Embarrassed, she finally convinced him with her answer, letting him slip the ring on her finger.

Her face flushed and she bowed her head so as not to look anyone in the eye. It must have worked, because no one made a commotion over what they had witnessed, but the banter would come sooner or later. It was a given.

It was Nora who quietly fussed over her, grabbing her left hand to admire the engagement ring, congratulating her and Jack as they took their seats with Hank and his wife leading the way in their assigned row, leaving open seats for Nate and Jack, who brought up the rear of the large group.

The comedy was wonderful, although she often sensed Jack watching her more than the show, catching him staring at her, smiling. She smiled back, giving his hand, already covering hers on the armrest, an assuring squeeze.

After the show, the group decided to walk the few blocks back to the hotel. Everyone was in a good mood, each of the crew grouping to their cabinmates, their conversation bantering back and forth between all of them. A few times, the guys would stop and give a short quick chase when a comment was too much about something. Jack and Tasha, silent and listening to all of them, walked in the 'mature section' of their group with Nora and Nate and Hank and Sybil, just behind the guys.

As their group dispersed to their own rooms, Jack opened their door. The irony was that the room had two queen-sized beds, compared to the one king-size bedroom they had shared in Anchorage together only six months earlier when she had first arrived in Alaska.

Jack, being the gentleman, let her go in first. When she turned around to ask him about that evening's sudden proposal being 'for real,' his answer was upon her mouth before she could ask as he pushed her up against the wall and gave her a long, passionate kiss that made her melt. The typical action that was ingrained in his nature still caught her off guard after a night of his genteel civility.

She gave in, letting pure joy envelop her body and soul. Unable to register the swiftness of his disembogued passion, drowning her in his need, she wondered if she had died and gone to heaven.

Hours later, sighing happily, Tasha snuggled up against Jack in one of the beds. She moved her left hand where she could see her newest treasure, sparkling in the sliver of light that slipped through the window from the streetlights outside. She smiled as she felt his whiskers caress the back of her neck, his breath warm against the back of her head, at first not hearing what he mumbled.

"Come again?" she asked quietly, turning enough to stroke his profile, only to have his hand catch hers when she reached his neckline. She turned the rest of the way to be flat on her back when Jack took her hand, looking at the ring he had bought her.

"Any regrets, Mrs. Lassiter?" he asked before kissing her on her temple.

She pursed her lips in contemplation, causing him to stop in his study of her ring finger to look back at her in concern, making her break into a big smile at him. "Not really. The journey started out rough...You certainly know how to give a gal a hard time...but, I think"—she made a moue—"it's been worth it."

"I guess I'll have to spend the rest of my life trying to make it up to you then," he told her huskily as he shifted himself over her form.

Tasha raised up to cup the sides of his face, giving him another sultry kiss. Jack groaned, pulling her to him, rolling them into another fun round.

CHAPTER TWENTY-FOUR

The C-47 interior's pressure changed as Jack closed and locked the main entry door. The Angelina's cockpit wiggled at the weight of Jack jumping into his pilot seat. "Everything set?"

"Almost," Tasha said, flipping a few more breakers from where she sat buckled in.

She nodded, then signaled to Hank outside that they were ready to start the engine. Jack went through the already memorized motions as Tasha went through the start-up checklist as backup verification.

It was late January, and watching Hank, outside in the elements, bundled up against the mid-morning darkness, made her shudder sympathetically in her seat. It was snowing lightly, one of the numerous days of just plain gray overcast skies and flurries. Even the harbor had partially frozen over with the more stable frigid temperatures.

The crew finally got their downtime and were working a bare minimum of three days a week. They only flew when necessary during the more frozen 'drier' times, and only to the outlying villages and airport stations to bring in basic supplies for the oil companies in the surrounding areas.

The imperfect flying weather was not icy nor gusty, but had the conditions that she needed to continue to practice in, along with gaining flight hours in the old twin-engine cargo plane. Jack decided to give Nick and Sam some time off since they flew a majority of the inclement weather flights over the winter months, pulling the lion's share of the work for the company until more of them were up to par, and Nate and Jack could feel comfortable with the less experienced of their crew.

Although Jack had nearly as many hours as Nick or Sam, he did not have the years of exposure to flying that either one of them had racked up. Jack had only been flying for about six years, with only the last two years learning it as thoroughly as he had. He took training—even his own training—seriously, and told Tasha he was always learning something about flying each day. Seeing her hesitation at his comment, he said, "Never be over-confident. It'll catch you off guard when you least expect it and kill you." He added with a smile, "Mother Nature will always win. Never try her patience."

"You may want to remind Nick about that statement," she told him.

Jack smiled at her. "Him"—he scoffed some—"I don't worry about too much, even though he comes off very cocky. That guy has been flying since he was fifteen years old."

"So, do you think it's a gift or that everyone has to constantly practice like me?" She never felt secure in learning fast enough to be ever truly proficient.

Jack mulled it over before answering her. "Everyone should practice, including those born with a gift for flying, Tasha."

"So Nick has the gift for it?" she asked, knowing in her gut that Nick, and even Sam, seemed to have it easier when it came to flying any aircraft so effortlessly.

"He has the aptitude for it, but I still see to it that he practices, but only with me or Nate. I don't want to deflate the man's ego. I sometimes think it's one of the reasons he stays up in the air so easily." He flashed his white teeth in his broad grin, his one dimple showing, neither denying nor supporting the naturally talented.

Tasha scanned the instrument panel before confirming it with the handheld GPS flight pad. It was her way of double-checking herself that all was matching with the instruments on the panel.

"You're unusually quiet, Tasha," Jack commented over the headsets once they were airborne.

"Just concentrating on the instrument panel. Flying over these mountains in these conditions usually makes me anxious. I think I prefer VFR conditions."

"We all do, Tasha. Who doesn't want to see the views?" he said, his hand resting easily on the throttles after they had gained the altitude necessary to clear the terrain to the northwest.

"You may want to adjust your heading more to the west by five degrees. I think the winds are stronger than reported at this altitude."

"Good...always keep me on the straight and narrow." She was not sure if he was meaning more than just their course.

They broke out of the cloud blanket at 7,550 feet and enjoyed the pinks and reds of the first morning's light low on the horizon. The sun's colors osculated certain cloud tops below them in its attempt to reflect its distant greeting.

They made McGrath within two hours, give or take a couple of minutes, against a forty-five-mile-per-hour headwind. However, by the time ground personnel unloaded the prior aircraft of its cargo, there was bad weather inbound. Jack, watching the western horizon and seeing the darker clouds building, decided to call it a day. He grabbed their flight bags, and suggested bunking in the pilots' quarters for the evening to wait it out.

"Good choice," said another pilot that had overheard them.

He said he had come in about an hour before them from Unalakleet. "Folks back home said the snow is coming down thick and the winds have picked up," he said, chewing on his jerky stick. "Said blizzard conditions, but then our town is right on the coastline."

Thankfully, Jack and Tasha had arrived earlier than most of the pilots there and Jack talked with the airport manager about having the Angelina refueled and then stored inside the main hangar with some of the other aircraft until the storm passed.

"That's going to be a pretty penny for Big Raven, Jack," Tasha noted.

"Trust me, it's worth it for this ol' gal." Neither of them wanted to deal with an older aircraft's finicky disposition after a night in the sub-zero temperatures, along with new layers of snow. "Besides, this is Nate's personal baby and best cargo hauler. She's our main money-maker."

At that Tasha raised an eyebrow. "I thought Lucy, the Grand Caravan, was his original baby."

"Actually, originally it was a Piper Cub. He traded it in for Lucy, and from that point on any plane that made him the most money automatically became the 'baby' of the Raven's fleet."

"Makes sense," Tasha said, both making their way through the various parked aircraft and then on down a long corridor. She let Jack lead the way since he was familiar with the airport.

"I notice that Nick and Sam like the Otter and the two Beavers," she said, but wanted to know if Jack had a personal favorite. "Do you have a favorite?"

He smiled. "I prefer Lucy," he said, meaning the Grand Caravan out in the harbor. "Until I ran across a new one, but she isn't a bird." He gestured to her.

"Why the Caravan?" she asked, but unfortunately they were interrupted.

"Hey Jack, who you got there?" A slender man matching Jack's six-four frame in a heavy winter coat came to greet them.

Tasha could smell the crisp, cold air coming off his coat and knew that he had just been outside.

"By the way, your aircraft is fueled and being towed into the hangar behind you as requested," he quickly added, not waiting on Jack to introduce her to him and pointing with his pencil before making a quick note on his clipboard.

"Thanks, Eric."

The two men happily clasped hands in greeting.

"How's Nate and the rest of your guys? I haven't seen much of you nor your crew this year. Haven't gotten many orders this way?"

"Not this year. I gotta work on securing more accounts here. However, Anchorage has us beat, with some of the newer and smaller aviation groups out there being able to airlift for less."

"Ah, not to worry. I'll keep spreading the word for you and Black Raven. You know most of these newer companies have a tendency not to last longer than a year or so. Nate's been at this for…what…how long? Ten, fifteen years?"

"Yeah, about fifteen, and hope to keep it that way, if not growing more. But Seward needs to start thinking about revitalizing our 'sinking airport.' I'm amazed that we can still do business when the spring flooding hits."

"Flooding?" Tasha asked in surprise.

Eric turned to her and smiled. "Okay…you are definitely new." He extended his hand to give her a warm welcome handshake.

Jack introduced Eric to Tasha. "This is the McGrath airport manager, Eric Stenson."

"Tasha, sir," she said as she took his hand. His smile and warm personality put her at ease, although she could tell he was uptight when it came to his job and keeping things under control, especially given the inclement weather coming soon.

"Sir? Oh my, I haven't been called 'sir' since leaving the Coast Guard." Eric smiled warmly at her. "Prior military?"

Tasha cocked her head in shock. Most would never think that women like her would have thought of serving.

"You must be fresh out," Eric added wryly. "Your stance, the other arm behind your back"—he pointed at her, and then indicated beneath his own chin—"your head held high."

Tasha blushed.

"Please don't tell me you still make squares," Eric jested.

"Squares?"

"It's a Marine thing," Jack expounded.

Eric pivoted on his foot in either direction in a short demonstrative militant walk, making her laugh when he told her, "Jack was still doing it when I first met him two years ago." Eric gave Jack a soft chuck to his shoulder. "But yeah, we finally broke him. Not as uptight as he used to be. Before you know it, he'll be wearing hippie clothing and have hair and a beard this long." Eric indicated to his gut.

"Speaking of which…" Eric inspected Jack, leaning forward, grabbing at his own chin. "Did you get a new look on the hair department, Jack?"

"Let's just say she wouldn't put up with it on the first day we met," Jack said, indicating Tasha.

"Wow! You got him to cut his beard and hair? I didn't think it was possible to convince him to do anything. Jack here can make a jackass look agreeable."

His comment sent Tasha into a fit of laughter.

"More like she cut half of my beard off."

Eric cocked an expectant smile and Jack waved a dismissive hand. "A long story, Eric."

"Ah, looks like we got all night with this incoming blizzard. But first I have to get the rest of the pilots that have landed settled in, and a few more planes inside that will be landing shortly." Then he turned to Tasha. "Nice to meet you, but before I go, I have to ask: which branch?"

"Army."

Then back to Jack, he said, "The Army's gotten a lot tougher than I gave them credit for…especially if she got you to cut your beard." Taking his leave, he said over his shoulder, "My hat is off to you." Eric chuckled at Tasha.

"Squares?" She cocked a half smile at Jack as she tried to visualize him doing 'squares.'

Jack took a few of the decisive military steps before executing a perfect corner at the next door just a few steps from them, opening the door to the pilots' sleeping quarters.

"Oh my, you haven't lost that," she admitted, walking over to him where he held the door for her.

"Never will, either," he said as she went past him into a large military-styled sleeping quarters filled with bunk beds and single beds, reminiscent of basic training.

"Semper Fi," she said under her breath, walking further into the room.

"Not the best hotel, but free," he added as his arm snaked around her waist, pulling her gently to him to give her a bear hug before deftly swinging their bags onto the lower bunk at the far side of the room.

Feeling like a kid, Tasha told him, "I claim the top bunk."

"I was thinking you would have wanted the bottom, since I'm taller. But then, you seem to have a preference—" Tasha didn't let him go there, giving him a light back-handed wallop to his gut, telling him to "behave." Jack chuckled.

"The restrooms are down the hall further, and then there are more out in the main hangar along the back wall." He sighed. "Otherwise, make yourself comfortable. It looks like we will be here for the night." Indicating with his thumb to the door, he said, "I'm going to go make a call to Big Raven to check in."

"Why not here?"

"Because cell reception isn't good in here," he said. Then, giving her a mischievous grin, he added, "and two, I can't concentrate on work when you are near me."

"Sounds like a personal problem to me." She smiled cockishly. "The others don't seem to have that problem with me," she told Jack off-handedly, referring to her co-workers, her thumb awakening her phone's screen.

Jack didn't answer, forcing her to look up and find him scowling.

"I figured all this time you were 'impervious' to my charms," she teased him with a minute wiggle of her derrière as she turned to clamber up to the top bunk, giving him her biggest smile.

Jack nabbed her before she could ascend any further, growling in her ear and then kissing the side of her head, giving her another bear hug she could easily have snuggled into before he shoved her away from him, spying more pilots about to enter the room. He watched them through the large window opening between the two darkening curtains that hung heavily on each side of the glass, looking out onto the hallway.

"I've got to stop." He shoved her gently to the bunkbed as the men came inside the massive bunkroom, jabbering amongst themselves.

Neither of them wanted to be considered an 'item' while on the job. Tasha knew how important it was to Jack to keep a professional image for Black Raven Aviation.

"Well then, go to it while I stay here. It'll be terrific to play a few games on my phone and catch up on some reading. A nap sounds good too."

He hesitated, and she gave him a dismissing wave once she was on the top bunk with her cell phone in hand. "I'll be fine, Jack," she encouraged him to go. "I'll help unload the plane when you get back."

"Nah, Eric's seen to the cargo getting unloaded. So rest here for a couple of hours. Eric will need me to verify and sign paperwork. I'll meet you here later."

She watched Jack's backside as he took his leave, and as he nodded a tentative greeting to the other pilots on his way out the door.

"All done here, Jack," said Eric, handing him a clipboard with paperwork to sign as the last of the power assist carts left with the rest of the cargo.

Jack took a last sweeping look at Angelina's empty interior before shutting the door and signing all the necessary forms.

Jack handed him the clipboard as he spied another familiar pilot, Dirk Bane. He had once been a Black Raven employee before Jack had joined the small company. Though he never worked with the man, Jack knew of the man and the negative tales that preceded him. Jack had only encountered him a few times. Those few encounters usually left Jack with his hackles instinctively raised.

"Ahhh…just great," Eric said sarcastically under his breath when he saw Dirk coming toward them. "Of all nights to have a thorn in my side," he commented as he turned to greet Dirk, hoping to quickly get rid of him.

Eric plastered a smile on his face. "Whatcha need, Dirk?"

Dirk noted Jack with those venomous dark eyes, not voicing a verbal greeting. He thumbed toward the outside of the hangar. "Need your guys to help unload some cargo before the storm hits." His voice was tainted from one too many cigarettes and drinks over the years.

"Okay, I have you next after True Star's bird is done. Might want to give them a little bit of time, with the extra birds coming in trying to beat the storm system."

"Sure—hopefully they can get to it before the snow falls. Got stuff that can't get wet," he said absently, pulling on his wispy thin goatee, although the rest of his face hadn't seen a razor for at least three or four days, his nails thick and yellowish with nicotine stains. He looked past Eric at Jack, sizing him up, before asking Eric another question. "You got any room for my bird tonight?"

"You want to hangar your bird?" It wasn't Dirk's style to request extra care with his bird. Normally, this man didn't care what he did with his owner's equipment. The only people who would employ Dirk were the smaller desperate businesses that were unable to afford most licensed pilots. Since the clash with Nate, he had become blackballed amongst many in the aviation community.

Eric lifted a few pages on his clipboard, checking, before telling him he might have some space left inside if they could just rearrange some of the current aircraft.

"Good," grunted a cantankerous Dirk. "Just be sure not to park my airplane next to this piece of junk." He chinned to the Angelina just past Jack. Dirk wanted to start a fight, where Jack just stood, his legs shoulder-width apart, arms folded over his chest, unbothered, although he kept Dirk in his sight, each of them the same height and build, literally pound for pound. The differences between them were the pride in upkeep in hygiene and their altruistic attitudes. "Don't need to have my aircraft parked near a piece of scrap metal."

Eric tried to assure him, "I'll do my best, Dirk, but cannot promise anything. There are other aircraft that have reserved a place inside already. Otherwise, if there's no space but near here, then I'll be sure to leave yours outside then." Eric gave him a big, bogus, customer service smile.

Dirk held Jack's gaze a little longer, neither caving in to the other.

"Sure, whatever." He gave Eric a dismissing hand wave as he turned his back on them to go to the small hangar door.

Eric exhaled heavily once Dirk was out of earshot. "Hate dealing with him." He turned back to Jack. "I'm surprised he's still flying, given that he was caught intoxicated while attempting to start an aircraft a few months back. Seems like he only got a slap on the wrist. Six months before that, Dirk was caught borrowing the owner's aircraft for his own personal purposes."

Jack raised an eyebrow at this new piece of information, but was not entirely surprised. He had known about Dirk's disservice to Nate and Black Raven Aviation. They had never caught Dirk on the drug trafficking back then, but they had been able to catch him on the 'extra side business' of supplying extra 'non-inventoried cargo' for which Dirk had pocketed the extra money. As soon as they had found out and turned him in with the proof, Nora and Nate had spent weeks trying to sort out the invoices and getting them corrected with their clients at the time.

"I better get going to check on the next aircraft." Eric said as his hip radio chirped, announcing another arrival and requesting ground crew help.

Jack turned back to the Angelina, where he decided to lock the side door. "Do you need the key, Eric?"

"Nope, I already have a copy from prior. It's best you hold on to yours this time. I know where I can find you if we need to move the Angelina later tonight. But I doubt it—I have every intent on leaving Dirk's plane outside to freeze tonight." Eric smiled, and then added, "Hey, go take Tasha out to eat at our 'finest' diner here at the hangar."

"It's your only diner," joked Jack, knowing about the hangar's mini cafeteria. It was not too horrible, but it beat going out into the weather to the nearest diner a few blocks down.

"On second thought, it might not be a good idea. Tasha may never eat here again," Eric reconsidered. "I think tonight its some sort of unidentifiable goulash." Then, he added, "I'll try to catch up with you two later, if you don't mind me joining you two."

"Sure," agreed Jack. "Just no more stories about me. I'm trying to make a good impression."

Eric cheekily grinned, knowing better.

Jack found Tasha asleep on the upper bunk, her back up against the wall, still sitting up. Her phone had dropped from her hands and was resting on top of her thighs, the screen dark. He gently nudged her awake, asking if she was hungry.

She stretched her arms as she yawned herself awake. "Are you kidding me? I'm famished. Even my energy bar didn't tide me over."

He smiled at her. "I figured it wouldn't." He helped her down from her perch. "McGrath does have a small cafeteria that is open. It's nothing like your home cooking, but it will do for now and I'm not sure if there'll be enough with the extra planes deciding to land and stay overnight during the blizzard."

"Blizzard?" she asked, surprised as he led the way between the bunk beds after leaving their flight bags on both beds, indicating to others that their bunk bed was taken.

"Yeah, the weather was deteriorating pretty quickly when I checked with the Flight Service Station a few hours ago. It's going to get nasty for about a day or so. We might as well hunker down."

"Not bad, I suppose. I could use the downtime." Tasha followed him to the hangar's café. It was easy to find, given the strong coffee aroma permeating the air. They had gone past a room that had a pool table, foosball table, plenty of chairs, and a few coffee tables strewn with old magazines, and a large flat-screened TV that had news images flashing across the screen on the far wall.

"If you don't like anything in the cafeteria, we could always make the walk to the local diner nearby."

"I'll tough it out here," she said, not liking the idea of having to walk outside in whiteout conditions.

Their meal was simple, keeping to the hot sandwiches and soup. Then they played a few rounds of Uno after Jack found a pack of cards on another table. Jack was ruthless again, winning three out of four games on her.

"Somehow I think you cheat," she told him as she shuffled the deck and then put the cards away in their case.

"Nope, it's just strategy. You have to think ahead a few plays with the cards you get. Never get impatient. You always have to be planning ahead."

"You don't like surprises, do you?" she asked, cocking a smile at him.

"Not entirely."

"Have you ever just done something on a whim? Ever in your life?" She placed her chin on her upturned hand, her elbow resting on the table, her other hand rotating the pack of cards on each of its pointy sides of the box. "Even once?" she asked when he didn't answer her right away. "You've got to *live* a little, especially when it comes to fun, Jack."

She sat back in her chair to stretch and then to rest against the chair's backing. He kept looking at something behind her, making her turn her head enough to look over her shoulder.

A large and not-so-pleasant-looking man was striding toward their direction, a sickening grin spreading over his scruffy-looking face. Turning her head back to him, she saw Jack's body stiffen, going to full alert. It was clear that he did not like this 'bush pilot.'

Tasha was certain he was just heading past them to the food bar when she felt a heavy 'paw' land on her shoulder, gripping it rather painfully, as the man came around their table, releasing her and coming to a stop adjacent to them both. The stale bar air surrounding the man finally assailed her nose and she leaned away to avoid inhaling the stench of old cigarette smoke. She backed opposite of where he stood and as far away as the back of her chair could let her.

"Wow, Jack! How did you entice this piece of sweet cherry pie into sharing your table?" the man asked, giving her a long, lewd glance. Without giving Jack a chance to answer, he went on. "Honey, if you want a real good time, I'm a much better choice than Jack here." He patted Jack's shoulder only once before Jack deflected his next advance with a hand, making it clear he was not welcome. He continued as he looked at Jack. "I can sure offer you some more fun than this young buck can."

Then to her, he said, "Just how high would you like to go?"

Tasha was rendered speechless, unsure of what to make of the nasty brazen man, a smile full of yellow stained teeth in front of her.

"Leave her alone, Dirk. Trust me, you're not her type," Jack said, crossing his arms, his eyes not leaving Tasha's, yet very much aware of Dirk's movements.

"Well, let me just ask her. I mean there is no way a woman would have dated you unless you *paid* her. Are you one of those girls, honey?"

"That's Lazar, not 'honey.' I tend to prefer aircraft over men. And last, no man could ever afford me, especially you, Mr...." The man did not even warrant the polite title, in Tasha's book.

"Just call me Dirk." His eyes appreciatively took her body in, making her skin crawl.

"Ah, Dirk, are you usually a jerk?" She crossed her arms, but it was more for defense.

"You've got a saucy one here, Jack." His smile became cockier at Tasha. "I like *this* one." Dirk gave her a wink as he took his leave of them. "I'll see you soon enough, sweet cherry pie."

She rolled her eyes at Jack. "Holy cow, I don't think I've seen a man so full of himself! Hell, he makes Nick look narcissistically modest in comparison!"

Her comment barely broke his scowl.

"Who *is* he, Jack? Do you know him?" she asked him in a lowered voice where she had leaned further over their table.

Jack growled, "Somewhat. Not personally, but I've heard the things he has done."

Tasha titled her head in expectation.

"But it's a long story."

"We've got all night," she reminded him. But his sudden dark mood scared her, and she decided not to push it, opting to lighten him up instead and get him to relax.

"Come on, Jack. I saw a pool table and it is calling our names. Besides, I definitely do not want to be here with two other open chairs at this table when this man decides to help himself to a seat."

At that he smiled and got up with her, and she noted how rigid his body moved, as if he was expecting an enemy attack at any moment.

Since they had eaten early, the pool table was still free. It was here that they were more of an even match in terms of outcome. At one point, as Tasha was lining up a shot, her back to the hallway window, Jack caught Dirk walking by with two other men in tow. Each of them had a beer bottle in their hand. He slowed down enough to make a lewd hand motion regarding Tasha being bent over the table. Jack was grateful that Tasha had worn her jeans and a bulky sweater instead of her usual leggings. However, with Tasha's looks and perfect curvaceous body, she was attractive in anything she wore.

Jack made a motion to go after Dirk, but he ended up laughing and moving on, taking a swig of his beer, not once coming in the room.

"Jack? Jack!" Tasha broke into his dark thoughts. "Are you going to play or forfeit your turn?"

"Yeah," he said, taking a glance at the table, seeing that she had knocked four of her balls into the pockets. It was going to be tough catching up to her on this round. He called the shot and started knocking in a few of his balls, catching up but not entirely giving it an earnest try, being more concerned over Dirk being up to no good.

"Hey, you okay?" she asked, noting his eyes had become dark with malice. She even noted how his 'hackles' had risen on his shoulders, as if she could see the bear's fur rising up for a fight just near the surface of his skin where his forearms were exposed, his muscles flexing.

"Yeah, just tired, and I need to check on a few things." He sighed heavily.

"Like what?" Tasha put her pool stick down on the table. "You want some help?"

"No," he said, not wanting to concern her about Dirk and his despicable habits. "It'll be on the way to Eric's office, and Eric said he had a possible new client for Black Raven to consider." He didn't look at her as he continued, lying to her for her own protection. "I'd like to get some more details before we retire for the night."

It was obvious to Tasha that Jack's mind was elsewhere again. Whenever he got like that, it was usually impossible to get his full attention until whatever it is was had been resolved or scrupulously planned out when it came to the job. She resignedly accepted his answer, although she swore there was something more going on. The trip should have been more relaxing, given the weather situation. There was nothing either of them could really do other than wait it out. The Angelina was hangared for the night. Secondly, back in Seward, there was little maintenance going on and no scheduled flights expected for the next few days. There should have been nothing to be concerned about.

This was a side of Jack she was going to have to accept. It was just as well. She wanted to get some more reading in anyways before retiring for the night. Nodding to him, she said, "Okay, Jack," twirling her engagement ring on her left hand. "Go take care of what you need to do. I'll see you back in the bunk room... soon?"

Noting her uncertainty by the way she played with her ring, he pulled her to him, giving her an assuring hug, and then quickly kissed her on the top of her head. He escorted her to the empty bunk room and saw to it that she had climbed up to the top bunk and was tucked in before leaving her to her reading. He was reluctant to leave her there by herself, but the room was empty and most of the pilots would be eating either at the local bar or at the cafeteria and then most likely hanging out in the game and TV room before retiring for the night. It would be hours before the first of them would show up, and he was certain he would be back before the first of the flyboys showed up to retire for the night.

He took off toward the main part of the hangar for the Angelina. Something instinctively felt afoot. He had nabbed one of the ground crew walking by him in the hallway, asking them if they had seen Dirk and the other two guys.

"Yeah, the assholes came by earlier. They decided to toss their empty beer bottles around like they were playing football in the hangar with all these parked planes, only to break a few of them, leaving a mess for us to pick up. The drunk bastards got broken glass everywhere. So watch your step. I think I got most of it."

Jack nodded. He made his way to the Angelina where she sat there silently resting. He scanned the open hangar space. The area was devoid of workers and pilots. He took a closer look, walking around the bird until he was satisfied that no one had disturbed or altered her. He took a short walk around the other parked aircraft, looking for anything unusual, and noted nothing. His gut instinct telling him that something was not quite right would not let him alone. When his gut did the talking, he could rarely sleep until whatever it was came into focus. Seeing more of the nighttime ground crew wandering in with various paperwork in hand, attending to their work, he decided that he could leave the Angelina on her own for the time being. He walked down the hallway and spied through the window of the sleeping quarters and found Tasha still reading on her phone. He kept moving on, not wanting to disturb her, and moseyed on to the other areas of the building.

He found Eric in his office working late and decided to stop in. Jack knocked on his door. "Working late?"

"Yeah, decided I need to stay this night until the storm passes," Eric replied, flipping a paper over on his desk. "I can't believe how many pilots we got in, and they're crazy enough to walk in this weather to get to the bar just down the street. The winds are increasing was we speak and it's coming down even heavier. We're expecting two to three feet tonight."

Jack walked over to the small window in Eric's office and peered out into the darkness. He could tell it was snowing by the few lights outside the building illuminating the falling powder. He could feel the cold seeping through the old glass window, his breath leaving a steamy fleeting impression as the cold glass quickly regained its original clear look.

"Yeah, this looks like only the beginning of it. Maybe the worst will be through the night. So far it seems quiet and uneventful," Jack said, thumbing back toward the hallway and the hangar. "However, your guys just finished cleaning up broken glass after Dirk and his two merry men went through. Strange that they went through the hangar though"—he made the comment more to himself—"but nothing else seemed amiss with the planes."

Eric didn't look up from his work. "Yeah, you heard about that? I'll be glad to get rid of him. Part of the reason I am staying behind tonight, other than I can use the time to organize and catch up on some paperwork." Finishing, he looked up. "I certainly don't trust the man." He closed the file folder on his desk, sighing as he tilted back in his office chair, stretching his arms above his head. "How come you are not with your new lady? I know I would be if I were you." He smiled at Jack knowingly.

Jack downplayed it for the moment. "I'm just letting her get some downtime to read and play her crazy phone games." Jack had come around from behind Eric's desk after looking out the window and had taken to leaning against the wall facing him as he thought about what to do next, unable to shake the feeling.

"Bookish?"

"Yeah." Jack half-smiled to himself.

"Good pilot?"

"She's getting there. Learns fast. I think we'll have her certified on all the aircraft by next fall. But got to keep her flying and get her confidence built up when it comes to handling the larger aircraft…It takes time." He shrugged a shoulder.

"Where'd did Nate find her?"

Half-laughing, Jack said, "Actually, she found us."

Eric cocked his head.

"We—Nate and I—thought we had hired an electrical guy named Tosh, only to find out Nora had mis-typed her name when we went to approve her for the job. Damn near killed her when she first arrived, although she did do some fairly good damage to my privates and my beard." He pawed his beard line flat.

Eric had put his foot up against the edge of his desk to keep his chair reclined, listening, but then dropped his foot at Jack's last comment. "Oh, do go on…This I would like to hear. You know, I got all night and it's not often we get to hang out together."

Eric opened his desk drawer, pulling out a glass whiskey bottle and two small clear glasses, pouring some of the golden liquid into each cup after offering some to Jack, where he initially declined.

"Aw—come on, Jack, relax. I normally don't drink this unless it's been a super rough week or the rare small celebration." Eric offered the small half-filled cup to Jack and he stepped forward, taking it. "You look like you could use a drink."

"I guess you're right, I'm feeling a bit off tonight. I guess I am letting Dirk get to me more than I should."

"Well, most men would have punched him in the face by now with what he said earlier today."

"I try not to lower myself to his level." Jack took another swallow, the second sending warmth throughout his entire body.

"You got patience, man." Eric sighed tiredly into his glass.

"Tasha told him off earlier this evening when he tried to harass her in the cafeteria."

"Oh yeah?"

"Thought I was going to have to be ready to break up a fight when she put him in his place, calling him 'Dirk the Jerk.'"

Eric laughed. "Wow, she's got spunk!"

"That she does."

"Well, I have one of my guys assigned to keeping an eye out on him for me while continuing his normal duty routines in the hangar. You know…for just in case and for my sake too.

"So, tell me more." Eric picked up the whiskey bottle again, offering Jack another round, but he declined, continuing to nurse the rest of his first drink. "We need to catch up. How's Black Raven doing?"

The two friends spent a couple of hours discussing each other's worlds, enlightening each other. Eric, a good man, had been helpful in the past to Jack when it came to providing a reference for Nate to hire him and always giving them business leads, each of them wanting to expand their careers. Both similar in age, military backgrounds, aviation goals, and physique, other than Eric being thinner than Jack's muscular build. Their conversation eased Jack, allowing him to get things off his chest, and eventually he took a seat in front of the desk.

They were interrupted by one of Eric's personnel needing to file more paperwork. Jack knew the time had gone by a little too long and he decided to retire for the evening, using the interruption as an excuse to take his leave. "I'll catch you in the morning, if you're not too busy or fast asleep," Jack joked with Eric.

Jack returned to the room to find it empty save for Tasha fast asleep in the top bunk. He decided it must be a party night down at the local bar for most of the pilots, considering the night hour. Usually there were more pilots catching up on their sleep. He grabbed his toiletry bag and took off for the restrooms down the hallway. The nightly ablutions would help him calm down now that the whiskey had spread her loving tendrils across the rest of his body.

He took his time, telling his reflection that he was too much of a worrywart at his age and needed to lighten up. Tasha was right: it was time to enjoy life. 'Smell the roses along the way,' as she always reminded him.

As he came out of the restroom, he heard a door click in the long corridor and thought that Eric had just come out of his office, but paused momentarily when he noted Eric's office door was already open, catching a glimpse of Eric standing and talking on his cell phone just inside his office's doorway.

Turning to go back to the bunk room, he noted one of the ground personnel hurriedly coming from the main hangar at the far end of the hall, past the bunk room. Jack stopped just before the door when the employee asked Jack if he had seen Dirk and the other two go past by him. Jack placed his hand on the doorknob, ready to open the door, and replied, "No one's been through here, and I just came out of the restroom that was empty. Maybe check—"

"What the hell—" the employee exclaimed, doing a double-take into the pilots' bunk room's window as he passed by the darkened sleeping quarters.

Jack's body went to full alert, glancing inside and seeing the shadowy figures huddled by Tasha and his bunk, their motions jerky and the sounds of a brawl growing. Jack dropped his toiletry bag, his fighting instincts kicking in and rage lending him speed and strength.

Tasha awakened to something strange. Not remembering her surroundings, she kept her eyes closed, too tired to move, then thinking Jack was back, retiring for the night, giving her a smothering kiss to the point where she could not breathe. He was being way too rough. Her eyelids flew open when her shirt was ripped partially from her body and she caught the smell of alcohol. She was too late realizing it was not Jack, but someone else who had multiple sets of hands on her as they ripped more at her clothes. She lashed out with her arms and legs, struggling.

Her movements only got her punched hard across her temple, another one landing on the opposite side just below her cheekbone, making her see stars in the dark as the pain seared in her head, bolting across her brain.

"Hold her down!" a gruff voice said. Her legs seemed caught up in material while her arms were forcefully held above her head, the weight of her assailant's arm against her forearm, making it feel like the bone in her upper arm was about to snap. "I've got to get ahold of her to get her down!"

She felt bile come up to her throat as she not only smelled old smoke but felt someone's mouth against her throat.

"Hold still so I can show you a good time—"

She snapped her head forward, headbutting the man.

A curse, and then, "Goddamn!" along with some noise in the dark, and her arms were momentarily free as she tried to get up and escape.

With the darkness and the daze taking over in her head, she wasn't fast enough to avoid the hands that came around her throat, pushing her back on the bed, squeezing her throat and cutting off her air supply, as her head was thrust deep into the pillow and mangled bedlinen. More jerking movements around her, and feeling her mattress sink around her body in various spots, she attempted to push her thumbs into the man's eye sockets as his grip loosened fleetingly around her throat, only to be hit again, the force so violent that her body bounced off the bed, unwelcome hands ripped off her, and she found herself landing face-down on the floor with feet scuffling all around her as she drew precious air back into her lungs.

She turned to look back up, and her vision swam as she detected a fight between several men: the sound of breaking glass and a dull thud of something hitting the opposite wall in the hallway. And then quiet surrounded her in the room, with the hallway's fluorescent light cutting a shaft in the darkness. Many of the bunks had been scattered. She scrambled to her feet, pulling herself up on a nearby single cot, and caught sight of Jack pounding her assailant from where he had dragged the man up against the wall, one hand wrapped around his throat as he pummeled him with his other fist.

She staggered out the door of the room, catching the doorjamb as the hall light momentarily blinded her. Eric ran past her toward them, another man in coveralls wrestling with the other man on the floor in addition to Jack beating the other man near senseless, yelling at him between the impact of his fist, "You touch her again and you die! Do you understand me?"

Eric grabbed the large zip ties that hung out the back pocket of his employee's coveralls, quickly making impromptu handcuffs for the first man that his worker had pinned down on the ground, giving the crewman instructions.

Tasha shook her head to clear it, only to make what injuries she had worse. She moved to help Jack, now realizing this had been her main assailant.

The horrible man was laughing, blood seeping between his nicotine-stained teeth. He grinned at her, trying to egg Jack on. "You see, she comes for me."

Tasha threw a hard punch at the man's jaw before Jack could, blood spewing on them both but mostly on Jack. Pain shot up her wrist and arm as she screamed "Fuck you, bastard!" and then fell back, letting Jack finish him off with Eric helping to grab ahold of Dirk, together slamming his inebriated body to the floor. Still in a daze, the room spinning, her heart racing to the point where her lungs couldn't keep up, she staggered back, noting her shirt in rags, and then quickly turned, walking shakily away from them toward the hangar.

Eric looked up as he zip-tied Dirk's hands behind his back. Dirk was too drunk to feel any pain, it seemed, as he laughed and spewed epithets at them. Jack picked up on the back of his head and smashed his face into the floor in one deft movement, stilling him.

"Whoa, Jack. That's enough!" Eric said, using his arm to block any further assault on the man under his knee. "I got him." He tried to thwart any more violence, seeing rampant rage in Jack's eyes. Eric got him to take a deep breath while encouraging him to go see to Tasha while he and his employee Brent dragged Dirk back to his office where he would hold the men for the sheriff to pick them up.

Dirk stirred as Eric and Brent hauled him into a half standing and dragging position between them. Dirk's movement incited Jack to lunge, forcing Eric to nearly drop his half of Dirk in an attempt to keep Jack from killing the man.

"Murder isn't going to fix this, Jack. And the last thing a Marine needs is a record, since us military guys are considered a walking weapon in the civilian sector." He set his hand on Jack's heaving chest, staying the raging bear in front of him. "Huh?" Eric nodded at Jack, getting him to back off. "Tasha's still alive, go check on her. Go find her for me?" Eric pushed him gently, encouraging him to go, promising him he would take care of Dirk and his pal, by pulling out his cell phone and placing a call. "You may want to clean yourself up first." Eric indicated to his face and shirt area for Jack to note on himself.

Jack did not want to let go, the blood still pounding in his ears, until he heard Eric mention her name. Turning slowly, he called for her. Getting no response only sent him running to the hangar. He stopped at the main room looking around for her. Seeing nothing, he dodged up and down the irregular aisles made by the various parked aircraft, stopping only momentarily to investigate hidden pockets around the desks and floor equipment. His panic rose when he did not hear her answer, still calling her name. He was worried that she had bolted outside into the raging blizzard when he shot past the outside door, hesitating, weighing options. It was like hunting down a wounded animal in the woods. *Wounded animals don't hide in open spaces, preferring protective enclosed spots to shield them*, he reminded himself. He decided to finish his hunt indoors, to the other set of doors along the back wall of the large hangar, where the restrooms lined the wall with locker rooms and shower areas for the pilots.

He opened every door, quickly peering inside, scanning rooms, asking a few pilots—when he encountered a few in the locker room—if they had seen a girl come in or go by. The answers, although some not appropriate given the situation, were all negative.

It wasn't until he came to the women's restroom and adjoining locker room that he found the door locked. He had forgotten that this was a more modernized hangar, with separate facilities. He sighed in relief at the whimpered 'no' and faint scuffling in the room beyond the locked door. Jack pounded on the door, telling her to unlock it.

He rested his forehead against the door, gathering himself, his palms leaving bloody smudge marks on the wood grain.

"Please, Tasha," he said between breaths. "It's just me." Jack slowed his labored breathing. "Unlock the door."

There was no sound from her.

He turned, using his head as the pivot point, laying his backside against the door and sliding down into a seated position, dropping his head between his arms where they rested on his bent knees. When Jack closed his eyes, there were various scenes flashing through his mind of walking amongst the dead bodies of his fellow teammates after the bombs had gone off or the ambush ended. He had failed again, and he let his conscience's voice scream the reminder of his inability to protect those under him with his earned name, *Suicide Jack*!

Suicide! The word made him cringe until he realized that he might not lose her to Dirk but to her own darkness if he did not get to her. Severely wounded animals gave up the will to live after being attacked. He scrambled to his feet using his whole body, slamming against the door, attempting to rip it from its metal frame, to no avail. "Tasha, listen to me, please say *something* if you won't let me in. I know you're hurt." He went on, reasoning with her. "I know you're scared. He's not going to bother you. Eric…Eric has him locked up until the sheriff can get here."

It was clear that she was not going to let him in, or maybe she was incapable of letting him in.

"Tasha, I need to see you. Let me in to *help* you, *please*."

He heard her weak "go away."

His heart cried out.

"I don't want anyone to see me."

His throat swelled on unshed tears. He choked them back, slapping the wood as he backed away, noting the metal reinforcement on the door handle matching the metal slip bolt that stubbornly held them apart, wondering.

"I don't care what you look like, Tasha. I need to see if I have to take you to the doctors." He dug for his wallet in his cargo pocket, relieved that it hadn't fallen out in the melee.

"No!" she yelled back at him. It was a scream of pain.

He slid the credit card between the door and the jamb, wiggling the plastic card until it was in place and he was able to push on the sliding locking mechanism, praying he would not break the card in the process, until he was able to pull the door open.

A trash can was on its side, either in her rage or in her attempts to block intruders. At the far wall, by the last wall-mounted sink, he found her huddled in the corner on the tiled floor. Her arms were clutched protectively around herself, her head down on her arms, and she was crying quietly. He stepped over the trash can, careful not to disturb it as he cautiously made his way to her.

Her wrists were red, and visible bruising could be seen on her upper and lower arms, her one hand cupping the other as if nursing it, her fine hair mussed, and there was a tear in her sweats along her upper thigh, exposing some of her fair flesh. But it was her tattered shirt that had got him the most. It was rendered useless in covering her.

The sound of the door clicking back into the lock made her head come up in horror, finding herself scrambling to stand up against the intruder, getting ready to fight again.

"Tasha! It's just me, you're okay."

She paused, then she screamed back at him, "It's not okay!" her fists rigid at her sides. "Go away!" She turned in shame, when he spied the imprints of Dirk's hand and fingers around her swan-like throat from where he had tried to choke her. He swiftly caught her up in his arms, gathering her to him as she fought him, letting her pummel him with her fists until she had nothing left save for a fresh wave of sobs.

He deserved it for not being there. He remained quiet, eventually squatting down with her in her private little corner just under the sink, getting her to sit on his lap and lie against him. They remained there for a long time, each of them gathering themselves. He was certain that Dirk would have killed her for not staying still as he tried to rape her. He was glad he had been able to save her but mad that he had not been there sooner and prevented it from happening. Jack could not even imagine what was going through her mind.

It was not until Eric had attempted to open the door, making Tasha jump, clawing at him to escape, that Jack hollered back to leave them be, as he cooed to Tasha to calm down, that it was only Eric at the door. She whimpered some, tugging at her shredded shirt to cover herself, this time able to hold back her tears, shaking her head no, that she wasn't ready to go anywhere. He tugged on her to indicate for her to come to him so that he could hold her. Hesitating, Jack encouraged her with a tug on her arm, making her flinch before she recovered and fell into his embrace, shaking, her nerves still rattled.

"How is she?" came Eric's voice from afar. "I have a med kit and I have asked for a doctor to come check her out. Problem is that the storm is hindering emergency personnel and we may not get either until tomorrow late morning."

"She's fine for now. Give us a few, will ya, Eric?" he said, ensuring that his voice would not scare his skittish moose.

"Yeah sure, if she's not in immediate danger medically from her injuries," Eric acquiesced reluctantly. "I mean, no broken bones or a concussion."

Jack lifted Tasha's chin to check her pupils, fighting her hands, whispering softly to calm her. Neither of her pupils were off size from the other, but the bruising on her temple by her eye and just under her opposite cheekbone were not only red but swelling, adding more reasons to personally kill Dirk. He took one of his thumbs to press on the swollen areas on her face, testing for possible bone fractures.

Tasha squirmed under his probing hands, slapping hard with her one good hand and thus reminding him that he needed to check the hand she had used to punch Dirk with. She pulled back from him, but he kept his grip firm on her, yet gentle enough not to hurt her.

"Tasha!" Jack told her in a harsh whisper. "I need you to pull yourself together! I'm just trying to see if you have any broken bones." He finally got her to let him look at her hand and arm. "Wiggle your fingers for me."

She wiggled them and then flipped a bird, wincing in that action.

There it was—he smirked—her first hint of anger coming back. *Good*, he thought, *fight, damn it*!

He protectively hauled her into him, snaking an arm around her shoulders before calling out to Eric.

"Just fetch me one of her shirts from our gear, some bags of ice for the swelling, and then be a good man and bring her a Coke in that fancy bottle of yours that you have in that office desk," he called, hoping Eric would get the hint to lace the soda. Jack needed to calm her, and the whiskey would be good to ease some of the physical pain.

"Ah…unh? Oh…never mind," Eric said, finally understanding what Jack was asking him to do. "Will do." They heard his footsteps fade from the door.

They both sighed heavily when he left. She kept jumping each time he moved, so he did his best to limit his movements. But he wanted to wash the blood off her hands and at the corner of her jaw where her skin had split.

"Tasha," Jack vied for her attention, getting her to go in the direction of the shower room. "I need to get you washed." He reached for an errant tress with a finger to lightly brush it away from her face, forgetting, making her reactively flinch when his hand came near her head. He opted to leave the errant blood-stained strand be for the time being, exhaling heavily.

She shook her head no.

"Why not?" he asked.

Her anxious eyes said it all as she backed away from his intended direction, looking back at a sink instead.

Of course. "All right, I understand." He gently encouraged her to get up. He took the lead when he realized how much blood had splattered all over his beard and face, spying his visage in the mirror. No wonder she was having issues with him. He did not recognize himself, this earlier version of him, the hardened face fresh from combat.

She refused to wash until he was done, having pulled a lot of paper towels to dry off. Her silence was killing him. He made sure to stand guard over her while she tentatively cleaned herself up, doing the same with a bunch of paper towels.

He got her to sit down on the floor as a knock sounded on the door, making her jump. However, this time she clung to his arm, still shaking.

"Tasha, listen, I've got to go to the door and get the bags of ice and your new shirt. I'll be back, I'm not leaving you or letting anyone else in, okay?"

She reluctantly let go, using her arms to cover herself again as she backed up against the corner wall where he had originally found her.

He quickly strode over, turned the lock, and slowly pulled the door ajar for fear of her escaping—although that was the furthest thing on her mind. But he wasn't taking any chances.

Eric peered in, searching for her. Jack backed up just enough to ease Eric's mind in letting him get a glimpse of her but not enough to let him in and ruin what sanctuary she had found.

"We've got the room straightened up again, if you are ready to go back there to sleep," Eric offered, talking just loud enough for just Jack to hear—or so he thought.

"I'm not sleeping. Not tonight," came her small, defensive voice.

"You got the other key?" Jack asked in a hurried whisper.

"You mean the plane's key?" Eric questioned.

Jack nodded affirmatively. "I'll take care of her and encourage her to come back out. I've got to get her to sleep. I'll need her to help fly the Angelina back home when the storm is over. Do me the favor of getting our gear inside the aircraft. We'll sleep in our sleeping bags tonight. I can lock the door from the inside and it may help her relax enough, knowing it's just us for now."

"Yeah, sure thing, I'll even throw in extra pillows for you two," Eric offered, grimacing at Jack's battered face. "Are you all right, too?" He handed over the glass whiskey container, filled nearly to the brim with soda, along with one of her shirts.

Jack nodded he was fine.

"One flight line special for the lady. Hope it helps," Eric added, peering back over to her, still concerned.

"By the way, Jack, the storm is raging outside. The sheriff's office called back saying it would be at least another ten hours before they will get here to take a report and haul him and his pal away."

"You didn't get the third guy?" Jack asked, now worried.

"Naw, he took off outside and hasn't come back so far. Hope he freezes to death. I got my guys standing by each entrance door waiting on him, should he return. I have another doing guard duty in my office over the other two. We have it covered for now. Just take care of her," Eric said, chinning over to Tasha.

Jack nodded. "Wake me when the sheriff arrives. It might take some time to convince her to sleep."

"All right, good luck, man."

It was near midnight when Jack got Tasha to drink about half the bottle. He tried to convince her to sleep in the cargo area of the Angelina.

"I'm not sleeping, Jack." Her determined words slurred from both the drink and the exhaustion that adrenaline had left behind.

He helped her up, dressed in her new shirt, and had her put her arm around his waist, getting her to walk and hold the two bags of ice that he had originally placed on each side of her face to keep the swelling down while they were in the bathroom. She finally began talking, but not much. She was very unhappy at not being able to pull herself together fast enough, much to his surprise, and was angry at herself for letting it happen, being caught off guard.

"I thought I was done with fighting and defending myself when I got back to the States. I did my part. Why do I need to defend myself against my own people? Why was he trying to kill me?" She asked these questions not necessarily to him. "I was stupid for letting my guard down."

"You were asleep, Tasha. It's no one's fault but Dirk's...and me," Jack added, snapping her attention back to him.

"You?" she asked, confused.

"I let you out of my sight and didn't do my job of protecting you."

There was a pregnant pause.

"Not really, you *did* warn me. You *always* do." She pondered her sore hand in her good hand. Looking back up at him, she said, "You were right...being the way you are...with our guys. But I have never felt...I have never felt them to be like that...that awful man." She pinched the bridge of her nose momentarily—he assumed either due to pain, tears, or a combination of both.

Jack tucked her into his body, hugging her protectively. "Oh Tasha..." he whispered, feeling even worse for being right.

When they got to the bathroom door, he had to pull on her to get her out there in the open space. "I've got you, Tasha. I'm not leaving your side...not tonight." He caught her scanning the area as he got her to the Angelina. They clambered up into her hold, where Eric and his crew must have done the extra work of getting a nice sleeping area set up for the two of them, away from the forward windows. The sleeping bags were rolled out, there were a few pillows for each of them, and there was extra padding underneath it all. He let go of her, encouraging to pick a spot, turning to lock them inside the Angelina for the night, although it wasn't truly lockable from the inside. The door latch's noise would be their first sign of entry by intruders, giving them a warning.

He turned to find she had gone to the aircraft's emergency kit, and he saw the aircraft's gun in her hand. She inspected the clip before locking it into place and taking it to her sleeping bag, closest to the door, tucking the gun under her pillow.

He sighed at her. "I'll be with you all night."

"I'm not taking a chance, nor will I mess up again." she said angrily, stuffing herself into the bag, adjusting herself inside but not closing her eyes, watching him take his spot next to her. Once he was settled, she rolled over, her back to him, watching the door.

"Tasha," Jack said softly, getting her attention so as not to scare her. "I'm going to put my arm around you, if you are okay with me doing so."

She nodded her consent, but still jerked when she heard the click of the gun's safety mechanism move as he put it on the far side of him, away from her.

"I don't want you shooting poor Eric by accident when he comes to wake us later today. I got you, just go to sleep, I'll stay up." Seeing that she was not going to comply, he added, "I'll wake you when I need some sleep, okay?"

Tasha turned her battered face to him. Her eyes searched his momentarily, not entirely convinced. He hugged her into his body, making sure to shield her as much as possible for tonight. As he watched her, it was not long until she was out, at first fidgeting in her movements as if she were trying to stave off the deep sleep or reliving the attack. Only did he let himself fall asleep when he noted her body had gone lax.

Their night was restless. A few times Tasha thrashed or whimpered, waking him. He would hug her back up to him, caressing her form through her sleeping bag, getting her back into a deeper slumber.

It wasn't until the next morning, when Eric had knocked on the door, alerting them, and began to open the latch, that they came to full alert. Tasha's hand accidently knocked the gun, causing it to skitter across the cargo floor. She scrambled for it with Jack grabbing at her to keep her from gaining a hold on it. He succeeded in wrestling her back to him.

As the door opened, the gun came to a halt at the opening, resting up against a raised portion of sheet metal. First Eric's face peered in, then a stranger's face, as they spied Jack holding down a skittish Tasha, his mouth close to her ear, reminding her that she was okay, keeping her enwrapped in his arm up against him.

"Jesus…" Eric said, eyeing the weapon in front of them. "Sorry for scaring you two."

The sheriff picked up the weapon in front of them, grunting to himself as he studied the offensive piece. "This sure would have hurt like hell before killing someone." The sheriff ensured the safety was on before returning the flare gun to Jack.

With his free hand, Jack reached around himself to find the other gun safely tucked under his bedding, before sighing at Tasha. Somehow in the middle of the night she had gotten up without him knowing it to dig through the aircraft's emergency kit and had retrieved the flare gun.

"Well, folks, when you are ready, I'll be waiting in Eric's office to take your statements," said the sheriff, first studying Jack, then Tasha a tad longer than he should have, making her turn her head away from his gaze.

Less than an hour later, they were both standing in Eric's office. The bunk room's broken window was gaping, but the glass on the floor had been removed. Tasha nearly bolted when she caught sight of a zip-tied Dirk in an office chair.

It took Jack's hand to steady her. They answered a few questions only after the deputy came in and took Dirk to either their car outside or to another location. The officer then moved to look at the bruising around her neck, making her instinctively step away.

"Whoa, young lady," the officer said, pacifying her with his hand. "Calm down, I'm not going to hurt you. But I do need to get a look at your neck since you seem to have some well-defined hand and fingerprints on that neck of yours. I would like to get some pictures and possibly prints lifted," he said, still squinting at the offending marks. He took a moment, looking at Jack's hands as if determining whether it may had been him that had attacked her, but decided otherwise the way Tasha had backed up against him, using him as a human shield. "I also need to get some photos of you, if there are any other bruises on you I need to be aware of."

Tasha offered her neck out to him first, visibly swallowing. The sheriff nodded to her before continuing with his work.

When he finished, he asked his last question to Tasha, which should have been obvious. "Do you want to press charges?"

Tasha nodded.

"I need a verbal confirmation, Miss Lazar."

Both Jack and Eric spoke at the same time.

"If she won't, I will—"

"I will for willfully disrupting my ground ops, making threats—"

The sheriff raised his hand and sighed at the two guys. "Just her."

"Yes," she answered. "But I don't want to be in court with that man. I don't think I can tolerate being in the same room."

"Duly noted, ma'am. But you may end up having to be there. No promises."

CHAPTER TWENTY-FIVE

By late afternoon, Jack and Tasha landed in Seward. They had to wait half the day until McGrath could clear the runways of snow, then wait their turn at the end of the runway to take off. Tasha fell back into what Jack called a near-normal mode when it came to flying home. She only flinched when she was caught off guard by a sudden movement on his part when he went to reach for the throttles as she was lowering the flaps. She apologized, making him huff to himself in dismay.

When Hank came out with the tug to hook on to them and tow them inside their hangar, she surprised him with a hand on his arm. "Jack, I really don't want to be seen by the others...at least for now. Is it possible to let me just go home now?" she asked, licking her lips in uncertainty.

"Yeah, Moose, I understand, but Nate already knows, and the rest...they'll know too. There's no shame," Jack told her, reaching out to caress the side of her battered face. "And yer still beautiful." He could see that had meant the world to her, as her eyes began to glisten. His contact with her was broken when the aircraft bumped over the threshold of the hangar.

"I'll be in the hall bathroom when you're done, and we can leave. I still prefer that no one sees me."

Hank had chocked their bird and come around to open the side door just aft of them. Tasha dashed from her seat, bolting past Hank just as he had finished lowering the steps.

"What the..." he muttered in surprise, seeing her run toward the hallway.

He looked at Jack. "You two have a fight, again?" he asked, and then looked back at her retreating form. "Why is her face all battered?" Hank nodded his head from side to side. "That better *not* have been you, Jack."

Jack gave him a gimlet eye. "Not this time." He sighed heavily. "Is anyone here today? Did we have any last-minute flights?"

"Nada on flights," he said, picking up Manny's Spanish, as Hank thumbed back to the aft part of the hangar, "but everyone's here today because Raven wanted hangar cleaning and parts inventory done. Will's coming through in another week to do our station maintenance check."

Not letting go on what he was able to observe, he asked again, "What's up with Tasha?"

"I'll explain, if you can round up the crew, minus Tasha, at the break table in less than five. I'm going to let Nate know we're back."

"Yeah, sure Jack." Hank turned quickly and ran as fast as an old, unfit man could.

Jack approached the small, spotlighted break table, noting all of them expectantly waiting. He was going to keep it short so that he could get Tasha home quickly. He was still angry. Angry at himself for not doing a better job of protecting her. But even angrier at Dirk.

"What's up, Jack?" Nick asked.

"Yeah, heard Tasha took a beating," chimed in Jarvis, slamming a fist into his other hand.

Jack placated them with his hand before beginning. "I'm going to make this quick and get her back home. But first thing first…make this yer cardinal rule when it comes to Tasha." Jack pointed at each and every one of them. "She does not *ever* go *alone* on any *overnight* trip. *One* of you will be with her at all times, including when you *sleep* with her!" Jack's anger made him slip up in his comment, and he rubbed his face in frustration.

In the stunned silence, a few of them looked at each other in confusion and then joked.

"Wow!" said Nick.

Hank snorted to himself, his arms folded over his chest.

"Er, I kinda like your sister more, Jack," came Sam's remark.

Manny was going to say something, as he pointed between Jarvis and himself.

"*Don't* even go there!" Jack barked at all of them. The joking eviscerated into dead silence at the break table. "What I meant was that each and every one of you will remain at all times at her side whenever you are out on overnight flights. You will guard her as if your life depended upon it! And that means sleeping with one eye open, within arm's reach of her…that is, if she even can *sleep* anymore!" He was nearly yelling at them in his fury.

"Good grief, man, chill!" came Nick, now serious as the rest of them. "Originally you kept her away from us as much as possible." He indicated to Jack with his hand. "What the hell went down in McGrath?"

Jack exhaled heavily, knowing it was best to explain and, let them know, but feeling it was not his place in that Tasha would have preferred that it not be public news. He paced back and forth the length of the table to quell his rage, giving them a summary of the past twenty-four hours.

"Ow!" she hissed at him when he applied a second and fresh bag of peas to her temple and eye area. He was happy that she no longer seemed to be jumpy with him, but he knew it was going to take a while before she would be back to her old self. She bounced back from her trials most of the time. He joined her on the sofa in front of the roaring fire, letting her lay her head on his lap so that she could rest her head on the bag of frozen peas while he helped her hold the other frozen bag against her cheekbone.

She groaned as he pulled the fur throw over her, hoping she would go to sleep again. But her eyes remained open, mirroring the hypnotic flames that kept her awake. Jack absentmindedly stroked her upper body, keeping the throw in place.

"I think you need some sleep."

"I can't…At least, not yet. My mind is…still racing."

"About what?"

"Just…just everything," she replied, tucking her good hand under her head, the ice pack becoming too much against her skin, sighing heavily. "That was not a good trip," she said off-handedly.

He smirked. "Ya think?"

It was the first smile he had seen since her attack.

He shifted, peering down at her. "There's the moose I have grown to love."

"I feel like one's on my face," she said, wincing as she smiled bigger at him. "Kiss me?" She lifted her head up expectantly.

He paused, but that ended up being the wrong move too.

"It's bad, isn't it?" She put her head back down and turned her face away from him.

But he gently moved her head, picking her up enough to meet halfway, and kissed her.

She pushed at him. "Don't…I don't need to gross you out."

"Nonsense, woman," he said, pushing her hair back from her face, smiling momentarily at her. "I'm just not sure what to do with you…without making you jump when I move…afraid to touch you because I'll bring back bad memories or worse…hurt you." He exhaled heavily at her. "I honestly don't know what to do with you other than be here next to you."

"I'm sorry, Jack." She shifted more to her back to look up at him. "I didn't mean to put you through this."

"Through what? It is not your fault." Then he added reluctantly, "Or even mine. But I don't like feeling helpless and not being able to protect you or those around me."

She smiled weakly at him, her hand reaching up to the side of his face. "You did protect me. You rescued me, you let me punch the SOB, and you didn't leave my side the rest of the time. A bit extreme, with you coming into the ladies' restroom every time I needed to use the facilities."

They laughed lightly together.

"You have done everything you could. I just need some time…to put myself back together. It's going to be bad enough when I have to show my face in two more days to the crew with"—she indicated her bruises, mostly at her neck and face—"having to explain what happened each time they ask me. If I tell them, they'll be stepping on eggshells around me for the rest of my life. I don't want that. I want it to be the way it was before. I don't want to be treated differently."

She looked back at the fire, turning some, her arm still too tender to stay put for long in any position. "I'm just not looking forward to all the questions."

"You won't have to answer them, Tash…I took care of that for you," he softly admitted, gently running his fingers through her hair, as if he was brushing it.

She twisted her head back to him in question.

"I told them what happened." He added, after seeing her expression, "They needed to know. And I have made a set of ground rules with all of them."

"You did what? No…no Jack, you didn't…"

"Hey, they know not to ask unless you volunteer the information."

"They won't come near me now! What did you threaten them with this time?"

"No…" he said, trying to get her to calm down and let him explain. "No threats. In fact, just the opposite, Tasha. You're going to find that they will be keeping a very close eye on you from now on, especially whenever you stay overnight at another airport. You do not fly alone unless it is a flight that you can be back to Seward in the same day."

"Oh," she said, raising an eyebrow at this new information, resuming her watch on the firelight coming from the fireplace. Then, as an afterthought, she said, "They are not going into the ladies' restroom with me when I need to go. I refuse."

She felt him huff out underneath her. "Certainly not! Even I have my limits with them when it comes to you," he said, and lightly grabbed her shoulder and squeezed it.

Two more weeks had gone by, and the Alaskan winter temperatures remained, leaving the company at a near standstill with the lighter workload. The most work they had was checking on the Grand Caravan down by the docks to ensure that the pontoons were ice free. The other task was changing the landing gear to skis on the Otter, for those airports that did not keep their runways free of ice and snow.

Tasha had resumed work as normal. Jack was impressed when she had stood up that first morning back with all of them at the break table's morning meeting. She had taken it upon herself to address them, being able to look everyone in the eye again, telling them she was fine, but to be sure that they did not 'sneak up on her' and that they should still act normal around her and feel free to touch her like normal but to understand from time to time, that she might initially flinch. She had looked at Jack. "The more normal you are around me, the faster I can overcome that bad night." She had pleaded with them all to give her a little time.

Emanuel had been the first to ask, "Can I give you a hug? You look like you could use one."

She had busted out laughing. "Of course!"

Manny had run around the table toward her, thus making the others chime in, wanting their hugs, too, until it became a giant group hug at the break table, causing Nate, who had shown up late, to hesitate in concern at the football huddle with Tasha in the middle. Jack had laughed as Nate gave him a questioning look, the *are you sure that's a good idea?* expression on his face priceless.

Jack had smiled at Nate, his arms folded across his chest, nodding that all was fine.

A few days later Jack was called into Nate's office. Nate had just gotten off the phone when Jack knocked casually on the office doorjamb. Nate indicated for him to have a seat, making sure that Jack closed the door before sitting down. Nora was not working in the office that day.

His interest piqued when Nate leaned back in his office chair, having the back wall help him stay balanced as he pondered a moment. Jack knew that when Nate had to think a moment before talking, what he had to discuss was extremely important. How long it took him to think depended on how serious the situation. And Jack noted it was getting worse by the second.

Nate suggested to him, "This is just between the two of us…for now." He sighed despondently before continuing.

"I just got a phone call late last night from Eric in McGrath." He let the chair swing forward, allowing him to put his forearms on his desk, clasping his hands in front of him. "According to him, the sheriff had to release Dirk Banes."

"You're kidding!" Jack exclaimed in surprise.

"Nope, someone paid for his bail. And they let him go." He sighed. "Thought you should know," he said, looking at him pointedly. "But I don't think it's a good idea that Tasha should know. Especially since she seems to have recovered some…at least physically. The emotional?" Raven gave Jack a questioning look, noting Jack's hand gripping and regripping the chair arms. "How is she, really?"

"She's good, Nate. For now." His voice was almost like a low growl in warning.

"Jack…now calm down," Nate said as he pulled at his chin and then resettled his train of thought. "I just got off the phone with the sheriff's department just to verify what Eric told me. Dirk still has to show up for court in September."

"That's nearly eight months from now! He could easily drop off the face of the earth by that time, Nate. Or worse, show up in Seward and finish what it was he wanted with her."

"I know, I know. But according to the department, Dirk is not allowed to go more than a hundred miles from their facility. What bothers me is that it still allows him to fly up to a hundred miles in any direction. Although it limits his current flight capabilities considerably."

"I'm surprised the FAA hasn't gotten in on this," came Jack.

"Unfortunately, they can't. It wasn't involving an aircraft."

"It involved a pilot," Jack shot back. "What about pilot-to-pilot situations?"

"It's something that we may need to ask William about—see if he can intervene or do something about it. McGrath is out of his jurisdiction. But maybe another FAA official can."

Jack, in his frustration, got out of his seat and ran a hand through his thick brown mane before resting both his hands on his hips, his usual stance when he was thinking or whatever it was that he did, not allowing the outside world to know what was going on inside his head.

"Jack, is there a way that you could let our boys know without her knowing? Do you think she's strong enough…just in case…you know…if Dirk did show up here?"

Jack's hand errantly wiped at his face, as if trying to wipe away the nasty thought that had just splattered on it. He nodded his head at Nate's concern. "Yes to the guys in our group and for not letting Tasha know. I don't need her back on edge, worrying about him showing up. But no to her not being ready should Dirk show up in Seward."

"She's a tough one, Jack. But I don't want to see her pushed beyond her limits and damaged for the rest of her life. These things…they can get to some women…" Nate did not go any further.

"Yeah, I know what you mean. She's been doing good, really good," he said, pacing some, "but she can put on a good show, too."

Nate's eyebrows arched at Jack's insight.

"She hasn't been skittish since her return to work. But from time to time I have notice her having…a momentary lapse…when she thinks I'm not watching." Smoothing his captain's beard on the one side, he continued thinking. "But she is much better than what I first witnessed watching over her in those initial days. It literally turned her into a wounded wild animal." Jack shook his head at the memory of the first twenty-four hours. Treating for shock is a difficult thing. It varies from person to person, but no one escapes its effect.

Nate continued. "Well, that last call was to the county department verifying his release and the steps we could take to prevent any engagement with that detestable man. Their answer was nothing until one of us or we encounter him again. And only if he is either bothering someone or jeopardizing something regarding our daily lives and flight operations! I think I am ready to kill him myself for what he nearly did to our business and reputation four years ago! I know we would have been a lot further ahead by now if it wasn't for that man. I've regretted hiring him ever since, and especially now that he has seen to it to come back in our lives."

"You can count me in on that sentiment. I know if I see Dirk, I don't think I could let him go. Not after what he did to Tasha, especially trying to strangle her when she began defending herself from being raped!" Turning some where he stood, Jack spoke in a low tone. "I truly believe no one would be worse off if he did die."

Nate nodded his head at him. "I know, son. But I don't need a fine man such as yourself, indicted for first-degree murder. Keep it clean, son." Nate added, "You know they gave him the benefit of the doubt because of the beating you gave him. It just sounds like we are going to see more of him than anyone would like."

Jack grunted unhappily. "Of course."

"Well, that's all for now. Thought you should know, and find a way to let the others know without Tasha knowing."

Taking his leave, Jack paused. "I'll make sure to bury the body where no one can find him," he said before he opened the door.

"I didn't hear that, Jack," Raven warned Jack's receding back side.

CHAPTER TWENTY-SIX

March was around the corner. Tasha was wishing for spring to be there but knew better. It seemed like winter was determined to stay, with all the thick drifts of snow and the steady temperatures hovering just in the teens. She was getting cabin fever between their home and the hangar, and needed to go somewhere, as restless as she felt. Having Jack at her side helped whenever she needed to get in more UV rays in the tanning booth. Lately, she had even been brave enough to go to that room alone—after making certain the room was locked—regaining some of her old confidence. But even the light therapy did not seem enough.

She was grateful that their workload had picked up with more flying contracts, but found Jack was not letting her get her flight hours in with the others. His excuse was that it was more important for her to be at the hangar.

It was only after Jack and Hank had seen to the task of getting the others airborne that she decided to confront him. She had found the pair talking, their Southern accents wafting on the air from Jack's office.

She knocked on his doorjamb before completely interrupting them. Both were leaning back in their chairs, relaxing, one of the few times she ever saw him relax from his duties. She had to give it to Hank: he was one of the few who could make Jack seem at peace, and she was grateful to him.

Jack sat up when she came into his office. "What's up, Tash?"

"I want to know when I get to go on the next flight."

"I'll get you on a flight soon."

"Is there anything coming up in the next week?" she pushed, looking back at his whiteboard.

Jack leaned forward on his elbows on his desk, curious. "Why so eager to leave?"

"Not eager, Jack. I just want more flight time to keep building on my ratings," she insisted. "The last thing I need to be is the weakest link in the company chain."

"You're not the weakest link in the chain, Tasha." Jack told her.

She gave him a dubious look.

"That would be me, Tasha," Hank admitted, clearing his throat, raising a finger at her. "I just don't fly, period. So you're not the last or the weakest, hon."

She smiled weakly at Hank.

"Why do you keep overworking the others then?" She leaned on the doorframe, still challenging Jack's authority.

"Did someone complain about being overworked?"

"No." She picked at her fingers. "But I feel left out." She looked back up at him. "It's time to put me back in the game or there's just no point in me being here, wasting the company money being idle."

Jack did not say anything. He picked up a pencil and idly tapped it on his desk calendar. "Funny that you say I need to stop and smell the roses, but I'm beginning to think you're the workaholic out of the two of us." Jack stopped his drumming when she didn't say anything. "You're not a waste on company resources. But I can give you work if you want. Nate could use a hand on getting his office organized."

She sighed. "That's not the point, Jack. It's flight time. You will have me on that next flight job." At her audacity in telling Jack what to do, Hank put down the front two legs of his chair, unsure if he should be staying or not.

She motioned for him to stay. "You can't keep me caged forever, Jack." She turned on her heel, taking her leave of them.

Hank gave him a low whistle, wiggling his toothpick between his teeth, as Jack leaned back again in his chair, putting his chin on his chest.

"You know she's right. Women usually are," Hank advised.

By the following week, Tasha found herself back on the flight schedule. All of them were day runs, and usually with one of the guys accompanying her. She did note that Jack did not let her go on the longer overnight flights or the flights that might have been delayed due to weather. The end of the first quarter was fast approaching and now the company would briefly see an increase in the number of flights. This in turn forced even Nate and Jack to pick up some of the flights. She accepted this, feeling that at least he was meeting her halfway in letting her log more flight hours. All the guys were supportive and genuinely happy to have her back flying. The more she flew, the more her mood elevated.

The biggest surprise for her was when Williams joined her on the Angelina. She had taken the co-pilot's seat and had almost buckled herself in when he told her to move to the pilot's seat.

"What? I've never been in that seat."

"Doesn't matter. Move over. Heard this trip would be an easy one today and we have terrific weather. Nice cold stable air to work with, Tasha. So scoot!" He jabbed his thumb at the pilot's seat.

She did as she was told and buckled in.

"So, where are we on the checklist?"

She looked at him a moment before answering. "In my case, from the beginning of the checklist, sir."

"Good answer." He smiled back at her. "Go ahead. Show me what you do."

They flipped through their flight plan and cargo paperwork, verifying their numbers. Thus she began her check flight for the old twin engine doing the Black

Raven's scheduled cargo run to Valdez and back.

After signing off on her paperwork, William looked at her and sighed. They both remained in the aircraft as Hank towed the Angelina back into their hangar. Tasha thought she had not passed, stealing a sideways glance at him. Will caught her gaze and she turned to look at him, waiting. When he still did not say anything, she asked, "What do I need to work on more in order to pass the twin engine?"

He just nodded imperceptibly, his lower lip jutting out as he thought to himself.

"Wow, it must be bad. How many things do I need to work on?"

He handed her the papers, giving her a chance to read them. "You need to work on your confidence when you're flying."

She ceased her scanning, letting him continue with her undivided attention.

"You got this. Take charge of your plane when you are flying. Own your plane, as I like to say."

"Wait..." she asked in confusion, going back and forth between the two papers. "This says I passed." She did not understand his reaction. "And this one too, for...ATP?" She stared at him, thus seeing his big, wide smile cracking across his face.

"Are you sure?" she questioned, the reality of it not sinking in at first.

"I'm sure about that"—William nodded to her, indicating to her paperwork—"but you lay a hand on my CJ3 by my office for another weird stunt like you pulled on me with my government-provided van and I'll just as soon make those revoked and voided." He gave her a warning look. "I don't even care if it is the President of the United States you are flying, the private jet is off limits."

"Yes, sir. I promise. I won't ask again under false pretenses."

"That's better. However, you may borrow the van again if needed, but keep returning it in better condition than it was before, like you and the rest of the team did the last time. I might get a new set of tires on that van yet," he joked with her.

She laughed. "That's going to be an expensive rental next time. I'll keep that expense in mind for the next client."

Thus, that afternoon, Tasha had passed not just her twin engine but her ATP rating. She filled out her paperwork, taking the papers to Jack's office where she found him cleaning up his desk for the day. He looked up expectantly, knowing she was excited by the large grin on her face. William had let him know she had passed everything earlier in his encoded reply of 'all good to go' to Hank on the radio. Jack came around his desk, spreading his arms wide to let her run to him for a big bear hug and a quick kiss. She was now licensed to be able to take paying passengers by herself, allowing her to do more flying for the company.

CHAPTER TWENTY-SEVEN

As the first week of March rolled in, Black Raven Aviation became more active with flying. The hangar seemed empty with everyone gone on their flights. Nick and Sam even pulled two flights per day a few times a week. Big Raven himself had taken on a more active role in flying, but Tasha suspected it was more of a chance for him to escape from his daily office work than it was to help lessen the burden of the extra flights. She saw little of Jack too, since their schedules did not match up. There would be nights when one would come home to the other one sleeping and then wake up to either one of them gone for the next scheduled run.

During this lonely period, she literally felt bereft of his presence, her body mirroring her feelings, getting sick on occasions, which she found to be unusual to be missing someone that much. *But maybe this is what being in love does to the human body*, she pondered dismissively.

It was in the morning on her day off, sitting in the cabin alone on the sofa, staring out the main window, holding a bowl of cereal in her hands, munching aimlessly while she let her mind wander that the window darkened unexpectedly with a large moving shadow. It was the moose, and trailing somewhat behind her, a new calf.

The moose paused when her spoon clinked in her bowl as she noted the beast. It had turned its massive head back toward the window, looking at her, snuffing the air a few times, blowing large swirls of visible air in the cold morning air. Then it ambled on.

Tasha felt blessed as she watched the mother and calf stroll by her view. Her spirit animal was showing her newborn how to forage. Ever protective of her baby....

Tasha suddenly felt ill again, nearly dropping the cereal bowl on the table, running toward the bathroom. Then it hit her as she flushed the toilet!

Never had she felt so certain as to what was really happening, given her odds and the circumstances. But she wanted to confirm it first, as she got dressed and headed to the pharmacy.

Thankfully, Tasha had all day and a night to herself to let the reality of her predicament sink in—only to have her mind racing, wondering how he would react. But she had to let him know, no note, no phone call. It had to be done in person and on the ground. Just the two of them.

Jack returned to their cabin late that evening, and she did her best to stay awake waiting for him on the sofa. But she had found herself in her old bed rather than his and he had already returned to work when she awoke.

She had heard his snoring from the other bedroom at one point during the night. It was obvious he was exhausted.

She decided to wait on telling him, wanting a more perfect moment when neither of them was rushed. However, a few more days went by and she was unable to withstand it. Tasha went in early to work to catch him before he took off on a cargo run for Pilot Point that day.

She entered the hangar, finding him finishing his manifest, banging on the plane twice to let Hank know he was ready to have his aircraft towed out to the tarmac while he took care of checking another plane nearby.

Jack greeted her with a big smile. "Hey there, Moose." He gestured to her to follow him.

She could see the tiredness etched in fine lines near his eyes. She sighed heavily, wishing that she could do more for him. But there were only so many of them and only so much time in one day, and each had their own schedules to stick to in order to keep flight operations running smoothly.

Tasha caught up to him on the far side of the second plane, out of Hank's sightline. Jack pulled her to him, giving her a bear hug and a fat kiss before releasing her and telling her, "I needed that."

He picked up his clipboard and opened the pilot's door, continuing his work, adding when she did not leave right away, "What's up?"

"Is there a way…" she asked hesitantly to his back side, wanting his full undivided attention, "…we can talk?"

"Yeah, what's on your mind?" he continued, checking the cockpit and then clambered down the step, turning to the side cargo door for his next check. "I'm listening."

Tasha could see he was busy thinking of other things, his mental checklist literally scrolling across his face. She knew and understood that he needed to be fully concentrating on his task.

"Well…when you get a little more than just five minutes and are not so busy," she said, deciding against telling him at the last second. The last thing he needed was to have his mind blown away with the news and then be distracted, missing something important—or worse yet, while flying.

"Sure." He stopped momentarily in his inspection, looking back. "Are you okay?"

She nodded, giving him an encouraging smile, feeling guilty to have bothered him at the busiest part of his day. "Yeah…it can wait. I'd rather talk when I have your full attention and when we have more time."

"We will, Tasha. We just have to get through this crazy week. Only one more day of this."

She nodded, spying Nick rounding the back end of the aircraft coming toward them.

"Hey, you two." Nick gave them a big smile. "I can't believe this week! This is nuts, man," he said, referring to Jack. "Can't you space these flights out better, Griswald?"

Jack finished up, double-checking the center of gravity numbers and then the cargo's security. "I'm trying, but we needed all the jobs we can get. It's like the beehive effect. When one customer wants something, then everyone else wants their flights scheduled at the same time." Turning to Nick, clasping him on his shoulder, he gave him a big smile. "But I have faith that 'Santa' can get it done in one day." Jack joshed Nick on his nickname. "I see that you made good time on the five a.m. flight."

"Yup." Nick was clearly proud of his time. "You got this one ready for me?" Nick indicated to the aircraft.

Jack handed him his papers, telling him he was good to go.

"You wanna come along, Moose?" Nick offered.

"Nope, I should be helping Manny finish loading his plane and get him on his way. And then I have my own nine a.m. flight to Quartz Creek to pick up Mr. Kernsey from his little ice-fishing trip. A real short one. An hour, hour-and-a-half flight, I suppose."

"That would be fantastic, Moose," said Jack. "Then I can get going now to Pilot Point and be back hopefully a little earlier this evening. We'll chat then?" he asked.

"Yeah. Sounds good," Tasha agreed, blowing it off and turning to head to the other planes. "I'll see ya," she told him over her shoulder, pausing, only to find him gone. To Nick she said, "See ya later, Nick."

Nick nodded, telling her, "Well, watch out. I see we have a snowstorm forming just northwest of us. Should hit late this afternoon. But you should be well ahead of it, getting to Quartz Creek and back before it's a worry."

"Okay." She appreciated the information.

By late lunch, she had completed her single-passenger airlift from the frozen upper lands and Kenai Lake. She too had made good time, she realized when pulling up to the hangar. She shut the engine down outside after Hank radioed her that he was still attached to the Otter inside the hangar.

Tasha came in through the side door, and Jarvis yelled to her to hit the hangar door opener. She complied as she took off her gloves.

"Thanks," he yelled back, getting into his bird for his flight.

She watched as Hank started the tug and helped watch the far wing as he towed the bird out onto the tarmac.

"I'll get your plane in a moment, Tasha," Hank yelled over to her as he drove by.

"No rush. I have to take a break a moment and I'll be right out to help."

Hank nodded, giving her a thumbs-up as he kept turning his head over his shoulder, making the adjustments in towing the plane out.

Having finished using the restroom for what seemed like the sixth time that morning, she grabbed a snack and a hot tea from the breakroom, grateful to Nora for bringing in more bagels to toast and cream cheese to thickly slather each side. When she was down to her last sip from her mug, she refilled her travel mug with more hot water. She grabbed the last half of the bagel, shoving it into her mouth, leaving the breakroom in time to get back to Hank, hearing Jarvis's prop noise fade outside from the hangar.

Tasha nearly slammed into Nora, almost adorning Nora's high-end fashionable sweater with her cream-cheese-covered bagel.

"Oh, *there* you are! I was hoping that you would still be here. Do you want to make another run?"

"Is it a one-day round trip?"

"Yes! And with our newest client! Mr. Reynolds just called and wanted to see if he could catch a flight today over to Valdez. Are you free? Otherwise I can wait on one of the boys to do it later, since everyone else is literally in the air."

"I sure can, if Mr. Reynolds is okay in a smaller aircraft and there are no other people coming with him and/or extra luggage. Give him a heads-up that the flight will take a little longer in *Tess*, the 185 Skywagon. I can get him up in the air within the hour if he drives himself down to our hangar."

"Terrific! I'll go call him to let him know." Nora put her hands together in gratitude.

"I'll be in Jack's office getting the weather report and flight plan set up. Hank can help me get the bird out on the tarmac."

Tasha found Hank already hooked up and ready to tow in her plane. She jogged over to him to cancel brining in the Cessna and instead asked him to get it fueled again and ready for a flight to Valdez for just her and one other client.

"Really? I didn't know we had another flight on the board today."

"Actually, we didn't, but Nora just asked if it was possible to fly this client out to Valdez and drop him off."

"He couldn't wait until tomorrow?"

"I didn't question it"—she shrugged her shoulders—"and Jack is always talking about getting as many flights in as possible. I'm the only one free at the moment. I'll be back before early evening, if not before Jack arrives."

"Well…okay." Hank was not entirely sure—at least not without asking Nate or Jack first about getting the last-minute flight in.

"Hank, it'll be fine. I'll be back before anyone else arrives, should the winds remain calm today. It's just a day trip."

"Well, Jack is real adamant on you doing just day trips only. Anything overnight he wants one of us with you at all times."

"Ah…so that's what's going on…"

"Tasha, he means well. But I have to agree with him since yer…er…um…"

Tasha pressed her lips together, smiling at him, and assured him she would be fine, especially a client like Mr. Reynolds.

Hank's eyebrows shot up at this information.

She nodded at him, saying "Yeah," her expression clear in stating *we can't afford not to take him.*

"All righty then, let's get her fueled." Hank said.

"Is there an extra emergency kit for him? And do you need an extra set of hands with fueling?"

"No to both. I can get one extra 'Emer kit' on board for you."

"Thanks, Hank. If I am not in Jack's office working on the flight plan, just find me in the sleeping quarters. I just want to get a quick nap in before he arrives."

It turned out to be an hour later when Mr. Reynolds arrived and was waiting by the bird. Hank had seen to waking her up after he had helped pre-flight *Tess* and helped the client get loaded into the co-pilot's seat. The power nap did her good.

They were airborne in minutes with the day's cold clear air. The weather was holding for at least another sixteen hours on their route, which would give her enough time to fly out, drop Mr. Reynolds off, take a short break while the aircraft was refueled, and return to Seward.

Mr. Reynolds kept her flight to Valdez interesting with all his bantering over their headsets. He was a natural talker, yet she was surprised he even bothered to want to know more about her. She did not find him a threat, given he had some years on her and she was certain she was well below his social status as a rich oil company man. She noted that he did not have a wedding band on. He must have noted her quick inspection, for he told her that he was a divorcee.

His first wife had left him because he was always away at work and she had found someone else to hang around with when he was not home. "Can't say I blame her." He looked out his side window as they flew by Storey Island to the south of them, rubbing his hands together between his knees as if he were cold. He looked at her. "Look, I'm simply curious about folks. Not trying to 'hit' upon you." He lifted a placating hand at her "However, I will admit I would have been honored if you even considered me as a possibility." Mr. Reynolds pointed to her left ring finger. "But I think I wasn't fast enough. Someone got to you first." He grinned, putting her at ease.

They made good time. Her tailwind was stronger than forecasted by the weather report she had obtained in Seward. However, it was going to make the journey back a lot longer. She wrinkled her nose at the thought that Jack might end up beating her back home. "Oh well, I guess a shorter break than I was hoping," she said under her breath.

She had line service top off her plane while she went in to get another weather update, a bite to eat, and a chance to rest her eyes and mind for about forty-five minutes in the lounge area. The lounge had two other pilots relaxing and reading magazines as they too were waiting for online service or someone to arrive. She helped herself to an overstuffed clay-colored leather chair and kicked back, closing her eyes.

The break ended when the linemen came in to let her know her plane was ready. She dropped her feet from the ottoman and got up to do another last-minute weather check. She saw it was not looking good, noting the growing snow system moving in over and north of Moose Pass in the Chugach Mountains stretching southwest to northeast and generally moving east toward her flight path. She made her decision as she watched the colored weather monitor and the storm system's movements; she could slip around it to the south if she had to.

Tasha, glad to be on her way home, did another thorough pre-flight including physically looking into the gas tanks to confirm they were full, and ensuring the caps were secure and all was in place inside. Once airborne, she settled into enjoying the flight, taking in the majestic views of snow-covered mountains and the interchanging light and deep blue coloring of the seawater below. Looking at some of the glaciers below made her feel cold, and she snuggled down as far as she could inside her coveralls and opened the aircraft's cabin air valve control to get more heat.

She was on the last leg of her flight, reaching the familiar Chugach Mountain range after being over water much of the time. She banked to her right and dropped down to the level of the cloud bases, heading for the inlet of King's Bay between the three mountains to her north, west, and south. From there she would follow the pass to the west and then southwest to Seward. Otherwise, she had to take the southern route past Chenega Island and Evans Island and out over Blying Sound and around the tail end of the mountain range.

Southward meant an additional thirty-five to forty miles or another twenty minutes of flight time. But Tasha was intent on making it back before Jack would land and finish for the day, and not flying over any more water than she had to. She opted for the shortcut to Nellie Juan Lake and through the mountain pass. She noted the snow system was still to the north of her, the clouds hugging persistently to the northern mountain ridge.

The clouds became thicker as she encountered the cloud patches on the southwestern edge of the snowstorm. Over the waters of Prince William Sound, she had cruised at 6,500 feet, staying under the overriding winds, and as expected, the wind became more westerly as she got closer to the Chugach Mountains and the approaching storm. It was going to be bumpy, but she was certain she could handle it and turned southwest over King's Bay.

She had made a general position call on Seward's frequency, letting folks know she was on her final leg of her flight and was entering the mountain pass from King's Bay. She adjusted her heading, aiming for the more southern pass toward Nellie Juan Lake, when she noted her left fuel gage indicator bouncing erratically. She sat up more in her seat, concerned. Her engine was still running smoothly and did not indicate any irregular operation. She switched tanks and noted that the right gauge remained steady while the left continued its erratic behavior. The condition was the same with the selector on the *Both* indicator.

Strange, she thought. She knew she had taken off with both tanks full and fuel caps secured.

But she was distracted by the terrain and the need to keep a sharp eye on it and her GPS map to avoid the jagged mountains defining her route. Tasha kept her altitude above the pass's lowest elevation, but the unsteady winds in the canyon became more turbulent, causing her to correct her path sharply, which caused the engine's RPM to drop suddenly before slowly returning to its cruise setting. The 'engine hiccup' made her reconsider her situation.

Tasha switched the fuel selector to the right-wing tank, sighing when the engine ran smoothly and the fuel gauge needle stabilized. But after a few minutes, the right tank began displaying the same issue, though the needle was not as erratic. She hoped it was just the instrument gauge going out.

She quickly assessed her options. She could try to turn around and look for a landing spot by the shoreline of King's Bay, but looking at her GPS, she realized she had gone too far into the narrow part of the pass, and with a lower 4,000-foot ceiling that had sunk below the surrounding peaks, she didn't want to risk climbing into the clouds and IFR conditions to make her turn. The thought of flying into cumulogranite did not appeal to her. She chuckled, though she did not feel calm or lighthearted, at remembering the aviation nickname stolen from the cloud name, cumulonimbus, but meaning a mountainside hidden in clouds. She wanted clear visibility and more room to make that turn.

She pushed ahead, switching the fuel selector back to *Both*, giving her the best chance for steady fuel flow to her engine by drawing half the needed flow from each tank. She was only minutes from Seward...not much more than thirty, given the increasingly strong headwinds and her slower airspeed so she could maneuver more easily between the steep mountains and under the thickening clouds.

Tasha chewed her bottom lip, keeping a wary eye on her instruments, making minimum directional changes to stave off the engine's sudden and bewildering tendency toward power loss. The last thing she needed was to make an impromptu landing on a snow-packed pass or in the middle of a mountain pass in a snowstorm. She held her speed and knew she was going to have to make another steep banking adjustment, first to the right and then to the left, before she would be on a steadier southwest course toward Nellie Juan Lake, where she would have more room to do a 180-degree turn back to King's Bay. But once she was over the lake, she would only be twenty-three statute miles from Seward and the point seemed moot.

Upon reaching the zigzag portion of the pass, she made her first turn and the engine lost power again, but as she rolled back to level from the turn, the engine RPM returned to the cruise setting. While making the second, opposite directional turn, the engine lost power again. As she rolled out, wings level and back in the center of the pass, the power returned, only a little slower that time. She noted, as expected, that she had lost some altitude in the turns.

To make matters worse, she was heading right into the oncoming storm as it continued its movement southeastward and the clouds that were sinking lower into the valley once they were free of the north mountain ridge. Her visibility worsened as she encountered the snowfall thickening into blizzard conditions.

In the back of her mind, she knew she had fuel—enough for another round trip from Valdez to Seward—but this was a fuel starvation issue. That meant something had to be blocking the fuel line and that something was messing with the fuel level indicators also, but it was the loss of engine power that bothered her. It bothered her a lot.

Carefully increasing the attitude, not wanting to trigger another power loss, she slowly climbed to regain her lost altitude. The next ten minutes were tense as she continued her narrow course, worrying that the engine would quit before getting there. It was nerve-racking. If she could get to the north end of the large lake, she would be able to breathe a moderate sigh of relief.

When she double-checked her position with her GPS, the sickening sound of engine silence occurred. As if she could not believe her ears, she looked through the windshield to see her prop free-spinning. A quick glance at the engine instruments confirmed manifold pressure was rising and RPM was under 2000 and decreasing, fuel pressure…zero. She absently trimmed *Tess* for best glide speed, and before she thought about it, she switched the second comm over to the emergency broadband but stopped before she thumbed her mic. Instead, she reselected comm one, calling Hank, telling him she had a failed engine, gave him her last known location, and her intent to make an emergency landing in the first clear area she could find. While one side of her brain managed her control of the plane, the other side searched the ghostly terrain through the decreasing visibility. At worst, she would end up in the river or crashing into the rugged terrain, missing the smoother, marshier places that existed below in the valley. The best was finding a spot that did not have any trees.

Visibility was down to a quarter mile in the blowing, heavy snowfall. As *Tess* sank in the bumpy air, she peered ahead for anything that looked like a white solid smooth spot, although looks could be deceiving. She held her course just off to the side of the river that would eventually lead her to the lake, hoping to reach a flat snow-covered area. Altitude was running out and she held her breath.

There! She exhaled. *I can make it*, she told herself encouragingly as she prepared for the short landing, slowing from glide speed to approach speed. *Am I too low? No, hold my spot*, she chided herself, remembering Jack's instructions. And she remembered her father's training, to fight against her body's automatic response to pull the nose up and create an inadvertent stall situation. Her training won out and she knew she could reach that spot. To make it over a copse, she partially dropped the flaps and kicked the rudder to slip around it at the last minute, the leading edge of her left wingtip clipping a few treetops, the impact creating an unnerving noise and shaking the entire plane. She dared not to look away, keeping eyes front, and white-knuckled the control wheel, doing her best to keeping the plane level before flaring for the landing.

Just a few hundred yards from her determined spot, she dropped the flaps, dumping altitude for the fast and short landing, where she tried to keep from flaring too soon but enough to keep her gear from being ripped off or her breaking her propeller as she touched the snow's surface. She managed a full stall landing as her aircraft ate what little space there was smooth enough to land, the wheels kissing the smooth surface. But the snow's appearance was misleading.

Tasha regained consciousness with a pounding headache near the top of her head, the soft electrical noise of the instrument panel cooling fan her only indication of first, being alive, and second, that she still had aircraft power on. She was not certain how long she had been out, touching the sore spot on her head, wincing, noting a smear of blood on her fingertips. It was not serious, she decided, as she looked for what she must have hit her head on. The GPS pad that was Velcroed to the yoke had fallen off, and she saw traces of blood on the edge of the pad where it lay on the passenger side floor, just out of her reach with her harness fastened.

She could not remember the time when she had started having fuel issues, having forgotten to look at the clock and to mark it on the GPS pad. Time was the least of her concern, noting it was 5:45 in the afternoon, and daylight was liminal.

She could not see out through her windshield, realizing snow was completely covering it, blocking her entire forward view. She peered out through each side window and saw the blizzard-like conditions of the gray landscape. *Well...*she thought to herself, *I landed right side up.*

She unbuckled her harness. What she could make out was that she had made it into a small clearing where the sides quickly sloped up into a dense tree line, the odd boulder or two being sentinels for the rest of the wooded area behind them. She was grateful that she had not run into a boulder. The passenger side view had more trees further past a snow-covered field, or possibly a frozen marshy area.

It must have been a while between landing and her regaining consciousness, for the cockpit's air was cold. But if the electrical was still on, she figured she had been out for less than thirty minutes. The electrical power on suddenly reminded her to act, attempting to use the radios while she could with the power she had left. She keyed the mic, reaching out to Hank, letting him or someone know she was all right and currently uncertain of the status of her aircraft. Tasha kept her voice as even as she could, choking back on her rising panic when she did not get a response, uncertain if anyone could or had heard her.

She switched over to comm two on the emergency frequency and called out to anyone listening. There was some crackle on the receiving side of the radio, indicating that comm two was working, although on second thought, why didn't she hear her own emergency locator sounding off in the background? *Didn't I land hard enough to set the ELT off?* She noted that the ELT light on her instrument panel was not flashing and knew the locator beacon was not working. *Flipping A*, she thought as she flipped the switch on, but still no flashing light.

She leaned forward, retrieving the handheld GPS pad off the passenger floor, and her vision seemed to lag when she bent over. She closed her eyes against the dizziness, flipping the pad right side up. She opened her eyes to look at a cracked screen, still grateful that it was displaying information. Reading her position, she tried each comm unit again, broadcasting her location to anyone listening. Still no answer. She decided to power down and preserve what precious battery power was left.

Tasha was able to keep her cool by thinking out the steps needed and organizing what she needed to do to hold out in the storm and stay alive until someone could reach her, remembering Jack's comment: *always know the next few hands ahead of time with the cards you're dealt.* She would be missed at least by nightfall when everyone else came in from their flights. She had already radioed Black Raven Aviation to tell them she was going down. *Did Hank answer?* She could not remember.

First thing first: she had to get to her ELT and make sure it could still work. If the switch on the box in the back was not operational, she would make it work by banging the living crap out of the orange box to set off the alarm.

Tasha pulled herself over her seat and got herself into the passenger section of the aircraft, where she was able to pull down on the rear seats and get to the baggage and cargo hold area of the plane. She found the small wall-mounted orange box along the extended baggage area after she moved the two emergency kits out of her way. There was no light flashing on the box, and the emergency kits had damaged the exposed wires going to her instrument panel. It now made sense to her as to why her indicator light on the instrument panel was not functioning.

Well, she could congratulate herself on not making a hard enough landing to set the ELT off, but it was certainly hard enough for her forehead. She winced at the painful throbbing, the pounding harder as she lay on her side and she flipped the switch on. Still no flashing light. She sat upright to ease the heartbeat she felt against her forehead before attempting to find something hard enough to beat on the locator box. Using her hand was not enough, and she feared her near frozen fingers would break in half during her beating attempts. She blew warm air over them and reached into her coat pockets for her gloves. She opened one of the emergency kits, searching for anything to leverage more force to her banging. Finding nothing, she checked the small tool bag and was able to find a small metal pry bar. She was still unable to set off the alarm after several swings in the limited cabin space. Her next attempt was to get it off the plane's sidewall and throw the box against a rock outside.

It took her a few moments, but she was able to get it released. She cradled the precious orange box to her as she fought her way back into the front seating area, resting a moment before opening the pilot's door. The cold air smacked hard against her exposed skin. The wind howled above her protected position, but close to the ground, in the space around the plane, it was relatively still, sheltered amongst the trees. The occasional gusts whipped around the taller trees and rock outcroppings, swirling down around the plane. She dropped down into the knee-deep snow and immediately found it difficult to walk. She was able to get out and far away enough from her plane to make a brief inspection, making note that *Tess* looked like she was still flyable—although she could not see the tires or anything forward of the wing struts, since she had buried that part in a snowdrift plowed up by her landing. The upper gear looked to be in good shape. The only damage she saw was a large ding in the leading edge of her left wing and a busted navigational light where she had struck a treetop on her way down. She found the right wing was undamaged, upon further inspection.

Taking a few more steps away to the nearest boulder, she tripped on something hard under the snow. She tapped her foot against the offending hindrance, only to realize it was another rock. Deciding that the bigger rocks were too far off in the cold, and the one she was stepping on was smaller and closer, it was wiser to dig through the foot or so of snow and just drop the ELT on the smaller one, simulating an impact.

After three tries, the light began flashing on the transmitter. She hurried back to the airplane, tossing the ELT back inside the cabin before quickly acquiescing to her bodily needs, grimacing at the notion of having to undress to do so, again wishing she was a guy at times.

She turned on the battery switch long enough to see if she could hear the ELT signal. She let out a grateful sigh when she heard that precious, obnoxious noise. Switching the frequency to Seward's airport, again she tried calling to Black Raven Aviation. Her only answer was the receiver's background noise. She powered down, saving what battery power she had left.

Then she remembered her cell phone, pulling it out of her flight bag in a hurry, as if hope would suddenly fly away on its own wings if she did not do everything she could to capture it and hang on to it. Her life depended on it more than ever. She pulled it out and turned it on to find that she only had fifty-eight percent battery life left and no signal. *Of course.* She was in a valley surrounded by mountains and out of direct line of sight to any tower. She texted her position and plight, hoping that the data might go through when she pushed the send button, but doubted it. It was worth a try. She turned it off to save the battery. After the snowstorm, she would climb one of the mountain slopes to see if she could get a cell signal then. Her hope muted for now.

She was alone for the night and until the snowstorm passed, whichever came first. She would decide in the morning on what to do next—either stay with the aircraft or figure a way to walk back on foot, in snow, up and downhill to the highway about twenty-six miles roughly due west and back a little to the north if she stuck to the pass. For the time being she was glamping overnight in her aircraft, striking a match to light the emergency candle for some light and what little heat it could muster. Last, pulling out two bundles and opening them, she wrapped the two thermal blankets around her.

Nick was the first to return with Jarvis, and Sam came in that afternoon around 4:30 p.m. Nick and Hank were busy towing the Beaver inside from where they had pulled up close to the hangar. Hank dropped the tow bar, setting off to retrieve the Angelina, and left Nick to chock his bird, finish his paperwork, and the shutdown checklist for the night.

"Man, some nasty weather brewing north of us. Looks like Crown Point and

Moose Pass are going to get about two more feet of snow tonight," Jarvis chatted idly.

"Just glad we had the Angelina to go over it. Otherwise we would have been spending a night out of town."

"Just as well—I could use a little R&R time away from here. At least I could've gotten some sleep," joked Sam. "I'm tired as hell today and can't wait to get into my bed."

"Me too. Unfortunately I have to hang out here a little longer," Hank stated.

"Yeah? Who's still flying?" asked Nick.

"Got Jack and Nate coming back around seven p.m. Tasha should be back around five thirty or six."

"Moose ain't back by now?" asked Sam, incredulously.

"No, she got back before lunchtime today from her first flight but ended up taking another last-minute flight to Valdez to drop off Mr. Reynolds."

"Manny went with her then?" asked Jarvis.

"No. Manny got back 'bout two thirty. He's off rounding up supper for us for tonight while we wait on Jack and Tasha to get back and load these two aircraft for tomorrow's flights."

Concerned, Sam continued, "Oh boy, you mean to tell us you let Tasha fly by herself with that client? A man, at that?" Sam's cheeks puffed as he blew out air, his hands pulled back on his long layers of dark brown hair. "Jack's going to be pissed, unless she makes it back before he does."

"Aw, guys, I think she'll be fine with Mr. Reynolds. Hell, I asked her if she could wait long enough for Manny to go along with her, but unfortunately Reynolds showed up first and she was eager to fly him out there and be back before Jack got back." He twisted his toothpick in his mouth with his thick mechanic's fingers before continuing. "He seems a decent feller. He certainly pays well enough."

"Well, I agree with you on that," said Nick. "But I still wouldn't want to be around if Jack finds out about it. You saw the way he went off a few weeks back after the McGrath incident. Jack hasn't let her do much unless one of us is with her."

"Tell me about it," stated Jarvis as he worked on logging his flight hours. "Always asking one of us where she is when he's lost sight of her. I'm ready to add a tracking device to her and add an app to my phone or his phone and make it easier on all of us."

This made them all laugh.

"Hey, Sam," Nick asked, "when you're ready, you want to go to the bar tonight and do a few rounds of pool?"

"Seriously? I'm beat, dude."

Nick pouted. "You wouldn't be if you weren't up half the night chatting and texting with Lela."

"Man, if I didn't know any better, Nick, I'd think you're jealous." Nick eyerolled him, and he added, "How about tomorrow night? I have a short flight tomorrow."

As the guys finished their paperwork, Manny came noisily charging through the human door with several bags hanging from each hand. "I've *got* dinner, Hank!" he yelled out a bit femininely, making Hank cringe his shoulders up around his neck and make a face at Jarvis.

"Jarvis, you need to straighten that boy out before I *do* something I'll regret in my homophobic moments."

"You have moments?" Jarvis questioned unbelievingly, knowing better when it came to Hank's all right-wing philosophy about life.

"It's…it's just not right. It's downright weird, I'm tellin' ya."

Jarvis snorted at Hank's discomfort.

"No, Hank. Weird is the day he comes in dressed up like Nora," Nick responded to Hank, egging him on.

Hank looked between Nick and Jarvis before ending back at Jarvis and giving him a *does he do that?* look.

"I think he nearly did that in Anchorage that night at the theater," Sam reminded Hank.

"Naw, man, that was him trying to be a Christmas tree!" Nick joked, jumping back to avoid Jarvis's backhanded swat. "Hey there, man, you might make your little man jealous!" Nick laughed at him. "Come on, let's check out what Manny brought Hank."

"You leave my dinner alone!" the grizzly old man warned.

"Come now, boys, you don't have to fight. I brought enough for *all* of us," Manny said, overhearing the last part of their conversation, proudly holding up five bags. "Thought we'd make it a night out at the hangar!"

"Nice going, Manny!" Nick smiled back at Hank. "Smells good." He rubbed his tummy as he pushed it out and bowed his back, trying to imitate Hank's beer gut.

Manny led the way like a Pied Piper to their break table at the back of the hangar, with Nick and Sam in tow and further behind, Jarvis and Hank. Eating there would allow them to hear the planes come in and possibly get in a few Nerf ball tosses in the hangar as they waited for the others to return.

Hank's radio squawked a few times, making him turn the volume down during their early dinner. Drake softly woofed a few times at him, and Hank thought it was peculiar that Drake had begun to beg while they ate. "I'll feed you as soon as we're back in Jack's office, Drake. Just wait yer turn." Drake whined a little.

It was not until Hank resumed his post in Jack's office by the main wall radio that he remembered to check his walkie-talkie, turning the volume up, and noted his radio needed a charging. He put the handheld radio on its charging station. Any aircraft chatter would be heard by the large wall radio. He sat down, picking up his *Fearin' the Banshee* book while the guys tossed the Nerf ball around in the near empty hangar after they loaded the cargo on the two planes scheduled to fly the following day.

"Hank!" squawked the radio system behind him. "This is Big Raven, I'm inbound and landing on the water in five minutes."

Picking up the mic, Hank answered, "Roger that, Nate. Do you need help in securing the plane?"

"No. I can get it. But I'll need a ride afterwards since Nora dropped me off earlier this morning."

"Okay, I'll send someone out to you. Manny brought all of us dinner. Yours is waiting when you get back."

"Great! See you shortly."

"Did I hear we have dinner ready?" came Jack's voice a few seconds later.

Hank laughed, picking up the mic again. "Good to hear your voice, Jack. What's your location?"

"I'm just behind Nate by fifteen minutes."

"Must be making good time to get back here before six," Hank said, and released the push-to-talk switch.

"A little, but not by much," radioed Jack.

Hank's gaze wandered over to the wall clock, doing an instant double-take at the late time and then feeling the pit of his stomach drop when he realized he had not heard from Tasha yet.

Not wanting to worry either of his bosses, he decided to tell them when they got back to the hangar.

Hank hurried out of the office, calling to the guys and asking if Tasha had landed or if they had gotten a phone call or message on their phones, as he swiftly pulled his cell phone out of his overalls cargo pocket to check. Hank had nothing and looked up at the guys gathering around him.

"What's up, Hank?" Sam asked, holding the Nerf ball and noting Hank's concern.

"Tasha hasn't arrived and there hasn't been one radio call from her. She was due over an hour ago. The other big problem is that Nate has just landed and moored *Lucy* out in the harbor and Jack is inbound in less than ten minutes."

Following Hank's lead with his phone, Sam asked, "Has anyone gotten a call or message?"

The guys all looked at their phones for voice messages and texts. One by one, each of them told Hank it was a negative. The group's concern grew, as did the increasing sound of Jack's plane coming in for a landing.

"Nick, Sam, go get Jack's plane with the tug. Jarvis, I need you to go pick up Nate at the harbor. Don't say anything yet until they are both back inside the hangar with us."

"What are you going to do, Hank?" asked Manny.

"You and I are going to radio out to her on two different frequencies—me

on the radio and you on your cell phone plus
everyone else's cell phone!"

The crew scattered accordingly after handing over their cell phones to Manny.

Jack sighed, glad that their busiest day was over. The next day's workload
would be lighter. Jack ran through the checklist as Nick and Sam came out to tow
him into the hangar. By the time the two flyboys chocked his bird, he was done.
All he had left was to fill out his paperwork, log his flight hours, and get his and
everyone else's paperwork together for Nate by the following morning, although
it would be Nora who would be logging everything into the computer system.

"Hey, Jack," Nick greeted.

"Working late?" Jack asked.

"Naw, we just got done with dinner and loading the two planes for
tomorrow's runs," Sam interrupted.

"Good, good." Jack took off toward his office, greeting Drake as his black
dog ran out to greet him.

"Hey man, take a break. Go get your dinner," Nick offered, trying to stall
him before he bounded in on Hank and Manny.

"Yeah, it's back on the break table," Sam encouragingly added.

Jack stopped and looked back at them. Drake barked in protest as he sat
down next to him, and suddenly Jack was alert to something not being right.
He waited on one of them to say something, but neither of them volunteered to
speak.

"What happened?"

Their pause was enough. His patience was thin, given how tired he was from
the long day and wanting to get home. He looked around the hangar but was
interrupted with the arrival of Nate and Jarvis, Nate rushing to Jack's office, then
spotting him in the middle of the hangar floor, calling out to him.

"Anything?" Raven asked.

Jack looked back at the two flyboys, giving them a questioning look,
deciding to leave them to go find out what happened. He quickly walked to Nate
and both headed to his office. "What's going on?"

"Not entirely sure." Nate jabbed his thumb over his shoulder at Jarvis. "He
refused to drive me back to my house, telling me my dinner was *too important* to
miss this evening." They bounded in on Hank messing with the radio recording
and Manny sitting at the desk covered with multiple cell phones, with a phone on
each ear.

"…inbound…" Crackling noise. "…entering the Chugach Mountains…
pass…" The recording played back the weak signal. "…via Nellie Juan Lake."
Moments later, Tasha was declaring an emergency, giving her last position in the

valley north of the lake, her voice steady but her panic underlying the intonation. Then, silence. Reality slapped Jack hard.

"When was this? How long ago?" Jack demanded, feeling nauseous, using his desk to steady himself as he dropped his paperwork.

"Not long, Jack," came Hank, waiting more on the recording feed. "That was at five twenty this afternoon."

"What? She should have been back hours ago if she left this morning, Hank," said Jack, interrupting him as he listened to the recording. "What is she doing that far east from Quartz Creek?"

"No, she took on another flight to Valdez early this afternoon."

"There wasn't a flight scheduled for that today…was there?" He looked at his whiteboard with the day's flight itineraries listed, reverifying what he had up there.

"This was a last-minute flight for Mr. Reynolds, and Tasha was the only one here at the time to take him," Hank told him.

"Was he with her?" Nate asked, concerned that he had two people on a downed aircraft.

"No, this was her return flight." Hank fast-forwarded the recording some since there was a long period of silence before the next soundbite. The static of the recording came online, stopping their conversation.

"Still when was she due back, Hank?" Jack persisted, pacing.

"She was due back around five or six this evening. Her first radioed message was at about five, and then her situation twenty minutes later. This is near six o'clock," he said as he pressed play again to listen if there was more.

There was a collective sigh in the room when Tasha's voice came through again. She was down, alive, trying to give out her coordinates, and finding out that the ELT was not working but would try to get it on in a few more minutes There was a lot of static noise interruption, making it hard to get all the coordinates down as Jack told Hank to replay the recording, motioning Nick to write the numbers down.

Nate's cell phone rang and he pulled it off his hip's clip. "Nate, here…Yeah, it's one of ours." He looked up as Jack and Nick worked on finding possible locations, with Hank adding in that she was north of the lake at the time figuring out speed and situation.

"Had to be nearby, it's somewhere in the valley," Hank said, pondering over the area map on the wall behind Jack's desk, pinning places.

Nate put his hand over his phone. "Will says an ELT has been going off about less than a half-hour, six to eight miles to the northeast of Nellie Juan Lake. However, neither we nor the search and rescue team can go out and search, due to the blizzard conditions in the area. Currently, visibility is zero, guys."

Jarvis looked up from his phone. "Weather is to be like that for the next twenty-four hours, with temps below freezing the entire time."

"Crap," came Manny, a visible shiver running through his body at the thought.

"No, we haven't heard from her any more, we just know she landed, at least not hard enough to set the ELT off until she herself started it, tried to give us coordinates, but connection seems bad...That would be great, I would like to borrow that equipment."

"Does anyone know what was on *Tess*?" Sam asked.

"She had the small tool bag and the one—"

Hank corrected Manny, interrupting him, "No...two emer kits for two people on this flight."

"Okay then, she should be good for at least a week if she can find some way to keep from freezing to death." Jack pulled anxiously on his beard. "But she's new and this is her first winter here..." he said, trying to remain calm with her being out there alone, praying that she had the common sense not to leave the plane.

Jack made the few other possible pinpoints on the map, then took a picture of it on his phone, making Nick and Sam take a photo of it too. "Nick, Sam, as soon as the weather blows over I want you two to get in the Beaver with William's ELT-locating equipment and a walkie-talkie set to my frequency. You will have to guide me in."

"How and with what, Jack?" Nate asked. "That's some really rough terrain over those mountains on foot. Bad enough in the summer, but wintertime?"

"Got it covered," he said, and dialed Chad on his cell phone.

"Chad, where are you?" Jack waited, listening. "Then tell the clinic you need the next few days off. We've got an emergency. I'll pick you up in a half hour. We're fetching your dogs and sled and some overnight gear." A pause. "You're going to get one hell of a training in this weather and through the mountain pass. I'll tell you more when I pick you up." Jack hooked his phone in his belt clip.

"You and Chad are going to go dog sledding up there?" Sam asked incredulously. "That's some rough terrain getting to Nellie Juan Lake."

"It's about twenty-six miles in, either from the highway or via a hop over the eastern ridgeline to the next bay and follow part way up the glacier and hook a slight right turn, traveling north," he said, coming over to the map again and tracing both directions. "If we come from the south, from Bly Sound, I'll have one of you guys dump us, the sled, and the dogs off here." He pointed to where the glacier melt met the bay waters. "Then, if the weather clears by then, I want you to continue to fly low to see if you can spot her plane, giving Chad and I better directions from the air."

Jack grabbed a walkie-talkie and a pair of fresh batteries.

"I'm calling the departure time at five a.m. tomorrow, weather permitting," Nate ordered while Jack grabbed other necessary items before heading out of the radio room and office. "I want you all flying in the daylight, in addition to giving that snowstorm a chance to move away from her area. Nick...Sam, get some sleep here at the hangar. I need you guys sharp. The last thing I need is three missing pilots!" Nate ordered.

"Jack, there's no point in going tonight," Raven told him, impressed with Jack's planning and rounding up the help but concerned about him leaving that night in the dark, and into blizzard conditions. "You need to get some sort of sleep before going."

"Not to worry, it'll take a good three hours just to get everything ready. I just need to get the Caravan readied in the morning, should Chad decide that is the easier route. Otherwise, it's my loaded truck on the highway up to the river just below Primrose." Jack smirked half-heartedly. "It's time to hunt for a lost moose." He gave Nate a smile, though his worry showed through, and he called for Drake to follow him.

"What about the rest of us?" Manny asked Jack, making him pause just outside his office, pointing to Hank and Jarvis.

"Go home. I'm counting on you two to get some rest because we have to stay on top of our flight schedule and rearrange some cargo to the other birds. There's only so much we can do for now, except hope that Tasha can keep her wits about her tonight and pray she stays safe."

Taking over, Nate nodded his head for Jack to take his leave, and said, "Hank and I have some radio monitoring do to for the rest of the evening. Maybe she can reach out to us." He scratched his salt and pepper hair. "...Why she hasn't used her cell phone is beyond me."

"Reception is scatty in the mountains, especially in a valley, boss," Jarvis suggested, adding, "I doubt she can get a call or can make a call. Maybe her cell phone is low on charge or she's keeping it in sleep mode to conserve power. I know I would until I could reach a place that showed stronger cellular signal." The younger crew members nodded knowingly at Hank and Raven, their attempts of lightening the dire situation for their older compatriots.

When Jack pulled up to the clinic, he found Chad waiting outside with a medical kit.

Jumping in, Chad asked, "What's up?"

During the drive to Chad's home, Jack explained the situation, telling him all that he knew. Then they discussed which route would be the best.

"Nellie Juan Pass is easier, but the route is longer. Not so many trees and more level ground along the river. That's not including the trip time on the highway north at this time of year," Jack said as he pulled into Chad's community.

"Isn't it snowing up there now?"

Jack nodded his head. "It's a blizzard. It'll be like that for another twenty-four hours. They're expecting another two feet of fresh snow."

"That's going to make it even harder for us to reach her." Chad stated. "Better add a few sets of snowshoes so we can pack down the snow in front for the team."

Jumping out on his side, Chad asked, "What's the other option on getting there, Jack?"

"Coming from the glacier side from the south with our ski-equipped plane. It's the best idea I have at the moment."

"Why not land on the lake with the plane in the harbor?" Chad questioned as Jack came around from the driver's side.

"We would be going in blind and we're not sure if the lake is entirely frozen or not." He sighed, but decided to keep that option open too, if the weather cleared faster than anticipated. "Come on, Chad, go feed your dogs while we get packing."

"When are *we* supposed to sleep?"

Jack gave him a pointed look.

"Never mind. I'll get Mom to make us a couple of thermoses full of strong coffee in the morning. But you must lay down and at least take a nap while we get our cell phones charged up. You and I will do much better in the first morning light. It will come by seven, and we'll leave an hour before that."

Seeing Jack's impatience, he held up a hand. "Relax, Jack, she's on the ground, alive. I think she can handle one night inside a plane by herself. She's smart and I've seen her fire a gun…and wield a knife. So let's pack and rest until six." Chad looked at his phone. "That'll give us at least six hours of sleep. I'll get the rest of my sleep while you drive."

Within two hours they had everything loaded in the back of his truck, save for the dogs. Chad opted for a spot four and a half miles below Primrose on the right of Seward Highway. Jack called Nate, telling them that it would be easier for him and Chad to go it alone for the time being, up through Nellie Juan Pass with the dogs. They would leave when it was daylight. Nate assured him that when the weather cleared enough, he would be sending Nick and Sam in to help locate the plane from above with the ELT tracker.

Before breaking the cell phone's connection, Jack asked, "Nate, have you heard anything?"

"No, not yet, son." The disappointment was heavy in his voice. Neither of them would be getting much sleep that night.

Chad shook Jack awake, indicating he was ready. They took off northbound, stopping by the hangar one more time and by Jack's cabin, picking up his camping gear with extra protective winter clothes. The trip was short with the snowplowed roads near town, but toward Primrose the snow steadily thickened. What would have been a twenty-minute trip turned into a forty-minute trip, with the snowfall increasing the further north they went. Jack pulled far over to the side of the road, double-checking his location with his phone. The storm was determined to hang on to the mountains as it reluctantly moved eastward.

They unloaded the dogs, setting everything up. Chad gave Jack a nod, indicating he was ready and to hop on. They took off, grateful that the marshes were frozen and the wet snow that had fallen there had compacted. The twenty-six miles in fresh powdery snow over the terrain was difficult as they went a little higher in elevation, stopping many times to stomp down a path for the dogs. Drake ran by their side the entire time. They had to break often, frustrating Jack, making the short twenty-six miles feel twice as long.

He figured, depending on finding a good snow trail to follow, at best, they could make it in a day. Worst-case scenario, it would take two.

Tasha awoke in her seat with a start. She had no idea what it was that made her wake up as she checked her flame on the emergency candle. It was still burning and about halfway used. She extinguished it to ration its use for when she needed it the most.

She looked at all her windows, only to find snow covering most of them save for a small peephole near the top of the passenger window. The storm had lightened up and it looked like morning light was breaking through. The interior of the plane seemed like a vacuum with its complete silence, no sound from anywhere. It was eerily quiet. Not even sound from the winds overhead.

Tasha decided to get out and knock the snow off, not just on her windows to be able to view her current world, but from the rest of the plane. She figured the snow covering the plane did not help make her visible to anyone searching for her, most likely by air. It was bad enough *Tess* was basically white on a white backdrop. The only contrasting color would be the vertical's logo and the three-color pinstriping on the either side of the aircraft. Next, she found one of the old red oil rags and tied it to the top propeller blade, hoping the color would signal anyone nearby that she needed help.

Doing as much as she could do to make herself visible, she attended to her needs as if she were bivouacking. Her plane was her shelter from the cold. She packed a handful of the cleanest snow she could find and stuffed it in a metal cup that she located in the emergency kit. She wanted some hot water and relit the candle, carefully propping the cup halfway over it inside the plane on the floor. She turned the GPS tablet on and toyed with her options.

Her first was to walk out of the valley, over the pass, and back to the Seward Highway. Twenty-six miles was not that bad and was doable. But the difficulty lay in the relatively unfamiliar terrain, the cold weather, deep snow, and the fact that she was now pregnant. In addition, she would have to make a large enough 'help' and a directional arrow showing her escape route from the wreckage out of good-sized rocks or tree limbs.

Option two was to remain put for the next two days to see if anyone would be searching for her. That she could easily do. She held out hope that maybe one of the guys would be flying *Lucy* or the Beaver to pick her up on Nellie Juan Lake. But she had to figure out if the lake wasn't frozen so they could land in the water—or, if frozen, was the ice thick enough to hold a plane with skis landing on its surface? Reaching the shoreline was a distance she could easily make and verify.

Having consumed her hot water, she decided to help herself to an energy bar for breakfast. Halfway through it, she found it did not sit well in her tummy. She left the half-eaten bar on the instrument dash and decided to work outside on making a large aerial 'help' sign on the ground. Physically moving around kept her warm and kept her occupied compared to sitting inside the plane doing nothing and fretting needlessly.

She shuffled through the snowdrifts, using her feet to catch any rocks that she could use while she spelled out 'help' in the snow near her bird. She was about halfway done when she spotted movement out of the corner of her eye near the tree line. She looked up only to realize a large gray wolf had been watching her. The one wolf became two and then three. In that instant she bolted for the plane, realizing that she was the prey.

She barely got into the plane and had the door halfway shut when the lead wolf snagged her coveralls' pant leg by her boot. She was able to use the door in her defense, slamming it against the wolf's head. The wolf yelped, letting go of her pant leg as she nearly pinned her leg in her panic to get the door closed. The wolf did not desist, pawing at the metal and glass of her pilot-side door, the aircraft shuddering under its weight every time it jumped up against the side of the aircraft, its jaws snapping at her.

She turned in her seat and grabbed the nine-millimeter from the emergency kit, switching the safety off as she watched the wolf jump up onto the aircraft's nose, pawing the front windshield, its claws scratching the glass, and she wondered if it and the thin metal would hold up against the lead wolf's assault. She quickly scanned for the others and found four of them, walking around, searching for an opening.

Take the enemy leader out and the rest will fall, she remembered from her Army training. She wondered if that technique would work on a pack of wolves. The last thing she needed was to shoot a hole in one of the windows, leaving what precarious protection from the cold and predators she had. She bided her time as the plane creaked under the wolf's weight clambering around on top, the noise of his paws giving her an idea of where the alpha was located. She prayed he would jump down and come near her side, where she could prop open her window enough to take a shot at him and discourage the others. It seemed like the minutes became an hour as the large beast clambered around before jumping back down on the ground and coming back to her door, standing on his hind legs to peer back at her through the glass. She screamed at the wolf, hoping to scare it. But the hungry canine was determined, baring its teeth at her as the pack circled the plane. A few of them tried to distract her by lunging at opposite sides of the plane, making the cabin shake under their weight.

It was when the half-eaten energy bar fell into her lap that she decided she could use that to her advantage.

She waited until the alpha wolf backed down onto all fours before turning the window lock. The noise garnered his attention and she nearly lost it when it lunged at her side again. The window flapped open a few times at the bottom, and she was grateful that whoever had designed the window had kept its movements to a minimum.

Collecting her wits in between the wolf's attempts of hopping up and down on its two legs, she was able to pitch the energy bar out a distance toward the rear to distract it and make it run to the 'offering.' She quickly took aim and shot the wolf in the neck, near its head. There was a yelp, but he did not drop as she had hoped; he turned and made a run at the window opening. Firing a second round, she stopped him before he made it. She scrambled to close the window, watching the others walk around before realizing that their leader had been killed. Two of them came up to nose at his heavy-coated carcass by her door.

She eventually exhaled her bated breath as she watched them finally move on to something less difficult to hunt, their figures disappearing one by one into the far tree line like ghosts.

As she let her pulse slow, she decided that it might not be a good idea to hike through the pass on her own, now seeing the threats up close. She also realized her stupidity of leaving a half-eaten energy bar inside the plane, causing the wolves to seek her out. She quickly gathered the other packaged food and put it back into the five-gallon bucket and secured the lid, sealing off any further food scents. The second bucket became her impromptu waste bucket, as she took out the other items such as a mid-sized knife, the other candles to burn along with the striker, and the flare gun, should she hear a plane fly overhead nearby. It was going to be a long day, and she silently called out to Jack with her thoughts to hurry up, hoping that he did not think she had died in the emergency landing. She was grateful that she had yet to tell Jack that she was actually two people. It would be less on Jack's conscience, knowing how sensitive he was losing people to unexpected deaths. She had to stay alive for him and not add to his inner fears and worry for those he led.

She looked back at the ELT in the back seat. The light was still blinking. There would be only two more days before it, too, would stop.

The thought of her red beacon of hope ceasing caused her to vomit into the empty bucket next to her, swearing she smelled blood, before passing out.

"We've got to give the dogs a break, Jack," Chad yelled to him from behind.

Again, Jack was tramping down the thick powdery snow that was still falling lazily from the gray sky through the canopy of the pine trees. It had been a full day of trekking through the pass. They were short of Nellie Juan Lake's southwestern end by eight miles, not including the nearly seven miles of the lake's length. They could have been there already under normal packed-snow conditions, where the dogs could have easily made eleven to twelve miles in one day. But there were no trails blazed for them.

Jack looked at his phone app, checking again how close they were to Tasha's plane. He imprinted the location in his memory should her beacon eventually fail. But they only had about a twenty-four-hour time frame left of the thirty-six total hours. He looked heavenward as he sighed, knowing that they had to stop for the day. If they did not, things could get uglier, with more problems, and the dogs could only do so much. He turned back to Chad. Over the dogs' barking and the trickling noise of the nearby river of snowmelt, Jack said, "Let's make camp."

He could see the surprise in Chad's face when he agreed to call it a day, as he walked back to him where he stood on the sled's runner board.

"Are you sure, Jack?" Chad asked. "They just need a break to rest and a chance to let me feed them."

Shaking his head, Jack's words were written with the white air he breathed out. "Yeah, I'm sure." He wiped the dusting of snow off his beard. "We need to stay strong in order to reach the plane and help her…" he said, meaning it more for himself than for all of them, including the dogs.

Chad noted his concern as he came around to untie their camping gear from the sled. "We'll get there. We'll find her." He did his best to assuage his friend's worry without the fear of finding her dead from exposure. But Jack had told him that she had reported in on landing fine and was alive before leaving earlier that morning.

Jack grabbed the one main large tent they had decided to bring with them. It was one of those newer, fancier ones where one could literally throw it up into the air and it would pop up on its own, and all they had to do was stake it down. Chad went to the task of feeding all the dogs, including Jack's dog, Drake. He pulled Drake off to the far side, away from his team, to give him what he normally ate instead of what his team ingested, telling Drake that he was doing good at keeping up with the rest of the pack, and might make a fine race dog yet. Chad patted him in gratitude. His breed was made to smell out folks who were in trouble in the snow. He got some relief at the thought as he watched Drake hungrily eat his food and then look up after he was finished, facing in the direction they were meant to continue on, sniffing the cold air.

"No, Drake. We need to take a break. We all do," he told the black Newfoundland.

As if understanding him, the dog reluctantly settled down in the snow, a small whimpering whine to him, but remained facing in Tasha's direction.

"Good boy, we'll get there."

Within the hour, they were settled in, including putting half of the team and Drake in with them in order to keep warm for the night. The snow gently tapped the tent's fabric until enough weight had built up and it would noisily slide off onto the ground around them outside. Neither said a word, the exertion of the day having taken its physical toll on both of their bodies, making deep sleep come fast. And short.

It was oh dark thirty when Jack roused Chad to get up and start packing up again. Dawn was not even close, from what he could tell by the air's scent. Normally he would fuss at Jack being up so early on a normal camping trip, but there was urgency and it had to be heeded as Chad tromped through the snow, gauging how much more snow had fallen. It was another four to six inches on top of the blizzard's two feet of fresh powder. It was going to be another long slogging day.

She regained consciousness a few hours later. Her body stirring her awake, shaking, uncomfortably cold. She lit the candle again, holding the container as the warmth spread, until her fingers could move again. She donned her gloves again.

She checked outside but the windows had fogged over, and she reached forward to wipe at the glass with the fore sleeve of her coveralls. More snow had fallen, but only a few inches. There were no wolves in sight that she could see, other than the lifeless pile of fur just outside her side of the plane.

The sight of the blood pool and the wolf's frozen, jagged death smile made her gag again. She twisted in her seat back to the co-pilot's side, where she emptily vomited light spume into the five-gallon bucket. Her stomach was empty since she wasn't eating much. But she was not hungry either, her exhaustion winning over any desire to eat. She was thirsty. But the idea of opening the door to grab a handful of snow to melt was not her idea of fun. But she had to spare what few bottles of water she had for the eminent hiking trip that she might have to take after her third or fourth day out there. She wanted enough supplies to take with her, should she be forced to leave her current shelter.

She double-checked her surroundings before inhaling deeply for courage—and to possibly be ready to be chased back inside her plane. The cold air that swirled in blew out her candle as she clambered down rather stiffly. Pain shot up from her ankle where the wolf had caught her legging. Her prior panic must have blocked out how much damage the wolf had done. No bones were broken, but it was still painful as she limped around her door toward the front of the plane to find the whitest and freshest snow possible, stuffing her cup full before climbing back inside.

As she got the candle lit and her snow to start melting, she pushed her seat as far back as she could and shifted to get her leg up, taking a look at the damage done. She cringed at the thought of having to undress in the cold. But it had to be done. Tasha found that it was mostly broken skin and it felt like she had over-stretched her ligaments from the weight of the wolf trying to pull on her foot. She noisily moved around to the first five-gallon bucket containing all the emergency supplies, digging around until she could find the mini medical kit. With it in hand, she twisted back and proceeded to dress her wounds. The twenty-some minutes of having her foot propped up and in the cold air seemed to make the redness and swelling go down, and she decided to rearrange her cramped living quarters to lie sideways for the day with her foot up on the co-pilot's seat.

From her new seating arrangement, she checked the ELT transmitter in the back seat for its reassuring red blinking light, the pulse of the light matching her heartrate when she had originally landed and the time after barely making it back inside the plane when the pack of wolves hunted her down. But she found her heart rate slowing as she stared at the pulsing light, sipping on her fresh cup of hot water, her thoughts roaming back to Jack, wondering if he was going mad at the thought of her possibly being dead.

This caused her to jerk back awake, realizing how much pain she would be causing him for her stupidity of not doing a more thorough pre-flight check. She wanted to go back out there to see if there was still gas in both wings, but without a stepstool or ladder and the current condition of her one ankle, there was no way she could make it on top of the aircraft to take a look and still be fast enough to get inside should the wolves return.

A tear slid down one cheek as her heart tore at the thought of causing Jack so much pain. She never wanted him to experience losing another person under his charge. She silently yelled out to him with her mind that she was fine, hoping that somehow he would sense it afar and cease worrying. Just mentally sending that message out made her head hurt, throbbing in the same place where she had hit it during the hard landing. She moved the candle back to the floor between the front seats and the back seat, hoping that the little warmth it provided would be more even. Between the various pains and the cold, she pulled her blanket around herself tighter and drifted back to sleep.

Her sleep was fitful between the dreams, her body's reactions to shake the cold off, and her bodily needs. At one point she woke up hungry enough to open a food packet and eat it. Because it was dark outside, she opted to open and use one water bottle, deciding she could refill it later if she had to make a hike back to civilization.

At dawn she awoke to the sudden sensation of wetness, unsure if the dream she remembered of fast-melting icebergs inundating her with floodwaters was real or not. She found she was only damp in her seat, and the smell of copper assailed her nose. She quickly got herself out of her coveralls and took off her damp leggings and then relieved herself the rest of the way over her one waste bucket. She was surprised to see blood on her hands when she was about to drop her leggings in another pile next to her overnight flight bag where she kept another day's clothing. She paused before wiping the blood off and then herself, putting on fresh attire before the cold could freeze her bare skin solid. The stained rag did not reassure her as her gut cramped again, making her nearly double over before she could finish dressing. She refused to look at what she could smell from the waste bucket. She quickly put the lid back onto the five-gallon waste bucket and did her best to redress the rest of the way. Mother nature had decided what was best for her at this time.

It's just as well, she supposed, grateful she had not told Jack. The least she could do was spare him that news should she make it back alive, hoping that her being alive would be enough for him and break that cycle of losing people under his 'command.' She did not need to add to it by telling him she had just lost a part of them. She would carry that to her grave if she needed in order to spare him further grief. Another guilt for her to shoulder for the rest of her life, all due in part to her ineptitude, she thought, sighing remorsefully to herself. She had failed him in more ways than one. She was angry but more sad—a sadness that turned into a massive empty void within her.

She checked the ELT light. Its flashing had become dimmer. She turned to wipe at the windows and peered up at the sky. It was still heavily overcast. She cried to let out some of the tension of her situation, and for the part of her she had just lost. The emotional release helped her back into another few hours of sleep. She had become overwhelmingly exhausted.

She awoke again, or so she thought, when she saw a grizzly bear walk in front of her plane. It looked back at her and she closed her eyes against the image like an ostrich trying to hide by sticking its head in the sand, forcing herself to remain still enough not to encourage the bear to rip open the plane to get to her. It was lifelike, hearing the heavy paws tread near her door and then hearing its breathing as if snuffing the air. She pleaded silently for the bear to just walk away and leave her be. But it was either the silence or her really waking from her dream that forced her eyes open. She noted movement by the tree line across the expanse of the field in the waning light of the day, surprised to see a grizzly walking past when she was certain that bears should still have been hibernating at that time of year.

They had found the plane in pretty good condition, other than a ding in the wing and a busted navigation light. It was surrounded by a pile of snow at the front, as if she had made a ploughed landing. There was blood on the snow by her door, the red trail leading to a wolf's dead body toward the rear of the aircraft and blood around the pilot's door. Both Chad and Jack jumped off the sled and rushed to the aircraft, wondering if Tasha had been hurt—or worse, had died from an animal attack. Jack, with his height and longer legs, made it to the door first through the thick snow.

Seeing an upright, bundled-up form sitting stock-still in the pilot's seat, he yanked the door open. His heart stopped at seeing the bloodstains on her coverall pantleg near her ankle, the cold-weather protective clothing torn either by teeth or claws near her work boots. She had not moved, and he feared the worst.

"Tasha!" he called, shaking her, trying to push her fur-lined hood back enough so he could see her face. "Tasha, wake up, come on girl, wake up!"

A languorous murmur came from her, her eyes opening at Jack's voice, over the protective black scarf covering her face from her eyes down, clearly not believing he was here. Jack sighed heavily with relief, nearly bursting in tears, hugging her to him, grateful that she was still alive after three days.

"You *are* real," her muffled response came in the down of his jacket. She was clearly exhausted. She was weakened, but more from the extreme cold, from what he could tell. She moved like a spineless ragdoll.

Jack backed away from her, noting dried blood smudged on her forehead too as her furred hood fell back. He pulled her hair away, noting a small cut and some bruising from where she must have hit her head when she landed. He checked her pupils again. She had taken one too many beatings to her head as of late.

"Yup, I'm here. Stay with me. Chad's here too." Then remembering, he yelled, "Chad!" getting his attention to whatever it was he was inspecting in the snow nearby at the front of the airplane.

Chad had noted and followed the bear prints in the snow.

Jack waved him over toward them. "Take a look at her before I move her to the sled. I'll get your med kit."

Chad did as instructed, making a quick assessment of her head and her ankle. He asked her if there were any other injuries, noting that there seemed to be a lot more blood than there should have been as he looked at first the front seats and flooring, and then the flooring in the back seating area.

She did not answer him, although she told him, "Damn wolf beat me to the plane before I could close the door fast enough." She pointed to the window latch, a gun sliding from her far hand and onto the floor. "Shot him from the window when he wouldn't stop jumping onto the side of the plane," she told him tiredly.

Jack returned with the med kit.

"I think he scratched the paint," she added, as Chad quietly cleaned her wounds and re-dressed them, telling Jack that was all he could do for her for the time being and she was readied to be moved.

To Tasha, he continued, "And you're more worried about the plane being scratched." Chad swore. "You aviation folks are true nutjobs, at times."

Chad shook his head at Jack, who was smiling for the first time since the night he had found out that Tasha's plane had gone down. "You need to talk to her about getting her priorities straightened out about crash landings when we get back. Her leg wound is going to need more attention when we get her back to the clinic." His eyes still noted the blood discrepancies in the plane's interior with the amount of visible body damage, especially in the bucket that Tasha had discretely resecured the loose lid, concealing it from him while he worked on re-bandaging her lower leg wound.

"It's a forced landing," Jack corrected Chad as he removed some of the snow off the propeller to inspect it, noting no damage there either. He stopped with some concern when Chad mentioned her leg needing more attention. Chad put him at ease that Tasha was fine and could travel. She was just going to need to get a better cleaning job and some possible stitches just above her ankle.

"You ready to get her out and onto the sled, Jack?"

"Yeah, but in a second, but only if she can wait a few seconds longer. Keep her sheltered from this cold breeze. I need to make a few mental notes," he said as he headed around the plane, inspecting it and then hefting himself up on the wing to look at the fuel, opening one cap, finding the one tank half empty—but there was plenty of fuel. Then he looked at the tail, control surfaces, and then did a quick dig of the tires where it looked like she had already tried to dig out the wheels some but must have gotten interrupted by the pack of wolves. He kept glancing back at her inside the cabin. Chad had closed the door to help keep her warm. There was a candle burning for heat. He noted the first emergency bucket torn apart where she had helped herself to some of the rations, her tin cup half full of water, with snow still melting along the cup's interior side. The flare gun she had on the dash of the instrument panel waiting, and he wondered if she had used it at all.

On his way to inspecting the other wing, he almost stepped on the area Tasha

457

must have been using as a latrine before the wolf attack, now understanding why she had the other bucket open with the lid on and on the floor of the co-pilot side and all its good and unopened contents spewed out over the rear seats near the other bucket. He stepped over the wolf's body. She had nailed the beast in the head with a bullet. He pulled himself up to check the other fuel tank, seeing that it too was about half empty. But there was still enough to make two trips home easily. *Strange*, he thought. The prop turned freely and there was no damage to it. He dug deeper around each of the tires and confirmed there was no damage to either.

Other than the dent in the leading edge, he accessed that the plane could be flown out, eventually. Jack noted the sound of running water. Tasha had managed to land just a few yards from the frozen river's edge in what he determined to be the marsh area further northeast of the lake area.

But that will be another day while the ground is still cold enough. They needed the surface hard for the plane to use as a take-off area. It would be tight. But he needed Nick's advice and a few more hands to help shovel a makeshift runway for the aircraft.

"Are you done yet?" Chad hugged himself against the cold breeze as he remained standing in the wing's shadow. "I want to get going. We only have so much daylight to get her out of here. You think Nick could land a float plane on the lake up a ways?" He looked up at the overcast gray skies and pointed off to a barely visible shoreline. Visibility was the best it had been in those last three days.

Jack nodded his head as he took out his handheld radio and called, telling them the good news.

CHAPTER TWENTY-EIGHT

"You're good to go, Tasha," the doctor told her, finishing his examination and treatment to prevent further issues. "But I would highly advise you to consider getting that operation. It just wasn't meant to be. I'm sorry, Tasha." He put a hand on her shoulder.

She nodded her head, refusing to sniffle in front of him.

"Get dressed, and I'll see that Chad or one of the flight line guys come pick you up." The doctor stopped at the door before turning the handle. "You did good to survive three days out in the cold, Tasha. No frostbite or other issues from this experience coming down the road to haunt you—physically, that is. For a greenie, you're a tough one." The doctor took his leave, giving Tasha the time she needed to get dressed in the clothes that Chad had gotten from their cabin.

Chad met her outside the examination room. She was grateful it wasn't Jack. She did not think she could face him. After the three of them returned and Jack was feeling confident with Tasha being in Chad's good hands, he had returned to work to see what could be done on getting their flights back on schedule and retrieving *Tess* from the wilderness.

Chad's concern showed clearly on his face. "You all right?" Chad noted her paleness and got her to a row of seats to let her rest a minute, taking a seat next to her.

He saw her fight back the tears that had threatened to spill as she nodded her head, indicating she was fine.

"It's not the end of the world, and Jack isn't going to be angry at you over that—"

Tasha sharply turned her head to face Chad, making him stop mid-sentence, her abject horrified expression along with her head shaking no.

"Seriously? Tasha! He doesn't know?" Chad asked, stunned. "Why didn't you tell him? For that matter, when…"

"I knew a few days before I flew out and was forced down." She squeezed his hand. "Chad, we've been so busy with flying these last two weeks that we have barely the time at home to be together, much less talk. I was going to tell him that day before he took off on his route…" She blew out a bated breath, a tear escaping and rolling down her cheek, leaving a sparkling trail on her winter-dulled skin. "He…" She paused, nodding her head. "…He was just so busy with everything that I couldn't interrupt him with this…" She waved her hand aimlessly in front of her. "The last thing he needed was to worry about something else, distracting him. I've caused him enough trouble as it is." She wiped at the errant tear, swallowing hard. "Hell, I create a situation everywhere I go lately… Even put his and your life on the line to come fetch me out in the middle of mountains!"

"Tasha." Chad got her to stop. "First of all, you're not trouble for him, save for his heart."

Tasha had her head down, her hair hiding her face.

"Tasha." Chad reached over to lift her chin and have her look at him. "You didn't risk our lives. Jack would move mountains to get to you." He encouraged her with a smile. "Me and the dogs, on the other hand, prefer running past or between them, as you well know. The dogs thought they were on a new racecourse."

Her mouth trembled as he spoke.

"Besides, it was some darn good training for the Iditarod in a few weeks."

Chad watched her laugh weakly, happy at getting her to lighten up on herself, as she put her hands to her mouth and then wiped at her nose with the back of her hand, sniffling.

"Let's get you home and let you rest," he offered.

But Tasha laid a hand on his arm, stopping him. "Chad…I don't want him to know. He doesn't need any more pain or disappointment from me…much less feeling like he lost someone under his management." She pleaded, "At least…not now. I need you to *swear* to me that you won't tell him."

"Only if you will…and from you," he said, persisting. "He *should* know, Tasha."

"Eventually, Chad." She nodded at him. "I just need to let things settle, I need some time to get a few things taken care of first…Promise me, Chad? Please?"

She could see he did not like it, but he reluctantly agreed, giving her knee a quick, assuring squeeze.

"Come on, Moose." He gave her a hand up. "Let's get you home and give you a heavy duty shot of pain meds. You need some sleep."

Tasha woke up several times intermittently during the next two days, only to find the cabin devoid of Jack. She found a note each time on the island countertop telling her he loved her, that he had to go back to work, to remain home resting, and that he would be home soon.

By day three, she went into work like normal, taking her car instead of walking. The cold weather was still too much for her after those three days out in the freezing wilderness.

"Hey, Moose! Whatcha doing back so early?" Hank greeted as she entered the hangar, then gave her a suspicious eye. "Aren't ya supposed to be at home resting?"

She smiled at him. "Yes, but I feel fine, Hank." Tasha looked around the hangar, a few planes missing here and there.

"Well, Big Raven is out on a delivery flight, along with Manny on another one out east. Jack and the rest of them took the Caravan and some tools to see if they could get *Tess* back here today. They've been shovelin' snow for a makeshift runway most of the morning."

"They got the fuel flowing again?"

"Yeah, the boys said the plane fired right back up like no problem after they put in a new battery."

"Then…why did the engine stop on me? I must have done something wrong." She was now wondering if she was going crazy.

"Nah, girl. Ya did fine. You did what ya had to. Once we get her home, we'll tear her down and figure out what's going on with her. William is going to want to do an inspection to finalize the incident report."

She gave him an ambiguous look.

"Moose, ya worry too much. It'll be fine." Hank patted her shoulder. His radio crackled with Nick announcing that they had already landed in the harbor and that Jack was just behind them, coming in for a landing.

"I've got to get ready for them, Tash."

"Can I come with you?" she asked hesitantly.

"Sure. Hop on, since ya got your coat on already." He gestured to the tug and hurried to the garage door button to open the main door. Returning, he jumped on the tug, where Tasha had already started the engine for him, and hustled them out onto the tarmac.

Tasha could see the landing light in the distance, the spot growing and forming the 185 Skywagon. At first she could not hear the engine, and then she did. It did not sound good, the engine cycling from full power to idle and back to full power, making her heart leap to her throat. It was doing the very same thing to whoever was flying it that it had done to her.

"Approaching final, but engine is acting like it's fuel starved," Jack's voice came over the radio.

She made a throat noise that even Hank noted, giving her a calming pat to her hand in her lap. "He's fine, Moose."

"…fuel gauges are going nuts…"

Nick, Sam, and Jarvis had just arrived, walking from the car over to the awaiting tug.

"Man, that's not sounding good," Jarvis commented.

"Yeah, he said it was spooling down each time he made a sharp turn but then resumed full power," added Sam.

"Was this happening to you, Moose?" Jarvis asked.

The engine's complete silence interrupted them. It didn't start back up. Jack was at least a half mile out from the end of the runway.

"Okay, problem. This will be a dead-stick landing," Jack radioed.

Tasha's hands in her fingerless gloves went up to her mouth, stifling a cry, a whimper, as the guys all went to full alert.

Nick hollered for Sam to go get the additional fire extinguishers from the hangar.

"On it!" he said, running toward the hangar.

"Hank, give me your radio." Nick's hand motioned for the device.

"Jack! Can you hear me?" Nick asked.

"Yeah, a little too loud and clear."

"Okay, funny guy, let's get your speed up. Lower that nose, you'll be coming in lower than normal but I'm certain you can make it."

"I'm taking the car down to the end of the runway just in case he ends up in the water," Jarvis told them all.

"Good idea," Nick said.

Jarvis took off for the car and drove down toward the end of the runway, staying along the edge so Jack had room to land.

They watched as Jack set up the glide.

The seconds ticked by too slowly as far as Tasha was concerned. Her most blatant fear reared its ugly head, its roar echoing in her mind. She was most likely going to lose him too, over her ineptitude of flying an aircraft that she should have checked more thoroughly—or at least tried to have flown the rest of the way, given that the engine could run again...until now. He was willing to die for her!

"Looking good, Jack," Nick encouraged. "Leave your flaps up. You've got the whole runway to get her stopped."

They could see Jarvis as he got out of the car and waited at the end of the runway by the water's edge.

Never has silence been so deafening, thought Tasha. She inwardly groaned, or so she thought, when Hank reached out hugging her to him, momentarily assuring her. He released her and got out of the tug, taking one of the fire extinguishers from Sam.

She got off the tug on her side and stood alone, her arms crossed tightly around her body in sheer fear.

Jack was really low. The plane's wheels looked like they would get hung up on the rocks at the end of the runway, possibly flipping the airplane upside down before he could get to the runway's smooth surface.

Why couldn't the tides have been out? There would be a sandy tidal area to land on. Tasha closed her eyes, praying fervently for him to remain alive—that she would do everything necessary to keep him alive, even if it meant leaving him to keep him safe, should he make it. She did not need another man's death on her hands.

She caught Jarvis jumping up and down, his arms waving wildly, and she realized he was signaling that Jack was over the end of the runway with his thumbs up.

"Yes!" Nick hissed into the walkie-talkie. "Drop flaps and flare!"

The plane dropped, bouncing heavily. The guys cheered, immediately high-fiving each other. Hank and Sam jumped onto the tug, with Nick hopping precariously onto the tug's hood. They had left the fire extinguishers with her in their excitement, hurrying out to hook up to the plane sitting at the end of the runaway, getting it cleared as fast as possible for other aviation traffic.

Tasha stood there until she could see Jack climb out of the plane, greeting the guys happily as they pulled up, laughing and smiling. Jack clasped forearms with Nick and they gave each other a bro hug, slapping each other's back.

Tasha looked skyward giving a big 'thank you' to whoever had listened to her prayer. It was time to fulfill her end of the bargain so that Jack would never risk his life for her again.

She turned, a fire extinguisher in each hand, and hauled them back into the hangar. Then she went to work on finding a new navigation light assembly to repair the one she had damaged in her forced landing.

When the guys towed *Tess* in, she had the cleaning equipment ready so that she could clean up her camping mess. As she was hauling the equipment to where they had chocked the bird, Jack stopped her, nabbing her to give her a big bear hug, happy to see her. *Who wouldn't be happy after a harrowing experience of landing without an engine?* She felt happiness swell inside her body as he swung her around, and then dissipate as he set her down on the ground. She smiled back, reaching up to touch his beard, stroking it for as long as she could to immortalize the sensation in her hand.

"You're supposed to be at home resting."

"So should you," she accused him. "That couldn't wait?" Tasha indicated to the plane with a cock of her head.

"We had some time and enough guys to help with shoveling to get her back up in the air and home. I now understand why you did what you did. I'm glad you played it safe. We are even going to make Nate even happier that we got his plane back in one piece—"

"And you," she interrupted. "You could have gotten hurt or worse…kil—"

"But I didn't." He grinned cheekily at her, kissing the palm of her hand that he laid on his chest after she had caressed his beard. "I'm still here. You're not getting rid of me that easily," he teased.

She gave him a Mona Lisa smile.

Jack took the bag of vacuum attachments from her, walking back to the aircraft, where Jarvis and Hank took to undoing the wing's fuel caps on each side to check inside the tanks.

Jack looked over his shoulder at her. "Give me an hour and we'll go home early?"

"Sure, I need to order a new light assembly anyways." She pointed to the damaged wing and turned to walk back to the room that contained all their manuals to look up the part and order it.

The week went by smoothly, and *Tess's* repairs were nearly done. Manny and Jarvis made short work on getting a new leading edge, and Tasha had just finished installing and testing the new navigation light assembly when she met Nate in the hallway on her way to the battery room.

"How ya doing, Tasha?" he asked.

"I'm doing good. We've got the plane finished. Repaired and cleaned." She looked down at the floor, not able to make eye contact in her shame of putting them all through hell and back.

"Good…good to hear that," he grunted in a fatherly fashion, nodding.

She did not look up until she realized he was standing there waiting. She had no idea what to say next to him, still uncomfortable with the past situation, before continuing with a weak statement to him. "Look, I just wanted to tell you how sorry I am for putting you and the crew through all that…" She waved a hand in the direction of the hangar. "I was stupid for not doing a more thorough job of checking before leaving Valdez—"

"Tasha," Raven said, grabbing ahold of her shoulder to make her stop, since she had her hands full with paperwork and her tool caddy. "Tasha. You did everything that you could." He sighed heavily, then indicated for them to go into her battery room by opening the door for her and letting her walk past him to deposit everything on the table.

"Take a seat, Tasha." He pulled out a stool for him to sit across from her at the table.

The door swung shut automatically, giving them the privacy to talk. She sat down, and before she could speak, he continued.

"Let me make this clear. You are not going to lose your job over this, if that's what you are concerned about." He unfolded his fingers and laid his hands on the table. "Things happen all the time when it comes to aviation. No matter how much we plan in advance, check, and double-check…things can still go wrong."

"But I could have—"

"Could have what? Tasha, you did everything you could do, and you did it right. You got yourself safely down, alive and in one piece." Nate interrupted her, trying to reassure her.

She placed a hand over her mouth, physically stemming her emotions, knowing she was no longer in one piece anymore, more like having lost pieces of herself in the past few weeks. Her emotions were threatening to overtake her now that there was more time to reflect.

"Secondly, I am very proud that you managed to land my airplane with very minimal damage." His aged blue eyes looked into hers. "In fact, you kept the plane in what we call 'rentable condition.' The boys managed to get her back home. I couldn't have asked for more, considering the situation.

"Last…" He pulled something out of his binder that he usually carried with him. "I don't know how you expected to see this"—he was digging items out of a plastic bag—"even with a flashlight, Tasha. But Jarvis and Manny found several of these inside the fuel tanks."

She gave him a questioning look as he produced the clear plastic pieces of what looked like a shredded milk container, only clearer.

"This was what was blocking the fuel lines and messing with the fuel indicator as they floated around in the tanks."

She crunched her nose up and exhaled against the fuel smell, asking, "What else is in there that would have fallen apart inside the fuel tanks?" Tasha handed the plastic pieces back.

"Nothing, Tasha. Absolutely nothing." Nate shoved the pieces back into the bag. He did not add anything else, not answering her mechanical question. But she was not going to push the issue either if he did not want to expound. She tried to discern what it was he was thinking, his face darkening, before he gave her an unexpected smile. Nate stood back up to take his leave.

"Sir?" she asked, stopping him at the door.

He turned back tentatively.

She licked her lips nervously. "I know this is maybe too early to ask, and I realize it's going to get busier, but is there any way…is there any way I can take some time off? Enough time to go visit my folks in Florida. I'm just not sure for how long."

At this, she had Nate's full attention.

She explained part of her reasoning for leaving based on medical leave, adding in the doctor's advice on some extra surgery, but not the full story behind it all, then adding, "It'll give me the time to think over a few things."

"You thinking of leaving us?"

"No. No, not entirely. Okay, I'm not sure what I want. But I need time."

He mulled it over, certain he was only going to allow her two weeks max, only to give her up to six months of 'family leave.' He added, "I really could use you here when tourist season starts back in full swing at the end of May. That's only a little under two months from now."

She nodded.

"When do you want to leave?" he asked gruffly.

"Within a day or two. As soon as I can get an airline ticket."

He nodded and opened the door, taking his leave.

A few days later, she 'hitched' a flight with Sam, although more like she was assigned to the flight. She stowed her bags on his plane outside where Hank had towed it minutes earlier. She was grateful that everyone had their assigned flights and that Jack had decided it was easier to break her back into flying again by making her double up with someone.

When she caught the assignment with Sam going to Copper Center and then onto Gulkana and back, she had asked him if she could be dropped off at the Anchorage Airport.

Sam raised his eyebrows at her surprise request.

"I decided to go on a quick vacation," she told him when he stopped by her cabin to pick her up. Jack had already taken off earlier that morning for his delivery flight. She added, "…need some time off."

"Already?"

"Yup."

"You already had three days out in the wilderness, nature watching," he joked, trying to get her to smile.

She did, but she knew it didn't reach her eyes and she cast her eyes away from him, pretending to be interested at something outside the car window.

"Where are you going?" Sam pressed, glancing over to her a few times as he concentrated on driving.

She shrugged her shoulders. "Thought I would make good on my promise to my mother to stop in and visit them and maybe go drive and see some folks I haven't seen since leaving for the Army. Most of all, soak up some warmth and sun. My last *vacation* was a tad bit cold for my tastes."

Sam laughed.

They chatted some more during the flight, and she steered him often to his favorite topic of his girlfriend, Lela. He dropped her off in Anchorage, where she would wait for the next three hours until her flight would leave. Twelve hours and two layovers later, she was unlocking her parents' door, letting herself in, and surprising her parents. She greeted them warmly but begged for her own bed so that she could recover from the jet lag.

From there, she had her father's help, desperately trying to spare her mother the full details of what she had gone through earlier and her intentions for the tubal ligation procedure. She was grateful to her father's quiet support and his strong arms wrapped around her, assuredly hugging her. She knew it was breaking his heart, yet he knew it was for the best to keep his daughter alive and healthy, too.

"Are you sure, honey?" he asked her, still concerned, and holding out hope three days later.

She nodded her head just as the aesthetician was about to put her under. "Yeah, I can't go through that again, Dad. It was just too pain…" she was telling him, falling asleep before she could finish.

He watched as the nurses wheeled her into the surgery room.

At two weeks later, she was still inside reading a book, moping. Her mind was not into her reading as she sat there and pondered, staring out the window. A knock came on her bedroom door, and her mother entered with someone in tow.

"Look who's here to see you, sweetie."

Tasha saw the old familiar sandy blond short-haired man and realized it was Artie, dropping her book aside on her bed as she got up to greet him.

She smiled brightly at Arthur, remembering her old high school and college friend. She gave him a quick hug before offering him her old desk chair as a seat and resuming her seat on the side of her bed by the window.

"Wow, you've changed!" Artie said.

"I have?"

"No, not really—just a paler shade of pale. My God, when was the last time you saw the sun?"

"Like forever, Artie!" her mother injected. "I don't think that place even knows what sun is."

"Yes, we do, Mother. You just happened to come visit me in the middle of winter when we have a lot grayer days." Tasha hoped her mother would take the hint and leave. She knew what her mother was up to, and it bothered her some that she was 'interfering' in her life again.

"Artie, you would hate it," her mother added, pulling at her necklace, hesitating on an errant internal thought, thumbing the beads on the chain in a worried manner before deciding, when neither of them said anything, to go make them all some lunch. Her mother winked at Artie before she turned her back on them to leave Tasha's room, softly closing the door.

"What's with the winking?" Artie thumbed over his shoulder to her door.

"Nothing, Artie…Just ignore it. She's still thinking we'll hook up one day."

"Seriously?" he chuckled, running a hand through his short, thick, sandy, sun-bleached hair. "So what's it like being Nanook of the North?"

Tasha snorted at his question. "Actually, quite nice. The mountains, the water, and all the glaciers are some of the most majestic vistas I have ever seen. I think you'd like it, but only in the summertime. But then, you'd hate it because you couldn't wear your flip-flops up there. You'd still be cold during our summers."

"Ah, no thanks." He picked aimlessly at his toes where he had crossed his leg over one knee. "I'll never give up the beach life. Love the sunshine way too much."

"So I can see from the tan," she noted, her hand gesturing to his deeply tanned skin. His body had filled out more, sporting a slight paunch, since the last time she had seen him. "And how's the hotdog wagon business these days?"

"Good. Really good. I'm up to ten carts and twelve girls."

At this she raised an eyebrow at him.

He wiggled a finger at her. "No, I haven't dated a single one of them."

"What'd you do, Artie, hire all the ladies from the downtown senior citizen's bridge club?"

"There's never been anyone remotely close to you, Tash."

This gave her pause, making her feel uncomfortable. She felt bad that she could never seem to see Artie in that way. Although they had lost their virginity together, wanting someone safe as they tasted and experienced life for the first time away from home and at college, it was nothing compared to the way she felt with Jack. Artie would always have a soft spot in her heart. Something that she would always treasure and carry with her as they went their separate ways on their own life's path. The same for Jack, although it was causing her too much pain this time around, causing her to hold a bated breath until the feeling subsided.

"Sorry, that was wrong of me to say that," Artie told her, pulling her from her thoughts.

"Oh...no...no, you're fine. I understand."

"You seem different." He switched legs over as he sat back in the chair. "I guess the military does really change you. Was it because you got wounded?"

"No, not really. I just lost a really *good* friend."

He raised an eyebrow on this, saying, "More than a friend." He knew her better than anyone else.

She pressed her lips into a tight, thin line, nodding. "You could say that. I had a severely misplaced crush on him. He was married...had a newborn and a pretty wife back home."

"And?"

She smirked at Artie. "Nothing happened between us. He was honorable." Artie was just way too easy to hang out with and tell him things. Nothing was secret between the two of them. "He died. He took the other two bullets that were meant for me." Her fingers picked at one of the printed flowers on her comforter. "It should have been me that day, Artie." She said the last statement a bit quieter in her flooding guilt.

"Lunch is ready!" came her mother's sing-song voice from downstairs.

He knew not to push her. Artie uncrossed his leg, placing both feet on the floor, leaned forward, and placed a hand on her knee. "Tell you what...Tasha... after lunch, how about letting me drive you around and let me take you to the beach, and we can talk more then? Your mother says you're not allowed to drive since your surgery. In addition, I think we need to get you outside and reacquaint you with the sun again."

He shook her knee as he got up. "Put your swimsuit on and a pair of shorts too. Bring a shirt in case we're forced inside during our normal afternoon showers. I'll meet you in the dining room and tell your mother that we're headed to the beach and walk around some of the new malls they've just built. That should keep her off your back for a while."

Artie hiked up his swim trunks around his waist as he stood there in front of her. "Let me guess, we're having grilled cheese sandwiches and tomato soup for lunch." He held her door open, allowing her to go first, letting her lead the way downstairs.

Tasha wrinkled her nose at him. "Knowing her, most likely."

Arthur ended up being a godsend and she was grateful to have someone to talk to other than her dad. Her spirit felt lighter after unloading all her experiences and her feelings to him. At first she was hesitant on talking about Jack, but Artie took it in stride.

"Ah, so *that's* why you're really home. Trouble on the northern frontier."

They had paused by the pier after clambering over a cement barrier and dropping down on the other side into the wet sand together.

"You really like this guy," he commented, forcing her head up from where she was watching the wet sand move, filling in the gaps between her depressed toes as she wriggled them in the heavy beige crystals. "Well, it's clear to me you're in love." He gestured to his face. "You always did wear your emotions on your sleeve, Tasha. You light up like a marquee just mentioning him."

"Problem is, I still have to work with him and yet tell him I can't be his wife. And it would darn near kill me to see him move on with another woman. But I cannot risk hurting him again, much less dying on account of me doing something stupid again. I know I scared him with nearly losing me when I had my forced landing out in the Alaskan wilderness, but the last thing I need to add is that I lost a baby on him. He doesn't need me to add any more grief on his plate. And I just can't handle it when he puts his life on the line for me. He shouldn't have to...not for me."

"Tasha, he rescued you. Not just because you're an employee, but because he *cares* about you. Men in love are supposed to *do* those kinds of *things* for the women they love. Love makes men do crazy things!"

"But women either drive them to it by being devious, or if they truly love them, keep them from doing stupid stunts like that that could get them killed! I'm trying to keep him from endangering himself over me. There are better pilots than me—people who will not cause as much trouble as I have done. He doesn't need the additional hassles. Honestly, I'm not worth it!"

Arthur gave her a poignant look before sighing. "Why don't you think you're worth it?"

"I'm not worth dying for—"

"Bullshit, Tasha. You are worth it," he told her, putting his hands on his hips. "You have so much to offer. Your love and affection, your looks, your intelligence, your practicality, your flight skills, and *oh-my-god*...your cooking..."

"But I can't give him any kids, and I am certain he will want at least one, Artie!"

"Has he said this, to you?" he asked. "Has he specifically told you he wanted kids?" When she did not answer him, he added, "I didn't think so. Tasha, you assume way too much about people. And now you're going to leave them behind over this little hang-up of yours?"

"No. It's not only my hang-up. I'm just trying to please everyone, you know…and I keep letting everyone down. And those I don't let down end up risking their life or dying for it!"

"Quit pleasing people, Tasha! You need to *please* yourself, *live your* life, not what *your mother* or anyone else wants, for Pete's sake! Stop beating yourself up over this guy who died saving you. He did what he thought was necessary! And in my book, he's a superhero for *saving* you, Tasha. Let him have his title and honor! Give us men something to look forward to." Artie ran a hand through his short blond hair. "Hell, I would love to be someone's hero! Us guys live for that one moment for that special someone! Otherwise, it's just not really living. *Can't* you see that?"

Tasha nodded, adding, "A little, but it's got to be a man thing, because it's so hard for me to comprehend the way you guys think at times. You make it sound like men have suicidal tendencies for the ones they love, Artie! I don't think I will ever be brave enough the way most men are. I wish I was stronger." Her hands aimlessly wrung each other, before she realized it was reflecting her inner turmoil to Artie and dropped them to her sides.

"I can't believe I am saying this when I would love for you to stay here with me. But don't leave what you love doing over this issue…these issues," he said, correcting himself.

"No, I can't leave them. I really like my job and the guys I work with. I love where I live now, even though I am certainly missing the Florida warmth and sunshine at times," she laughed. Then on a more somber note, she continued. "But I need to find a way to protect Jack from me. Even if it means breaking off our personal side of the relationship. I love him too much to let him risk his life for me again, and he doesn't need to go through what I just did. I would only be adding to all the hurt he carries."

Her feet stayed firmly in the sand, letting the water repetitively surge and envelop her lower calves. The water was normally too cold for her tastes at that time of year. It was early spring and the Gulf waters wouldn't be nearly warm enough for her for in another month or so. But the cold water did not stab her with a million ice picks as it did in Resurrection Bay. She wondered if she would eventually turn into a snowbird, thinking the Florida winter waters were warm enough for her to swim in.

As if reading her thoughts, Artie noted, "Christ, Tasha, there was a time you would never have stuck your feet in this water at this time of year."

She moved to get out of the cool water.

They continued to walk the beach, but up along the drier sand.

"Well, I think the guy would be crazy to let you go over a small…well…not so small thing for *you*…but over a wound that left you unable to have children. You had to do what is best for you. It isn't the only thing in a relationship or marriage that holds it together."

Together they stopped on the sand, where a large broken conch shell lay.

"Tell you what: if he doesn't accept it when you finally tell him and you find yourself unable to stay up in the North, then you've always got me…you know I'll take you in. But you're going to have to help me work a wagon a few days a week."

She gave him a playful slug to his shoulder, and he acted like he was hurt, grabbing his shoulder, telling her, "Man, the Army gave you superhuman strength that you're obviously not aware of." Arthur was big into superheroes and comic books, which made him an eternally geeky teenager in her eyes, reminding her of all the fun they used to have back then. But somewhere she felt like she had grown up, where he seemed to be the eternal Peter Pan. The thought made her smile. And he did have a way of making her smile, even when she felt she was at her worst.

CHAPTER TWENTY-NINE

"Sit down, Jack," Nate ordered him once he was in his office. "I've got something interesting to show you, son."

He pulled out his cell phone, swiped and clicked his screen, pulling something up for Jack. "I got this in from the Valdez airport. It's one of the airport's flight line monitoring cameras and it caught this…" Nate handed him his phone and indicated for Jack to start watching the video.

He watched as their lone Skywagon was towed back in by a fuel worker and parked near several other aircraft. Once the lineman left with the tug, another man appeared, with a hoodie on and carrying a mini-stepladder. He looked around several times, as if ensuring the coast was clear. Jack watched as the man stepped up on the ladder and opened the fuel cap on the wing tank, dumping something into the opening, and then put the cap back on. He took his time walking around to the other side to do the same thing to the other wing tank, as if it was his airplane and he was preforming a pre-flight check. It was when the man scurried away facing toward the perched camera that Jack recognized him.

"Dirk!" Jack growled to himself, swearing, but Nate heard him.

"Yup, we now have the evidence to finally pin something on him. He's the reason Tasha's plane had trouble. William and I are going to prosecute him for tampering with an aircraft with the intent to destroy property and murder one of our own. So I need you to keep yourself under control when it comes to Dirk. Do not give the justice system any further reason not to prosecute him to the fullest extent and beyond a reasonable doubt."

"Did they catch the bastard?" he asked.

"They've rounded him up yesterday. As we speak he's back in jail, without bond until his initial hearing."

"Well, that will keep him safe from me for now. How did you secure this feed?" Jack asked, returning Nate's phone and asking him to send it in a text message to his phone. "When did you suspect?"

"Oh, I knew something was strange when Jarvis and Manny drained the fuel and found all this clear plastic debris the day after you boys brought the plane back. I took it to William to have it inspected and tested. And in turn, he pulled some FAA and Homeland Security strings and got the Valdez airport to hand over their security camera recordings."

Nate shoved his phone back in his belt clip. "I even showed Tasha what we found, but didn't tell her about what we suspected since we both agreed not to tell her about them releasing Dirk a few days after his first attempt to hurt her. However, I don't think she put two and two together. She's still blaming herself for everything, along with being shaken after those three days out in the snow-packed valley. Can't say I blame her being as young and not having more than about four…what…five years flight experience? Intermittent at that." Nate looked at Jack to verify what he had suspected.

"Yeah," Jack wiped his damp palms on his pants. "But there was something else eating at her. I know my dead-stick landing scared her to death. It upset her."

"Can't say I blame her. I'm glad I wasn't there to witness it either. I have enough gray hairs, son. Don't need any more."

Jack pressed his lips together, and Nate slapped his one hand down on his desk, changing the subject.

"So how is she? You've talked to her?"

"Honestly, I don't know, and I'm worried. She won't answer her phone, she hasn't returned a single call—or a text, for that matter." Jack exhaled heavily. Standing up, he shoved his hands into his pockets and paced some just behind his chair. "I can't even remember what it is that I did to possibly upset her three weeks ago."

Nate had leaned back in his desk chair, tipping it back against the wall. He put a hand to his chin, only to rub his jowls before asking cautiously, "You two didn't have a fight or anything before she left?"

Jack shook his head no. "She was gone before I even knew she was taking time off." His hand rubbed at the back of his neck, and then he looked at Nate, asking, "Did she tell you anything?"

"Not really." He was not sure how much Jack knew, so he did not say much. Nate was a big believer in holding people's confidences and wanted to keep that intact. Though he wondered what Jack did know. "She just told me that she wanted time to think and spend time at home in Florida with her parents."

"Her parents?" Jack asked incredulously.

"I know, I know. Tasha can barely put up with her mother, but it seemed to me she loves her dad. She's definitely a daddy's girl," Nate said, a wistful smile on his mouth.

Jack knew Nora and Nate had always wanted a girl, and he was certain that Tasha had filled that void in their lives for them.

However, Tasha was breaking not just his heart, but Nate's and the rest of the crew's. It was not the same without her. She had made a niche in those past few months. His fingers caressed her ring in his pocket, where he had kept it since he had discovered that she had left it behind on the desk in her room. She had cleaned her room and nearly packed up all her things, he thought. Nearly everything was either in her duffel bag, knapsack, or in the plastic milk crates in her closet. It was all waiting, in limbo, just like him—waiting to see whether she was going to be staying or leaving on a whim. Every day he came home, though her car was still parked outside, the first thing he did was check her room to see if anything had disappeared or if she was back.

"Well, I'm sure she'll be back, Jack," Raven added, although it sounded like he was also just hoping she would.

"She didn't tell you how long?"

"No, son. Just that she needed some time to rearrange some things back home."

He still had no answer, and it was not like Raven not to know a specific date, much less not tell Jack when it was he expected her to return.

Jack left Nate's office to return to his task of scheduling the next week's flights. The work helped to distract him, but they were having another lull in flight requests and the idle time was killing him.

Another week passed, and the following Wednesday he decided to meet up with the crew at the local bar. Entering the darkened tavern, he let his eyes adjust and located the crew at their usual table along the adjacent wall. Chad was with them, too, waving him over. Nick was the only one not sitting with the group. He was up at the bar trying to hit on a pretty redheaded woman. She wasn't a local, since Jack did not recognize her and redheads weren't that common in Seward.

As he took his seat at the end of the booth, he saw the woman slap Nick's face. The guys commented among themselves, and betted money slid around between them on Nick either scoring—or quite clearly losing—the gal at the bar. Jack smiled at his feeble attempt, currently feeling very much like Nick.

"Told ya he wouldn't," Sam said to Jarvis sitting across from him, taking a sip of his beer.

"Just what is that man saying to get slapped like that?" Jarvis mused, "Sure hope it wasn't something stupid and making the rest of us look like losers."

"We're not losers. She's just stuck up…" Manny contended.

"Now, now, now, guys. Mind yer manners and yer cussing and you all may end up lucky to have a nice girl." Hank facetiously buffed his dirty nails on his coveralls. "You guys could be as lucky as me and my missus."

"Lucky?" Jarvis said in surprise. "Man, I think yer wife is trying to kill ya with her cooking!" His comment made Hank stop in his manicure.

Several *hear, hears* were made between them all.

"It's that bad?" Chad asked Jack quietly away from the group's small talk, looking at Jack for confirmation.

At first he didn't answer, taking a long draw on the beer that Nick placed in front of him as he reclaimed his seat. Jack noted one side of Nick's face was still red, before Jack nodded his head, yes.

"Seriously, I thought y'all liked her cooking! Jack, help me out here!" Hank interrupted Chad and his side discussion.

"Hell, even Drake backs away from it, Hank. And the dog is as honest as one can get!" Jack jested some, although his heart wasn't entirely with the group. It had been stolen by a moose that had gone south.

Laughter erupted along the guys with a few high fives.

"Well…" Hank said, taking another swig of his beer, burping, and then stating on a more serious note, "I sure do miss someone else's cooking."

A couple of low 'yeahs' were said. Manny spoke up after a gravid pause. "When's she coming back, Jack?"

He shrugged his shoulders as he shook his head. He took another long swig, until he realized their expectant faces were waiting on an explanation for Tasha's absence.

Only Chad was looking down at his lap.

Jack looked at Sam, knowing that he was the one that had given her a lift to Anchorage. "I don't know why she left. Have you all asked Sam, since he was the last to see her?" Jack's voice took on an accusatory tone.

"Hey, man, you assigned her to my plane and delivery route. She hopped in, asking for the drop-off at Anchorage, and it was on my way to my route that day. Like I told you before, she didn't explain why. Only that she wanted a vacation."

"It's an awfully long vacation if you ask me," said Nick. "Hell, I don't…I don't think any of us get that much time off," he added, making a petulant statement toward Jack.

"Guys!" Chad interrupted. "You have to remember she just had a hell of a time out there on her own and she's new to flying. Am I right?" he asked, trying to smooth over the tension.

"Yeah, there was a lot of blood in that bucket along with…ahem…human waste when we cleaned the plane," said Jarvis.

"Blood?" Jack asked. "Like in bloody rags or bandages?"

"No, man," Jarvis said, taking another sip. "The contents darn near made Manny and I sicker than a dog when I asked him to toss the bucket in the main trash bin outside. That wolf must have gotten her good. Damn near looked like a massacre had taken place."

Jack looked at Chad, catching something in his eyes before Chad looked away. He suddenly knew there was something he wasn't saying. Jack took a long last swallow of his lager, glaring at Chad the entire time. He watched Chad's body stiffen under the heavy weight of his gaze.

"Chad, just how bad was it?" asked Sam.

Jack was grateful for him voicing one of his questions. Now that he thought about it, Chad and he had not talked since they had rescued her. But he had been extremely busy trying to keep the flight schedules on track while *Tess* was under repairs.

"Now, guys, she's fine and she's just sporting a few more stitches on her lower calf from the wolf attack. It just looks bad," Chad said, shifting rather uncomfortably in his seat, not daring to look Jack in the eye once as he told the others.

"How much blood?" Jack asked Jarvis, knowing Chad was not going to tell him, and not like he would have known or seen this bucket. But he sensed Chad was hiding something.

"Like I said, there was a lot. But it's not like I really looked closely, since it was making me queasy."

Jack got up as if he was going to grab another beer.

"Hey Jack," Nick called out, getting halfway up to catch him, "grab me another one." Nick reached into his pocket for his wallet when Jack exploded into pure action, nabbing Chad from his seat when Nick moved out of the way.

Jack hauled Chad up by his shirt collar, knocking bottles over on the table in the process, and threw him up against one of the posts separating the booths, placing his forearm against his throat, putting him in a choke hold. It was easy to do, given Chad's diminutive size compared to Jack's.

"*What* are you *not* telling me?" he growled, their faces inches apart.

Chad's hands clawed at Jack's massive arm that lay against his throat as Jack pushed on him, trying to make him spew what he knew.

"Whoa—"

"Jack!"

"Easy there, man!" came a few of the guys' comments all together.

"Have ya gone mad, man?" Hank came up to his side as the others tried to help free Chad and pry Jack off.

Jack ignored him. "Tell me!" Jack yelled at him, making Chad flinch. "Why's she really gone?"

Chad tried to say something, but couldn't against Jack's arm pressure.

"Jack, ease up on him," Hank encouraged at his ear. "Let him talk."

Chad's body slid down the post a bit, and he coughed and sucked in air. Jack still didn't take his arm away, bodily shaking off his crew with his shoulders. Sam remained by Chad's side, though, ready to get entangled should Jack follow through with a killing. The crew gave the two of them expectant looks, not entirely sure why Jack would attack his best friend or what else they didn't know about Tasha.

"What's wrong with her?" Jack made an assertive motion.

"She's fine, Jack...honestly."

Jack hauled him back up against the post and laid into him. But his crew managed to pull back on him to let Chad speak.

"She made me swear! She made me swear...*not* to say a word to you! I begged her to tell you. She needs to tell you herself!"

"What?" His face twisted to the side some, glancing at his crew, but keeping his attention locked on Chad. "What was she *supposed* to tell me?"

"It has to come from her," Chad insisted.

This caused Jack further anger, knowing it was impossible to get her to talk when she was several thousand miles away, halfway around the world and down by the equator, and not answering her phone.

"Well, she's not here!" He applied more pressure to Chad's throat. "Tell me,

God damn it!"

That time Chad was quick enough to get his hands in between Jack's arm and his neck to hold back on the pressure. "I…she *made* me swear…and it goes against patient confidentiality policies…Ungh!"

That time it took Hank, Jarvis, and Nick to get him off, letting Chad slide down the post to the floor.

Sam gave Chad a hand back up into the booth and protectively sat next to him, blocking Jack's access to him. "You okay, man?" asked Sam, looking back over his shoulder at Chad, the two of them wary as the three guys struggled against Jack's impatient angry strength.

"Yeah," Chad said, his hand massaging his sore neck.

"Man, I think you better tell him. Jack's in full berserker mode. Tasha's anger will be less compared to Jack's," Sam reasoned with him.

Chad finally nodded. Sam gave them all a two-finger sharp whistle, getting them all to stop in their struggle.

"Okay, Jack," Sam said, "here's the deal. You sit down civilly and don't lunge at Chad, and he said he will tell you."

On second thought, Chad spoke up. "It would have to be for only Jack to hear." He was being protective of Tasha's request, looking at the rest of the guys, swallowing hard, realizing he had just put himself at the mercy of Jack's volatile anger.

The four men stopped midway, Hank laying a passive restraining arm on Jack.

Sam leaned back toward Chad, not looking over his shoulder, and keeping an eye on the heaving beast in front of him. "Is that wise, man?" He voiced his concern between them. "I can usually hold my own pretty well, but Jack here can best me in a fight." When Chad did not answer, Sam twisted in his seat and looked at him, seeing him twist his nose and lips in thought.

"Stay, then," Chad sighed heavily. "But if and when Tasha returns, I will need every single one of you in my defense of breaking my promise to her."

Sam gave him a half-cocked smile at the thought of Chad being more scared of Tasha than Jack. He then turned, giving a *come here* wave to the guys. The group rearranged themselves accordingly, with one on each side of Chad and Jack, ready for any more explosive reactions.

Nick waved off the waitress when she asked if they needed anything, telling her to take away all the beer bottles—a good thought on his part, now focusing on the sit-down Western showdown…minus the guns, of course.

Sam knocked Chad's knee with his, getting him to start.

Chad swallowed hard, not looking at Jack, and instead chose to look at the others, reminding them what he was about to tell him could make him lose his job at the clinic—not to mention his life if Tasha found out. "When she was out there those three days…" Chad paused. "…she lost…a part of her." The air thickened over their table. Chad looked at Jack's piercing gray blue eyes, adding "…and a part of you."

There was a sudden vacuum of air loss over their table that left them in a void of silence.

He continued. "She tried to tell you earlier, but she said that you were too busy to give her any time with your workload…she was afraid of having your… 'mind blown,' as she put it, and for not wanting to have you distracted from your work and flying."

"Oh *hombre, definitivamente voy a estar enfermo*," came Manny's small voice, breaking the long, noiseless pause as the truth hit Jack, all of them noting his shoulders moving back and slumping, all his anger evaporated.

"You're not the only one going to be sick, Manny," came Jarvis.

"We could've all been uncles," came Hank's quiet afterthought.

"But…" Jack whispered, still trying to process the information. "The military doctors told her she wouldn't be able to"—his face contorted in confusion, pain, and sadness—"because of the bullet wreaking havoc on her insides…" He cocked his face away from Chad in disbelief.

"Well, it happened," Chad told him. "Unfortunately she could not go full term, and never will if she got pregnant again. She had to decide, and so she left. It would be cheaper in the lower forty-eights to get it done."

"Get what done?" Jack asked.

"A sterilization procedure. A tubal."

"Why would she think I'd be angry…and…and leave because of that?"

His guys all gave him a pointed look at having to rescue Chad from him.

"I would never!" he hissed lowly at them.

"I know you wouldn't," Sam said, defending Jack.

"She was more upset at herself than…" offered Chad.

"She made the decision?" Jack interrupted. "Why not…me…I mean, us?"

"Because you are not married to her, Jack…not yet."

Chad took the time to explain further. Jack's eyes watered with unshed tears. He leaned forward, placing an elbow on the table, putting his hand over his mouth, speechless. Then he dropped his face into his hands for a long time, sitting there quietly, putting the rest of the guys in an awkward position. None of them recollected ever seeing Jack lose his alpha dominance before—at least not in front of them. There had never been a moment of weakness that exuded from him. Even when they had thought Tasha was lost to them for good, Jack still plowed forward, not taking no for an answer until he had seen her with his own eyes.

When Jack recovered, sighing heavily, he dragged a hand down his face and then absently laid his beard flat against his jawline a couple of times before he asked, "So she's back home? In Florida?"

"I believe so." Chad shrugged. "She would need someone to assist her for a while…and then a couple of weeks to heal with no heavy lifting."

"Her dad," he said flatly.

"Are we good?" Chad asked cautiously, making Jack look him in the eye.

"Yeah," Jack said, sitting up more and back to his normal self. "I need a beer." He looked to the others as they nodded tentatively.

Nick got the waitress's attention and motioned for another round at their table.

Jack gave his buddy a sorrowful apologetic look, adding "Sorry."

Chad, still uncertain, told him, "You made me break a promise. My word. But apology accepted."

The mood of the place was downright dismal the following week. The winter weather stubbornly remained. His guys were unusually quiet at their daily work as Nate wandered between the planes on the hangar floor casually checking things. Jack had told him that past Friday of what he had learned, from all people and places, from his friend Chad. It was then that he had told Jack that he had granted her medical leave request but was not entirely sure as to why and was asked to not say anything to Jack. That she would have rather it be private for the time being. Nate said he had argued with her, saying Jack should know, so he thought. However, she had reminded him that they were not married yet, nor did she owe anyone an explanation.

Now, Raven understood her reasoning. It was a touchy subject, but in her case understandable, given her past injuries and the current circumstances. He was grateful that she was helping the company save on medical costs by returning to the lower forty-eights. It was disheartening that she had gone about it alone and would not let Jack in to be of some comfort and assistance.

Jack wasn't *that* busy at the expense of family and friends. Then again, he knew of Tasha's stubbornness at not talking with Jack the past few weeks. Her only responses back were the weekly texts to Nate stating she was fine and healing. He wanted to text back that she needed to talk with Jack, but it was not his place to get involved between the two of them.

By the following Monday, at the morning meeting, he let Jack finish instructing the guys on their expected duties and writing on the whiteboard. The sense of 'something off' in the break area would have even been noticeable to a stranger walking upon them. Nate looked at the whiteboard. There were only four flights for the week: one for each day, save Wednesday. He studied the board, keeping the guys in limbo at the table and Jack patiently waiting beside him, in his usual military 'at ease' stance.

"Hank!" Nate barked, still looking at the whiteboard.

Hank perked up at the end of the table.

"You think us two old men could handle this workload like we did in the old days?"

Hank looked at the guys, not too sure what to make of his question, but answered, "Yeah, boss, I know we could still handle it. Why?"

Nate turned in his spot to take in his view of his guys sitting at the break table, half awake and clearly despondent.

"Well, you don't fly and I do…and I think all of our boys here, including Jack here, need a vacation."

"*Qué?*" came Manny.

"Huh?" came Jarvis.

"Yes!" exclaimed Sam and Nick, high-fiving each other.

"For real?" asked Jarvis.

"How long?" asked Manny.

"What's our work schedule for next week, Jack?" asked Nate.

Jack looked at his clipboard he had held behind him as he waited, flipping a page up. "There's not really another flight until the following Wednesday."

"Where to and what plane?"

"The Angelina. Juneau."

"Anything after that?"

"A few day-trippers, and the first cruise ship of the season is expected to arrive by Saturday."

The Raven nodded, taking in the information given him, mumbling, but still audible to Jack, and the two guys sitting closest to where he stood overheard him. "God, this is going to cost me on fuel." He dragged a hand down on his lower face, pulling some on his middle-aged jowls.

There was a long pause.

"Guys, here's the deal…you're all taking the Angelina to Florida until Tuesday morning! Angelina has the longest range and will need the least number of stops. You will all take turns flying nonstop except for refueling to…to…" Raven hesitated.

"Palm Harbor?" Jack filled in, realizing where this was leading.

"Yes, Palm Harbor! You will all pay for your own lodging and food. All of you are going Moose hunting—"

"Wait? Hunh—"

"—with Jack."

"There's moose in Florida?" Manny asked, but Nate clarified.

"Jack, I need my Sparky back. Go get her and bring her back, one way or the other."

The guys excitedly jumped up from their seats at the prospect of flying to Florida.

"Go get packed—lightly, I remind you—and be ready to leave in the hour."

The younger boys took off, leaving just Nate, Jack, and Hank.

"Oh Jack, and on a side note, make a return flight plan to include a stop at these coordinates on your way back. They know you will be arriving in a few days." Nate handed him a piece of paper with some coordinates and a radio frequency on it. Jack frowned at them when there was no airport identification. At least, not one that he could discern. Jack looked back up in question at Raven and was about to ask Nate what the stop was all about when Nate interrupted him, adding, "It's about your ability to follow through with what we have talked about in the past; about you being able to move up and eventually take over Black Raven Aviation." This had Hank's full attention. Nate caught this and shook his head indicating he would tell Hank of his plans later and in private.

"When you arrive, you will be meeting my one of my family members there, my niece, Helen. They restore war birds. I need the Angelina checked over since they specialize in old birds at the Ghost Ranch. Besides, while you are there, talk to Helen's son. His name is West and I think he can help the two of us out in making this become a reality for you. I know you have been trying son with most of Alaska's banks. But it's time for someone to give you a chance at this financially." Nate dismissed him by waving him off while taking a seat near Hank, getting a load off his feet.

"Now, scoot, Jack. Start making a flight plan and the weights, including the extra fuel tanks you will need to install on the Angelina.

"Coffee?" Hank asked, offering more from his thermos as Jack turned and hurried away.

Knowing better, Nate said, "Nope. I'm just gonna sit here a moment and pray this works."

Hank smiled. "It will. The boys will help keep Jack from messing up."

"Did you want to go along?" Nate offered.

"Missus would be pissed if I went without her. Plus, you need my help and I don't like to fly. And most of all, anything over sixty-five degrees makes me sweat and I hate sweating at my age. Especially if there's beach sand involved. It makes me itch."

The two men laughed.

CHAPTER THIRTY

Artie felt the temperature drop in the large shadow that had fallen across his hotdog wagon. He was giving one of his girls a lunch break and the customer he had just served had taken off with his order moments before. Arthur looked up at the giant man standing in front of him. He wore dark sunglasses, plain navy swim trunks, an unbuttoned Hawaiian fifties-styled shirt that was way out of date and style, and sported thick auburn hair on his head, along with hair on his chest and a heavy five o'clock shadow clinging to his square jawline—a pinkish jawline that had not seen sun in a while. This man carried some serious chest scars and was obviously not your typical clean body-building Florida beach boy. The man was menacing looking, as he looked back at him.

"Ah…What can I get ya?" he asked with a quick, hard swallow, plastering on a wide customer service smile.

"Are you…Artie?"

"Ah…yeah." Artie prayed to himself that this wasn't another jealous boyfriend or wife-beater of one of his girls. The last thing he needed that day was another fight, defending one of his workers. He wiped his hands on the towel. "Why?"

"Where is she?" the man asked, looking around Artie.

"You mean Maureen? She's off taking her lunch. Want me to leave her a message?" Artie pointed at the man's cell phone. "Why not call her yourself?"

The man's head snapped back at him and he abruptly leaned forward some, telling Artie, "No."

Artie watched the man scan the immediate area behind him. "No? As in she's—"

"No, as in wrong girl, and no, as in she's not answering her cell phone."

"Well, *Joe*," Artie said rather sarcastically, "like most smart people, she probably didn't carry a cell phone to the beach, and I don't know which girl you are referring to. I have twelve of them working for me. And at this point, I don't think telling you where to find one of my girls would be a good idea, especially if she's not answering your calls," Artie told him with bravado, contradicting what he really felt, being the typical coward. He put a fist on his hip and stood up taller, nearly missing the man's height by a mere two inches, he figured, sizing him up. "It would seem to me she doesn't want to be with a man like you."

"Like me?"

Artie was glad when he saw other people coming toward his cart, hoping that they would come to his aid should the man start anything.

"Look, I'm tired of defending my workers from their jealous boyfriends and women-beaters. You're nothing new, man. Give it up," Artie told him, pointing past him to the other customers coming closer. "If you don't want to order a dog, then let these guys order theirs. I won't tell you where she's at if you're going to disrupt my business."

The man lunged, but the four other guys behind him jumped on his back, holding him back.

"Whoa, calm yourself!" said one of them.

Artie had jumped back, letting his cart block the man's charge to him. But seeing the four guys helping him out only boosted Artie's confidence, and he took a step forward. "Besides, why would I let you hurt another girl?" He acknowledged their help as they pulled the man away some distance. "Thanks, guys."

The littlest guy came forward, prancing toward him rather effeminately. Artie found it difficult to believe this man was with the others.

"Yes, I would like to order two of your hotdogs—one with the works, and the other with just cheese and jalapeños. Then, I will ask for my friend again," the Latino said as he jabbed his thumb at the guy who had just tried to attack him. "Where can we find Tasha?"

"I don't have a girl named…" He stopped and looked back at the man being held back by the other three guys. The man shook off their hands and they reluctantly let go.

"You know this guy?" Artie asked.

"Yes." The demure calypso guy smiled at him. "Please, where can we find her?"

Artie swore he batted his eyelashes, making him back away, a bit disturbed and uncomfortable.

"We're not here to hurt her."

Artie looked back at the first man. "So, you're Tasha's Jack?"

He nodded.

To the others, he continued, "Then who are you all?"

"Let's just say we're the cavalry, should things go even further south," said Nick.

Artie smiled. "Then you're the others she works with? I've heard a lot about you all." He dropped his money box inside and locked up the wagon. "Come on"—he gestured for them to follow—"she's over here. But I'm not entirely sure of the reception you'll get…" He nodded to Jack. "…especially him."

Jack cocked his head.

They followed Artie over to a lone concrete pier, away from the crowds of beachgoers, where two metal beach lounges and a large blanket in between had staked out a spot on the white expanse of sand. A woman lying face-down with a protective hat over her head from the bright sun's rays was obviously napping.

The group let Artie and Jack go forward when Jack gave them an imperceptibly dismissive hand motioning them to wait.

"Hey, Tash," Artie called when he got close enough to her for her to hear him.

"Hmm?" she said without lifting her head up, shifting her heels up more as she stretched her long legs.

Artie put a finger to his lip at Jack and indicated for him to take a seat on the other lounge.

"That was a fast lunch break," she commented off-handedly from under her large hat.

"Well, not really. Just wanted to check back with you to see if you needed more water."

"I'm fine, but I could use some help spreading more sunscreen on my back side, Artie."

"Yeah, sure."

Jack gave him a hostile look when he found the bottle.

"Seriously, SPF fifty? I didn't know they went that high, Tash," he told her, chatting to hide their movements, placating Jack by handing him the tube of sunscreen.

Jack began slathering the lotion onto Tasha's back, grateful at the opportunity to touch her again, ensuring him she was really there after all those weeks. The initial smearing of lotion was electric as he made familiar contact with her skin, which was flawless other than the marring of her bullet wound and the new redness of the claw marks just above her ankle. He was grateful it would not scar on her in the long run, knowing how sensitive she was about her flaws.

He didn't say anything as he enjoyed the pleasure of sliding his hand over her body, forgetting everyone else. He took his time, making sure to work the lotion in just under her bikini's halter strings, making her shoulders stiffen momentarily as he let his hand slide on her curves to the swell of her hips, stopping inches from her bottom. Squeezing the tube for more, he shifted in his seat, making the lounge creak under his weight, and worked his way up from her ankles on the backs of her golden legs to her buttocks. It was when he let his fingers slide under the suit's material that she shook his hand off with her bottom, turning her front side toward him defensively. "Artie, you touch me like that again and so help me—"

She was stunned at seeing Jack in his aviator sunglasses with just a five o'clock shadow, smiling.

"You'll do what?" asked Jack. "Because if you *let* him touch you like I just did, I'll do what I did to the last guy who tried."

"Hey now…peace, bro," came Artie, unsure if he needed to back away or to help Tasha escape this madman.

Jack decided for him, looking annoyed that he was still there. Artie got the tacit message and left.

"What are you doing here?" she asked, as she kept studying this new face of his. "Don't you have work?"

"Yes…but it can wait for a few days," he said, dropping the tube of lotion on the blanket between them.

They both watched as the tube rolled toward another one of her books before saying anything.

"I think we need to have that talk you wanted so badly that day." He clasped his hands in front of him as he sat forward on the lounge with his elbows on his knees.

"Did you always have that shirt?" she asked, the question catching him off guard.

He refused to look down at the old, thin, and faded Hawaiian shirt. "Yes, but that's not part of the discussion you wanted to have."

"Just how old is that shirt, Jack?"

He gave her a riled look.

"It looks like something my dad would have worn back in the day."

She let her eyes drink in his entire body. It was the first time she had ever seen him dress in less than a pair of jeans and a long-sleeved Henley shirt. Her eyes met his underneath his dark sunglasses and followed where his gaze had landed. Then she realized she had turned too far, and he could see the large square bandage just below her navel. She moved to conceal it but was too late. His hand reached out to stop her, and his other hand moved to touch her, the palm of his hand protectively covering the small incision that the bandage hid. He didn't say anything. She kept waiting for his anger to explode, but it never came. She looked back at him, unable to read his face through his sunglasses, other than what looked like sadness, and it broke her heart to see him like that. He knew. But how much did he know? she wondered.

"Jack…I had…I had to."

"Why didn't you say anything? Before you left. I could have gone with you," he interrupted her.

"You were too busy. You had enough on your plate already without me giving you any more issues to contend with—much less more grief." Tasha tried to hide her shame by turning her belly away from him and donning a filmy cover wrap around her middle before turning completely around, sitting sideways on the lounge chair to face him.

"Tasha, all you had to do was just say 'stop.' I'm not *that* busy to ignore you…us." He pointed to himself. "You're a part of my life, at least…" He dug into his swimsuit's pocket and pulled out her ring to see. He paused, as if unsure, before continuing, but in a different direction. "The least you could have done was leave me a Dear John letter, explaining why." Jack sat back up to run a hand through his hair's thick layers.

"I didn't want to hurt—"

"This didn't?" he challenged her. "Leaving without a word? Not answering any of my calls?"

She sighed heavily. "Jack, it was painful enough for me as it was. Especially when I found Mr. Right." She tried to look past the dark lenses and into his eyes. "You didn't need any more pain…or guilt. You've had enough losses in your life. I certainly didn't help when I crashed the plane and then you nearly killing yourself getting it back to the airfield. I won't let another man die because of me…because of my stupidity and ineptitude at not checking more thoroughly…"

"Tasha, about that—"

He was interrupted by the gang. Nick, Sam, Jarvis, and Manny made their way over to stand behind Jack.

"What?" she exclaimed, as she barely recognized them out of context of where she normally saw them. Each of them was in bathing suits according to their personality. And as always, Manny, being the exception, outshone them all with his gold necklace, fancy swimwear, matching sunglasses, a large woven sombrero, and the white zinc oxide on his nose. It was the footlong in his hand that made her laugh.

"Wow, girlfriend, work that body. Simple black bikini works well on you… mm, mm, mm!" He took a bite of his dog.

Tasha smiled at them. "Where's Hank?" she asked, then remembered. "That's right, he doesn't fly. Is the boss here too?"

"Nope, they stayed behind to keep the place running for the time being," Sam commented. "Minimal work this week, though the two old geezers will be hopping trying to get it all done."

"I gotta say thank you for getting us a Florida vacation compliments of Black Raven Aviation," Nick told her. "The girls"—Nick's face tracked a gorgeous, tanned blonde that went by—"are just fabulous."

"Did you check out the one at hotdog cart?" Manny chinned over to Artie's cart in the tree line.

Jarvis burped. "I think I'm going to have heartburn."

"Well, you shouldn't have eaten yours so fast!" Manny reprimanded him with a light backhand to his chest.

She smiled as Nick and Sam gave those two some space behind Jack. She tilted her head at all of them, wondering, "How long are you all here for?" She looked back at Jack, but he didn't say anything.

"Well, for eight days, as long as you two keep arguing over whatever it is that we know you'll be arguing about," Manny said.

"Wait! What?" she asked.

"Make it seven days, we need a day to fly back," Nick corrected.

"Six, preferably five, since Jack is going to make a pitstop in his Louisiana hometown to let me see Lela." Sam put a heavy hand on Jack's shoulder, reminding him of his promise.

Jack made a momentary grimace in annoyance at the thought of Sam and his little sister.

"Okay," she added cautiously, unsure of what to say next when she noted a small rope, like the kind used on sixties-styled lamp bases for the natural home décor of the time. "Why are you holding a piece of rope, Jarvis?"

He looked down at it as if he had forgotten he was holding it, before giving it to Nick. Manny chirped up, telling her, "The rope is for you if Jack fails to woo you back and/or you two can't solve your differences in that time period."

"Hunh?" She was clearly astounded. Her jaw dropped and then she pulled herself together, saying, "You mean to tell me you're going to kidnap me and take me back to Seward?"

"Kidnapping is such a strong word, Tasha," Nick told her rather disdainfully.

"Yeah, kidnapping means you're taking someone away from their home and loved ones...not the other way around, where we're taking you back home," Sam added, grinning.

"More like hog-tie you until you straighten out," offered Jarvis. "He's been a bear all this time without you, and he's driving the rest of us mad."

She looked back at Jack, catching him smirk before he dropped it and lifted his hand without looking at them, telling them, "Guys...give us a moment more, will ya?"

"Yeah..."

"Sure..."

"All right..."

As they all replied at the same time, Sam added, "Go easy on him...and... hurry up, Tasha! I want to see Lela." To Jack, backhanding the back of his shoulder, and with a cheeky grin, he added, "Yell if you need us to bring the rope back, buddy."

"You wouldn't dare!" Tasha barked at Sam.

Sam just smiled over his shoulder at her. The crew had taken their leave of them, giving them the space Jack and Tasha needed, while they amicably taunted each other on the beach.

"Jack won't let you..." She looked back at him for his support and found none, as he peered over his sunglasses at her, with an expression clearly stating *try me*.

"Fine." She crossed her arms.

But before she would let Jack talk, she told him, "First of all, I had no intention of leaving Seward"—she raised an index finger—"because I like my job and the crew." Tasha raised the next finger. "Second, I needed time to heal and I wanted some warmth after freezing my arse off waiting for you to rescue me."

Jack noted that she had a finger to go, trying not to let her see his mirth now that she was talking and not giving him the silent treatment. "And?" Jack prompted her.

"Third, I had to decide on how best to protect you from hurting yourself because of me..."

Jack quickly slipped the ring back on her finger, making his silent point to her, and waited as she stared at her ring, not entirely certain on what to say next. But he finished with, "The best way *to protect* and *not hurt* me is for *you* to be *with* me, Tasha. By my side as Mrs. Less-Than-Perfect." He raised his eyebrows at her in question.

She didn't say anything, but he saw the tears well up in her eyes. He slid off his lounge chair and fell to both his knees in front of her, to be eye level with her, reaching out to stroke the side of her face, saying sadly, "Oh, Tasha...I don't want a Mrs. Right or Perfect. Those women are impossible to live with, much less live up to their standards."

She sobbed a half laugh. "But I failed you—"

"No, you didn't fail me except in one way—"

Tasha inhaled sharply, expecting him to say something about losing their baby.

"...you left without a word, and without letting me be a part of your life, in whatever you choose to do or wherever you go."

She gave him a confused look. "What about me losing...about me not being able to provide you a—"

His hand cupping the side of her face became firm, making her look at him as he told her, "It *would* have been nice, Tasha. But it doesn't break the deal between us. It's not the only thing in life to be considered successful. Besides"—Jack jerked his head toward the gang out of earshot of them—"who needs kids when you have those guys around?"

Tasha fell into gales of laughter at the suggestion, and at having watched them from time to time in the background as Jack had wooed her back. She put the back of her hand to her mouth to stifle her mirth.

After having eaten, the guys roughhoused a bit between them all, each taking their turn joking with one another. Only Manny had set up their beach spot in the sand. The crew had decided to play in the water. Manny joined them, having had found a hot pink inflatable lounger to lie on in the water until Sam splashed him and Nick flipped him over into the water like a shark attacking a mini skiff. Jarvis floated on his back, spitting ocean water up into the air like a fountain.

"Seriously, Tasha. *They're* your family. Our family. And we'll have our hands full with keeping up with them and the business. Nate and Nora felt like they lost a daughter when you left. They adore you. We need you and want you to come back."

Jack let his hand slide from her face to enclose her hands in his, asking, "What more of a family could you ever want? None of us are perfect. We're all flawed. But each of us fills a gap in each other, as we continue to grow and expand in our little Artic group."

"But what about my mistake in handling the plane's engine failure, Jack? I don't think you or Nate will ever have faith in me again to fly alone."

"Now that is entirely a different story."

"What? Why?"

"Someone set you up for failure on that one, Tasha."

"What?" she exclaimed, dumbfounded. "But who and why?" she asked.

"Trust me on this? I will tell you everything on the way back home."

She cocked her head at him.

"Will you come back?" Jack asked.

She nodded yes, and fell into him, her wide-brim hat sliding off her head, letting him enwrap her with his strong arms.

Jack nearly sobbed in his relief of her answer. He kissed the top of her golden head as she held on tight to him. He sucked in all the sunshine she had contained in her, enjoying the warmth she was feeding him, making him come alive after all those cold and empty weeks without her. He did not dare let her go until he could feel whole again.

When he was certain all was good, he became aware of everything around him, including the faint conversation of the crew behind him. "Lose the rope, Sam. Jack's got his moose."

There were a few whistles and some clapping, and then Jarvis told them, "Let's hit the water again, guys! I want a full week here, and I intend to use every moment of it in the sun and surf!"

"Better not! He promised me we could see Lela!"

Their voices trailed off as they ran back to the breakers.

A thought came to him as he loosely held her. He thought he remembered it from reading it somewhere, and the words finally came easily to him. Jack released her enough to look at her and said, "My plane is Seward bound. If you care to join me, we can follow the northern lights to the last star on the right—the North Star. The journey will be long, for that I am certain, with a few bumps here and there on the northern wild frontier, but with the cold air I expect a lot of smooth sailing among the winds and the clouds, the tall mountains, sea, and the great land below. I know we will be held aloft by our crew and friends often, but more so, I hope you will always be by my side, each of us guiding each other as we navigate our journey together."

EPILOGUE

"Hi, Dad," Jack said as his father opened the door to him and the expectant gang behind him.

His burly father studied every one of them in turn, like the old Marine sergeant he was. He was never openly friendly, always on guard, and it seemed no one would ever meet his expectations.

"*Who* are *these* people, Jack?" His father did not move to let them into their home.

"I told you I would be dropping by to visit everyone, Dad."

"You didn't bother to let me know how many to expect," he said rather sharply to Jack. His gaze dropped to Tasha standing perkily next to him, military tall and proud, before she extended her hand and introduced herself to him.

Just behind his father came a woman's familiar voice. "Tasha? Tasha, is that you and Jack out there?" Lela happily appeared, eager to know just who her father was inquisitioning, as she worked her way around his recalcitrant body. When she spied Jack and Tasha, she squealed in delight. "I knew it! I knew it! Jack asked you! You're engaged!" She jumped up and down in front of Jack and alternately hugged them. Then she spied the rest of their crew and saw Sam.

"Sam!" Lela exclaimed, and ran to him, jumping into his arms and wrapping her legs around his waist in pure joy as he nearly stumbled with the speed of her impact, twirling together with the weight of her excitement.

His father's jaw dropped. It was one of the few times Jack saw his father fit to be tied before his anger started to flood over his daughter's lack of inhibitions in public.

To distract his anger, Jack said, "Dad, meet Tasha, my wife to be." He followed his father's gaze, looking back over his shoulder at his sister and Sam's entwined greeting, far from appropriate behavior, to his dismay. "And possibly your new son-in-law, Sam," Jack added somewhat apologetically to his father, until Tasha elbowed him to behave.

The older version of Jack flexed his jaw in annoyance at what he was witnessing in front of him. Finally, his grizzly voice connected with his facial movements. "So I see...I think."

"May we come in, sir?" asked Tasha, pulling her sticky, hot shirt away from her body in Louisiana's already hot, humid morning. "The sun is a tad strong at this hour for me, and the first leg of our flight was long and way too early of a start to get here," she told him in her best charming Southern voice.

Still trying to process everything, he reluctantly stepped aside, letting them in. Jack and Tasha led the way with the others in tow, coming in one by one, each of them doing their own greeting according to their personality. Jarvis nodded politely and quietly in greeting, like anyone of mixed and questionable race would do in a predominantly white southern neighborhood of questionable intentions. Manny curtsied as if he were a girl, flashing Jack's father his biggest white toothy grin. Nick said 'hello' and gave him a mock salute, with Lela barely giving Sam a chance to properly introduce himself, as she clung tightly to him.

Jack's father closed the door, nearly horrified by what he had let his son bring into their home, as he watched all of them file into the large sitting room. Tasha, Nick, and Jarvis took their seats on one of the two large, long sofas. Lela had other ideas, and she yelled for her mother to come meet Sam first, and then the others.

Manny lagged after them, taking in the Southern décor of the old, refurbished plantation home, walking very effeminately in his normal bright and flashy attire as he sighed in matching feminine delight between the dining room's and the front sitting room's décor.

"There's something seriously wrong with that one, son," his father grunted quietly to Jack, his arms folded and legs shoulder-width apart, like the drill sergeant he was for so many years in the Marine Corps.

"Let's just say 'don't ask and didn't see,' Dad," Jack said as they watched Manny twirl in place as he took in the high, mural-painted ceilings.

By that time, Jack's mother had come out of the adjoining kitchen and into the dining room to greet his flight line crew. As for his mother, he did not worry about her acceptance when it came to his unusual crew.

"Jack?" she called out when her eyes landed on him. She ran to him and hugged him for a long time. "Is it true?" she asked. "You finally found your happiness? Where is she?"

Jack extended a hand to introduce Tasha, using her Army military rank in hopes of winning his father over too.

From the corner of his eye, he caught his father's surprised expression that slowly melted, as he did, when Tasha flashed that big smile of hers at him the way she had to Jack not so long ago, realizing it was when he had first fallen in love with her.

FOUR MONTHS LATER

"Your wife's coming. She just got in early this morning, Jack," Nick told him as he nosed over his shoulder by the shoreline's parking lot.

Jack turned to note Tasha coming down the gangway over to them at the end of the pier for their annual hypothermia training. He gave her a brief smile before resuming the checklist of equipment and attendance, where the guys formed a semi-circle in front of him, as a wary and not-so-happy captive audience. Again, the guys were all huddled close to the edge of the pier, as if 'Captain Jack,' along with his trusty sidekick Mr. Hank, was about to gangplank all of them.

He felt Tasha lovingly squeeze his upper arm as she caught up to him and said, "Here, and reporting for duty." She let her hand slide down his arm as he lifted his arm to lightly swing her hurriedly back into the gang. He was eager to get the training done that day, his thoughts momentarily distracted by Tasha's return and memories of them the night before she had left for her supply run to Cold Bay. He felt her weight grow heavier as he realized too late that she was using his arm leverage more than he was hers. Within the next second, in Tasha's smooth fighting move, he found himself propelled by his own weight over to the pier's edge, momentarily balanced on one foot, teetering between the concrete and the water below, until Nick grabbed his clipboard, that minuscule bit of mass, causing him to end up tumbling over and falling into Resurrection Bay's cold summer waters.

When he surfaced, he could hear his crew's hoots and hollers along with some clapping. He was pretty certain they were high-fiving each other too. He looked up at all their faces peering down at him in smiles. Tasha yelled down to him, "Thought you could use some brushing up on your own training, Jack!"

The water was definitely shockingly cold, but he had grown relatively used to it—yet it could still kill him if he stayed in long enough. He swam deftly over to the ladder. Their faces disappeared from his sight and he heard some hurried and jumbled conversations.

Tasha knew she would catch hell for her subterfuge, especially when she caught the evil glint in his eye when his gaze landed on her face above him. He swam seemingly unfazed by the cold water, as if he was built for that environment. *He is a bear, and bears do well up North!* she thought to herself.

"Dang, I don't think the cold water is bothering him. He's like a polar bear enjoying a pleasant swim," Tasha commented more to herself, not realizing some of the crew had heard her.

"You betcha, sister. We didn't give him his bear nickname without good reason!" Nick told her.

"Get ready guys!" She ordered as Jack begin to climb the ladder from below. "Grab the blankets!"

On the pier, Hank was busy laughing too hard to be of use to anyone, and the guys scrambled getting the thermo blankets readied.

"Where are you going, Tasha?" asked Sam.

Knowing she had to hurry to 'vamoose,' she quickly yelled her excuse as she sprinted back to the parking lot. "I gotta go get his truck started and get the heater going." But she had every intention of escaping Jack and his wrath.

His old truck gave her fits, not wanting to start on the first turn, and she cursed it, noting how fast Jack was able to climb out, the guys barely throwing all the blankets on his sopping wet form before he took off running after her, closing the distance to the truck quickly.

She was finally able to get the truck running and the heater on, but was unable to put the truck in gear fast enough to make her escape. He landed on his truck's hood, his weight shaking the vehicle, startling her, as he quickly let himself in. She forgot that he had left his truck unlocked on both sides.

"Oh no you don't, Moose!" Jack huffed out heavily as he slid in and snared her in a very cold and wet bear hug on the front bench seat, pulling them out of view of the truck's windshield from their crew outside, who were following them with the emergency gear box.

Tasha screeched but could not stop laughing at what she had successfully done for the entire crew. Payback!

They could still hear Hank bellowing with laughter outside.

Jack did his best to hold on to her as she struggled to get away from him, making sure she was getting just as wet as he was, the old truck rocking easily on its well-worn out springs.

"You're getting me all wet, Jack!"

"You're my safety buddy, remember? You're supposed to snuggle up to me and help me regain my body heat!"

"I think I do *that* after we have you stripped out of your wet clothes!" she retorted.

He moved around on her more, tickling her in the process and making her squeal in delight.

Together they heard the guys outside loading up the box in the back of Jack's truck, and Nick say, "Oh look you all, if the truck's a-rocking don't come a-knocking!"

"Let me see!" said Manny.

Jarvis elbowed him to stay put.

Hank knocked on the driver's window, and Jack allowed Tasha an arm out to roll down the window.

"You two good to go?" he asked, peering in on the two of them lying across the bench seat, Jack pinning her down with his entire body.

Before she could scream 'help me,' Jack answered for them with a wide grin. "Yup, just warming up in here."

Hank clicked his tongue, his toothpick wiggling off to the side of his mouth. "Well, don't take too long. The boys want to take the test and go home."

"Just tell them to go on home and I'll test them on Monday morning." Tasha wiggled some to escape his grasp, but he held on tight as he continued. "I've got some retraining to follow up on."

"All righty, then," Hank said, winking at Jack.

"Wait! Hank!" she tried to get him to rescue her, but Hank ignored her.

"Make sure he learns his lesson well, Tasha," Hank added with a smile, his toothpick swapping sides in his mouth. "See you both on Monday. Stay warm." He patted the truck's window frame before leaving.

Jack to continue his soppy assault on Tasha, who was still laughing hard in his arms. He was bound to make sure his Moose would not feel left out on all the sogginess he could share with her in Seward.

The End

Eight's Warning
(Somewhere in the beautiful Colorado Rockies)

For those readers who are interested in reading more about the investor who helped Tasha and Jack afford to buy out Nate's Black Raven Aviation company and the secret life of restoring old war birds, a millionaire called West and his crew on the secluded Ghost Ranch, you should read Eight's Warning and its sequel, Charlie's Promise by Aidan Red.

It is a thrilling drama about Charlie Basset, whose life began hiding from her abusive past, but found love, family, and a new purpose in life on the ranch. However, her picture in a newspaper magazine reawakened her past and troubles began anew.

To order copies of Eight's Warning and Charlie's Promise books, go to
www.AidanRedBooks.com

Other books by C.A. McJack

Fate's Twisted Circle – Vol I: *The Unraveling*
Fate's Twisted Circle – Vol II: *The Weaving*
The Other Side of the Flip

PREVIEW

An excerpt from *Fate's Twisted Circle*

THE NOISE OF THE FIGHT GREW LOUDER, thus pulling Abbey's concentration from the research in front of her. It had been several nights since she had her first open conversation with Evelyn, and so far she encountered no rumors.

Each night, like clockwork, Abbey came in for her evening meal while, at the same time, she worked on her laptop to come up with building ideas and business concepts, tally purchasing costs, and go over the legal paperwork from Mr. Benjamin Nevin. She peered over the top of her laptop screen at the source of the commotion across the main floor toward the billiard tables.

The burly man with near shoulder-length black hair and well over-grown beard that covered his jawline in a thick and black mass started to threaten the gangly woman with just his sheer size. The rail-thin woman stood as tall as she could muster just over the man's chest. Overall, she was mousy in upkeep and coloring. Her hair was a dull color between dark blonde and light ash brown. Her skin was pale, almost see-through, and lacked the luster of good health due to lack of nutrition, which was apparent in her protruding bones just underneath the skin that jutted from the oversized clothing she was wearing.

The woman kept up with her argument in regard to their kids though one could tell she was scared of him, as if she had been beaten by him in the past. In fact, Abbey could place a sure bet that the bruises that peeked out from under her loose clothing were, indeed, from previous beatings.

Most of the patrons had yet to arrive at the bar. The few that were there stayed quiet and watched from their shadowy perches. Evelyn looked a bit tense, as she usually did when this particular man arrived at the tavern.

Abbey had asked about him some time ago, mainly to inquire about Evelyn's sense of discomfort whenever he was around. But all she got was that the "man was just a local bully." He never tore anything up on her and always paid his tab. So she couldn't complain about him much since he was a paying customer though it was not her place to say anything about the way he would take things out on his wife and their kids.

It was obvious that this was the wife who was imploring him to return home and watch their kids while she went to work tonight.

If the man was compliant, she doubted he was in any condition to watch over their kids from his demeanor and the multiple empty pints of beer that lined the far half wall near where he and his aloof buddies were standing around the billiard tables, playing a few rounds.

Abbey's body had gone on alert as soon as she heard the intensity of the arguing. When the shouting grew more severe and the man flipped the woman's hand off him as she grabbed at him imploringly, Abbey slipped quietly from the center of her booth to the edge of the table, ready to cross over to the woman just in case the man's inclination was to ram a fist down her throat.

Abbey, knowing the man was almost twice her size, began to look around the room for possible weapons to help defend herself, though she was pretty sure she could take him out without any weapons given the man's drunken state. The empty mug in her hand would not be enough to clout the man. But she could use it to hide her real intentions by attempting to go fetch another drink. She spied the two claymores on the adjacent wall from her, above the fireplace mantle of the tavern. She could reach them and still be in time for the situation off to the left of the fireplace.

Thankfully, the tavern was rather long and narrow at the point where she sat and where the fireplace was located. Only three tables in the recessed area from her booth were in her way for reaching those weapons should the need arise. *Spoken too soon,* she thought as the ensuing argument reached a tipping point.

The woman grabbed the man's arm again only to have him turn on her like a wild animal intent on killing his annoying prey. He ended up shoving her forward and off balance, and he began to beat her with his pool stick.

Abbey leapt to her feet, jumping from her vantage point, literally running across the tabletops, nearly toppling a few chairs and tables in the process. She grabbed one of the claymores from its perch on the wall and kicked the man in the seat of his pants in one blurred motion, like a silent panther.

The burly large man fell forward nearly crushing his wife on the floor. She had managed to escape the full-weight impact on her form though one leg remained trapped by his chest and shoulder.

The stunned man wondered how he fell over. The action barely registering in his mind, he made the motion to continue his assault on the poor woman in front of him. Standing behind him, Abbey slipped the edge of the claymore's blade along the front side of his neck, careful not to draw blood just yet.

Quietly commanding in a threatening tone, Abbey said, "I would think twice before you lift your hand against her again."

The man leaned forward to take another swipe at his wife, but Abbey moved the sword enough to draw some blood and applied more pressure, the point of the blade on his neck making an indention on the bearded skin of his throat. This forced the man to shift upward and backward onto his haunches to relieve the pressure of the blade against his neck.

The room was deadly quiet as the patrons waited on each opponent's next move. She could hear not only her beating heart but his labored breathing and the whimpering of his wife. The beaten woman, stunned and relieved from the onslaught, scrambled from her self-protecting fetal position to scoot herself up against the farthest wall, away from and out of reach of her enraged husband.

The blood began dripping down the man's neck and seemed enough to bring the man back from his intoxicated rage a bit.

"If it's a fight ye be wanting, then why don't we even the playing field, sir." As if on second thought, she added, "But I can't really call you a sir—much less a man since you like to beat women for your entertainment." Abbey emphasized *sir* and *man* in a harsh and derogatory way. "Because everyone knows real gentlemen, much less a man, don't beat women. So what shall we call you, buddy?"

497

asked Abbey, the last word dripping in sarcasm.

He grumbled something that she could not hear, and he began to make a motion to move again.

Abbey shifted quickly with him, responding, her adrenaline still high from the sudden rush to rescue the woman from a certain public beating. "I didn't quite catch what you said. It must be that you don't have any balls either, or I would have heard your comment." She heard some light nervous laughter from the pub's gathering night crowd. "What a shame, I would have had fun making you a eunuch."

Behind her, she began to hear the patrons hushed whispers and comment on her brave talk, daunting the man.

It was a very insulting comment, but Abbey was still vibrating with anger from watching the man beat his wife with a pool stick. The man moved in an attempt to take Abbey by surprise. She stomped on his upper back, forcing the man to lie flat on his stomach, her military boot applying pressure, holding him down. She drew the sword across his neck, keeping it in contact with his skin so that he would know that the weapon was still there and ready.

"I would suggest, Mr. . . . uh . . . Mr. . . . ." She placed her free finger upon her lips as if trying to recall the name that still was never mentioned.

"Rolf!" wolfed the man with his face still pressed to the floor, his reddened beefy cheek pressed into the dark wooden flooring, distorting his facial features into a melted look.

Abbey dropped the act. "Mr. Rolf, I would suggest that you stand up and turn around slowly, or you might just risk losing a finger or, possibly, another important limb." In a more lowered conversational but psychotic tone, she added, "I'm a little shell shocked from the war, you see? I tend to be a wee bit jumpy at times." Abbey let the claymore drag across the back of his neck, drawing a longer blood line but not enough to seriously hurt him, as she backed up, staying out of his arms' and fists' reach.

His buddies, stunned by Abbey's adept quickness, began to close in from behind and around Rolf. She quickly spun around, taking a few steps forward, swinging the sword at them, commanding, "Oh no you don't!" Rolf had been about to get up when she just stepped back on him, forcing him back down face first onto the floor.

The men fell back some but were still intent on taking her out although none of them sure what to expect next given her demeanor.

Through the pregnant pause, she switched over to a more polite tone though her posturing was definitely aggressive and on the defense.

"Now would you looky here. I see one wife beater and three guys who think they are man enough to take me . . ." She paused for effect as she turned around to announce their thoughts to the rest of the customers. "Me, just little ol' me, on for a fight!" she added in a Southern accent. "I'd never thought I would see the day when it took four big bullies to try to take out a little lady like me." She feigned a fluttering of her eyelashes like a Southern belle, with her free hand to her throat in a similar Southern gesture.

Dropping her hand from her throat and returning to her normal terse voice, she said, "Usually, it's men fighting over me and not with me back where I come from." More nervous laughter erupted, and a few jeers were thrown at them.

The other three started to charge when her back was slightly turned to them, but she quickly swung the sword at them again, in a sweeping wild arc, making them jump back in alarm and questioning her sanity.

Abbey looked at the sword, regarding it for a moment, and then commented loud enough to the patrons in the pub, "I wonder how this works . . . Hmm . . ." Like a baton twirler, she twisted her wrist enough to let the blade flash around dangerously close to the men wanting to charge her. The men backed up, and Rolf grunted underneath her boot's increasing pressure as she stood on the man's back, leaning in toward them in a menacing manner.

Abbey placed a finger on her lips as she thought about it a bit to the amusement of the gathering patrons. Then exaggerating her posture, as if a sudden thought just occurred to her, she leaned closer to the man named Rolf.

"Hey, Rolf! Yes, yes, Rolfie . . . Let's make this a level playing field, shall we?" She kicked for him to get up, making him grunt.

As he got up and faced her, Abbey twiddled the sword back and forth in the dim light of the room, making the blade's flat sides flash to egg on Rolf.

"Since you like to fight just women"—more laughter erupted from the crowd behind her—"why don't you and I play with these two wonderful swords that Evelyn has here. Evelyn?"

Abbey paused and asked in a feigned sincere tone of voice, "Evelyn, is it all right if I take these two swords and have some fun here with my newest BUDDY, Rolf?" She emphasized her new term for Rolf. "I promise not to break anything in the pub. We will take it outside, and I promise to return them shortly." Her voice was still light and bright with politeness dripping from each word.

No answer. Abbey looked over to the bar area to see Evelyn just standing in shock, terrified at the scene Abbey was creating, hesitating, and nodded her head rather quickly. Evelyn's demeanor oozed her irresolution of it all. Abbey gave her the biggest grin she could muster to help reassure Evelyn's uneasiness.

It was like being on stage and acting out a Shakespearian scene. The rest of the men in the pub eagerly shook their heads, and a few of them had begun placing bets.

God, I hope one of them has enough decency to stop the fight before she manages to get herself killed by this man, she thought. *But then again, it would take care of all my issues,* she thought to herself. Otherwise, jail was not an option for her as of yet, and in the end, she lost her doubt by not caring about her own welfare anymore.

She could hear Rolf's men shuffle, and she whipped her head around quickly and gave them a hard look. They stopped in their tracks. Only Rolf slowly smiled at her, like a starved wolf eager to chase a rabbit. She lifted a silent eyebrow of "*Yes?*" in return. Rolf wiped his neck, smearing the blood that Abbey had drawn, giving him an even more alarming countenance.

"How do I know you fight fairly?" he growled.

"How much fairer do you want me to become, Rolf?" asked Abbey, keeping it light as possible against his darkness. She quickly added, "You are already fighting a woman half your weight and size, the only way I could make it any fairer to you is to slice what possible manhood you have and still let you have your very own sword that Evelyn has so kindly granted us to play with." She threw a quick smile back over her shoulder at Evelyn.

He flinched a bit out of a man's instinct to protect the family jewels. Grumbling he stepped forward slowly and Abbey backed up, every nerve on end standing for any possible tricks. She swung her sword and popped the other sword out of its hooks to let it land on the floor in front of him. The heavy metal clattered on the dark wooden flooring at his feet. He grinned slowly this time as he bent over, picking up the sword. Not once did his eyes leave her face, warily watching her.

As Rolf slowly stood back up, he said, "How do I know you don't carry a concealed weapon on you?" He pointed to her military fatigues and her boots. She checked herself out in an exaggerated manner, with her lips pressed together as if seeing the outfit for the first time making her figure look fat, thus causing more mirth from the patrons behind her.

Like a strung-out crack addict, she swung her head at him and said, "Fine!" She laid her sword down on the table behind her, and she pulled out her leatherman from her belt loop and placed it on the table. Then her short army knife concealed just in the inside of her boot followed, and then she took off the outer blouse of her fatigues and her standard-issue brown sweater, leaving her with just her brown T-shirt, her trousers, and her boots on.

By this time, the four men were looking more amused than ready to fight at her antics. The crowd behind her gave her catcalls for the semi-striptease act.

"Well, I do have one problem, Rolf."

"Eh?" he grunted like a six-foot-four-inch enraged bull, which he looked like. All she needed was the red cape to flash.

"I just can't take off my hands, I simply need them to hold my sword!" she said, throwing her hands up in exasperation. This was the red flash of the cape as Rolf lunged with his sword at her.

Abbey rotated out of the way, deftly picking up her sword as Rolf scored the table where she was standing just moments with his blade, before knocking her personal effects off the table and scattering them on the floor near the base of the next freestanding table. She was backing up quickly, trying to get him to follow her outside where she could have better footing and the room to wield the sword.

Her senses on overdrive, she could feel the crowd parting behind her, getting ready to get out of the way of the impending fight.

Scolding him like a misbehaved child, she said, "Now, Rolfie! Shame on you! Look what you did to Evelyn's table! Now you will owe her not just the beer tab but a new table. And let's talk about fair fighting now!" She clicked her tongue and continued to back to the door.

Quickly, she eyed a man in the crowd and pointed to him and motioned for him to grab her weapons that had spilled on the floor and to hold them for her while she kept Rolf occupied.

The man, shaking, didn't move at first, clearly not wanting to get involved in the impending action, but then conceded to retrieve them. The man nervously picked up her personal items and scurried off to the side, disappearing within the crowd. Abbey wanted those items of hers as far away from the three other big men as possible, in case they decided to help Rolf.

Noting one man at the door, ready to fling it open, she continued to taunt Mr. He-Man. "Here are the rules," Abbey said loudly, ensuring that everyone could hear.

"We fight until the first one is pinked, you understand? Because I would really hate to clean up your mess. It would ruin my vacation here, you know? Besides I have had enough fun killing a whole bunch of people these past few years in the desert. My black belt here has no more room for another notch mark." Abbey deftly indicated to her waist where her trousers were held up by the typical black web mesh belt. "It gets boring after a while, the killing of men, though I know it would greatly improve mankind's gene pool without you in it."

More ruckus from the patrons.

That was the final straw, and Rolf lost it. He charged her and she artfully dodged him as he went sailing through the entry door of the tavern, and she in turn spurned him on with a swift kick to his buttocks on the way out, causing him to lose his balance again, falling on the cold and damp street outside on his face.

The customers cheered and commenced to follow Abbey out the door to watch the ensuing sword fight. It was obvious that Rolf didn't know how to fight fair, and thus she was going into the fray with a temper. That was not good for the fight. She had to keep a level head on her shoulders.

On her way out, she threw dirty looks at the other three men to make sure that they didn't attempt to interfere in their fight. They hesitated but still followed only to join the congregating crowd outside.

Rolf rolled over and stood up, eyeing her thoroughly with his red glare as he shook his head to free some of the water droplets from his face and hair fringes. She thanked her lucky stars for learning the art of sword fighting back in college and thus took her time counter parrying Rolf's strokes and, by going with the flow of gravity, always stroking downward, adding to her strength.

She was walking slowly in circles, hoping to keep Rolf off balance in his drunken state. Letting him attack first, she let Rolf wear himself out, thrusting his sword at her, and she in turn would counter the attacks. Deftly, she would deflect the strokes and swipes from her body, and at one point, she was able to knock his sword out of his hand with such force that the sword skittered into the crowd along the wet pavement, its path making a clearing in the crowd.

The noise of the crowd helped to keep her focused on just Rolf. Though in times when Rolf paused to catch his breath and balance, she would check the crowd for the other three men who were in support of Rolf. She caught Alex's face within the crowd and smiled at him. But only to have her face nearly cut with one of Rolf's sword strokes.

She spun on her boots' heels, missing the latest swipe of his sword, and promptly smacked Rolf again on his buttocks with the flat side of her blade, enraging him further.

She began to kick him more, hoping to wear him out and personally satisfy her need to put him in his place for beating his wife. She knew that he was intent on stabbing her and not pinking her, so she needed to wear him down enough for him to cry mercy.

Though the fight must have only been about ten to fifteen minutes long, it felt longer when Abbey's blood raced, and she was in the middle of it. Judging from Rolf's size and muscle mass, she knew she would be in for the long haul.

GREG HEARD THE RINGING OF METAL AND A CROWD JEERING and could not believe what he thought he was hearing before he reached the pub. In the late dusk of the oncoming night, he could see the crowd under the streetlights just in front of the tavern. Every once in a while he would see flashes of light glinting off metal surfaces.

Greg stepped up his pace toward the crowd, intent on trying to see what all the commotion was about. There were extremely few fights in Ullapool. One occurred every once in a blue moon, but usually the local police would take care of the two individuals in the middle of the brawl.

But there were no police around, and the fight must have just started, he figured.

He saw Evelyn at the entrance of her pub with a dish towel balled up to her mouth in an unmistakable sign of distress. She watched from her perch on the tavern's steps from the distance, her eyes wet with tears. Normally, Evelyn would not give a crap when two men dogged it out as long as it was outside her tavern.

Upon reaching the edge of the crowd, he pushed his way forward using his shoulder. His height helped him catch a glimpse of his father and Alex among the crowd farther around the circle. With folks still hindering part of his view, Greg made his way toward them and asked Alex what exactly was going on when he saw the flash of a sword come down and the rattle of metal sliding across the pavement.

Next he heard Sergeant McCaffree's clear American-accented voice, though loudly commanding, saying, "Just give it up and admit that you lost! All you have to do is apologize to your wife for your behavior! I'm getting bored here fighting you!"

Stunned, Greg's jaw dropped, and he looked at Alex for verification of who he just heard and for what he just saw. Alex excitedly nodded his head, verifying who was fighting who and with what. He had a fistful of money in his hand. No one had ever seen the likes of this type of fighting.

"Bets are two to one in favor of Sergeant McCaffree Greg!" exclaimed Alex excitedly.

Having gained some sort of composure, Greg asked his father and brother, "Have ye both lost yer minds!"

"Nooooo! The American is really good at it!" chimed his elderly father, his brother nodding with him in agreement. "I havena had this much fun since the late '50s!"

Greg stepped closer to get a better view and saw how Sergeant McCaffree walked deliberately and slowly in circles as if she was a panther playing with a large rodent. He saw Rolf crawling on his knees toward the sword that had dropped to the pavement, and Greg could smell the reek of ale on him from where he stood. Abbey waited patiently for him to reach it.

He saw blood on Rolf's neck and wondered if Abbey had done that to him. Rolf charged her, and he jerked to go to her defense only to see her dodge the charge, the sword flashing under the lamppost's light, and smack Rolf's backside with the flat of her blade. He heard the crack to his buttocks and inwardly grimaced.

He watched in fascination just like what he had caught his brother and father doing earlier. It was quite clear that Sergeant McCaffree still had the upper hand. She was cool as a cucumber. It was unnerving yet exciting to him. *How many women do I know that could fight like that and with a sword much less? Did the United States Army still train their soldiers to fight with swords?* he wondered.

She wore her fatigues but was stripped down to her brown T-shirt and cargo pants now. The shirt was damp with the night's heavy moisture, and the fabric clung, molding to her breasts and to her waist where her shirt was tucked into her pants. Her black belt accented her small waist, holding her trousers in place, not that she needed it with the swell of her hips. She wasn't sweating profusely like Rolf was, but he could see the moisture gleaming on the skin of her arms, neck, and face. When her back was toward them all, her fatigues flowed over her hourglass shape, down her long legs to her brown boots, where her trousers were tucked in a sharply folded in traditional military style.

The way she fought was almost seductive. No, it was perverse seduction, he thought. No wonder the United States Army employed women to fight. A man might die happy under such a beauty if he was a sadomasochist!

He felt his cock stiffen, and he swore at himself. He was one of them, he thought, much to his annoyance.

Rolf lunged at her again, and the blades clashed with a loud ring and then with a grating sound as they slid against each other. The continuous clashing of the blades made the metal sing its rusty old song in the night air. She was good on her defense, allowing each blow to slide to either side of her as she met each of Rolf's strokes. At one point, Rolf gained an upper hand, and she wasn't able to deflect his sword to any direction. Rolf stepped forebodingly closer, using his height, weight, and strength against her, trying to push her down, knocking her off balance. Rolf began to gloat under his heavy breathing. Though Rolf's back was to him, Greg knew Rolf had to be smiling over his soon-to-be victory.

Greg couldn't see her through Rolf's large frame, but in one swift instance, he did see Sergeant McCaffree's leg come up in a crushing blow to Rolf's groin as she held him off her and then just as quickly, with the same leg and foot, kick him on his outer leg just below his knee, knocking him completely down like a bowling pin.

He heard the crowd gasp as one man in unison to Rolf's pain. Rolf landed like a large Scot pine to the ground, the sword falling free from his hand as he tried to gasp for air.

Like a medieval knight, Sergeant McCaffree kicked his claymore aside. With her sword point down on the pavement, she braced herself with her sword as she kneeled on one knee, just near Rolf's head. Lying on his back, Rolf stared into the misty night sky above, trying to recover from the pain she had just inflicted on him below the belt.

Her voice took on a bizarre note of tenderness when she asked, "Rolfie boy—Rolf—if you can hear me, I truly think you need to call an end to it. You fought well. Anytime you think you need to hit or have the urge to fight another woman again, you just come down and see me, OK?"

No answer.

"Not your wife. Agreed?"

Rolf tried to make a sound as he inhaled but couldn't. Sergeant McCaffree took it for an agreement, said "good," and patted his shoulder.

Greg watched her stand up and pick up the other sword, swinging both of them, one in each hand, as if she was ready to take on the next combatant, even giving the crowd a challenging look before walking away to the tavern. The crowd cheered now sure that the fight was over.

Money passed between hands, and it snapped him out of the surrealistic scene he just watched. He moved in the crowd and saw Alex and his dad collecting win money from their placed bets. He snorted disgustedly at them both as he pushed his way to Evelyn at the entrance door.

He watched Abbey hand Evelyn the two claymores and say something to her as if in reassurance, and she went into the pub. Evelyn had held out the claymores as if they were possessed by a demon. By the time he reached the door, he reached out to Evelyn's arm to help guide her into her pub, taking both claymores in his other hand and to see what damage had been done.

Greg had never seen Evelyn so speechless and in such shock until tonight. He took a look at the empty pub only to see that the room had remained intact. Not a glass broken or a chair or table broken or upended, save for the one in the middle of the floor. He saw that the fireplace's wall stood empty of its decor, which he currently held in his hand.

Greg returned the claymores to their place above the fireplace as he searched the large room for the sergeant. She wasn't to be found at first. *Where did she go?* he wondered. He noted that her laptop was still at her usual booth, but no sign of her.

He heard a sound only to discover that Rolf's wife was still holding herself, terrified from tonight's earlier attack. She lay huddled up against the far wall behind the pool table, and he immediately crossed over to her direction to check on her.

"Nadine, are you all right?" he asked, checking her out for cuts and bruises. She shirked away from him, screeching out her fear of him.

Greg didn't try to reach for her again. Instead he crouched down, getting on her eye level and waited for her to calm down. He sighed his frustration in not being able to help. Nadine continued to shiver as her thin arms remained wrapped protectively around her folded legs.

"Of course not, would you be if a two-ton elephant came to pound down on you?" Her voice came out cold and angry from behind him.

The sergeant stood there with a couple of wet rags and one with ice within its folds. She must have been in the kitchen getting the items while he had placed the swords back on their hooks and had located Nadine in the far corner.

Greg was going to answer her when she told him bluntly, "Move."

He did so more out of shock than her command. She came down to Nadine's level to hold the ice pack to her temple and eye. Greg continued to watch her administer to the battered woman, reminding him of something vaguely familiar. He reflected on how she must have been made of something not quite human. But then didn't his brother, Alex, just finish writing a song about her, the Valkyrie?

Aye, he thought to himself; she was a Valkyrie. There was no doubt after what he just encountered outside. *How in the—*

"Greg, don't just stand there. Get me some more ice and a glass of water." She looked over her shoulder at him when she didn't hear him move. "I mean now not later, Greg." He moved to retrieve what she requested only to hear Nadine jump from his movements, and Sergeant McCaffree cooed to her that she was safe.

From behind her, Abbey heard Evelyn's shaky voice say, "She can stay with us. I'll . . . I'll . . . have one of my daughters go fetch her kids and bring them here." Abbey nodded her thanks and let Evelyn take over her administrations on Nadine. Greg returned with the glass of water and the extra ice bags for Nadine and handed them over to Evelyn, knowing that he could not do anything for Nadine until she could trust a man's presence again, especially given her current state.

Sergeant McCaffree was walking toward him, and he reached out, grabbing her elbow, to stop her. She didn't flinch when she stopped, but her expression registered surprise at him for touching her. He could still feel her pulse banging away from her earlier exertions and noted that she was just as affected inside while showing her coolness on the outside.

Having regained her composure, she looked up at him with a hard expression of *"what"* on her face. Her angry silence was deafening. Greg let go of her, recognizing the fight still simmering just behind her dark green eyes. He would wait until she was in more control.

He watched her pick up her sweater and jacket and her fatigues from one of the tables and then walked over to her booth to grab her laptop. She turned, looking at Greg for a long moment. Their gazes locked. Then something flickered behind her eyes, and she looked past him and spoke to Evelyn.

"Evelyn, if you would be so kind, please just tab my order for the night and be sure to get that elderly gentleman to return my other two," she paused, looking at Greg, "items to me. That is, the other two possessions I had on me earlier to help even out the fight."

"I'll make sure you get them back, Sergeant," Greg interjected.

She saw Evelyn nod her head at her to guarantee that everything would be fine.

Without wavering, she broke her gaze with Greg and turned sharply on her heels to leave.

Abbey reached her room without hassle from the crowd or from the local police. The crowd must have dragged off Rolf and dispersed before she walked out the door of the pub.

She was shaking badly from the fight and was grateful for the solitude of the dark wet street. She didn't know what possessed her to do what she did. For the first time in a long time, she felt exhilaration. She crossed her room in two strides to pop two pills from the prescription sleep aids on her night table.

She then stripped down and wrapped her bath towel around her, grabbing her toiletry, to go shower off and try to calm herself down enough to sleep tonight. Her body was still vibrating from the rush of the fight.

In the shower, standing under the hot water, she half cried and half laughed to herself until she was spent. She gathered herself together, starting to feel the effects of the sleeping pills, and headed back to her room.

She locked the door and promptly lay down before the room tilted precariously and to let the darkness encompass her to the black dream world.

About the Author

C.A. McJack was born and raised in San Juan, Puerto Rico and in Central Florida and the west coast of Florida since the mid-1970s. In 1998, after their service time in the U.S. Army, she and her husband have been residing in Wichita, Kansas.

She holds a Bachelor's in Fine Arts from the University of South Florida and an Associates in Aviation Applied Science from Broomfield, Colorado. She joined the US Army shortly after graduating from the University of South Florida, working as a flight line avionics technician with temporary assignments working as a photojournalist for the Fort Hood Sentinel Newspaper. She continued working in the civilian sector as a Flight Line Avionics technician for over 15 years for Cessna Aviation. Fate's Twisted Circle was her first novel published a few years later after the "great layoffs of 2008."

During that time, her second passion for remodeling homes had kept growing as she worked alongside her husband as a real estate investor and remodeler. Currently, it is her primary job that she loves doing.

In turn, her passion led her to write her second book called, The Other Side of the Flip. This book explains what to expect as a house-flipper and a landlord in the city of Wichita, Kansas. However the advice is still applicable in other parts of the nation for novices to intermediate real estate investors. She presents not just the good but the bad that comes with working in this profession.

Seward Bound, her most recent fictional novel, focuses on the adventures of a young female war veteran who decides to take a chance on making a living and a home on the edge of the Alaskan wilderness. She not only learns more aviation skills but ends up finding love and a new family.

For more information on her latest works, from artworks, fabric arts, and stories, or to leave a message or comment, go to *www.facebook.com/camcjack*

Seward Bound